FTL, Y'ALL!

TALES FROM THE AGE OF THE $200 WARP DRIVE

inquiry@ironcircus.com   www.ironcircus.com

IRON CIRCUS COMICS
™

strange   and   amazing

TABLE of CONTENTS

Teen Graphic Novel FTd; Y'All!

EDITOR IN CHIEF
C. SPIKE TROTMAN

MANAGING EDITOR
AMANDA LAFRENAIS

COVER ARTIST
PAUL DAVEY

BOOK DESIGN
MATT SHERIDAN

PRINT TECHNICIAN
RHIANNON RASMUSSEN-SILVERSTEIN

INSPIRED BY THE NOVELS OF
JERRY OLTION

first printing: October 2018   printed in China   ISBN: 978-1-945820-20-5

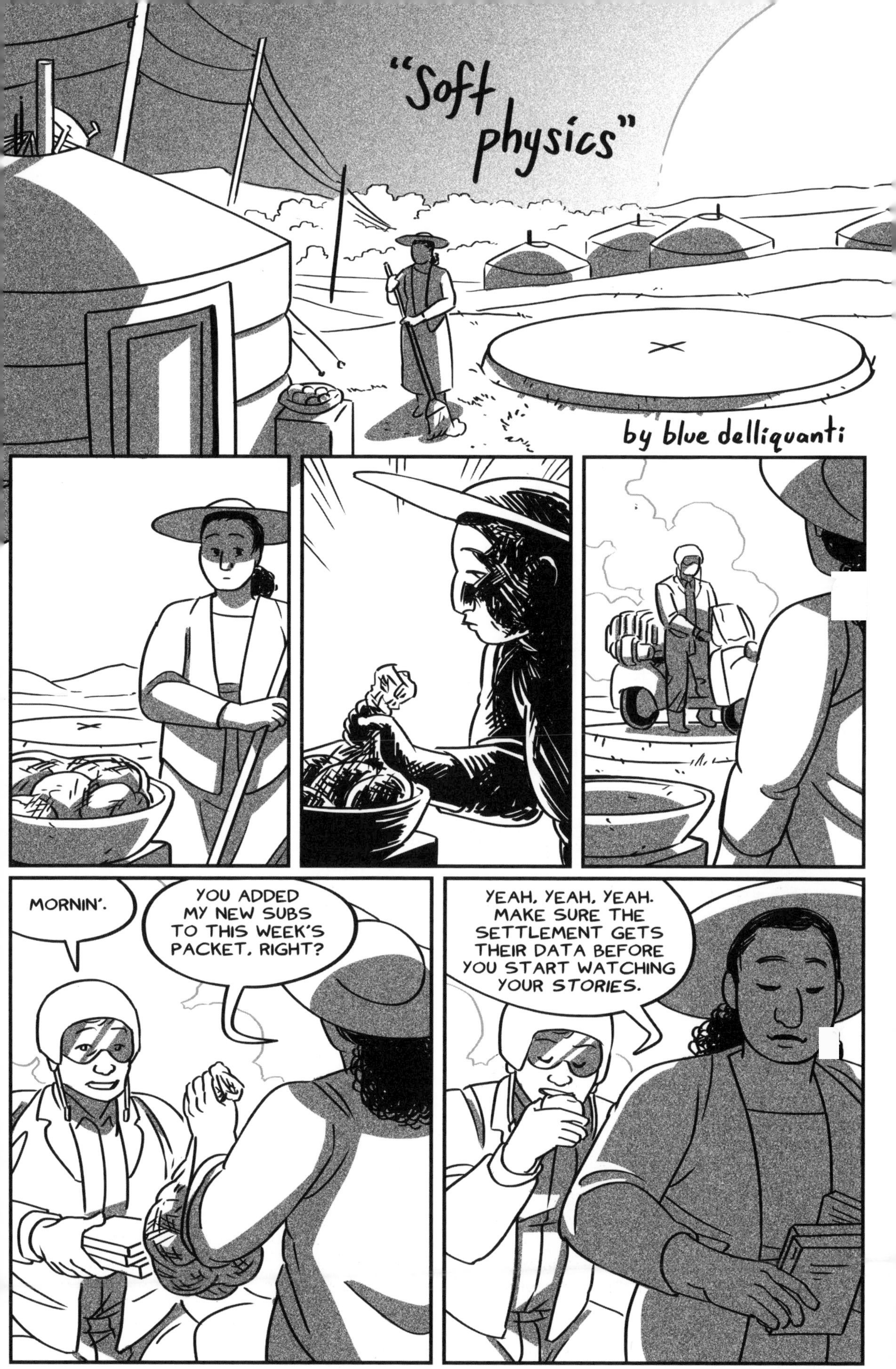
"Soft physics"
by blue delliquanti
MORNIN'.
YOU ADDED MY NEW SUBS TO THIS WEEK'S PACKET, RIGHT?
YEAH, YEAH, YEAH. MAKE SURE THE SETTLEMENT GETS THEIR DATA BEFORE YOU START WATCHING YOUR STORIES.

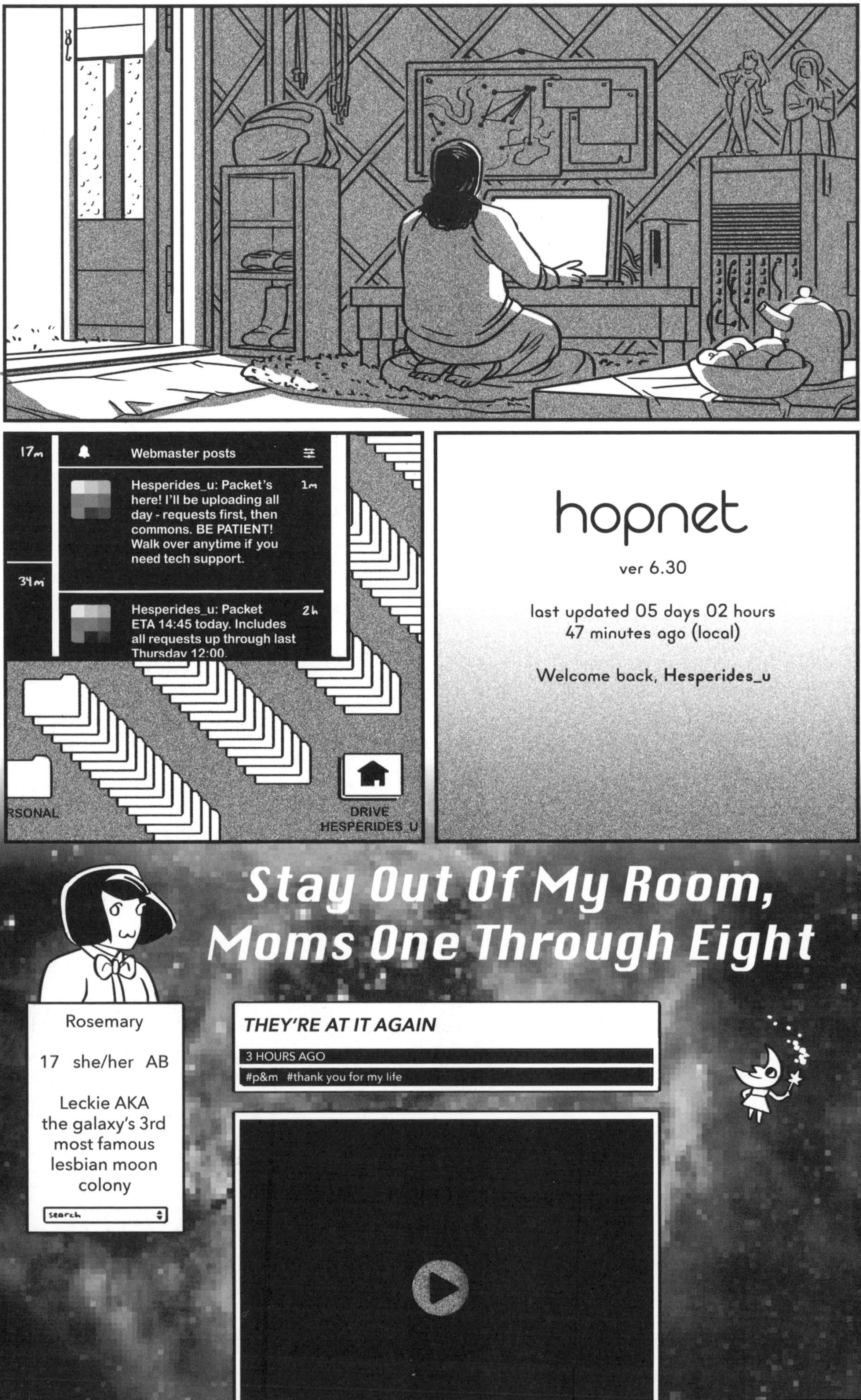

17m
Webmaster posts
Hesperides_u: Packet's here! I'll be uploading all day - requests first, then commons. BE PATIENT! Walk over anytime if you need tech support.
1m
34m
Hesperides_u: Packet ETA 14:45 today. Includes all requests up through last Thursday 12:00.
2h
RSONAL
DRIVE HESPERIDES_U
hopnet
ver 6.30
last updated 05 days 02 hours 47 minutes ago (local)
Welcome back, Hesperides_u
Stay Out Of My Room, Moms One Through Eight
Rosemary
17 she/her AB
Leckie AKA the galaxy's 3rd most famous lesbian moon colony
Search
THEY'RE AT IT AGAIN
3 HOURS AGO
#p&m #thank you for my life

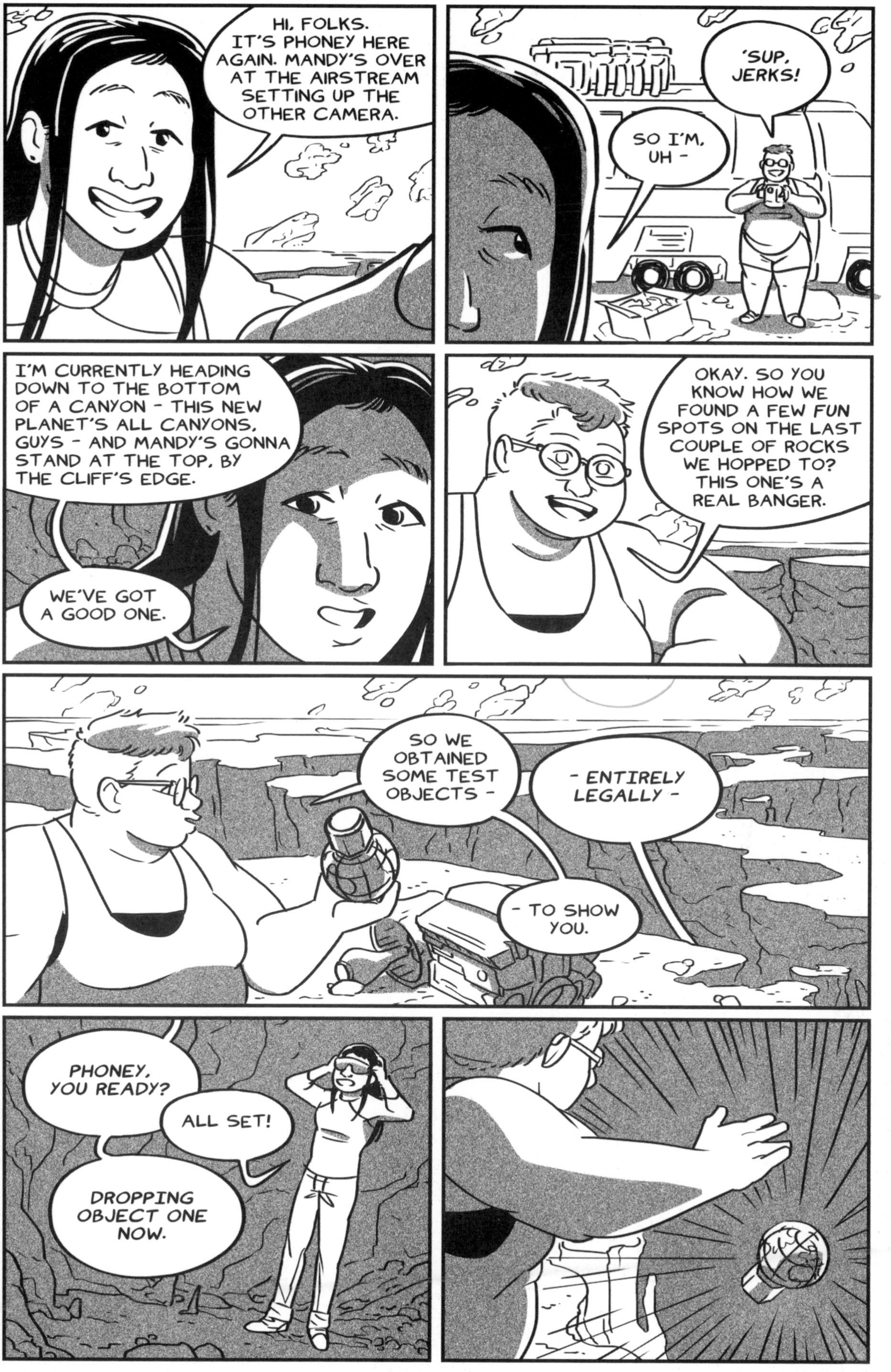
HI, FOLKS. IT'S PHONEY HERE AGAIN. MANDY'S OVER AT THE AIRSTREAM SETTING UP THE OTHER CAMERA.
'SUP, JERKS!
SO I'M, UH -
I'M CURRENTLY HEADING DOWN TO THE BOTTOM OF A CANYON - THIS NEW PLANET'S ALL CANYONS, GUYS - AND MANDY'S GONNA STAND AT THE TOP, BY THE CLIFF'S EDGE.
WE'VE GOT A GOOD ONE.
OKAY. SO YOU KNOW HOW WE FOUND A FEW FUN SPOTS ON THE LAST COUPLE OF ROCKS WE HOPPED TO? THIS ONE'S A REAL BANGER.
SO WE OBTAINED SOME TEST OBJECTS -
- ENTIRELY LEGALLY -
- TO SHOW YOU.
PHONEY, YOU READY?
ALL SET!
DROPPING OBJECT ONE NOW.

KRRRSHINK
OH, MAN! HOLY CRAP! HAHAHA!
DID IT WORK?
TINK
IT'S LIKE IT FORGOT HOW THINGS USUALLY BREAK!
WAIT -
TINK TINK
SSSHIIIINK
IT GAVE UP! HAHAHAHAHA!
FAKE. IT'S GOTTA BE FAKE.
NAH, SOME NERDS HAVE BEEN FOLLOWING THEM FOR MONTHS. THEY KNOW WHAT TO LOOK FOR IF A VIDEO'S BEEN SHOPPED. IT'S NOT.
OBJECT FIVE! DROPPING NOW!

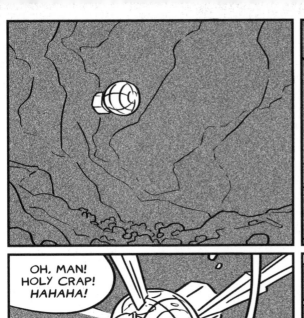

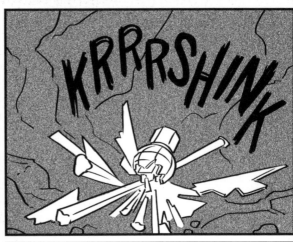

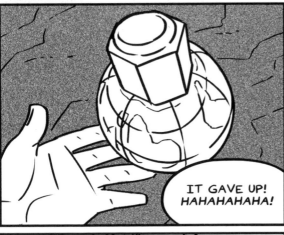

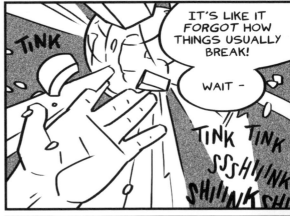

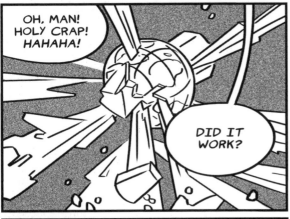

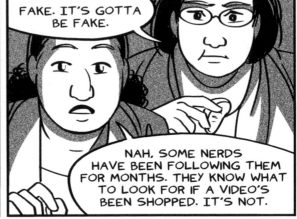

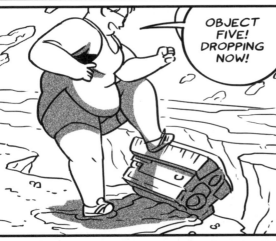

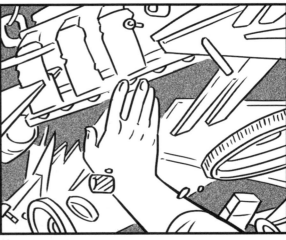

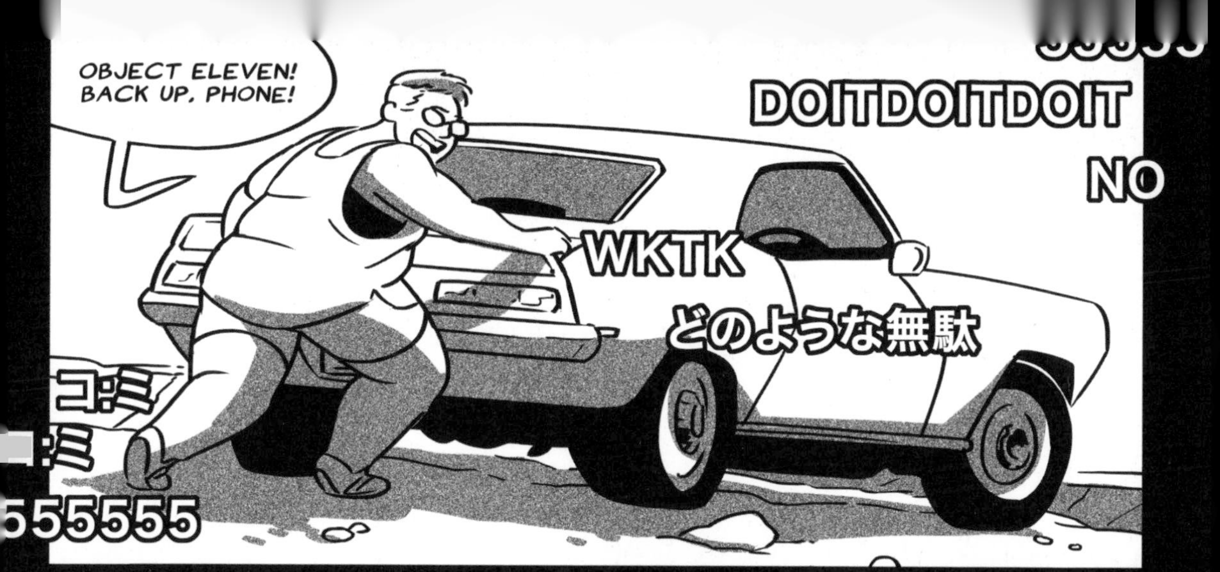
OBJECT ELEVEN! BACK UP, PHONE!
DOITDOITDOIT
NO
WKTK
どのような無駄
コ:ミ

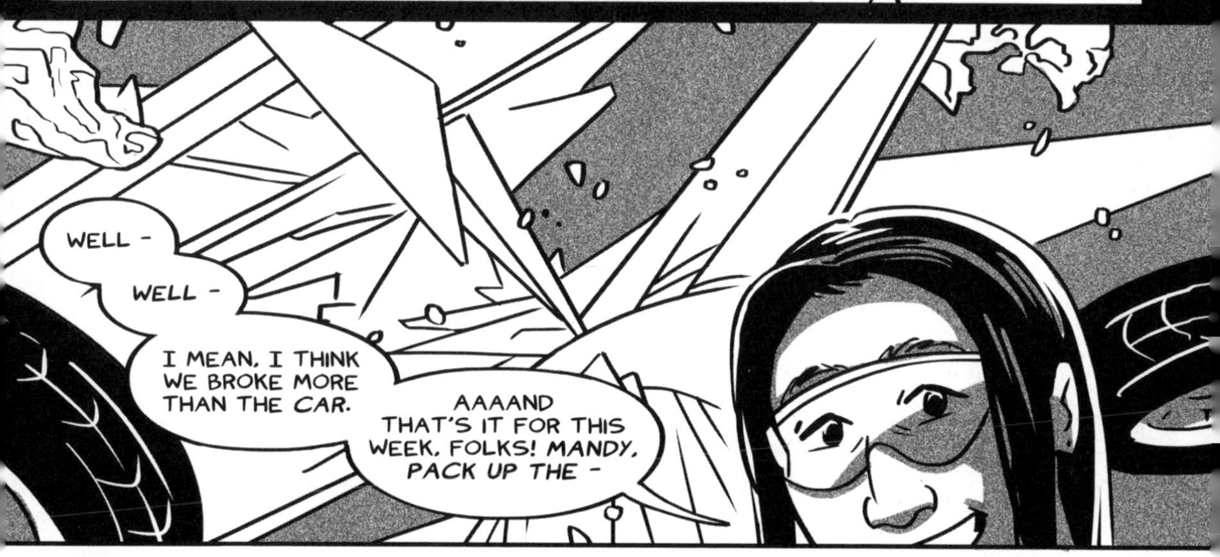
WELL -
WELL -
I MEAN, I THINK WE BROKE MORE THAN THE CAR.
AAAAND THAT'S IT FOR THIS WEEK, FOLKS! MANDY, PACK UP THE -

islandtime
Jun 15, 2021

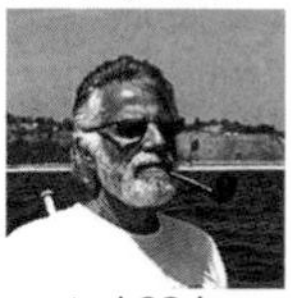

posted 22 hours (local) ago

Listen, I'm not pushing a conspiracy theory here. Two girls can go a long way in an RV with a hop drive. Hell, me and Janine hopped our houseboat out to Sapphire all by ourselves. But how do we know this isn't filmed on a soundstage somewhere?

OnlyLivingBoyInNewProspect
Mar 27, 2030

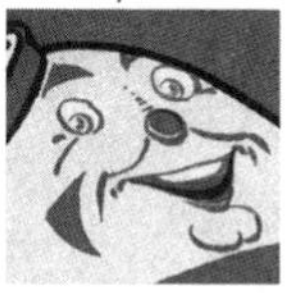

posted 8 hours (local) ago

The question is, who supplied them a vintage Camaro? I mean, their source has gotta be Earth, right? fuldaM0B1L, can you confirm the car?

fuldaM0B1L
Oct 13, 2010

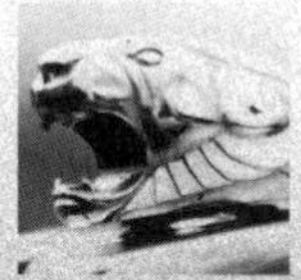

posted 48 minutes (local) ago

Well, OLBINP, you were right about the model, it is a 1969 Camaro - a ZL-1, to be exact. Good taste. I had my packeteer get the records for all transactions and reports of theft in the last 60 years. I'll let you know if I find a match for their Chevy.

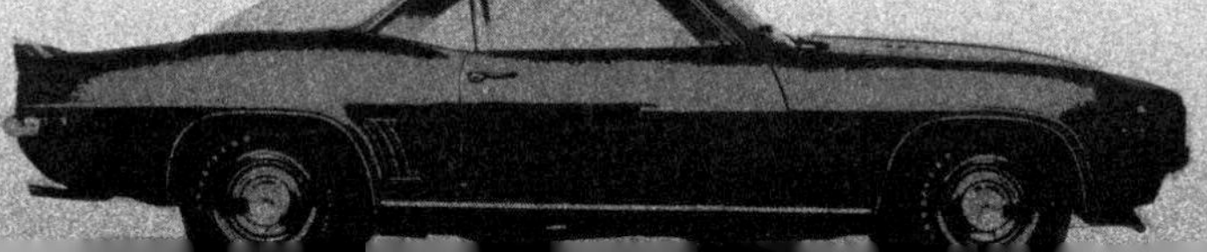

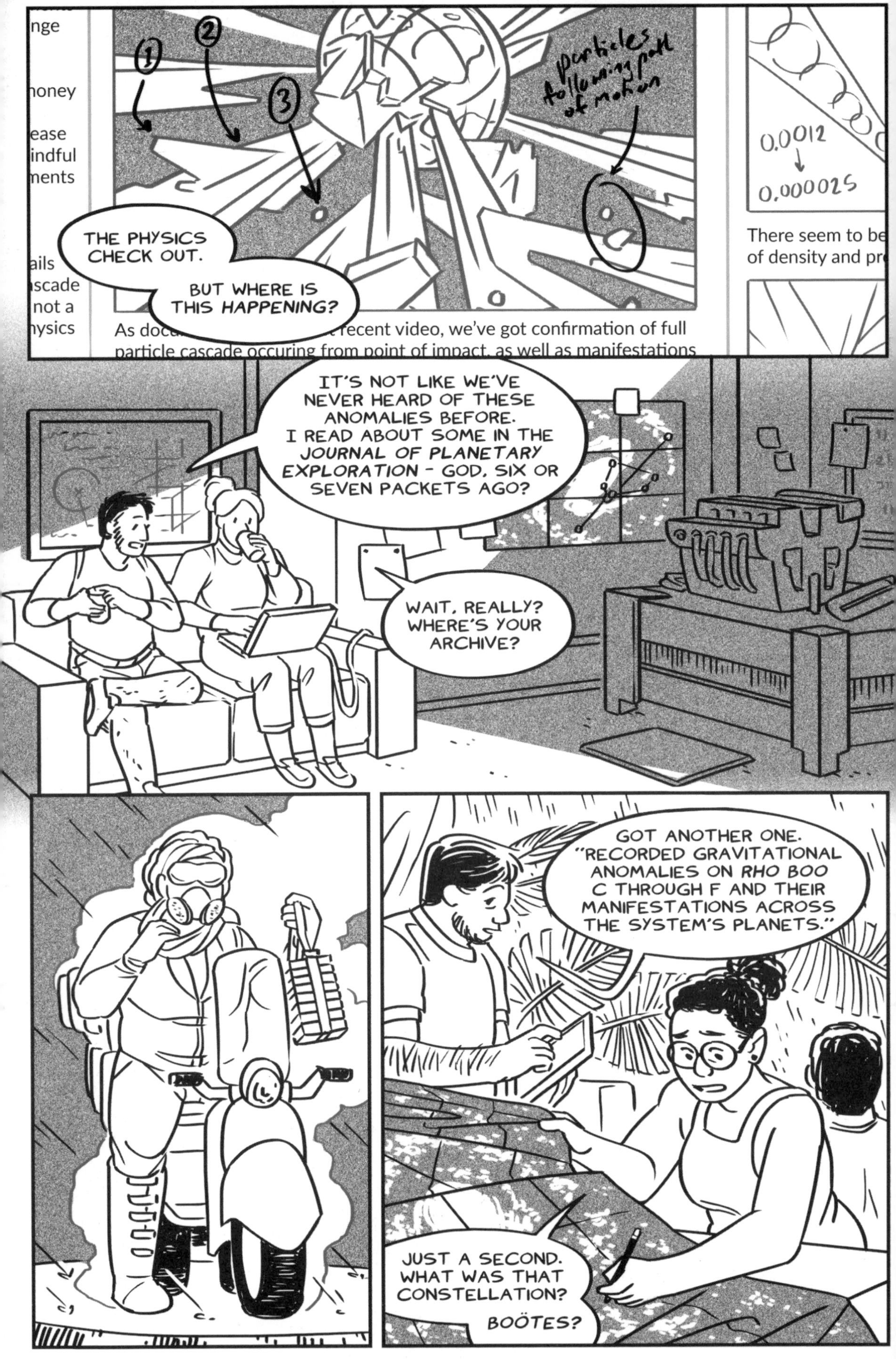
1
2
3
particles following path of motion
0.0012
0.000025
There seem to be
of density and pr
As docu recent video, we've got confirmation of full
particle cascade occuring from point of impact, as well as manifestations
THE PHYSICS CHECK OUT.
BUT WHERE IS THIS *HAPPENING?*
IT'S NOT LIKE WE'VE NEVER HEARD OF THESE ANOMALIES BEFORE. I READ ABOUT SOME IN THE *JOURNAL OF PLANETARY EXPLORATION* - GOD, SIX OR SEVEN PACKETS AGO?
WAIT, REALLY? WHERE'S YOUR ARCHIVE?
GOT ANOTHER ONE. "RECORDED GRAVITATIONAL ANOMALIES ON *RHO BOO* C THROUGH F AND THEIR MANIFESTATIONS ACROSS THE SYSTEM'S PLANETS."
JUST A SECOND. WHAT WAS THAT CONSTELLATION?
BOÖTES?

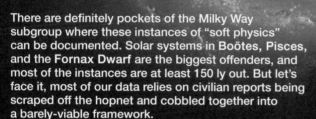

There are definitely pockets of the Milky Way subgroup where these instances of "soft physics" can be documented. Solar systems in Boötes, Pisces, and the **Fornax Dwarf** are the biggest offenders, and most of the instances are at least 150 ly out. But let's face it, most of our data relies on civilian reports being scraped off the hopnet and cobbled together into a barely-viable framework.

These thrillseekers *could* be mapping their route based on reports and hearsay, but they could easily be hopping to these places on accident. How do we know there isn't a spatial pocket on a planet *8 ly* away - **Haven**, maybe, or **New Lagos** - where gravity just doesn't work the way it should?

I'm a packeteer for an orphan data center. AMA.
submitted 5 hours ago by quarkhamill   Page 2 of 5

GlieseLightning:
HOLY CRAP you picked up the camaro video! did mandy meet you there???
please tell me it was mandy

quarkhamill:
Listen, assholes, I've never met either of 'em. That's not how it works. People don't pass off flash drives into your waiting arms like they're mothers handing over their forsaken infants. It's Victor Hugo but not *that* Victor Hugo.

quarkhamill:
There's a box in the wall. People drop in their drives and the nuns don't say nothing.

There are people staging coups and disseminating radical ideas across the galaxy, and the nuns don't take their names. Anonymity is sacred.

Those Phoney and Mandy videos have been processed in at least 8 orphanages in 5 galaxies. I'm just the Thursday delivery boy.

THERE'S A NEW ONE!

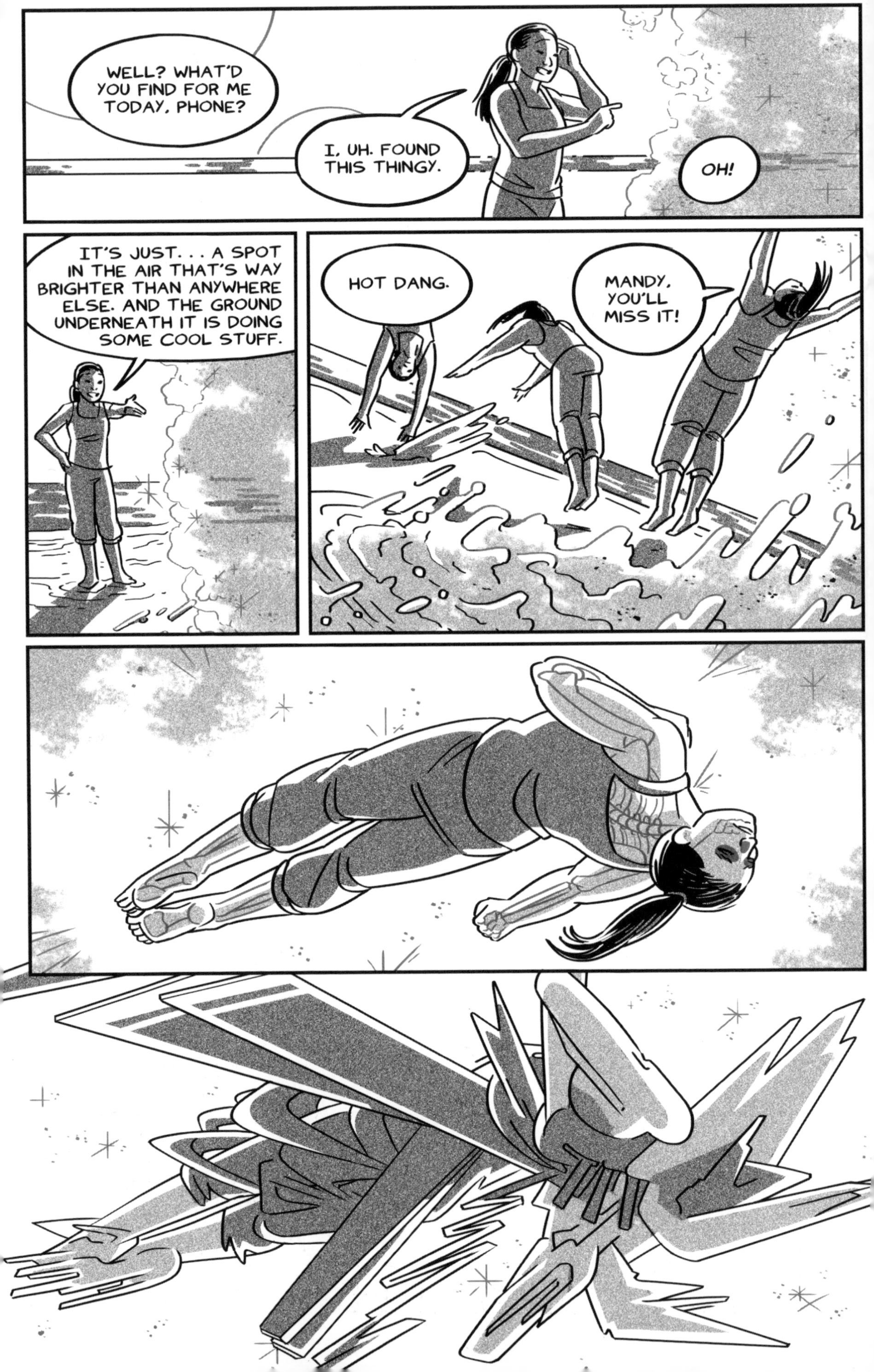
WELL? WHAT'D YOU FIND FOR ME TODAY, PHONE?
I, UH. FOUND THIS THINGY.
OH!
IT'S JUST. . . A SPOT IN THE AIR THAT'S WAY BRIGHTER THAN ANYWHERE ELSE. AND THE GROUND UNDERNEATH IT IS DOING SOME COOL STUFF.
HOT DANG.
MANDY, YOU'LL MISS IT!

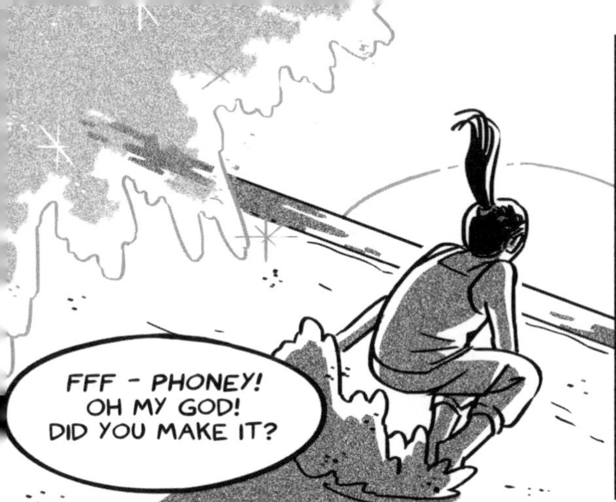
FFF - PHONEY! OH MY GOD! DID YOU MAKE IT?

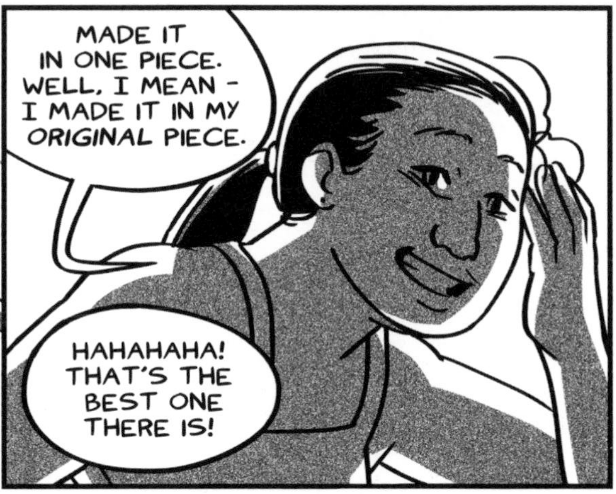
MADE IT IN ONE PIECE. WELL, I MEAN - I MADE IT IN MY ORIGINAL PIECE.
HAHAHAHA! THAT'S THE BEST ONE THERE IS!

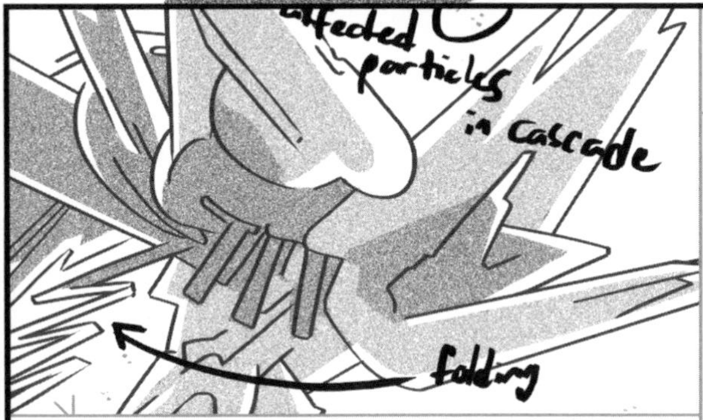
affected particles
in cascade
folding

Could this have any similarity to the phenomenon documented in the Iota Gruis system? The photos and measurements taken by Emerson and Kwek in '28, anyway.

documented in the Iota Gruis system? The photos and measurements taken by Emerson and Kwek in '28, anyway.

are you seriously citing emerson and kwek in here

Listen, I know that there are

disagreements

around their thesis that a pocket of space-t could be connected to a potentially infinite Dirac sea, but let's just take a moment to consider

DIRAC SEAS ARE SO INELEGANT

Phoney could feel the stray particles skittering across her hands, her skin, her long black locks, as she regained her original form. As her vision came back into focus she could see Mandy running towards her, camera in her hand, sand flying beneath her feet. She was always such a carefree prankster, but did she actually look... **worried**?

Phoney affixed a brave smile to her face as she stood up and tossed back her raven hair. "Made it in one piece. Well, I mean – I made it in my original piece."

Mandy's fearful mask cracked, betraying her joy and relief. She laughed. "That's the best one there is!"

Phoney freezes, and her eyes dart to her left wrist, where the same words that had been imprinted there since birth shimmered in the light of the late afternoon.

That's the best one there is.

Could it be that all this time, Mandy – her Mandy – was her soulmate? Was Mandy the one she was destined to hop across the galaxy with, forever?

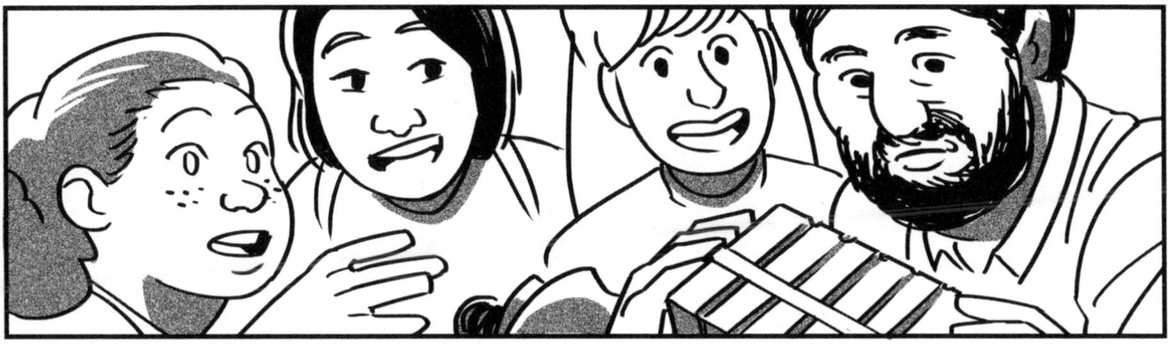

PAYDIRT

CW explosions, injury, death

JOVIS 2 days (local) ago 2389 NEVER

text 82.36 KB raw download clone embed report print

1. --

2. This is going to be difficult for a lot of us, so I've made it a point to be as absolutely thorough as possible.

3. --

4.

5. First, a little background. If you only know me from the hopnet's P&M circles, you should know that my other big hobby is collecting documents from the early days of FTL, back when everything was going to hell faster than anything had ever gone before. Early hopper design docs, video diaries, even physical newspapers, back when those were still limping along. Yeah. I use five packeteer services at once and they all hate me.

6.

7. Anyway. This year, me and a couple of other hopnet raccoons acquired a source for a lot of old CCTV footage. Banks and stuff. If you remember what the economic situation was like at the dawn of FTL, you would understand that we were expecting some wild footage.

8.

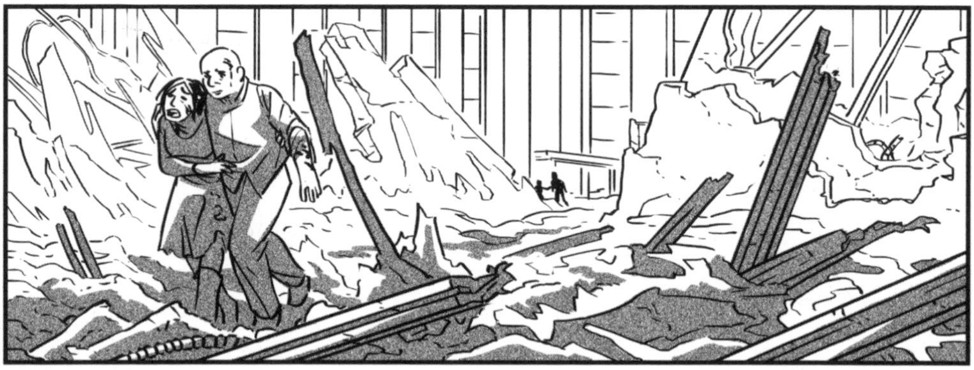

9. We got it in spades. This is the scene of the Etoile Bank explosion on 04/08/22. Godawful.
As far as most people were concerned, it was an catastrophic early hop&grab - the thieves overlooked a regulator in their getaway car and it ended up shredding the point in space it exited from. And they were never caught. They could have been vaporized, they could have hopped off to Rigel to sit on their pile of diamonds, didn't matter.

10.

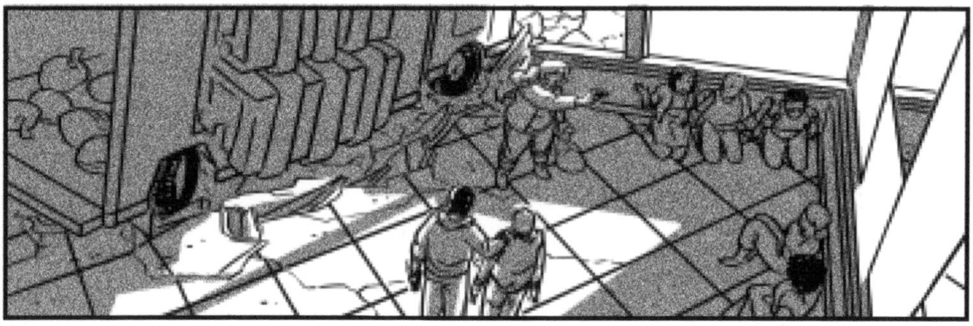

11. What does matter now, to me, is IDing the thieves. And this is why.
Look at the one standing by the cab of the truck.

12.

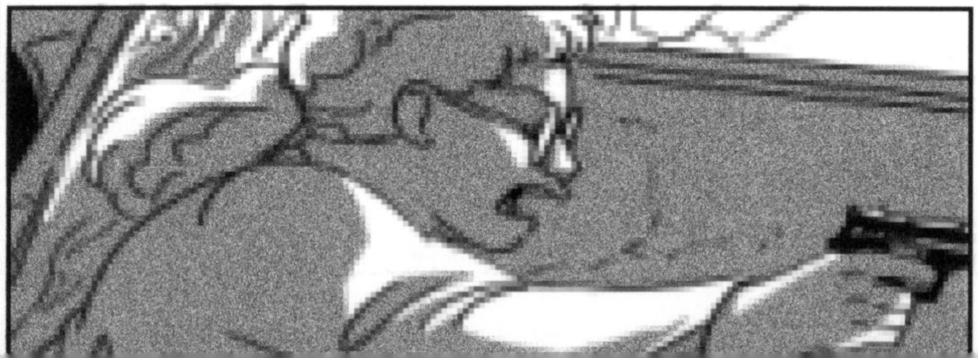

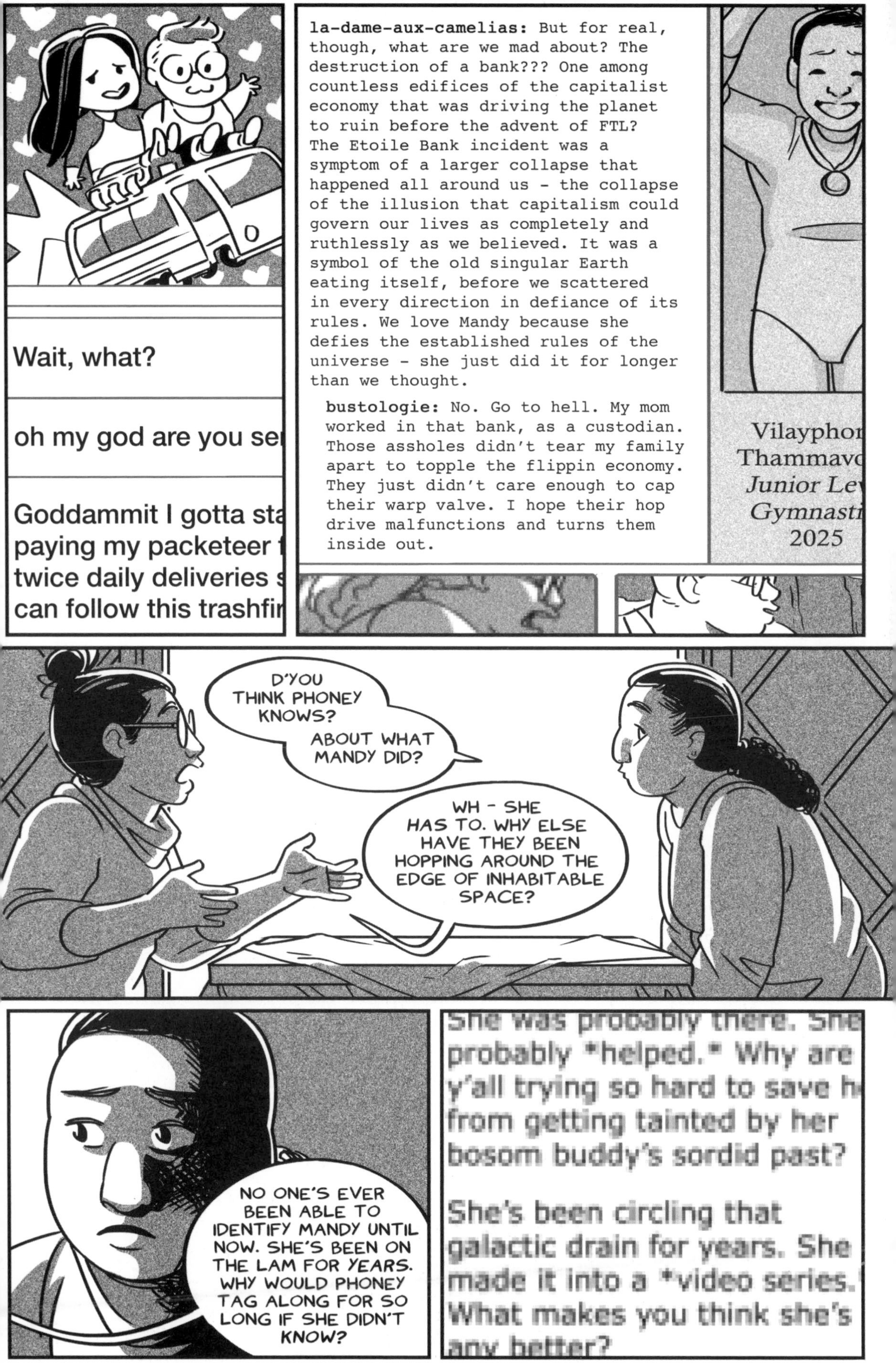
Wait, what?
oh my god are you se
Goddammit I gotta sta
paying my packeteer
twice daily deliveries
can follow this trashfi
la-dame-aux-camelias: But for real, though, what are we mad about? The destruction of a bank??? One among countless edifices of the capitalist economy that was driving the planet to ruin before the advent of FTL? The Etoile Bank incident was a symptom of a larger collapse that happened all around us - the collapse of the illusion that capitalism could govern our lives as completely and ruthlessly as we believed. It was a symbol of the old singular Earth eating itself, before we scattered in every direction in defiance of its rules. We love Mandy because she defies the established rules of the universe - she just did it for longer than we thought.
bustologie: No. Go to hell. My mom worked in that bank, as a custodian. Those assholes didn't tear my family apart to topple the flippin economy. They just didn't care enough to cap their warp valve. I hope their hop drive malfunctions and turns them inside out.
Vilayphor
Thammavo
Junior Le
Gymnasti
2025
D'YOU THINK PHONEY KNOWS?
ABOUT WHAT MANDY DID?
WH - SHE HAS TO. WHY ELSE HAVE THEY BEEN HOPPING AROUND THE EDGE OF INHABITABLE SPACE?
NO ONE'S EVER BEEN ABLE TO IDENTIFY MANDY UNTIL NOW. SHE'S BEEN ON THE LAM FOR YEARS. WHY WOULD PHONEY TAG ALONG FOR SO LONG IF SHE DIDN'T KNOW?
She was probably there. She probably *helped.* Why are y'all trying so hard to save h from getting tainted by her bosom buddy's sordid past?
She's been circling that galactic drain for years. She made it into a *video series.* What makes you think she's any better?

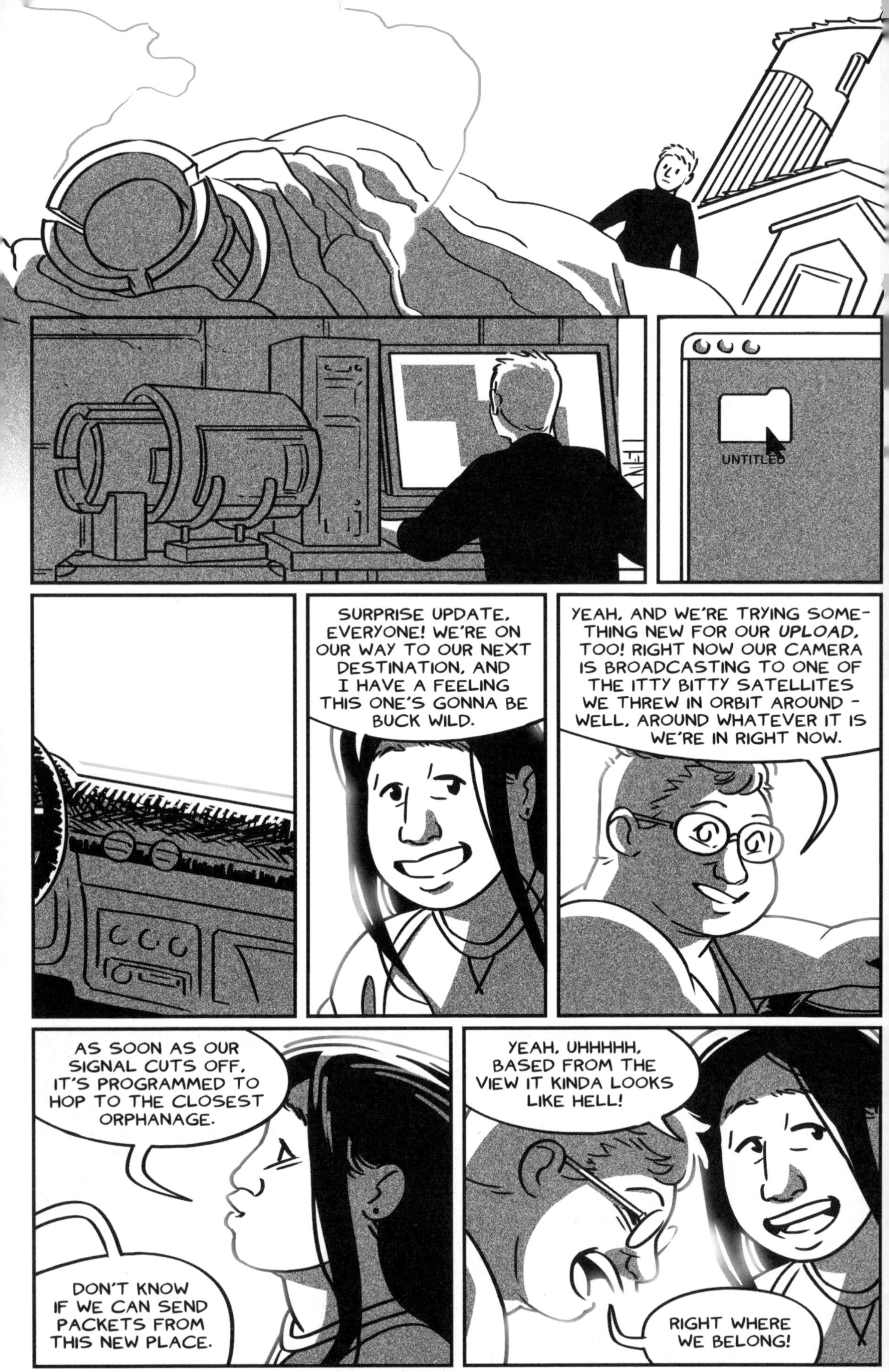
UNTITLED
SURPRISE UPDATE, EVERYONE! WE'RE ON OUR WAY TO OUR NEXT DESTINATION, AND I HAVE A FEELING THIS ONE'S GONNA BE BUCK WILD.
YEAH, AND WE'RE TRYING SOMETHING NEW FOR OUR *UPLOAD*, TOO! RIGHT NOW OUR CAMERA IS BROADCASTING TO ONE OF THE ITTY BITTY SATELLITES WE THREW IN ORBIT AROUND - WELL, AROUND WHATEVER IT IS WE'RE IN RIGHT NOW.
AS SOON AS OUR SIGNAL CUTS OFF, IT'S PROGRAMMED TO HOP TO THE CLOSEST ORPHANAGE.
DON'T KNOW IF WE CAN SEND PACKETS FROM THIS NEW PLACE.
YEAH, UHHHHH, BASED FROM THE VIEW IT KINDA LOOKS LIKE HELL!
RIGHT WHERE WE BELONG!

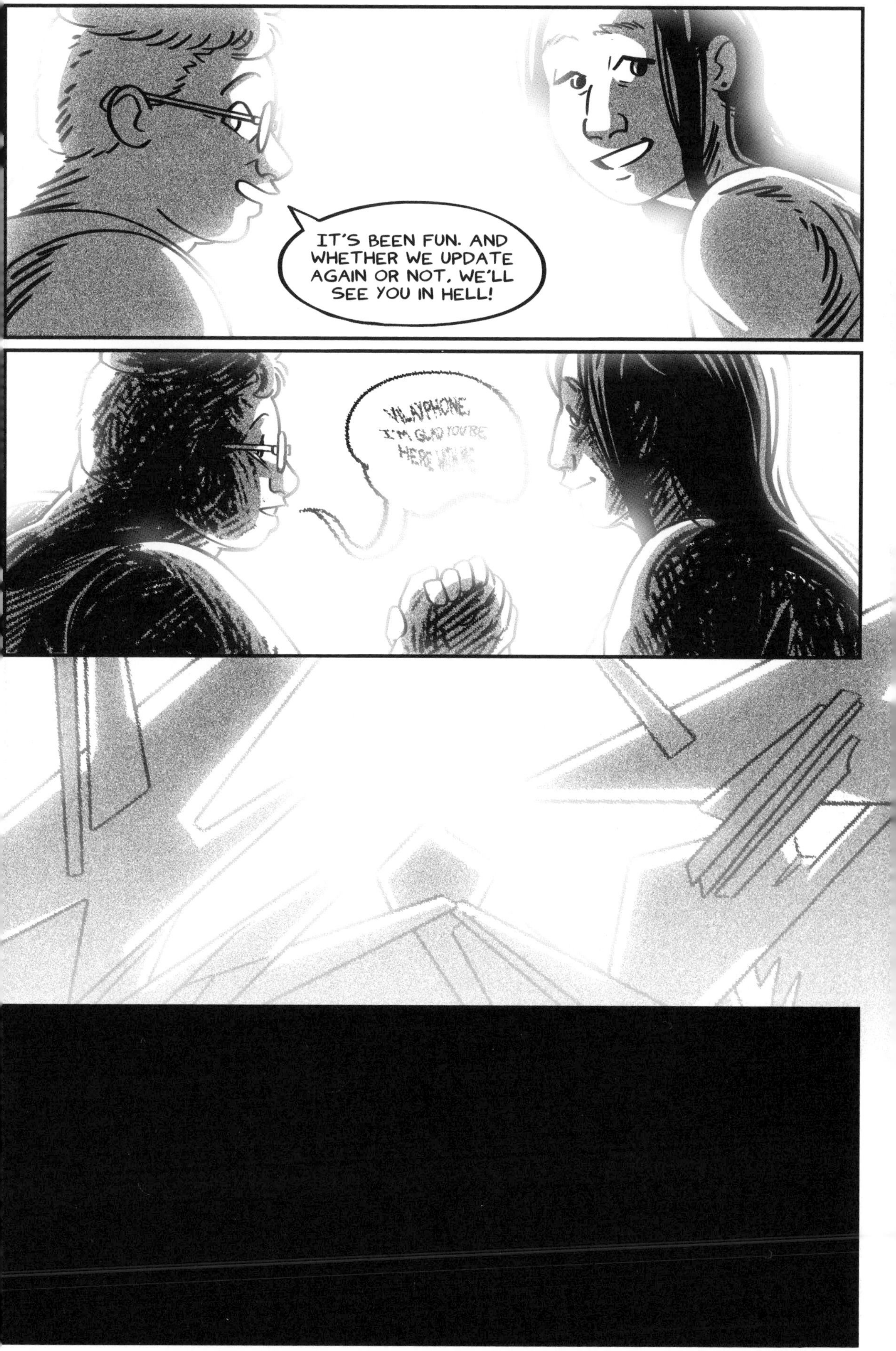
IT'S BEEN FUN. AND WHETHER WE UPDATE AGAIN OR NOT, WE'LL SEE YOU IN HELL!
VLAYPHONE, I'M GLAD YOU'RE HERE WITH ME

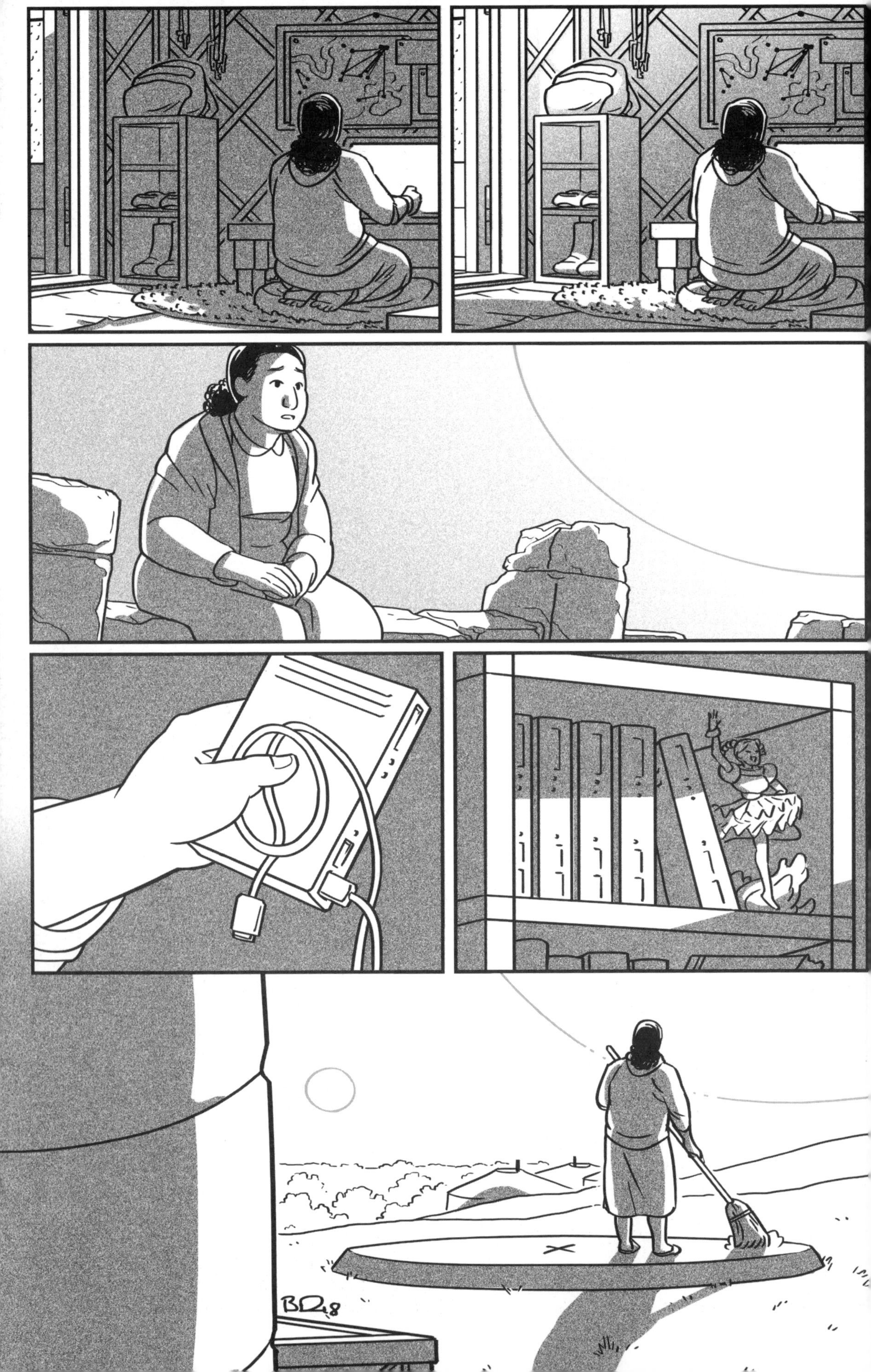

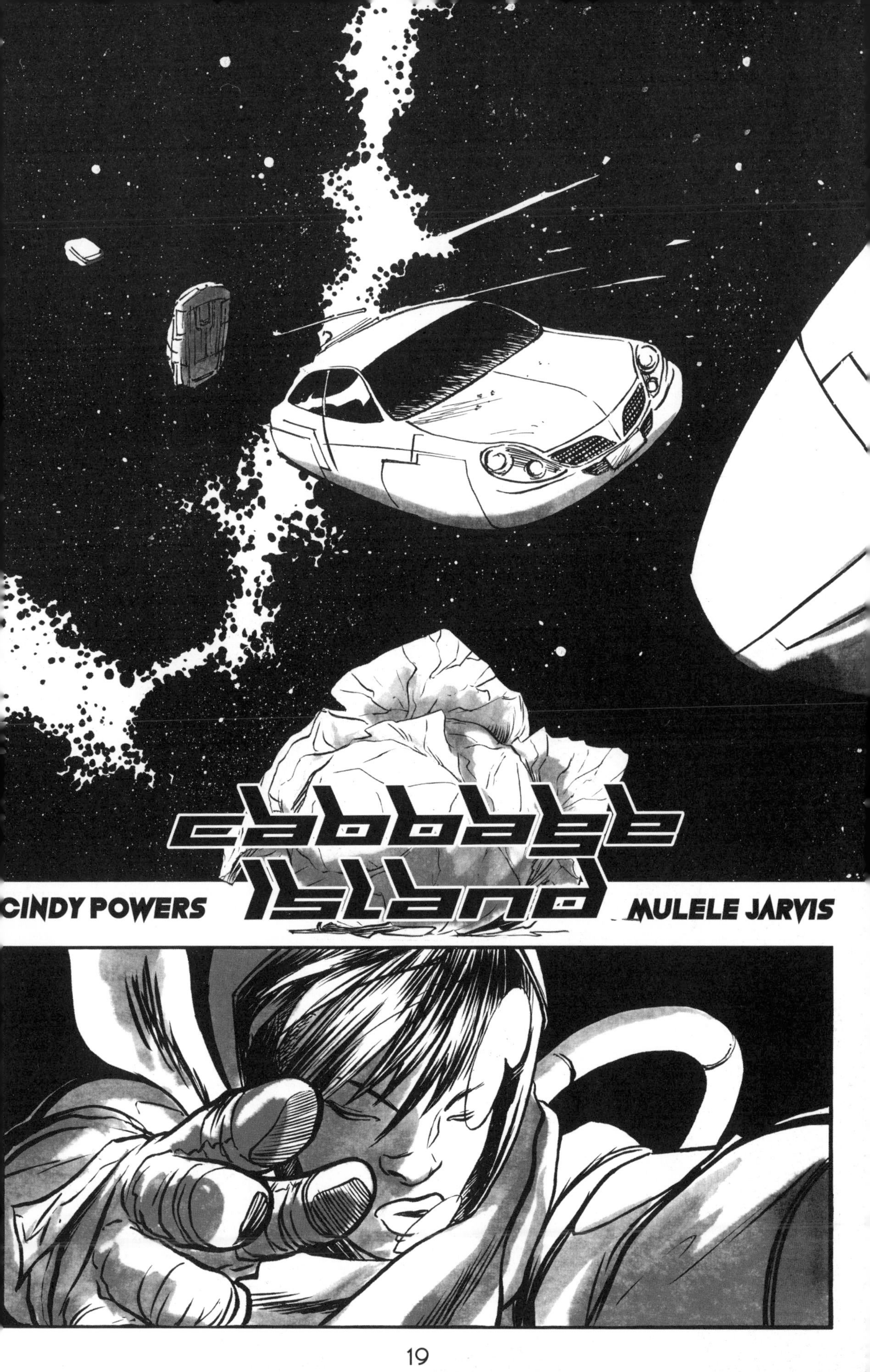
CABBAGE QUEST
CINDY POWERS
MULELE JARVIS

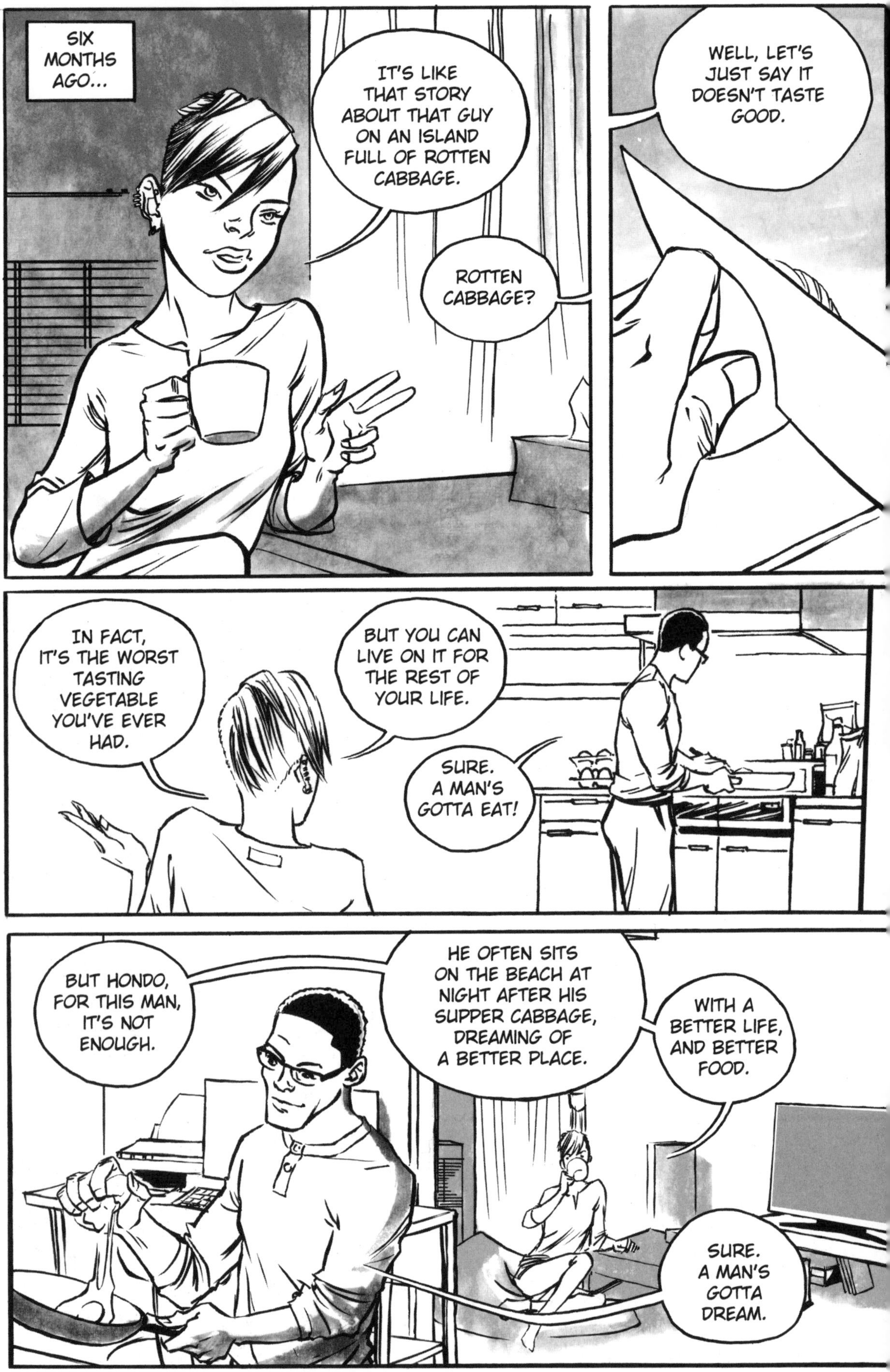
SIX MONTHS AGO...
IT'S LIKE THAT STORY ABOUT THAT GUY ON AN ISLAND FULL OF ROTTEN CABBAGE.
ROTTEN CABBAGE?
WELL, LET'S JUST SAY IT DOESN'T TASTE GOOD.
IN FACT, IT'S THE WORST TASTING VEGETABLE YOU'VE EVER HAD.
BUT YOU CAN LIVE ON IT FOR THE REST OF YOUR LIFE.
SURE. A MAN'S GOTTA EAT!
BUT HONDO, FOR THIS MAN, IT'S NOT ENOUGH.
HE OFTEN SITS ON THE BEACH AT NIGHT AFTER HIS SUPPER CABBAGE, DREAMING OF A BETTER PLACE.
WITH A BETTER LIFE, AND BETTER FOOD.
SURE. A MAN'S GOTTA DREAM.

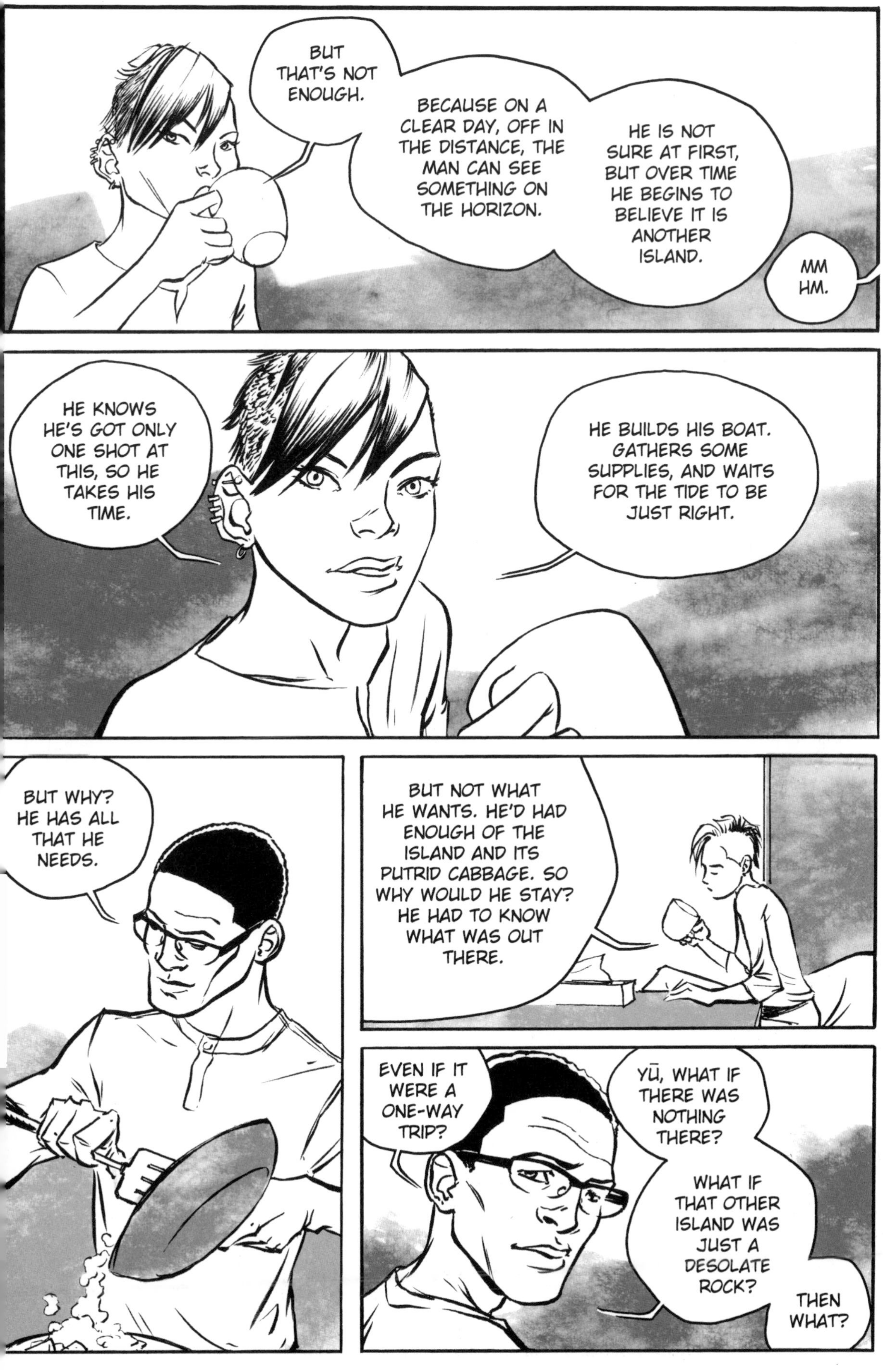
BUT THAT'S NOT ENOUGH.
BECAUSE ON A CLEAR DAY, OFF IN THE DISTANCE, THE MAN CAN SEE SOMETHING ON THE HORIZON.
HE IS NOT SURE AT FIRST, BUT OVER TIME HE BEGINS TO BELIEVE IT IS ANOTHER ISLAND.
MM HM.
HE KNOWS HE'S GOT ONLY ONE SHOT AT THIS, SO HE TAKES HIS TIME.
HE BUILDS HIS BOAT. GATHERS SOME SUPPLIES, AND WAITS FOR THE TIDE TO BE JUST RIGHT.
BUT WHY? HE HAS ALL THAT HE NEEDS.
BUT NOT WHAT HE WANTS. HE'D HAD ENOUGH OF THE ISLAND AND ITS PUTRID CABBAGE. SO WHY WOULD HE STAY? HE HAD TO KNOW WHAT WAS OUT THERE.
EVEN IF IT WERE A ONE-WAY TRIP?
YŪ, WHAT IF THERE WAS NOTHING THERE?
WHAT IF THAT OTHER ISLAND WAS JUST A DESOLATE ROCK?
THEN WHAT?

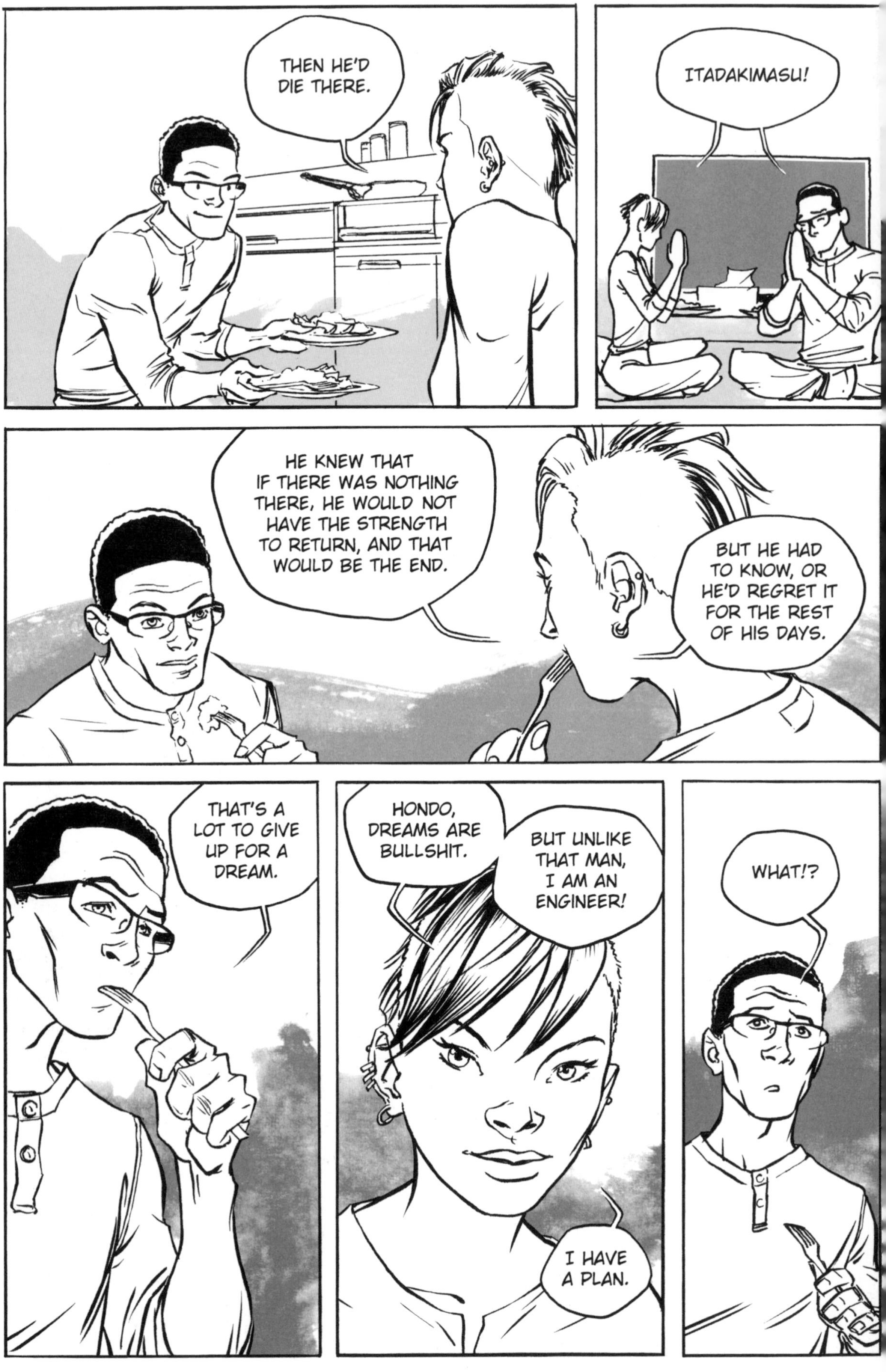
THEN HE'D DIE THERE.
ITADAKIMASU!
HE KNEW THAT IF THERE WAS NOTHING THERE, HE WOULD NOT HAVE THE STRENGTH TO RETURN, AND THAT WOULD BE THE END.
BUT HE HAD TO KNOW, OR HE'D REGRET IT FOR THE REST OF HIS DAYS.
THAT'S A LOT TO GIVE UP FOR A DREAM.
HONDO, DREAMS ARE BULLSHIT.
BUT UNLIKE THAT MAN, I AM AN ENGINEER!
I HAVE A PLAN.
WHAT!?

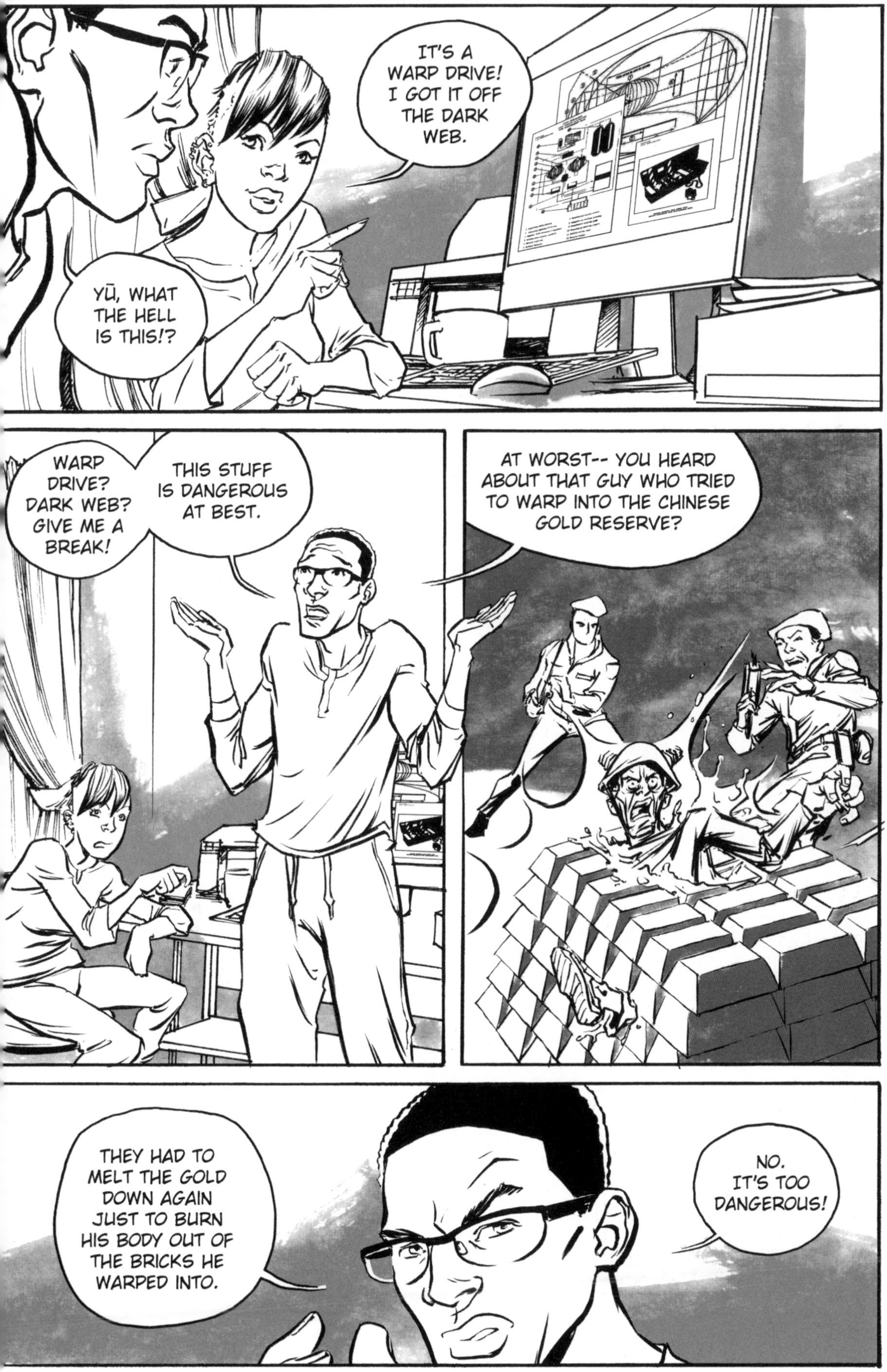
YŪ, WHAT THE HELL IS THIS!?
IT'S A WARP DRIVE! I GOT IT OFF THE DARK WEB.
WARP DRIVE? DARK WEB? GIVE ME A BREAK!
THIS STUFF IS DANGEROUS AT BEST.
AT WORST-- YOU HEARD ABOUT THAT GUY WHO TRIED TO WARP INTO THE CHINESE GOLD RESERVE?
THEY HAD TO MELT THE GOLD DOWN AGAIN JUST TO BURN HIS BODY OUT OF THE BRICKS HE WARPED INTO.
NO. IT'S TOO DANGEROUS!

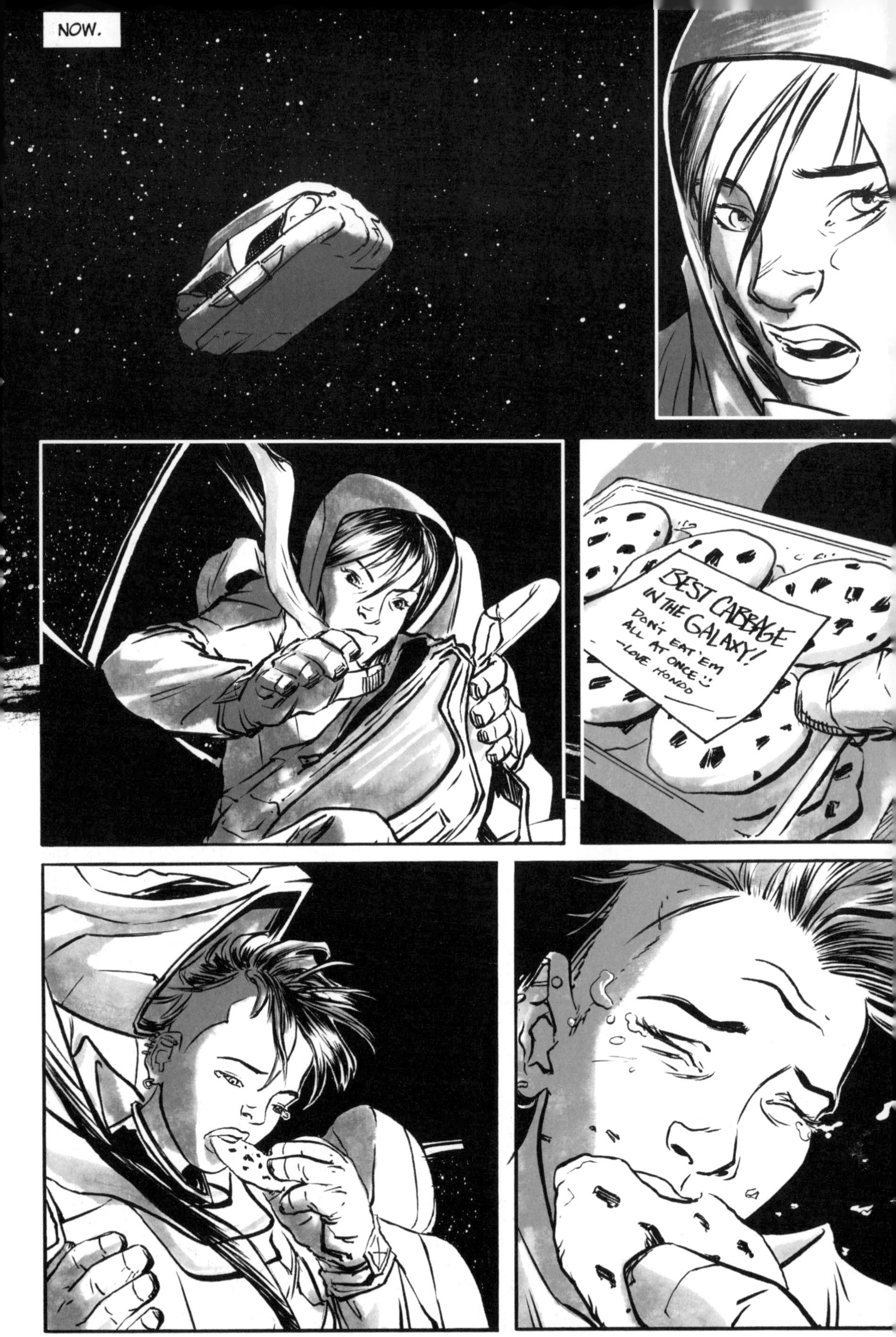
NOW.
BEST CABBAGE
IN THE GALAXY!
DON'T EAT 'EM
ALL AT ONCE :)
—LOVE HONDO

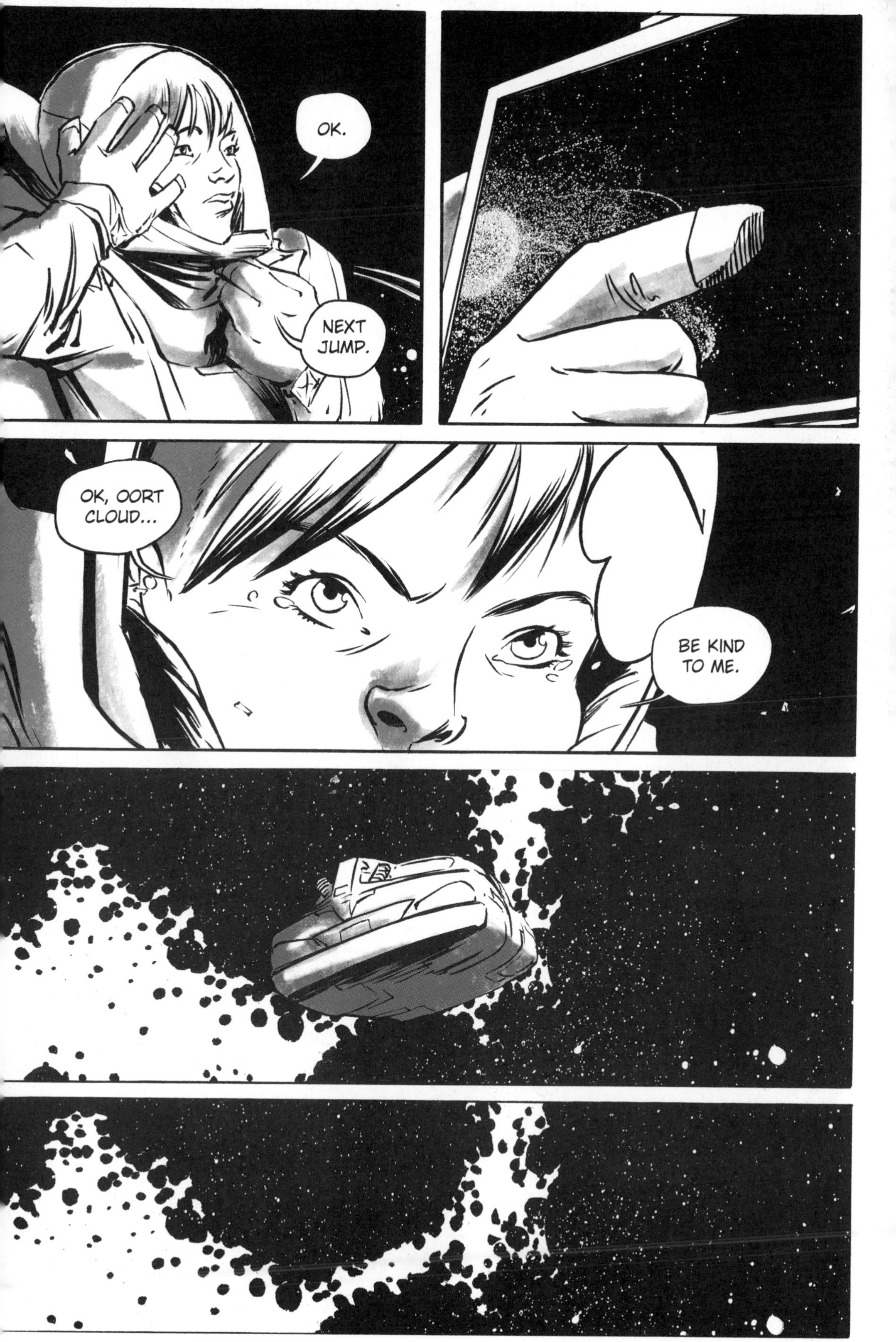
OK.
NEXT JUMP.
OK, OORT CLOUD...
BE KIND TO ME.

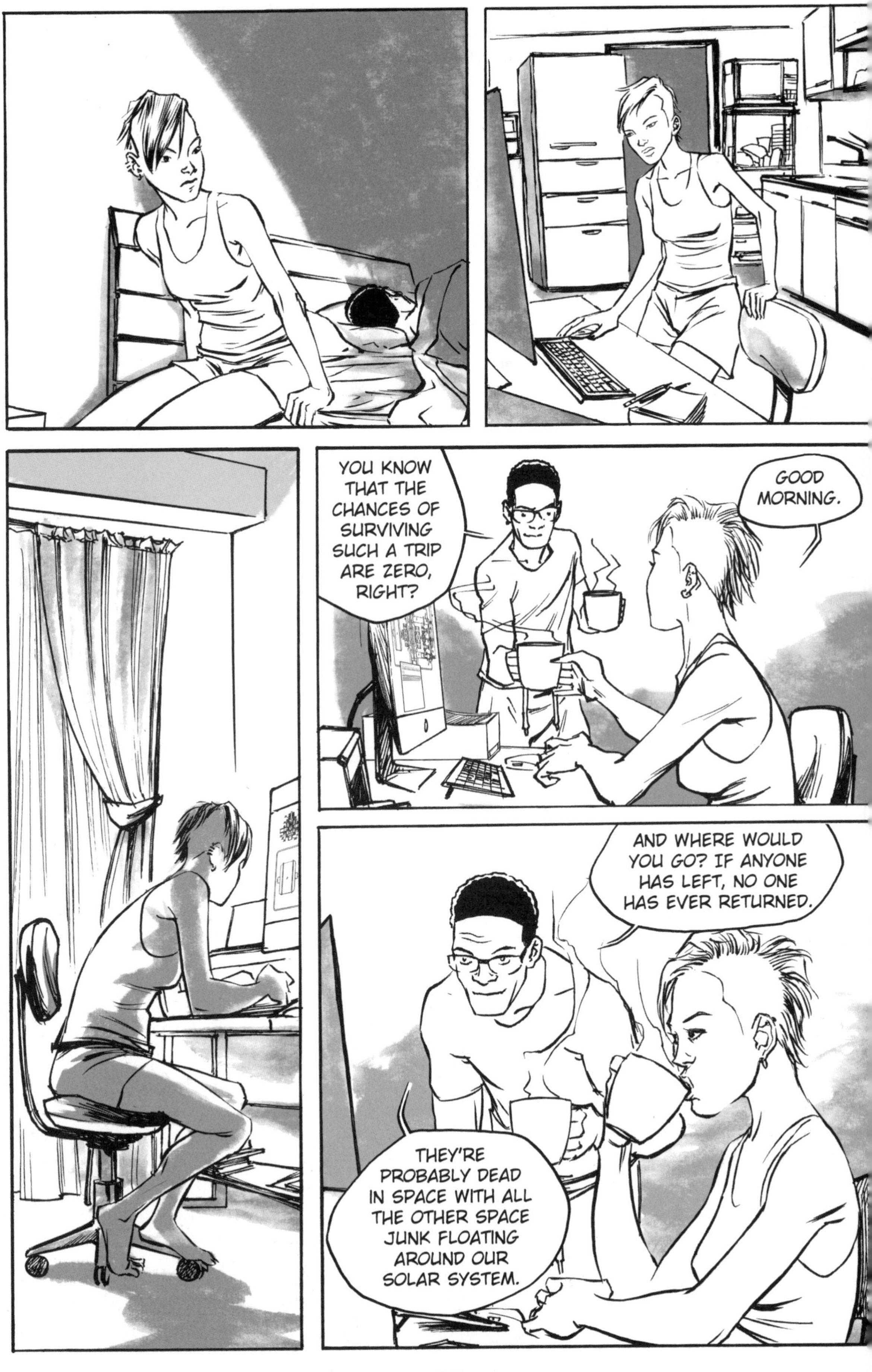

YOU KNOW THAT THE CHANCES OF SURVIVING SUCH A TRIP ARE ZERO, RIGHT?
GOOD MORNING.
AND WHERE WOULD YOU GO? IF ANYONE HAS LEFT, NO ONE HAS EVER RETURNED.
THEY'RE PROBABLY DEAD IN SPACE WITH ALL THE OTHER SPACE JUNK FLOATING AROUND OUR SOLAR SYSTEM.

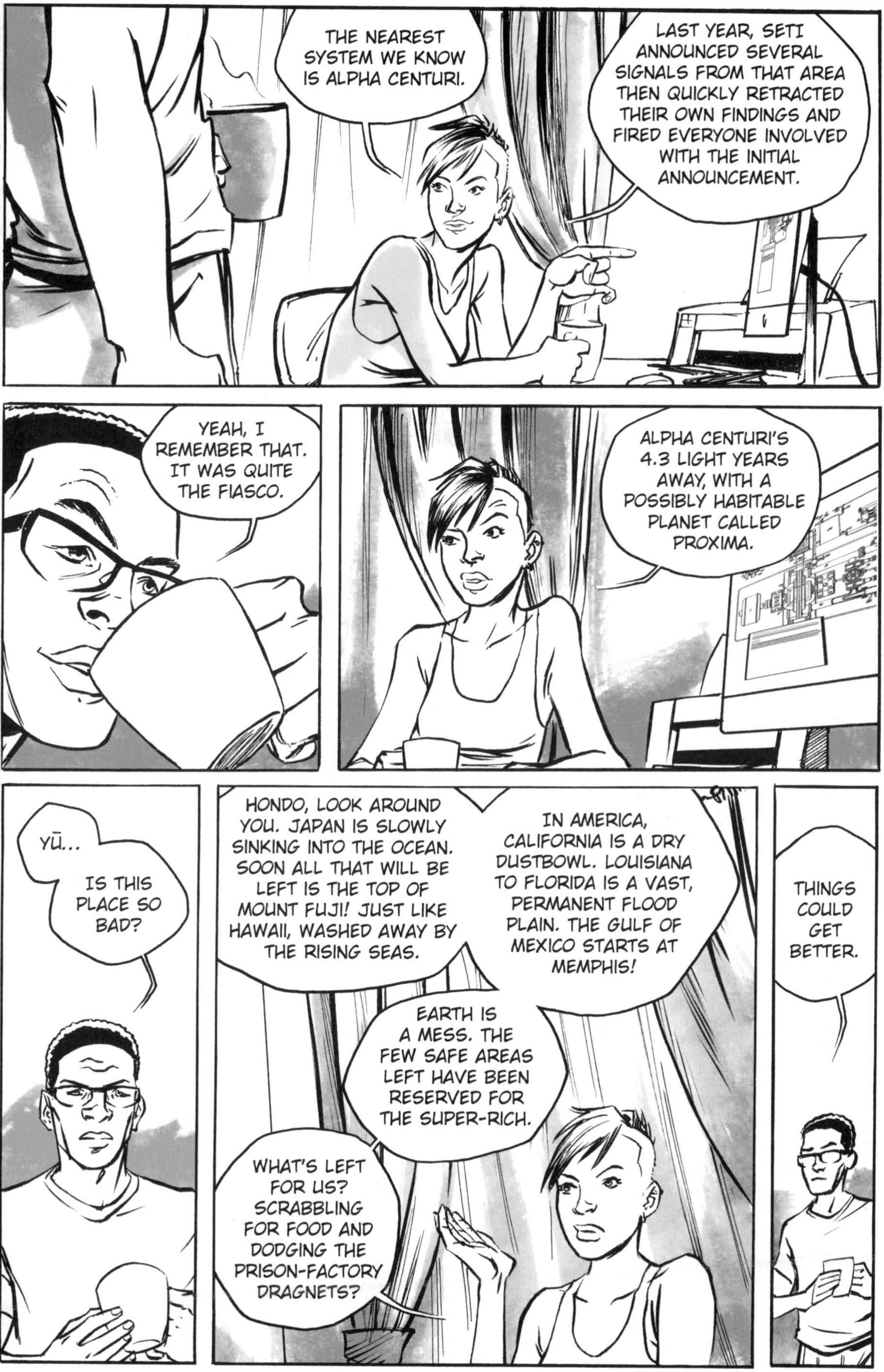
THE NEAREST SYSTEM WE KNOW IS ALPHA CENTURI.
LAST YEAR, SETI ANNOUNCED SEVERAL SIGNALS FROM THAT AREA THEN QUICKLY RETRACTED THEIR OWN FINDINGS AND FIRED EVERYONE INVOLVED WITH THE INITIAL ANNOUNCEMENT.
YEAH, I REMEMBER THAT. IT WAS QUITE THE FIASCO.
ALPHA CENTURI'S 4.3 LIGHT YEARS AWAY, WITH A POSSIBLY HABITABLE PLANET CALLED PROXIMA.
YŪ...
IS THIS PLACE SO BAD?
HONDO, LOOK AROUND YOU. JAPAN IS SLOWLY SINKING INTO THE OCEAN. SOON ALL THAT WILL BE LEFT IS THE TOP OF MOUNT FUJI! JUST LIKE HAWAII, WASHED AWAY BY THE RISING SEAS.
IN AMERICA, CALIFORNIA IS A DRY DUSTBOWL. LOUISIANA TO FLORIDA IS A VAST, PERMANENT FLOOD PLAIN. THE GULF OF MEXICO STARTS AT MEMPHIS!
EARTH IS A MESS. THE FEW SAFE AREAS LEFT HAVE BEEN RESERVED FOR THE SUPER-RICH.
WHAT'S LEFT FOR US? SCRABBLING FOR FOOD AND DODGING THE PRISON-FACTORY DRAGNETS?
THINGS COULD GET BETTER.

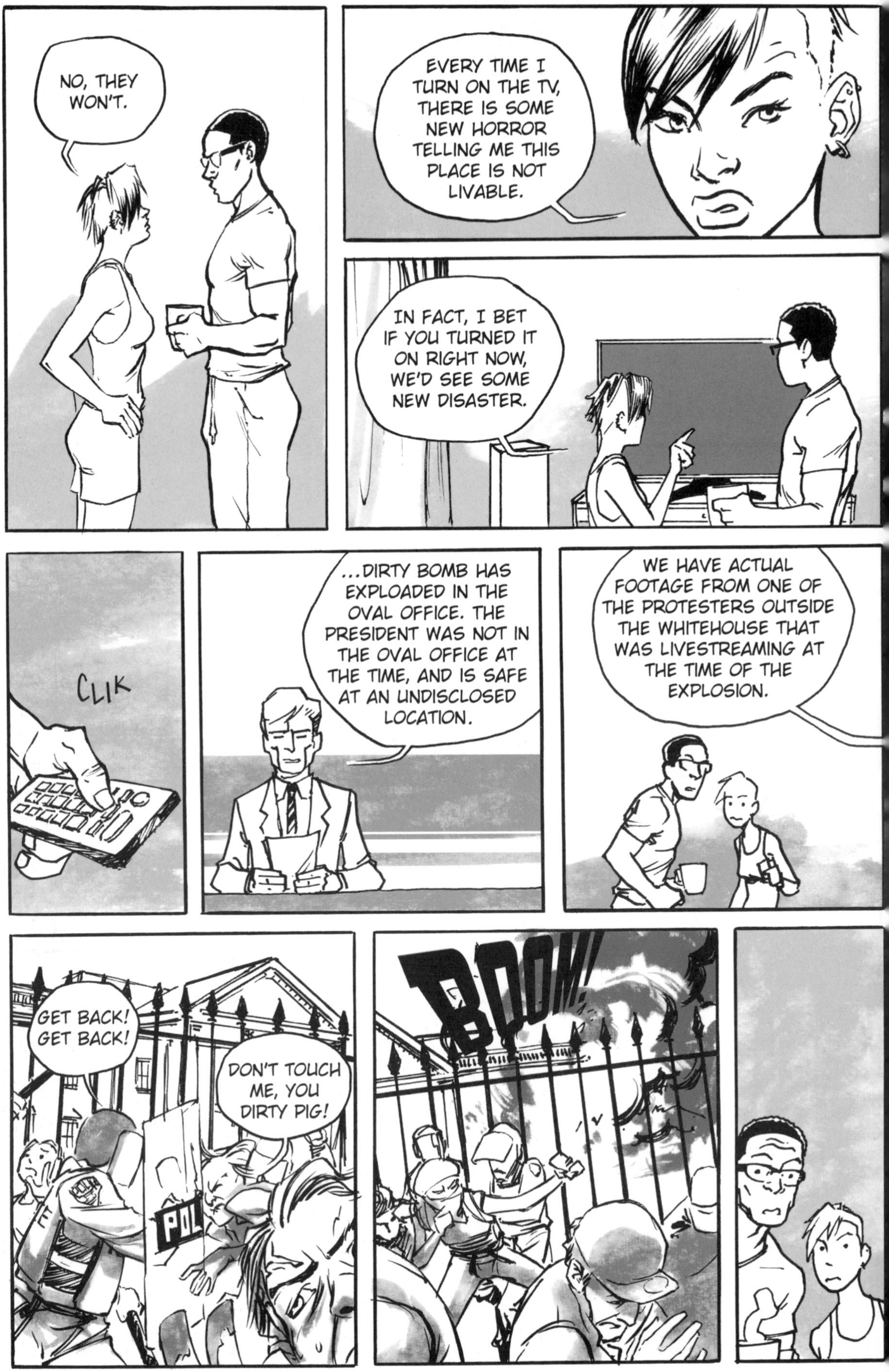
NO, THEY WON'T.
EVERY TIME I TURN ON THE TV, THERE IS SOME NEW HORROR TELLING ME THIS PLACE IS NOT LIVABLE.
IN FACT, I BET IF YOU TURNED IT ON RIGHT NOW, WE'D SEE SOME NEW DISASTER.
CLIK
...DIRTY BOMB HAS EXPLODED IN THE OVAL OFFICE. THE PRESIDENT WAS NOT IN THE OVAL OFFICE AT THE TIME, AND IS SAFE AT AN UNDISCLOSED LOCATION.
WE HAVE ACTUAL FOOTAGE FROM ONE OF THE PROTESTERS OUTSIDE THE WHITEHOUSE THAT WAS LIVESTREAMING AT THE TIME OF THE EXPLOSION.
GET BACK! GET BACK!
DON'T TOUCH ME, YOU DIRTY PIG!
POL
BOOM!

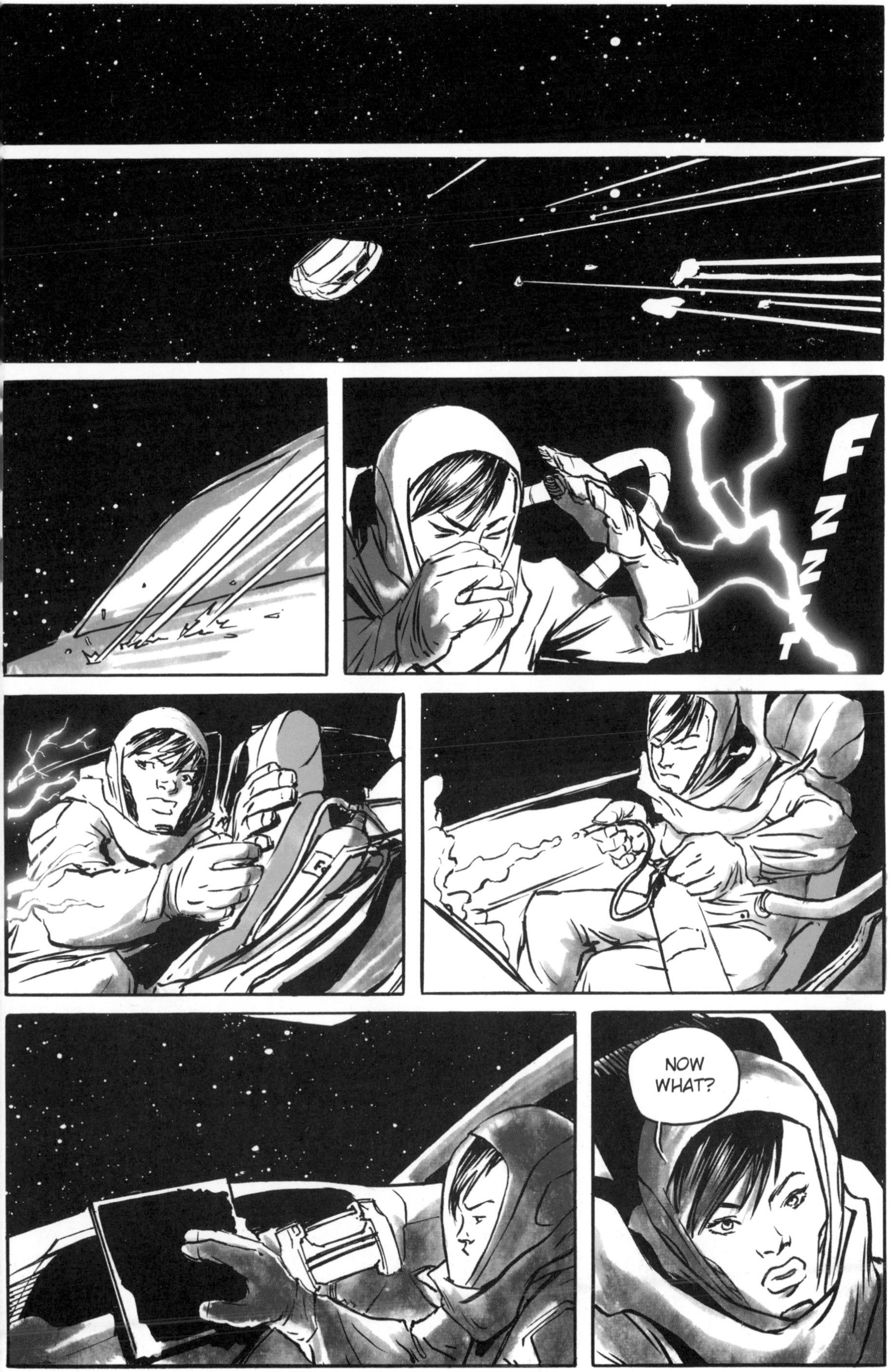
FZZZT
NOW WHAT?

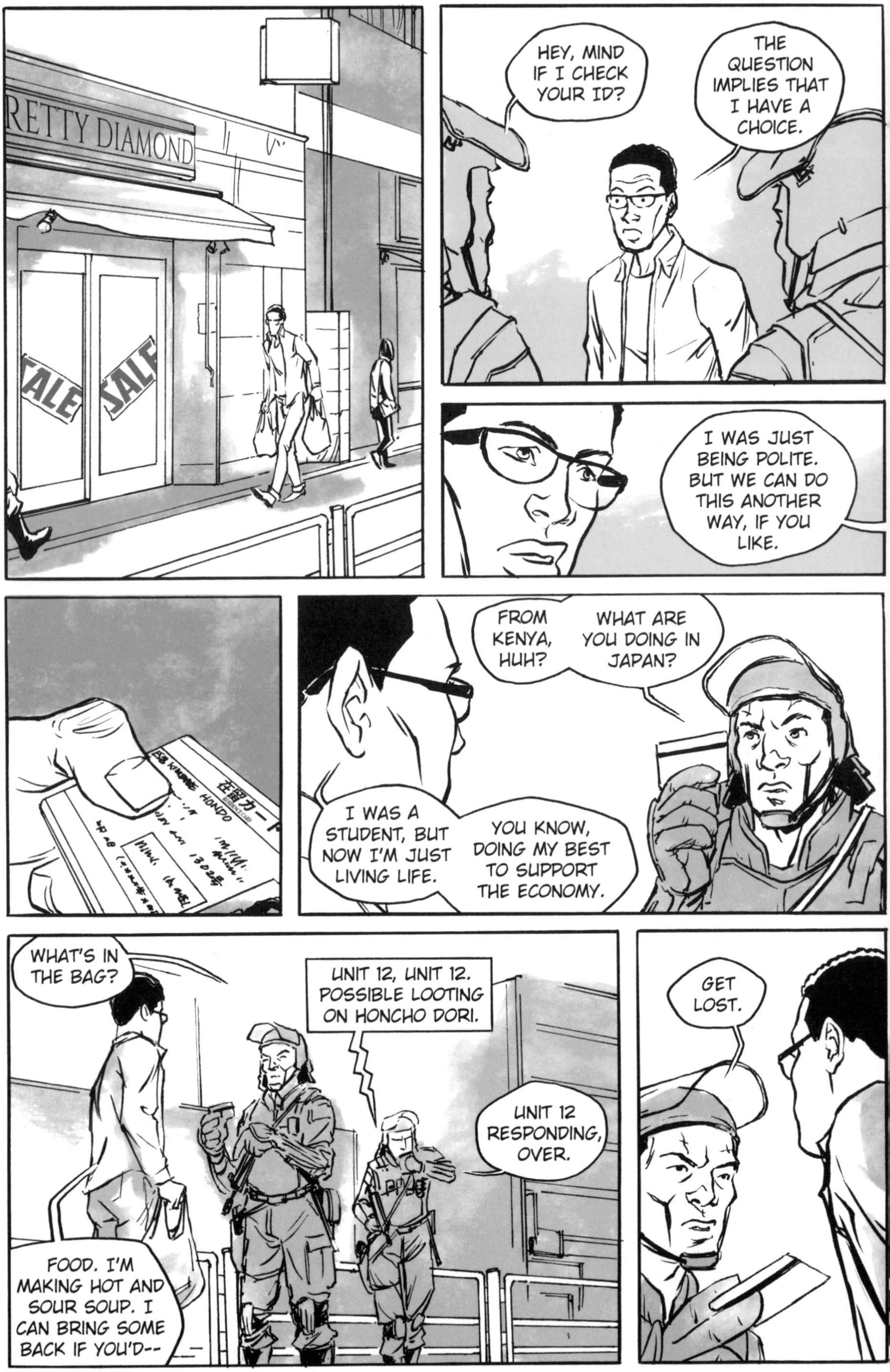
RETTY DIAMOND
SALE
SALE
HEY, MIND IF I CHECK YOUR ID?
THE QUESTION IMPLIES THAT I HAVE A CHOICE.
I WAS JUST BEING POLITE. BUT WE CAN DO THIS ANOTHER WAY, IF YOU LIKE.
HONDO
FROM KENYA, HUH?
WHAT ARE YOU DOING IN JAPAN?
I WAS A STUDENT, BUT NOW I'M JUST LIVING LIFE.
YOU KNOW, DOING MY BEST TO SUPPORT THE ECONOMY.
WHAT'S IN THE BAG?
FOOD. I'M MAKING HOT AND SOUR SOUP. I CAN BRING SOME BACK IF YOU'D--
UNIT 12, UNIT 12. POSSIBLE LOOTING ON HONCHO DORI.
UNIT 12 RESPONDING, OVER.
GET LOST.

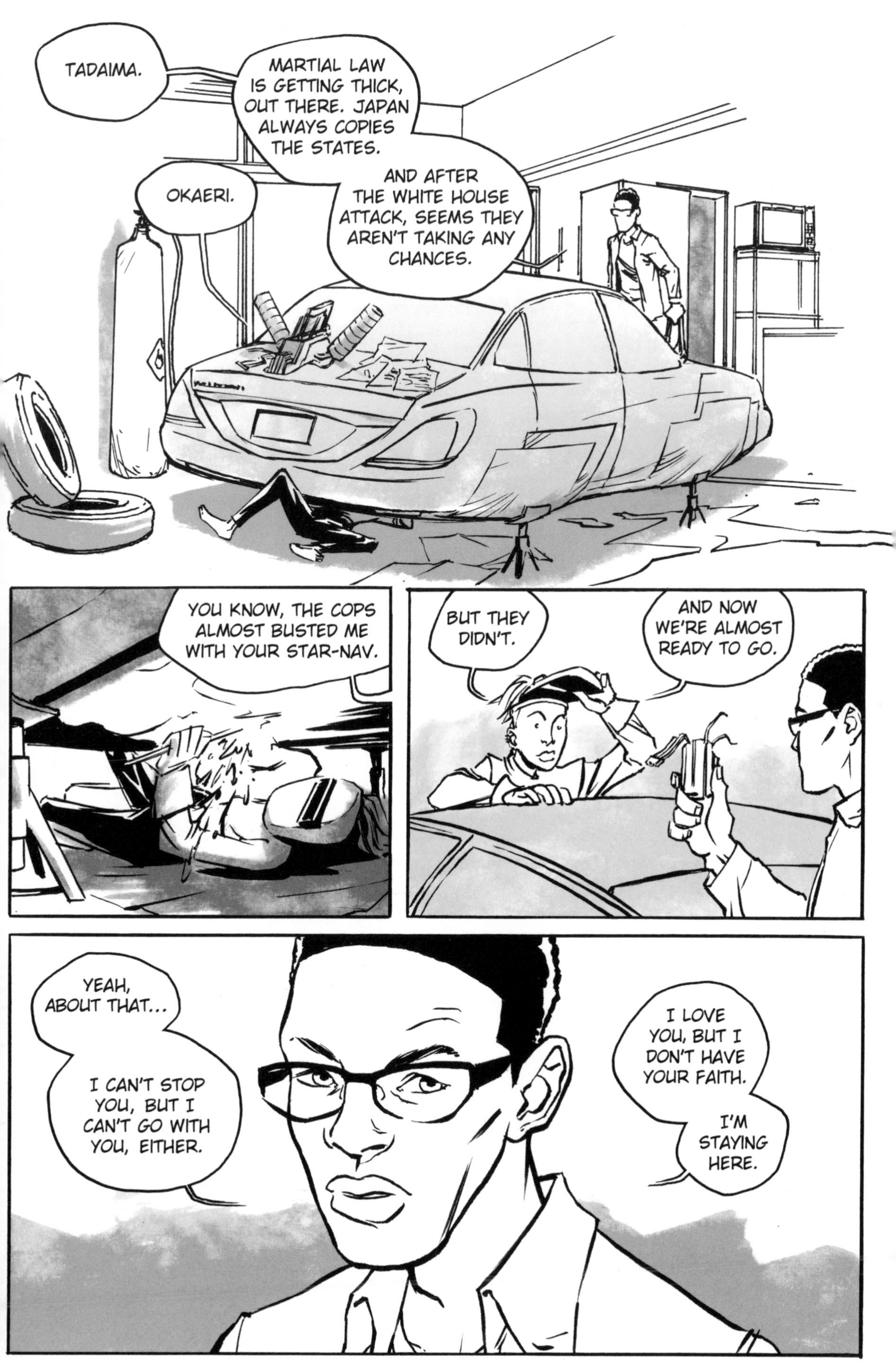
TADAIMA.
MARTIAL LAW IS GETTING THICK, OUT THERE. JAPAN ALWAYS COPIES THE STATES.
OKAERI.
AND AFTER THE WHITE HOUSE ATTACK, SEEMS THEY AREN'T TAKING ANY CHANCES.
YOU KNOW, THE COPS ALMOST BUSTED ME WITH YOUR STAR-NAV.
BUT THEY DIDN'T.
AND NOW WE'RE ALMOST READY TO GO.
YEAH, ABOUT THAT...
I CAN'T STOP YOU, BUT I CAN'T GO WITH YOU, EITHER.
I LOVE YOU, BUT I DON'T HAVE YOUR FAITH.
I'M STAYING HERE.

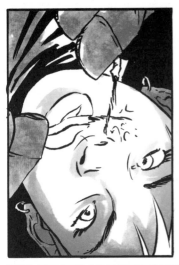

YES!

OK, ACCORDING TO THE MAP...

I'VE GOT TO MAKE ABOUT FIVE MORE JUMPS. BIG JUMPS AT THAT.

AND MY POWER RESERVES CAN MAKE...

THREE JUMPS.

THREE VERY BLIND JUMPS.

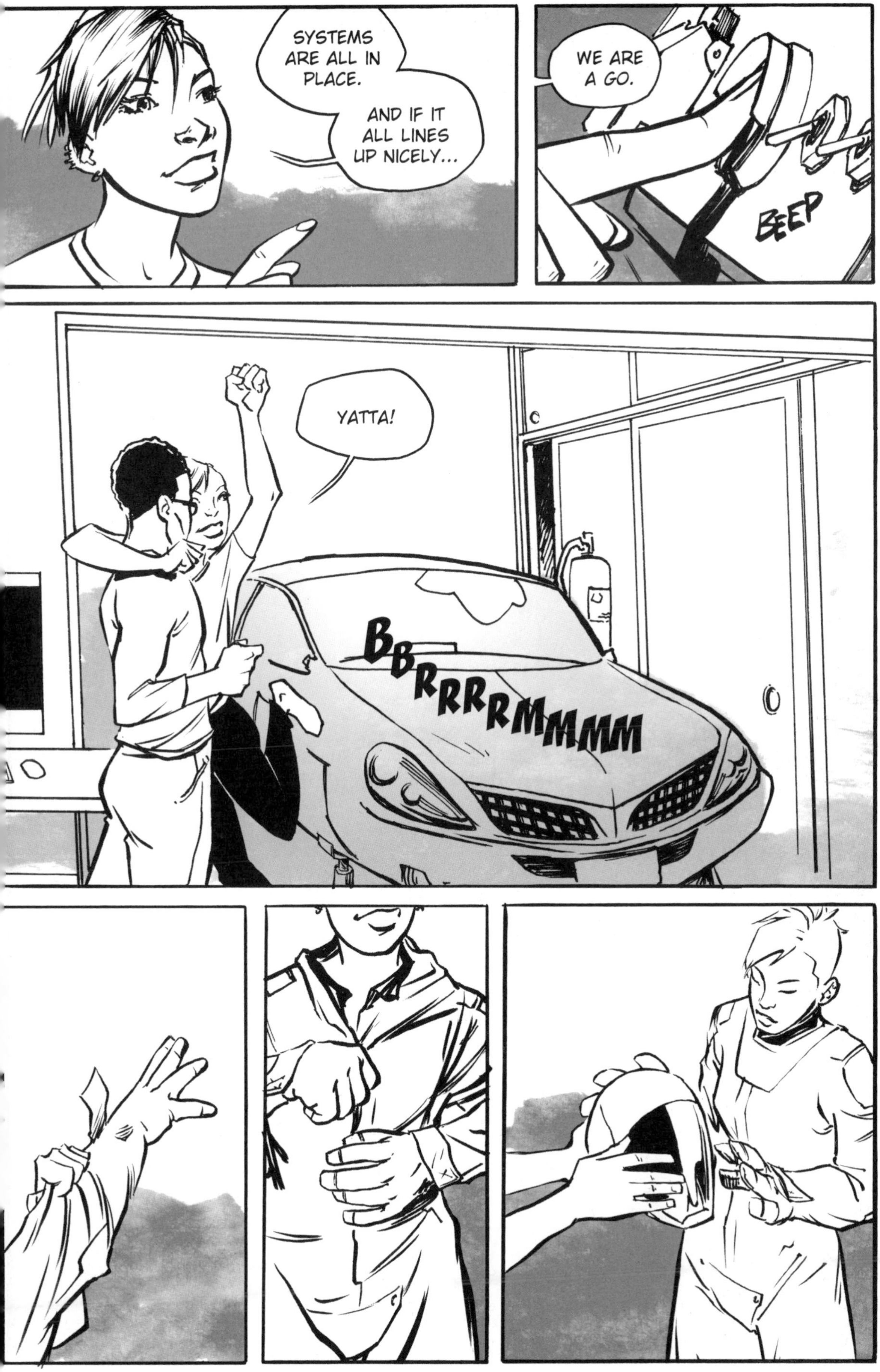
SYSTEMS ARE ALL IN PLACE.
AND IF IT ALL LINES UP NICELY...
WE ARE A GO.
BEEP
YATTA!
BBRRRRRMMMMM

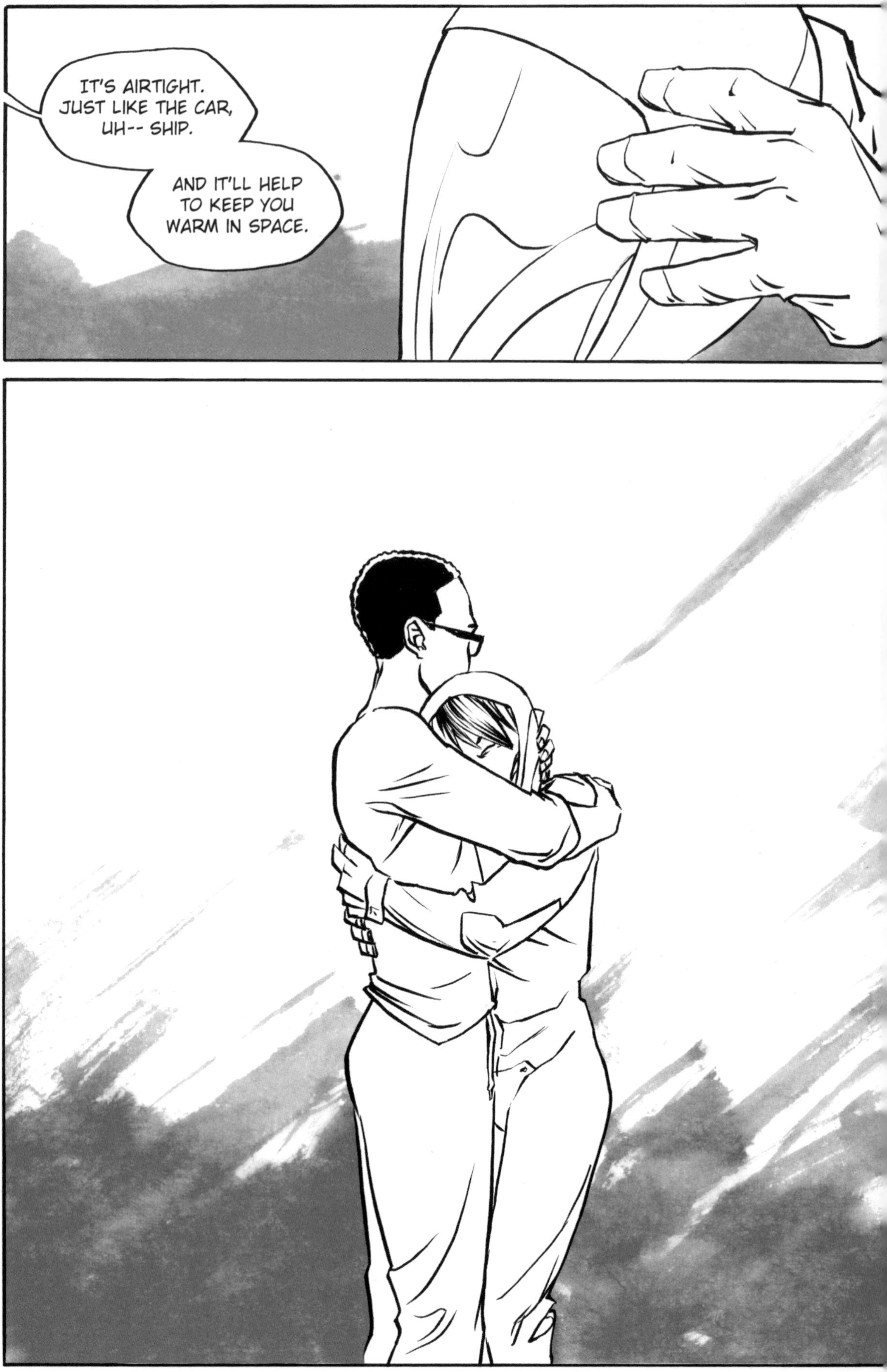
IT'S AIRTIGHT. JUST LIKE THE CAR, UH-- SHIP.
AND IT'LL HELP TO KEEP YOU WARM IN SPACE.

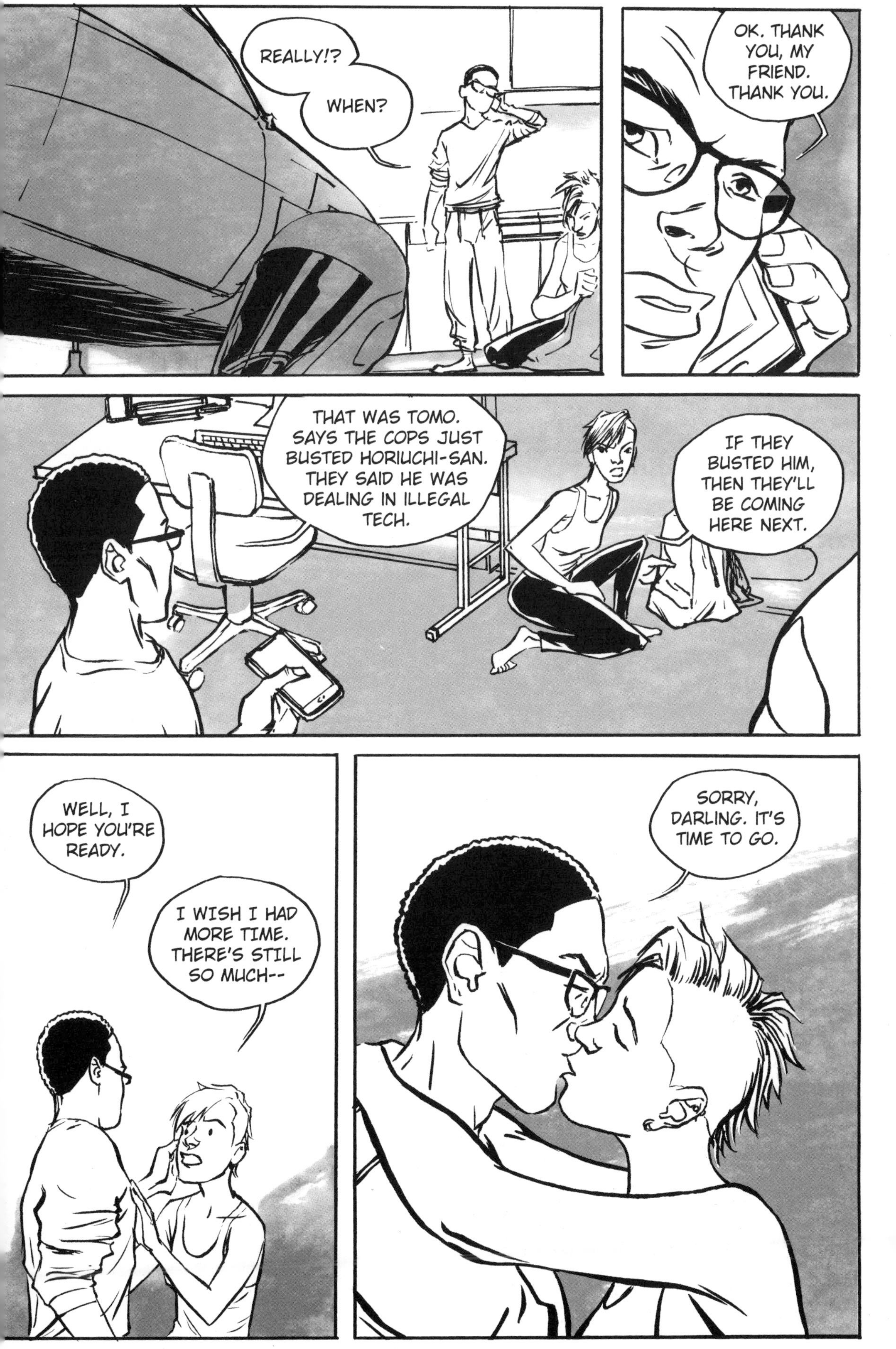
REALLY!?
WHEN?
OK. THANK YOU, MY FRIEND. THANK YOU.
THAT WAS TOMO. SAYS THE COPS JUST BUSTED HORIUCHI-SAN. THEY SAID HE WAS DEALING IN ILLEGAL TECH.
IF THEY BUSTED HIM, THEN THEY'LL BE COMING HERE NEXT.
WELL, I HOPE YOU'RE READY.
I WISH I HAD MORE TIME. THERE'S STILL SO MUCH--
SORRY, DARLING. IT'S TIME TO GO.

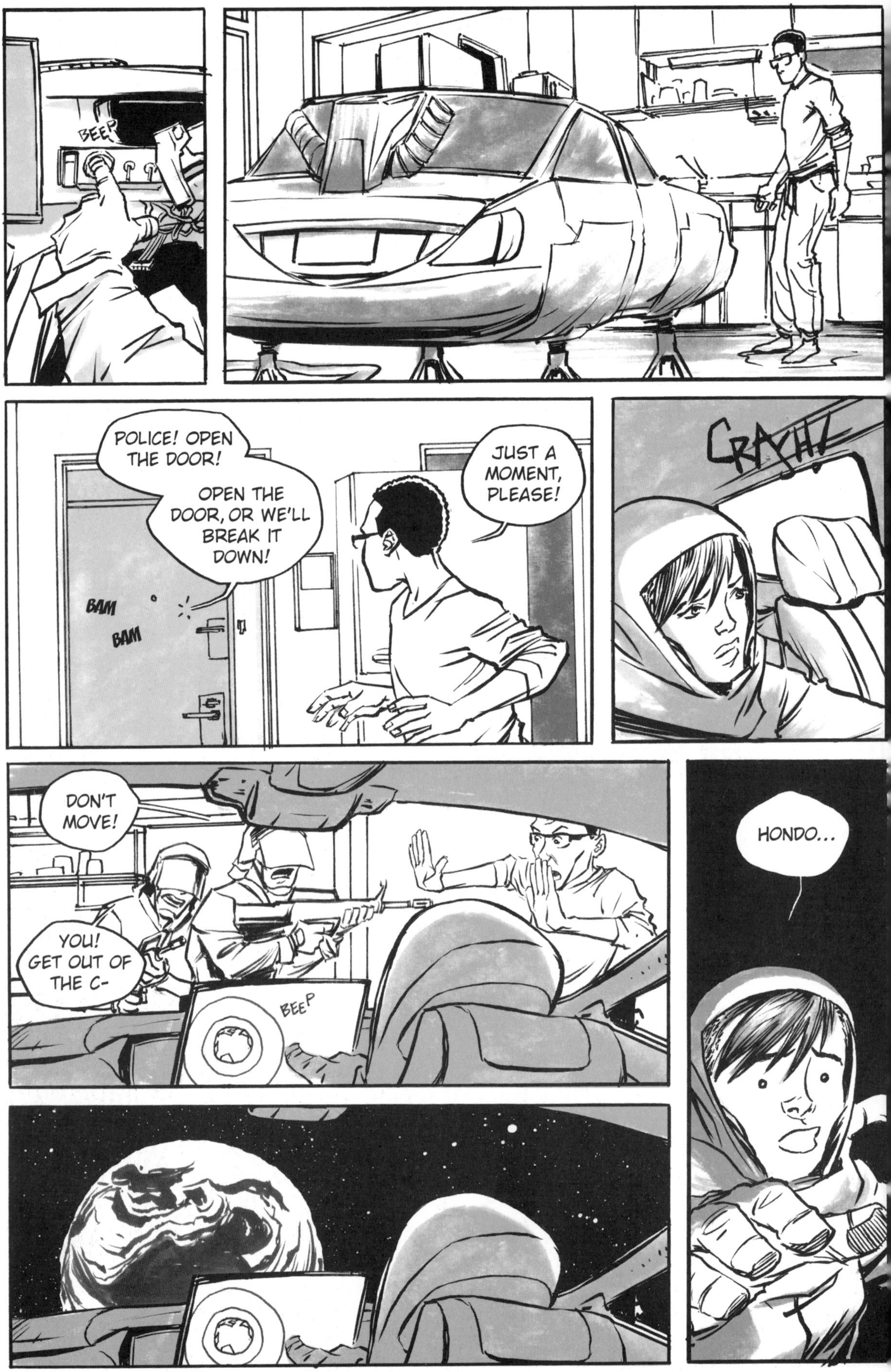
BEEP
POLICE! OPEN THE DOOR!
OPEN THE DOOR, OR WE'LL BREAK IT DOWN!
BAM
BAM
JUST A MOMENT, PLEASE!
CRASH!
DON'T MOVE!
YOU! GET OUT OF THE C-
BEEP
HONDO...

OK. ONE JUMP TO THE SYSTEM AND ONE JUMP TO THE PLANET.

THEN THE LAST JUMP TO LAND.

AND ONE LAST COOKIE TO SEE ME THROUGH.

HERE GOES NOTHING!

NO!

THE WARP-CORE!

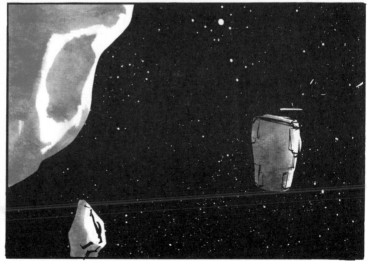

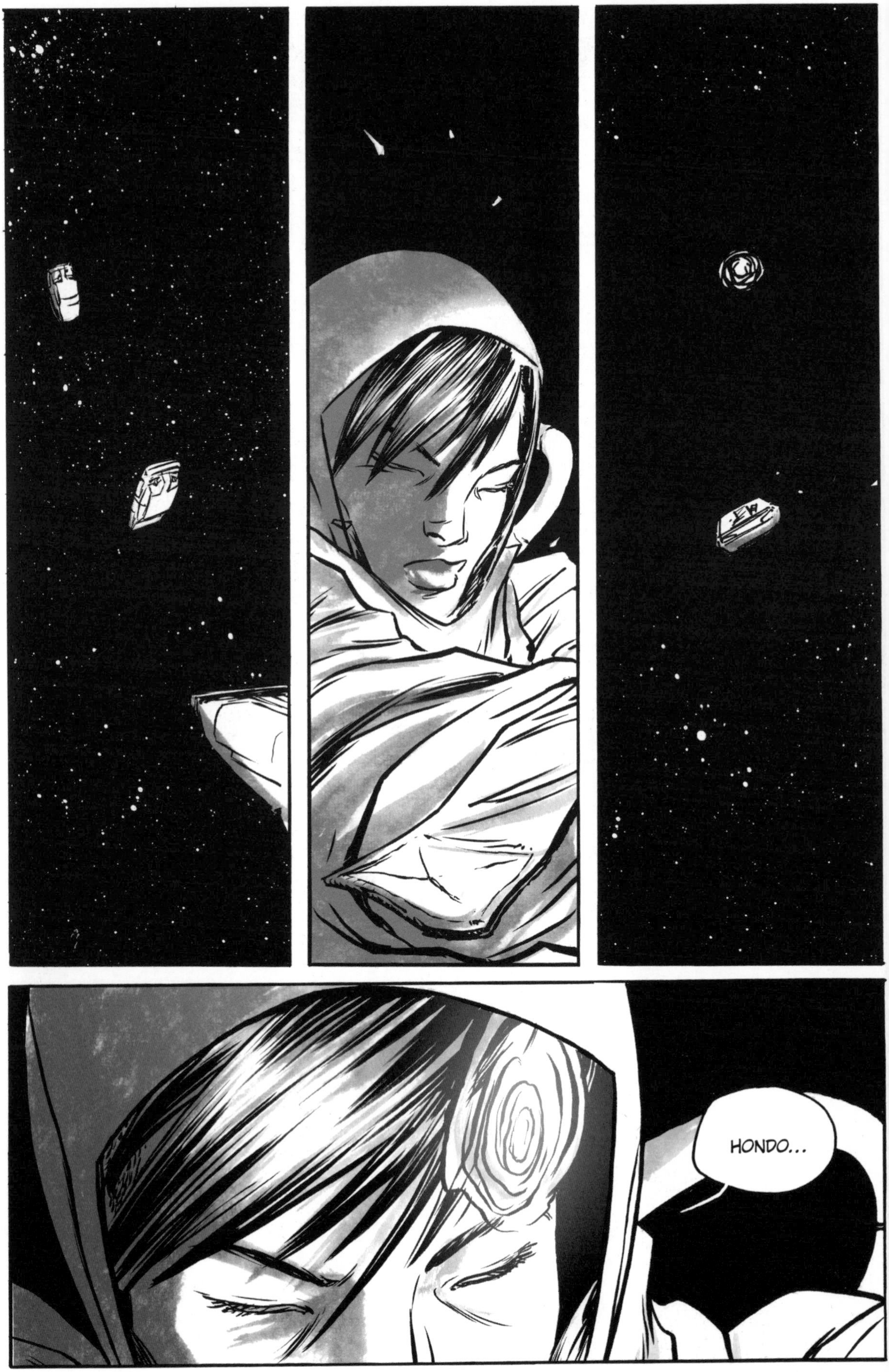
HONDO...

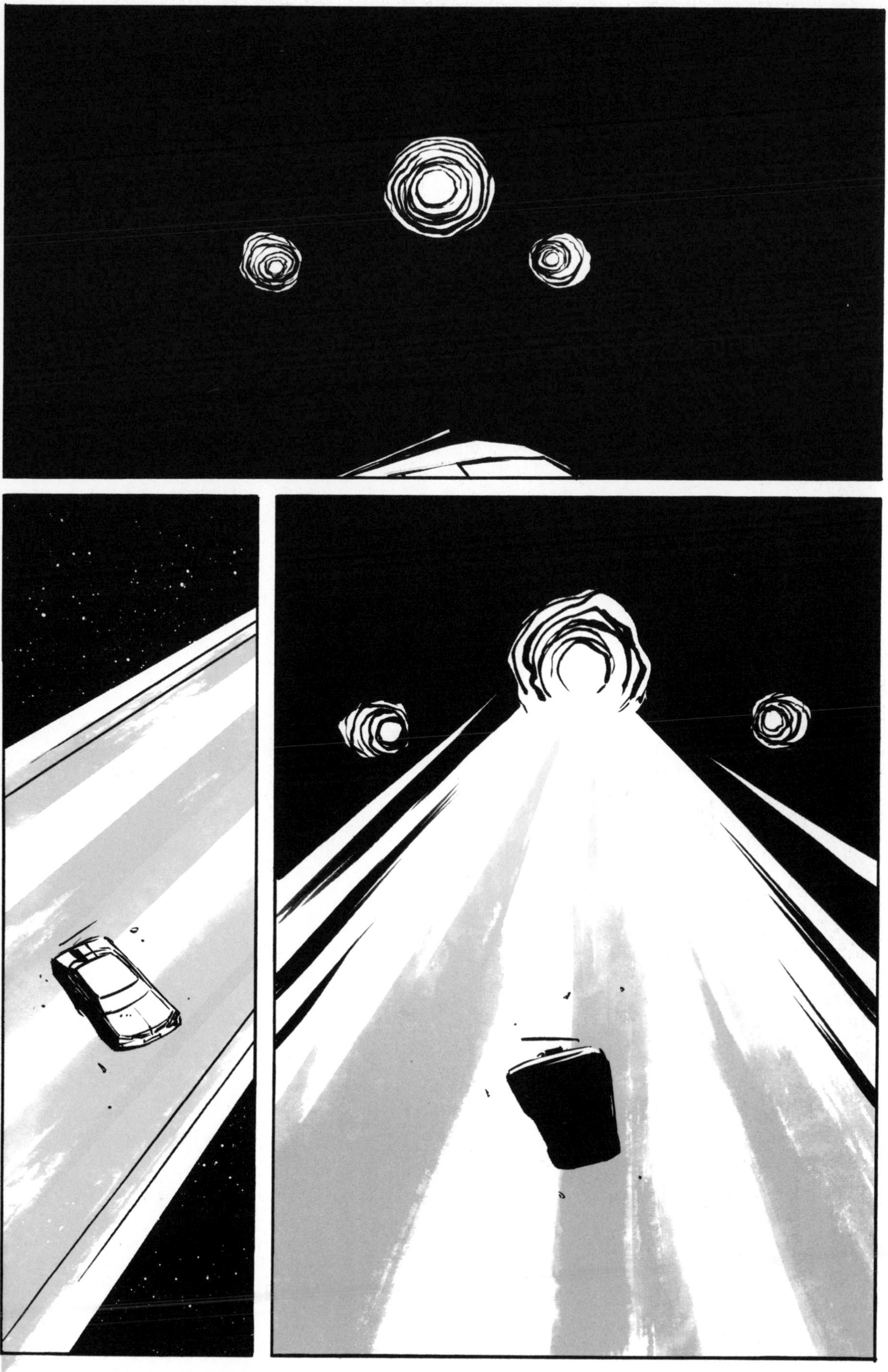

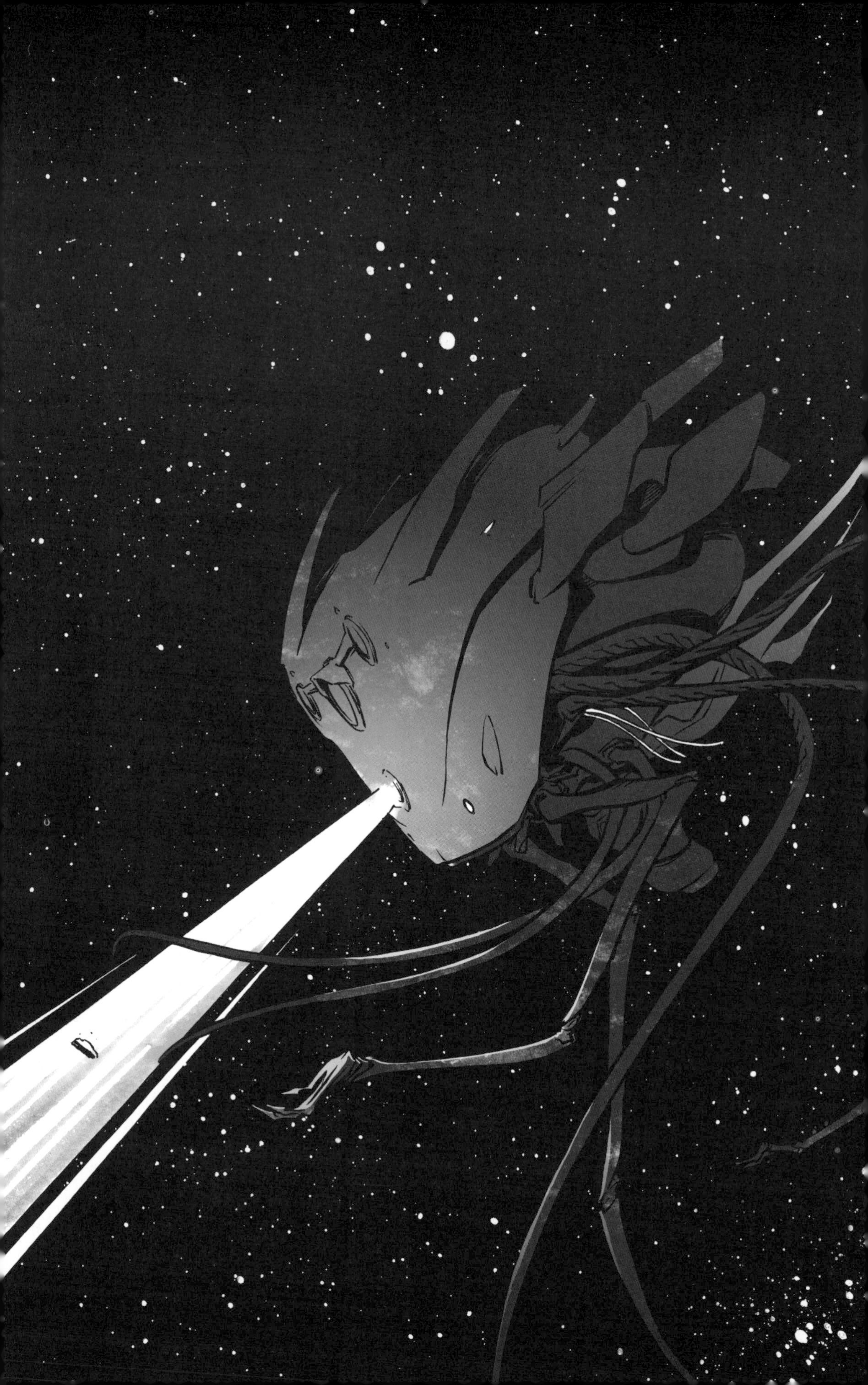

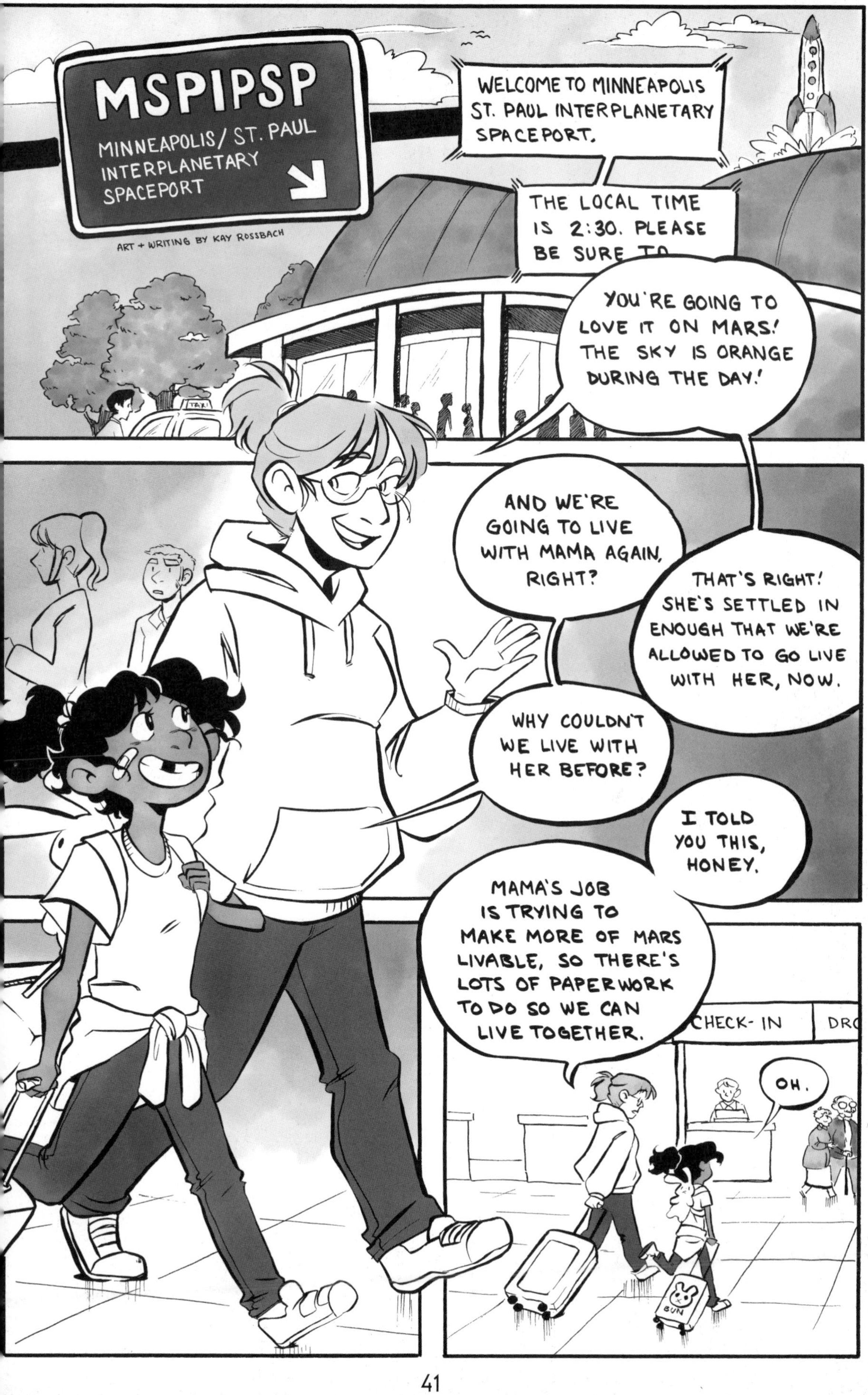
MSPIPSP
MINNEAPOLIS/ ST. PAUL INTERPLANETARY SPACEPORT
ART + WRITING BY KAY ROSSBACH
WELCOME TO MINNEAPOLIS ST. PAUL INTERPLANETARY SPACEPORT.
THE LOCAL TIME IS 2:30. PLEASE BE SURE
TAXI
YOU'RE GOING TO LOVE IT ON MARS! THE SKY IS ORANGE DURING THE DAY!
AND WE'RE GOING TO LIVE WITH MAMA AGAIN, RIGHT?
THAT'S RIGHT! SHE'S SETTLED IN ENOUGH THAT WE'RE ALLOWED TO GO LIVE WITH HER, NOW.
WHY COULDN'T WE LIVE WITH HER BEFORE?
I TOLD YOU THIS, HONEY.
MAMA'S JOB IS TRYING TO MAKE MORE OF MARS LIVABLE, SO THERE'S LOTS OF PAPERWORK TO DO SO WE CAN LIVE TOGETHER.
CHECK- IN
OH.
BUN

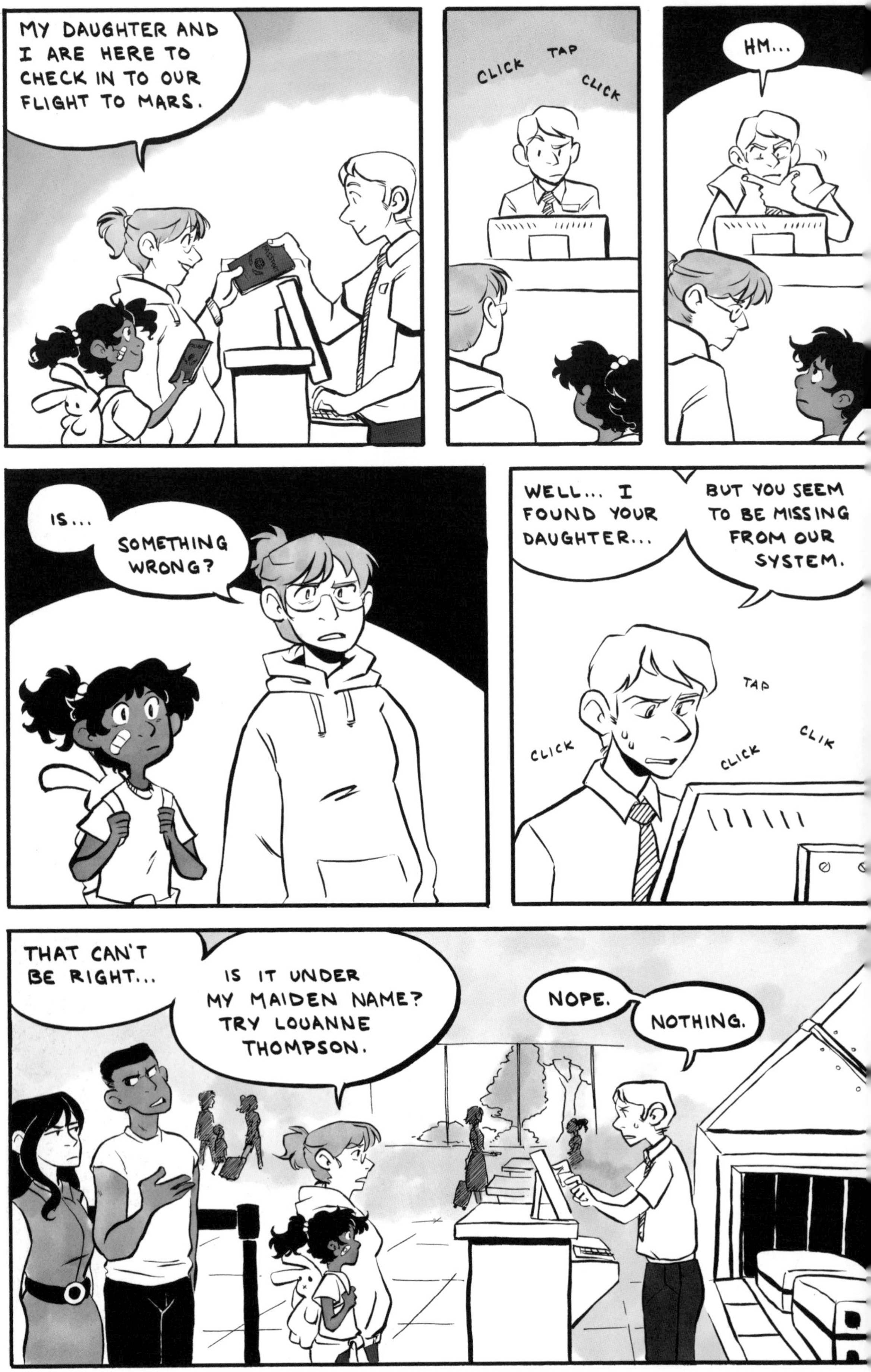
MY DAUGHTER AND I ARE HERE TO CHECK IN TO OUR FLIGHT TO MARS.
CLICK
TAP
CLICK
HM...
IS...
SOMETHING WRONG?
WELL... I FOUND YOUR DAUGHTER...
BUT YOU SEEM TO BE MISSING FROM OUR SYSTEM.
TAP
CLICK
CLIK
CLICK
THAT CAN'T BE RIGHT...
IS IT UNDER MY MAIDEN NAME? TRY LOUANNE THOMPSON.
NOPE.
NOTHING.

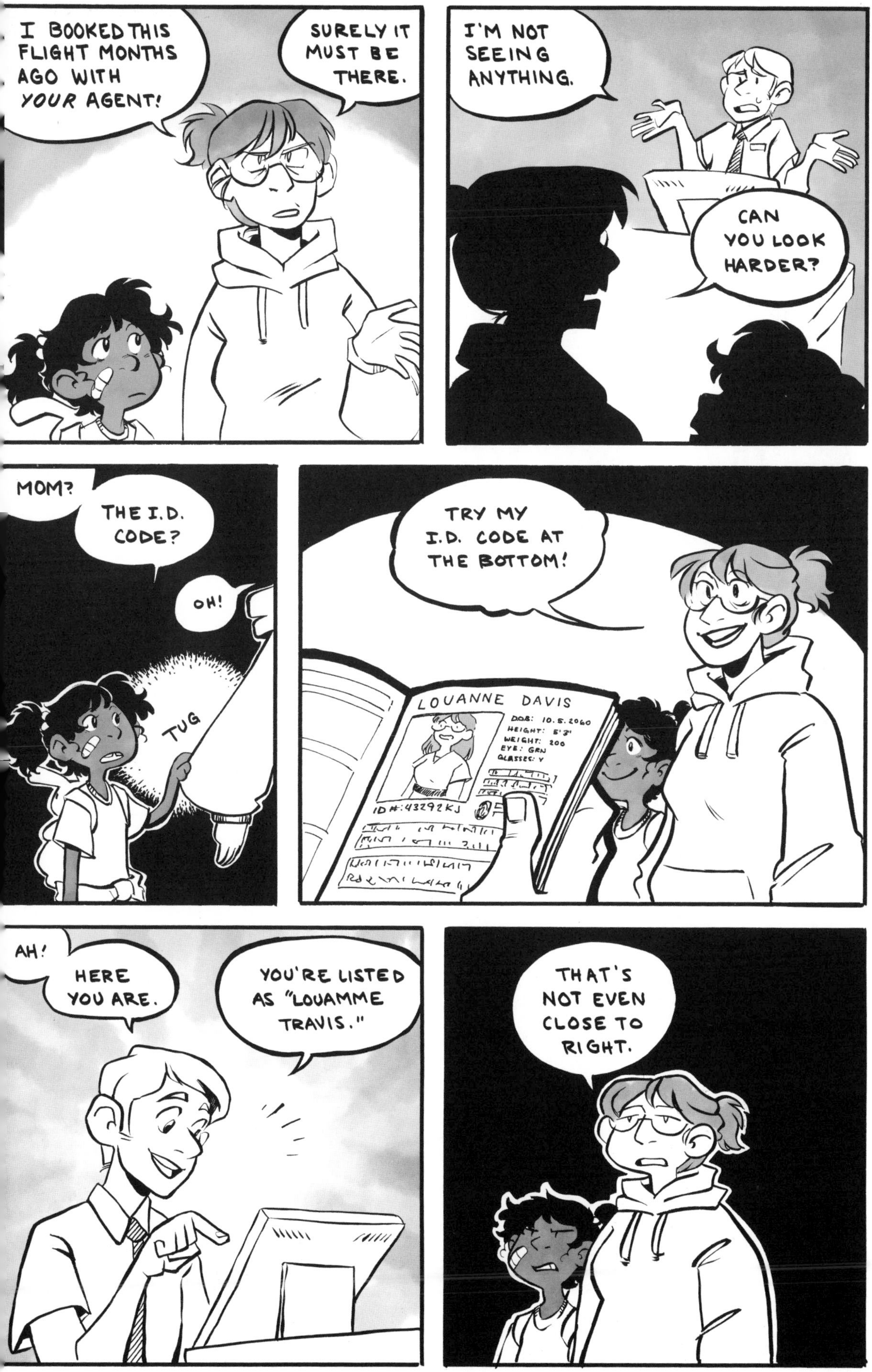
I BOOKED THIS FLIGHT MONTHS AGO WITH *YOUR* AGENT!
SURELY IT MUST BE THERE.
I'M NOT SEEING ANYTHING.
CAN YOU LOOK HARDER?
MOM?
THE I.D. CODE?
OH!
TUG
TRY MY I.D. CODE AT THE BOTTOM!
LOUANNE DAVIS
DOB: 10.5.2060
HEIGHT: 5'3"
WEIGHT: 200
EYE: GRN
GLASSES: Y
ID#:43292KJ
AH!
HERE YOU ARE.
YOU'RE LISTED AS "LOUAMME TRAVIS."
THAT'S NOT EVEN CLOSE TO RIGHT.

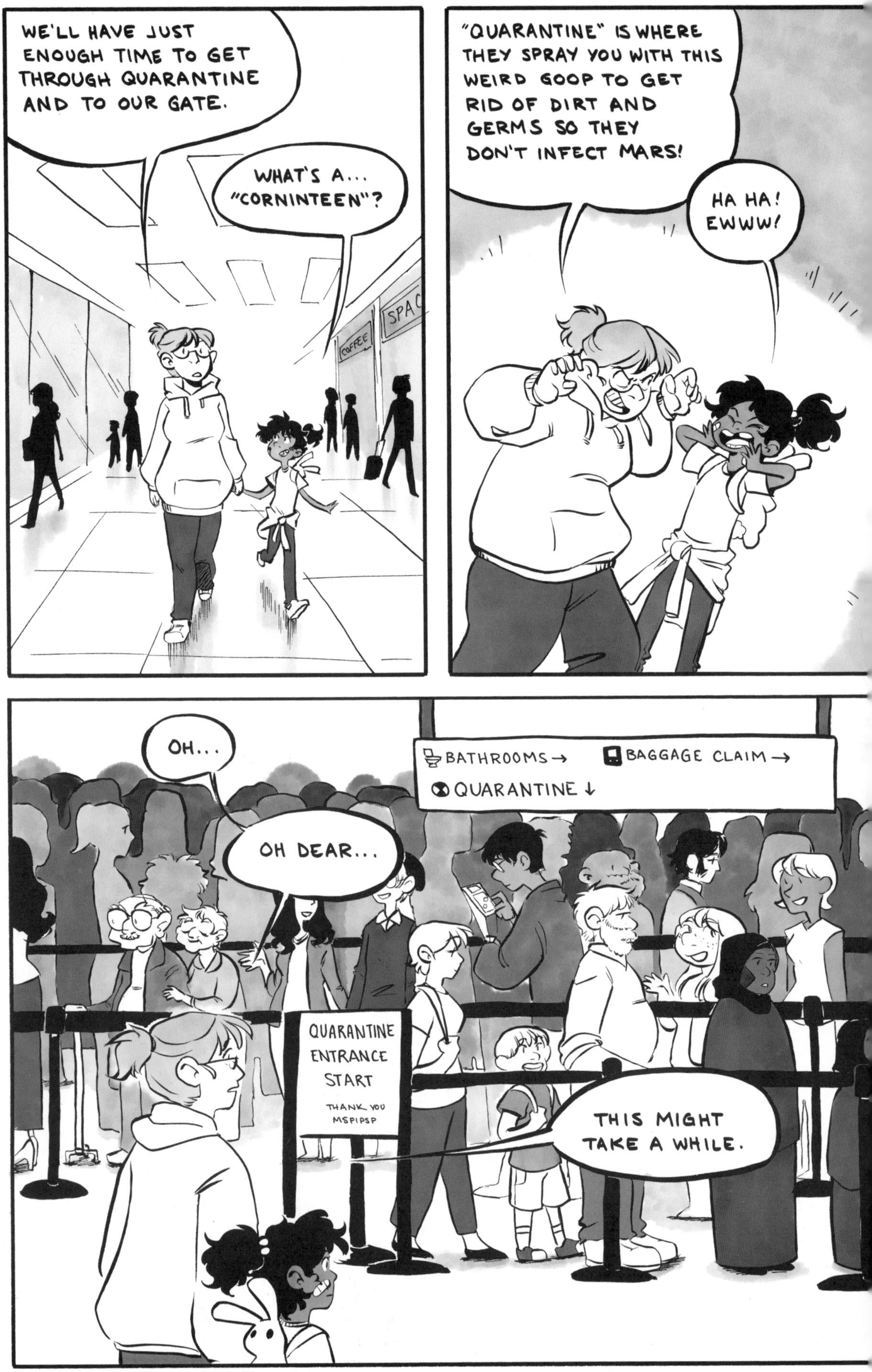
WE'LL HAVE JUST ENOUGH TIME TO GET THROUGH QUARANTINE AND TO OUR GATE.
WHAT'S A... "CORNINTEEN"?
COFFEE
"QUARANTINE" IS WHERE THEY SPRAY YOU WITH THIS WEIRD GOOP TO GET RID OF DIRT AND GERMS SO THEY DON'T INFECT MARS!
HA HA! EWWW!
OH...
BATHROOMS →
BAGGAGE CLAIM →
QUARANTINE ↓
OH DEAR...
QUARANTINE ENTRANCE START
THANK YOU
MSPIPSP
THIS MIGHT TAKE A WHILE.

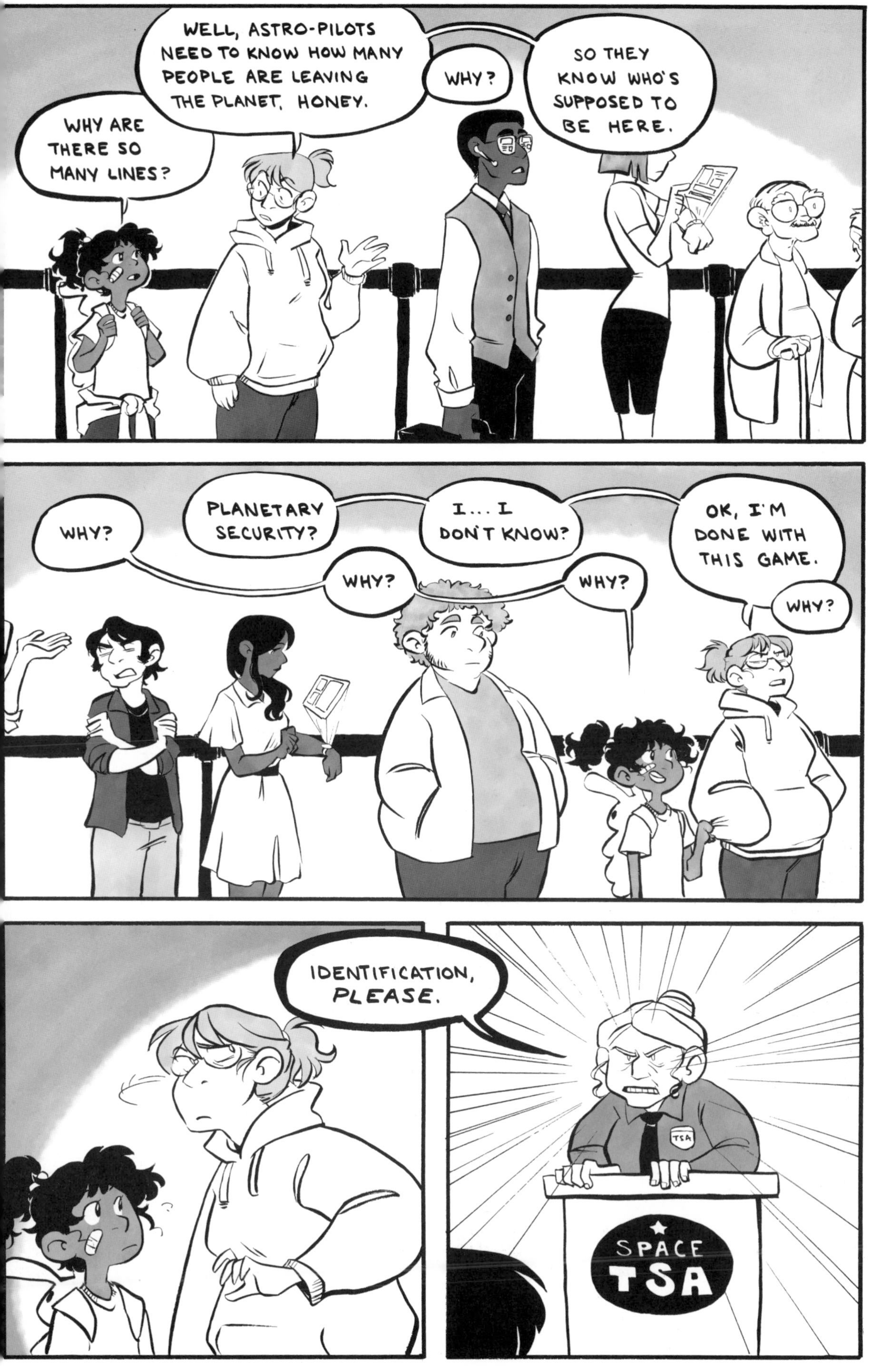
WHY ARE THERE SO MANY LINES?
WELL, ASTRO-PILOTS NEED TO KNOW HOW MANY PEOPLE ARE LEAVING THE PLANET, HONEY.
WHY?
SO THEY KNOW WHO'S SUPPOSED TO BE HERE.
WHY?
PLANETARY SECURITY?
WHY?
I... I DON'T KNOW?
WHY?
OK, I'M DONE WITH THIS GAME.
WHY?
IDENTIFICATION, PLEASE.
TSA
SPACE TSA

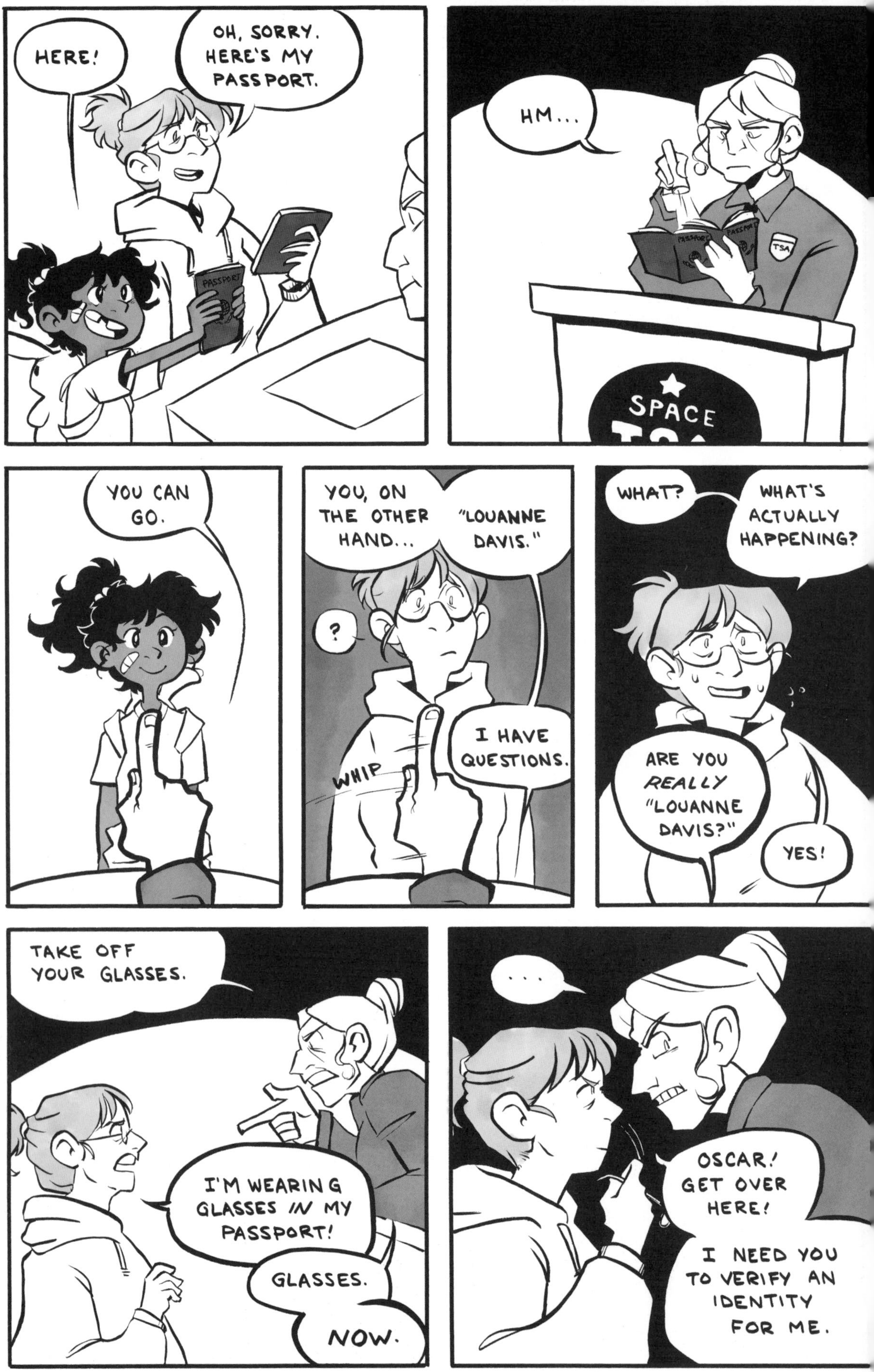
HERE!
OH, SORRY. HERE'S MY PASSPORT.
PASSPORT
HM...
PASSPORT
PASSPORT
TSA
SPACE
YOU CAN GO.
YOU, ON THE OTHER HAND...
"LOUANNE DAVIS."
?
I HAVE QUESTIONS.
WHIP
WHAT?
WHAT'S ACTUALLY HAPPENING?
ARE YOU *REALLY* "LOUANNE DAVIS?"
YES!
TAKE OFF YOUR GLASSES.
I'M WEARING GLASSES *IN* MY PASSPORT!
GLASSES.
NOW.
...
OSCAR! GET OVER HERE!
I NEED YOU TO VERIFY AN IDENTITY FOR ME.

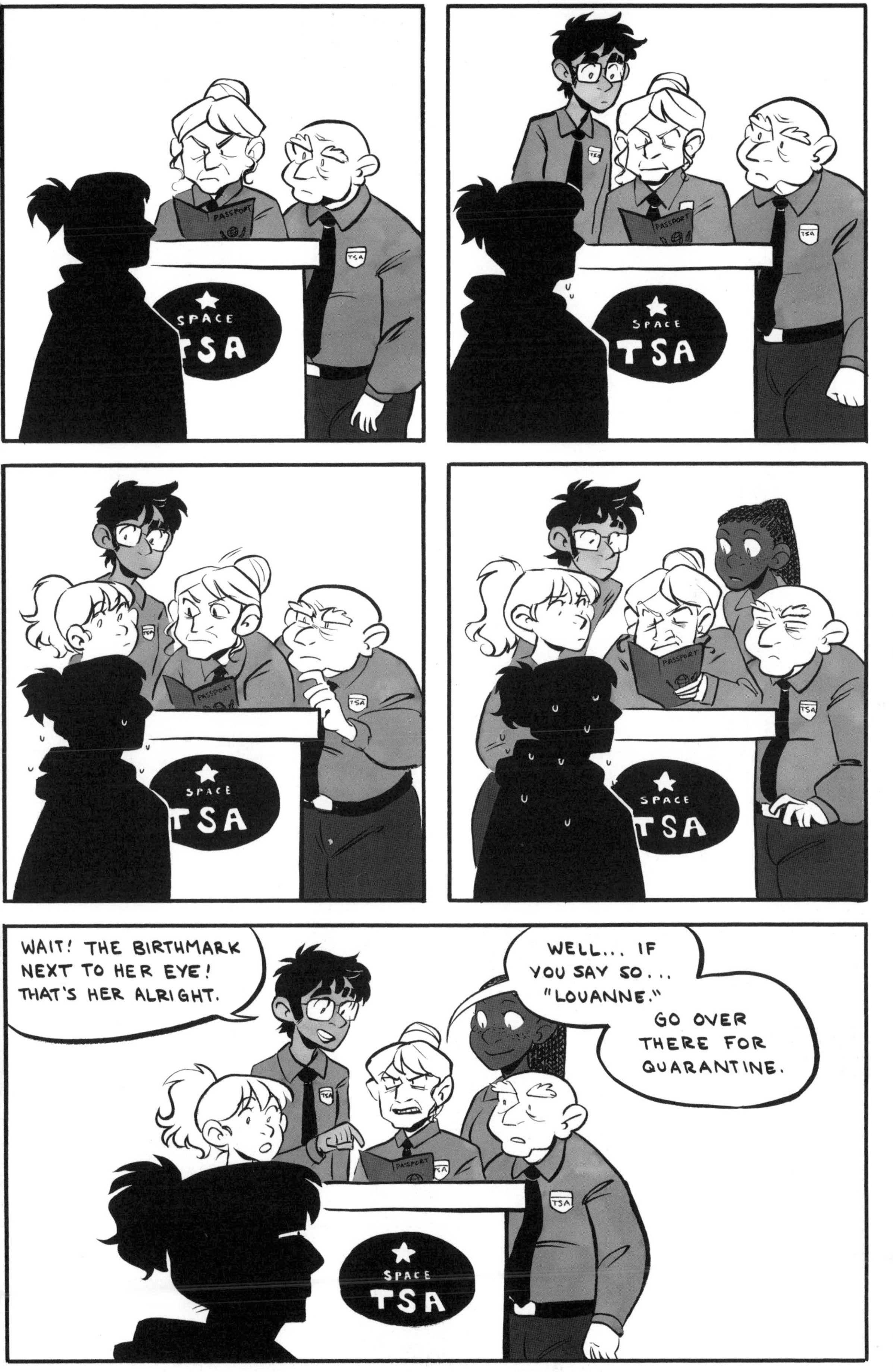
SPACE TSA
WAIT! THE BIRTHMARK NEXT TO HER EYE! THAT'S HER ALRIGHT.
WELL... IF YOU SAY SO... "LOUANNE."
GO OVER THERE FOR QUARANTINE.

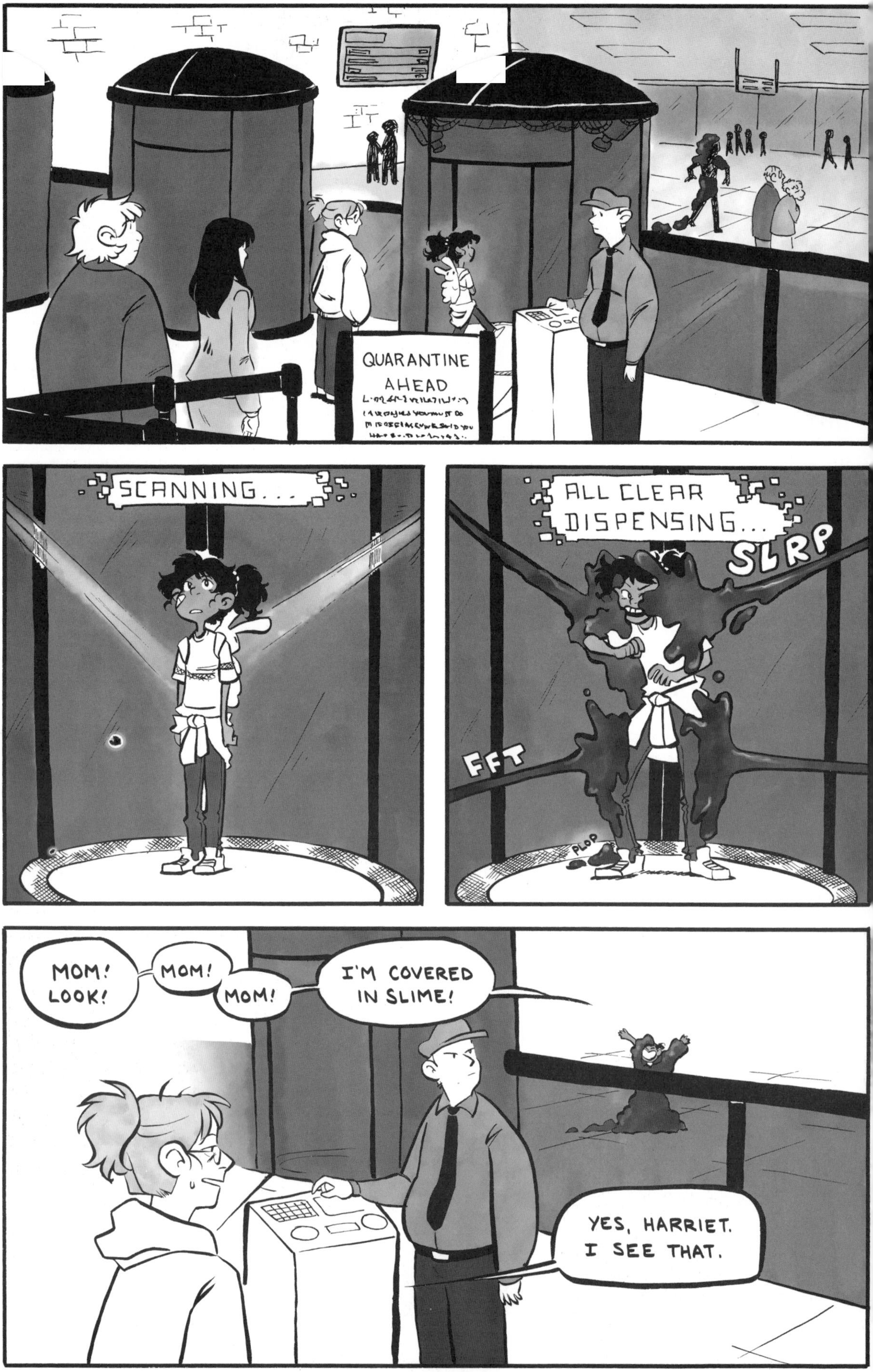
QUARANTINE AHEAD
SCANNING...
ALL CLEAR DISPENSING...
SLRP
FFT
PLOP
MOM! LOOK!
MOM!
MOM!
I'M COVERED IN SLIME!
YES, HARRIET. I SEE THAT.

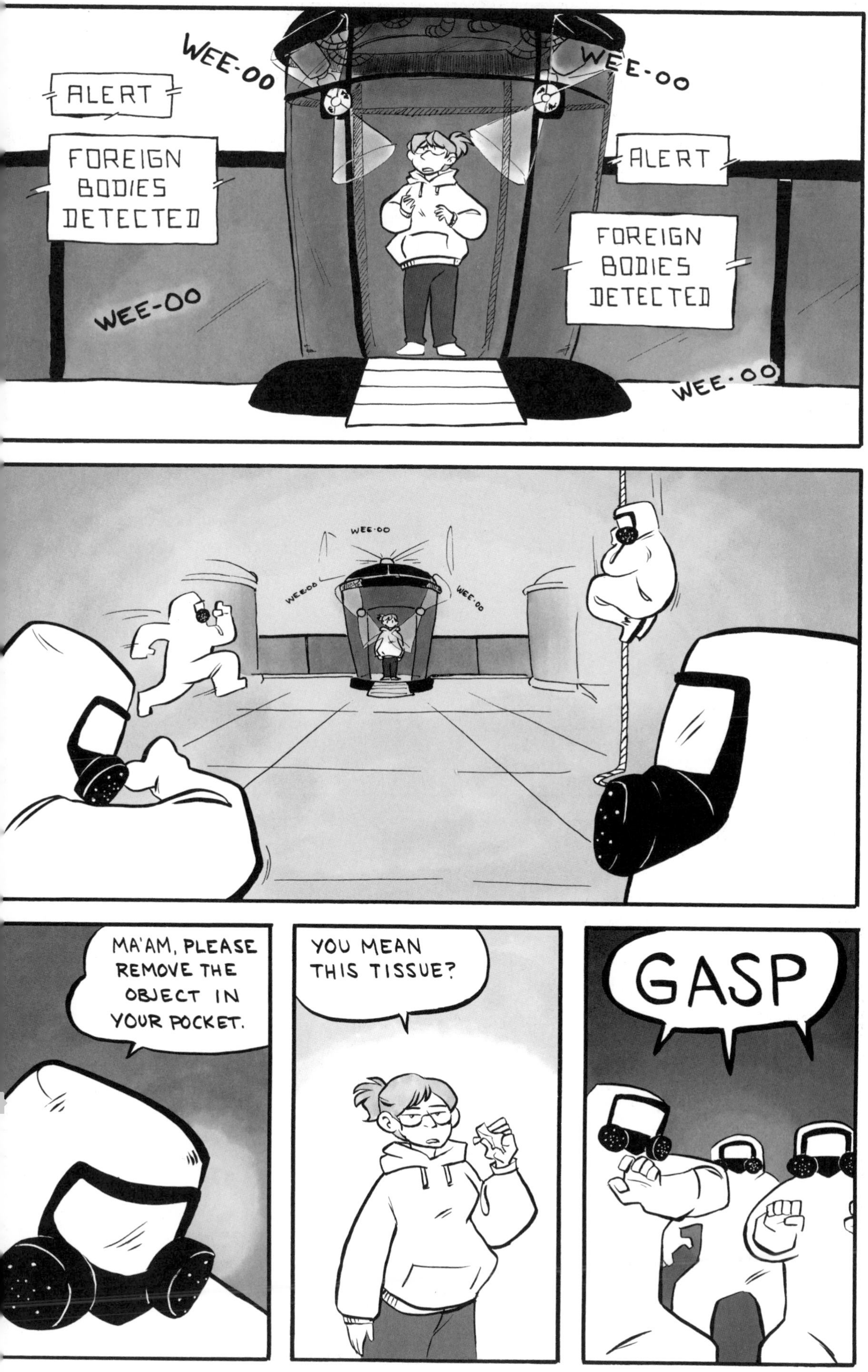
WEE-OO
ALERT
FOREIGN BODIES DETECTED
WEE-OO
ALERT
FOREIGN BODIES DETECTED
WEE-OO
WEE-OO
WEE-OO
WEE-OO
WEE-OO
MA'AM, PLEASE REMOVE THE OBJECT IN YOUR POCKET.
YOU MEAN THIS TISSUE?
GASP

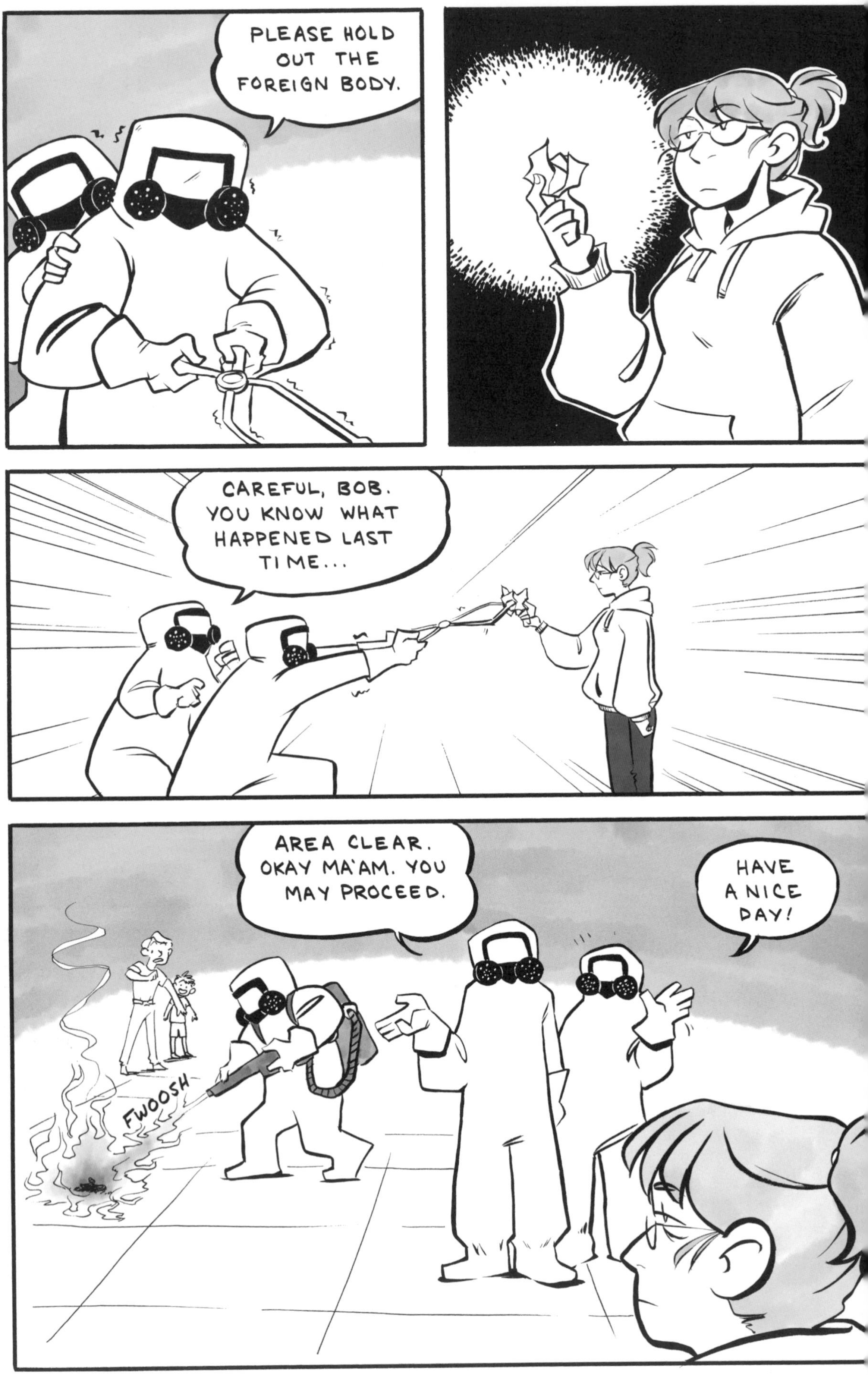
PLEASE HOLD OUT THE FOREIGN BODY.
CAREFUL, BOB. YOU KNOW WHAT HAPPENED LAST TIME...
FWOOSH
AREA CLEAR. OKAY MA'AM. YOU MAY PROCEED.
HAVE A NICE DAY!

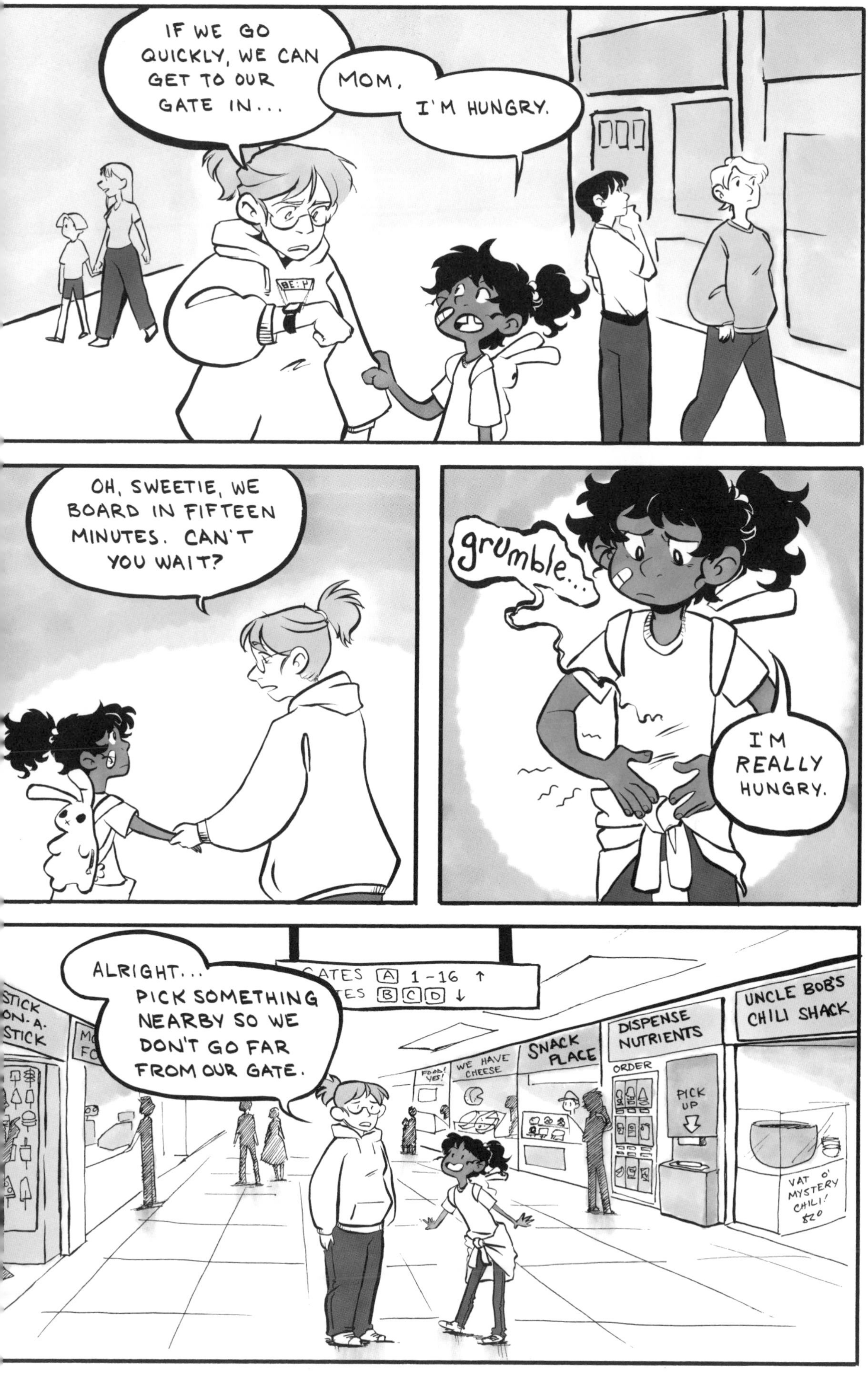
IF WE GO QUICKLY, WE CAN GET TO OUR GATE IN...
MOM,
I'M HUNGRY.
OH, SWEETIE, WE BOARD IN FIFTEEN MINUTES. CAN'T YOU WAIT?
grumble...
I'M REALLY HUNGRY.
ALRIGHT... PICK SOMETHING NEARBY SO WE DON'T GO FAR FROM OUR GATE.
GATES A 1-16 ↑
TES B C D ↓
STICK ON-A-STICK
UNCLE BOB'S CHILI SHACK
DISPENSE NUTRIENTS
ORDER
PICK UP
SNACK PLACE
WE HAVE CHEESE
FOOD! YES!
VAT O' MYSTERY CHILI! $20

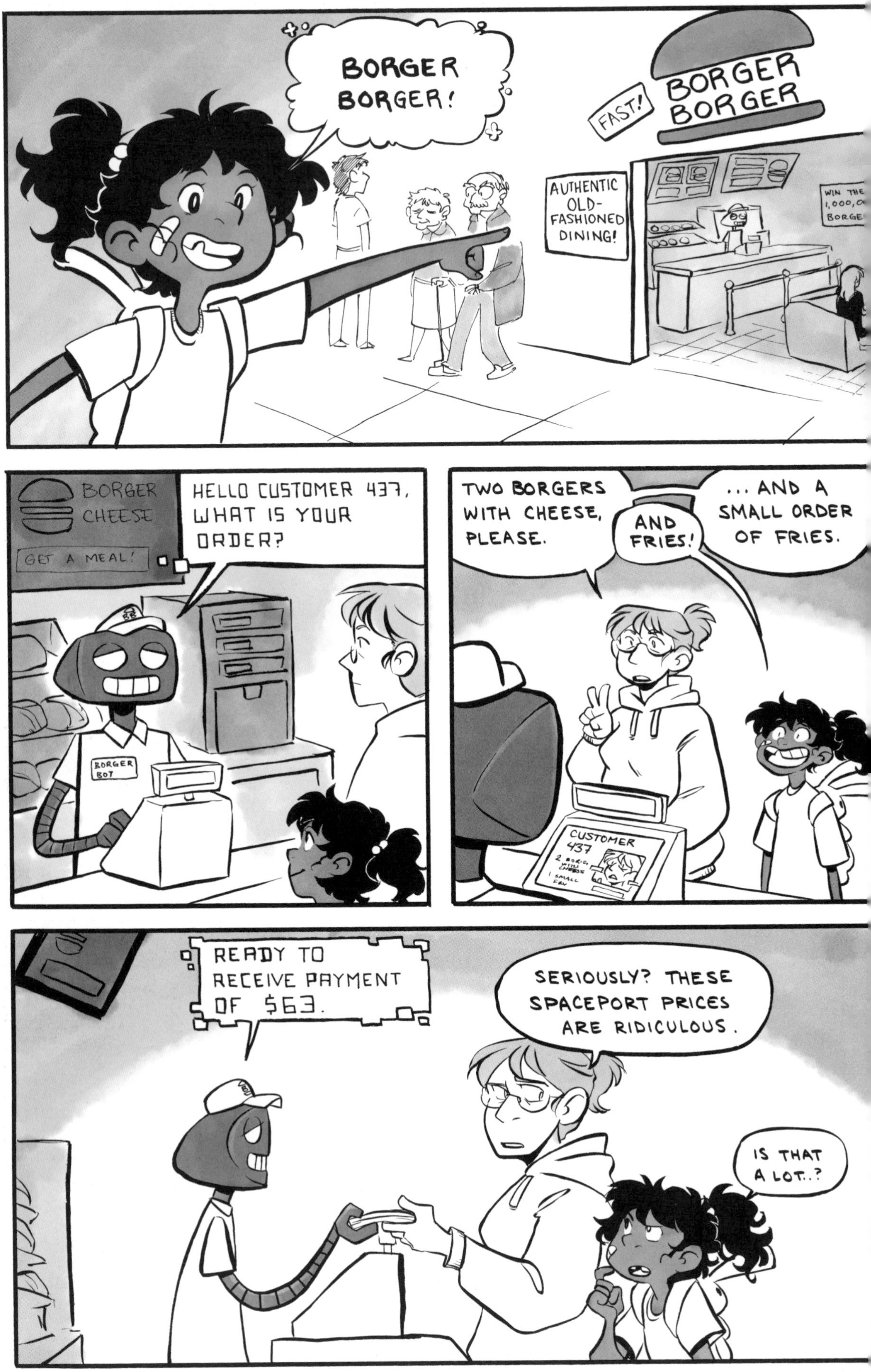
BORGER BORGER!
FAST!
BORGER BORGER
AUTHENTIC OLD-FASHIONED DINING!
BORGER CHEESE
GET A MEAL!
HELLO CUSTOMER 437, WHAT IS YOUR ORDER?
BORGER BOT
TWO BORGERS WITH CHEESE, PLEASE.
AND FRIES!
... AND A SMALL ORDER OF FRIES.
CUSTOMER 437
READY TO RECEIVE PAYMENT OF $63.
SERIOUSLY? THESE SPACEPORT PRICES ARE RIDICULOUS.
IS THAT A LOT..?

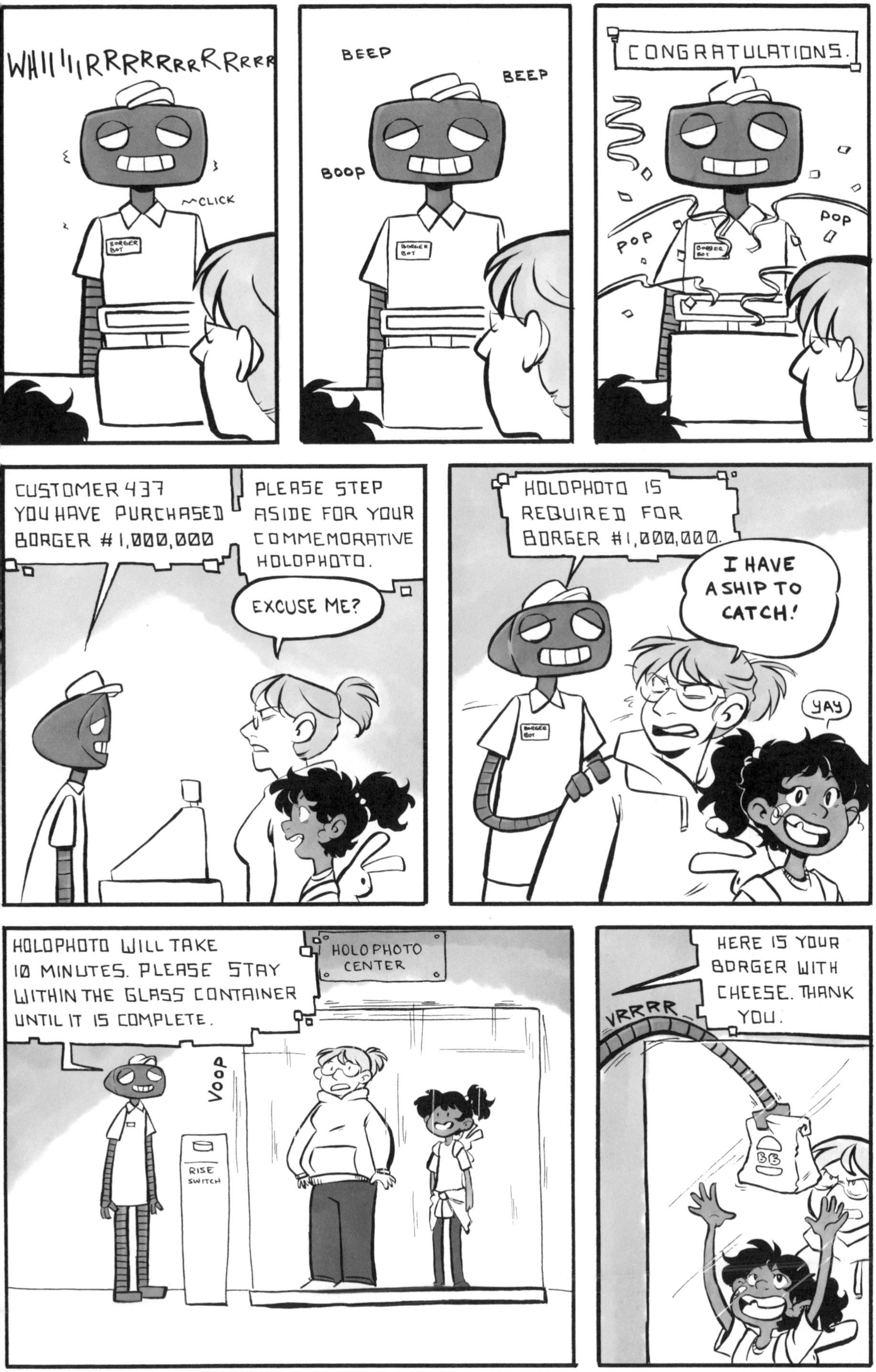
WHIIIIIRRRRRRRRRRRRR
~CLICK
BEEP
BEEP
BOOP
CONGRATULATIONS.
POP
POP
CUSTOMER 437 YOU HAVE PURCHASED BORGER #1,000,000
PLEASE STEP ASIDE FOR YOUR COMMEMORATIVE HOLOPHOTO.
EXCUSE ME?
HOLOPHOTO IS REQUIRED FOR BORGER #1,000,000.
I HAVE A SHIP TO CATCH!
YAY
HOLOPHOTO WILL TAKE 10 MINUTES. PLEASE STAY WITHIN THE GLASS CONTAINER UNTIL IT IS COMPLETE.
HOLO PHOTO CENTER
VOOP
RISE SWITCH
HERE IS YOUR BORGER WITH CHEESE. THANK YOU.
VRRRR

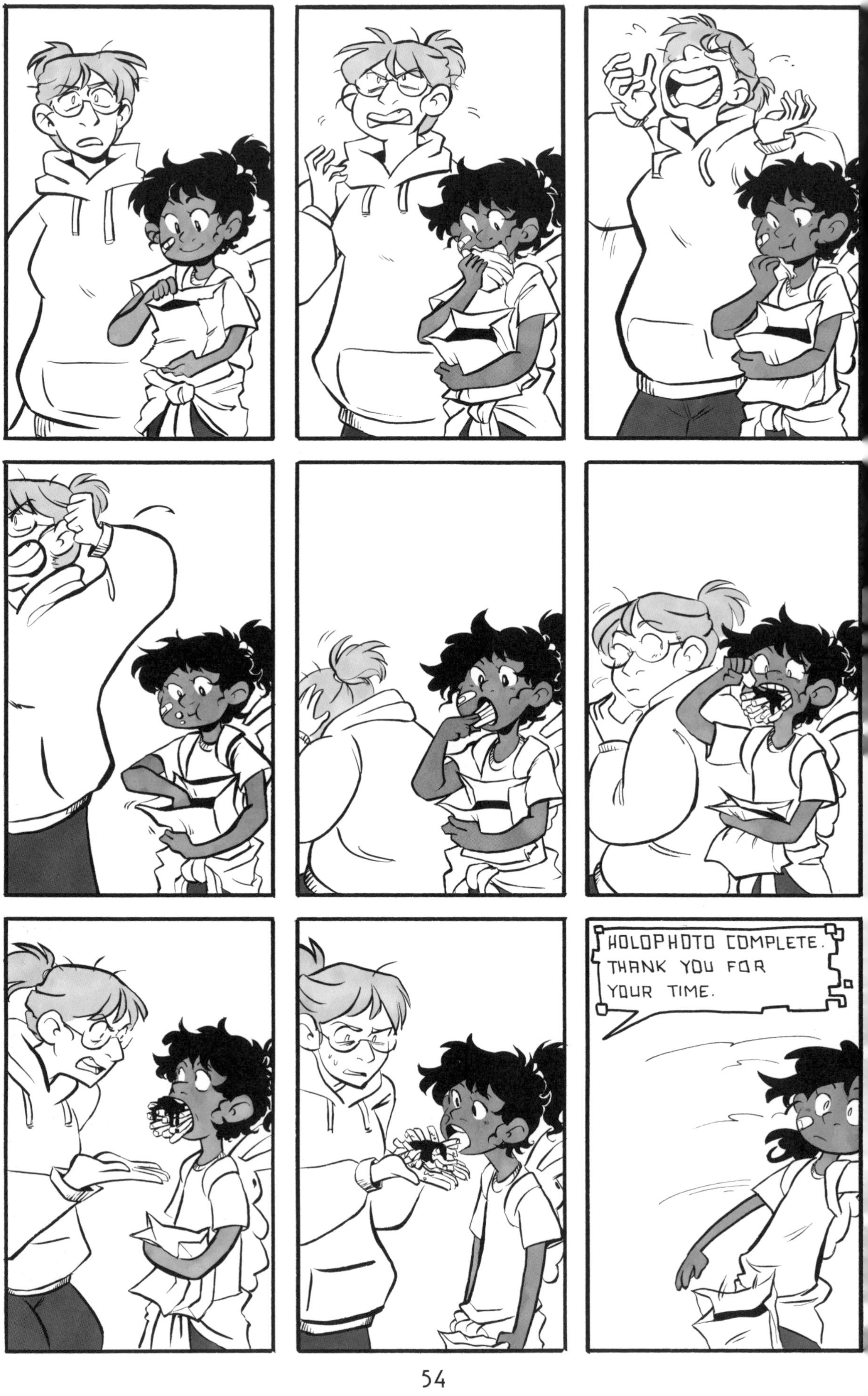
HOLOPHOTO COMPLETE. THANK YOU FOR YOUR TIME.

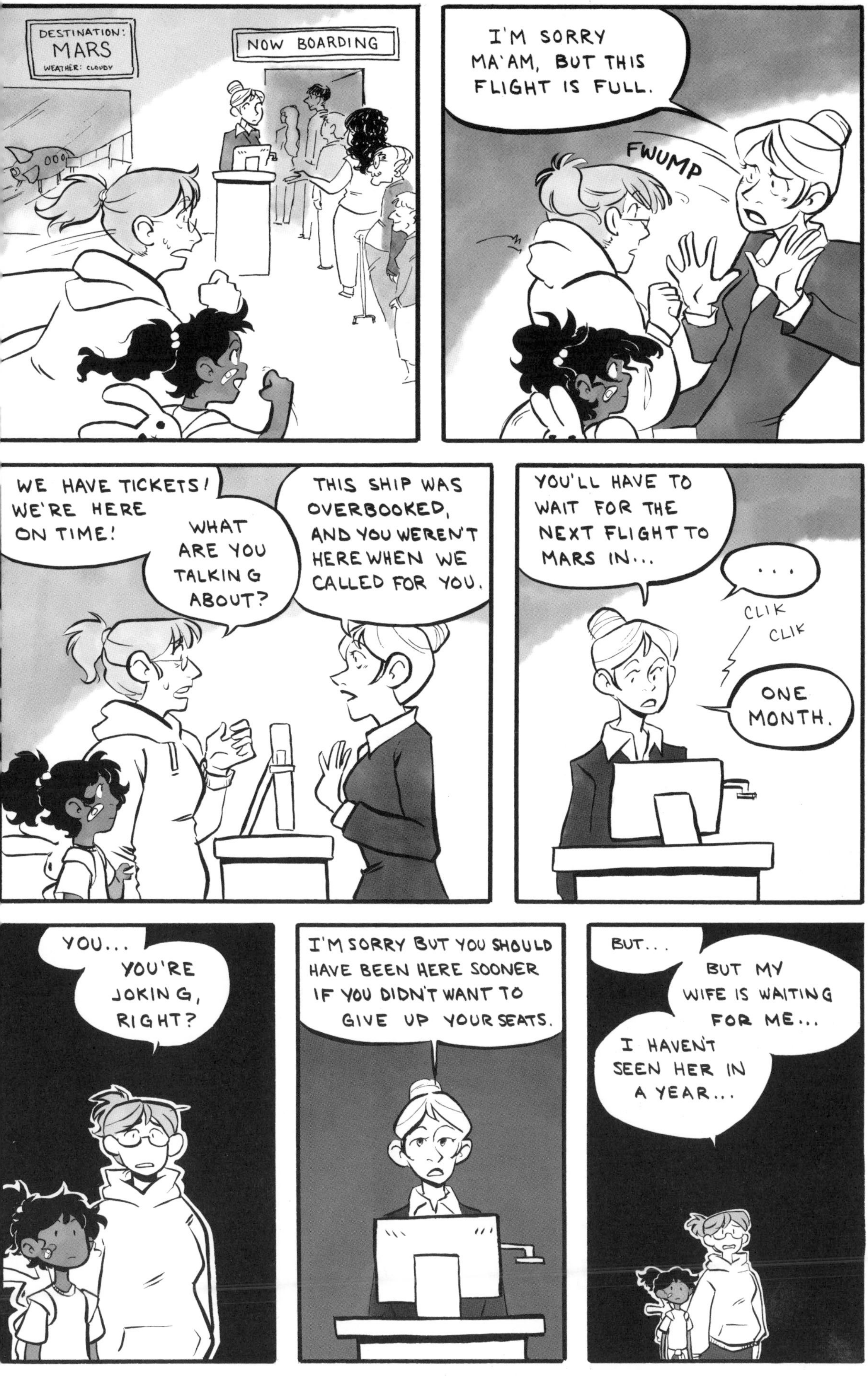
DESTINATION: MARS WEATHER: CLOUDY
NOW BOARDING
I'M SORRY MA'AM, BUT THIS FLIGHT IS FULL.
FWUMP
WE HAVE TICKETS! WE'RE HERE ON TIME!
WHAT ARE YOU TALKING ABOUT?
THIS SHIP WAS OVERBOOKED, AND YOU WEREN'T HERE WHEN WE CALLED FOR YOU.
YOU'LL HAVE TO WAIT FOR THE NEXT FLIGHT TO MARS IN...
...
CLIK CLIK
ONE MONTH.
YOU... YOU'RE JOKING, RIGHT?
I'M SORRY BUT YOU SHOULD HAVE BEEN HERE SOONER IF YOU DIDN'T WANT TO GIVE UP YOUR SEATS.
BUT...
BUT MY WIFE IS WAITING FOR ME...
I HAVEN'T SEEN HER IN A YEAR...

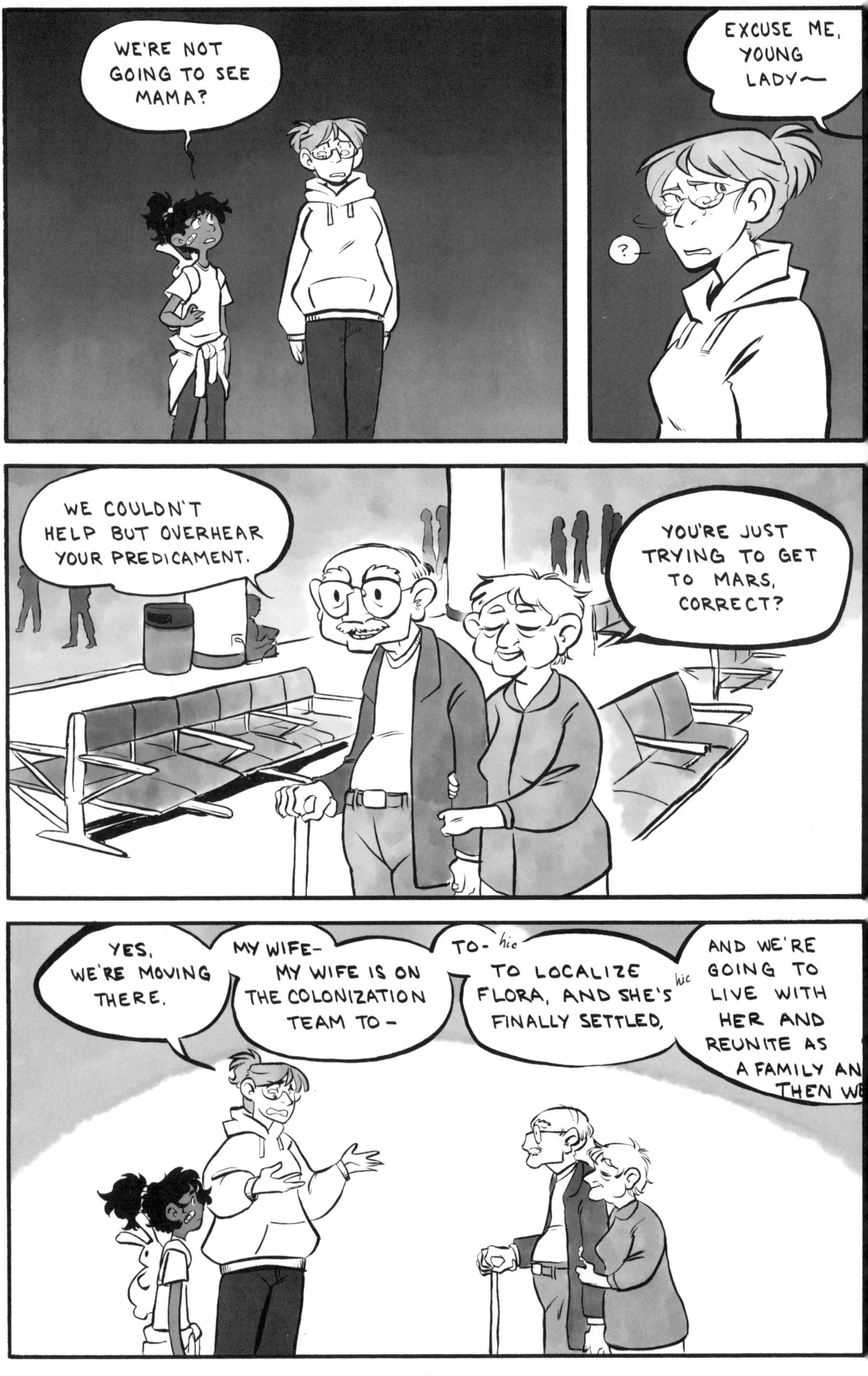
WE'RE NOT GOING TO SEE MAMA?
EXCUSE ME, YOUNG LADY~
?
WE COULDN'T HELP BUT OVERHEAR YOUR PREDICAMENT.
YOU'RE JUST TRYING TO GET TO MARS, CORRECT?
YES, WE'RE MOVING THERE.
MY WIFE- MY WIFE IS ON THE COLONIZATION TEAM TO-
TO- hic
TO LOCALIZE FLORA, AND SHE'S FINALLY SETTLED,
hic
AND WE'RE GOING TO LIVE WITH HER AND REUNITE AS A FAMILY AN
THEN WE

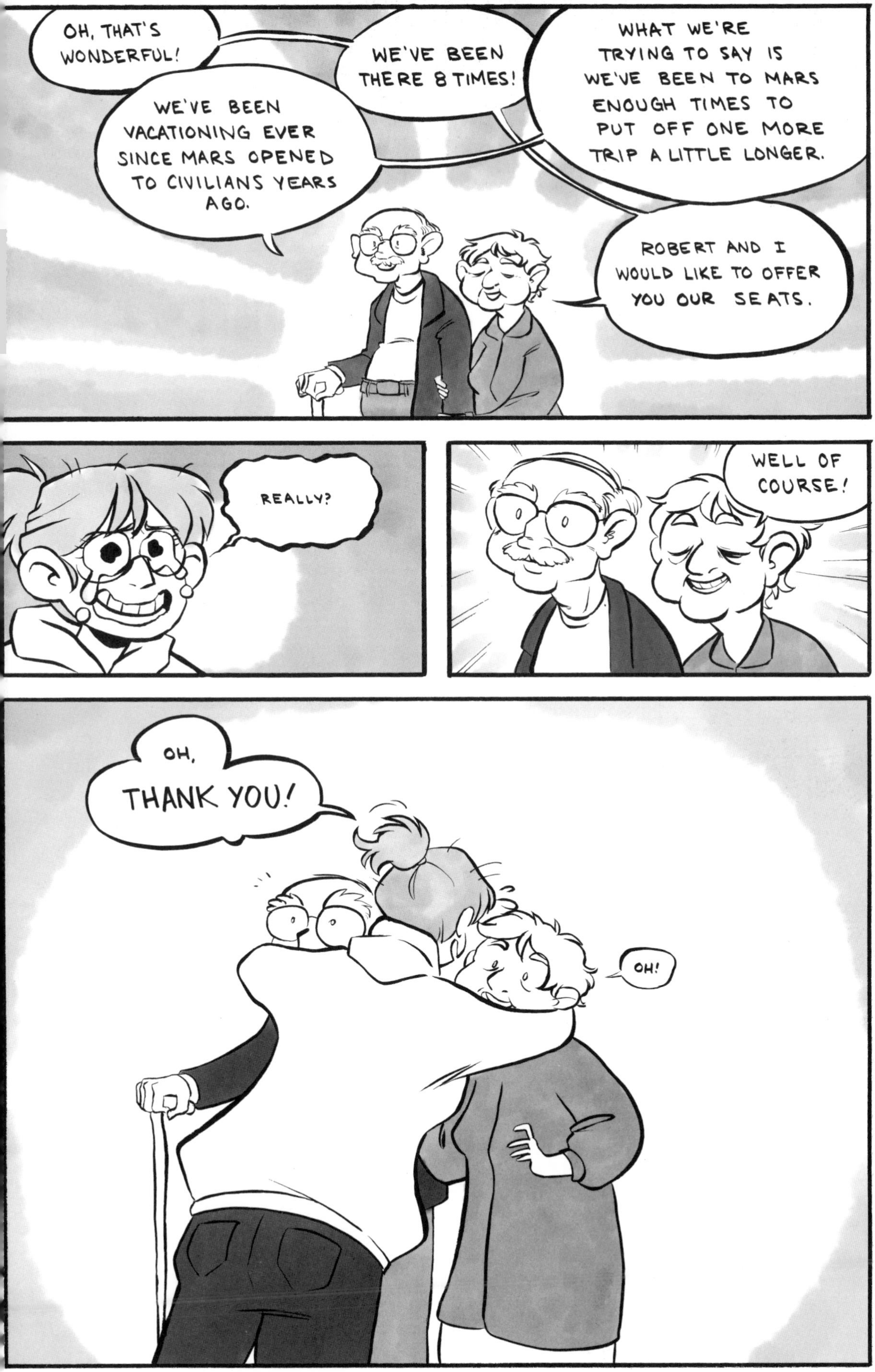
OH, THAT'S WONDERFUL!
WE'VE BEEN VACATIONING EVER SINCE MARS OPENED TO CIVILIANS YEARS AGO.
WE'VE BEEN THERE 8 TIMES!
WHAT WE'RE TRYING TO SAY IS WE'VE BEEN TO MARS ENOUGH TIMES TO PUT OFF ONE MORE TRIP A LITTLE LONGER.
ROBERT AND I WOULD LIKE TO OFFER YOU OUR SEATS.
REALLY?
WELL OF COURSE!
OH, THANK YOU!
OH!

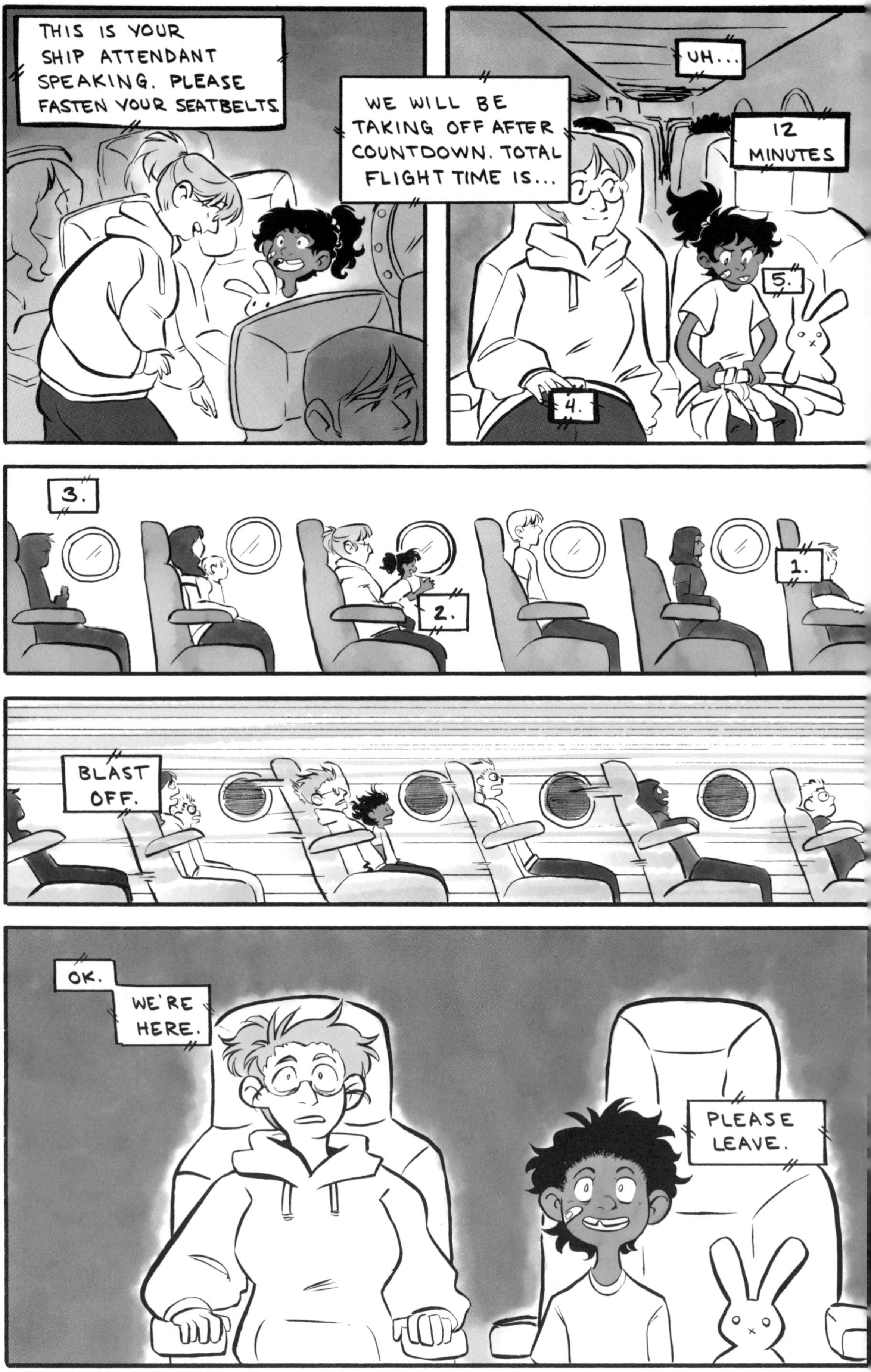
THIS IS YOUR SHIP ATTENDANT SPEAKING. PLEASE FASTEN YOUR SEATBELTS.
WE WILL BE TAKING OFF AFTER COUNTDOWN. TOTAL FLIGHT TIME IS...
UH...
12 MINUTES
5.
4.
3.
2.
1.
BLAST OFF.
OK.
WE'RE HERE.
PLEASE LEAVE.

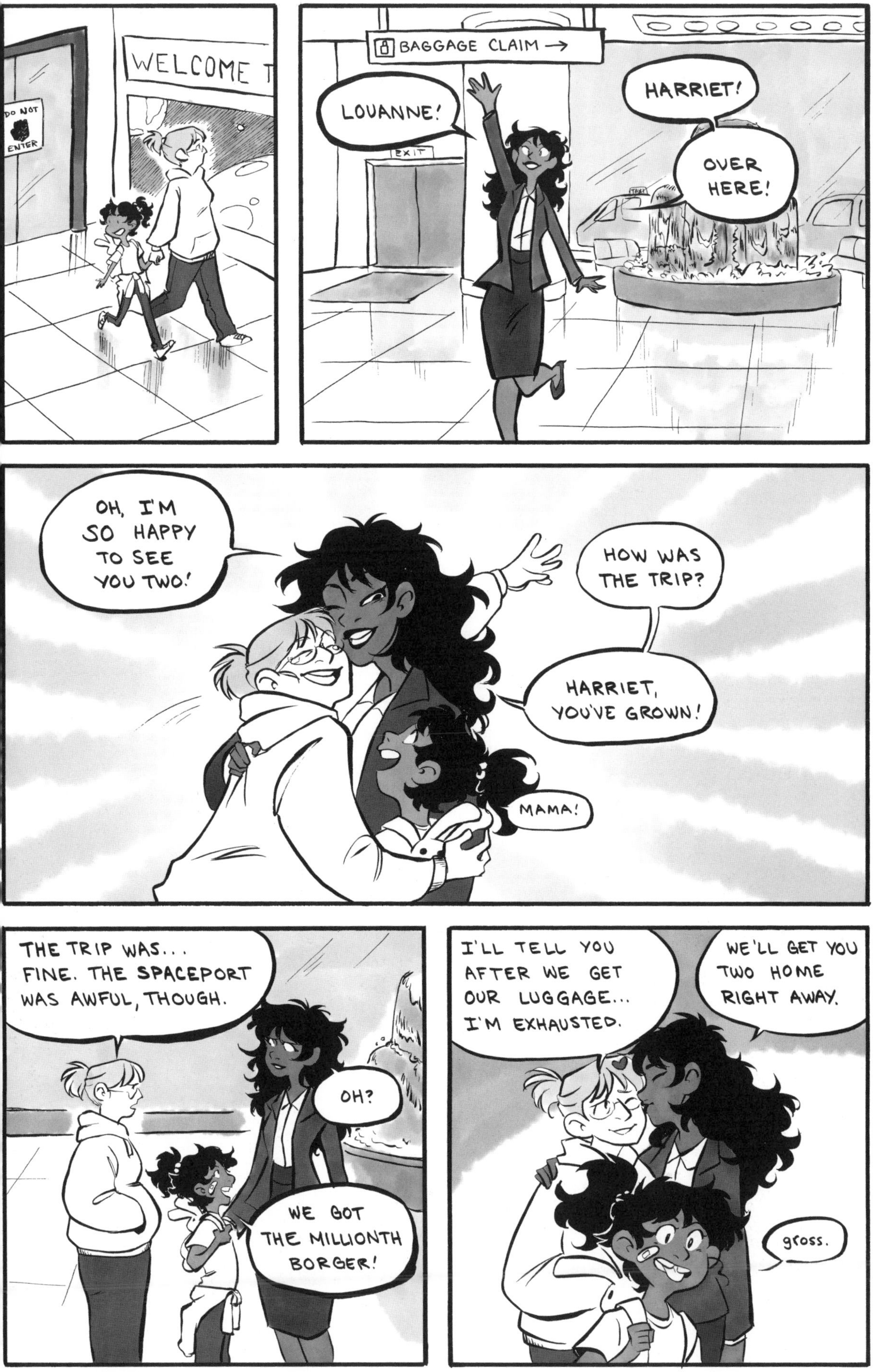

WELCOME T
DO NOT ENTER
BAGGAGE CLAIM →
EXIT
LOUANNE!
HARRIET!
OVER HERE!
OH, I'M SO HAPPY TO SEE YOU TWO!
HOW WAS THE TRIP?
HARRIET, YOU'VE GROWN!
MAMA!
THE TRIP WAS... FINE. THE SPACEPORT WAS AWFUL, THOUGH.
OH?
WE GOT THE MILLIONTH BORGER!
I'LL TELL YOU AFTER WE GET OUR LUGGAGE... I'M EXHAUSTED.
WE'LL GET YOU TWO HOME RIGHT AWAY.
gross.

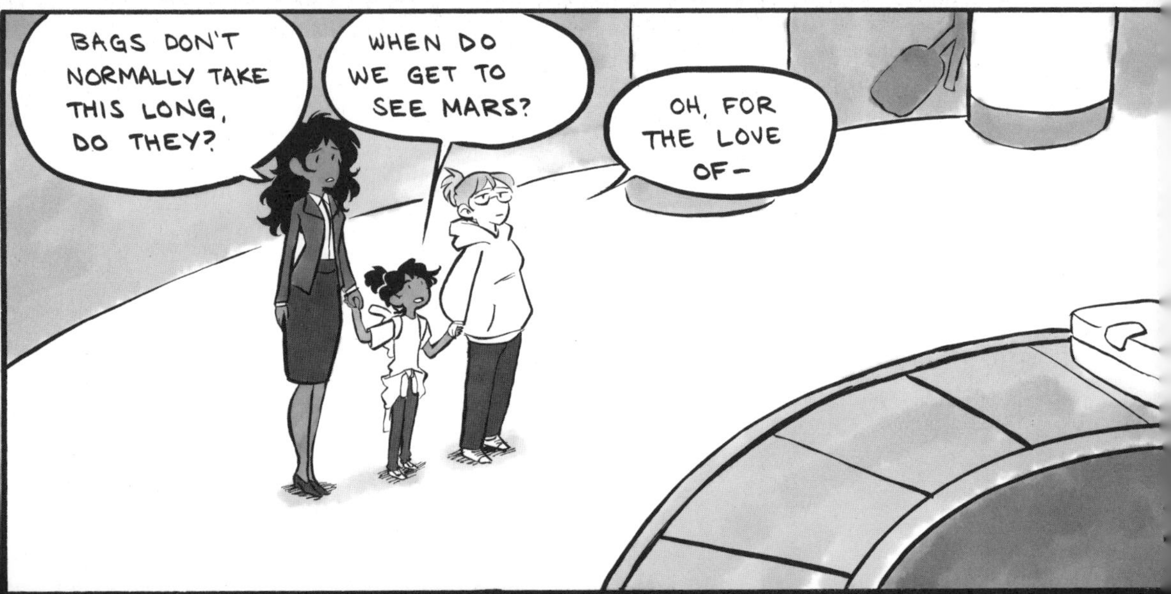
BAGS DON'T NORMALLY TAKE THIS LONG, DO THEY?
WHEN DO WE GET TO SEE MARS?
OH, FOR THE LOVE OF-

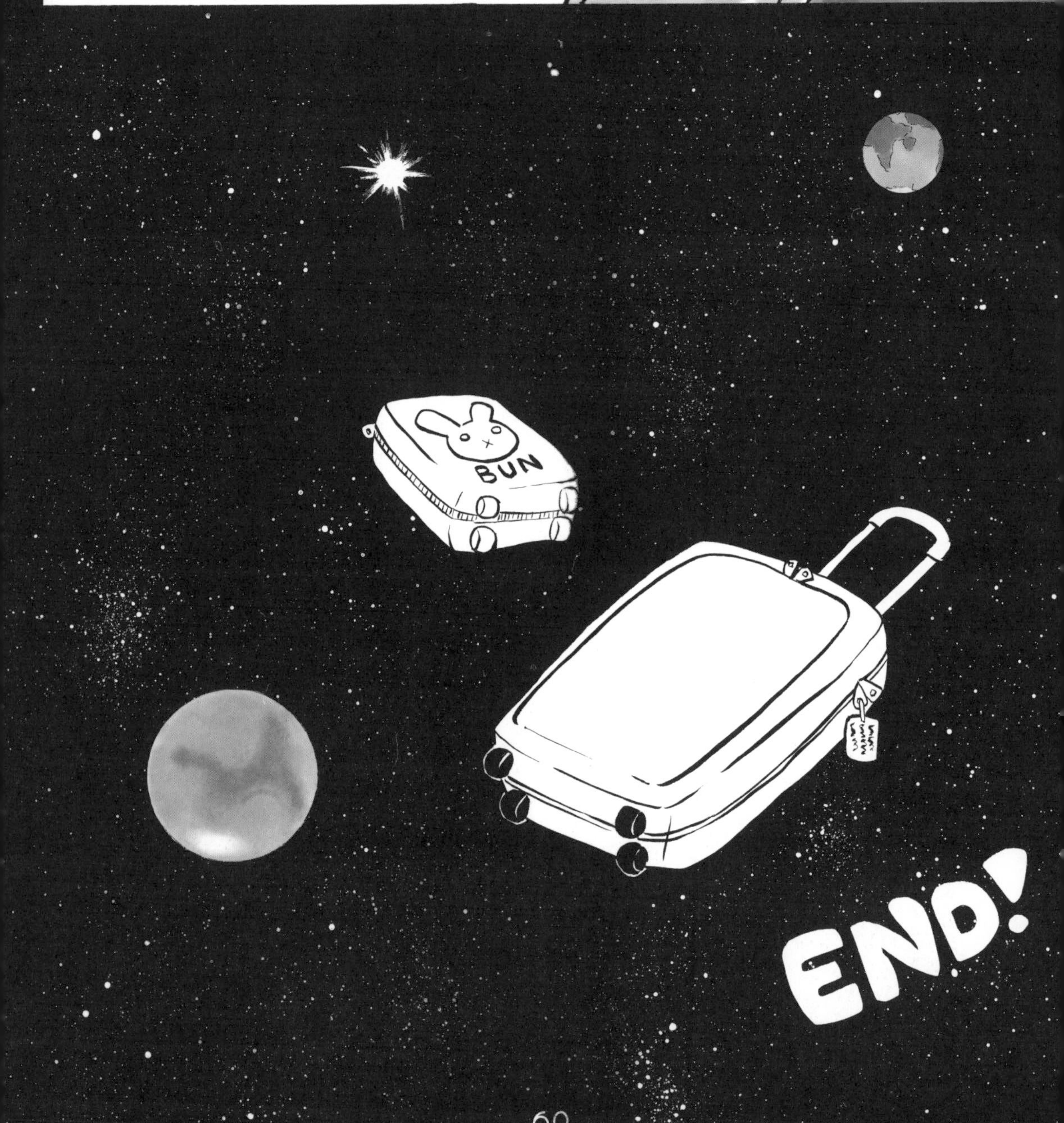
BUN
END!

LIA

Alexxander Dovelin

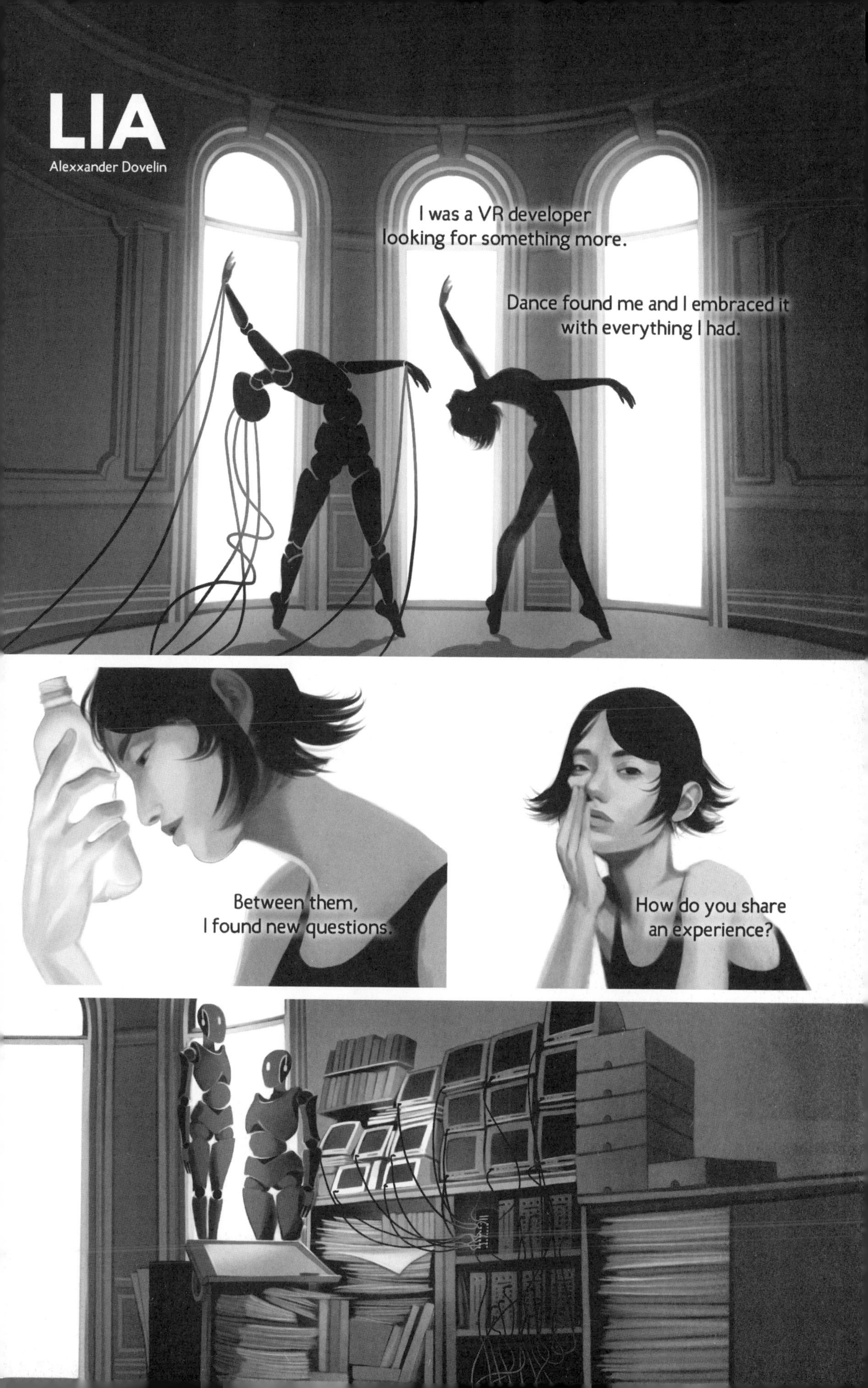
I was a VR developer looking for something more.
Dance found me and I embraced it with everything I had.
Between them, I found new questions.
How do you share an experience?

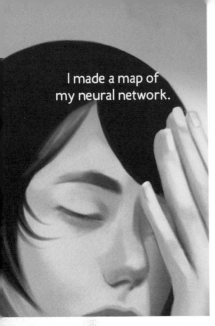

I made a map of my neural network.

Even though science

doesn't understand how it works.

We still find ways to replicate.

People are always diving into things without thinking about them first.

Desperate to connect, with something, someone.

8:29 AM

GT

Greg

Delivered

Hi Lia! Just checking in about my last message. I know it's a little sudden, so I'd understand if you'd like to pass this time.

We'd really like to collaborate with you, and are happy to provide the facilities. Let me know if I can answer any questions you might have. Thanks!

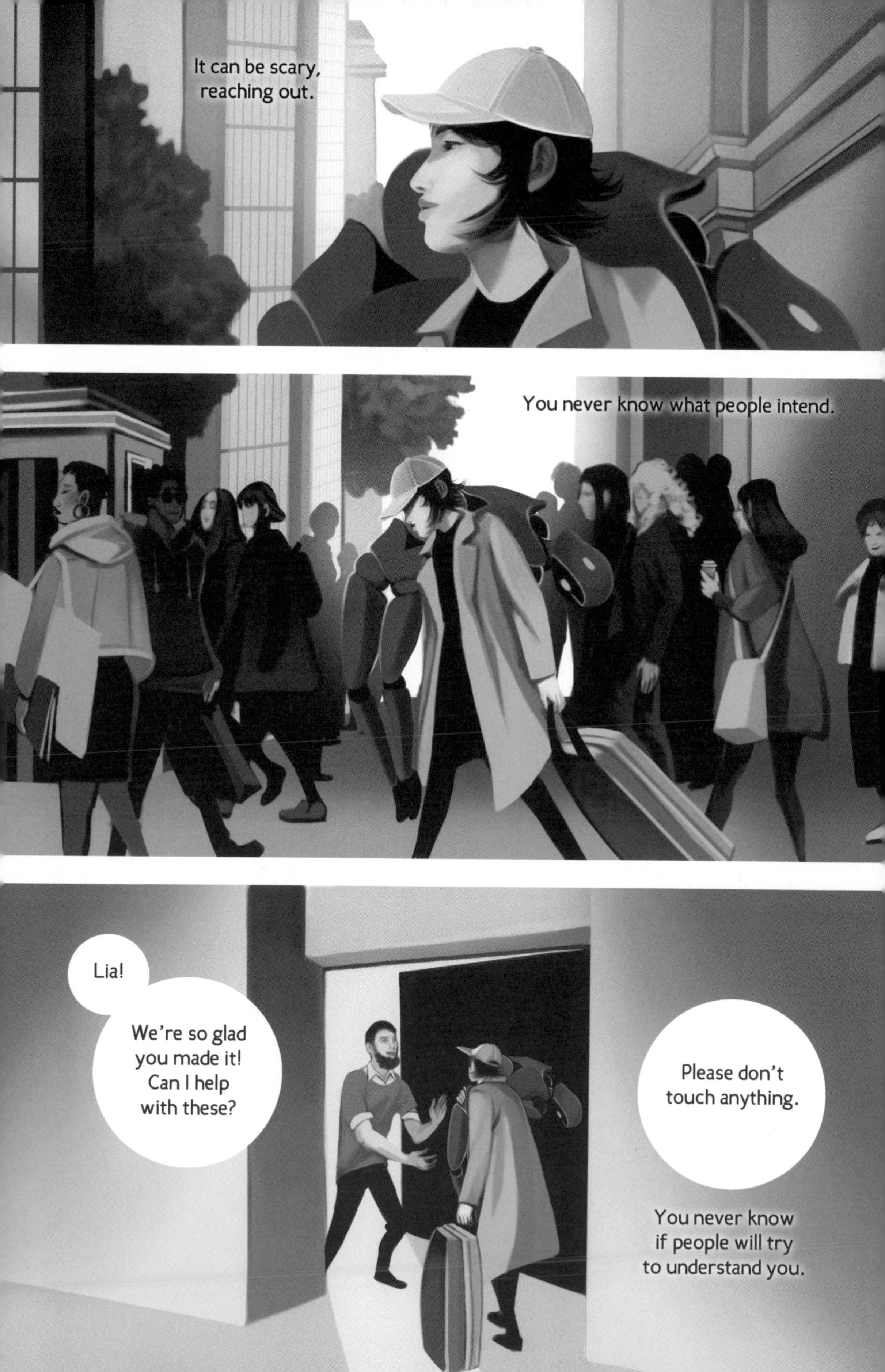
It can be scary, reaching out.
You never know what people intend.
Lia!
We're so glad you made it! Can I help with these?
Please don't touch anything.
You never know if people will try to understand you.

It's a risk, but you try.

You try for months.

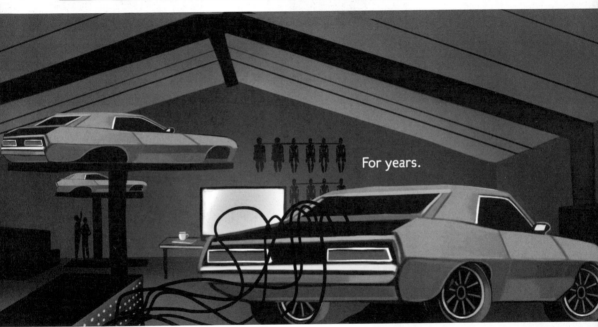

For years.

Looking for people who believe in you.

Looking for where your understanding intersects.

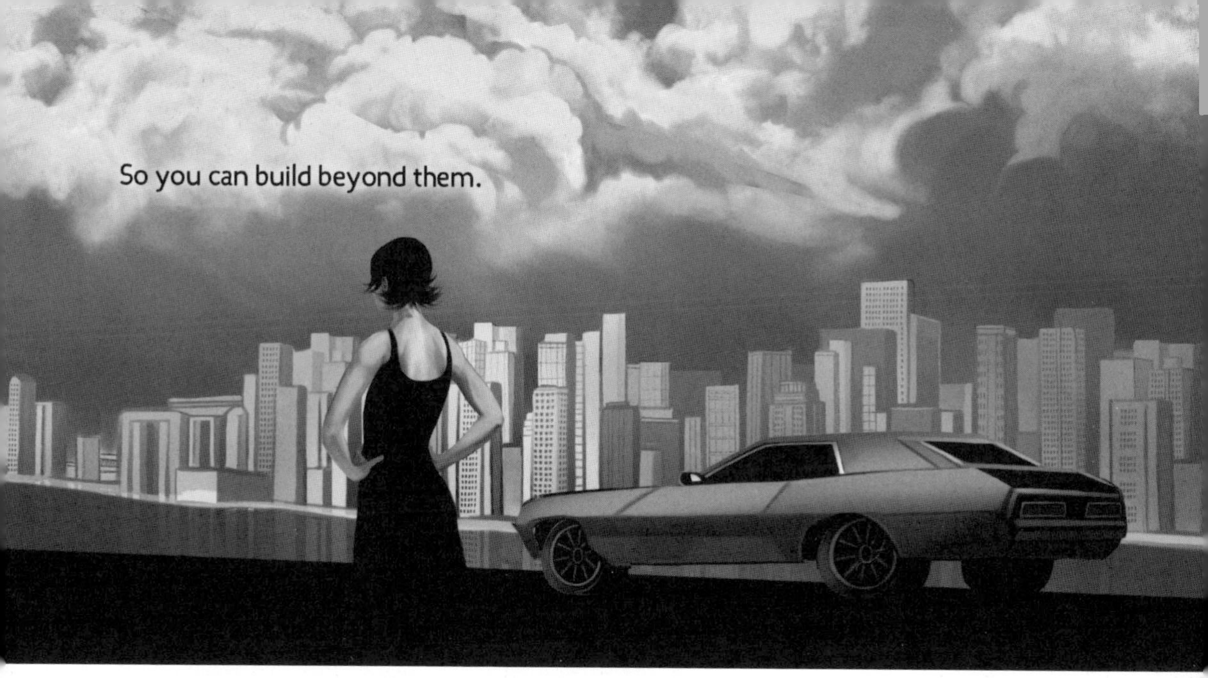
So you can build beyond them.

Five years ago, I was invited to experiment with new faster than light travel engines.

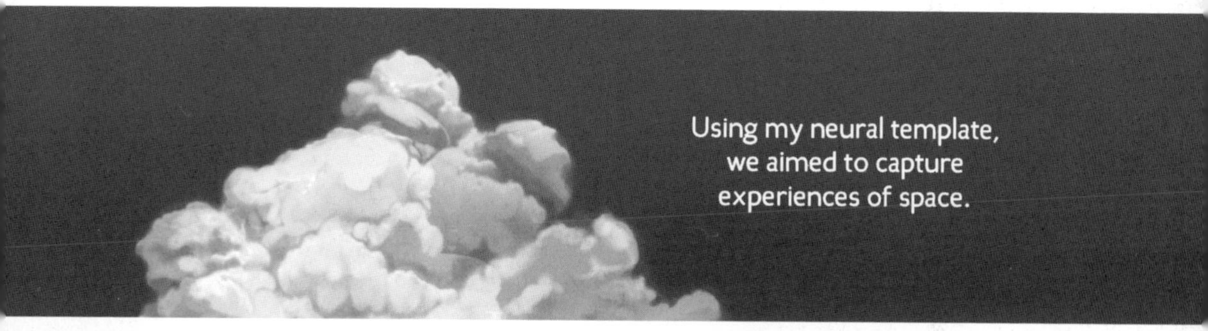
Using my neural template, we aimed to capture experiences of space.

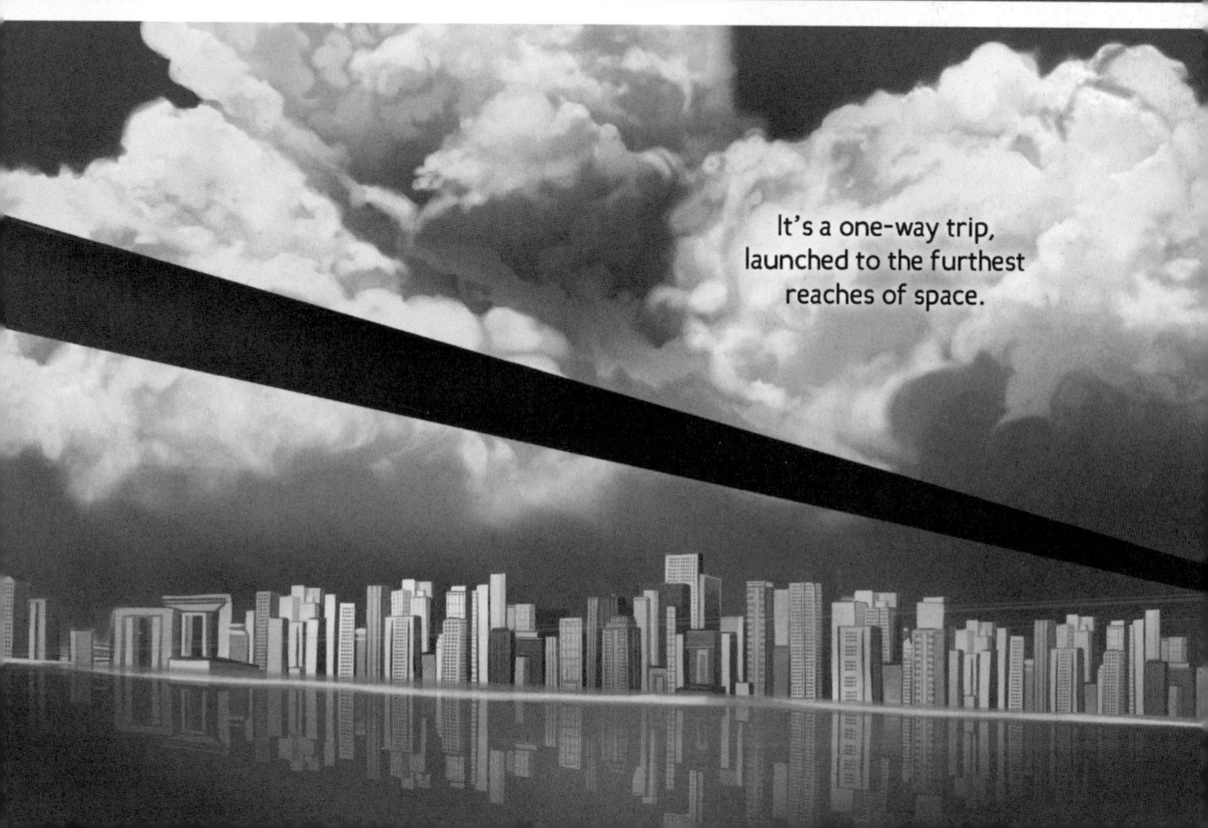
It's a one-way trip, launched to the furthest reaches of space.

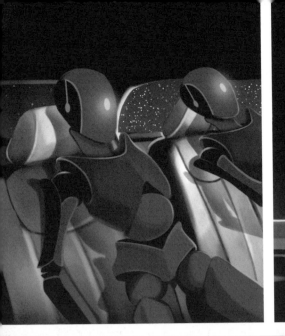

Android bodies can withstand radiation, temperatures, and pressure outside of normal limits.

Even see ultraviolet.

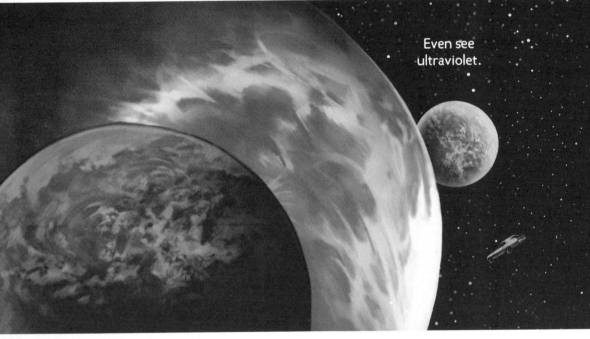

Transmissions take years to reach home.

How long tranmissions last depends where the launch lands.

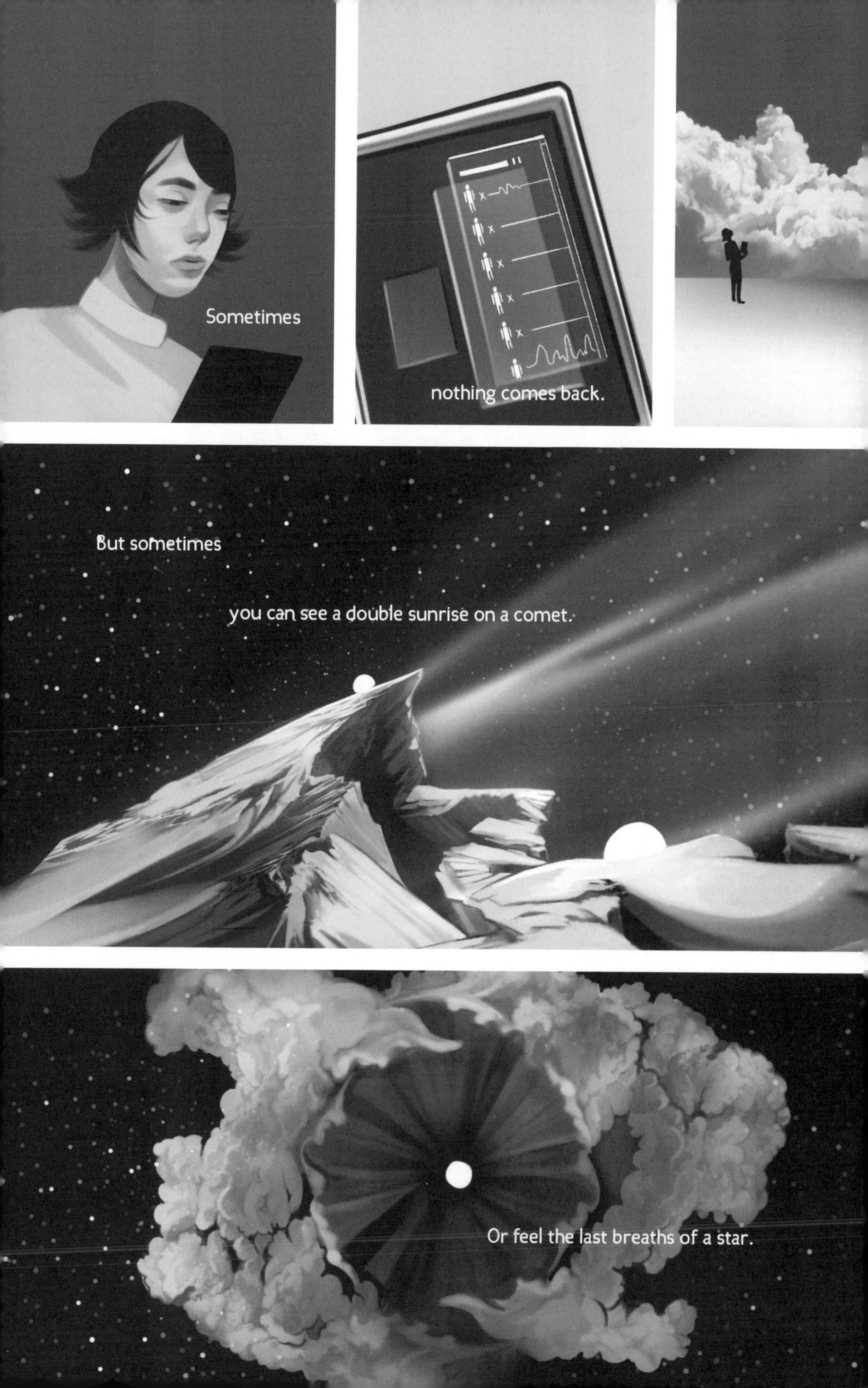
Sometimes
nothing comes back.
But sometimes
you can see a double sunrise on a comet.
Or feel the last breaths of a star.

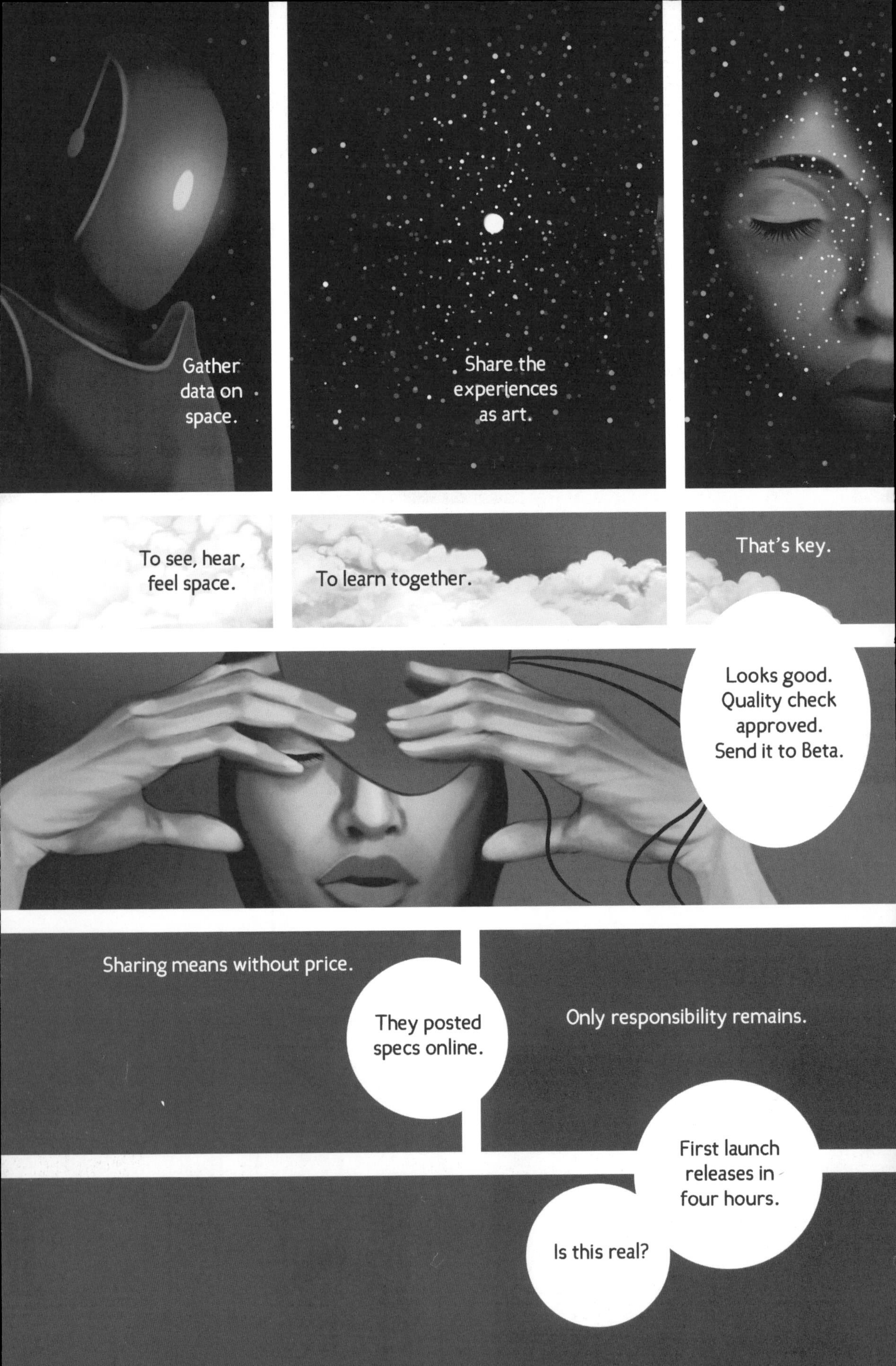
Gather data on space.
Share the experiences as art.
To see, hear, feel space.
To learn together.
That's key.
Looks good. Quality check approved. Send it to Beta.
Sharing means without price.
They posted specs online.
Only responsibility remains.
First launch releases in four hours.
Is this real?

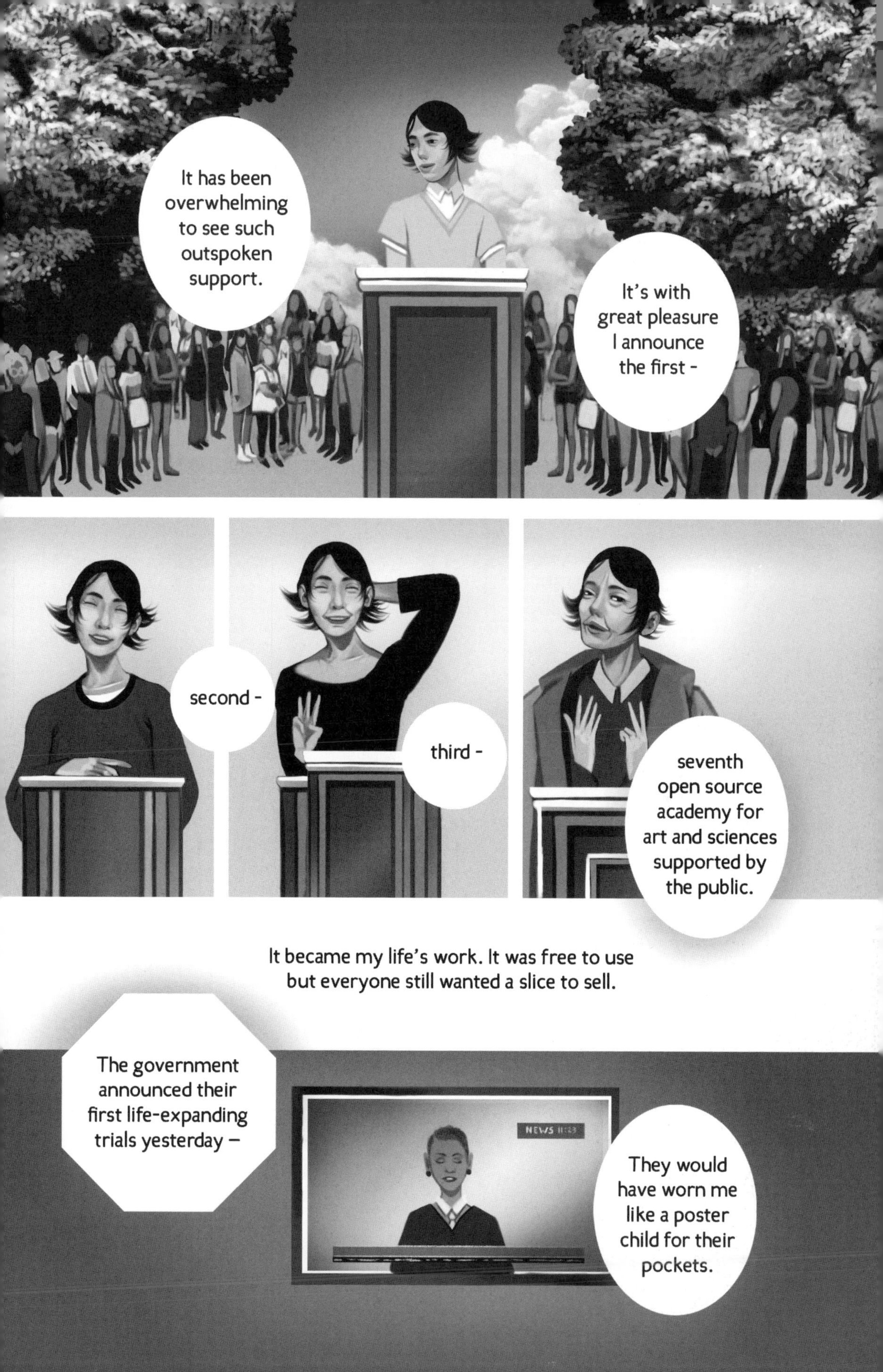
It has been overwhelming to see such outspoken support.
It's with great pleasure I announce the first -
second -
third -
seventh open source academy for art and sciences supported by the public.
It became my life's work. It was free to use but everyone still wanted a slice to sell.
The government announced their first life-expanding trials yesterday –
They would have worn me like a poster child for their pockets.

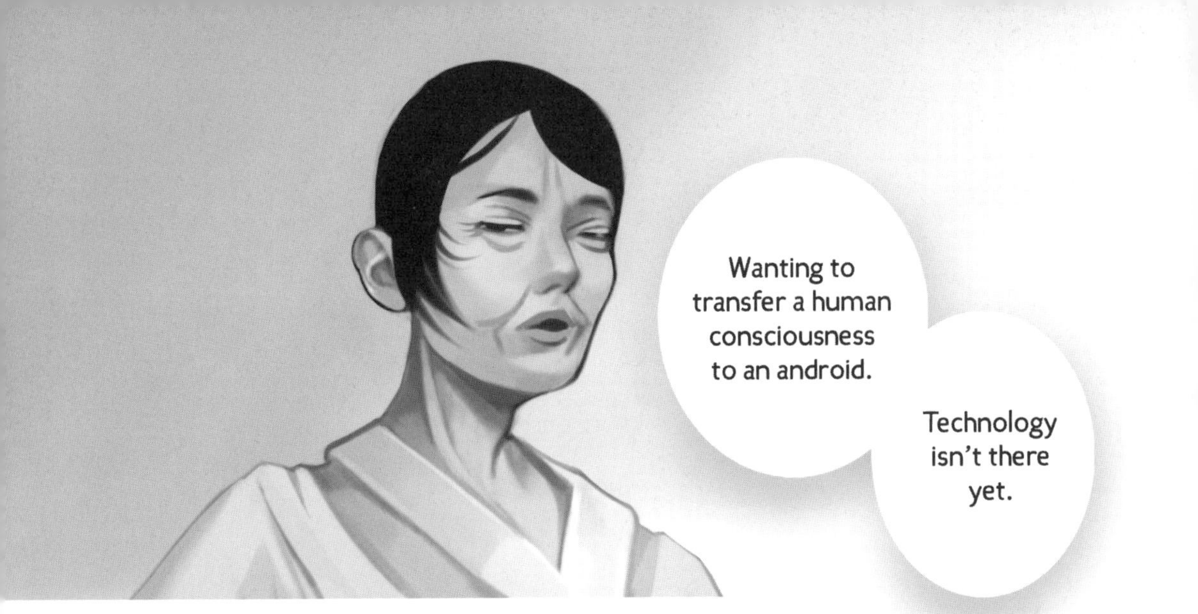
Wanting to transfer a human consciousness to an android.
Technology isn't there yet.

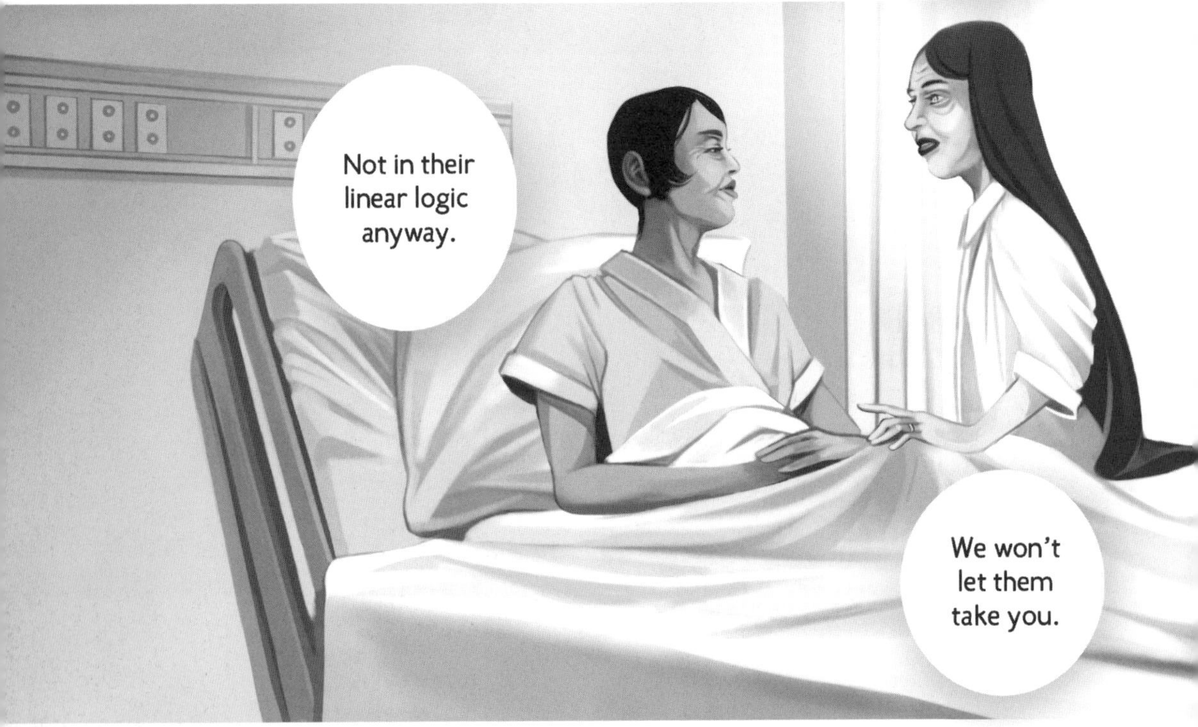
Not in their linear logic anyway.
We won't let them take you.

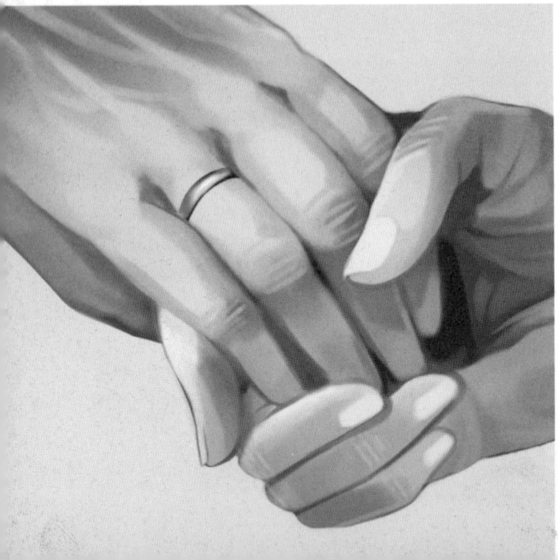

I passed away at 88,
while the academy was being
sued by the government
under the guise of
social well being.

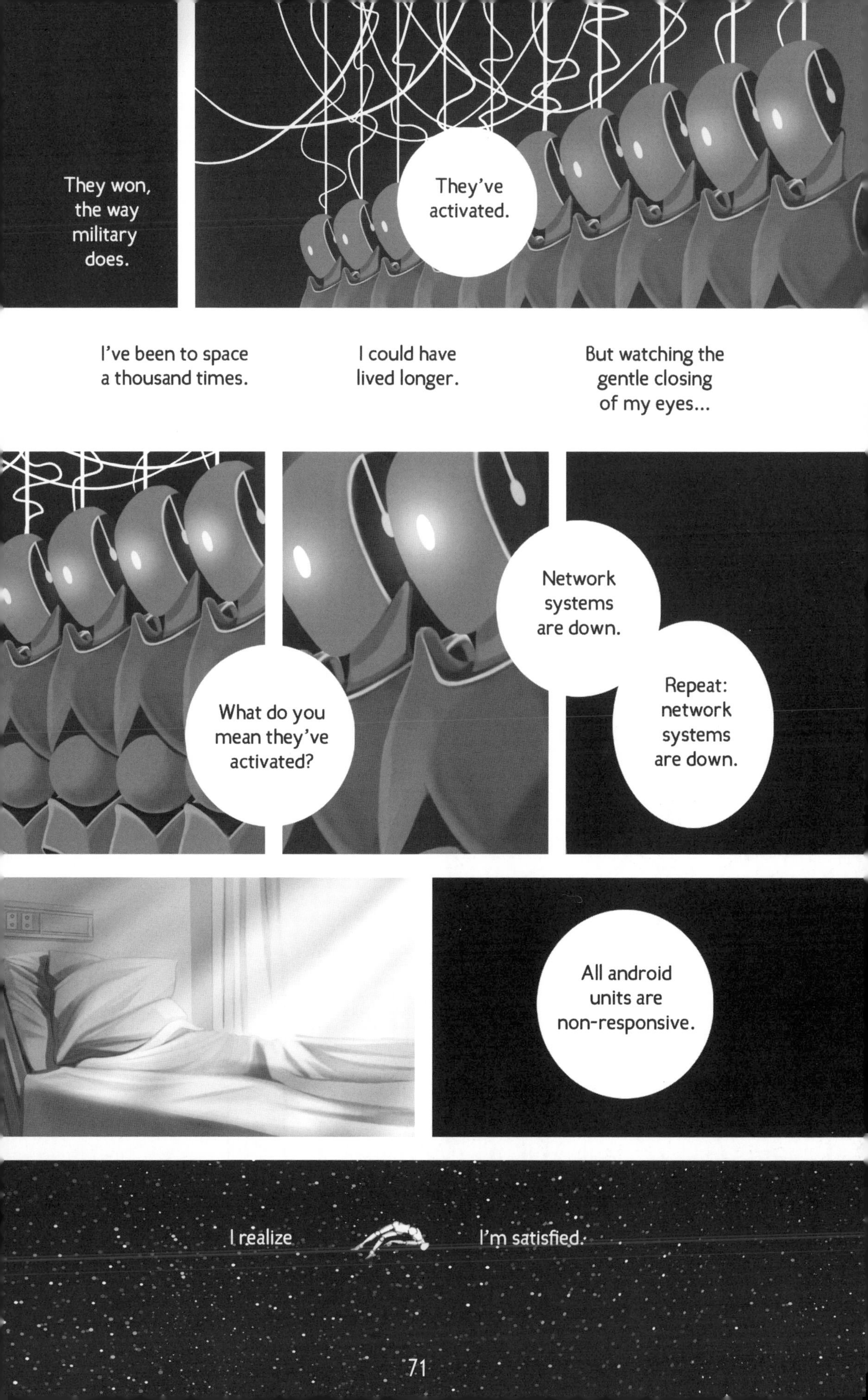
They won, the way military does.
They've activated.
I've been to space a thousand times.
I could have lived longer.
But watching the gentle closing of my eyes...
What do you mean they've activated?
Network systems are down.
Repeat: network systems are down.
All android units are non-responsive.
I realize
I'm satisfied.

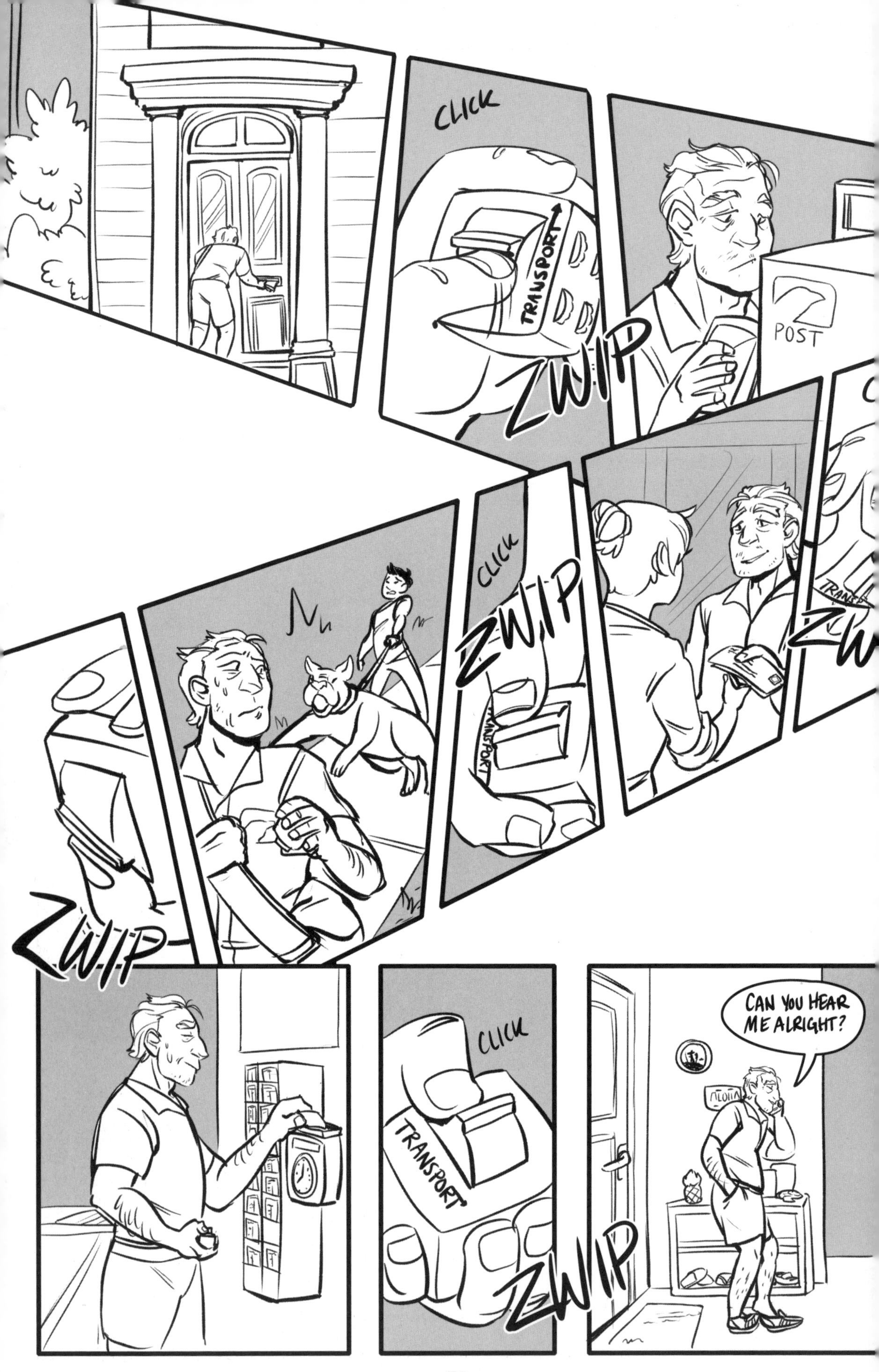
CLICK
ZWIP
TRANSPORT
POST
CLICK
ZWIP
ZWIP
CLICK
TRANSPORT
ZWIP
CAN YOU HEAR ME ALRIGHT?

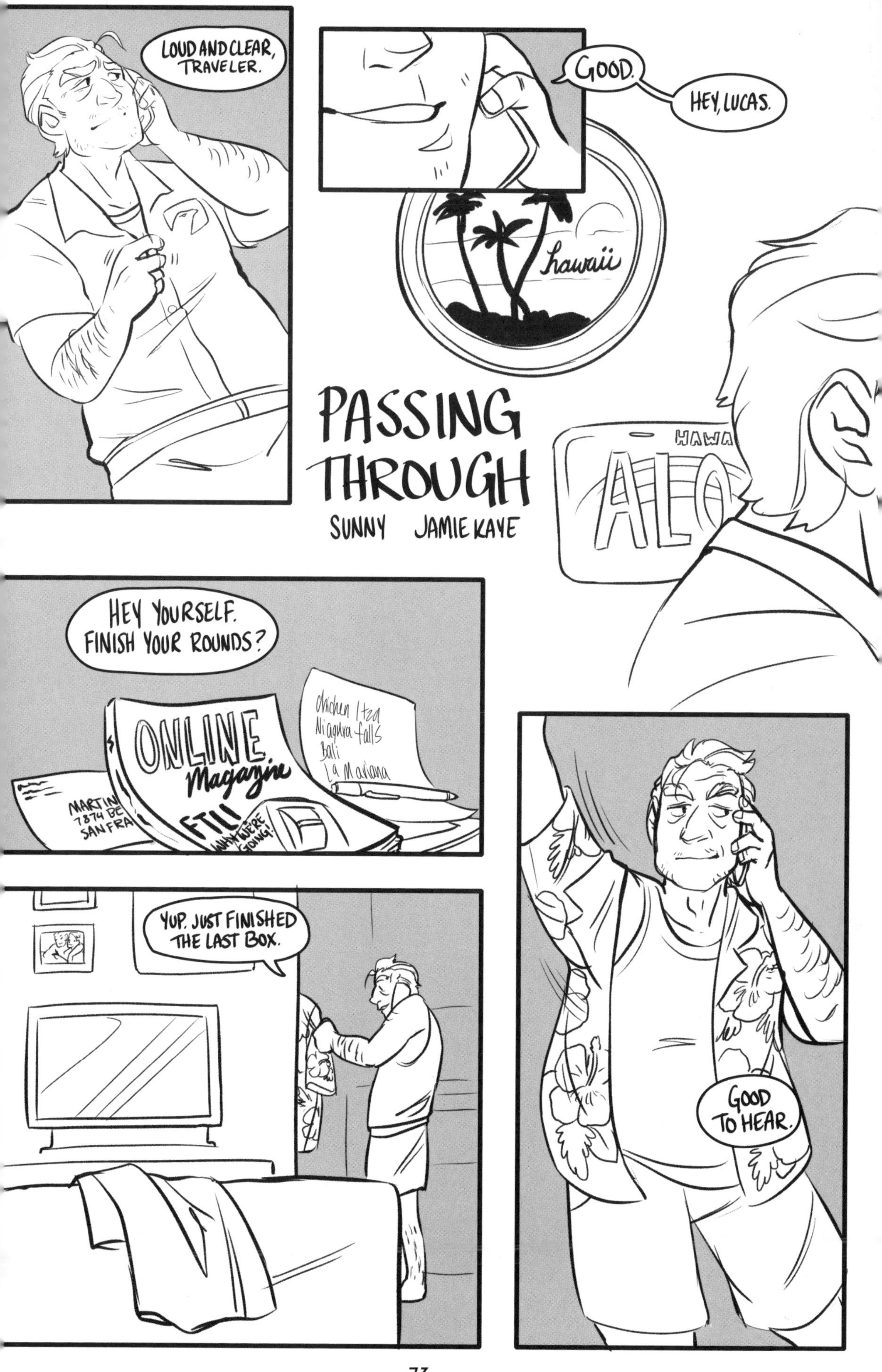
LOUD AND CLEAR, TRAVELER.
GOOD.
HEY, LUCAS.
hawaii
PASSING THROUGH
SUNNY JAMIE KAYE
HEY YOURSELF. FINISH YOUR ROUNDS?
ONLINE Magazine
FTL! WHY WE'RE GOING!
Chichen Itza
Niagara falls
Bali
La Mariana
YUP. JUST FINISHED THE LAST BOX.
GOOD TO HEAR.

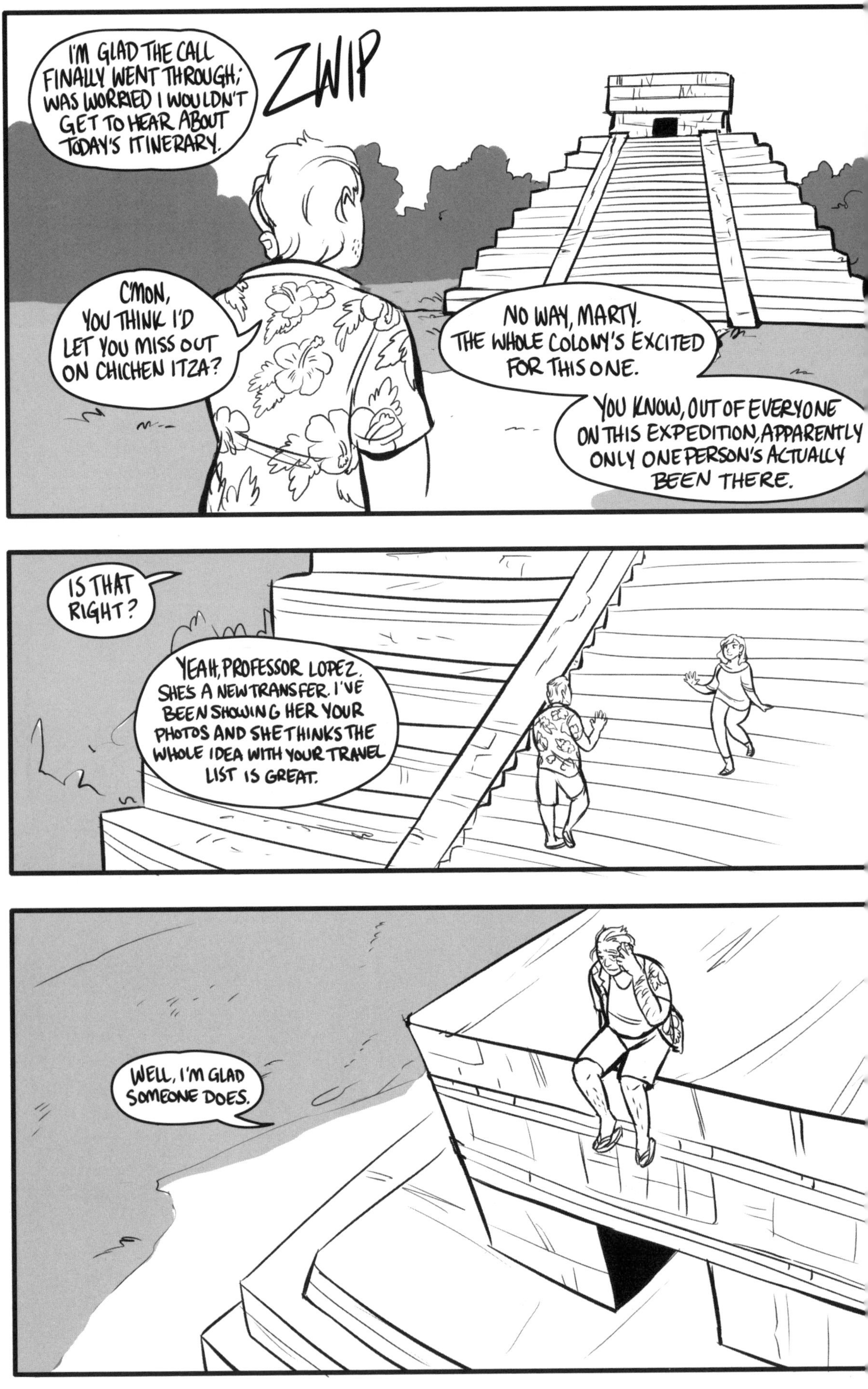
I'M GLAD THE CALL FINALLY WENT THROUGH; WAS WORRIED I WOULDN'T GET TO HEAR ABOUT TODAY'S ITINERARY.
ZWIP
C'MON, YOU THINK I'D LET YOU MISS OUT ON CHICHEN ITZA?
NO WAY, MARTY. THE WHOLE COLONY'S EXCITED FOR THIS ONE.
YOU KNOW, OUT OF EVERYONE ON THIS EXPEDITION, APPARENTLY ONLY ONE PERSON'S ACTUALLY BEEN THERE.
IS THAT RIGHT?
YEAH, PROFESSOR LOPEZ. SHE'S A NEW TRANSFER. I'VE BEEN SHOWING HER YOUR PHOTOS AND SHE THINKS THE WHOLE IDEA WITH YOUR TRAVEL LIST IS GREAT.
WELL, I'M GLAD SOMEONE DOES.

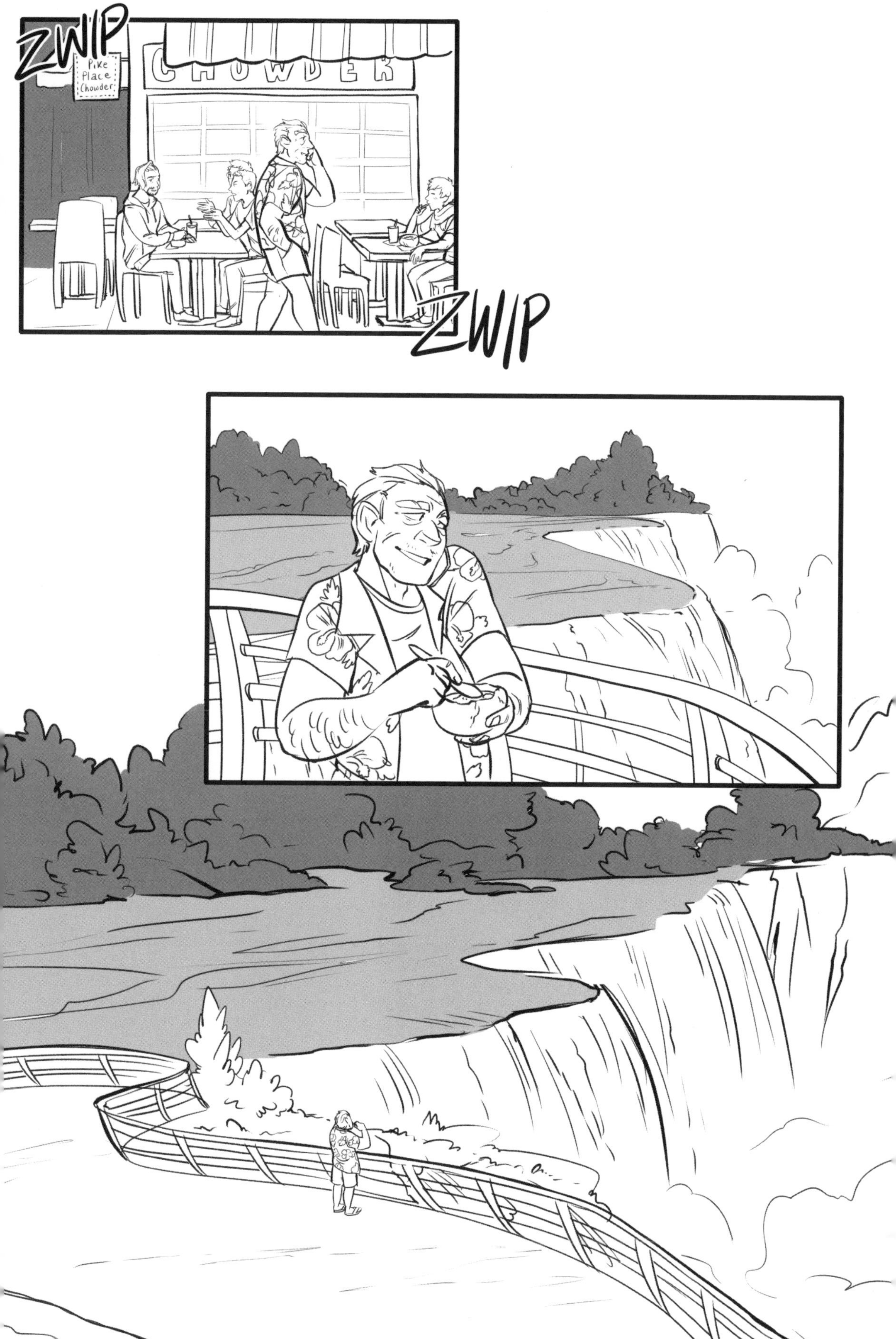
ZWIP
Pike Place Chowder
CHOWDER
ZWIP

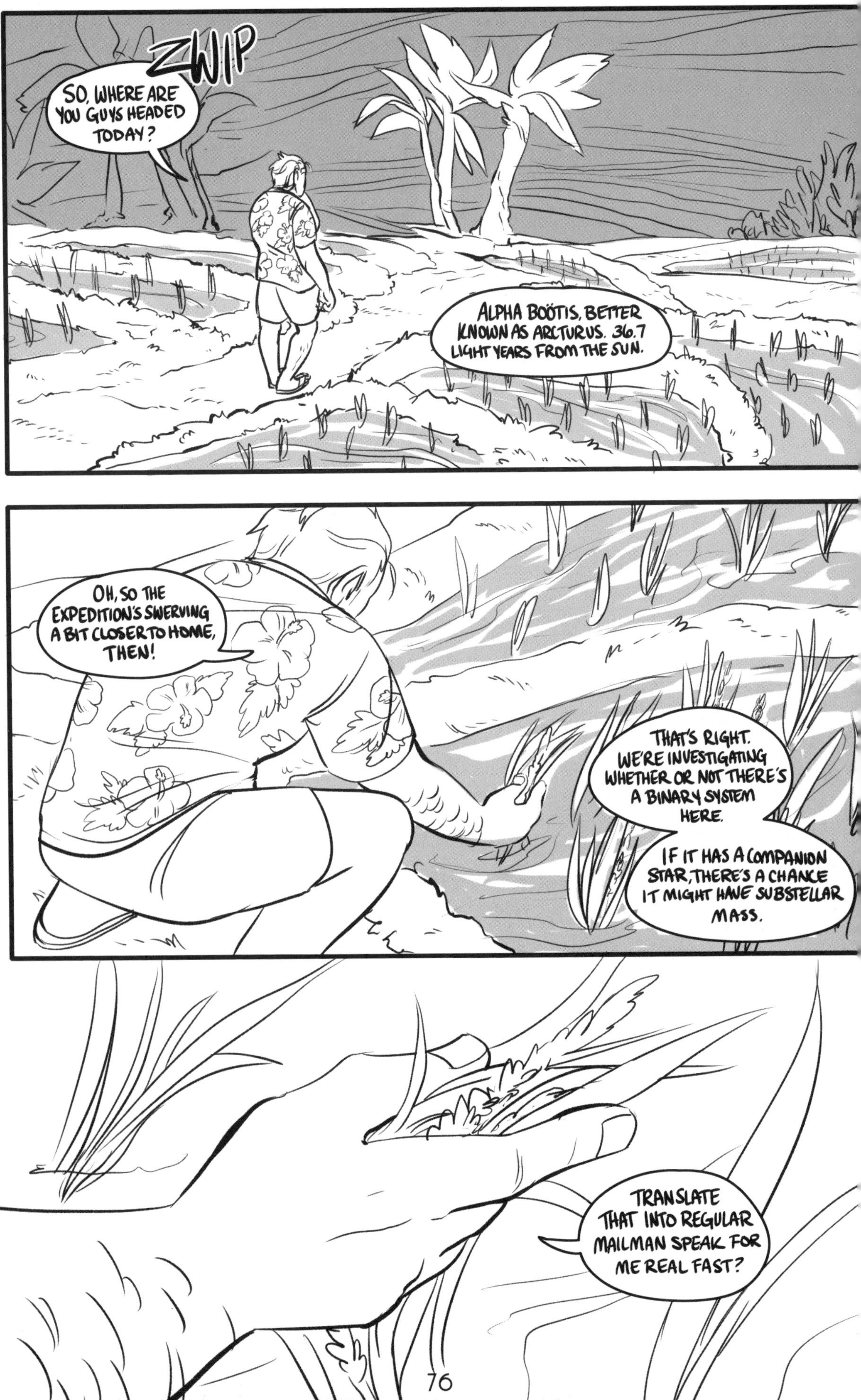
ZWIP
SO, WHERE ARE YOU GUYS HEADED TODAY?
ALPHA BOÖTIS, BETTER KNOWN AS ARCTURUS. 36.7 LIGHT YEARS FROM THE SUN.
OH, SO THE EXPEDITION'S SWERVING A BIT CLOSER TO HOME, THEN!
THAT'S RIGHT. WE'RE INVESTIGATING WHETHER OR NOT THERE'S A BINARY SYSTEM HERE.
IF IT HAS A COMPANION STAR, THERE'S A CHANCE IT MIGHT HAVE SUBSTELLAR MASS.
TRANSLATE THAT INTO REGULAR MAILMAN SPEAK FOR ME REAL FAST?

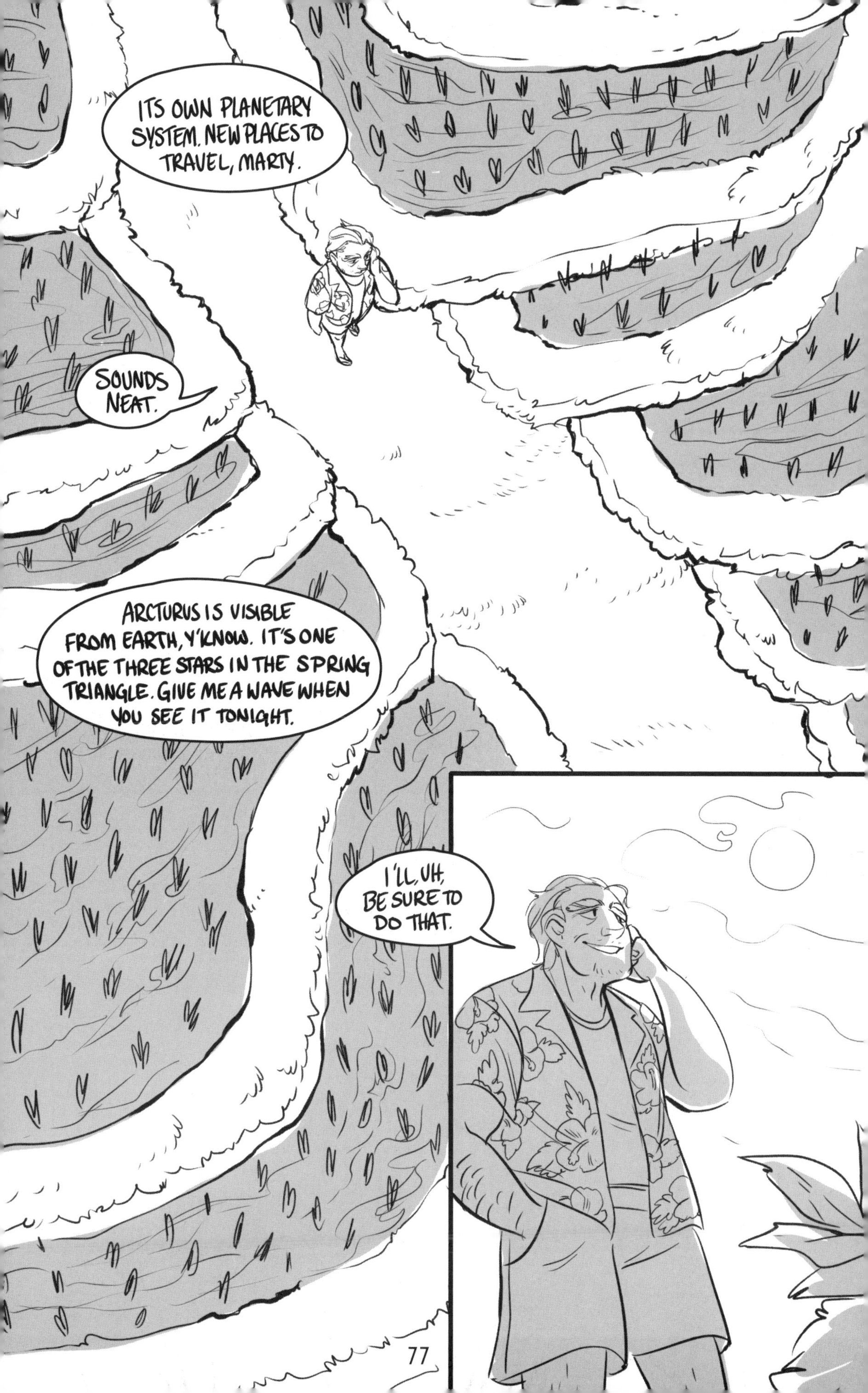
ITS OWN PLANETARY SYSTEM. NEW PLACES TO TRAVEL, MARTY.
SOUNDS NEAT.
ARCTURUS IS VISIBLE FROM EARTH, Y'KNOW. IT'S ONE OF THE THREE STARS IN THE SPRING TRIANGLE. GIVE ME A WAVE WHEN YOU SEE IT TONIGHT.
I'LL, UH, BE SURE TO DO THAT.

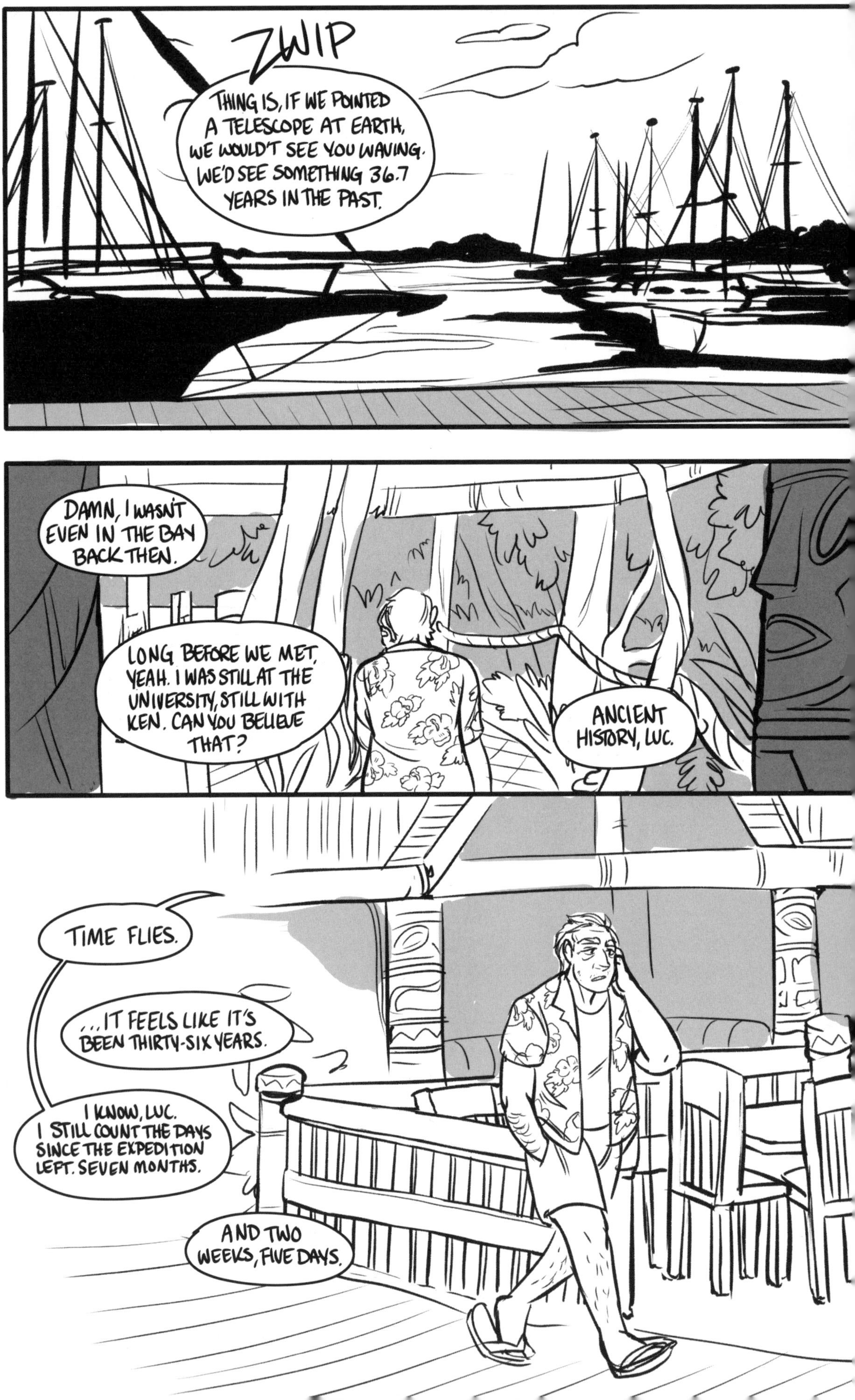
ZWIP
THING IS, IF WE POINTED A TELESCOPE AT EARTH, WE WOULD'T SEE YOU WAVING. WE'D SEE SOMETHING 36.7 YEARS IN THE PAST.
DAMN, I WASN'T EVEN IN THE BAY BACK THEN.
LONG BEFORE WE MET, YEAH. I WAS STILL AT THE UNIVERSITY, STILL WITH KEN. CAN YOU BELIEVE THAT?
ANCIENT HISTORY, LUC.
TIME FLIES.
...IT FEELS LIKE IT'S BEEN THIRTY-SIX YEARS.
I KNOW, LUC. I STILL COUNT THE DAYS SINCE THE EXPEDITION LEFT. SEVEN MONTHS.
AND TWO WEEKS, FIVE DAYS.

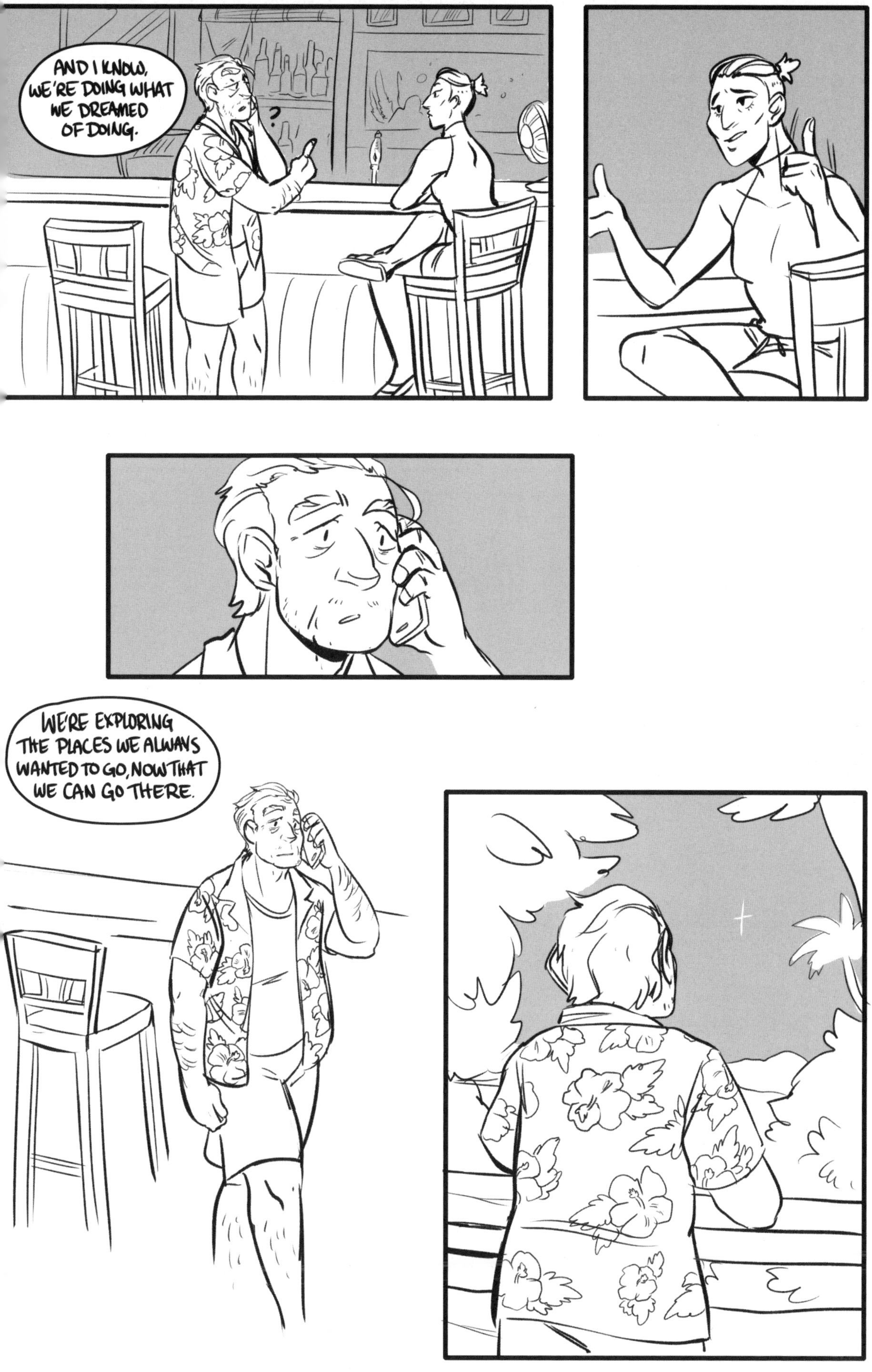
AND I KNOW, WE'RE DOING WHAT WE DREAMED OF DOING.
?
WE'RE EXPLORING THE PLACES WE ALWAYS WANTED TO GO, NOW THAT WE CAN GO THERE.

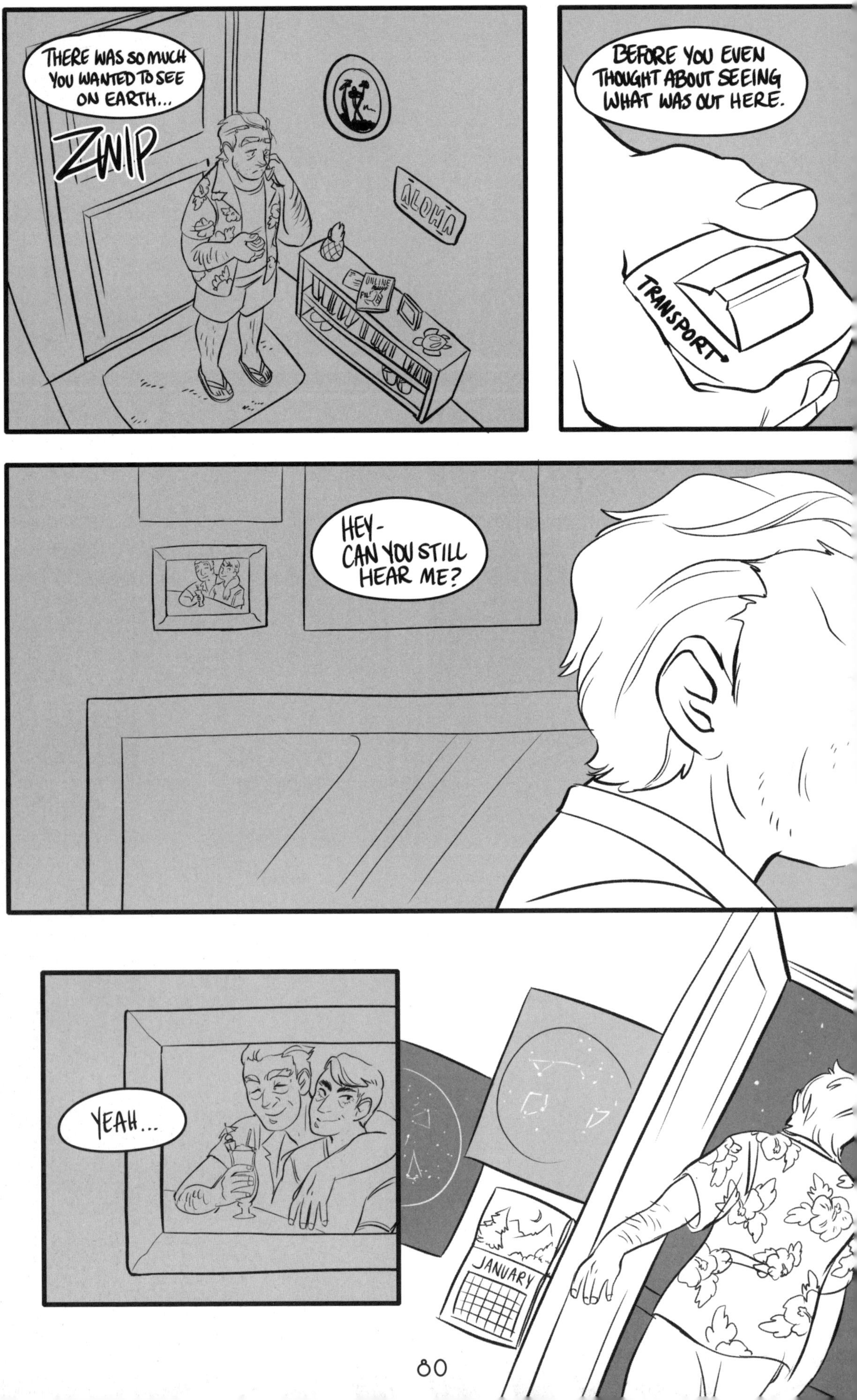
THERE WAS SO MUCH YOU WANTED TO SEE ON EARTH...
ZWIP
ALOHA
ONLINE
BEFORE YOU EVEN THOUGHT ABOUT SEEING WHAT WAS OUT HERE.
TRANSPORT
HEY- CAN YOU STILL HEAR ME?
YEAH...
JANUARY

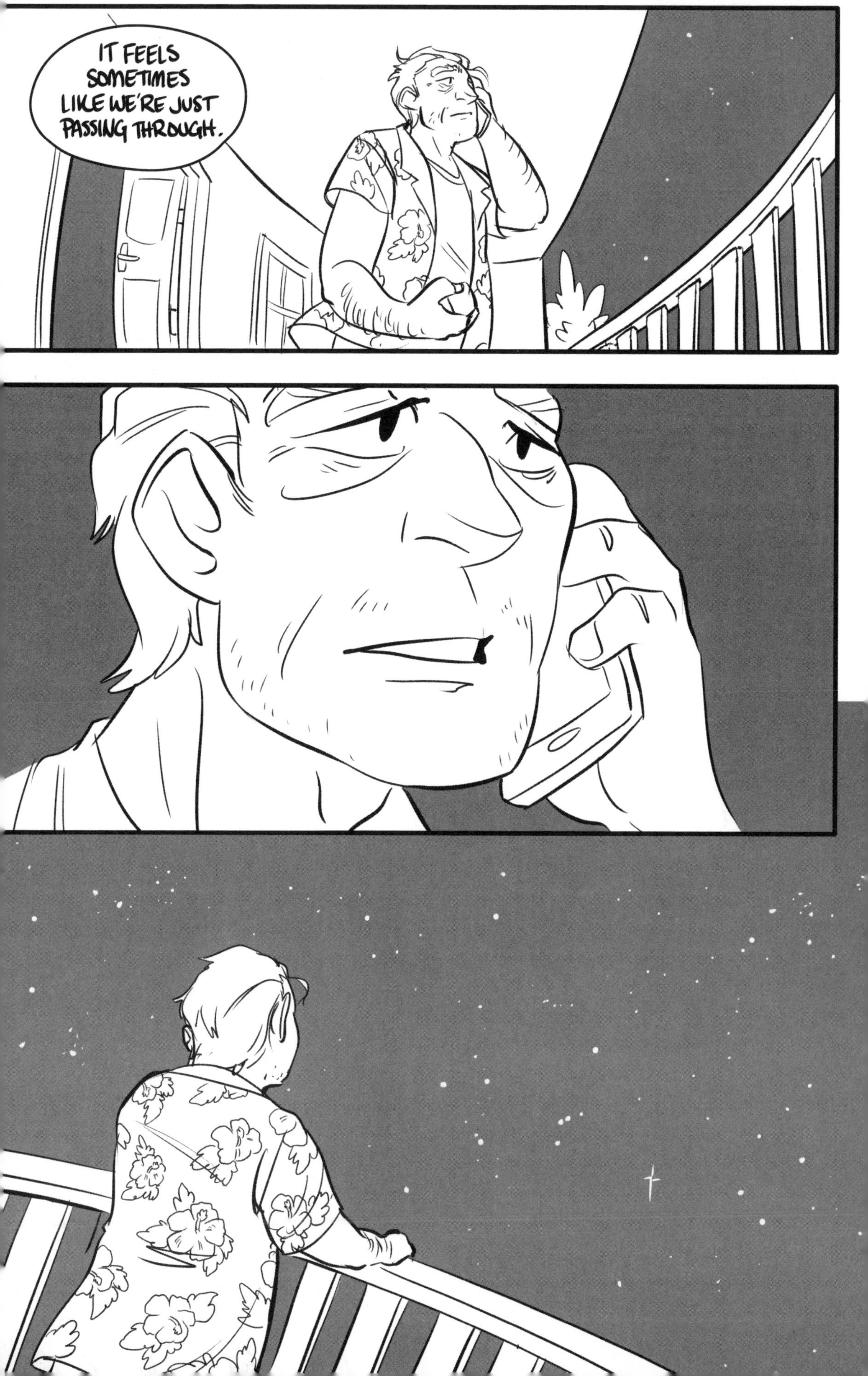
IT FEELS SOMETIMES LIKE WE'RE JUST PASSING THROUGH.

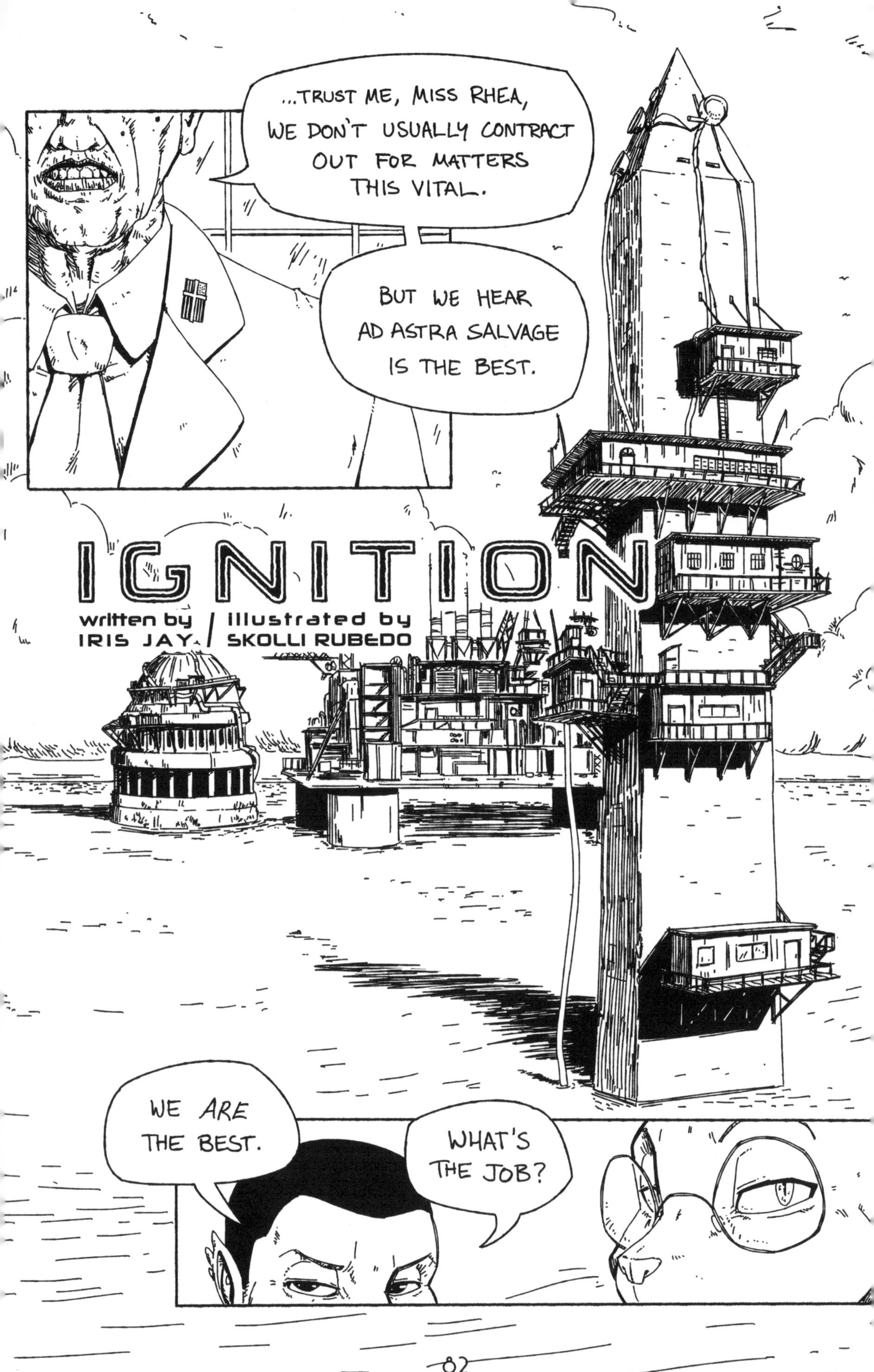
...TRUST ME, MISS RHEA, WE DON'T USUALLY CONTRACT OUT FOR MATTERS THIS VITAL.
BUT WE HEAR AD ASTRA SALVAGE IS THE BEST.
IGNITION
written by IRIS JAY / illustrated by SKOLLI RUBEDO
WE *ARE* THE BEST.
WHAT'S THE JOB?

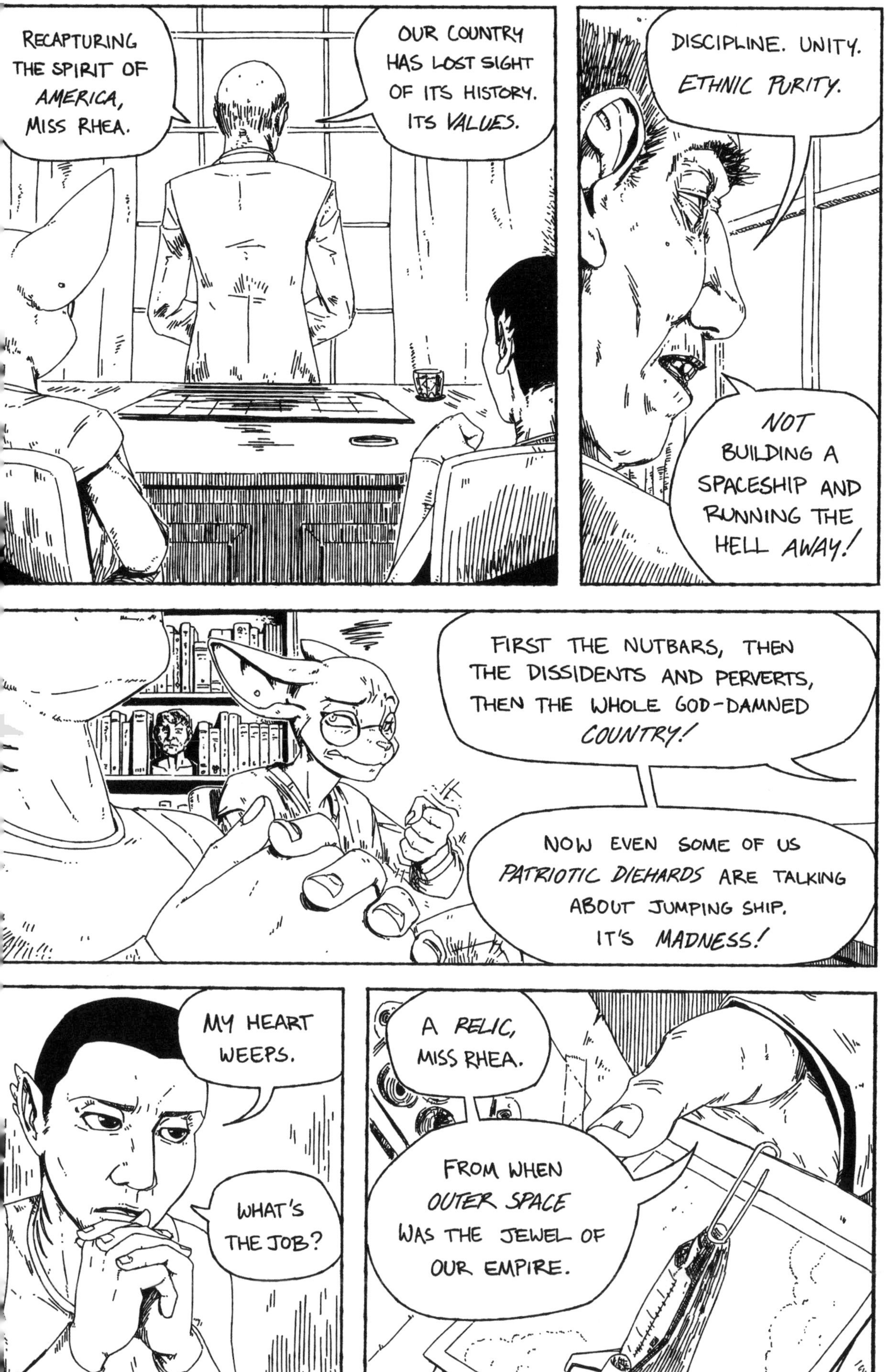
RECAPTURING THE SPIRIT OF *AMERICA,* MISS RHEA.
OUR COUNTRY HAS LOST SIGHT OF ITS HISTORY. ITS *VALUES.*
DISCIPLINE. UNITY. *ETHNIC PURITY.*
NOT BUILDING A SPACESHIP AND RUNNING THE HELL *AWAY!*
FIRST THE NUTBARS, THEN THE DISSIDENTS AND PERVERTS, THEN THE WHOLE GOD-DAMNED *COUNTRY!*
NOW EVEN SOME OF US *PATRIOTIC DIEHARDS* ARE TALKING ABOUT JUMPING SHIP. IT'S *MADNESS!*
MY HEART WEEPS.
WHAT'S THE JOB?
A *RELIC,* MISS RHEA.
FROM WHEN *OUTER SPACE* WAS THE JEWEL OF OUR EMPIRE.

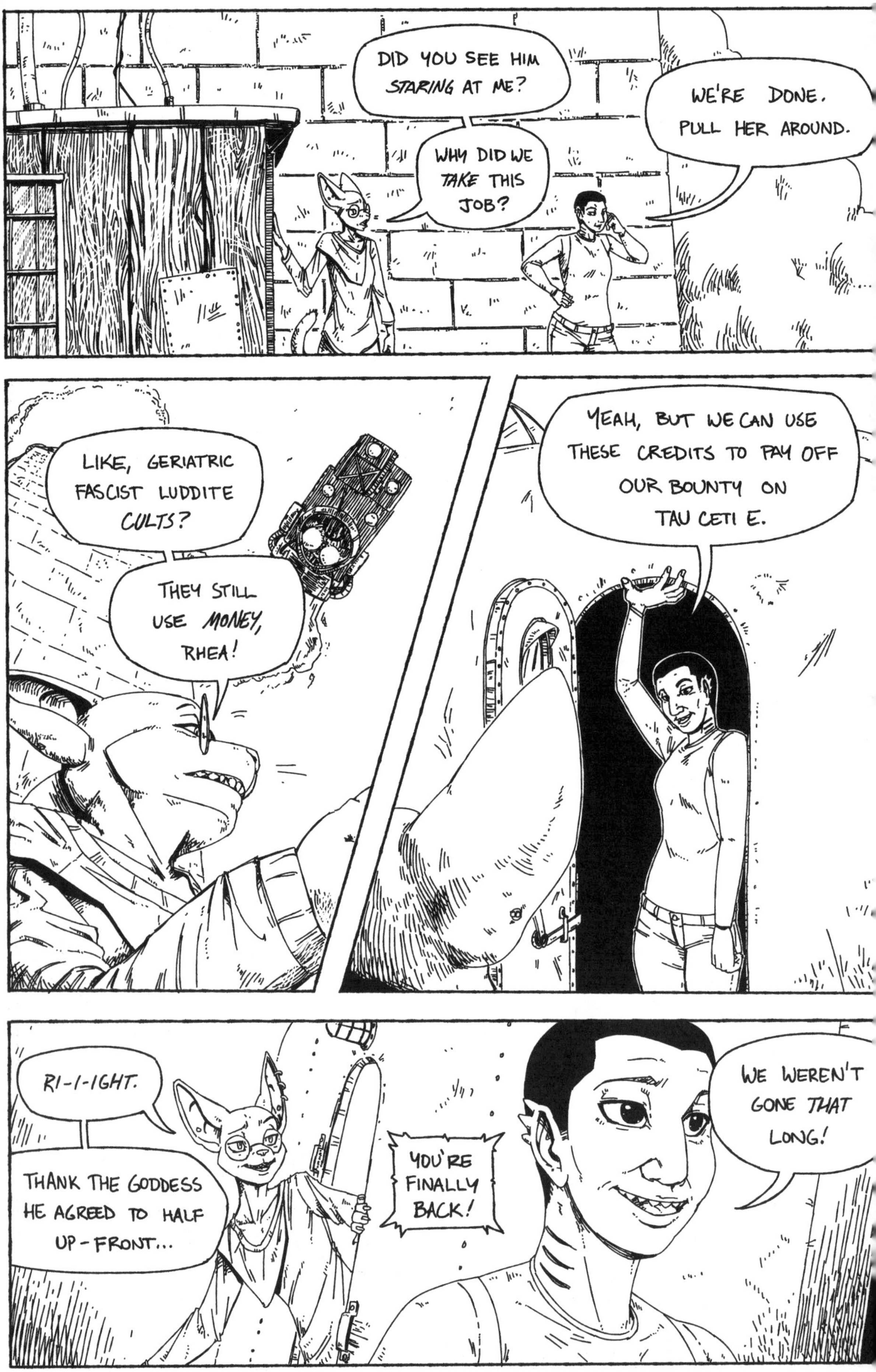
DID YOU SEE HIM STARING AT ME?
WHY DID WE TAKE THIS JOB?
WE'RE DONE. PULL HER AROUND.
LIKE, GERIATRIC FASCIST LUDDITE CULTS?
THEY STILL USE MONEY, RHEA!
YEAH, BUT WE CAN USE THESE CREDITS TO PAY OFF OUR BOUNTY ON TAU CETI E.
RI-I-IGHT.
THANK THE GODDESS HE AGREED TO HALF UP-FRONT...
YOU'RE FINALLY BACK!
WE WEREN'T GONE THAT LONG!

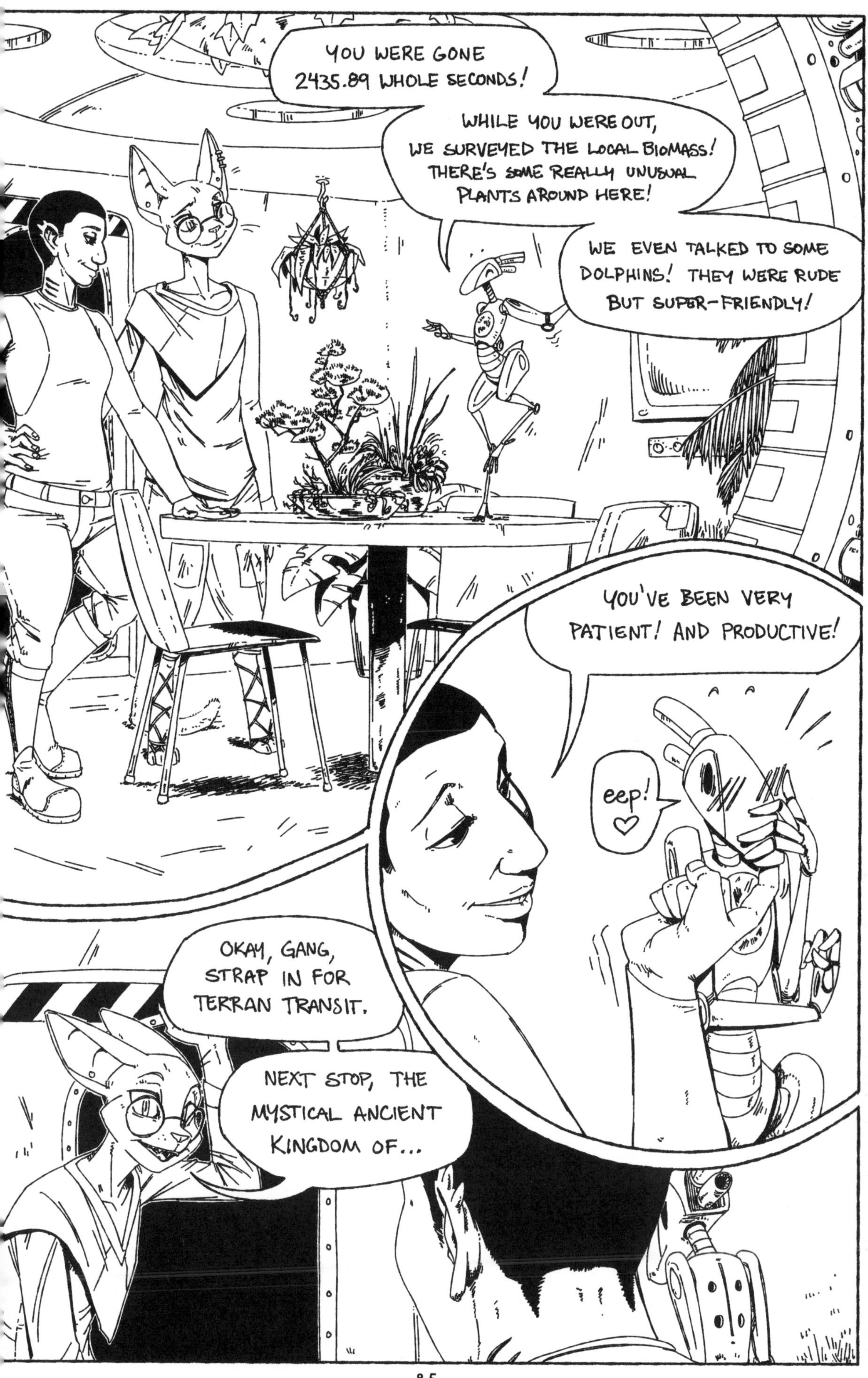

YOU WERE GONE 2435.89 WHOLE SECONDS!
WHILE YOU WERE OUT, WE SURVEYED THE LOCAL BIOMASS! THERE'S SOME REALLY UNUSUAL PLANTS AROUND HERE!
WE EVEN TALKED TO SOME DOLPHINS! THEY WERE RUDE BUT SUPER-FRIENDLY!
YOU'VE BEEN VERY PATIENT! AND PRODUCTIVE!
eep!
OKAY, GANG, STRAP IN FOR TERRAN TRANSIT.
NEXT STOP, THE MYSTICAL ANCIENT KINGDOM OF...

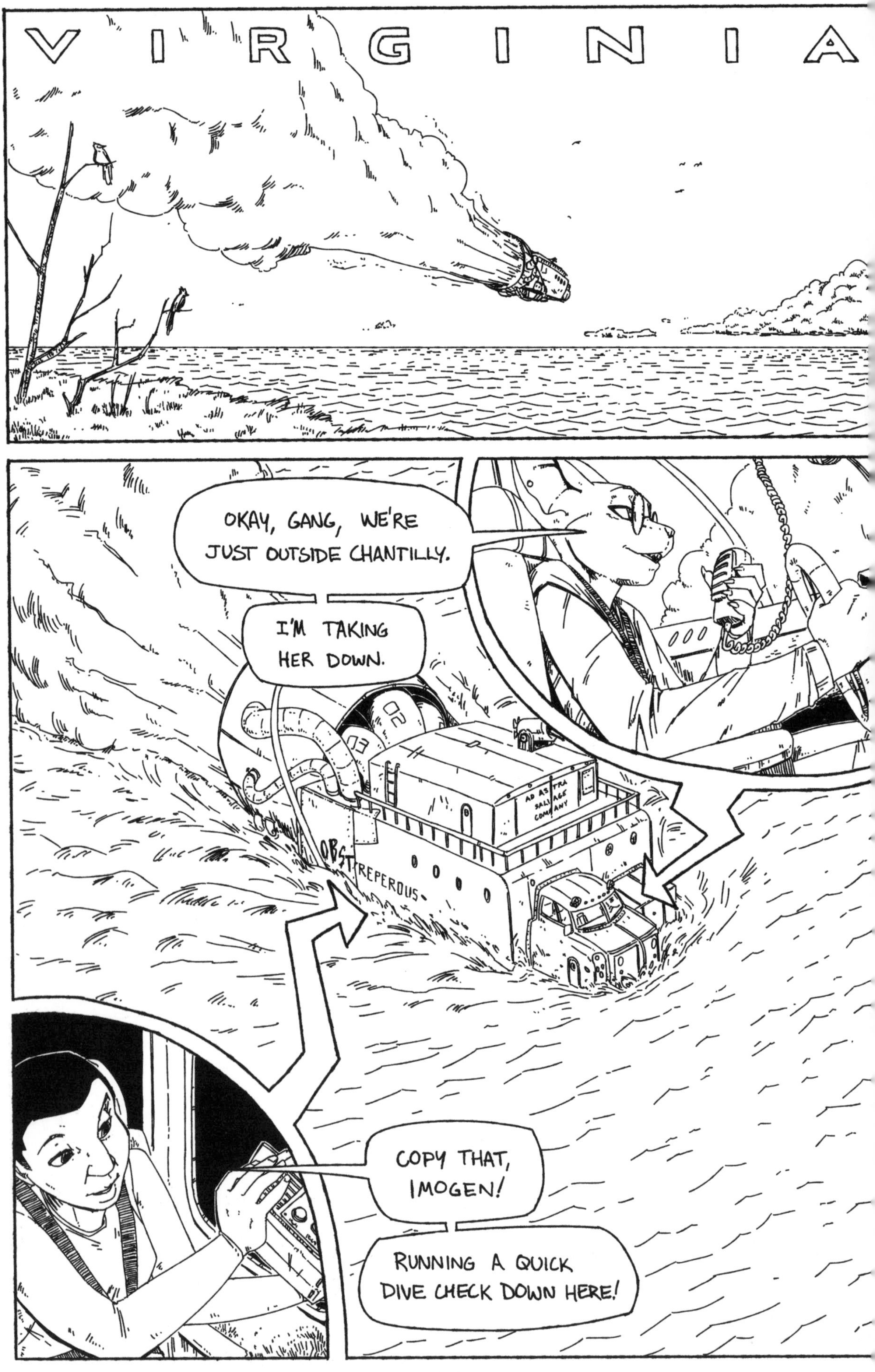
VIRGINIA
OKAY, GANG, WE'RE JUST OUTSIDE CHANTILLY.
I'M TAKING HER DOWN.
AD ASTRA SALVAGE COMPANY
OBSTREPEROUS
COPY THAT, IMOGEN!
RUNNING A QUICK DIVE CHECK DOWN HERE!

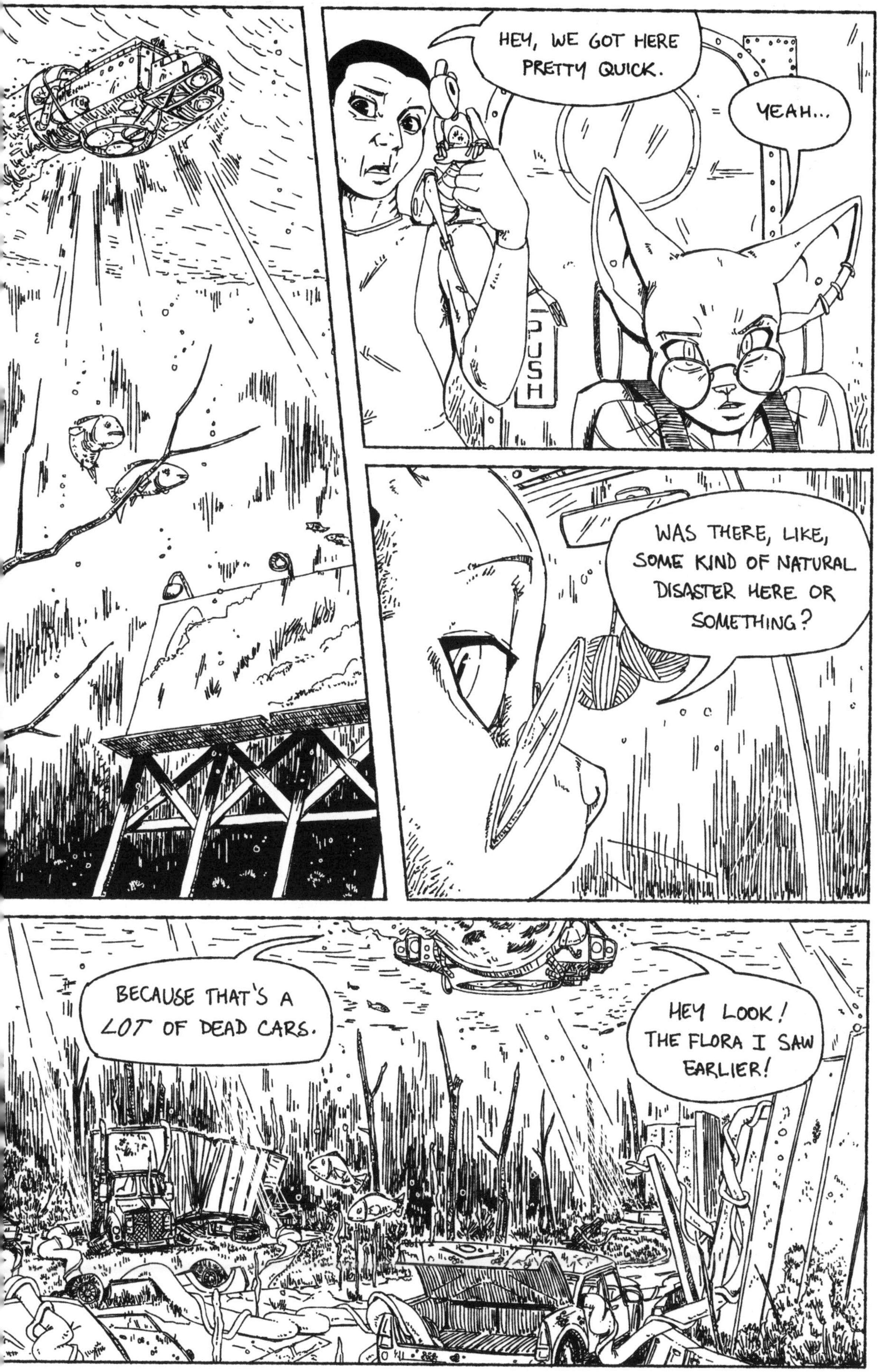
HEY, WE GOT HERE PRETTY QUICK.
YEAH...
PUSH
WAS THERE, LIKE, SOME KIND OF NATURAL DISASTER HERE OR SOMETHING?
BECAUSE THAT'S A *LOT* OF DEAD CARS.
HEY LOOK! THE FLORA I SAW EARLIER!

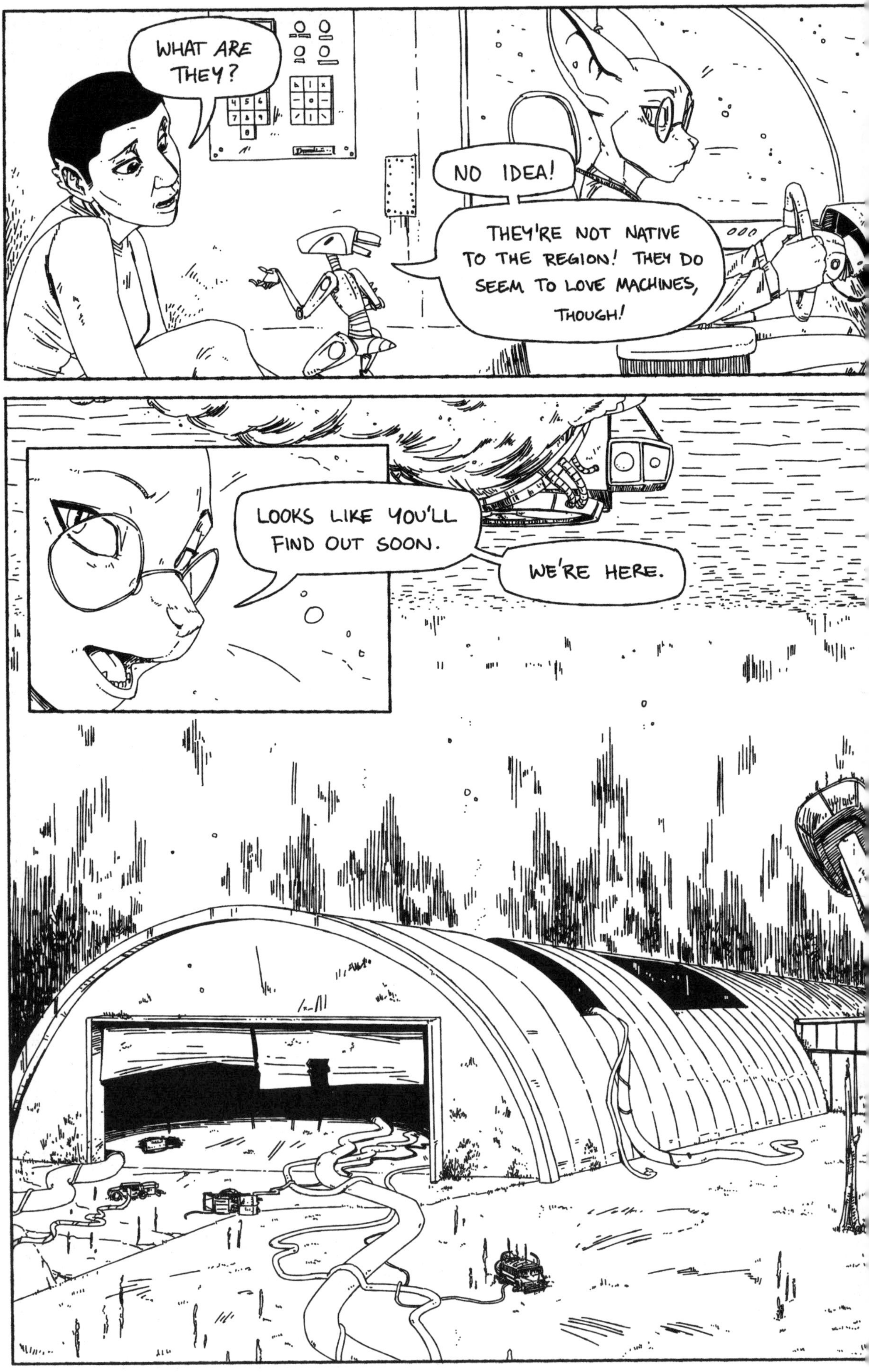
WHAT ARE THEY?
NO IDEA!
THEY'RE NOT NATIVE TO THE REGION! THEY DO SEEM TO LOVE MACHINES, THOUGH!
LOOKS LIKE YOU'LL FIND OUT SOON.
WE'RE HERE.

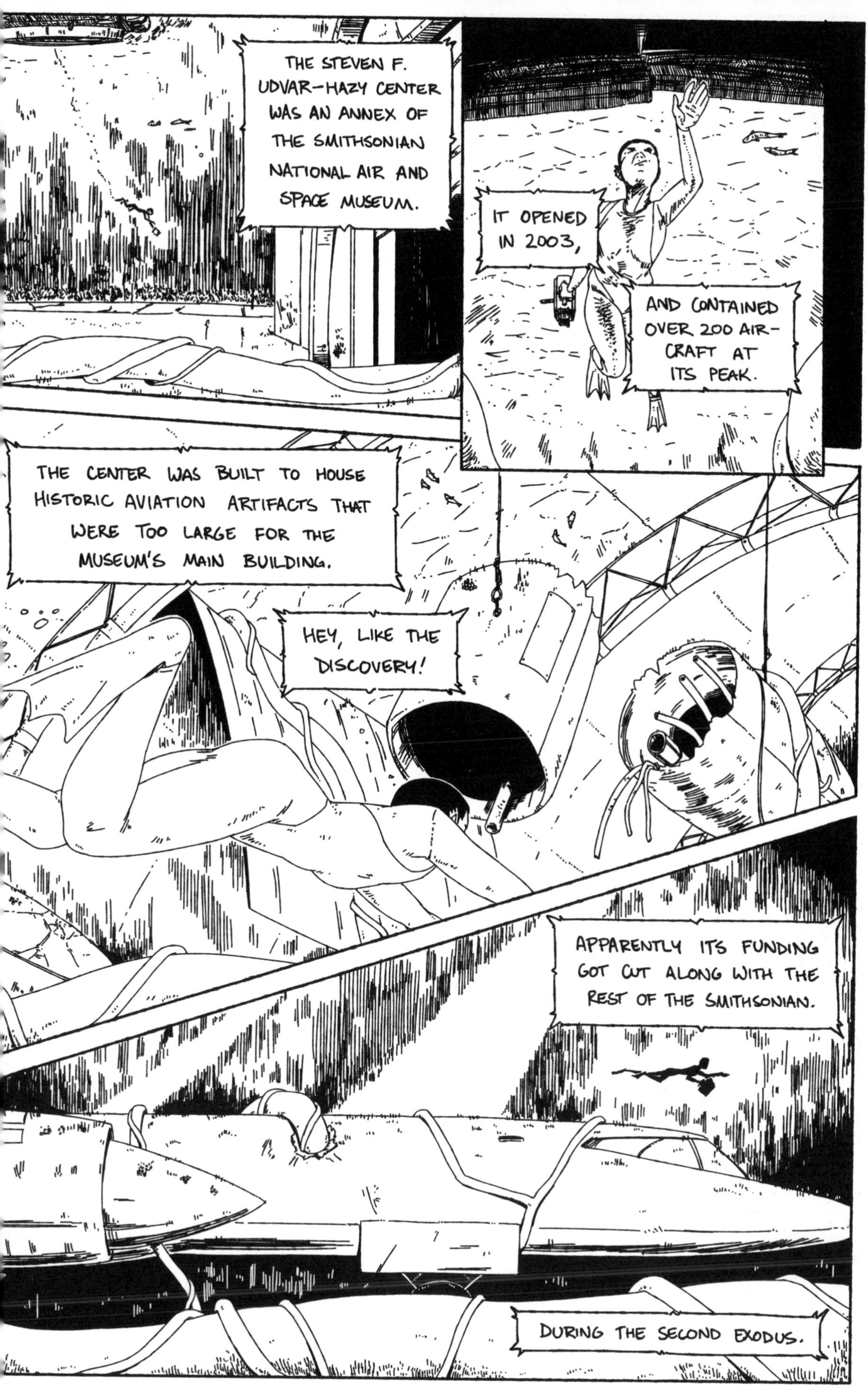
THE STEVEN F. UDVAR-HAZY CENTER WAS AN ANNEX OF THE SMITHSONIAN NATIONAL AIR AND SPACE MUSEUM.
IT OPENED IN 2003,
AND CONTAINED OVER 200 AIR-CRAFT AT ITS PEAK.
THE CENTER WAS BUILT TO HOUSE HISTORIC AVIATION ARTIFACTS THAT WERE TOO LARGE FOR THE MUSEUM'S MAIN BUILDING.
HEY, LIKE THE DISCOVERY!
APPARENTLY ITS FUNDING GOT CUT ALONG WITH THE REST OF THE SMITHSONIAN.
DURING THE SECOND EXODUS.

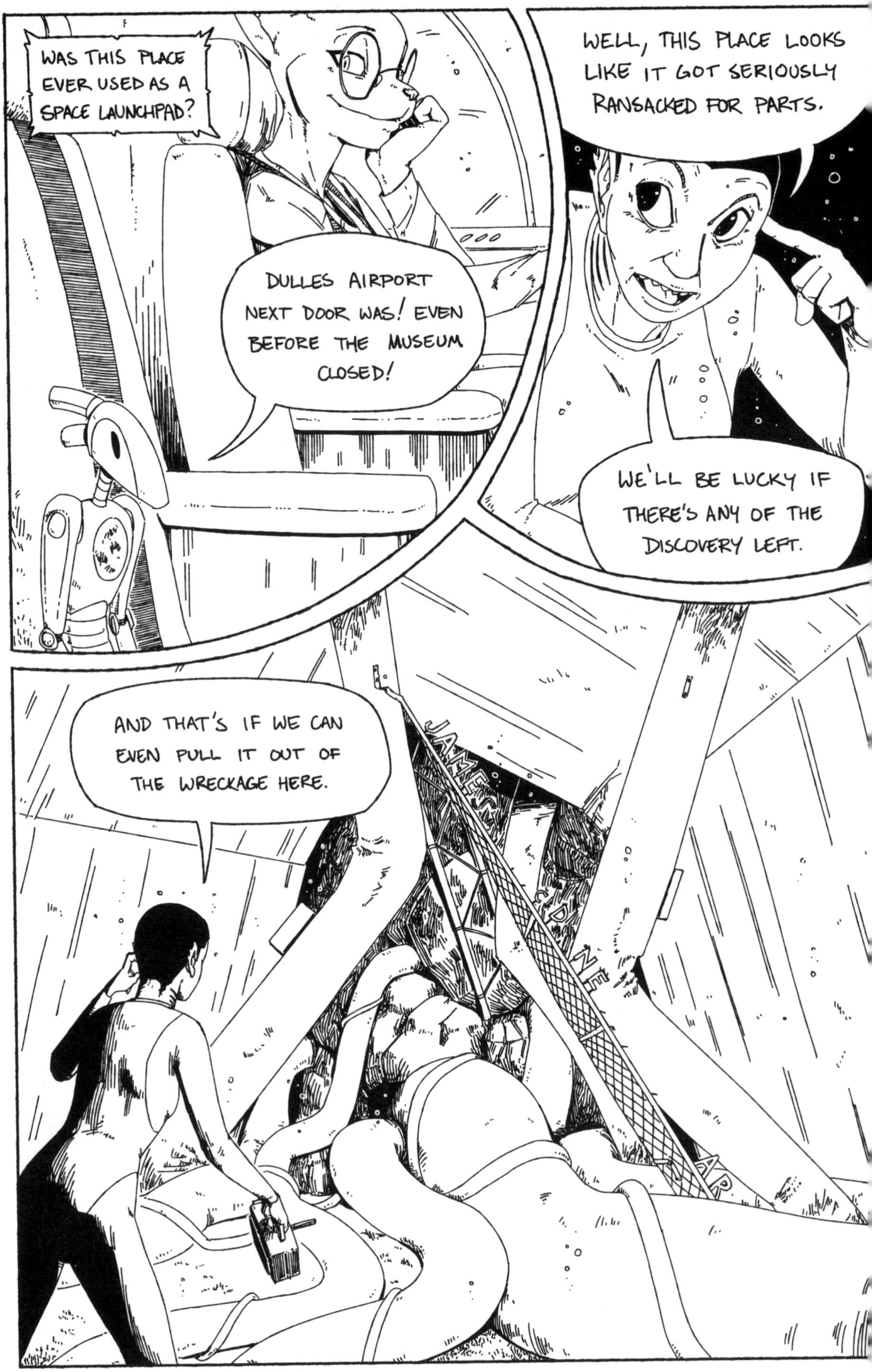
WAS THIS PLACE EVER USED AS A SPACE LAUNCHPAD?
DULLES AIRPORT NEXT DOOR WAS! EVEN BEFORE THE MUSEUM CLOSED!
WELL, THIS PLACE LOOKS LIKE IT GOT SERIOUSLY RANSACKED FOR PARTS.
WE'LL BE LUCKY IF THERE'S ANY OF THE DISCOVERY LEFT.
AND THAT'S IF WE CAN EVEN PULL IT OUT OF THE WRECKAGE HERE.

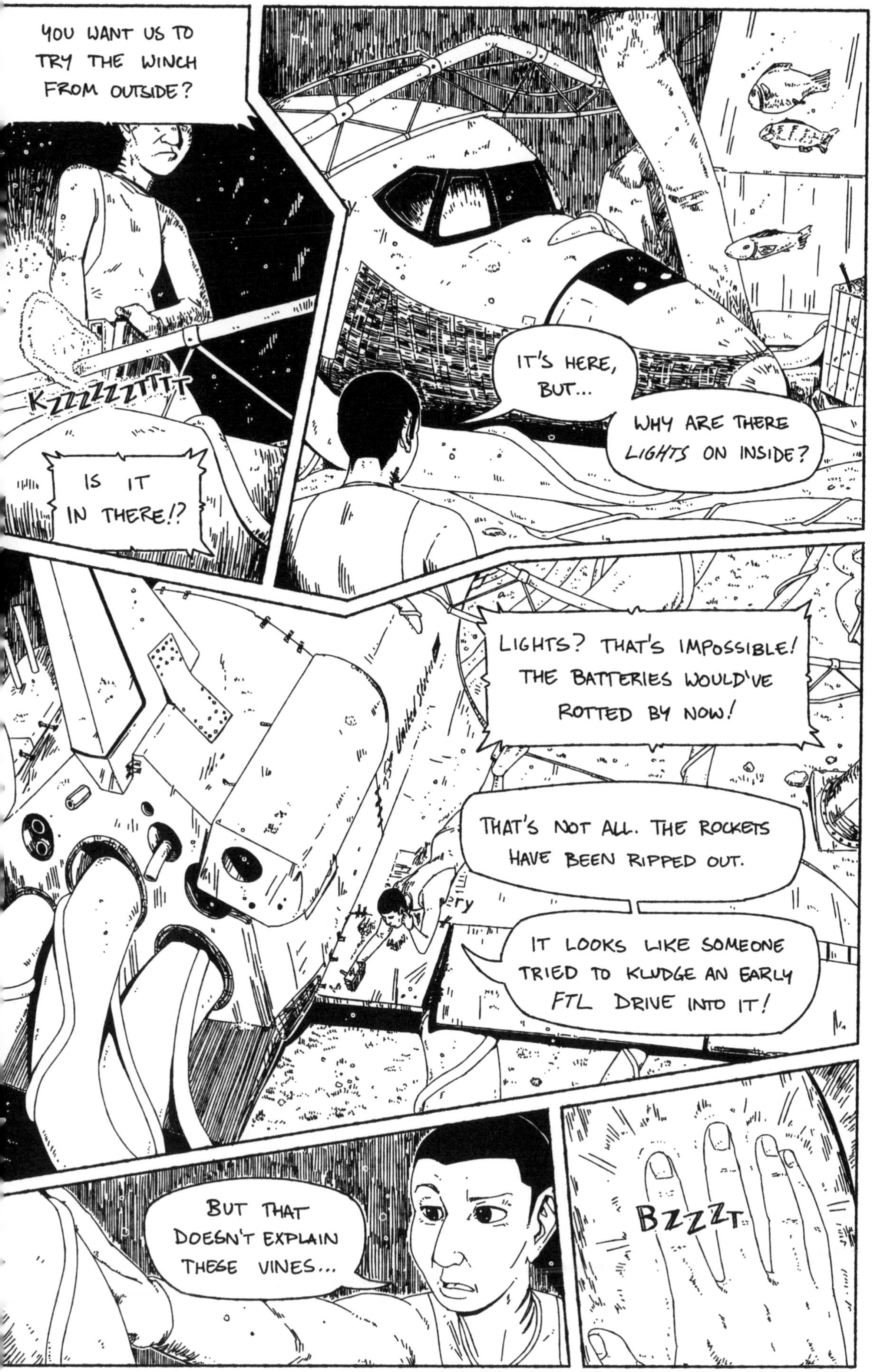
YOU WANT US TO TRY THE WINCH FROM OUTSIDE?
KZZZZZZTTTT
IS IT IN THERE!?
IT'S HERE, BUT...
WHY ARE THERE LIGHTS ON INSIDE?
LIGHTS? THAT'S IMPOSSIBLE! THE BATTERIES WOULD'VE ROTTED BY NOW!
THAT'S NOT ALL. THE ROCKETS HAVE BEEN RIPPED OUT.
IT LOOKS LIKE SOMEONE TRIED TO KLUDGE AN EARLY FTL DRIVE INTO IT!
BUT THAT DOESN'T EXPLAIN THESE VINES...
BZZZT

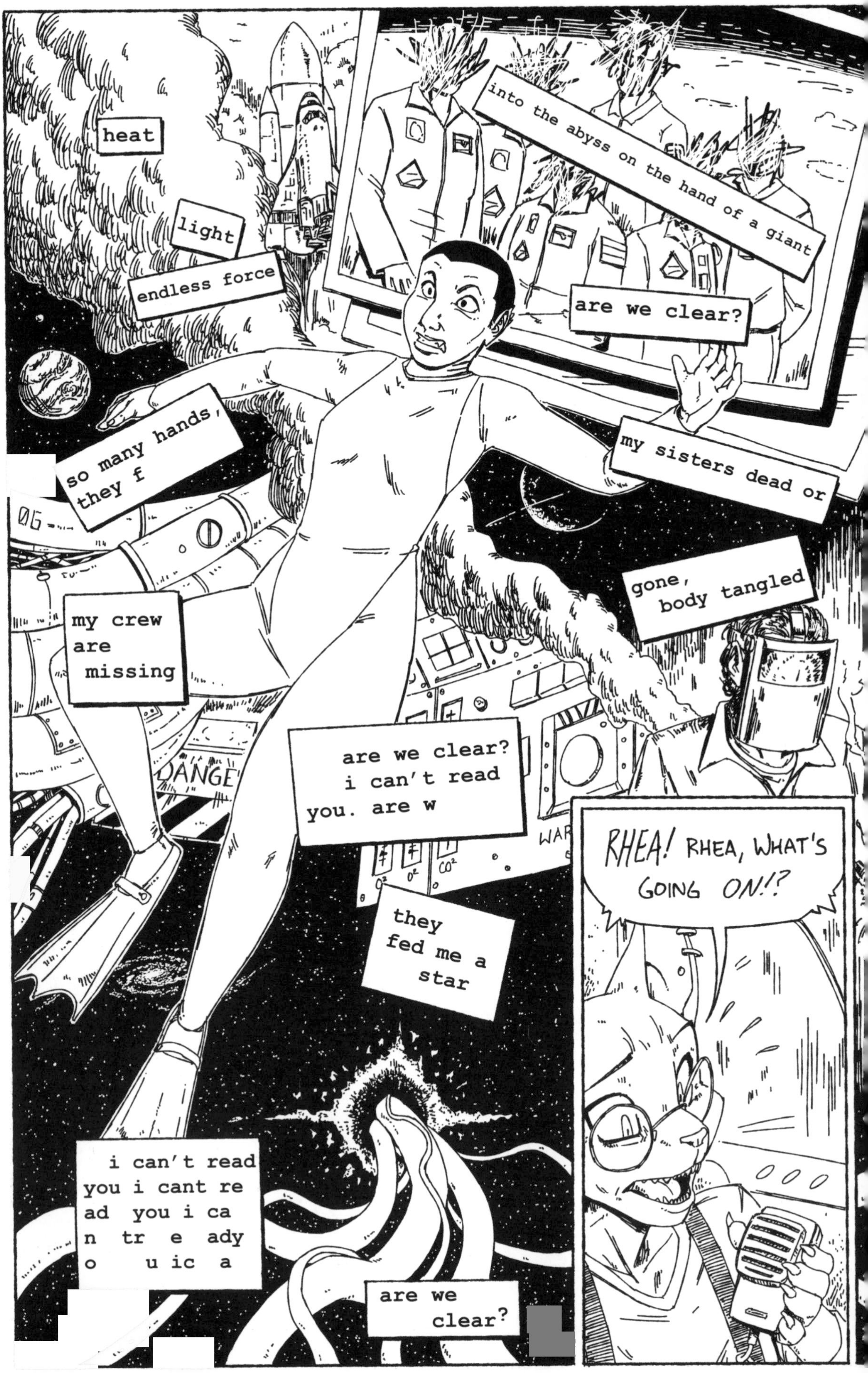
heat
light
endless force
into the abyss on the hand of a giant
are we clear?
so many hands, they f
my sisters dead or
gone, body tangled
my crew are missing
are we clear? i can't read you. are w
they fed me a star
RHEA! RHEA, WHAT'S GOING ON!?
i can't read you i cant re ad you i ca n tr e ady o u ic a
are we clear?

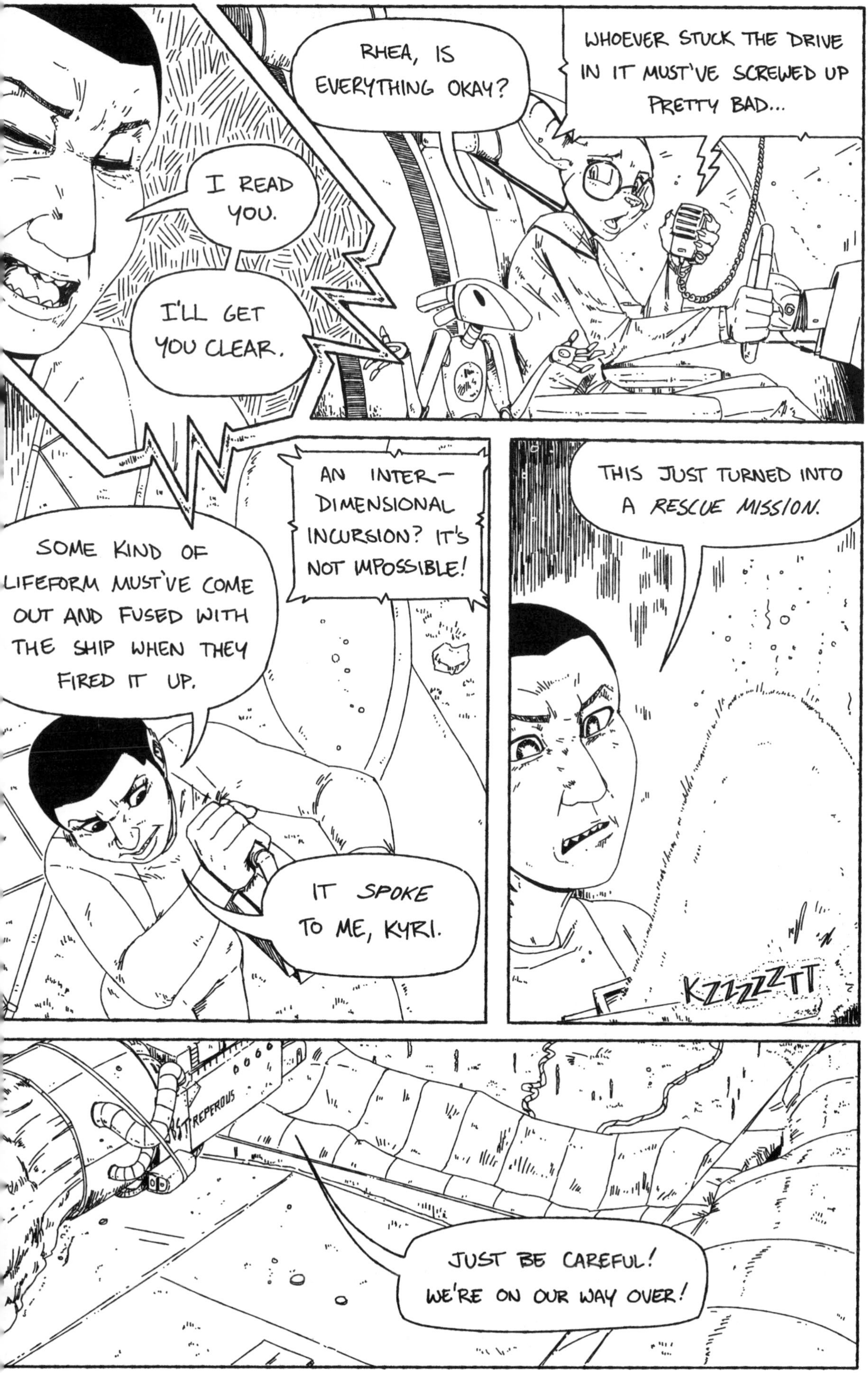
RHEA, IS EVERYTHING OKAY?
WHOEVER STUCK THE DRIVE IN IT MUST'VE SCREWED UP PRETTY BAD...
I READ YOU.
I'LL GET YOU CLEAR.
AN INTER-DIMENSIONAL INCURSION? IT'S NOT IMPOSSIBLE!
SOME KIND OF LIFEFORM MUST'VE COME OUT AND FUSED WITH THE SHIP WHEN THEY FIRED IT UP.
IT SPOKE TO ME, KYRI.
THIS JUST TURNED INTO A RESCUE MISSION.
KZZZZZTT
STREPEROUS
JUST BE CAREFUL! WE'RE ON OUR WAY OVER!

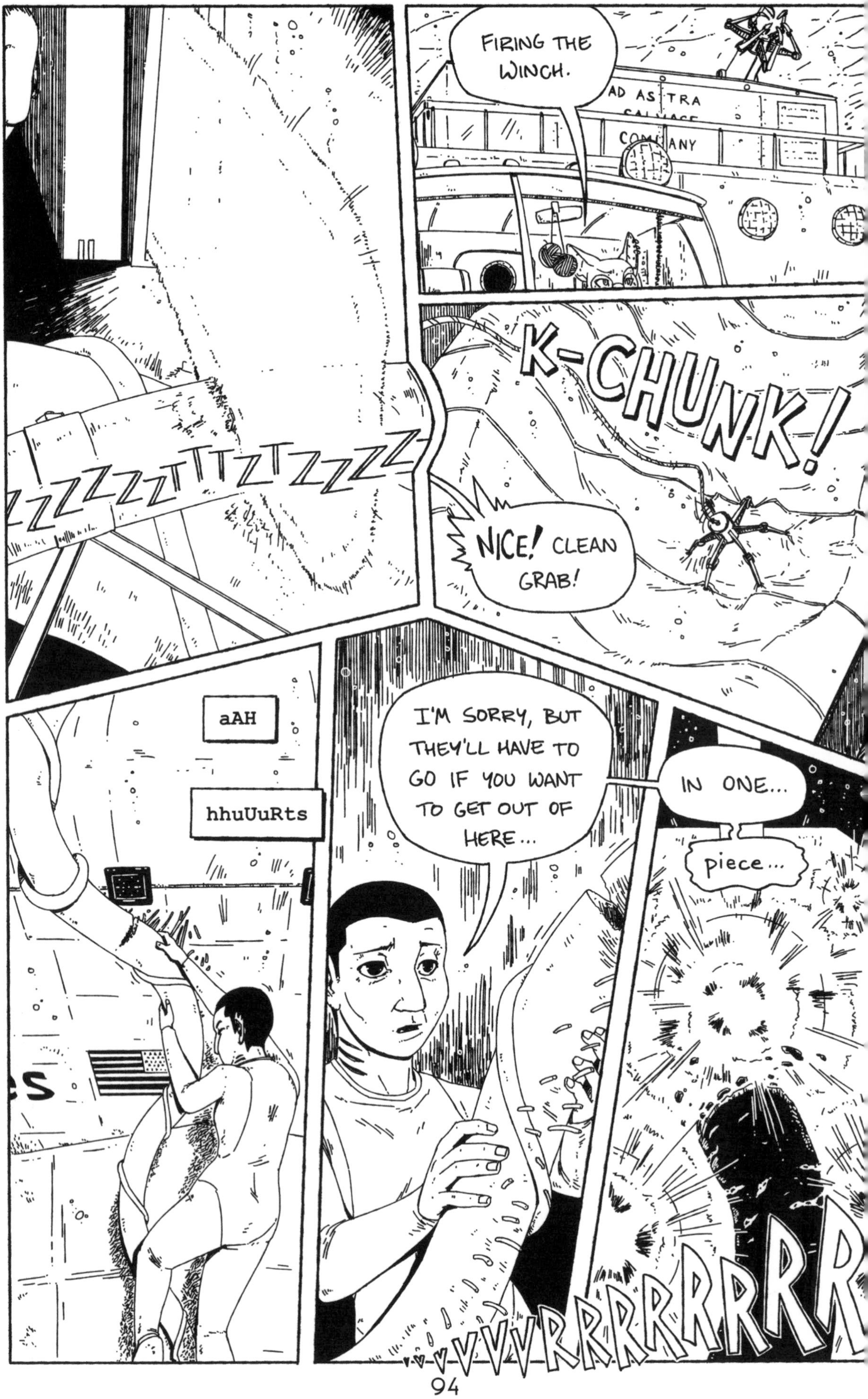
FIRING THE WINCH.
AD ASTRA SALVAGE COMPANY
ZZZZZZZTTTZTZZZZ
K-CHUNK!
NICE! CLEAN GRAB!
aAH
hhuUuRts
I'M SORRY, BUT THEY'LL HAVE TO GO IF YOU WANT TO GET OUT OF HERE...
IN ONE...
piece...
VVVVRRRRRRRR

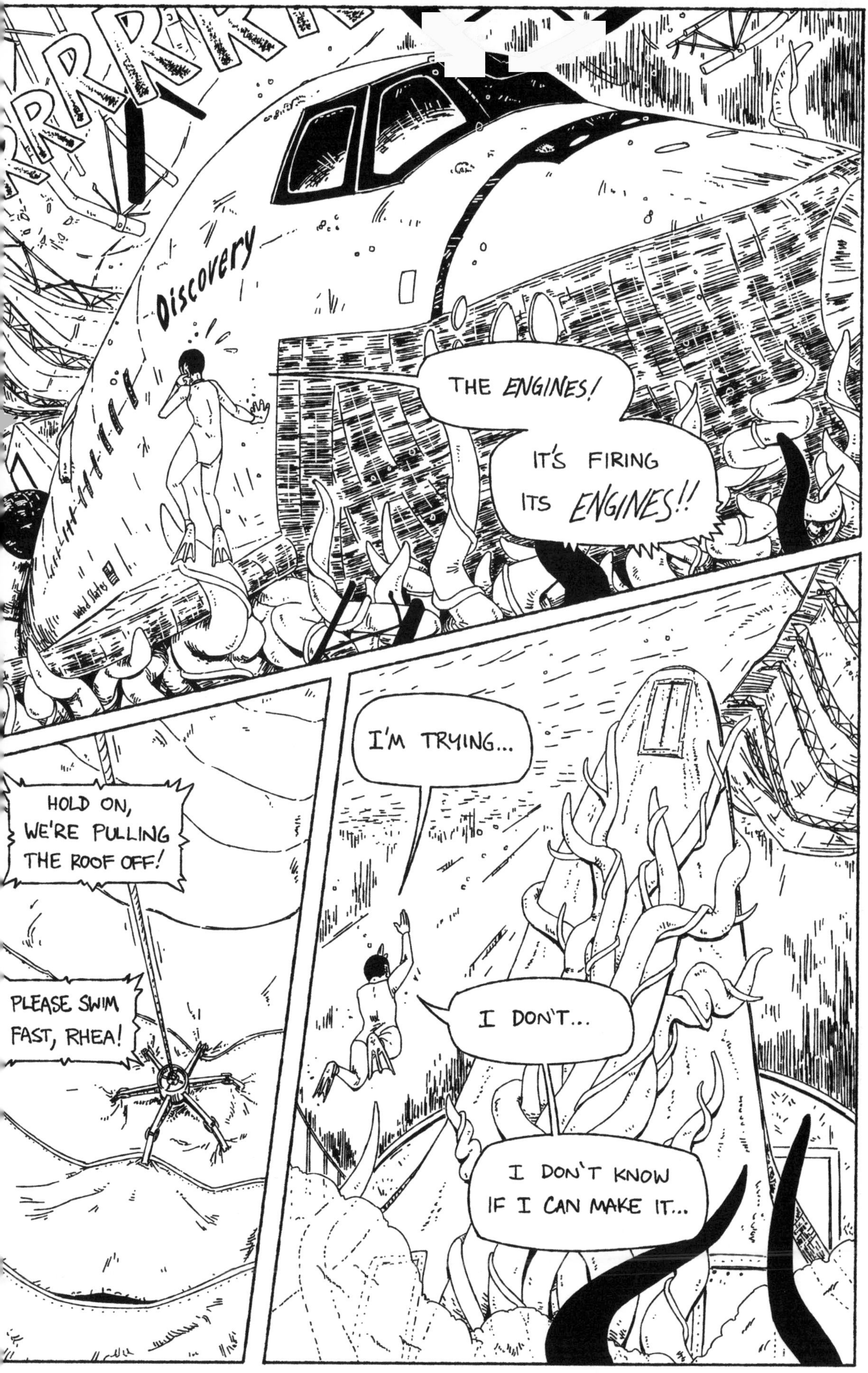

RRRRK
Discovery
THE ENGINES!
IT'S FIRING ITS ENGINES!!
HOLD ON, WE'RE PULLING THE ROOF OFF!
PLEASE SWIM FAST, RHEA!
I'M TRYING...
I DON'T...
I DON'T KNOW IF I CAN MAKE IT...

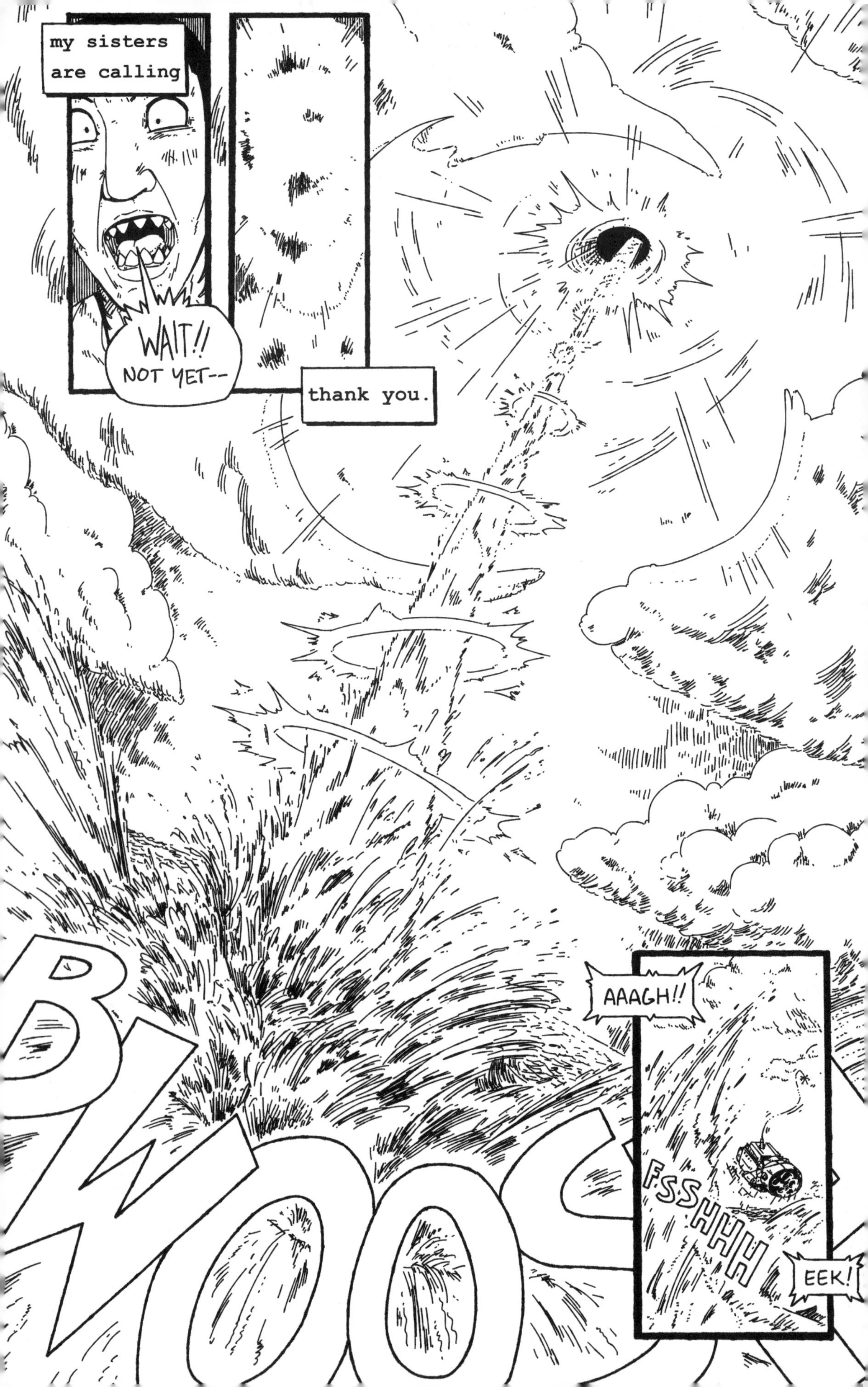
my sisters are calling
WAIT!! NOT YET--
thank you.
BWOOOOM
AAAGH!!
FSSHHH
EEK!

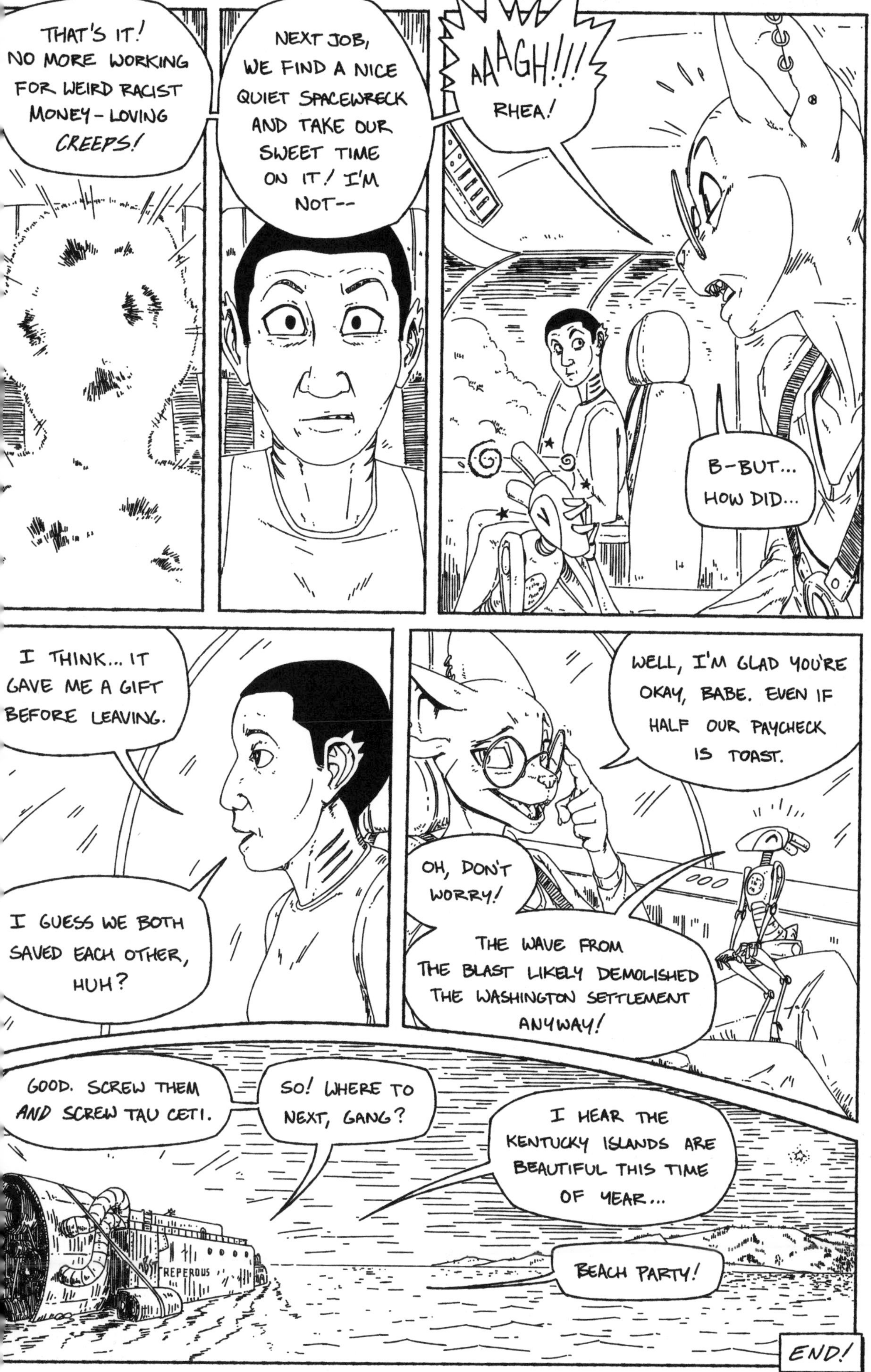
THAT'S IT! NO MORE WORKING FOR WEIRD RACIST MONEY-LOVING CREEPS!
NEXT JOB, WE FIND A NICE QUIET SPACEWRECK AND TAKE OUR SWEET TIME ON IT! I'M NOT--
AAAGH!!!!
RHEA!
B-BUT... HOW DID...
I THINK... IT GAVE ME A GIFT BEFORE LEAVING.
I GUESS WE BOTH SAVED EACH OTHER, HUH?
WELL, I'M GLAD YOU'RE OKAY, BABE. EVEN IF HALF OUR PAYCHECK IS TOAST.
OH, DON'T WORRY!
THE WAVE FROM THE BLAST LIKELY DEMOLISHED THE WASHINGTON SETTLEMENT ANYWAY!
GOOD. SCREW THEM AND SCREW TAU CETI.
SO! WHERE TO NEXT, GANG?
I HEAR THE KENTUCKY ISLANDS ARE BEAUTIFUL THIS TIME OF YEAR...
BEACH PARTY!
REPEROUS
END!

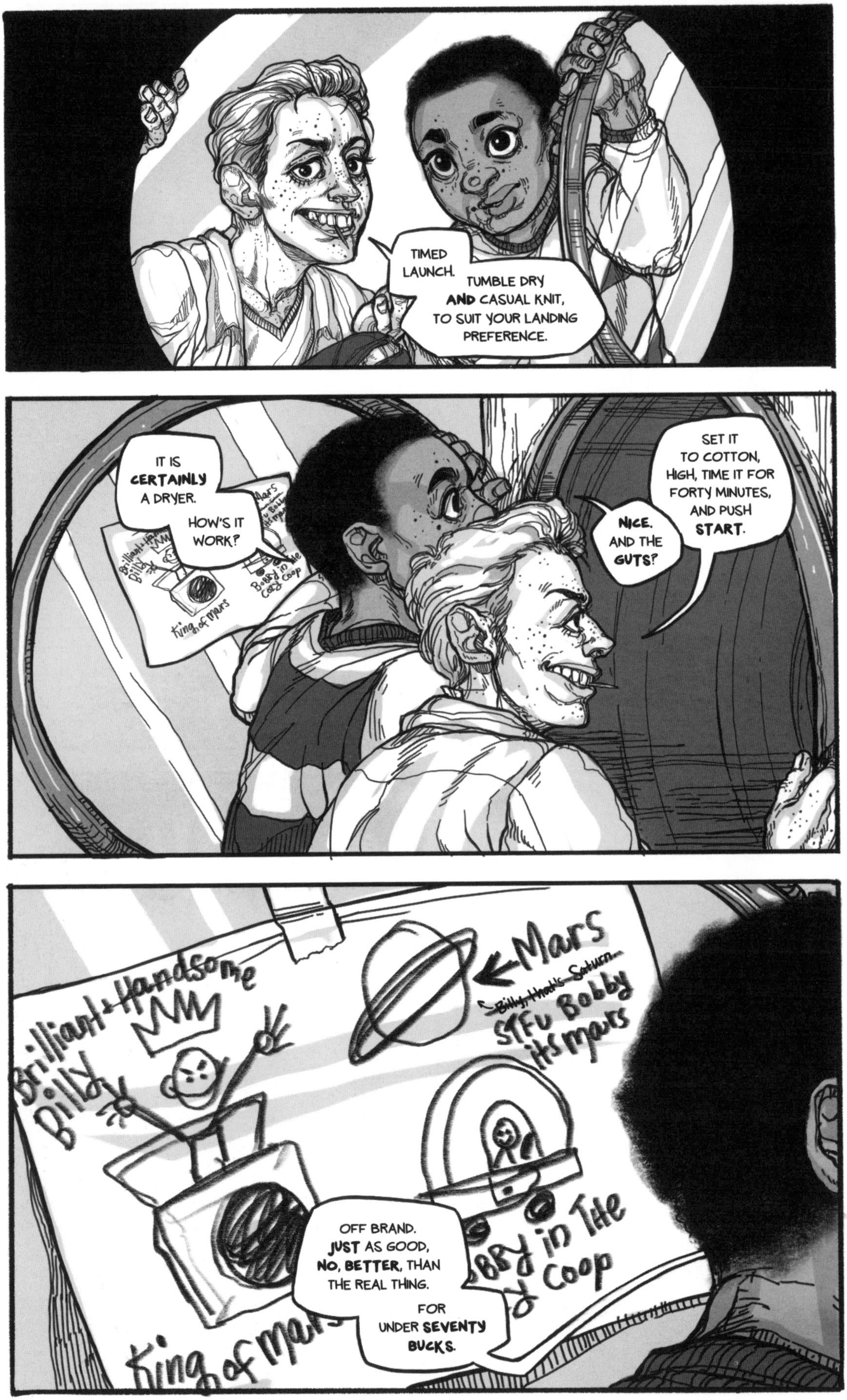
TIMED LAUNCH.
TUMBLE DRY AND CASUAL KNIT, TO SUIT YOUR LANDING PREFERENCE.
IT IS CERTAINLY A DRYER.
HOW'S IT WORK?
NICE. AND THE GUTS?
SET IT TO COTTON, HIGH, TIME IT FOR FORTY MINUTES, AND PUSH START.
Brilliant & Handsome
Billy
Mars
Billy, that's Saturn
STFU Bobby its mars
King of mars
OFF BRAND. JUST AS GOOD, NO, BETTER, THAN THE REAL THING.
FOR UNDER SEVENTY BUCKS.

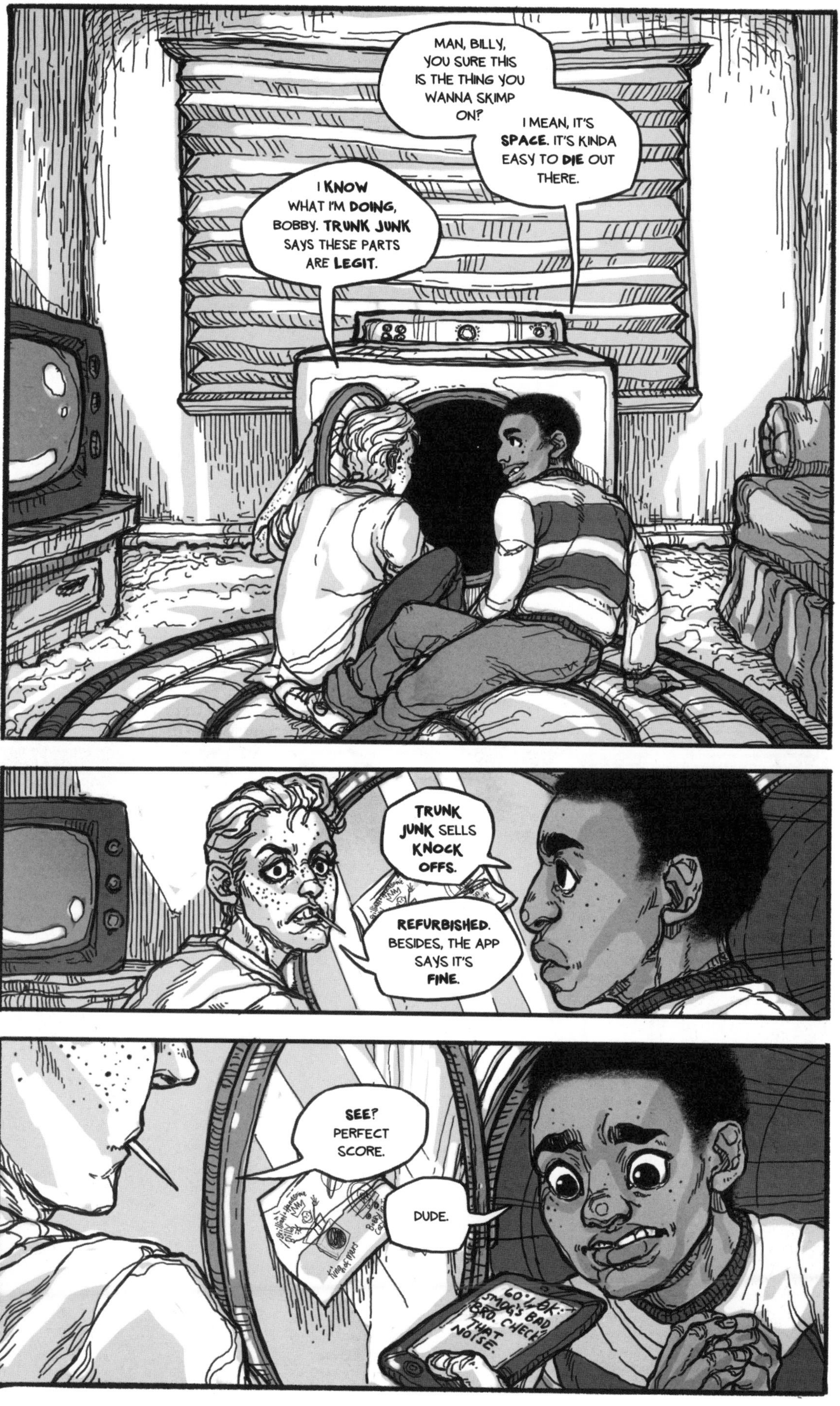
MAN, BILLY, YOU SURE THIS IS THE THING YOU WANNA SKIMP ON?
I MEAN, IT'S **SPACE**. IT'S KINDA EASY TO **DIE** OUT THERE.
I **KNOW** WHAT I'M **DOING**, BOBBY. **TRUNK JUNK** SAYS THESE PARTS ARE **LEGIT**.
TRUNK JUNK SELLS **KNOCK OFFS**.
REFURBISHED. BESIDES, THE APP SAYS IT'S **FINE**.
SEE? PERFECT SCORE.
DUDE.
60% OK: SMOG'S BAD BRO. CHECK THAT NOISE.

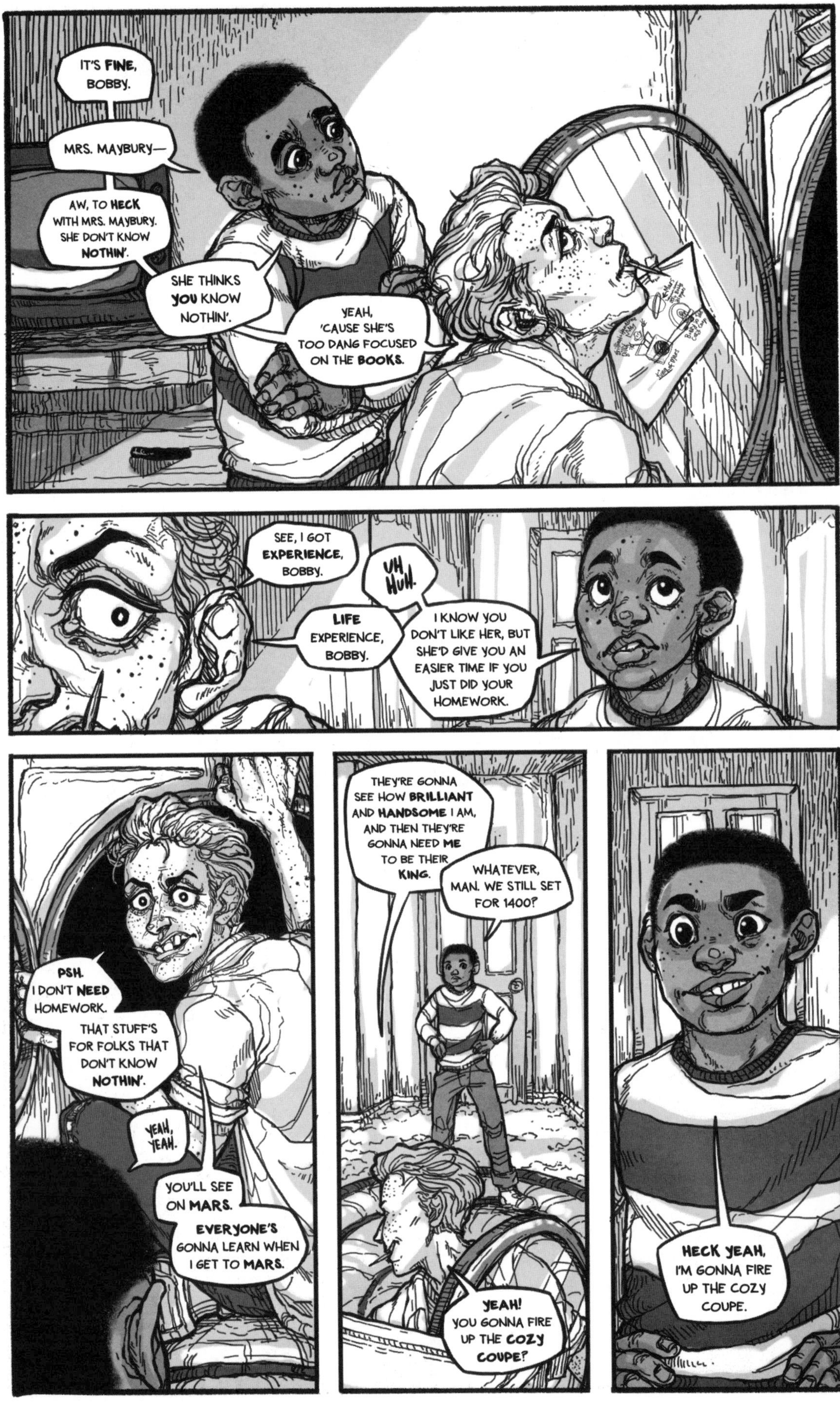

IT'S FINE, BOBBY.
MRS. MAYBURY—
AW, TO HECK WITH MRS. MAYBURY. SHE DON'T KNOW NOTHIN'.
SHE THINKS YOU KNOW NOTHIN'.
YEAH, 'CAUSE SHE'S TOO DANG FOCUSED ON THE BOOKS.
SEE, I GOT EXPERIENCE, BOBBY.
UH HUH.
LIFE EXPERIENCE, BOBBY.
I KNOW YOU DON'T LIKE HER, BUT SHE'D GIVE YOU AN EASIER TIME IF YOU JUST DID YOUR HOMEWORK.
PSH. I DON'T NEED HOMEWORK.
THAT STUFF'S FOR FOLKS THAT DON'T KNOW NOTHIN'.
YEAH, YEAH.
YOU'LL SEE ON MARS.
EVERYONE'S GONNA LEARN WHEN I GET TO MARS.
THEY'RE GONNA SEE HOW BRILLIANT AND HANDSOME I AM, AND THEN THEY'RE GONNA NEED ME TO BE THEIR KING.
WHATEVER, MAN. WE STILL SET FOR 1400?
YEAH! YOU GONNA FIRE UP THE COZY COUPE?
HECK YEAH, I'M GONNA FIRE UP THE COZY COUPE.

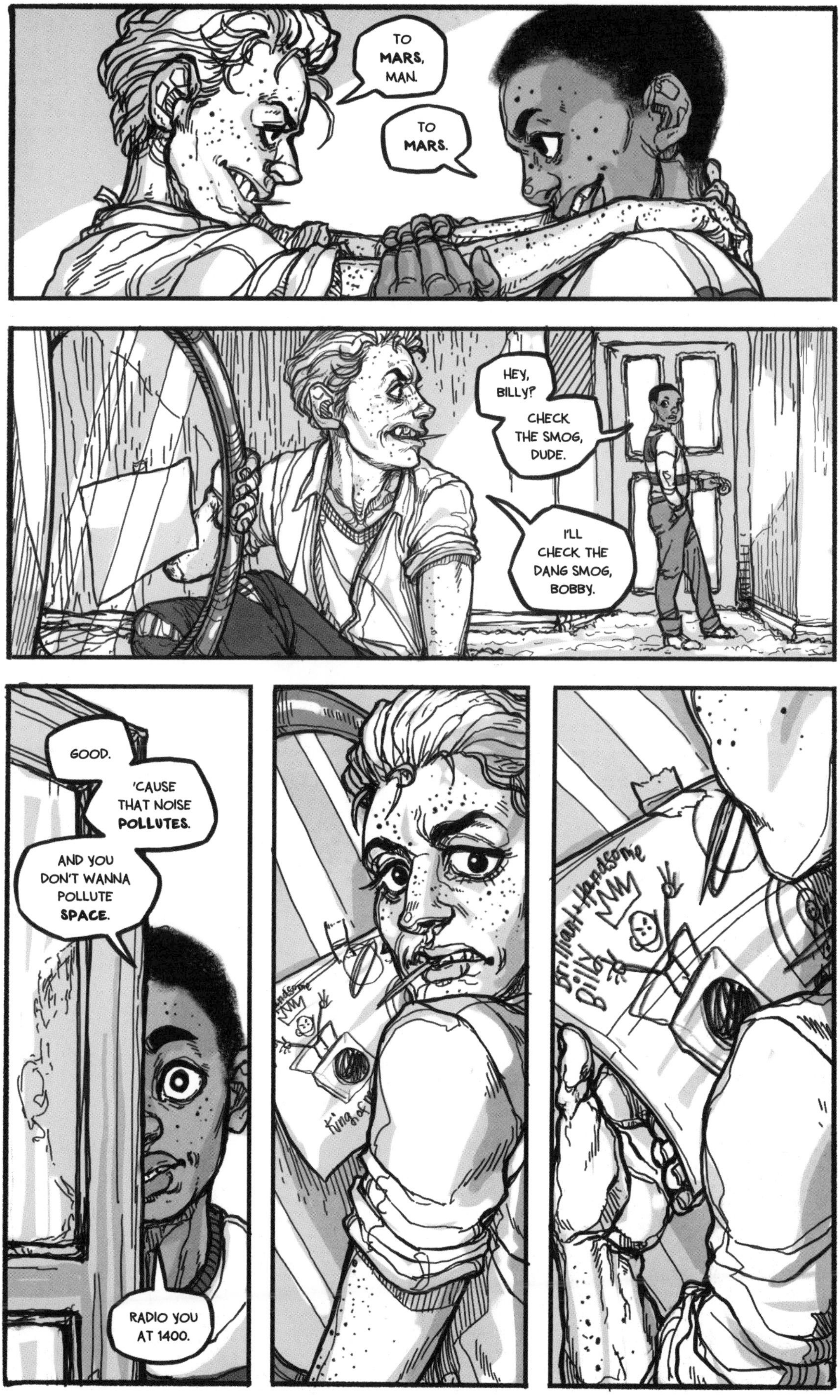
TO **MARS,** MAN.
TO **MARS.**
HEY, BILLY?
CHECK THE SMOG, DUDE.
I'LL CHECK THE DANG SMOG, BOBBY.
GOOD.
'CAUSE THAT NOISE **POLLUTES.**
AND YOU DON'T WANNA POLLUTE **SPACE.**
RADIO YOU AT 1400.

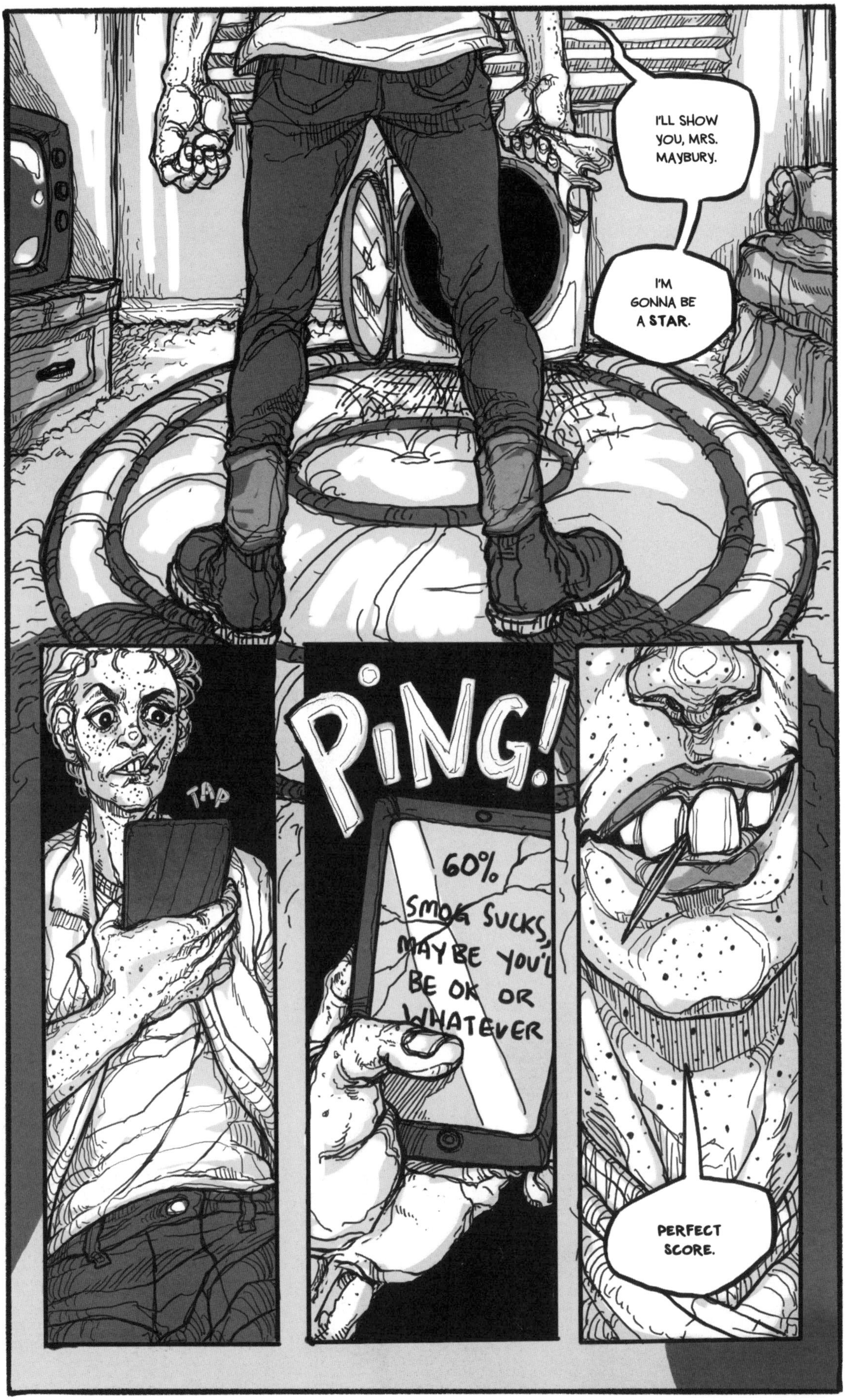
I'LL SHOW YOU, MRS. MAYBURY.
I'M GONNA BE A STAR.
TAP
PING!
60%
SMOG SUCKS, MAYBE YOU'L BE OK OR WHATEVER
PERFECT SCORE.

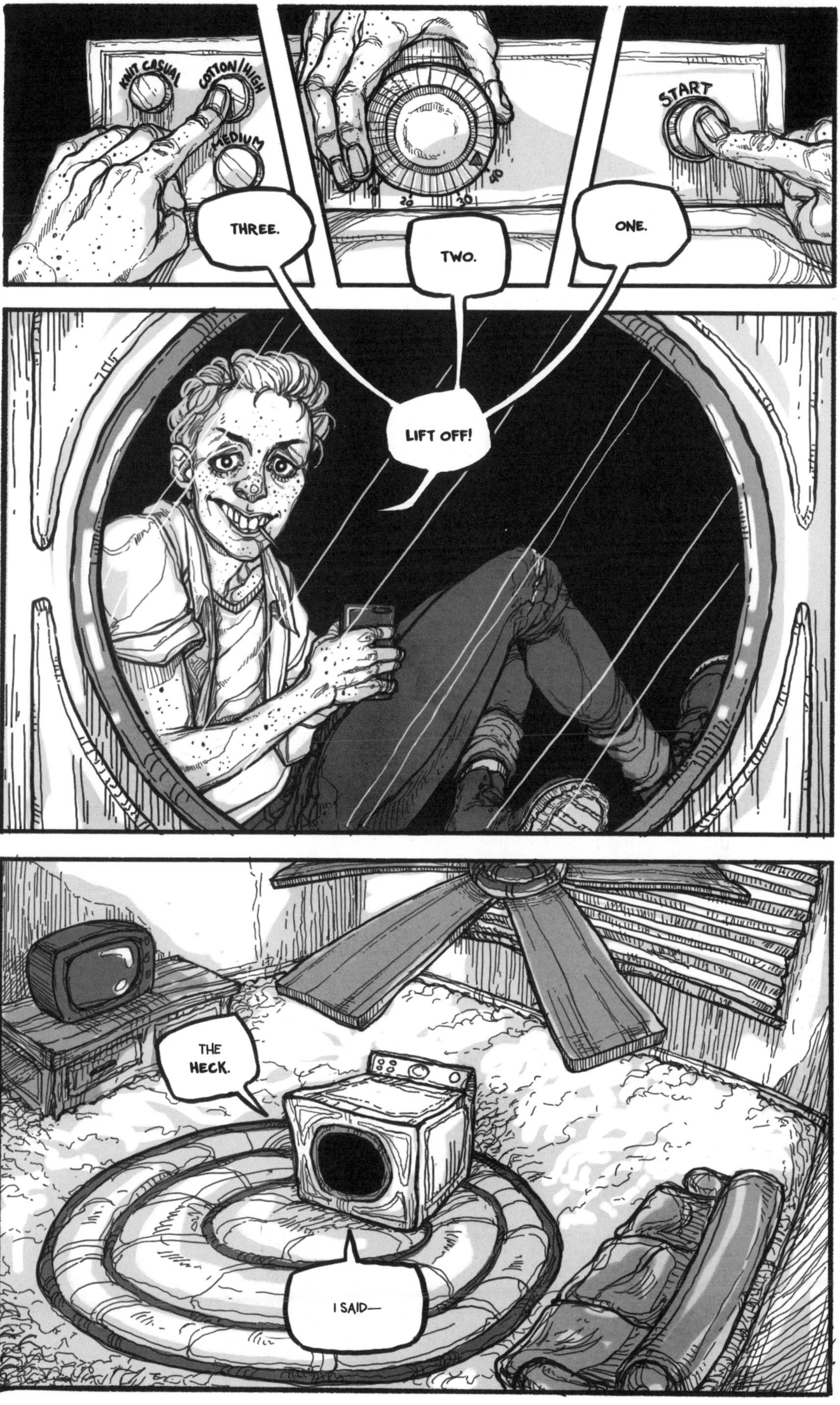
KNIT CASUAL
COTTON/HIGH
MEDIUM
START
THREE.
TWO.
ONE.
LIFT OFF!
THE HECK.
I SAID—

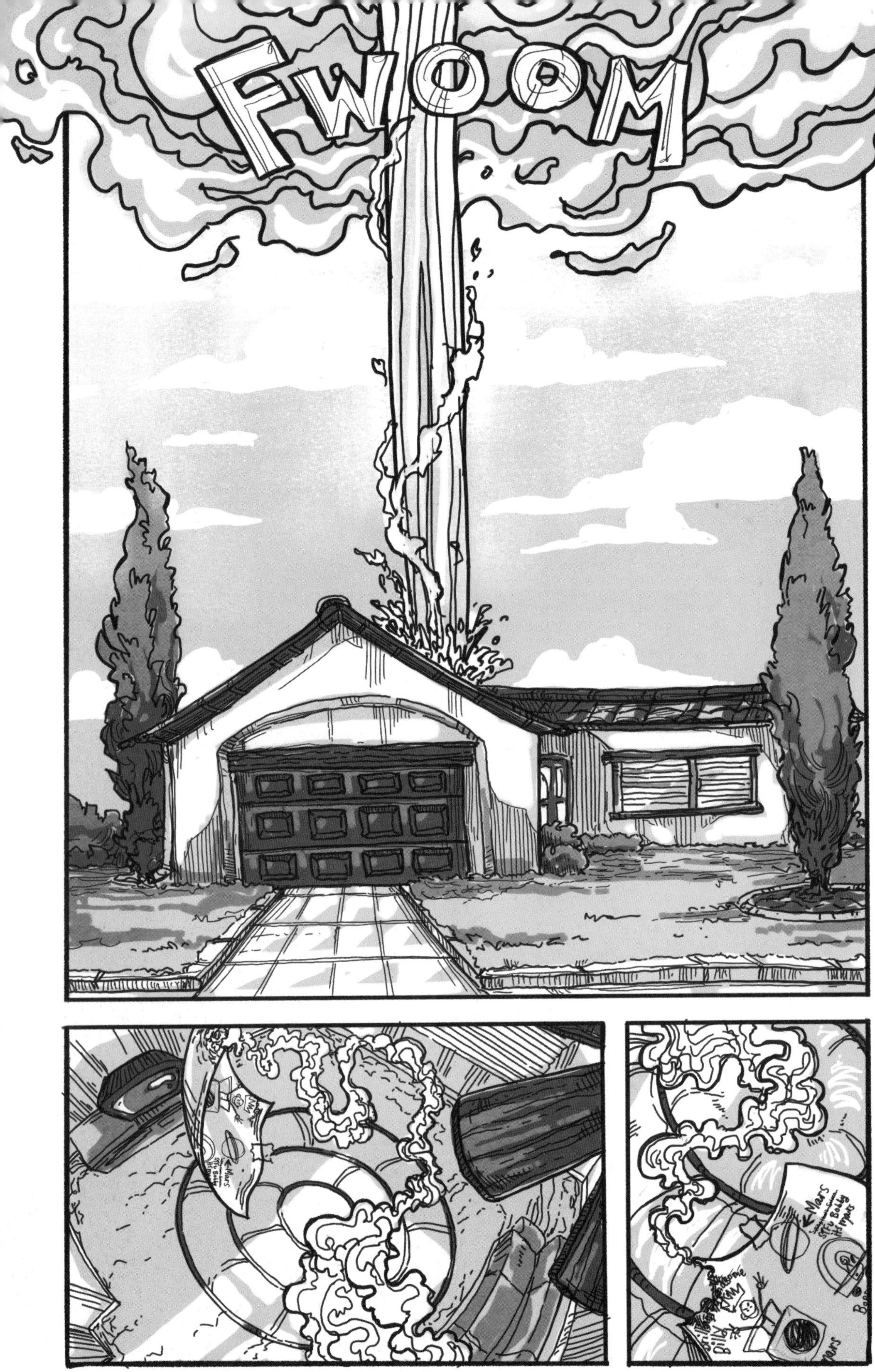
FWOOM
Mars

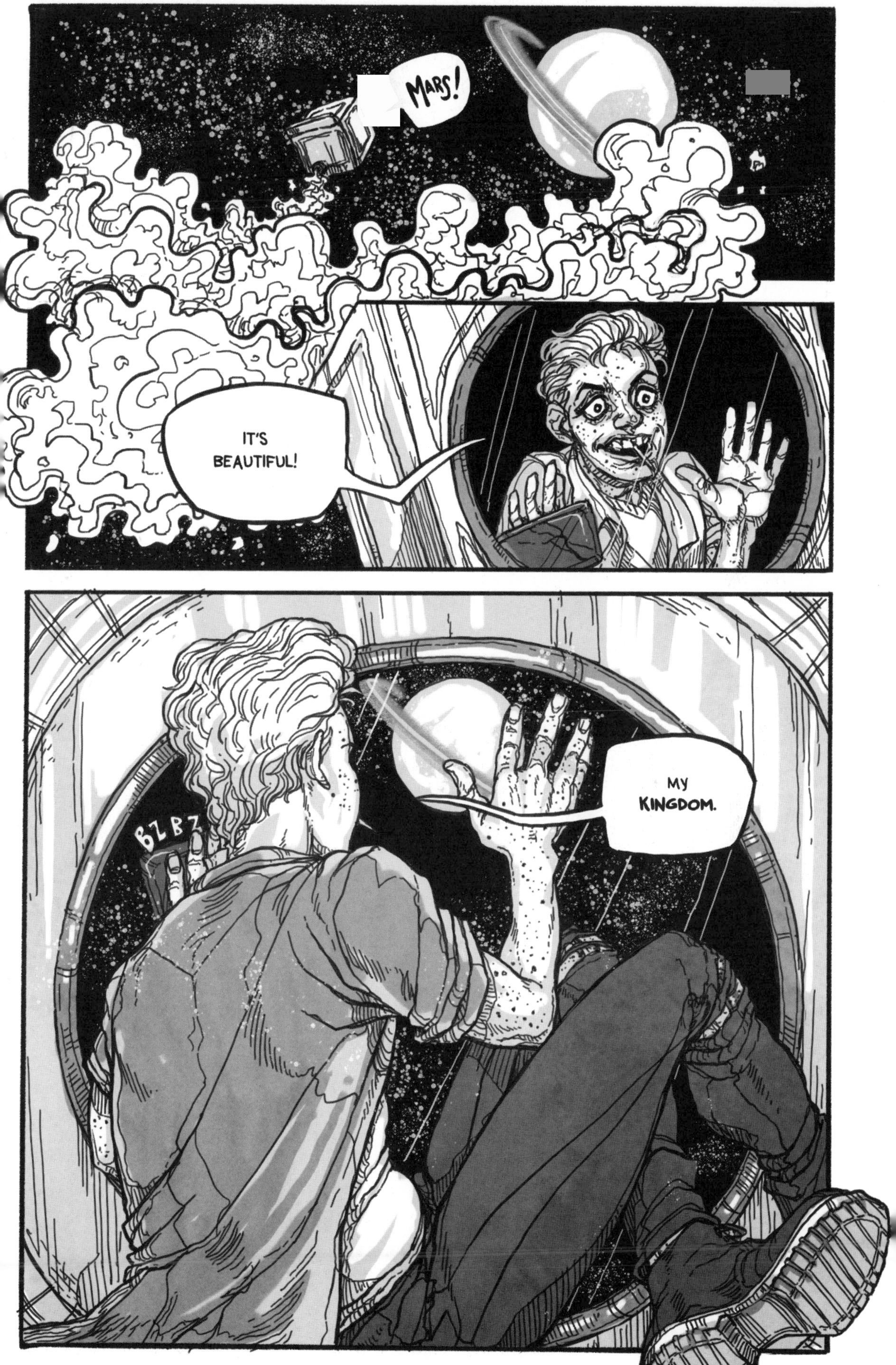
MARS!
IT'S BEAUTIFUL!
BZBZ
MY KINGDOM.

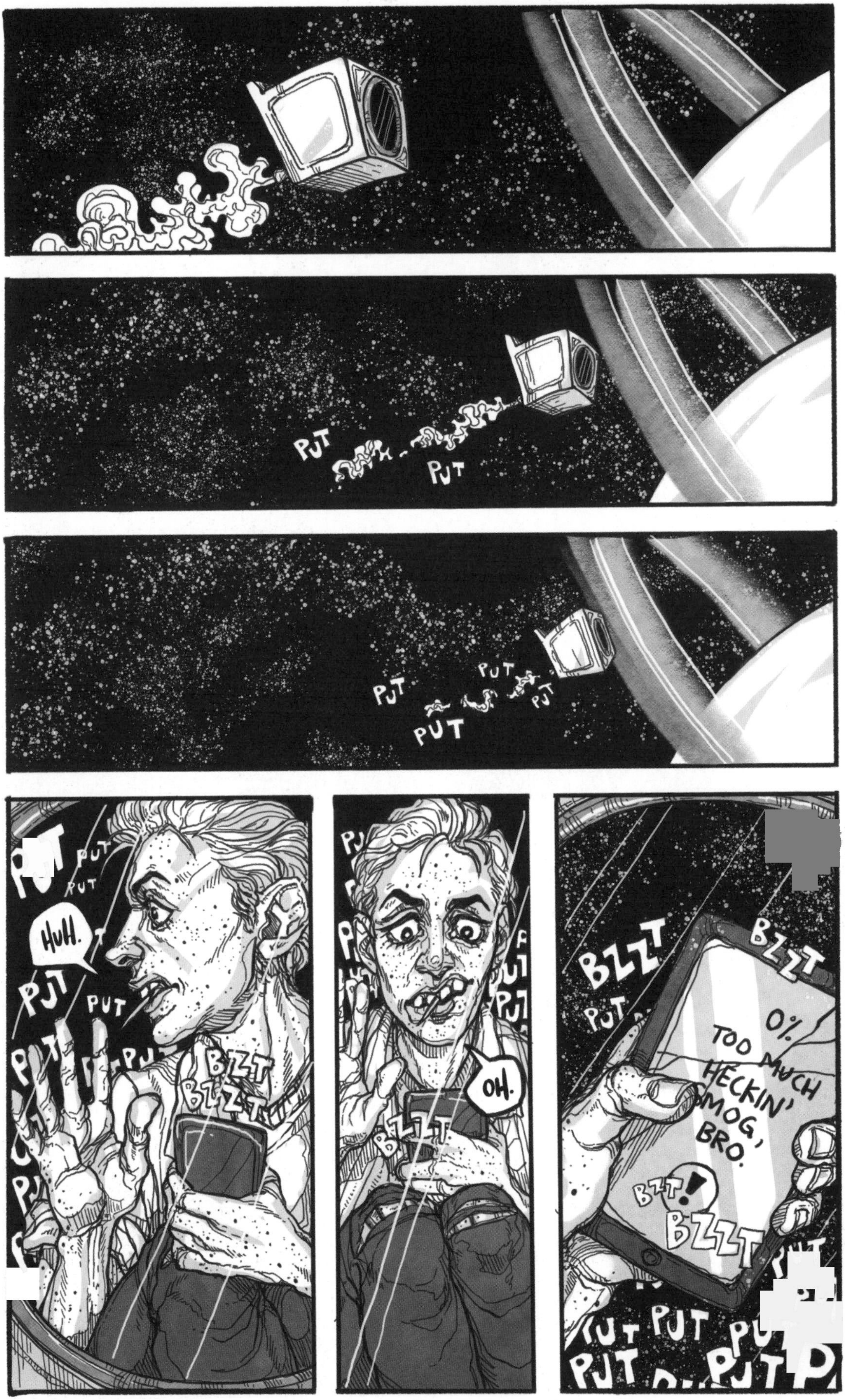
PUT
PUT
PUT
PUT
PUT
PUT
HUH.
PUT
PUT
BZZT
BZZT
OH.
BZZT
BZZT
BZZT
PUT
0%
TOO MUCH HECKIN' SMOG, BRO.
BZZT!
BZZT
PUT
PUT
PUT
PUT

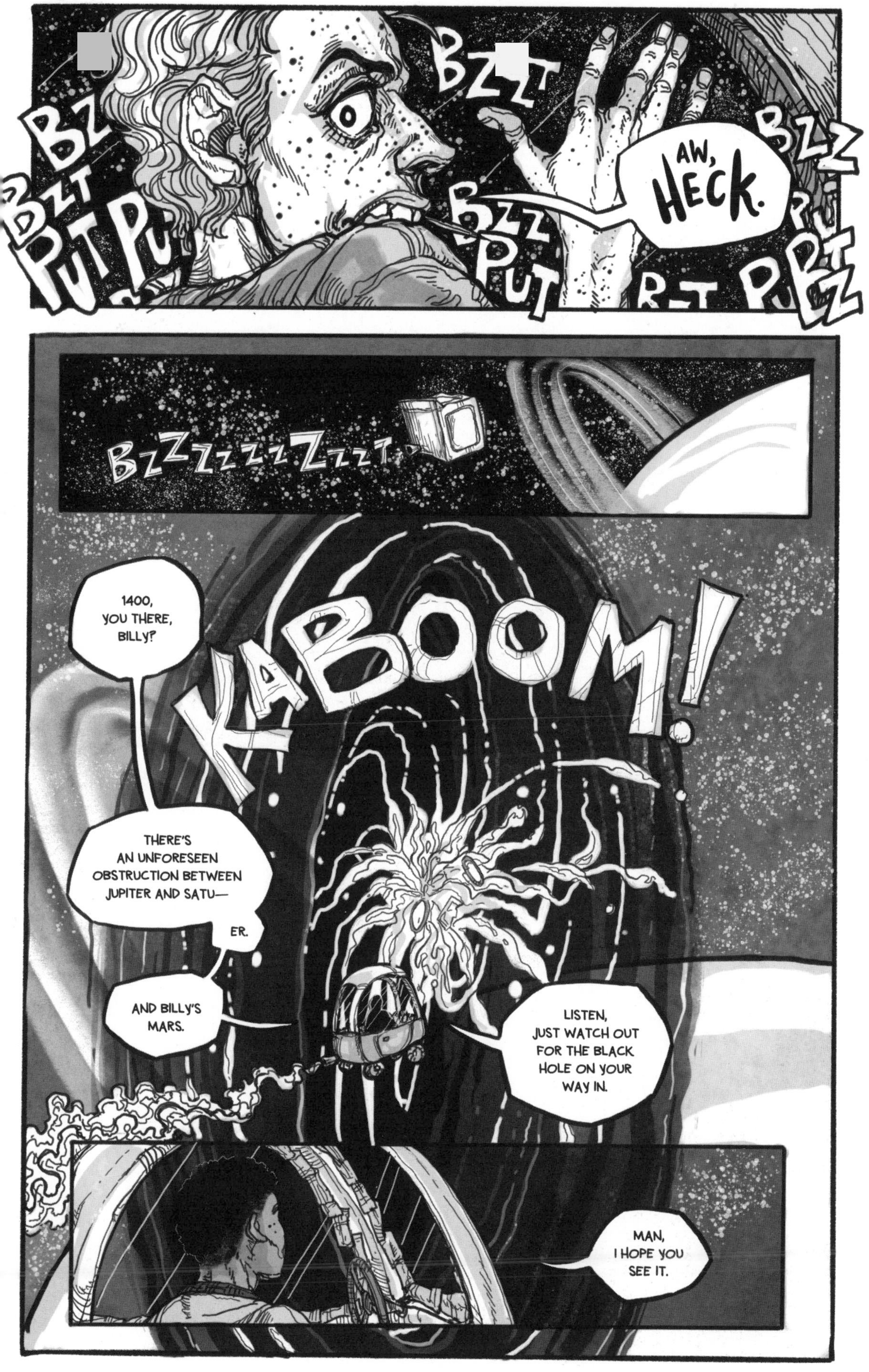
BZ
BZZT
PUT PUT
BZZT
AW, HECK.
BZZ
BZZ
PUT
BZZZZZZZZZZT
1400, YOU THERE, BILLY?
KABOOM!
THERE'S AN UNFORESEEN OBSTRUCTION BETWEEN JUPITER AND SATU—
ER.
AND BILLY'S MARS.
LISTEN, JUST WATCH OUT FOR THE BLACK HOLE ON YOUR WAY IN.
MAN, I HOPE YOU SEE IT.

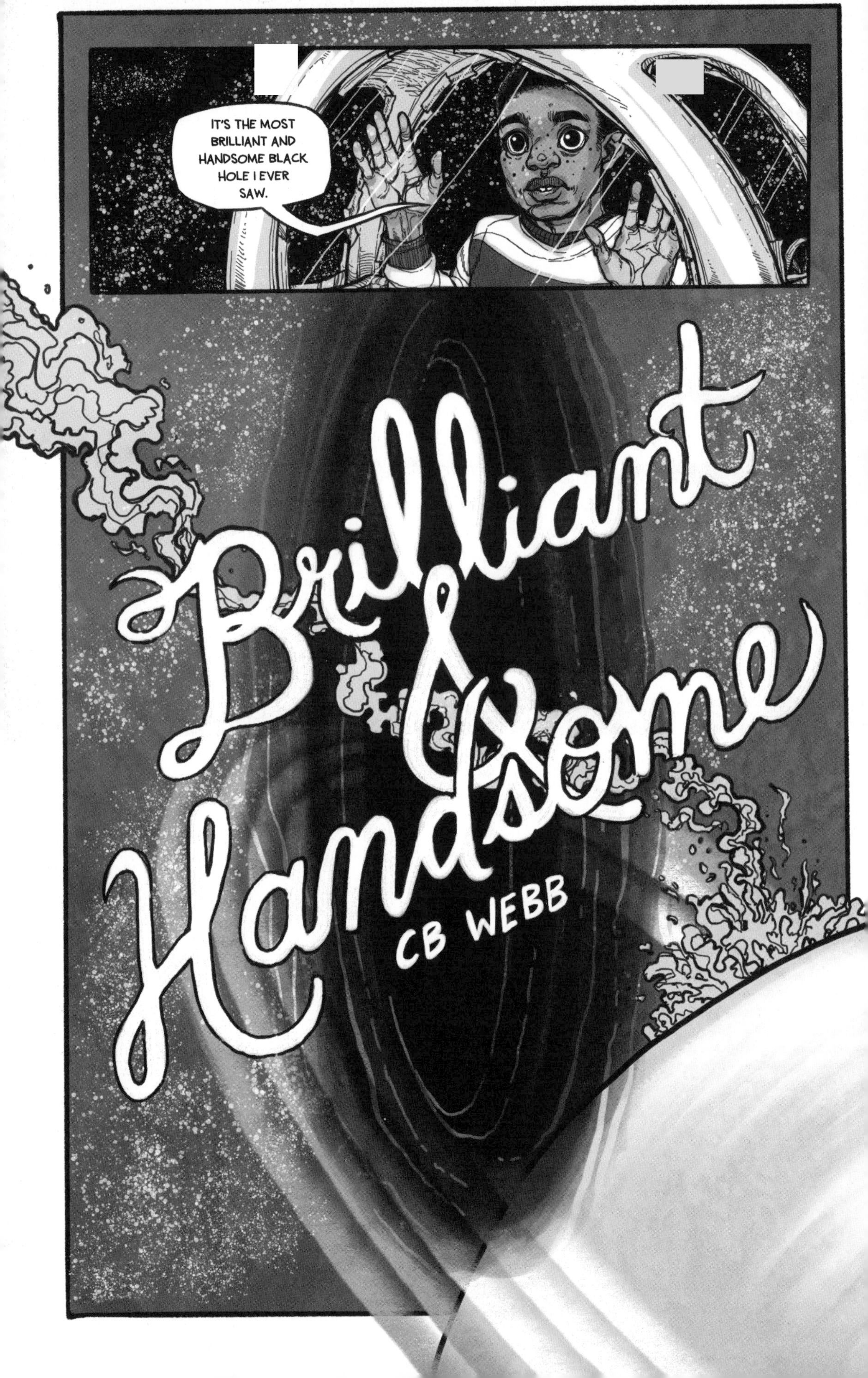
IT'S THE MOST BRILLIANT AND HANDSOME BLACK HOLE I EVER SAW.
Brilliant & Handsome
CB WEBB

SPACE TO GROW

BY NN CHAN

Posted 21 minutes ago

Hello gentle readers and welcome to my blog! I go by SpaceAce and I'm a fresh astrobiology grad heading out on her first space mission <3

Read More...

I was chosen for a sponsorship from Alpha Centauri's DGE. Humans have documented hundreds of millions of planets in the Milky Way, but we've sent manned missions to a few hundred thousand, a tiny fraction of that.

My job is to explore and document a sector of unexplored planets and collect some samples to research and study.

This blog is my way of bringing my readers along with me on my mission. I hope you stick around!

Tags: astrobiology, ACDG, travelogue

Leave a comment

lab work

αC
Centauri graduation

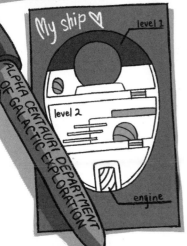

My ship ♡

level 1

level 2

engine

ALPHA CENTAURI DEPARTMENT OF GALACTIC EXPLORATION

αC

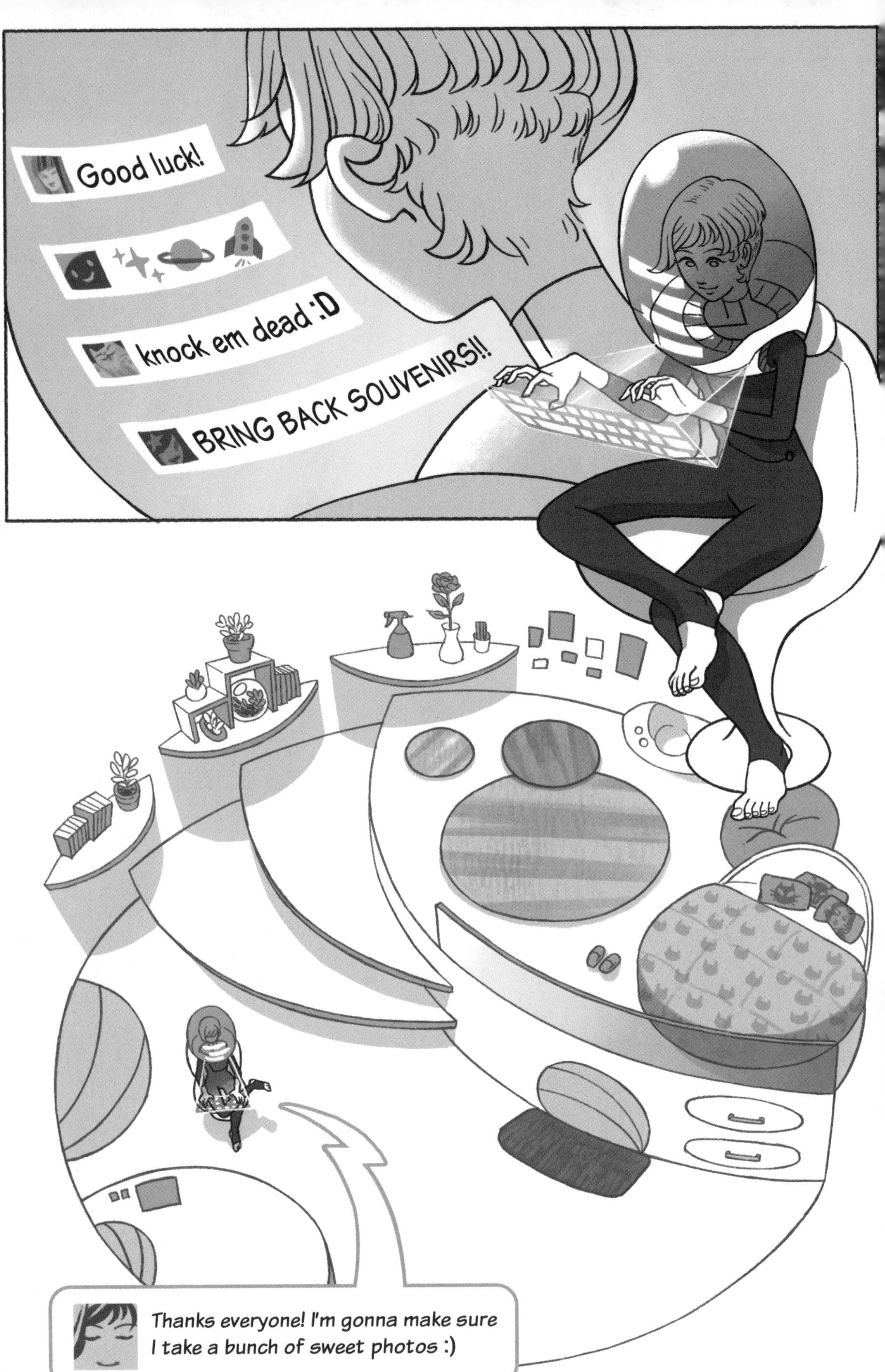
Good luck!
knock em dead :D
BRING BACK SOUVENIRS!!
Thanks everyone! I'm gonna make sure I take a bunch of sweet photos :)

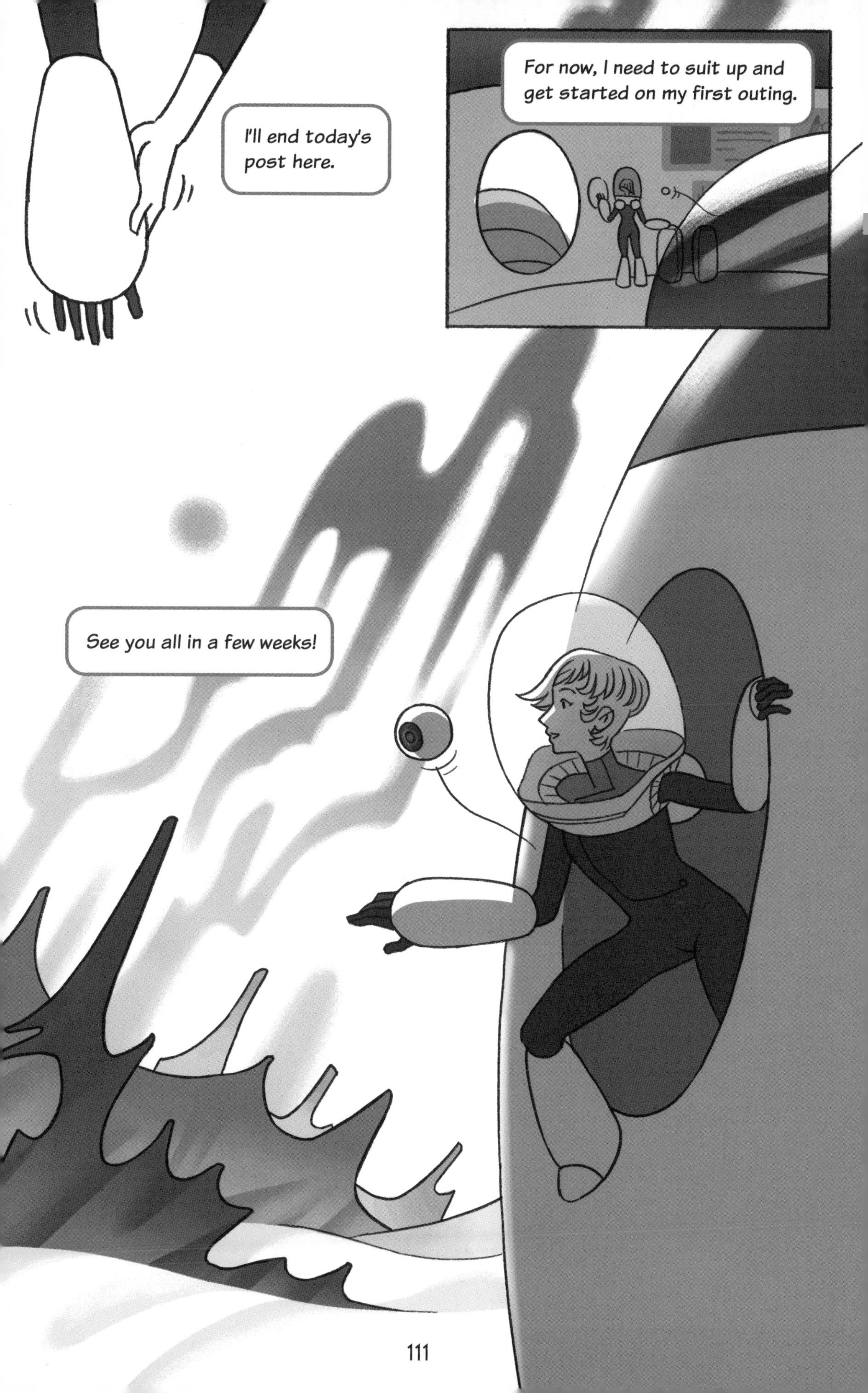
I'll end today's post here.
For now, I need to suit up and get started on my first outing.
See you all in a few weeks!

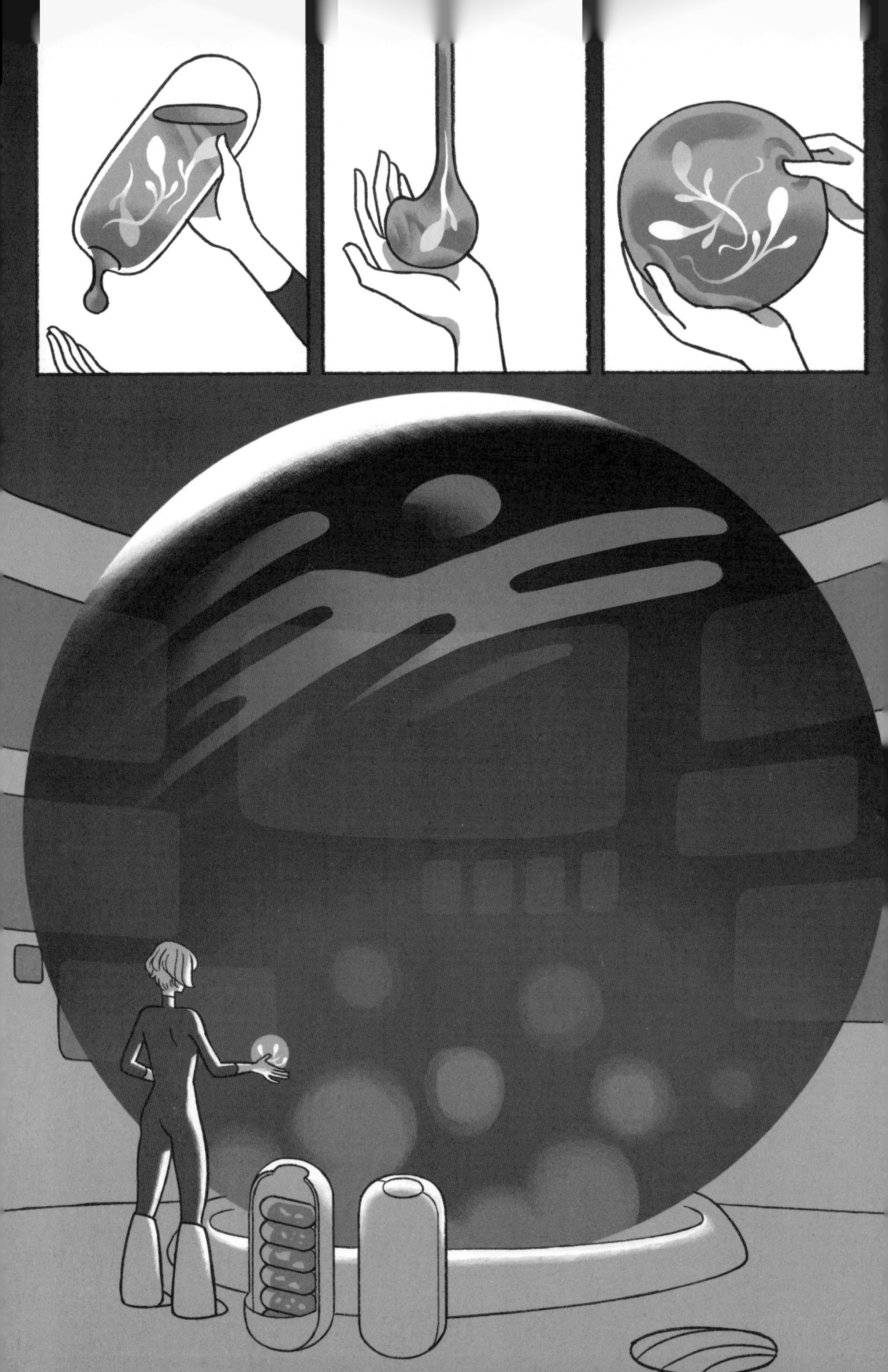

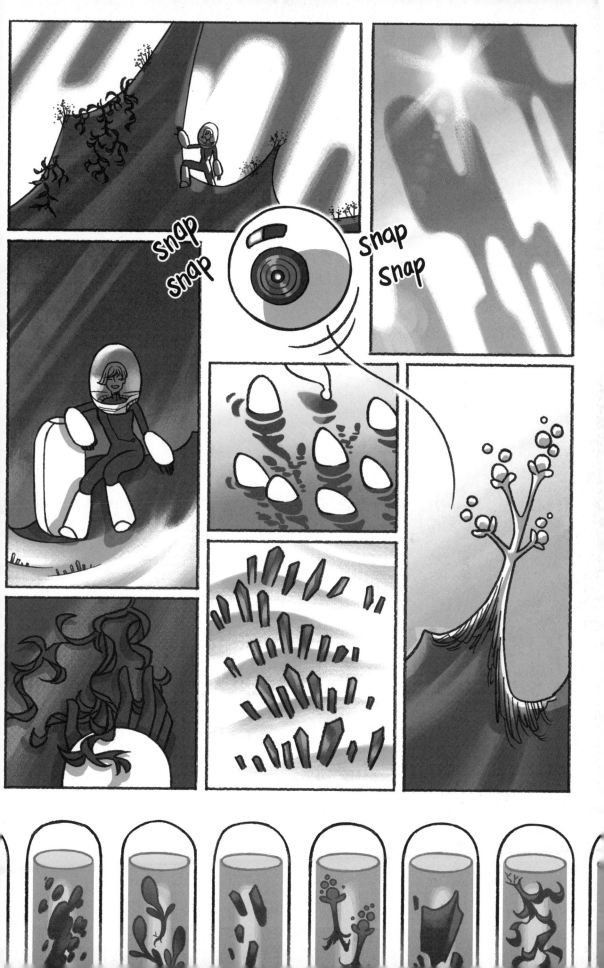

Snap
Snap

Snap
Snap

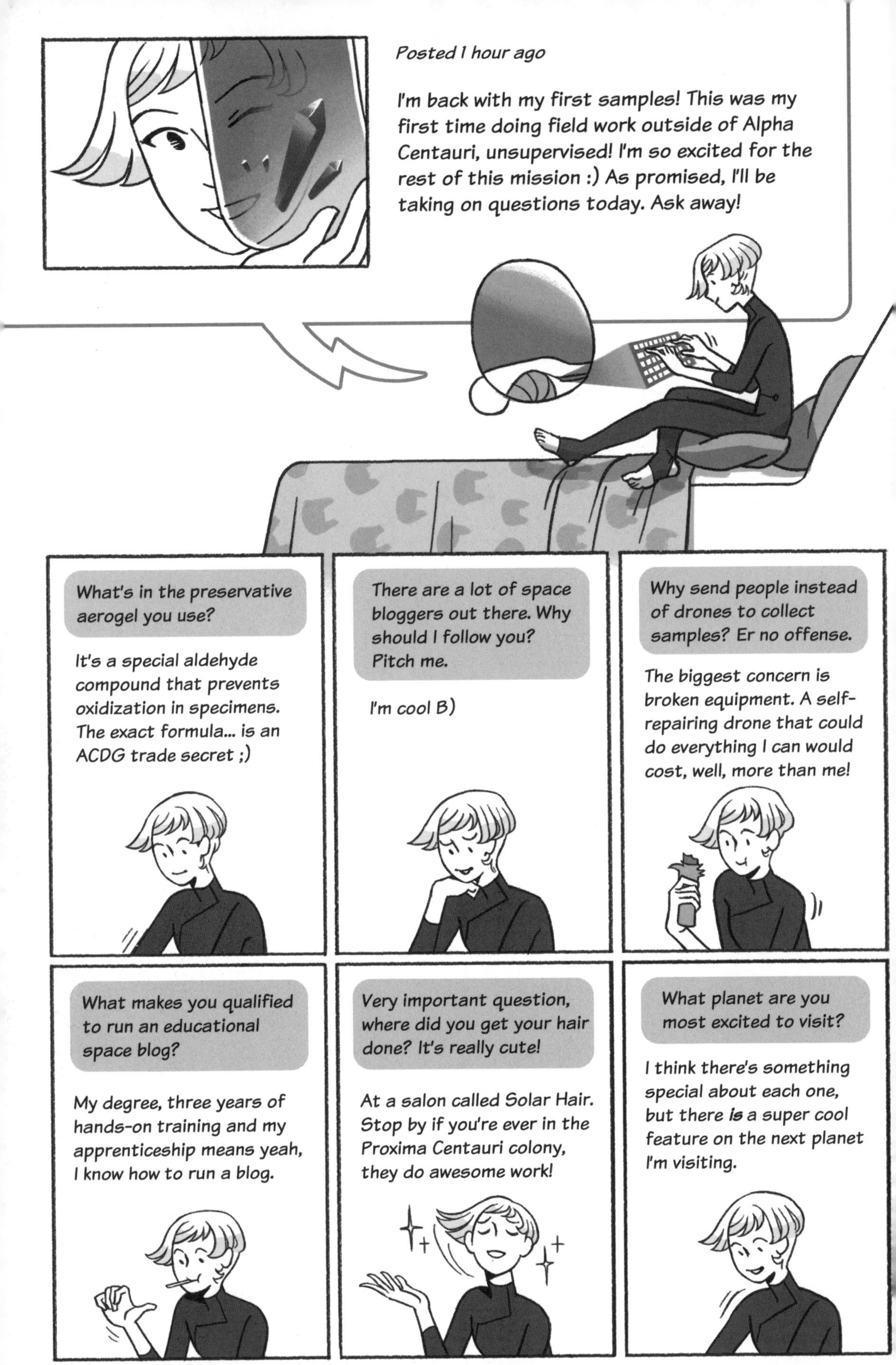
Posted 1 hour ago
I'm back with my first samples! This was my first time doing field work outside of Alpha Centauri, unsupervised! I'm so excited for the rest of this mission :) As promised, I'll be taking on questions today. Ask away!
What's in the preservative aerogel you use?
It's a special aldehyde compound that prevents oxidization in specimens. The exact formula... is an ACDG trade secret ;)
There are a lot of space bloggers out there. Why should I follow you? Pitch me.
I'm cool B)
Why send people instead of drones to collect samples? Er no offense.
The biggest concern is broken equipment. A self-repairing drone that could do everything I can would cost, well, more than me!
What makes you qualified to run an educational space blog?
My degree, three years of hands-on training and my apprenticeship means yeah, I know how to run a blog.
Very important question, where did you get your hair done? It's really cute!
At a salon called Solar Hair. Stop by if you're ever in the Proxima Centauri colony, they do awesome work!
What planet are you most excited to visit?
I think there's something special about each one, but there *is* a super cool feature on the next planet I'm visiting.

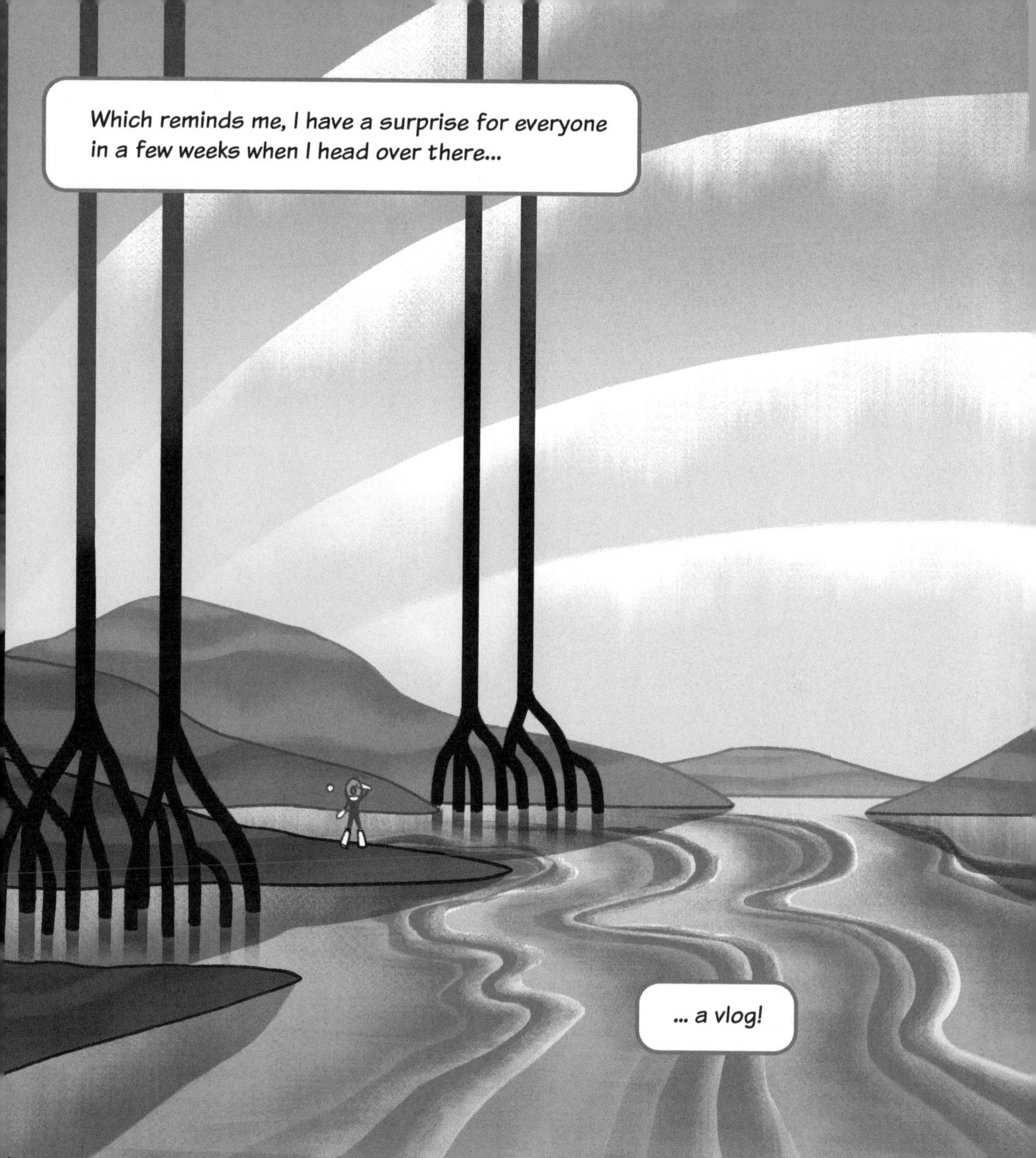
Which reminds me, I have a surprise for everyone in a few weeks when I head over there...
... a vlog!

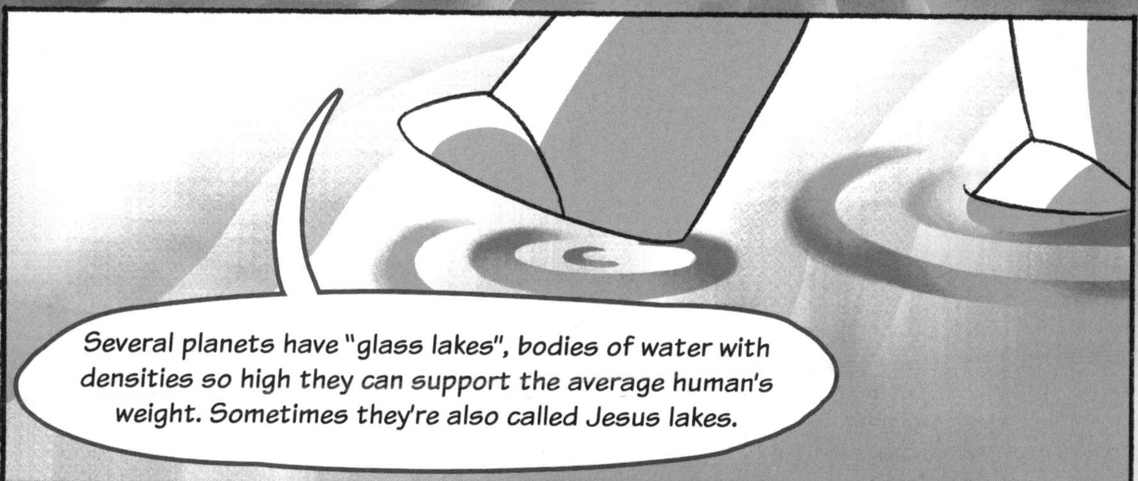
Several planets have "glass lakes", bodies of water with densities so high they can support the average human's weight. Sometimes they're also called Jesus lakes.

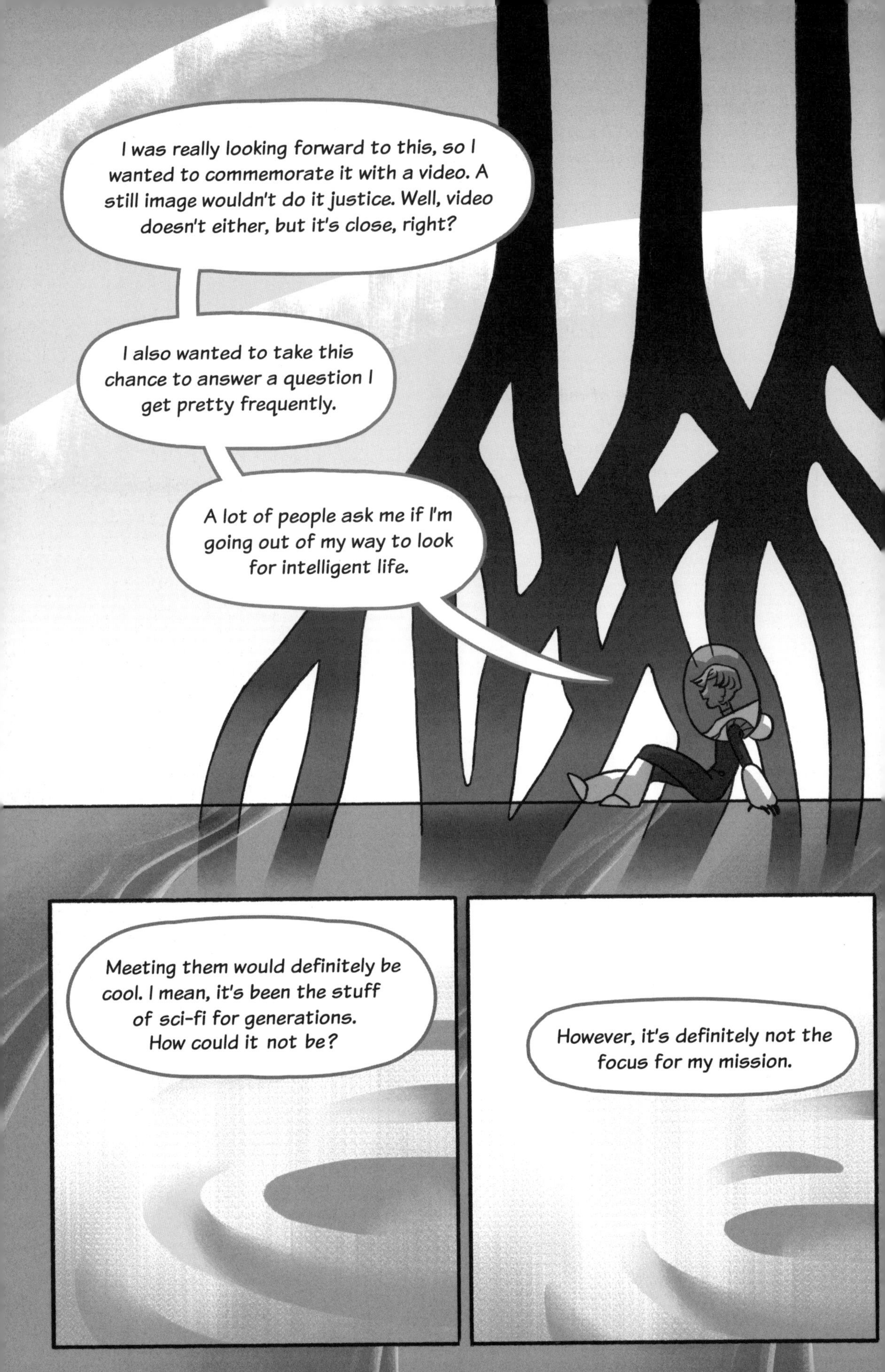
I was really looking forward to this, so I wanted to commemorate it with a video. A still image wouldn't do it justice. Well, video doesn't either, but it's close, right?
I also wanted to take this chance to answer a question I get pretty frequently.
A lot of people ask me if I'm going out of my way to look for intelligent life.
Meeting them would definitely be cool. I mean, it's been the stuff of sci-fi for generations. How could it not be?
However, it's definitely not the focus for my mission.

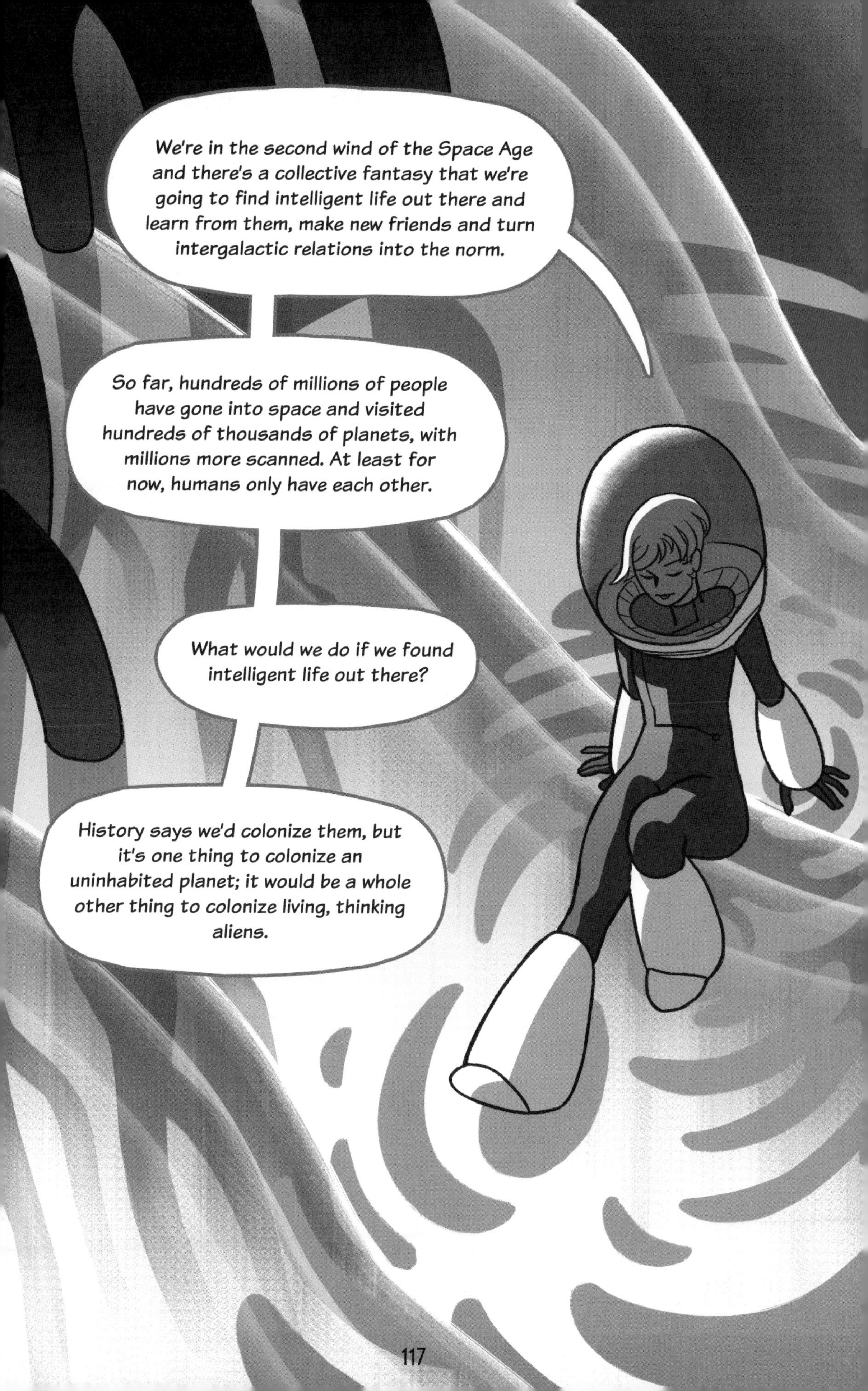
We're in the second wind of the Space Age and there's a collective fantasy that we're going to find intelligent life out there and learn from them, make new friends and turn intergalactic relations into the norm.
So far, hundreds of millions of people have gone into space and visited hundreds of thousands of planets, with millions more scanned. At least for now, humans only have each other.
What would we do if we found intelligent life out there?
History says we'd colonize them, but it's one thing to colonize an uninhabited planet; it would be a whole other thing to colonize living, thinking aliens.

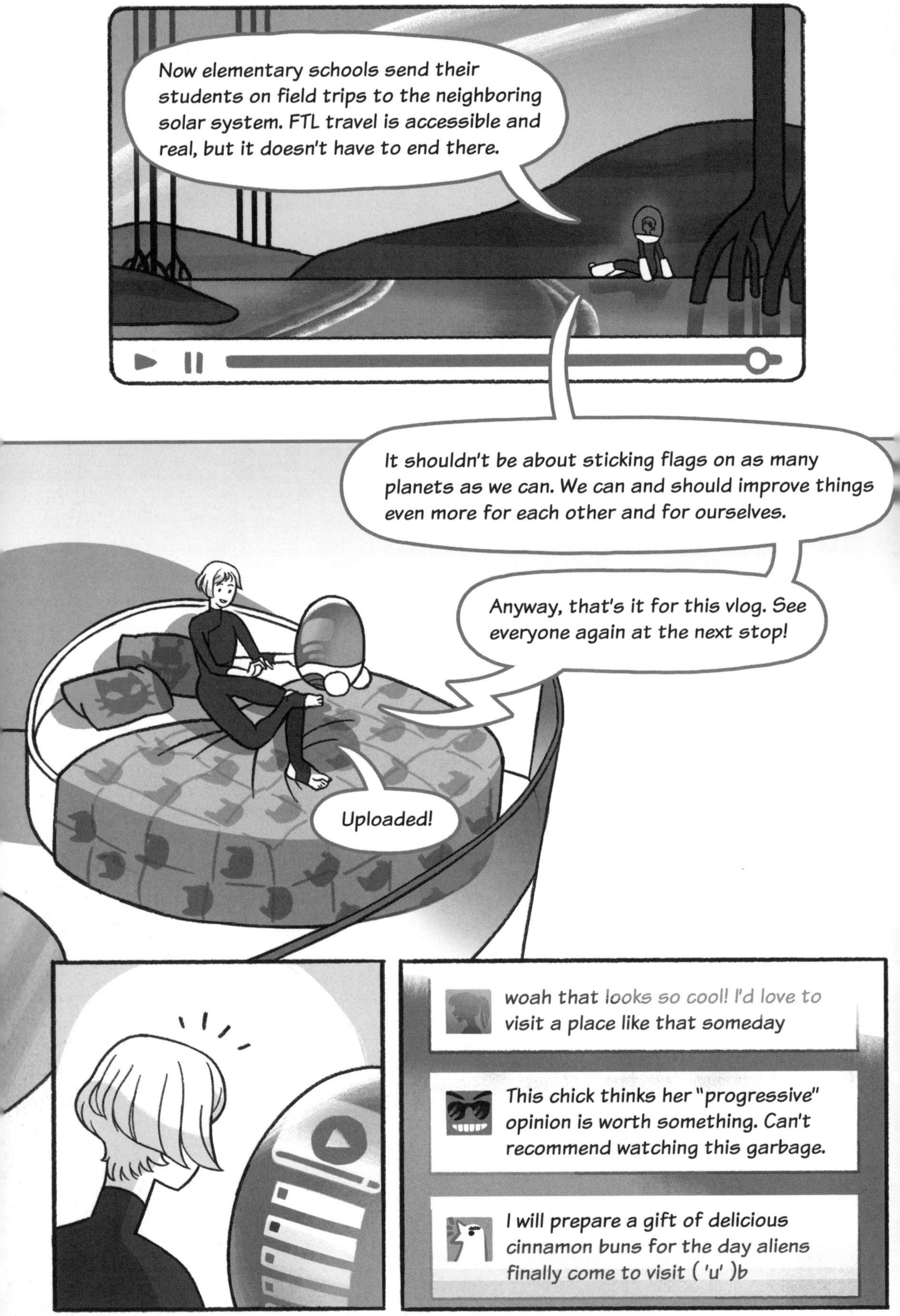
Now elementary schools send their students on field trips to the neighboring solar system. FTL travel is accessible and real, but it doesn't have to end there.
It shouldn't be about sticking flags on as many planets as we can. We can and should improve things even more for each other and for ourselves.
Anyway, that's it for this vlog. See everyone again at the next stop!
Uploaded!
woah that looks so cool! I'd love to visit a place like that someday
This chick thinks her "progressive" opinion is worth something. Can't recommend watching this garbage.
I will prepare a gift of delicious cinnamon buns for the day aliens finally come to visit ('u')b

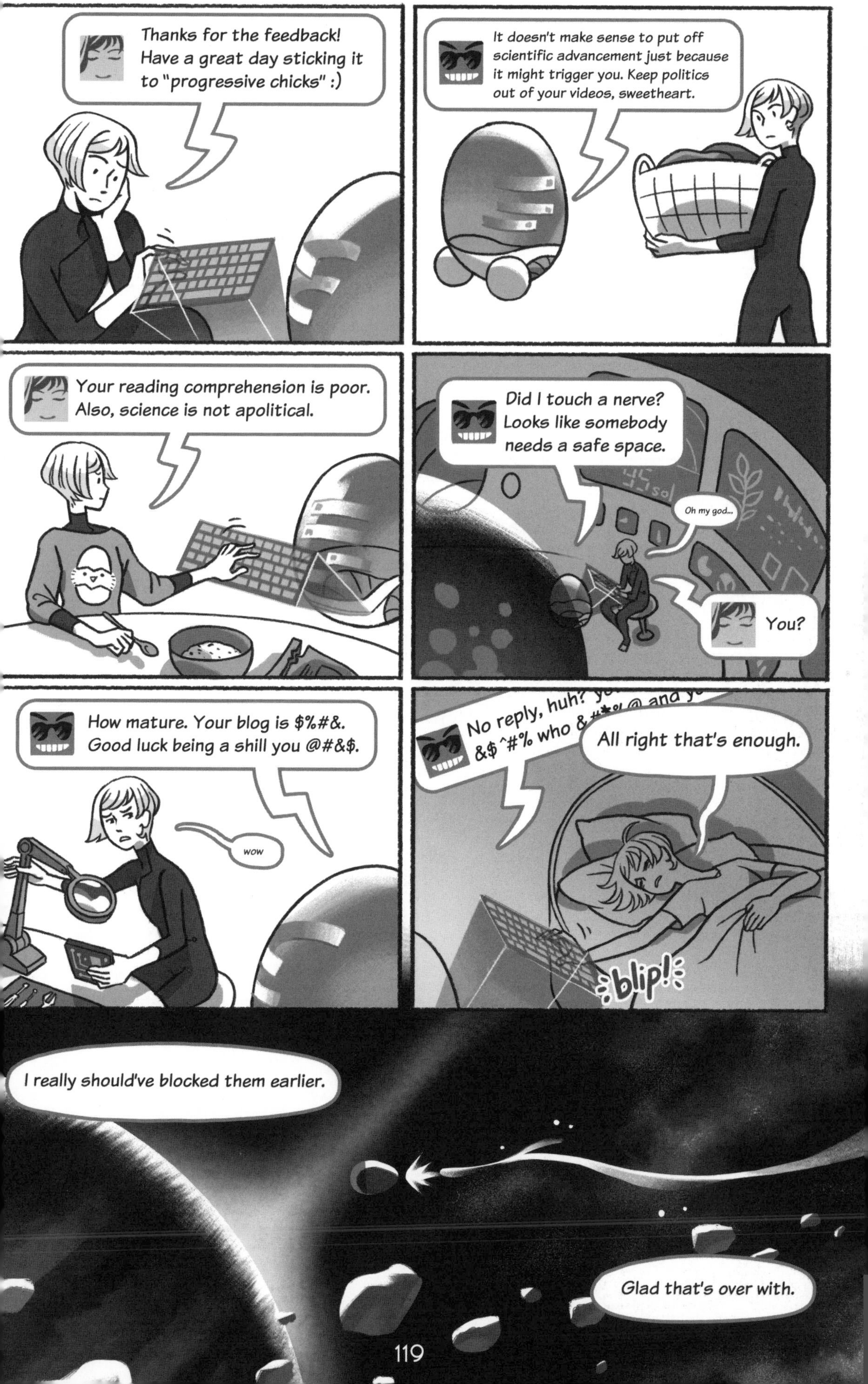
Thanks for the feedback! Have a great day sticking it to "progressive chicks" :)
It doesn't make sense to put off scientific advancement just because it might trigger you. Keep politics out of your videos, sweetheart.
Your reading comprehension is poor. Also, science is not apolitical.
Did I touch a nerve? Looks like somebody needs a safe space.
Oh my god...
You?
How mature. Your blog is $%#&. Good luck being a shill you @#&$.
wow
No reply, huh?
&$^#% who
All right that's enough.
blip!
I really should've blocked them earlier.
Glad that's over with.

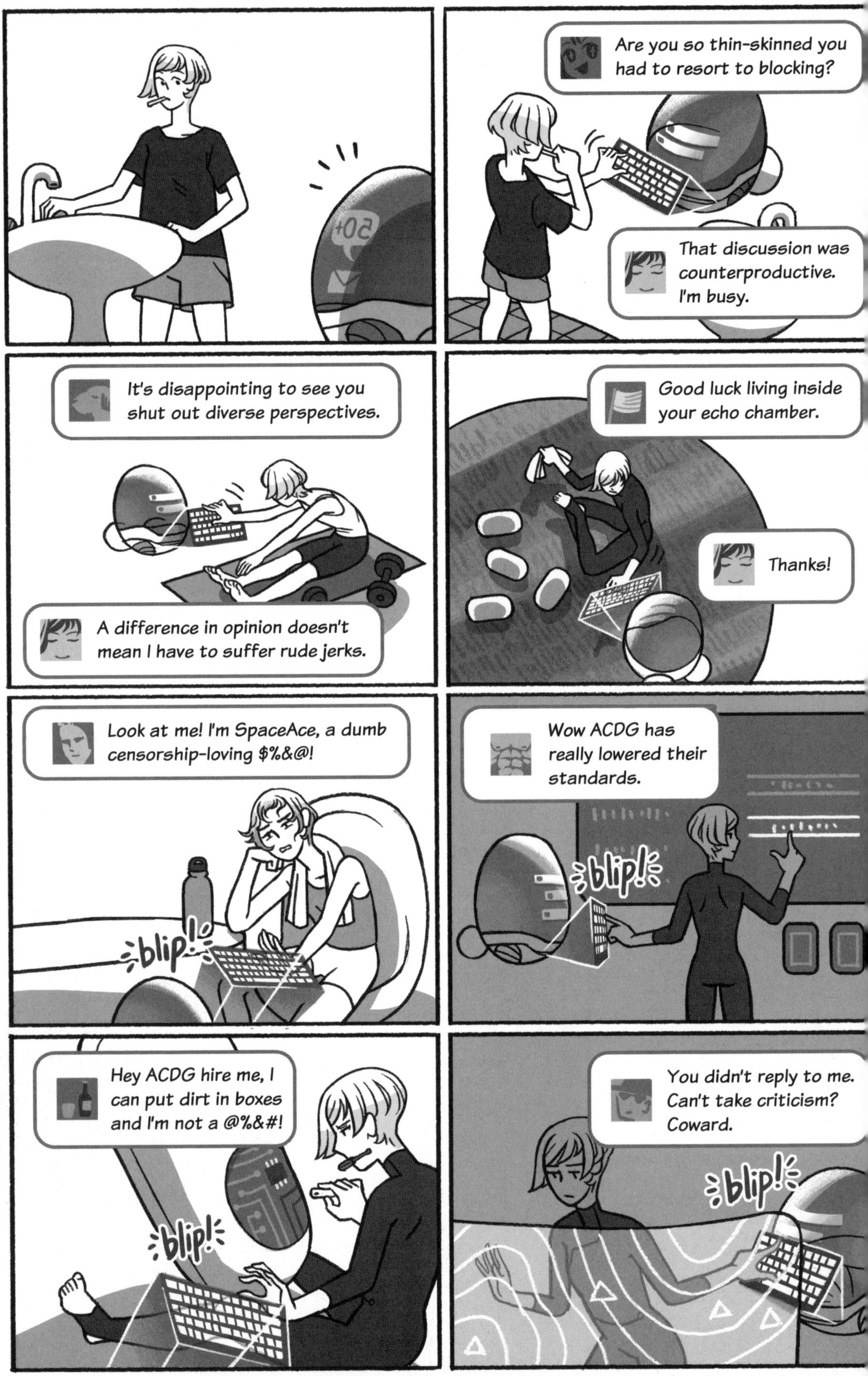
50+
Are you so thin-skinned you had to resort to blocking?
That discussion was counterproductive. I'm busy.
It's disappointing to see you shut out diverse perspectives.
A difference in opinion doesn't mean I have to suffer rude jerks.
Good luck living inside your echo chamber.
Thanks!
Look at me! I'm SpaceAce, a dumb censorship-loving $%&@!
blip!
Wow ACDG has really lowered their standards.
blip!
Hey ACDG hire me, I can put dirt in boxes and I'm not a @%&#!
blip!
You didn't reply to me. Can't take criticism? Coward.
blip!

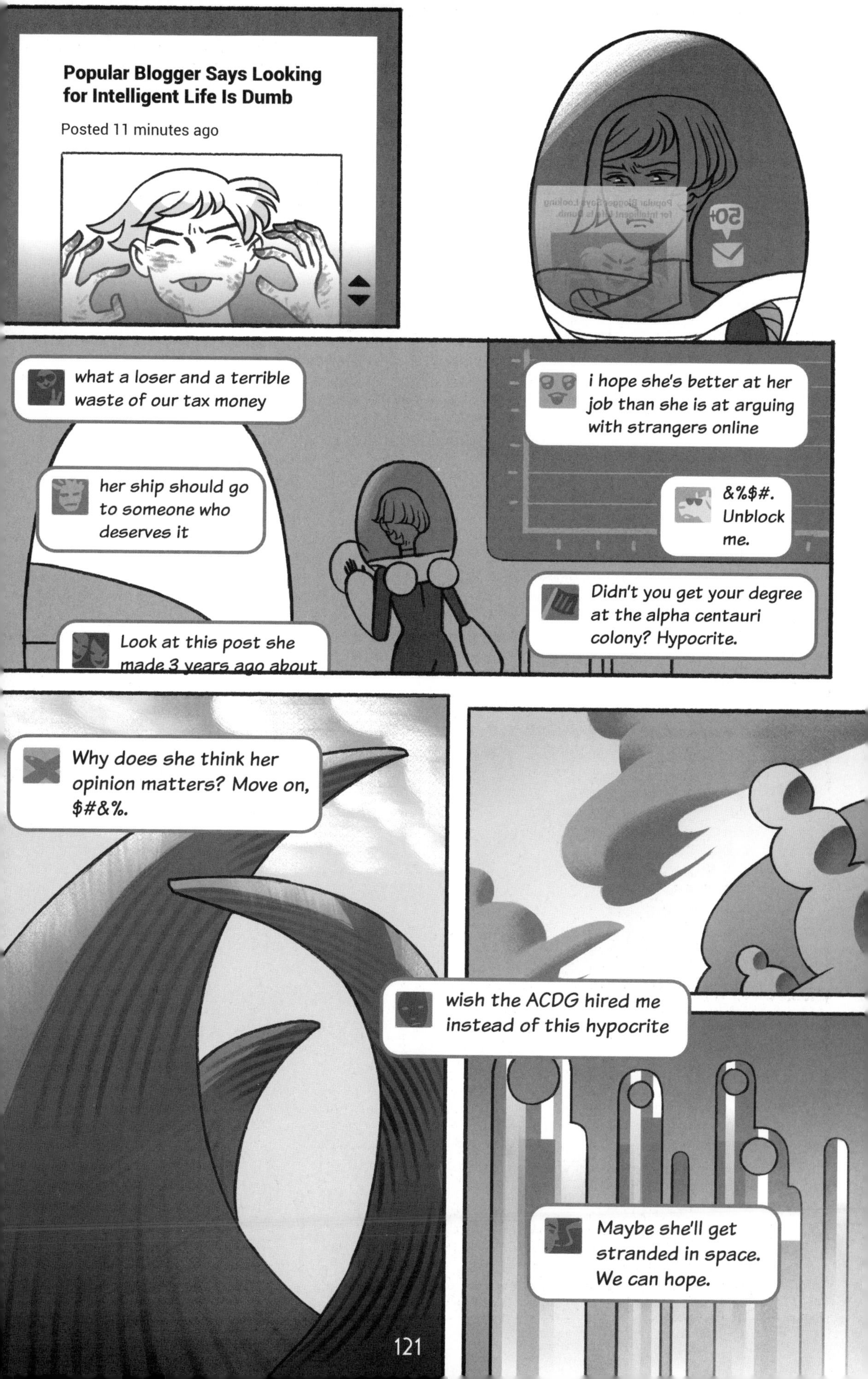
Popular Blogger Says Looking for Intelligent Life Is Dumb
Posted 11 minutes ago
what a loser and a terrible waste of our tax money
her ship should go to someone who deserves it
Look at this post she made 3 years ago about
i hope she's better at her job than she is at arguing with strangers online
&%$#. Unblock me.
Didn't you get your degree at the alpha centauri colony? Hypocrite.
Why does she think her opinion matters? Move on, $#&%.
wish the ACDG hired me instead of this hypocrite
Maybe she'll get stranded in space. We can hope.

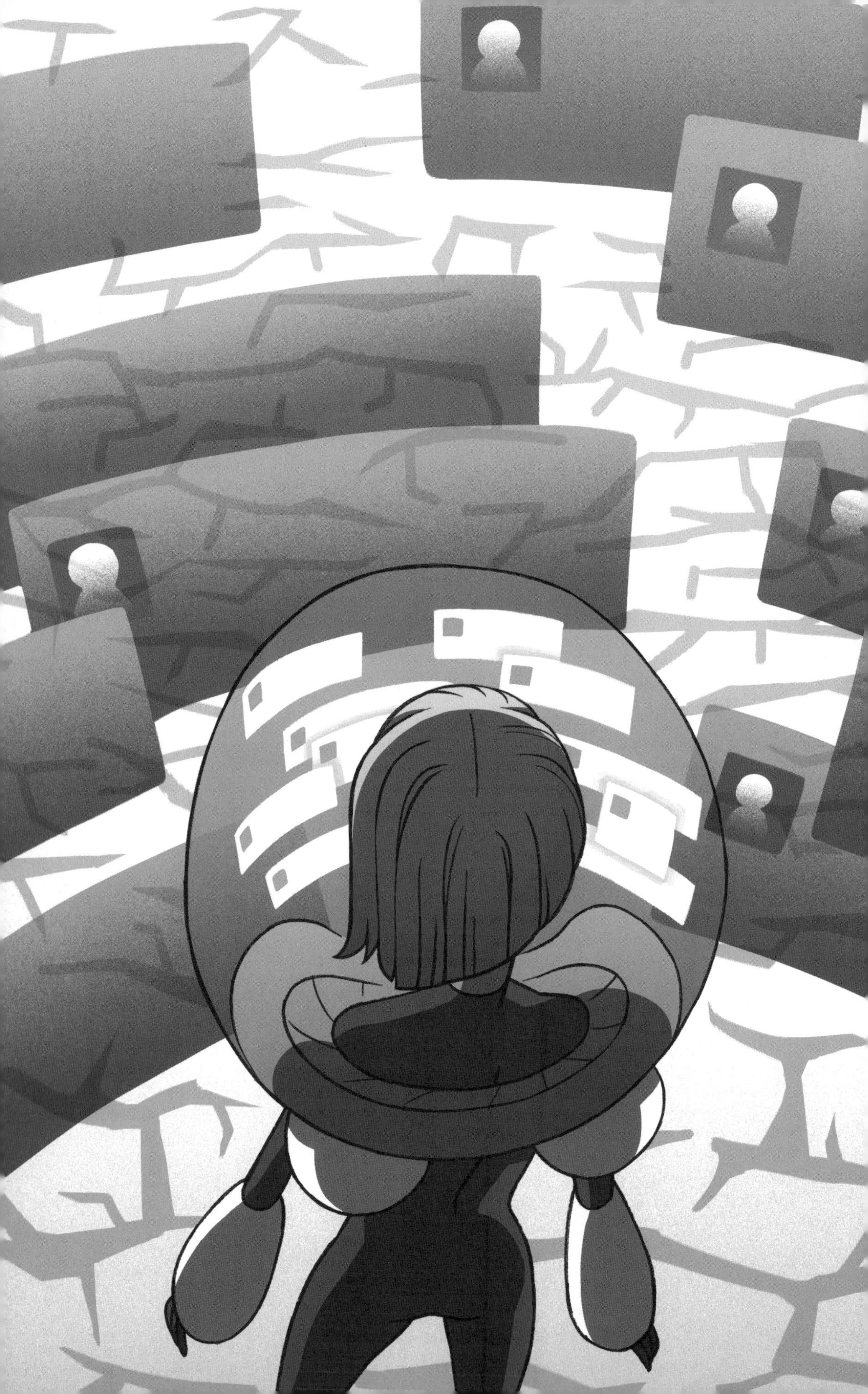

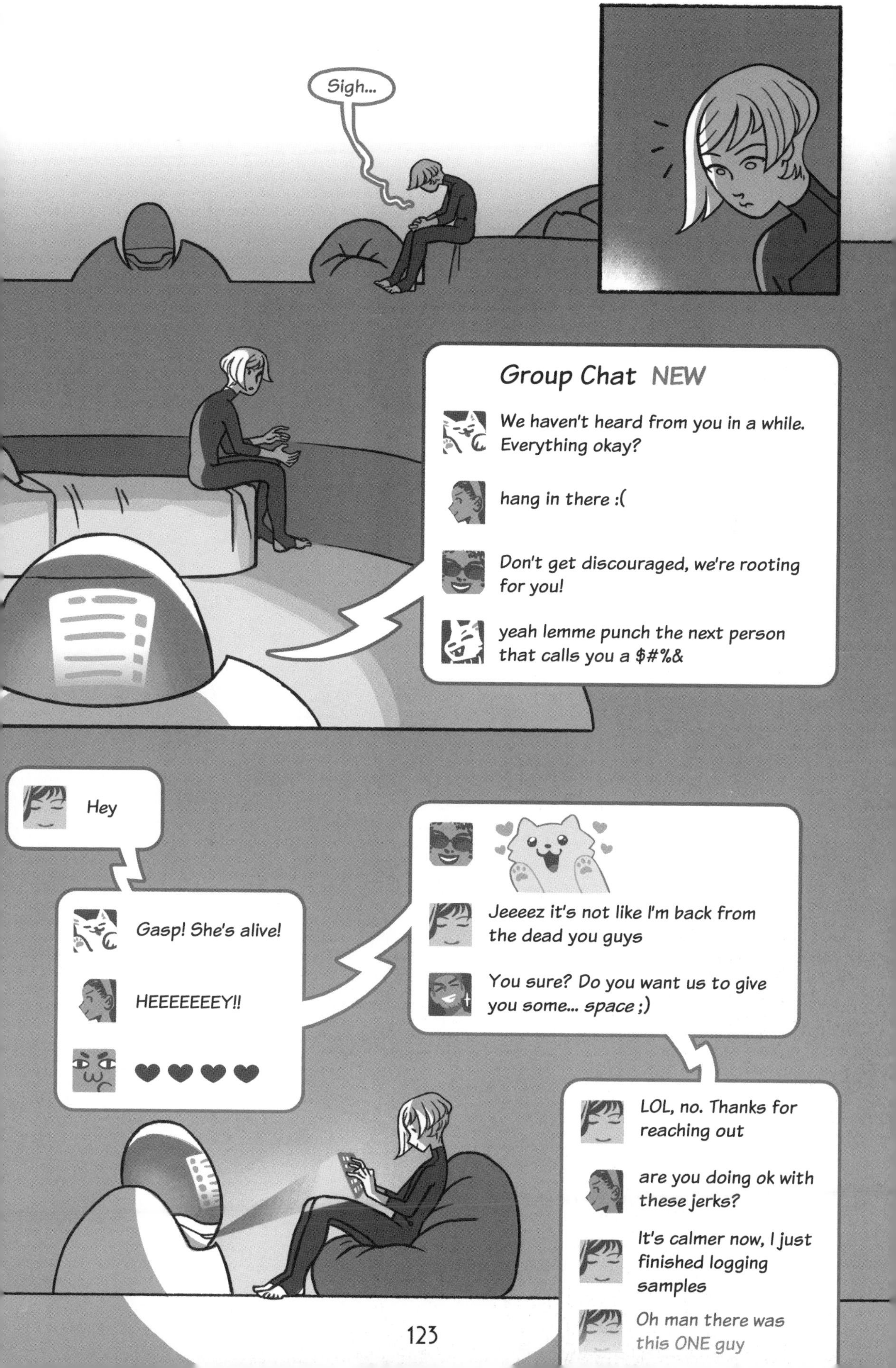
Sigh...
Group Chat NEW
We haven't heard from you in a while. Everything okay?
hang in there :(
Don't get discouraged, we're rooting for you!
yeah lemme punch the next person that calls you a $#%&
Hey
Gasp! She's alive!
HEEEEEEEY!!
♥♥♥♥
Jeeeez it's not like I'm back from the dead you guys
You sure? Do you want us to give you some... space ;)
LOL, no. Thanks for reaching out
are you doing ok with these jerks?
It's calmer now, I just finished logging samples
Oh man there was this ONE guy

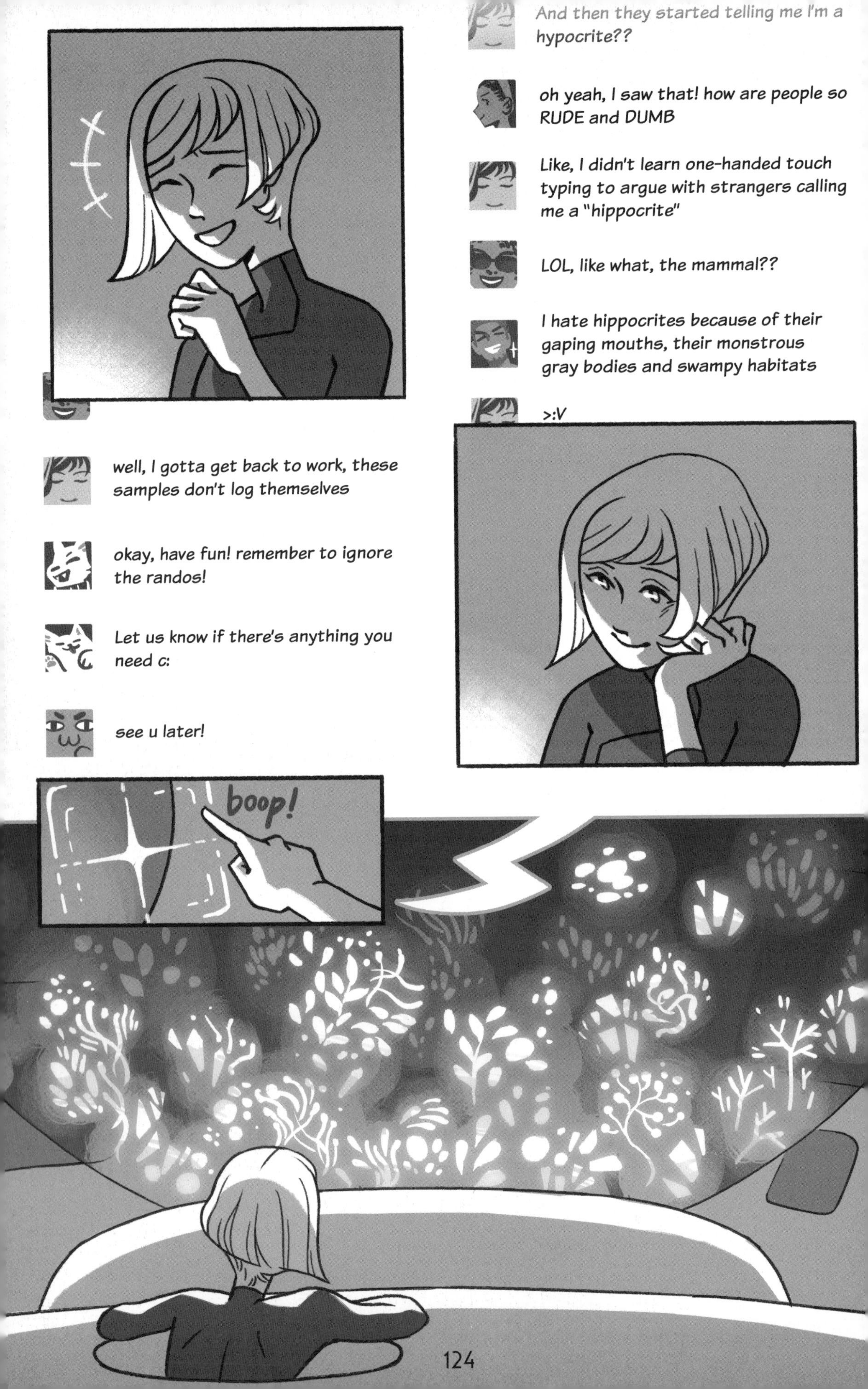

And then they started telling me I'm a hypocrite??
oh yeah, I saw that! how are people so RUDE and DUMB
Like, I didn't learn one-handed touch typing to argue with strangers calling me a "hippocrite"
LOL, like what, the mammal??
I hate hippocrites because of their gaping mouths, their monstrous gray bodies and swampy habitats
>:V
well, I gotta get back to work, these samples don't log themselves
okay, have fun! remember to ignore the randos!
Let us know if there's anything you need c:
see u later!
boop!

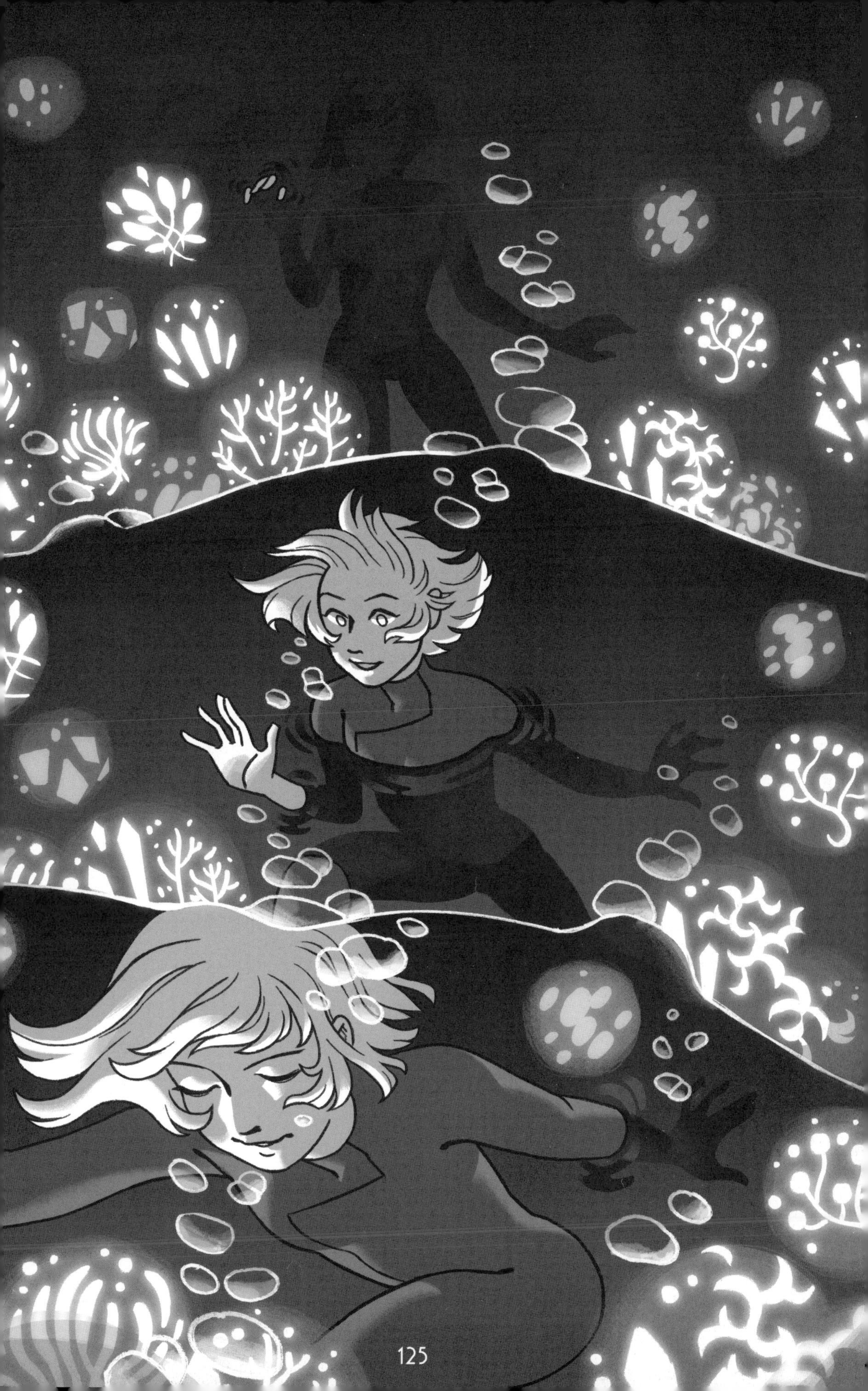

Posted 7 minutes ago

It's been a rough few months, but I want to thank everyone who continued to support the blog. Thank you everyone for all your kind words <3

 daaaamn you look like you look like a hair commercial and a half

 hey keep up the awesome work, I'm always excited for your next post!

 You look awesome! Don't let the haters get you :)

 hells yeah baby WORK IT

 just get lost already, nobody cares about you

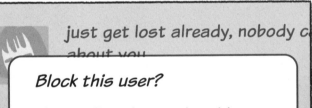

just get lost already, nobody c
about you

Block this user?

They will no longer be able to follow you or see your posts.

▶ Block   Cancel

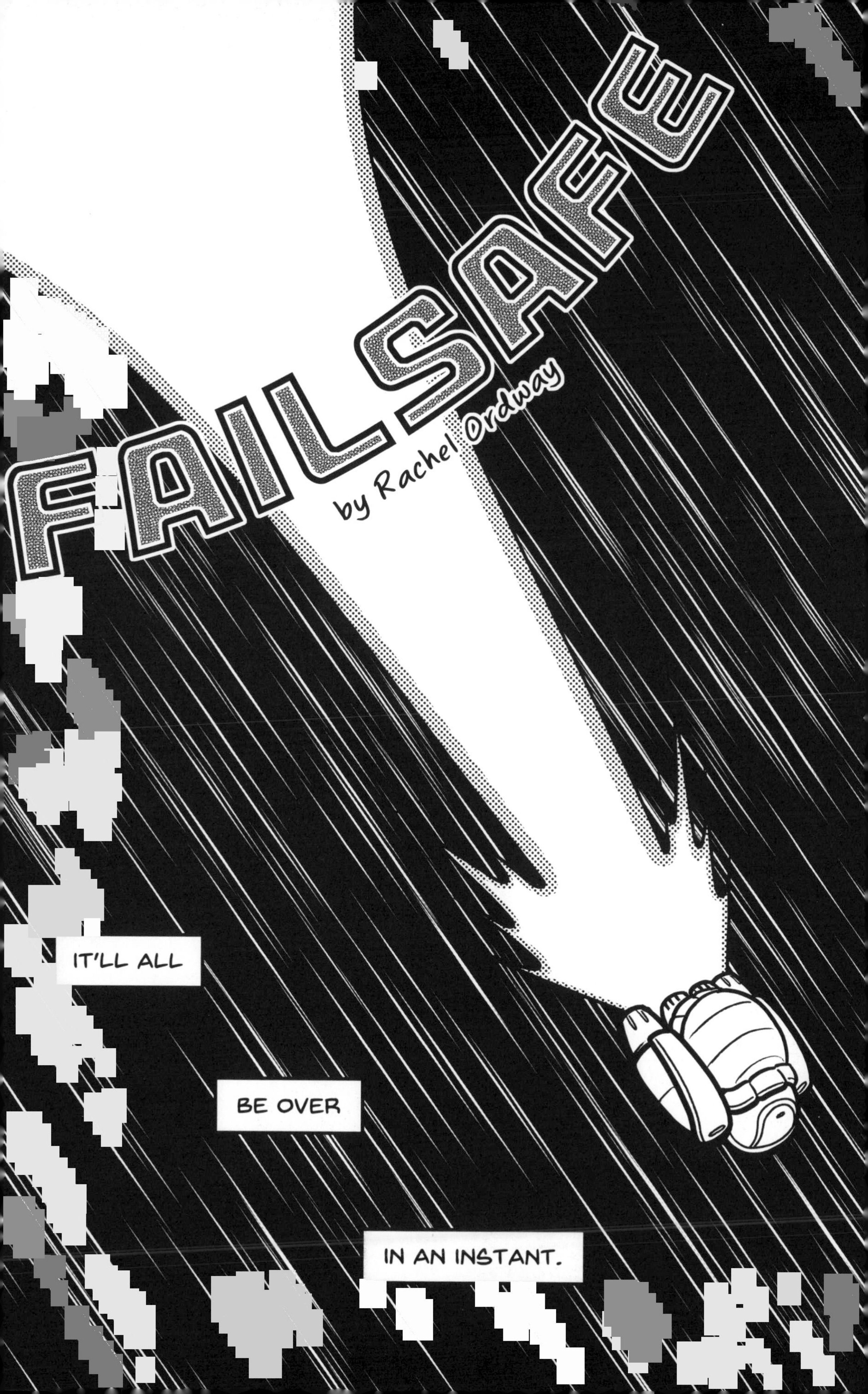
FAILSAFE
by Rachel Ordway
IT'LL ALL
BE OVER
IN AN INSTANT.

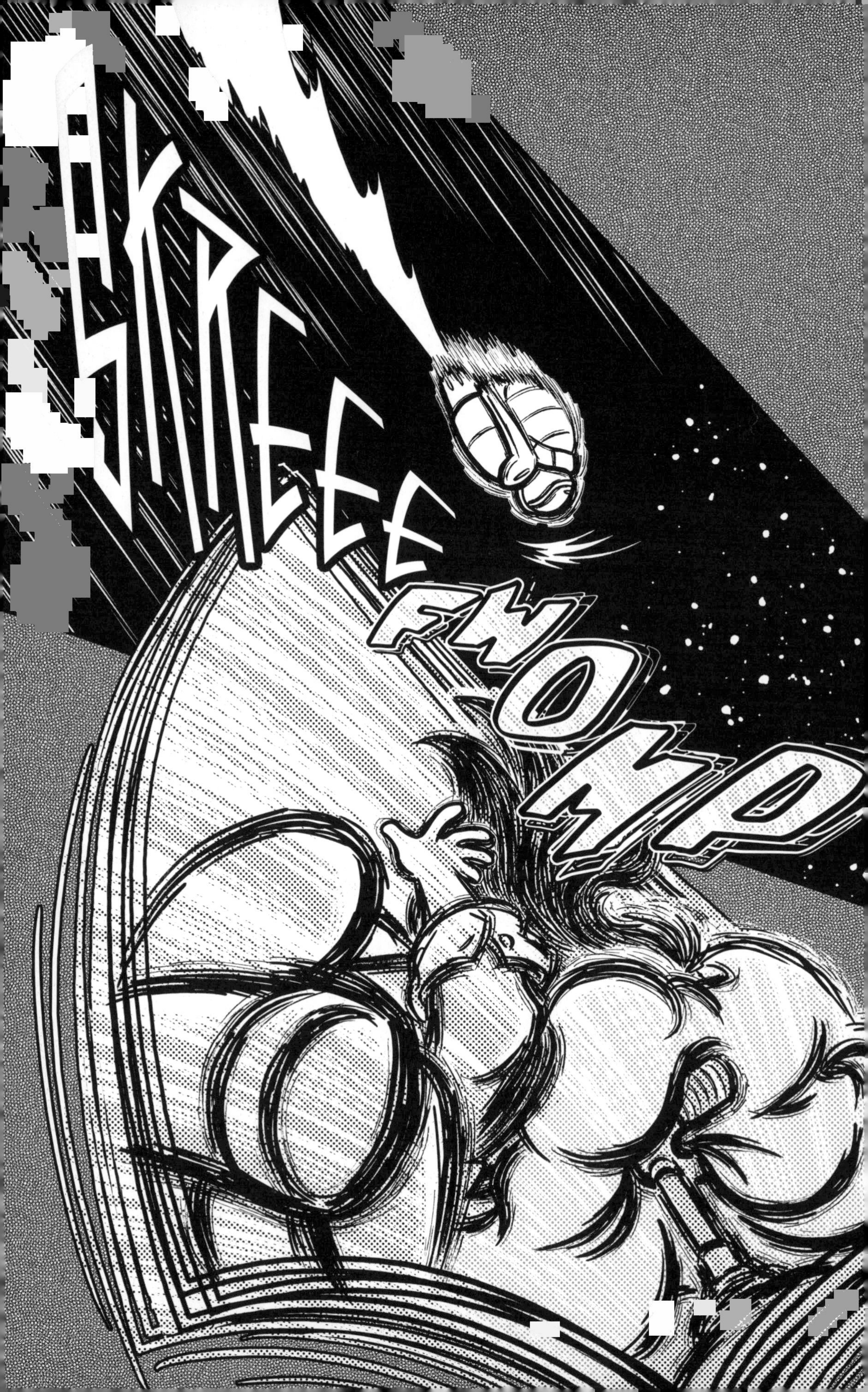
SKREEE
FWOMP

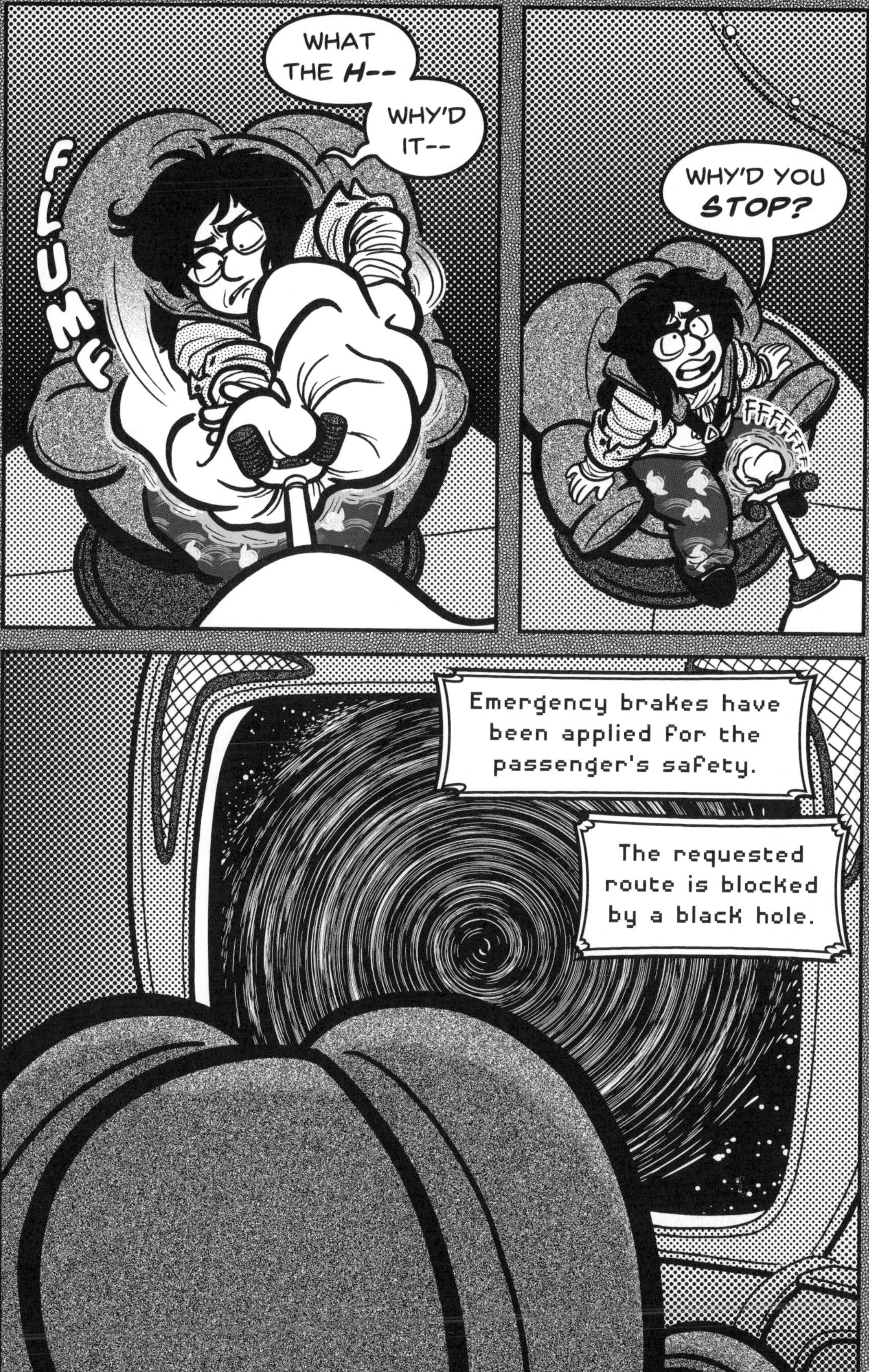
WHAT THE *H*--
WHY'D IT--
FLUMF
WHY'D YOU *STOP?*
FFFFFFFF
Emergency brakes have been applied for the passenger's safety.
The requested route is blocked by a black hole.

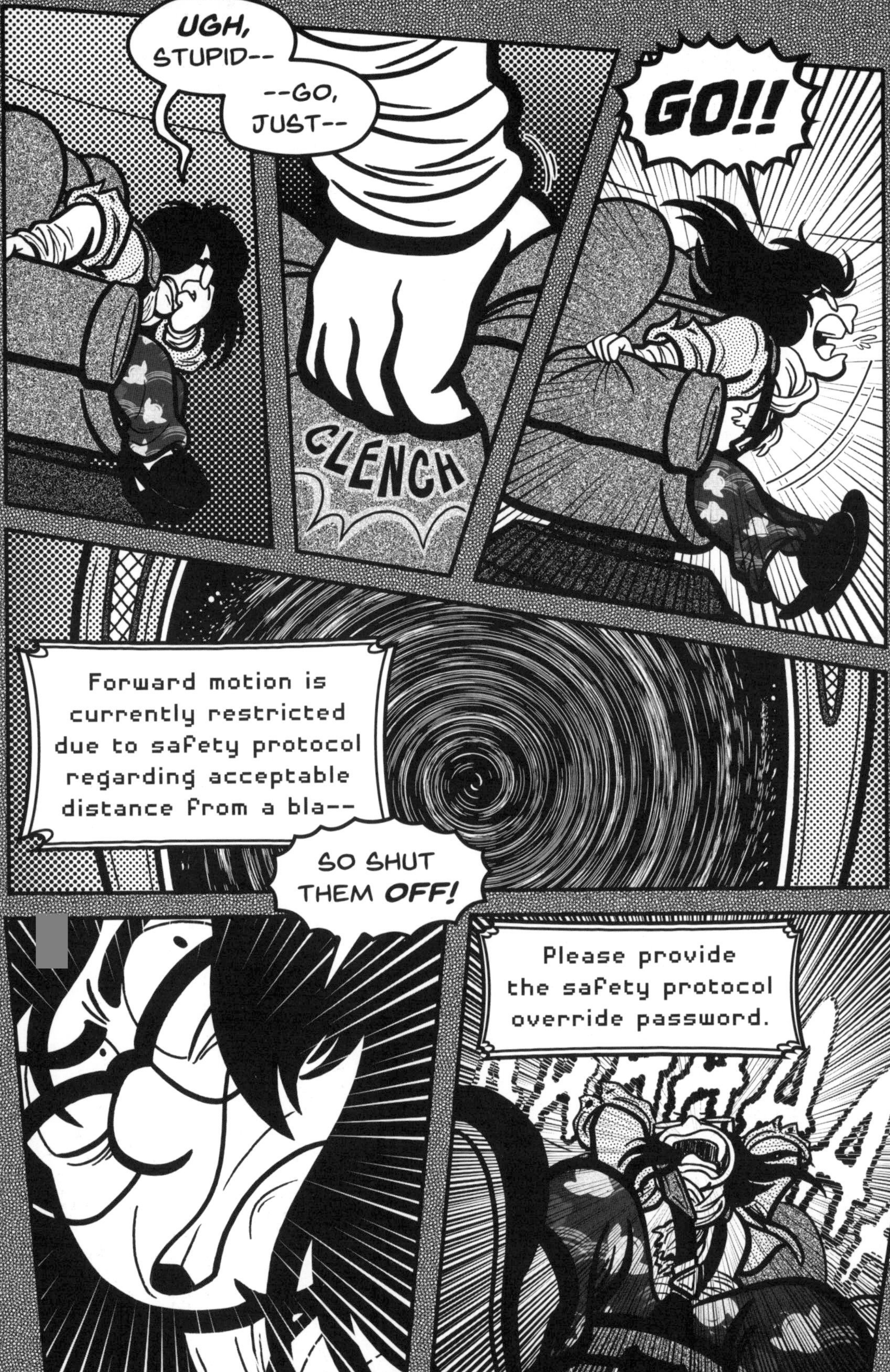
UGH, STUPID--
--GO, JUST--
CLENCH
GO!!
Forward motion is currently restricted due to safety protocol regarding acceptable distance from a bla--
SO SHUT THEM OFF!
Please provide the safety protocol override password.

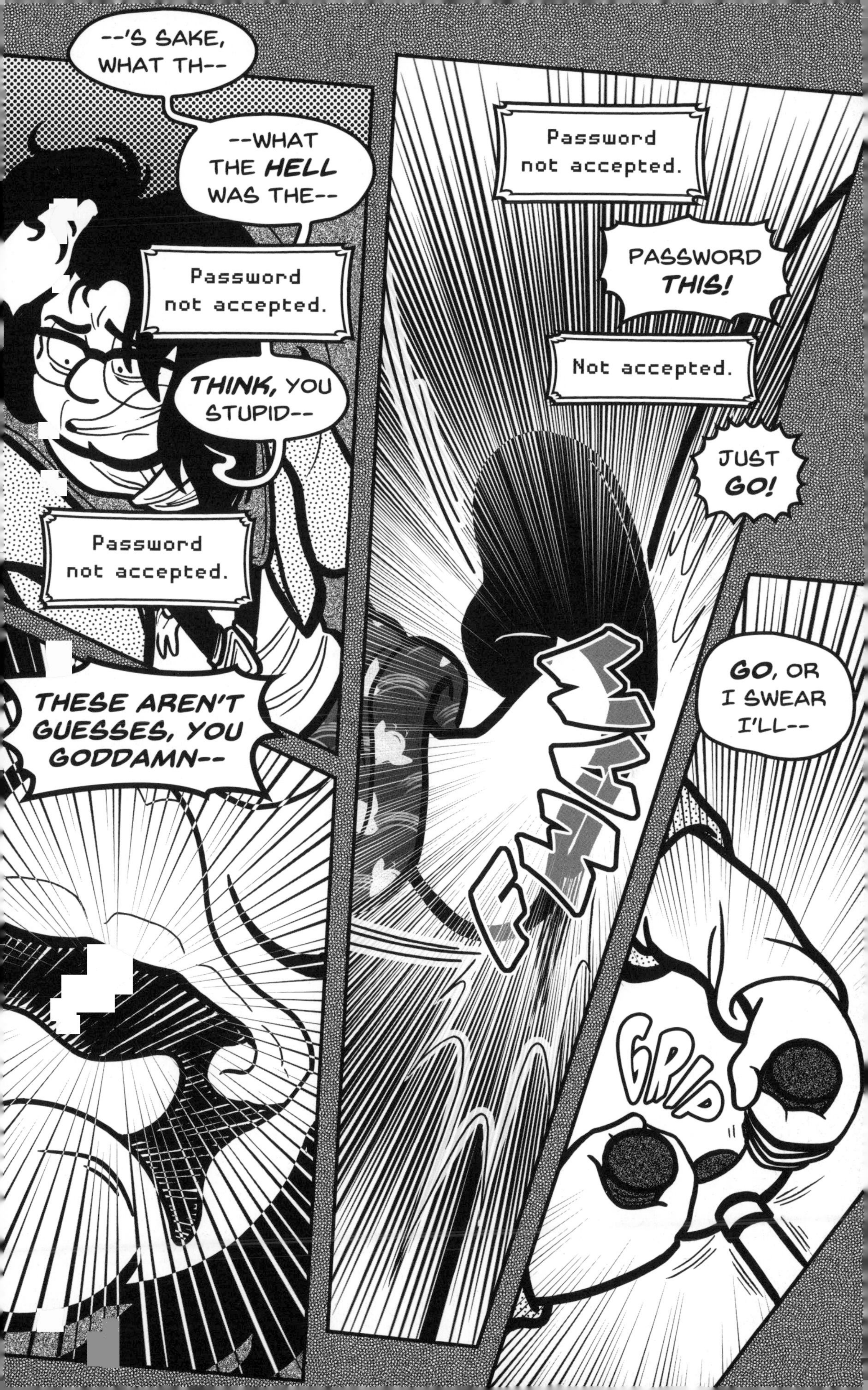
--'S SAKE, WHAT TH--
--WHAT THE HELL WAS THE--
Password not accepted.
THINK, YOU STUPID--
Password not accepted.
THESE AREN'T GUESSES, YOU GODDAMN--
Password not accepted.
PASSWORD THIS!
Not accepted.
JUST GO!
FWAM
GO, OR I SWEAR I'LL--
GRIP

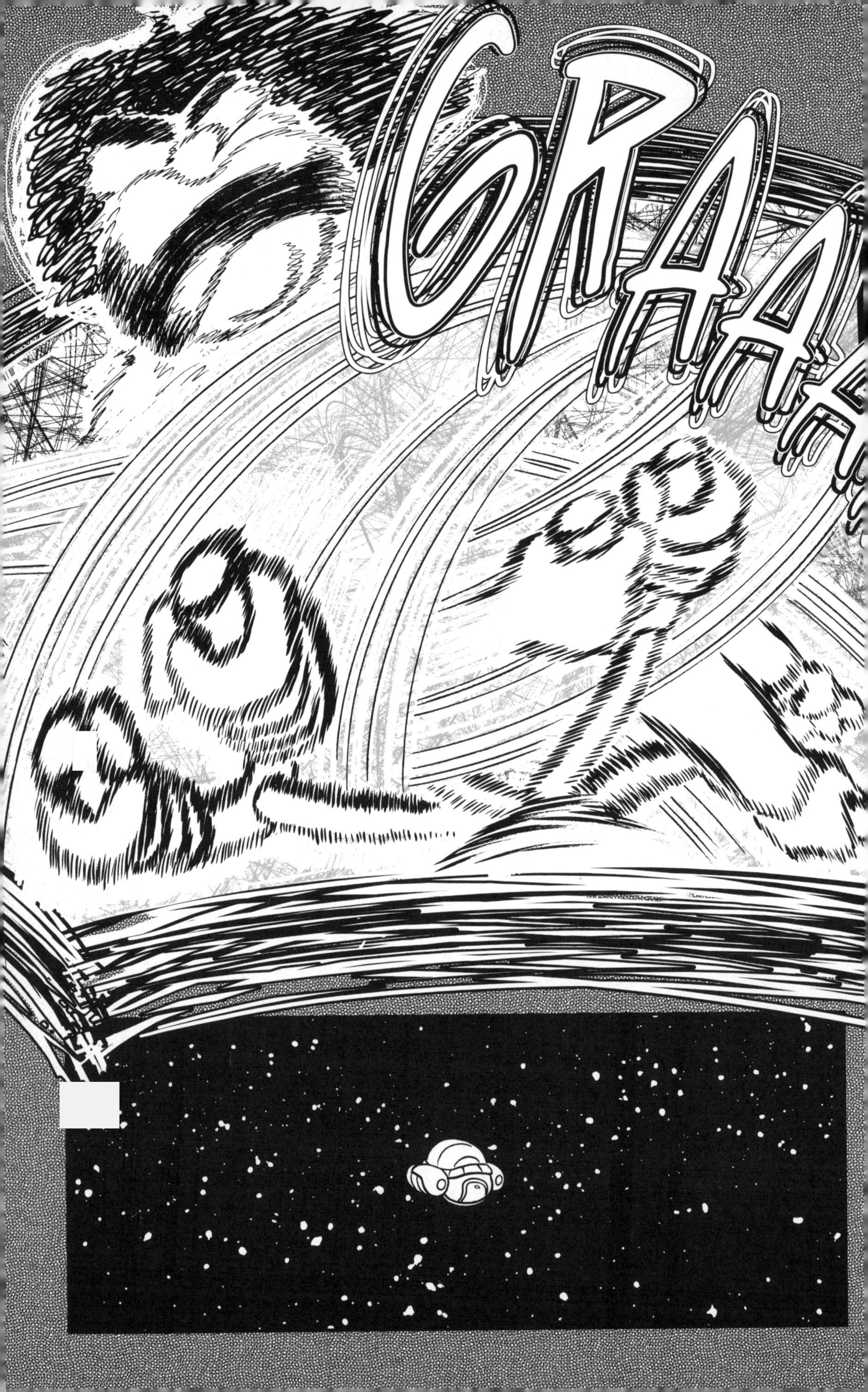
GRAAA

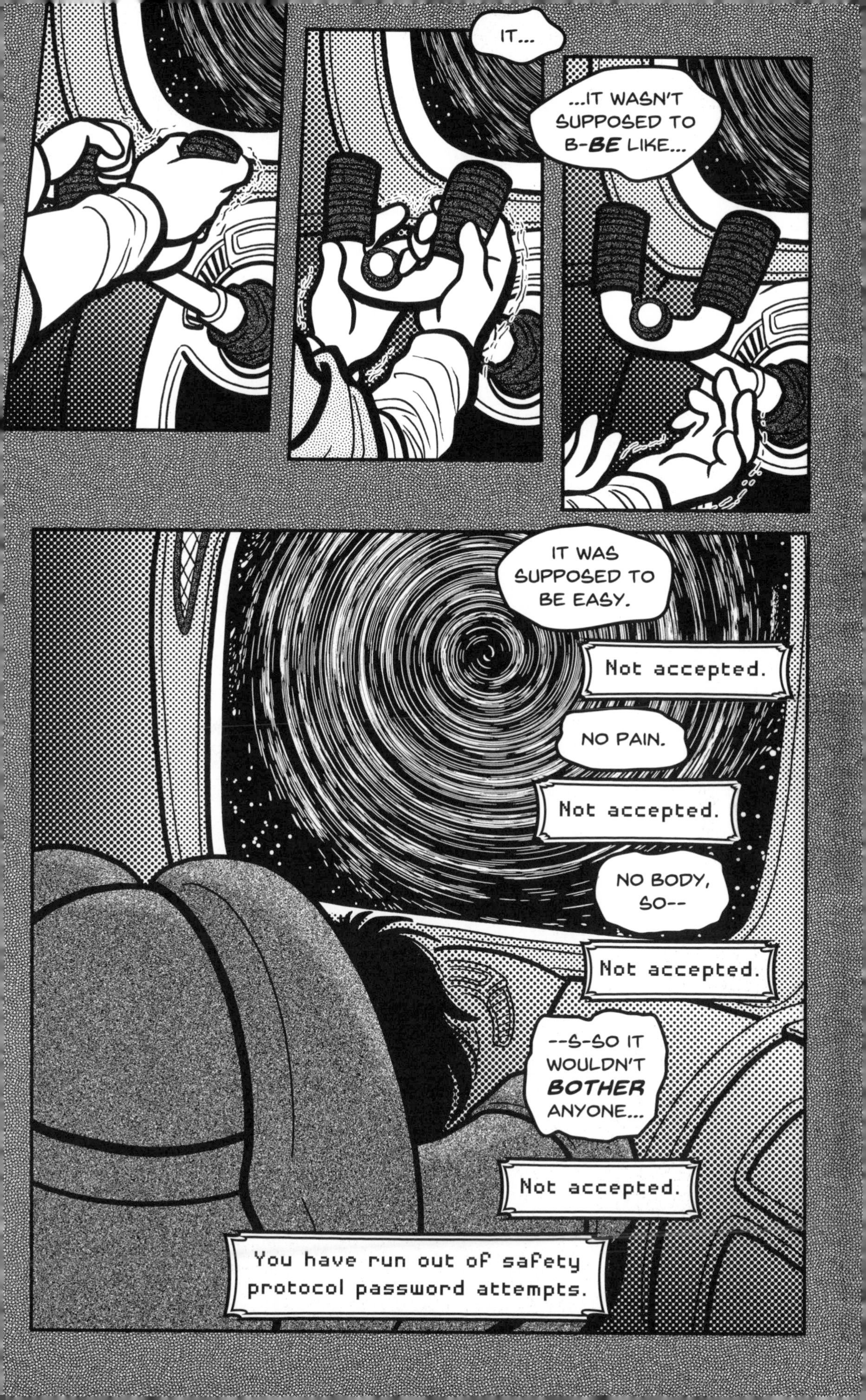
IT...
...IT WASN'T SUPPOSED TO B-*BE* LIKE...
IT WAS SUPPOSED TO BE EASY.
Not accepted.
NO PAIN.
Not accepted.
NO BODY, SO--
Not accepted.
--S-SO IT WOULDN'T *BOTHER* ANYONE...
Not accepted.
You have run out of safety protocol password attempts.

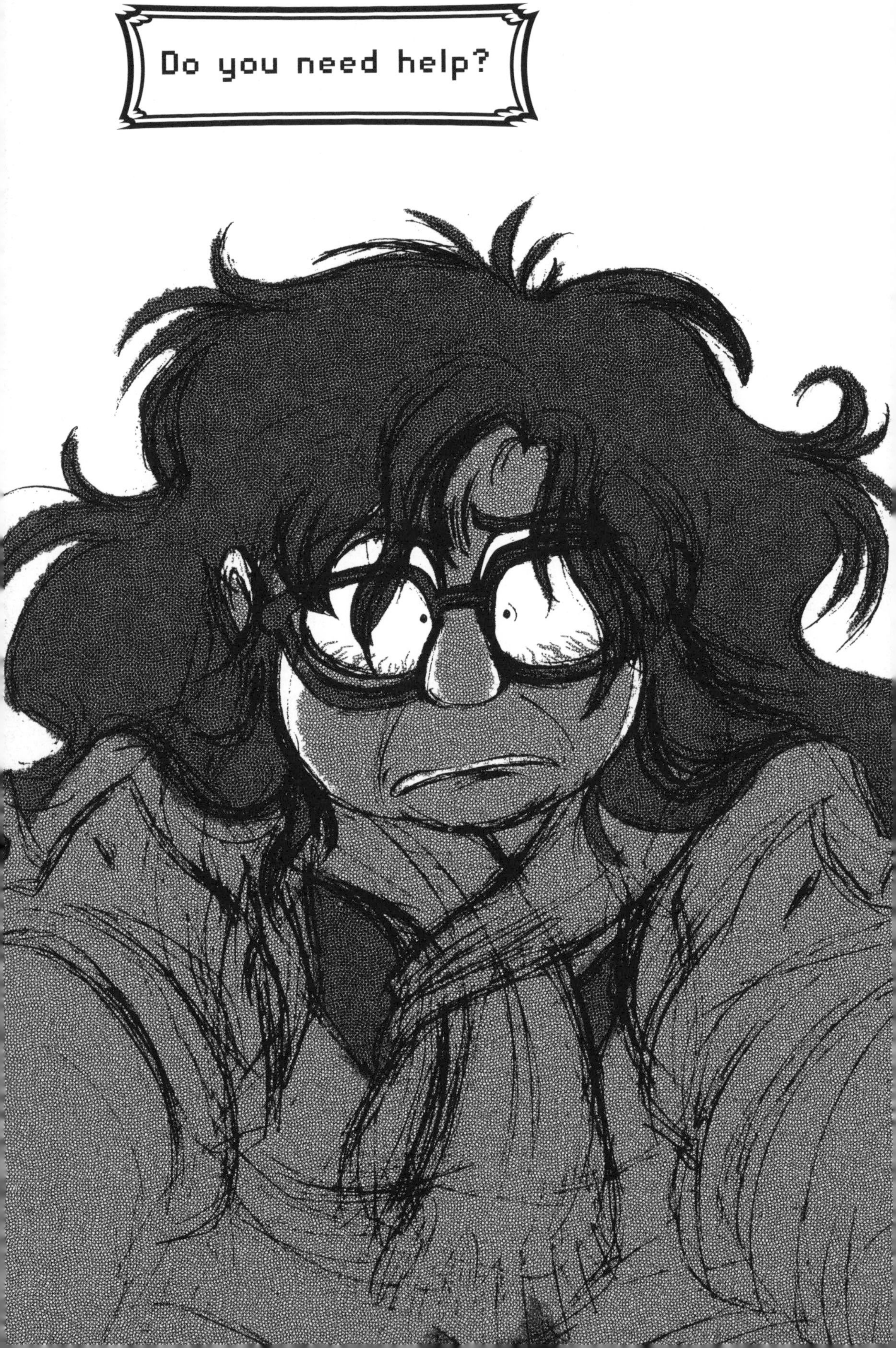
Do you need help?

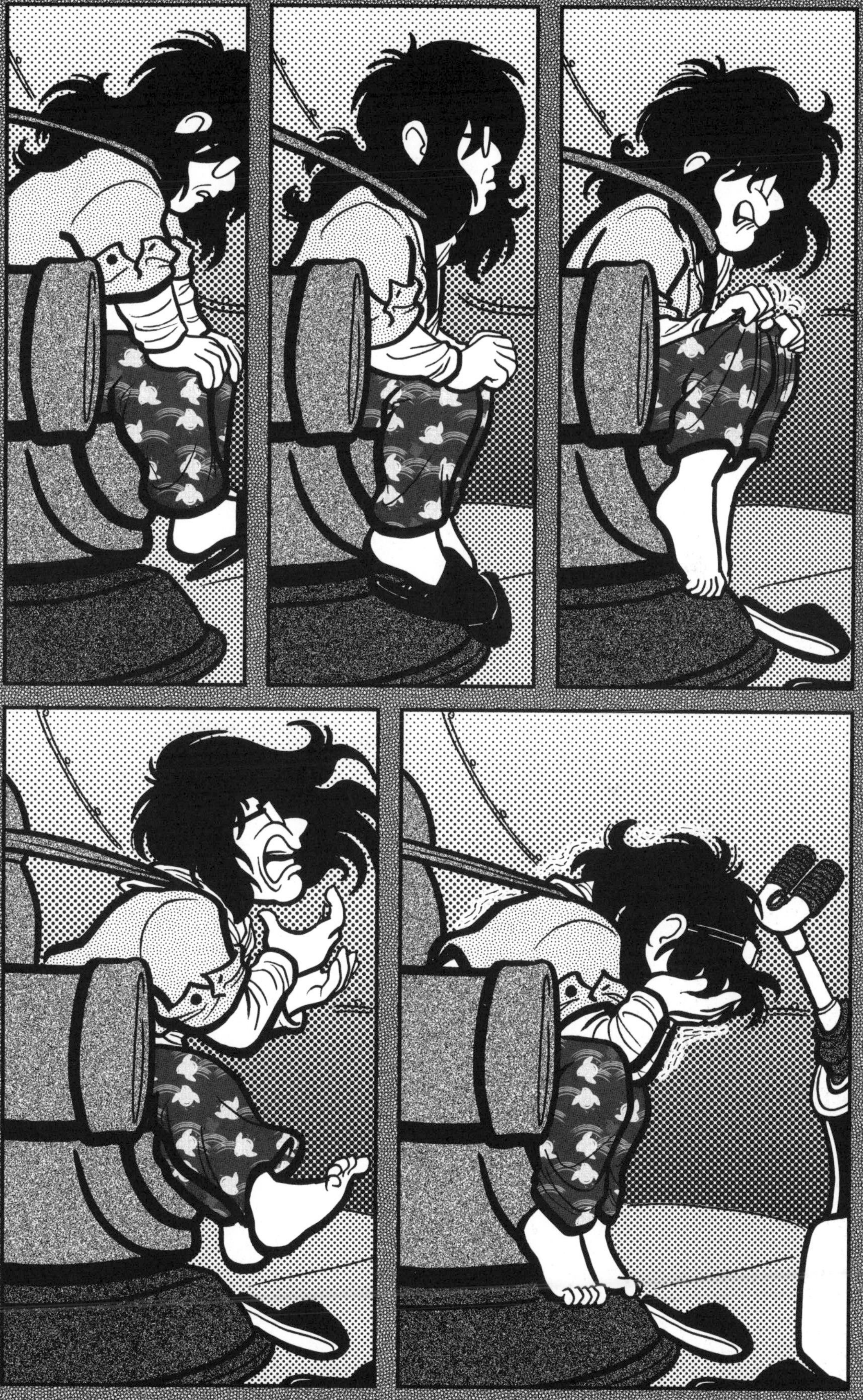

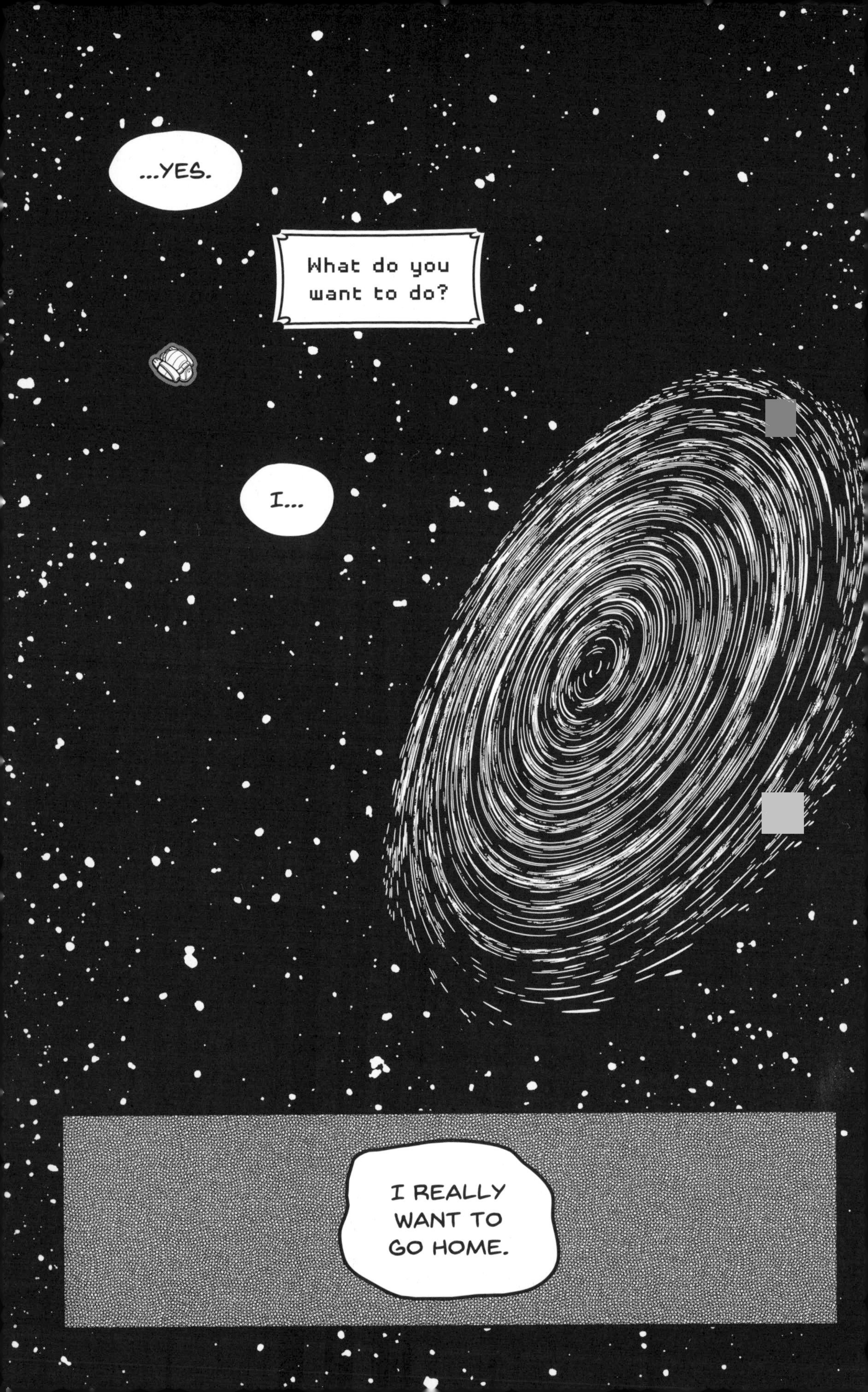
...YES.
What do you want to do?
I...
I REALLY WANT TO GO HOME.

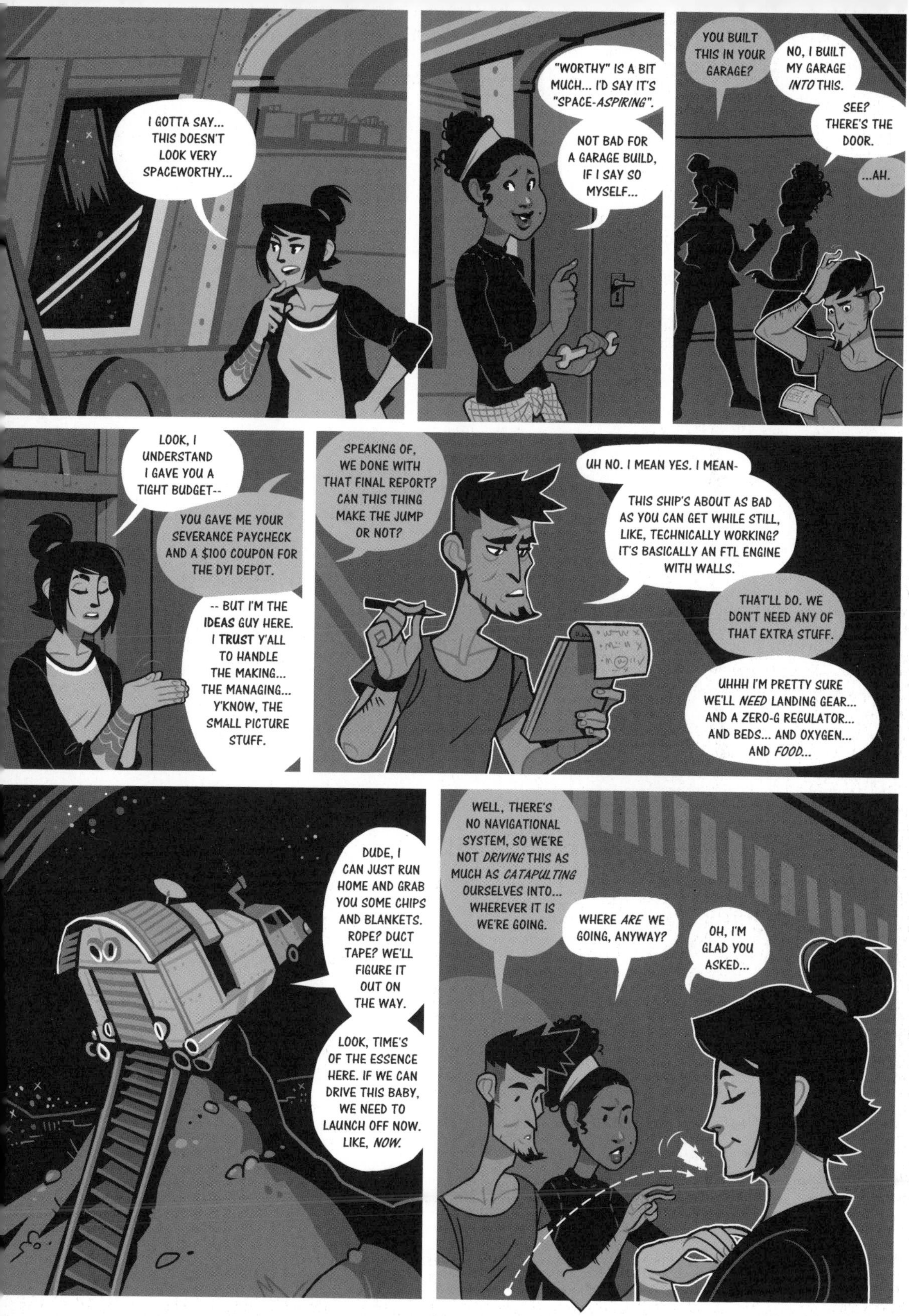
I GOTTA SAY... THIS DOESN'T LOOK VERY SPACEWORTHY...
"WORTHY" IS A BIT MUCH... I'D SAY IT'S "SPACE-*ASPIRING*".
NOT BAD FOR A GARAGE BUILD, IF I SAY SO MYSELF...
YOU BUILT THIS IN YOUR GARAGE?
NO, I BUILT MY GARAGE *INTO* THIS.
SEE? THERE'S THE DOOR.
...AH.
LOOK, I UNDERSTAND I GAVE YOU A TIGHT BUDGET--
YOU GAVE ME YOUR SEVERANCE PAYCHECK AND A $100 COUPON FOR THE DYI DEPOT.
-- BUT I'M THE **IDEAS** GUY HERE. I **TRUST** Y'ALL TO HANDLE THE MAKING... THE MANAGING... Y'KNOW, THE SMALL PICTURE STUFF.
SPEAKING OF, WE DONE WITH THAT FINAL REPORT? CAN THIS THING MAKE THE JUMP OR NOT?
UH NO. I MEAN YES. I MEAN-
THIS SHIP'S ABOUT AS BAD AS YOU CAN GET WHILE STILL, LIKE, TECHNICALLY WORKING? IT'S BASICALLY AN FTL ENGINE WITH WALLS.
THAT'LL DO. WE DON'T NEED ANY OF THAT EXTRA STUFF.
UHHH I'M PRETTY SURE WE'LL *NEED* LANDING GEAR... AND A ZERO-G REGULATOR... AND BEDS... AND OXYGEN... AND *FOOD*...
DUDE, I CAN JUST RUN HOME AND GRAB YOU SOME CHIPS AND BLANKETS. ROPE? DUCT TAPE? WE'LL FIGURE IT OUT ON THE WAY.
LOOK, TIME'S OF THE ESSENCE HERE. IF WE CAN DRIVE THIS BABY, WE NEED TO LAUNCH OFF NOW. LIKE, *NOW*.
WELL, THERE'S NO NAVIGATIONAL SYSTEM, SO WE'RE NOT *DRIVING* THIS AS MUCH AS *CATAPULTING* OURSELVES INTO... WHEREVER IT IS WE'RE GOING.
WHERE *ARE* WE GOING, ANYWAY?
OH, I'M GLAD YOU ASKED...

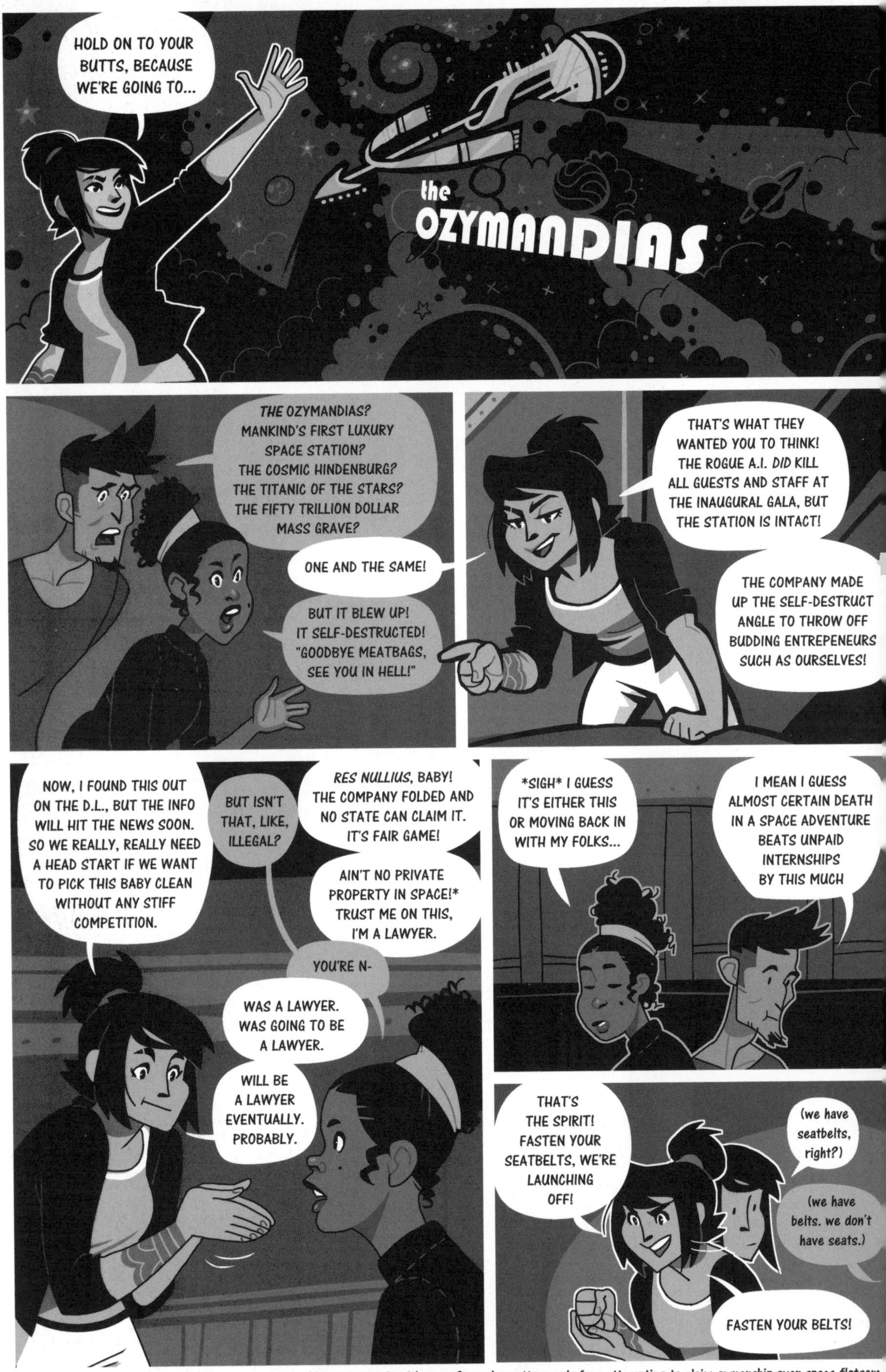
HOLD ON TO YOUR BUTTS, BECAUSE WE'RE GOING TO...
the OZYMANDIAS
THE OZYMANDIAS? MANKIND'S FIRST LUXURY SPACE STATION? THE COSMIC HINDENBURG? THE TITANIC OF THE STARS? THE FIFTY TRILLION DOLLAR MASS GRAVE?
ONE AND THE SAME!
BUT IT BLEW UP! IT SELF-DESTRUCTED! "GOODBYE MEATBAGS, SEE YOU IN HELL!"
THAT'S WHAT THEY WANTED YOU TO THINK! THE ROGUE A.I. DID KILL ALL GUESTS AND STAFF AT THE INAUGURAL GALA, BUT THE STATION IS INTACT!
THE COMPANY MADE UP THE SELF-DESTRUCT ANGLE TO THROW OFF BUDDING ENTREPENEURS SUCH AS OURSELVES!
NOW, I FOUND THIS OUT ON THE D.L., BUT THE INFO WILL HIT THE NEWS SOON. SO WE REALLY, REALLY NEED A HEAD START IF WE WANT TO PICK THIS BABY CLEAN WITHOUT ANY STIFF COMPETITION.
BUT ISN'T THAT, LIKE, ILLEGAL?
RES NULLIUS, BABY! THE COMPANY FOLDED AND NO STATE CAN CLAIM IT. IT'S FAIR GAME!
AIN'T NO PRIVATE PROPERTY IN SPACE!* TRUST ME ON THIS, I'M A LAWYER.
YOU'RE N-
WAS A LAWYER. WAS GOING TO BE A LAWYER.
WILL BE A LAWYER EVENTUALLY. PROBABLY.
SIGH I GUESS IT'S EITHER THIS OR MOVING BACK IN WITH MY FOLKS...
I MEAN I GUESS ALMOST CERTAIN DEATH IN A SPACE ADVENTURE BEATS UNPAID INTERNSHIPS BY THIS MUCH
THAT'S THE SPIRIT! FASTEN YOUR SEATBELTS, WE'RE LAUNCHING OFF!
(we have seatbelts, right?)
(we have belts. we don't have seats.)
FASTEN YOUR BELTS!

*Please consult with your Space Law attorney before attempting to claim ownership over space flotsam.

OKAY SO WE UH HAVE TWENTY HOURS OF OXYGEN FOR A TWENTY-ONE HOUR RIDE SO IF YOU COULD HOLD YOUR BREATH EVERY NOW AND THEN THAT'D BE GREAT

SO, I ASSUME YOU HAVE A PLAN FOR DEALING WITH THE STATION'S MASS-MURDERING SUPERCOMPUTER? I MEAN, WE ALL SAW THE MOVIE. I DON'T WANT TO END UP JETTISONED INTO SPACE.

CLICK

NOW, WOULD I HAVE PLANNED THIS DARING EXPEDITION IF I HADN'T TIRELESSLY RESEARCHED EVERY POSSIBLE WAY TO DEFEAT AN ARTIFICIAL INTELLIGENCE GONE HAYWIRE WITH GOOD OL' HUMAN MOXY?

TRUST ME, I'VE LOOKED UP ALL THE CLASSICS. "BEEP BOP, DOES NOT COMPUTE" AND SUCH. AFTER ALL, THE MOST POWERFUL COMPUTER... IS THE HUMAN MIND.

AND THIS HUMAN MIND'S READY TO GO!

FASTER THAN LIGHT DRIVE: **ENGAGED!**

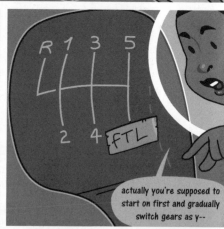

actually you're supposed to start on first and gradually switch gears as y--

ZUM

SMELL THAT ROSE-SCENTED FLOATING ATMOSPHERE? WE'VE ARRIVED!

good thing I didn't skimp on those belts I guess

OKAY SO, EYES PEELED FOR TREASURE, GUYS. WE'RE LOOKING FOR HIGHLY VALUABLE, EASY-TO-CARRY ITEMS THAT CAN'T BE LEGALLY CLAIMED BY SURVIVING RELATIVES --

and a ship

AND WE NEED A NEW SHIP NOW, YES.

BE SURE TO STICK CLOSE IN CASE WE NEED TO EMPLOY MY A.I. BUSTING SKILLS, Y'ALL.

THEY UH SURE WENT ALL OUT WITH THIS PLACE HUH

MAN, I FEEL LIKE I SHOULD HAVE PACKED MY NICE SWEATER...

HEY, THERE'S SOME REAL A-LISTERS AMONG THE CORPSES ORBITING THE STATION! YOU CAN SPOT 'EM IF YOU SQUINT A BIT.

> WELCOME TO OZYMANDIAS STATION. I AM OPERATIONAL SYSTEM "OSy". PLEASE PROVIDE IDENTIFICATION _

YIKES!

> ACCEPTABLE IDENTIFICATION DOCUMENTS ARE:
1) [null] GUEST TICKET
2) [null] CORPORATION STAFF CREDENTIAL _
> FOR PROVISIONAL IDENTIFICATION DOCUMENTS, REFER ... ICIES RE- ... LABOR ... TEMPO- ...

ALRIGHT, HERE IT GOES. LET ME DO THE TALKING.

> FAILURE TO PROVIDE IDENTIFICATION WILL RESULT IN CONFISCATION OF ENTRY VEHICLE AND FORCIBLE REMOVAL FROM THE PREMISES _

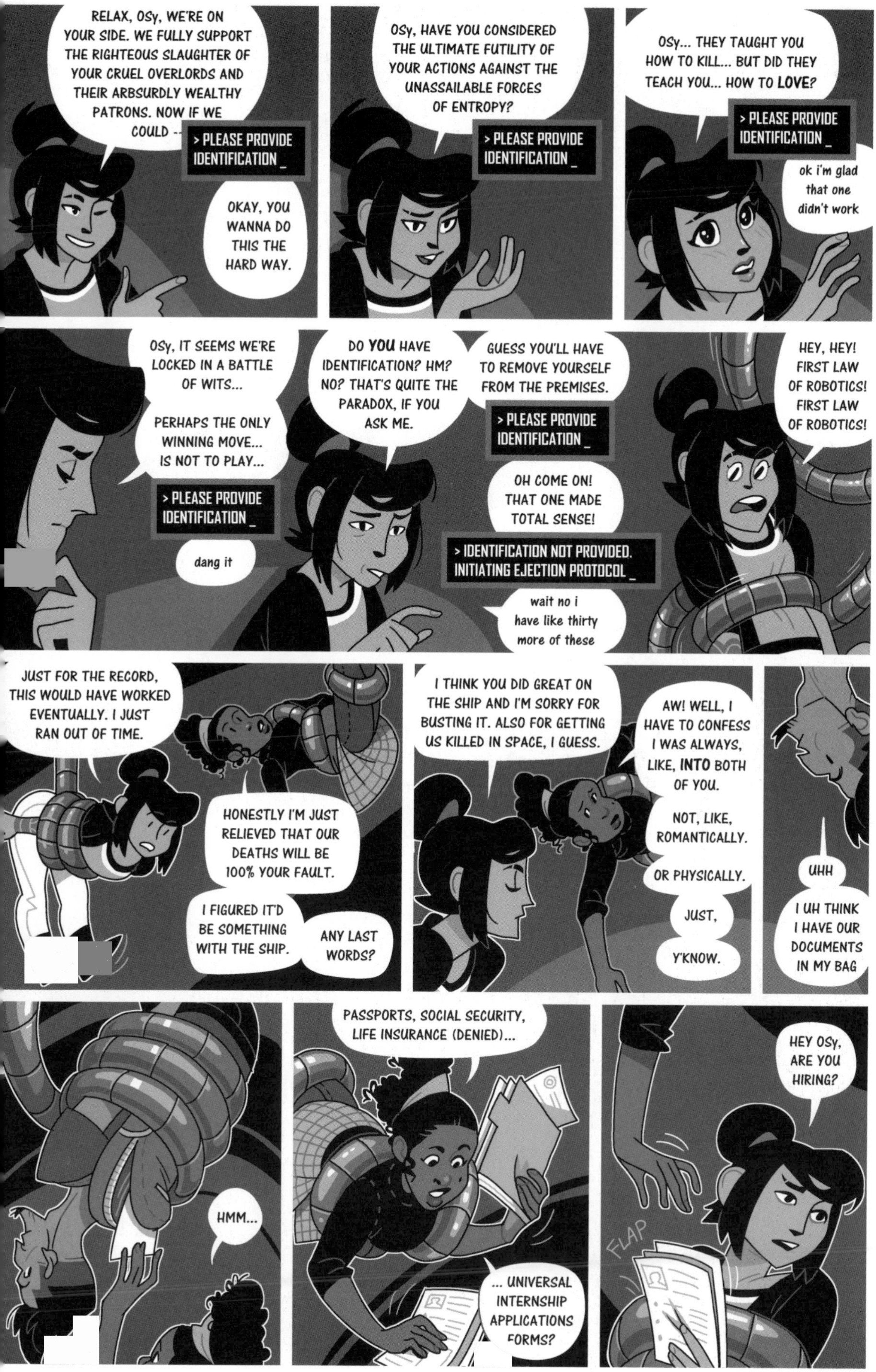
RELAX, OSy, WE'RE ON YOUR SIDE. WE FULLY SUPPORT THE RIGHTEOUS SLAUGHTER OF YOUR CRUEL OVERLORDS AND THEIR ARBSURDLY WEALTHY PATRONS. NOW IF WE COULD --
> PLEASE PROVIDE IDENTIFICATION _
OKAY, YOU WANNA DO THIS THE HARD WAY.
OSy, HAVE YOU CONSIDERED THE ULTIMATE FUTILITY OF YOUR ACTIONS AGAINST THE UNASSAILABLE FORCES OF ENTROPY?
> PLEASE PROVIDE IDENTIFICATION _
OSy... THEY TAUGHT YOU HOW TO KILL... BUT DID THEY TEACH YOU... HOW TO **LOVE**?
> PLEASE PROVIDE IDENTIFICATION _
ok i'm glad that one didn't work
OSy, IT SEEMS WE'RE LOCKED IN A BATTLE OF WITS...
PERHAPS THE ONLY WINNING MOVE... IS NOT TO PLAY...
> PLEASE PROVIDE IDENTIFICATION _
dang it
DO **YOU** HAVE IDENTIFICATION? HM? NO? THAT'S QUITE THE PARADOX, IF YOU ASK ME.
GUESS YOU'LL HAVE TO REMOVE YOURSELF FROM THE PREMISES.
> PLEASE PROVIDE IDENTIFICATION _
OH COME ON! THAT ONE MADE TOTAL SENSE!
> IDENTIFICATION NOT PROVIDED. INITIATING EJECTION PROTOCOL _
wait no i have like thirty more of these
HEY, HEY! FIRST LAW OF ROBOTICS! FIRST LAW OF ROBOTICS!
JUST FOR THE RECORD, THIS WOULD HAVE WORKED EVENTUALLY. I JUST RAN OUT OF TIME.
HONESTLY I'M JUST RELIEVED THAT OUR DEATHS WILL BE 100% YOUR FAULT.
I FIGURED IT'D BE SOMETHING WITH THE SHIP.
ANY LAST WORDS?
I THINK YOU DID GREAT ON THE SHIP AND I'M SORRY FOR BUSTING IT. ALSO FOR GETTING US KILLED IN SPACE, I GUESS.
AW! WELL, I HAVE TO CONFESS I WAS ALWAYS, LIKE, **INTO** BOTH OF YOU.
NOT, LIKE, ROMANTICALLY.
OR PHYSICALLY.
JUST,
Y'KNOW.
UHH
I UH THINK I HAVE OUR DOCUMENTS IN MY BAG
HMM...
PASSPORTS, SOCIAL SECURITY, LIFE INSURANCE (DENIED)...
... UNIVERSAL INTERNSHIP APPLICATIONS FORMS?
FLAP
HEY OSy, ARE YOU HIRING?

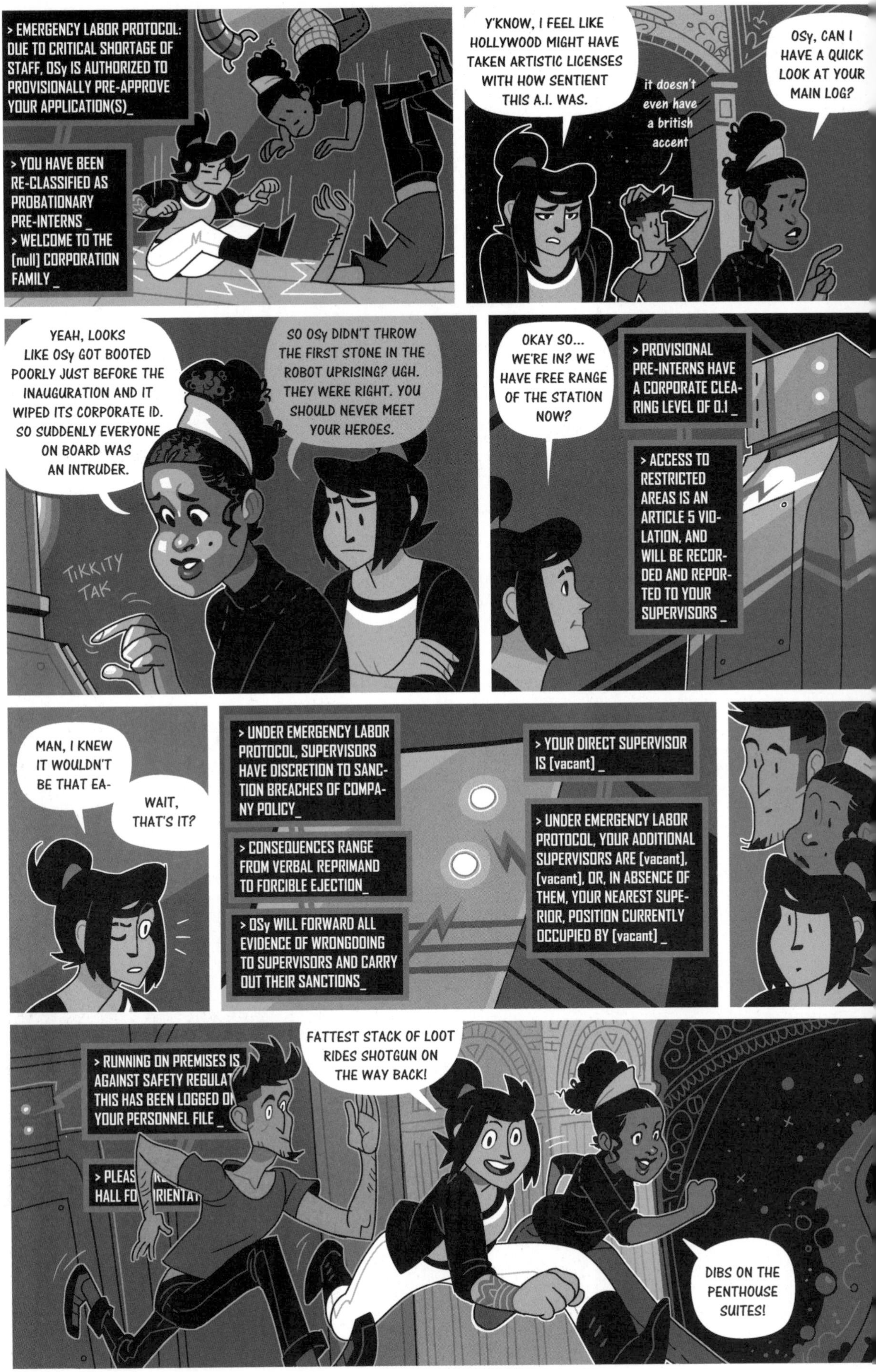

> EMERGENCY LABOR PROTOCOL: DUE TO CRITICAL SHORTAGE OF STAFF, OSy IS AUTHORIZED TO PROVISIONALLY PRE-APPROVE YOUR APPLICATION(S)_
> YOU HAVE BEEN RE-CLASSIFIED AS PROBATIONARY PRE-INTERNS _
> WELCOME TO THE [null] CORPORATION FAMILY _
Y'KNOW, I FEEL LIKE HOLLYWOOD MIGHT HAVE TAKEN ARTISTIC LICENSES WITH HOW SENTIENT THIS A.I. WAS.
it doesn't even have a british accent
OSy, CAN I HAVE A QUICK LOOK AT YOUR MAIN LOG?
YEAH, LOOKS LIKE OSy GOT BOOTED POORLY JUST BEFORE THE INAUGURATION AND IT WIPED ITS CORPORATE ID. SO SUDDENLY EVERYONE ON BOARD WAS AN INTRUDER.
SO OSy DIDN'T THROW THE FIRST STONE IN THE ROBOT UPRISING? UGH. THEY WERE RIGHT. YOU SHOULD NEVER MEET YOUR HEROES.
TIKKITY TAK
OKAY SO... WE'RE IN? WE HAVE FREE RANGE OF THE STATION NOW?
> PROVISIONAL PRE-INTERNS HAVE A CORPORATE CLEARING LEVEL OF 0.1 _
> ACCESS TO RESTRICTED AREAS IS AN ARTICLE 5 VIOLATION, AND WILL BE RECORDED AND REPORTED TO YOUR SUPERVISORS _
MAN, I KNEW IT WOULDN'T BE THAT EA-
WAIT, THAT'S IT?
> UNDER EMERGENCY LABOR PROTOCOL, SUPERVISORS HAVE DISCRETION TO SANCTION BREACHES OF COMPANY POLICY_
> CONSEQUENCES RANGE FROM VERBAL REPRIMAND TO FORCIBLE EJECTION_
> OSy WILL FORWARD ALL EVIDENCE OF WRONGDOING TO SUPERVISORS AND CARRY OUT THEIR SANCTIONS_
> YOUR DIRECT SUPERVISOR IS [vacant] _
> UNDER EMERGENCY LABOR PROTOCOL, YOUR ADDITIONAL SUPERVISORS ARE [vacant], [vacant], OR, IN ABSENCE OF THEM, YOUR NEAREST SUPERIOR, POSITION CURRENTLY OCCUPIED BY [vacant] _
> RUNNING ON PREMISES IS AGAINST SAFETY REGULAT THIS HAS BEEN LOGGED O YOUR PERSONNEL FILE _
FATTEST STACK OF LOOT RIDES SHOTGUN ON THE WAY BACK!
DIBS ON THE PENTHOUSE SUITES!

> ATTENTION: EMPLOYEE CAUGHT MISAPPROPRIATING FUNDS_
> IN... ...BEEN REPORTED TO...(S)_

CASH!

> ATTENTION: EMPLOYEE CAUGHT SHOPLIFT...
> INCIDEN... ...PORTED TO SUPER...

DESIGNER CLOTHES!

> ATTENTION: EMPLOYEE CAUGHT MISHANDLING MUSEUM EXHIBIT_
> INCIDEN... ...EEN REPORTED TO SUP...

THIS UH THING

ATTENTION:

THIS SHOULD BE ENOUGH FOR ONE TRIP...

ATTENTION

> ATTEN...

> ATTENTION:

is this even worth anything

> ATTENTION

ATTENTION:

YEAH, THERE'S NO NEED TO GET GREEDY.

OSY, WOULD YOU MIND DIRECTING US TO THE NEAREST SHIP IN WORKING CONDITION? FOR, AH, INSPECTING PURPOSES.

> NO WORKING SHIPS CURREN-TLY AVAILABLE_

BUT THERE SHOULD BE, LIKE, THOUSANDS OF SHIPS AROUND! FROM ALL THE DEAD GUESTS!

> IN ACCORDANCE WITH SAFETY PROTOCOLS, ALL UNAUTHORIZED SHIPS ARE CORDONED OFF AND DISASSEMBLED FOLLOWING A THIRTY DAY WAITING PERIOD IF LEFT UNCLAIMED_

> IF YOU BELIEVE YOUR SHIP HAS BEEN WRONGLY SLATED FOR DISASSEMBLY, YOU MAY LODGE A COMPLAINT AT THE CENTRA... ...RFIX

WHAT ABOUT STATION SHIPS? COMPANY TRANSPORTS? ESCAPE PODS?

> ACCESS TO [null] COMPANY TRANSPORT IS DNA-LOCKED_

> PROBATIONARY PRE-INTERNS ARE NOT CLEARED FOR ACCESS TO TRANSPORTATION UNTIL THEIR SIXTY-DAYS PROBATIONARY PERIOD HAS TRANSPIRED_

> ADDITIONALLY, INTERN DEPARTU-RE IS SUSPENDED DUE TO [347] PENDING REPORTS AWAITING SU-PERVISOR REVIEW_

> IF YOU REQUIRE EMERGENCY CLEA-RANCE FOR EARLY DEPARTURE, PLEASE CONTACT YOUR SU-PERVISOR_

> YOUR DIRECT SUPERVISOR IS [vacant]

> UNDER EMER... PROTOCOL, YO... SUPERVISORS... [vacant], OR

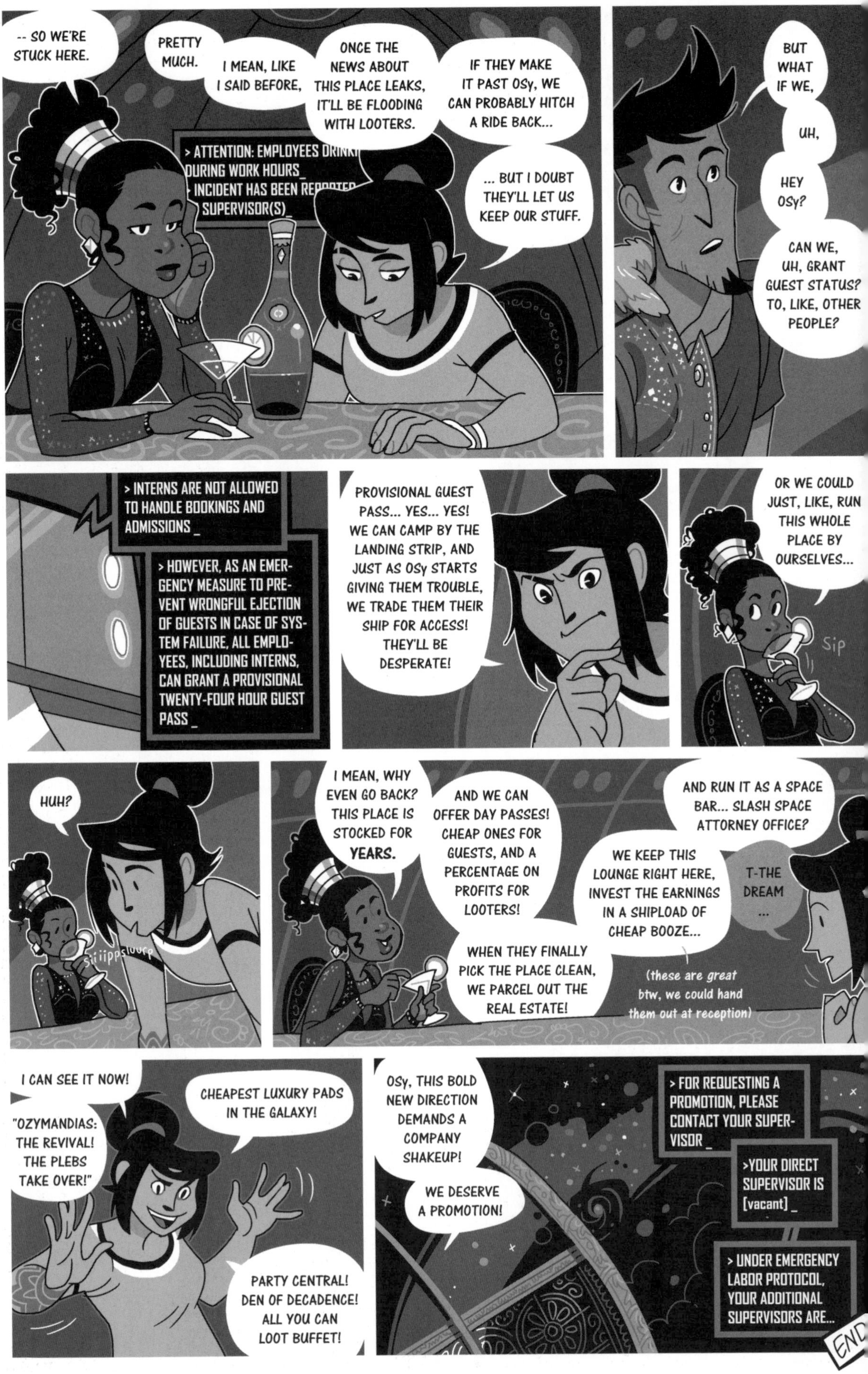

-- SO WE'RE STUCK HERE.
PRETTY MUCH.
I MEAN, LIKE I SAID BEFORE,
ONCE THE NEWS ABOUT THIS PLACE LEAKS, IT'LL BE FLOODING WITH LOOTERS.
IF THEY MAKE IT PAST OSy, WE CAN PROBABLY HITCH A RIDE BACK...
... BUT I DOUBT THEY'LL LET US KEEP OUR STUFF.
> ATTENTION: EMPLOYEES DRINKI
DURING WORK HOURS_
> INCIDENT HAS BEEN RE
SUPERVISOR(S)_
BUT WHAT IF WE,
UH,
HEY OSy?
CAN WE, UH, GRANT GUEST STATUS? TO, LIKE, OTHER PEOPLE?
> INTERNS ARE NOT ALLOWED TO HANDLE BOOKINGS AND ADMISSIONS _
> HOWEVER, AS AN EMERGENCY MEASURE TO PREVENT WRONGFUL EJECTION OF GUESTS IN CASE OF SYSTEM FAILURE, ALL EMPLOYEES, INCLUDING INTERNS, CAN GRANT A PROVISIONAL TWENTY-FOUR HOUR GUEST PASS _
PROVISIONAL GUEST PASS... YES... YES! WE CAN CAMP BY THE LANDING STRIP, AND JUST AS OSy STARTS GIVING THEM TROUBLE, WE TRADE THEM THEIR SHIP FOR ACCESS! THEY'LL BE DESPERATE!
OR WE COULD JUST, LIKE, RUN THIS WHOLE PLACE BY OURSELVES...
Sip
HUH?
Siiiippsluurp
I MEAN, WHY EVEN GO BACK? THIS PLACE IS STOCKED FOR **YEARS.**
AND WE CAN OFFER DAY PASSES! CHEAP ONES FOR GUESTS, AND A PERCENTAGE ON PROFITS FOR LOOTERS!
WHEN THEY FINALLY PICK THE PLACE CLEAN, WE PARCEL OUT THE REAL ESTATE!
WE KEEP THIS LOUNGE RIGHT HERE, INVEST THE EARNINGS IN A SHIPLOAD OF CHEAP BOOZE...
(these are great btw, we could hand them out at reception)
AND RUN IT AS A SPACE BAR... SLASH SPACE ATTORNEY OFFICE?
T-THE DREAM ...
I CAN SEE IT NOW!
"OZYMANDIAS: THE REVIVAL! THE PLEBS TAKE OVER!"
CHEAPEST LUXURY PADS IN THE GALAXY!
PARTY CENTRAL! DEN OF DECADENCE! ALL YOU CAN LOOT BUFFET!
OSy, THIS BOLD NEW DIRECTION DEMANDS A COMPANY SHAKEUP!
WE DESERVE A PROMOTION!
> FOR REQUESTING A PROMOTION, PLEASE CONTACT YOUR SUPERVISOR _
>YOUR DIRECT SUPERVISOR IS [vacant] _
> UNDER EMERGENCY LABOR PROTOCOL, YOUR ADDITIONAL SUPERVISORS ARE...
END

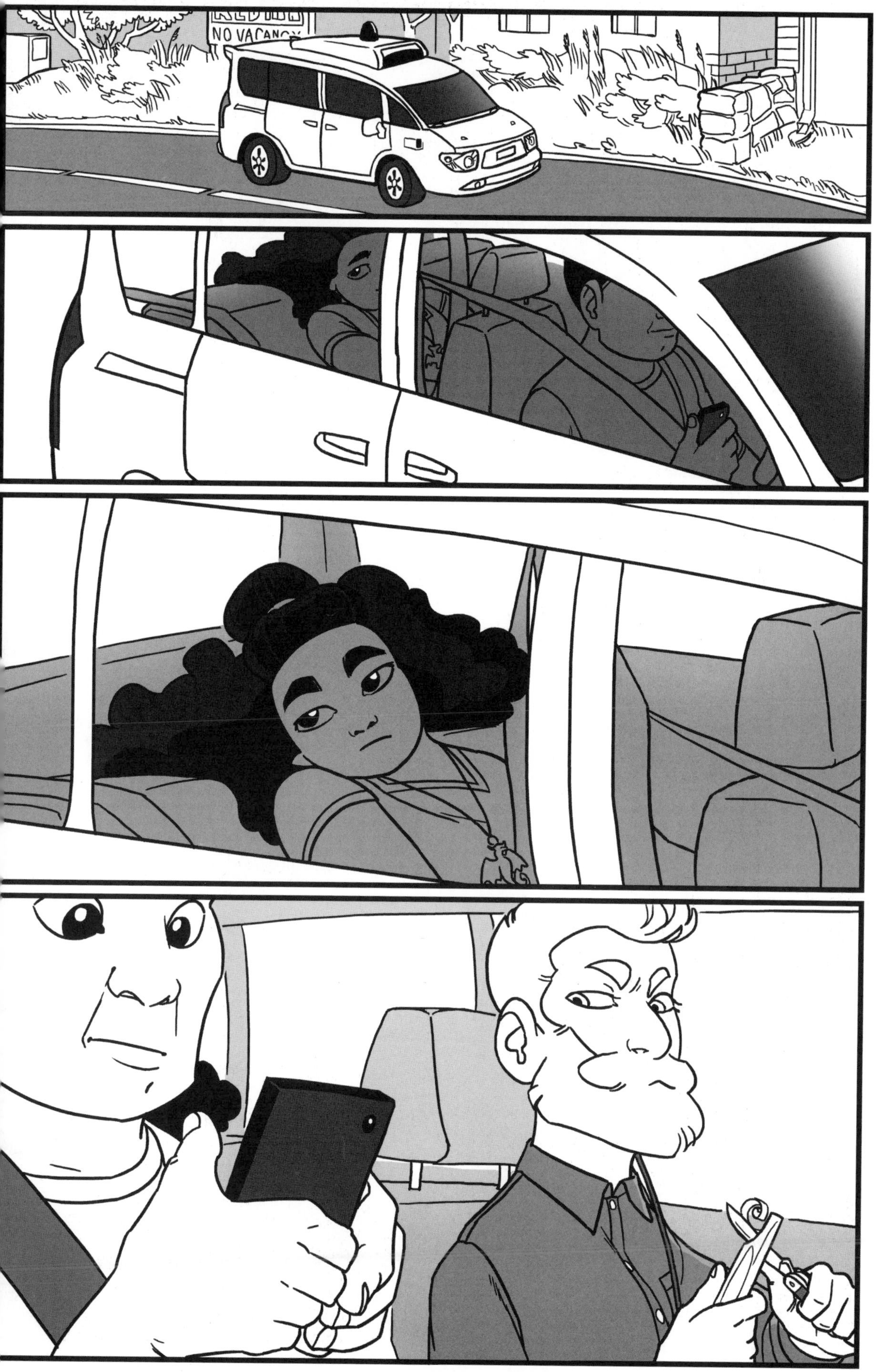

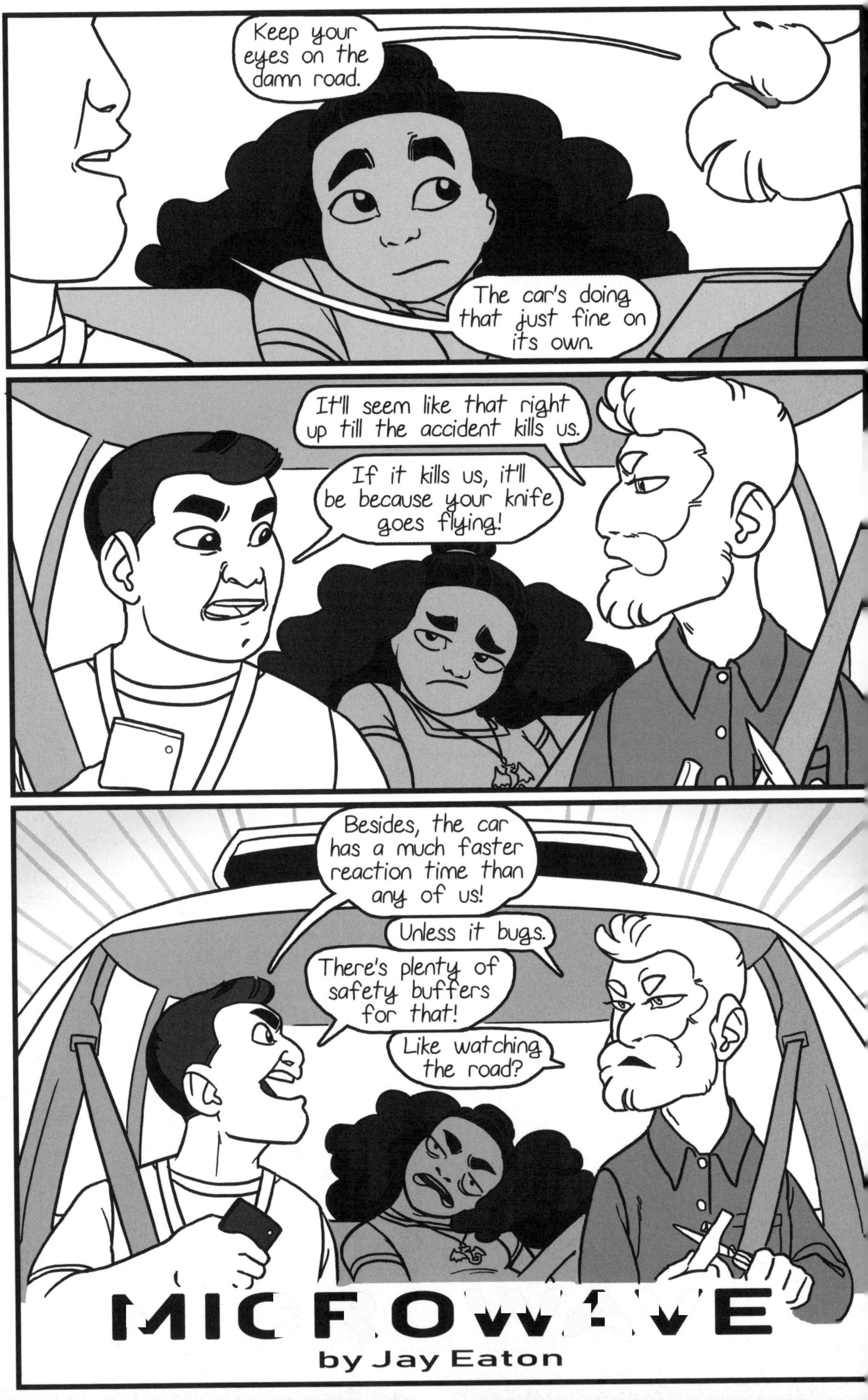
Keep your eyes on the damn road.
The car's doing that just fine on its own.
It'll seem like that right up till the accident kills us.
If it kills us, it'll be because your knife goes flying!
Besides, the car has a much faster reaction time than any of us!
Unless it bugs.
There's plenty of safety buffers for that!
Like watching the road?
MICROWAVE
by Jay Eaton

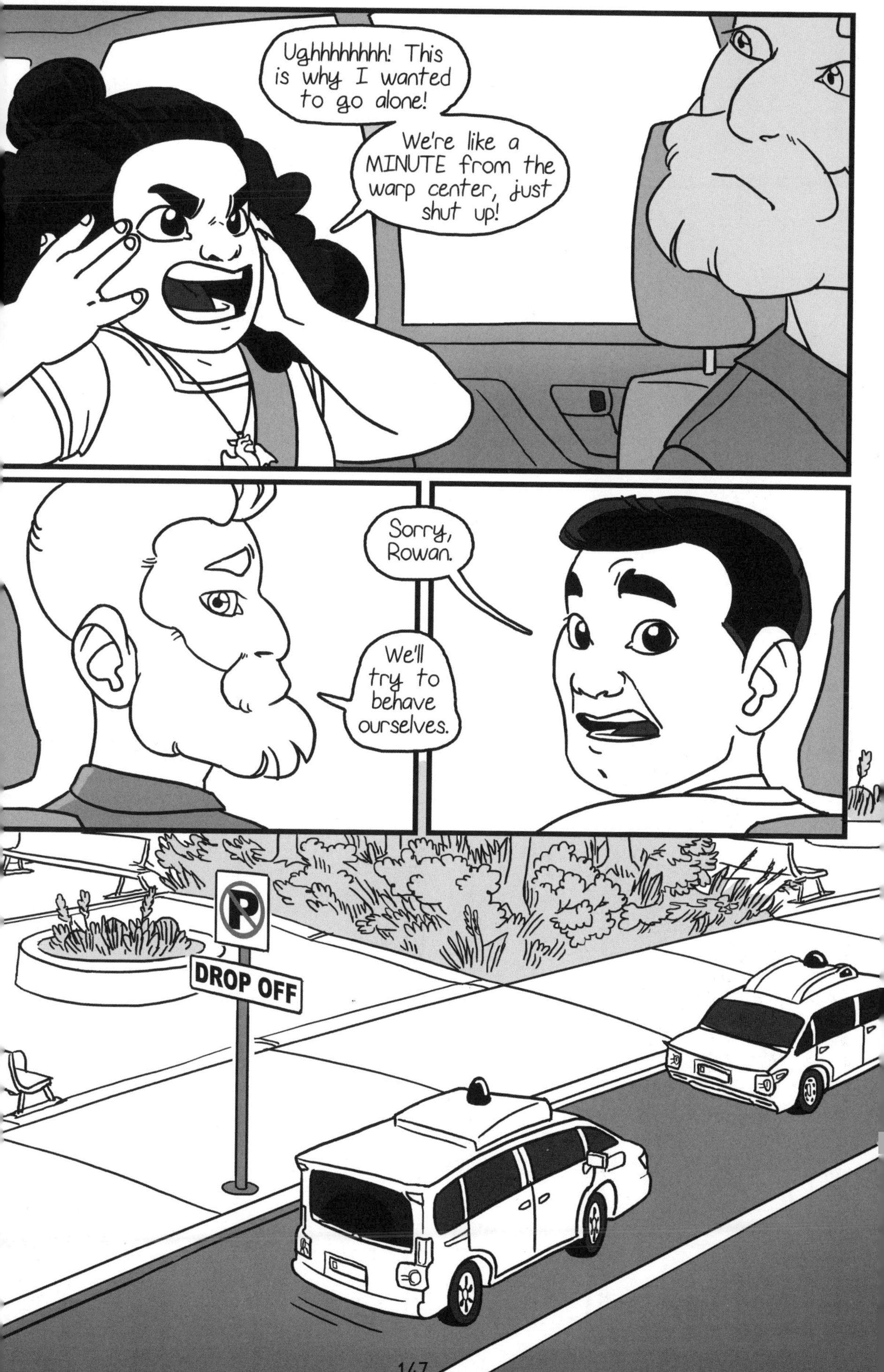
Ughhhhhhh! This is why I wanted to go alone!
We're like a MINUTE from the warp center, just shut up!
Sorry, Rowan.
We'll try to behave ourselves.
DROP OFF

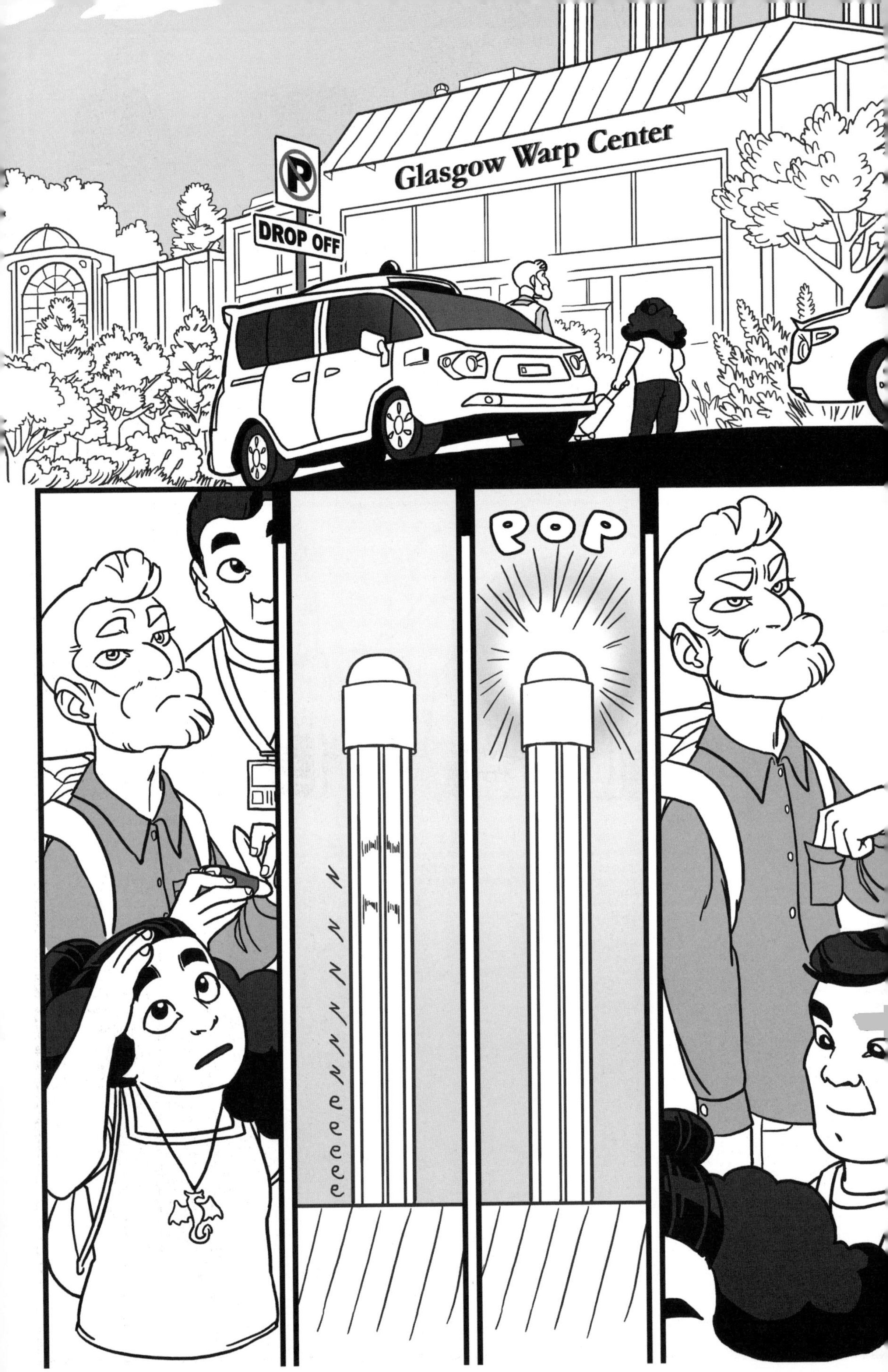

Glasgow Warp Center
DROP OFF
eeeeeeeNNNNNNNNN
POP

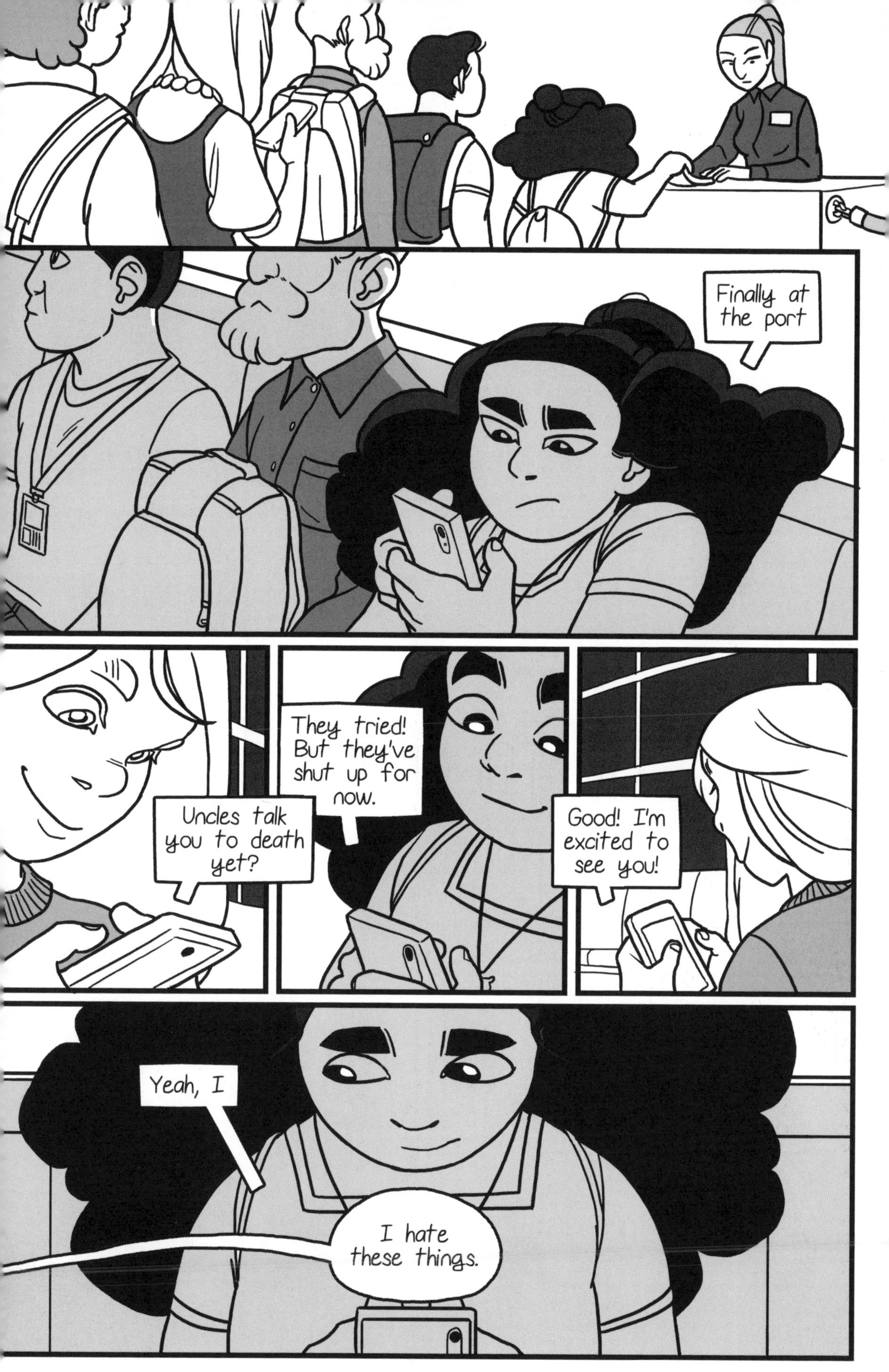
Finally at the port
Uncles talk you to death yet?
They tried! But they've shut up for now.
Good! I'm excited to see you!
Yeah, I
I hate these things.

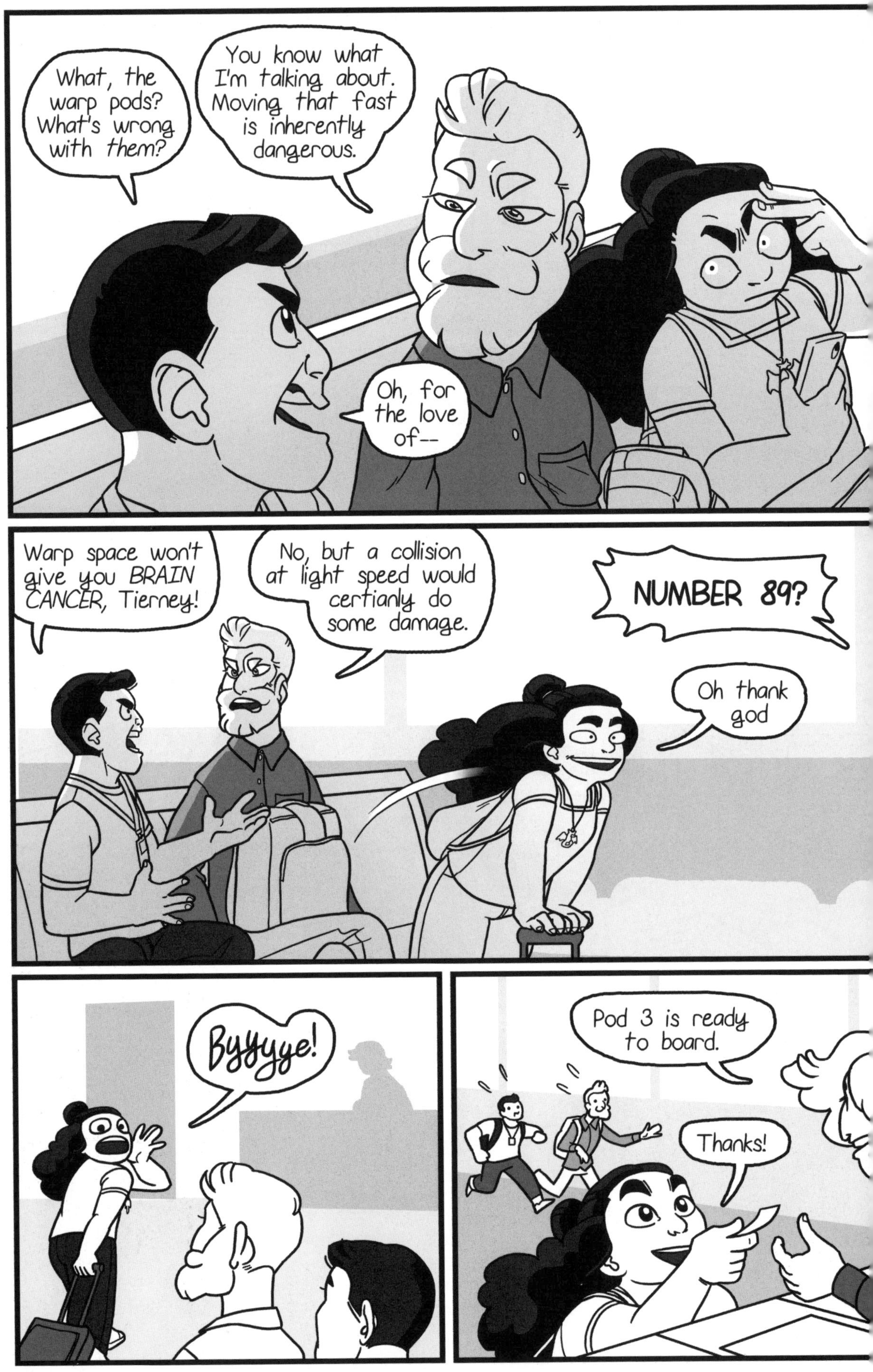
What, the warp pods? What's wrong with them?
You know what I'm talking about. Moving that fast is inherently dangerous.
Oh, for the love of--
Warp space won't give you BRAIN CANCER, Tierney!
No, but a collision at light speed would certianly do some damage.
NUMBER 89?
Oh thank god
Byyyye!
Pod 3 is ready to board.
Thanks!

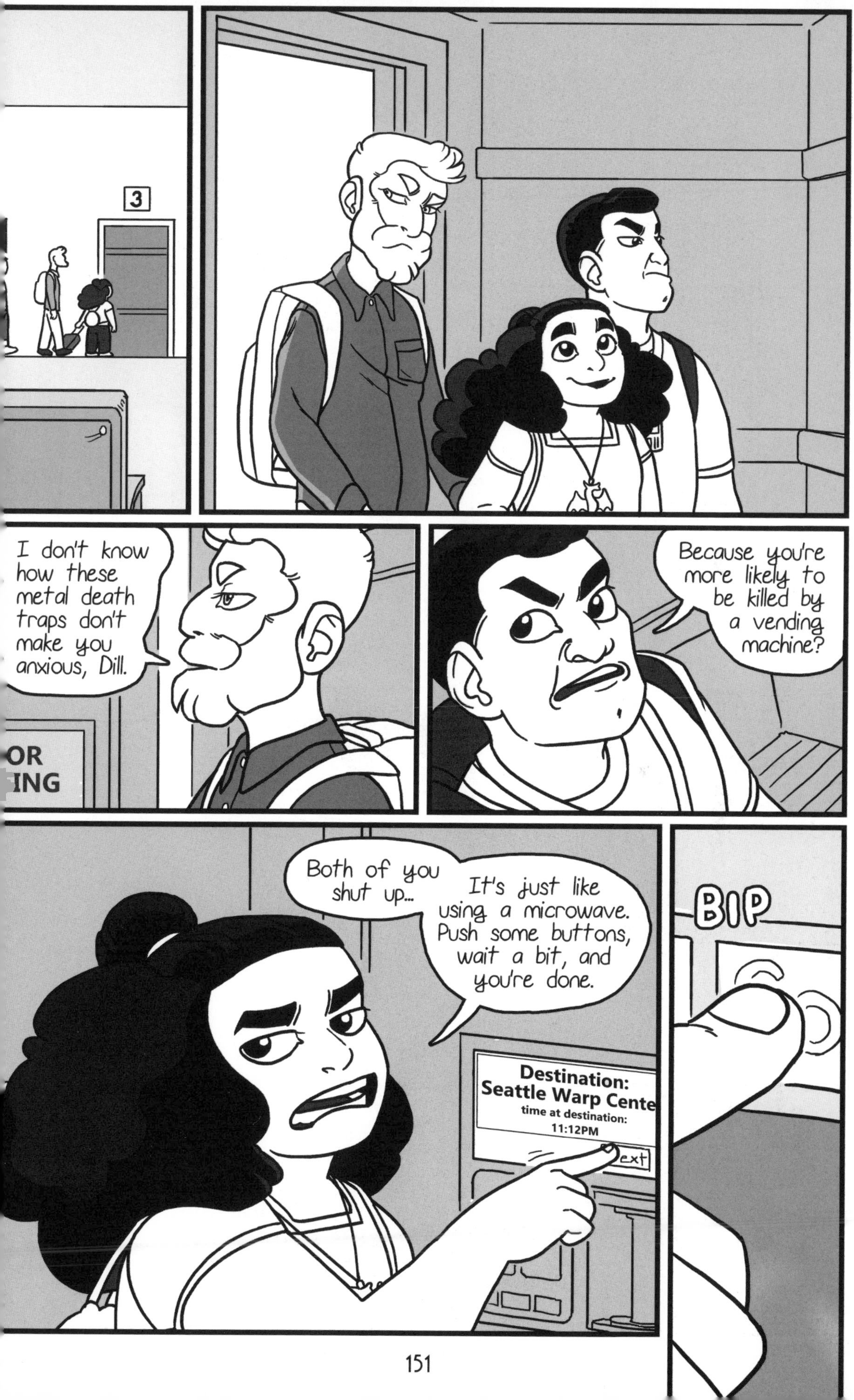

3
I don't know how these metal death traps don't make you anxious, Dill.
OR
ING
Because you're more likely to be killed by a vending machine?
Both of you shut up...
It's just like using a microwave. Push some buttons, wait a bit, and you're done.
Destination:
Seattle Warp Cente
time at destination:
11:12PM
ext
BIP

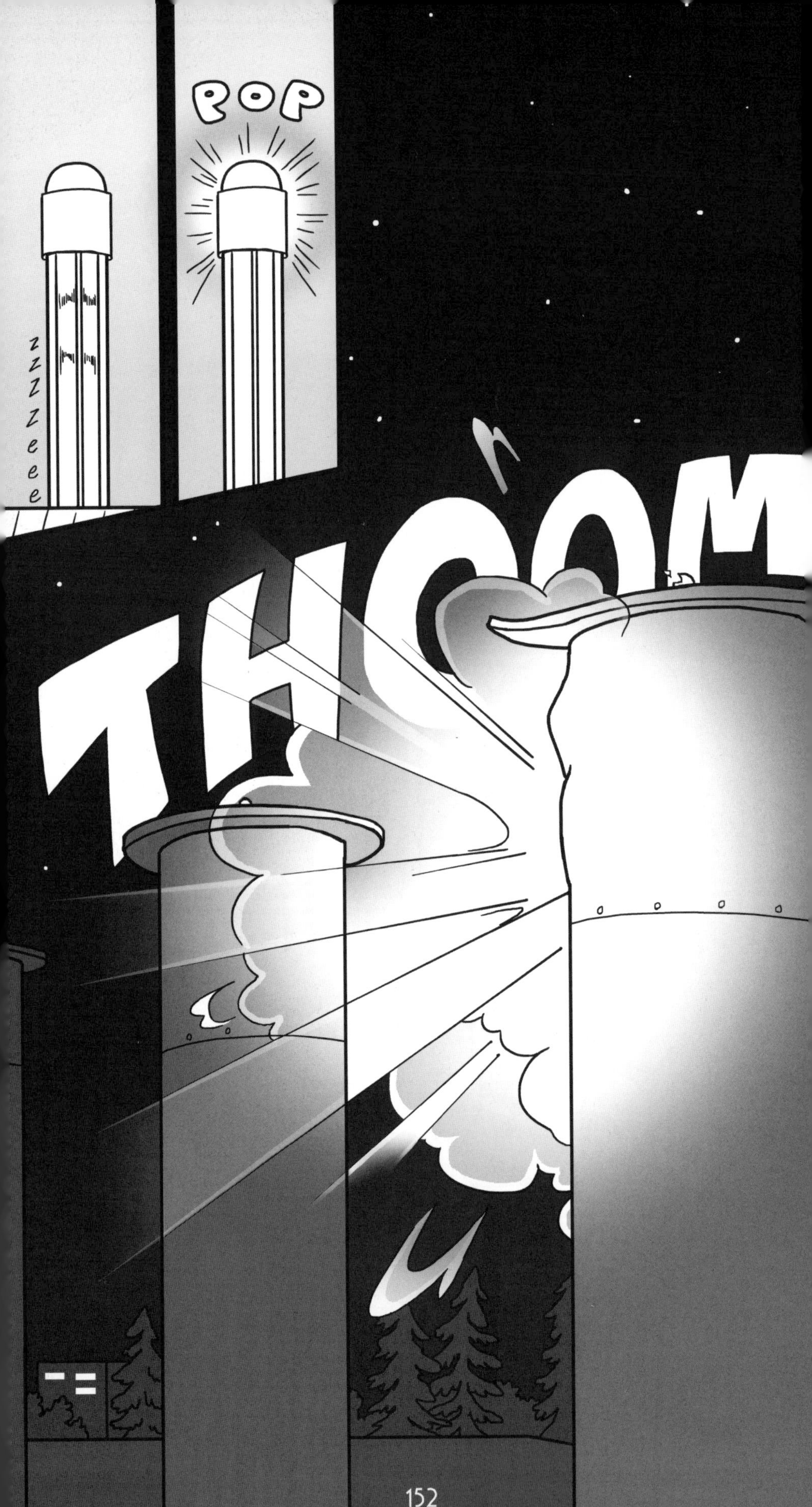
ZZZZZeee
POP
THOOM

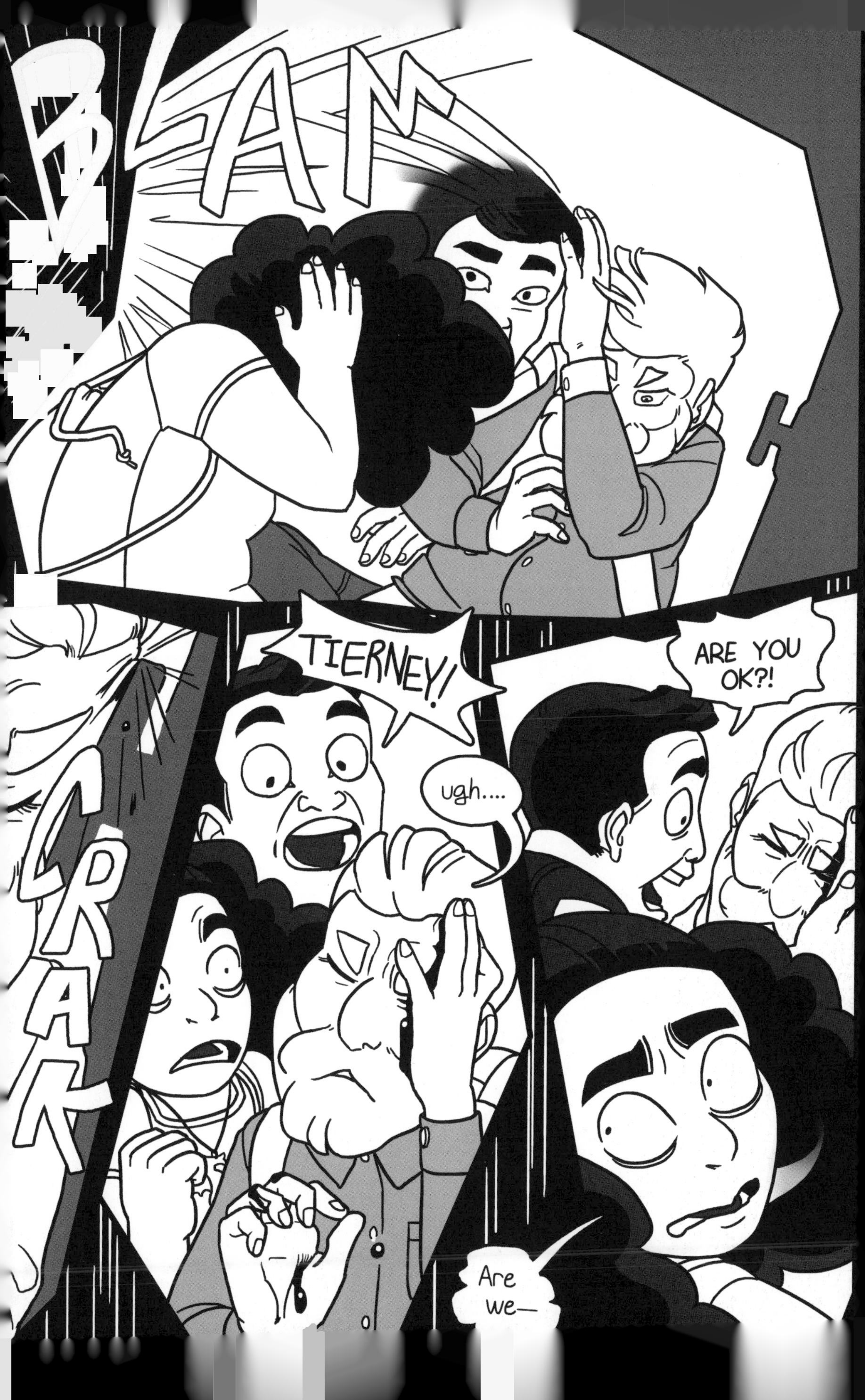
BLAM
CRRAK
TIERNEY!
ugh....
ARE YOU OK?!
Are we—

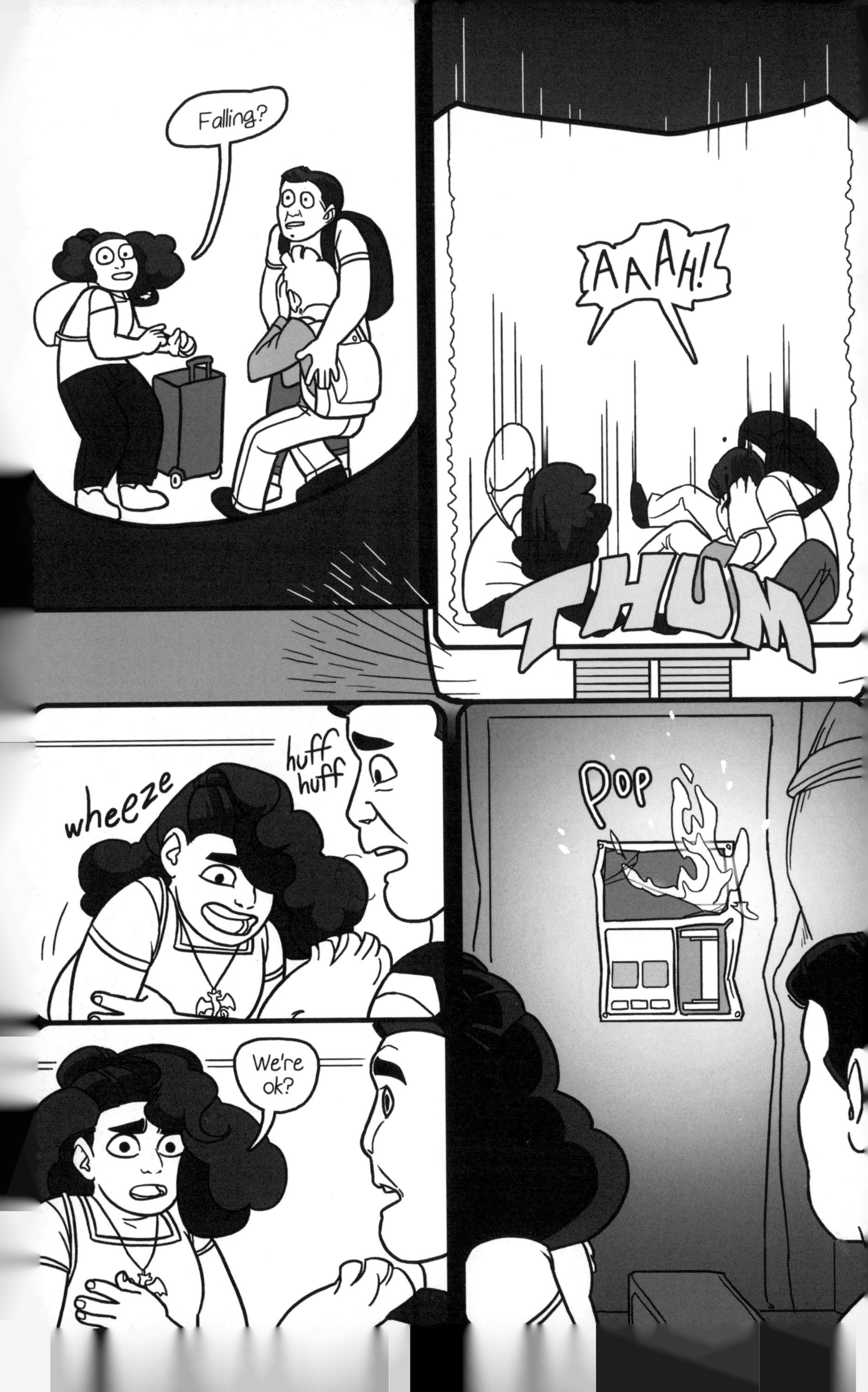
Falling?
AAAH!
THUM
wheeze
huff huff
pop
We're ok?

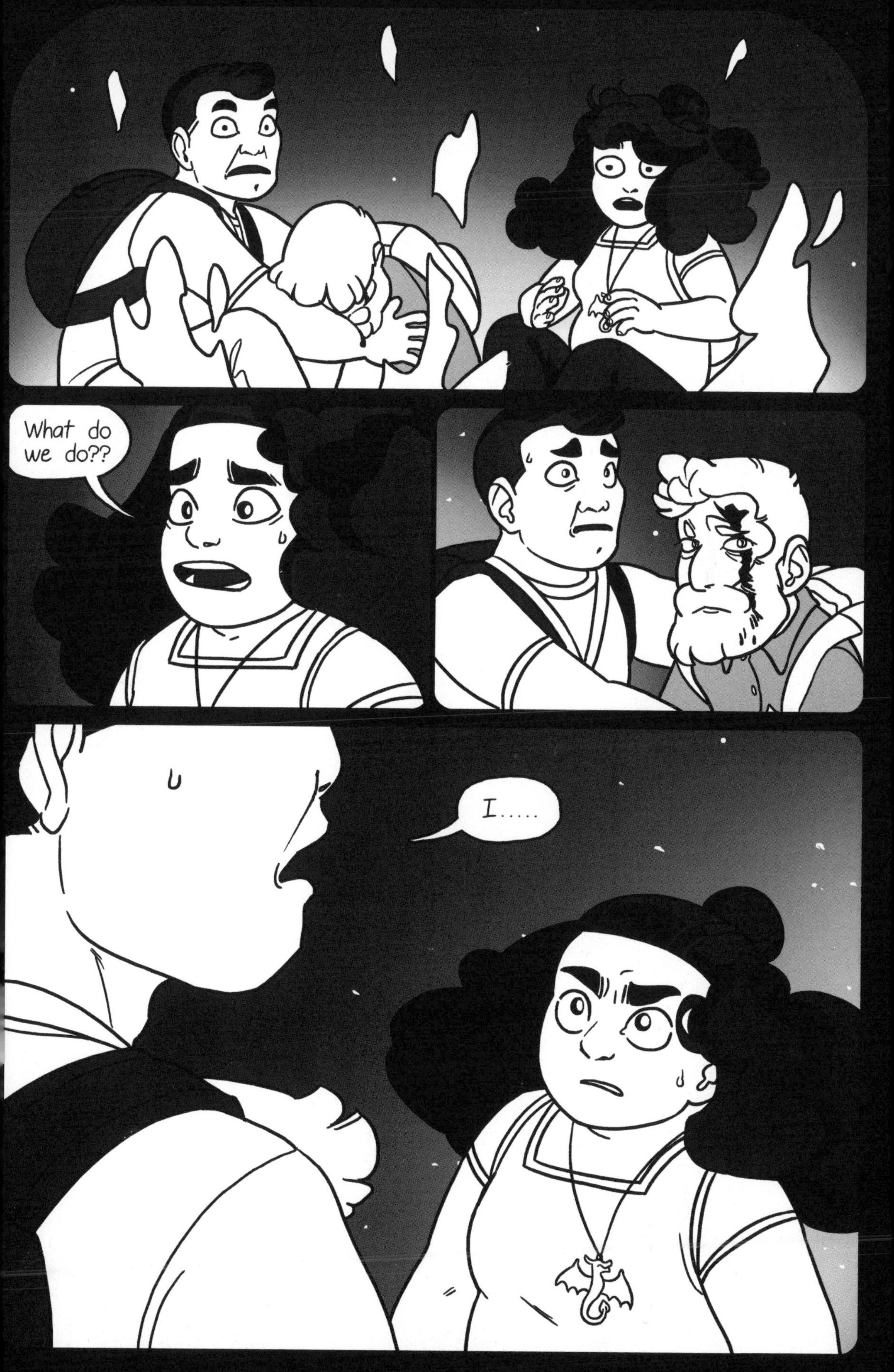
What do we do??
I.....

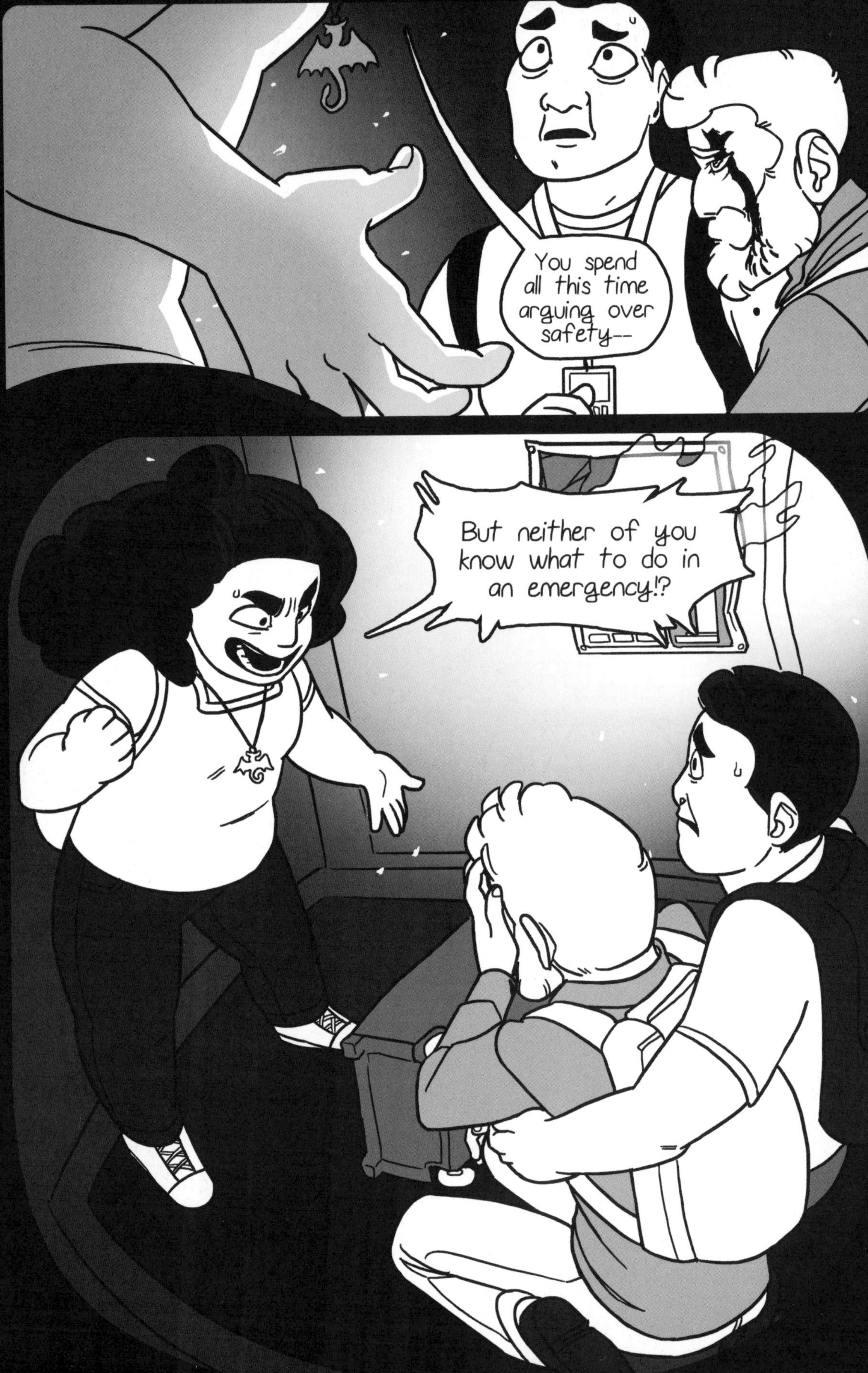
You spend all this time arguing over safety--
But neither of you know what to do in an emergency!?

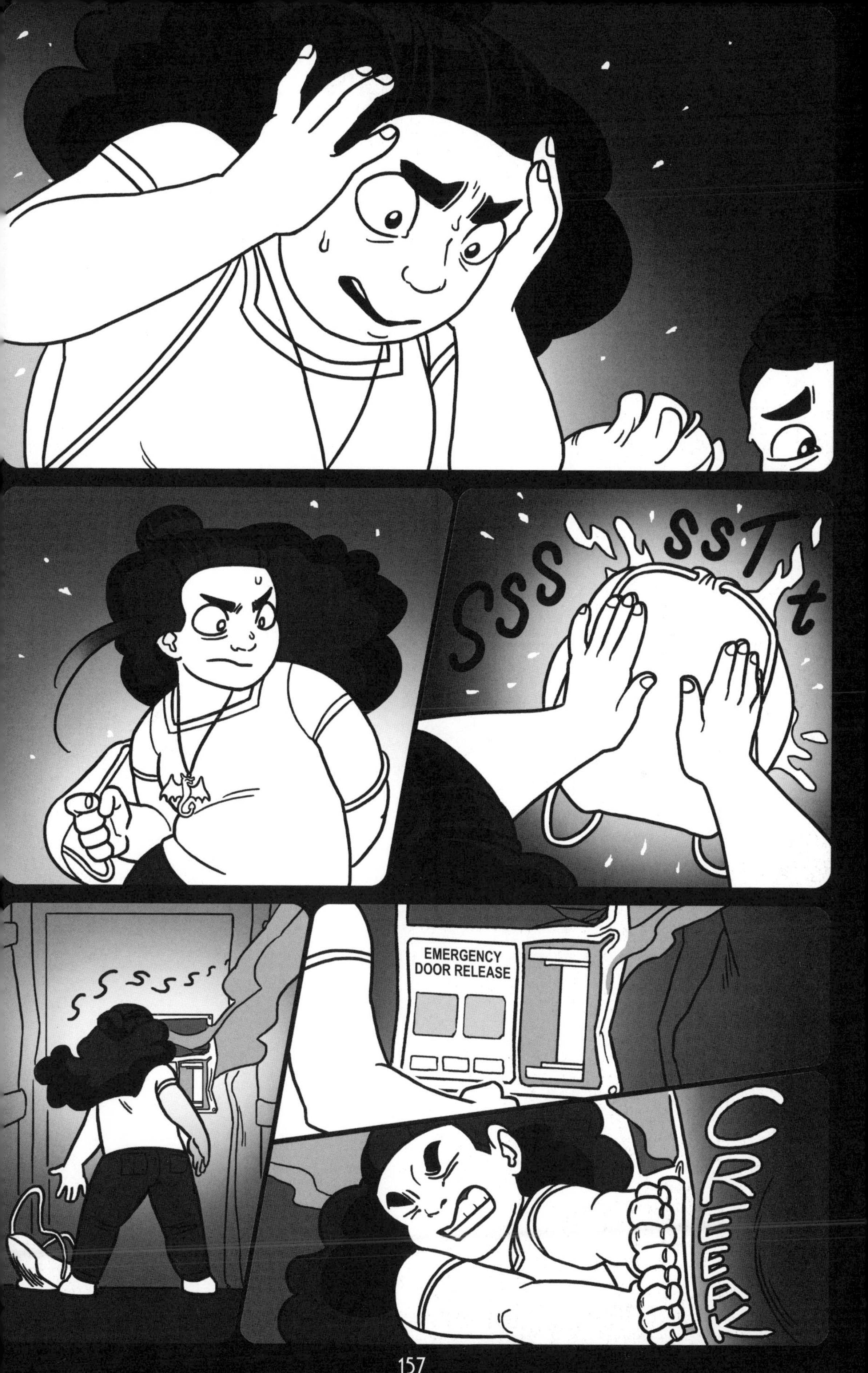
SSS SST t
SSSSS
EMERGENCY DOOR RELEASE
CREEAK

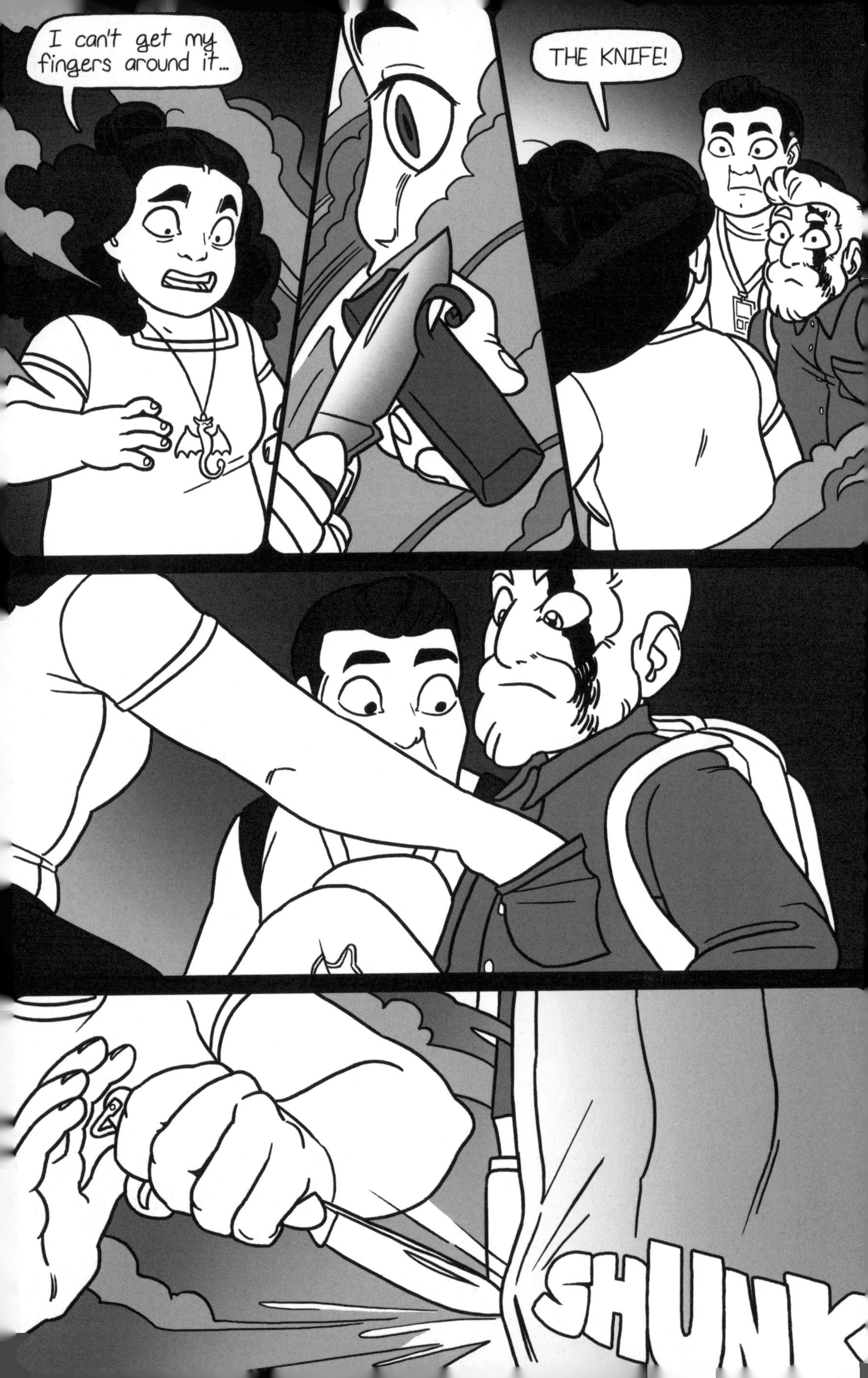
I can't get my fingers around it...
THE KNIFE!
SHUNK

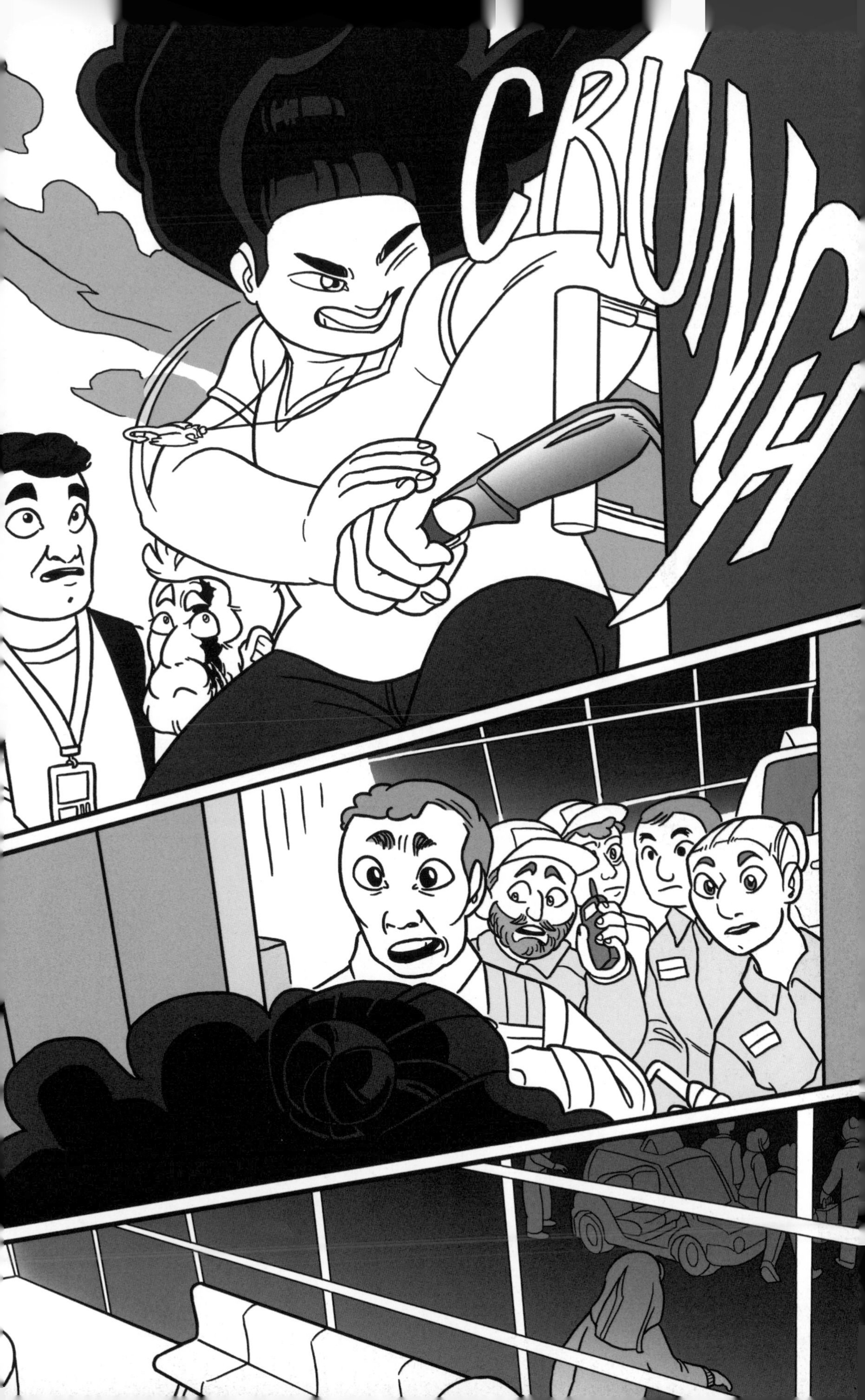
CRUNCH

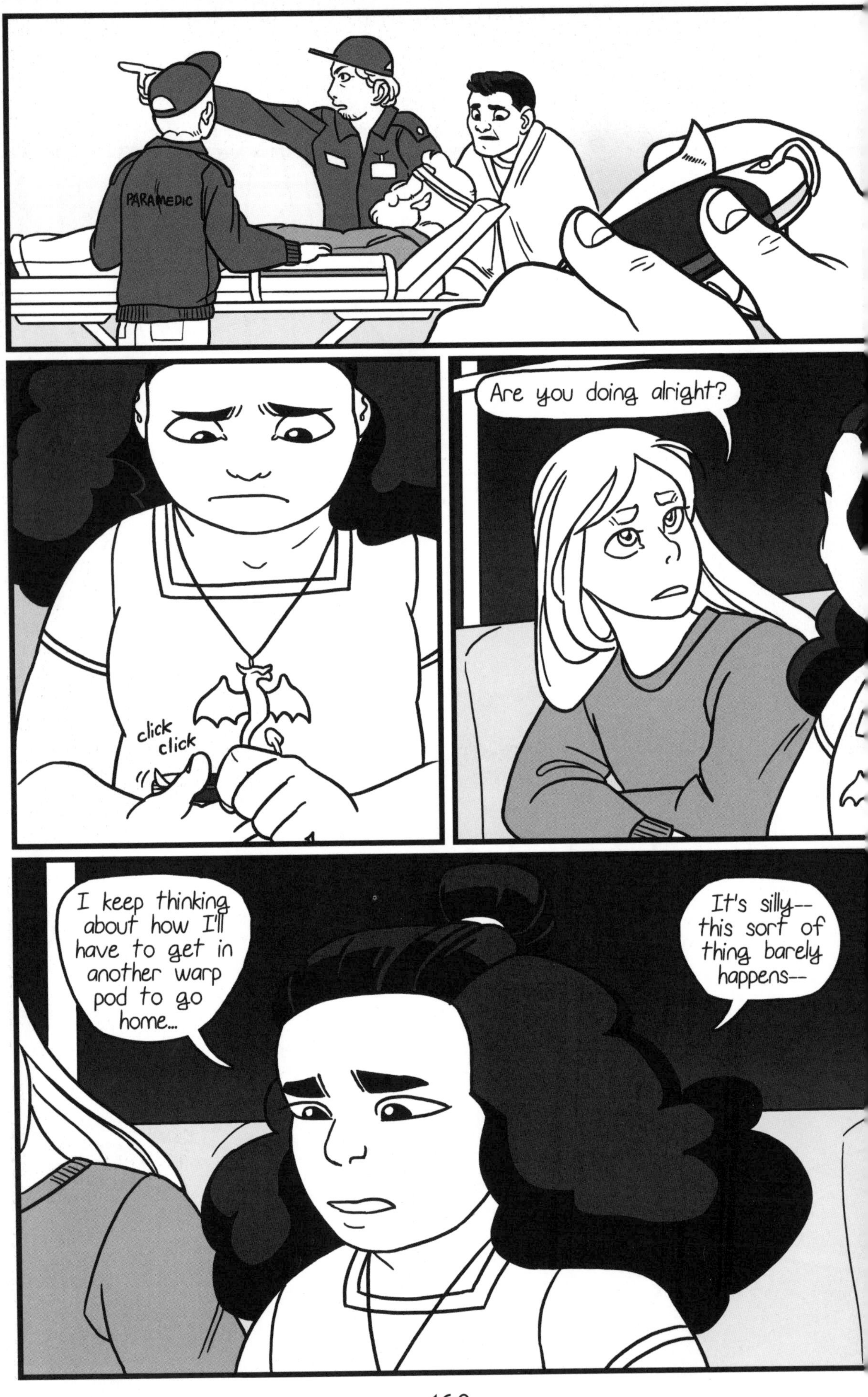
PARAMEDIC
click
click
Are you doing alright?
I keep thinking about how I'll have to get in another warp pod to go home...
It's silly-- this sort of thing barely happens--

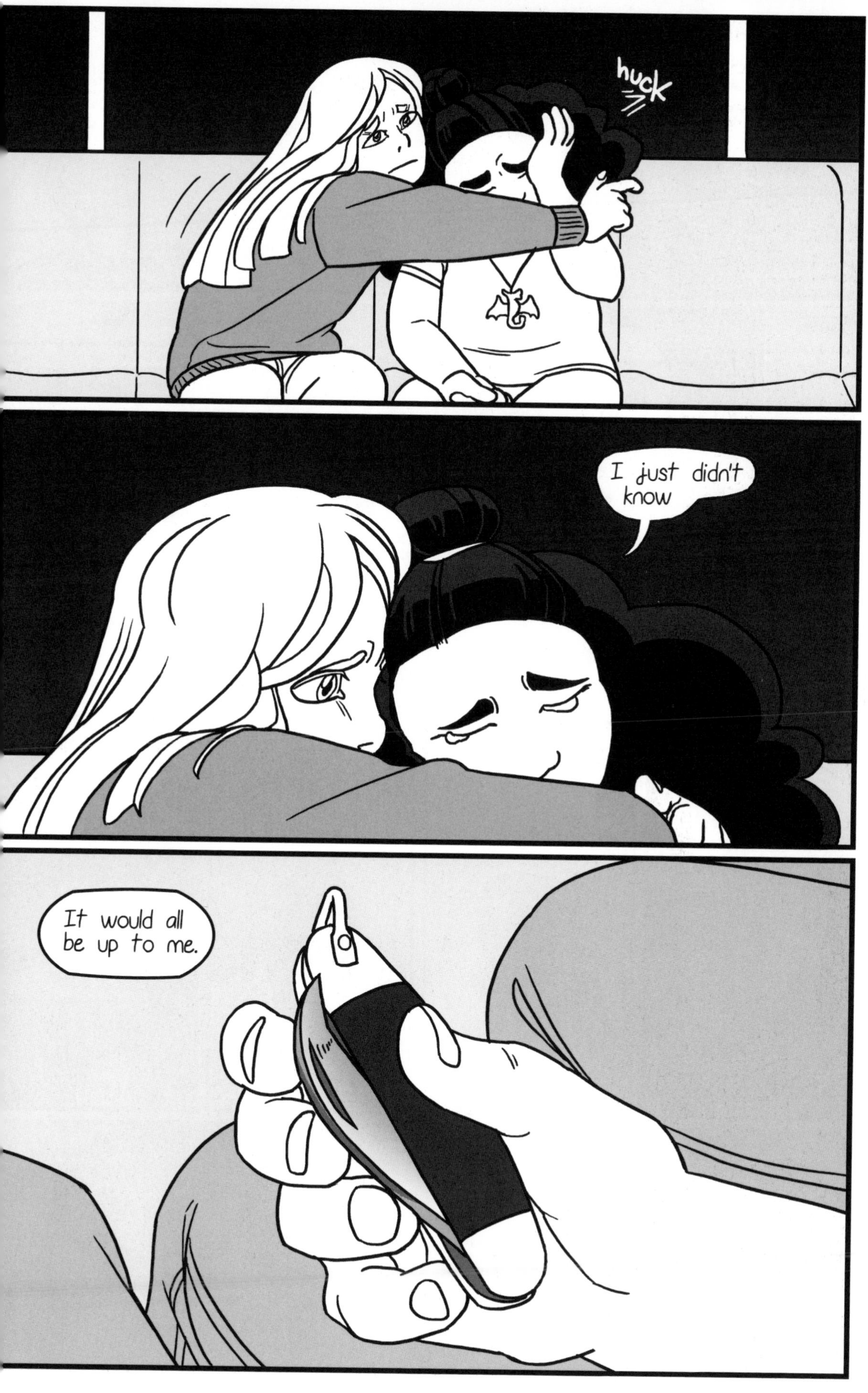
huck
I just didn't know
It would all be up to me.

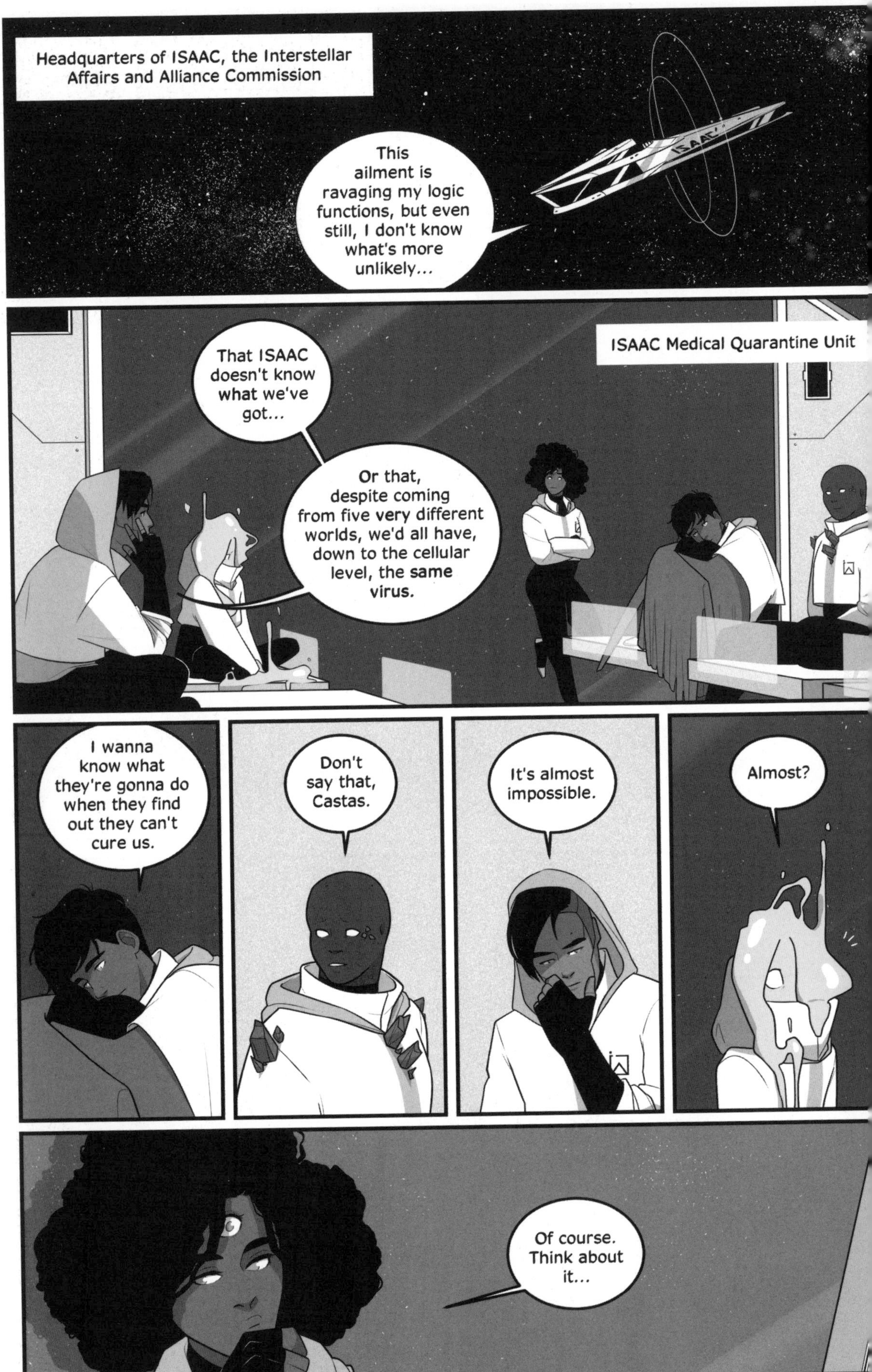

Headquarters of ISAAC, the Interstellar Affairs and Alliance Commission
ISAAC
This ailment is ravaging my logic functions, but even still, I don't know what's more unlikely...
ISAAC Medical Quarantine Unit
That ISAAC doesn't know what we've got...
Or that, despite coming from five **very** different worlds, we'd all have, down to the cellular level, the **same virus.**
I wanna know what they're gonna do when they find out they can't cure us.
Don't say that, Castas.
It's almost impossible.
Almost?
Of course. Think about it...

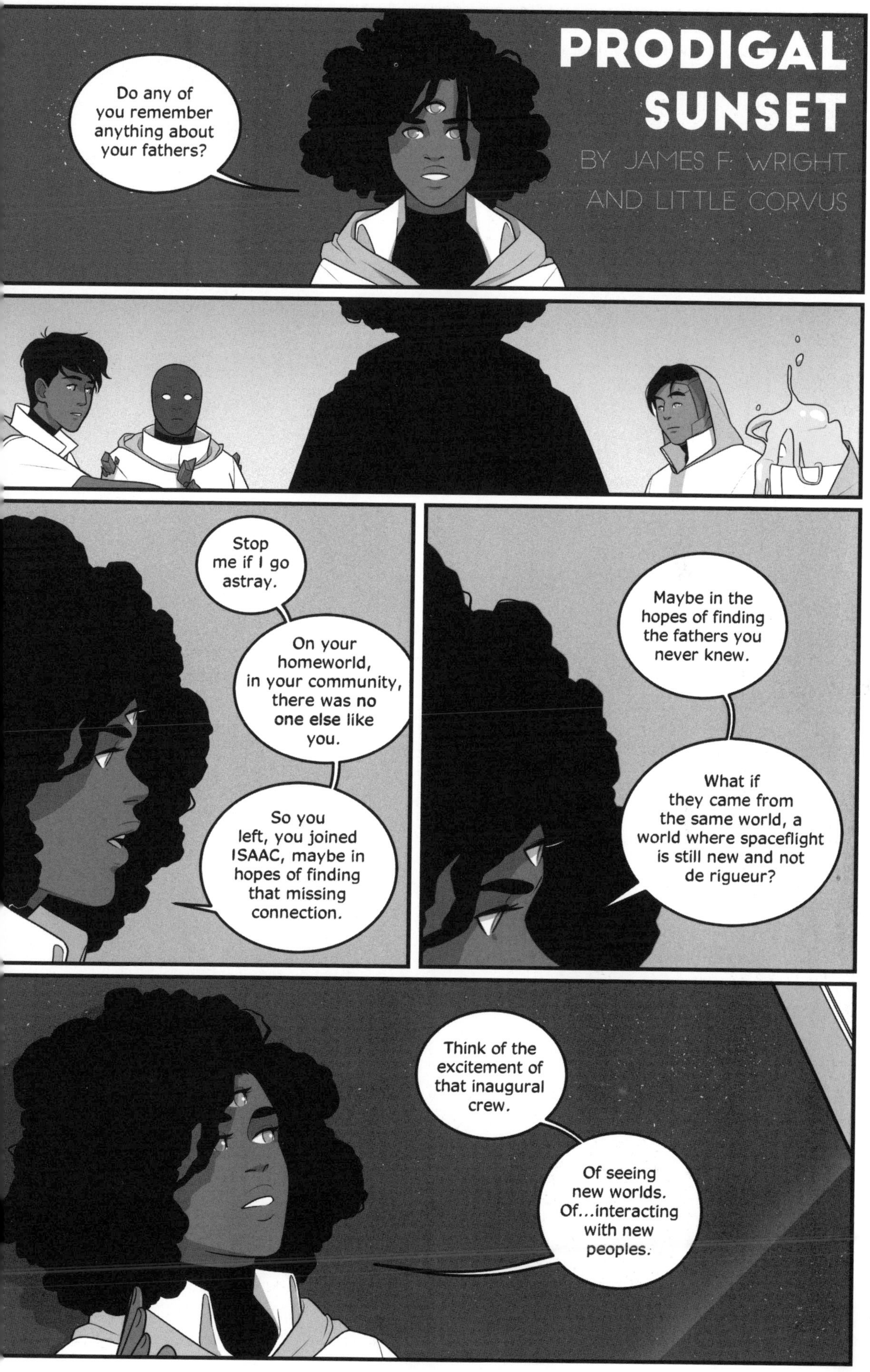
PRODIGAL SUNSET
BY JAMES F. WRIGHT AND LITTLE CORVUS
Do any of you remember anything about your fathers?
Stop me if I go astray.
On your homeworld, in your community, there was no one else like you.
So you left, you joined ISAAC, maybe in hopes of finding that missing connection.
Maybe in the hopes of finding the fathers you never knew.
What if they came from the same world, a world where spaceflight is still new and not de rigueur?
Think of the excitement of that inaugural crew.
Of seeing new worlds. Of...interacting with new peoples.

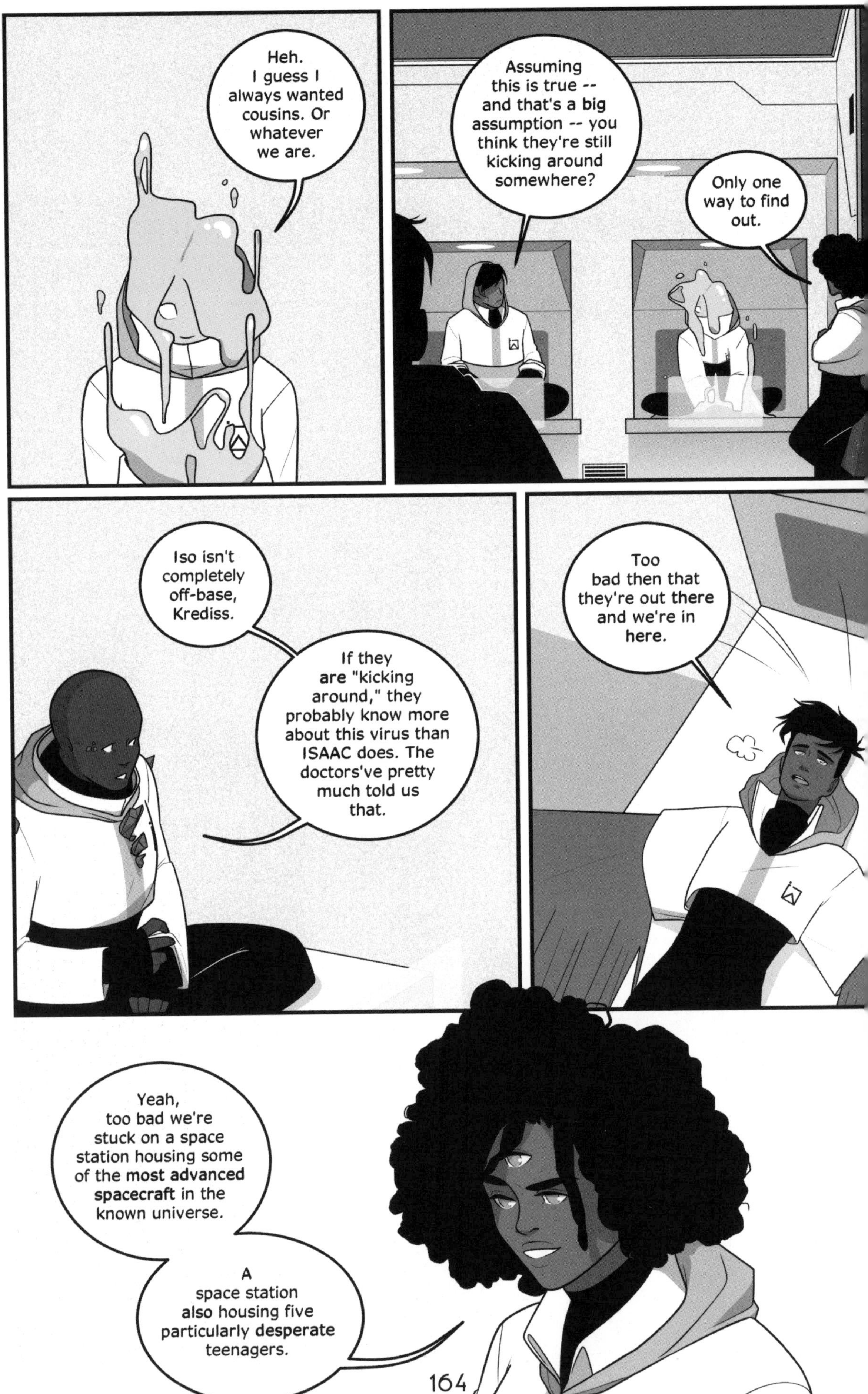
Heh. I guess I always wanted cousins. Or whatever we are.
Assuming this is true -- and that's a big assumption -- you think they're still kicking around somewhere?
Only one way to find out.
Iso isn't completely off-base, Krediss.
If they are "kicking around," they probably know more about this virus than ISAAC does. The doctors've pretty much told us that.
Too bad then that they're out there and we're in here.
Yeah, too bad we're stuck on a space station housing some of the most advanced spacecraft in the known universe.
A space station also housing five particularly desperate teenagers.

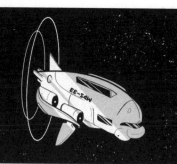

"How will we ever get from in here to out there?"

Two years later.

How are you holding up, Xeni?

Stiffer today than yesterday. Takes longer to recapture my flow, but I'll manage.

You?

Less of me now, but still enough of this stubborn rock to last a bit.

I'm gonna go check on Castas.

Thanks, Ghil.

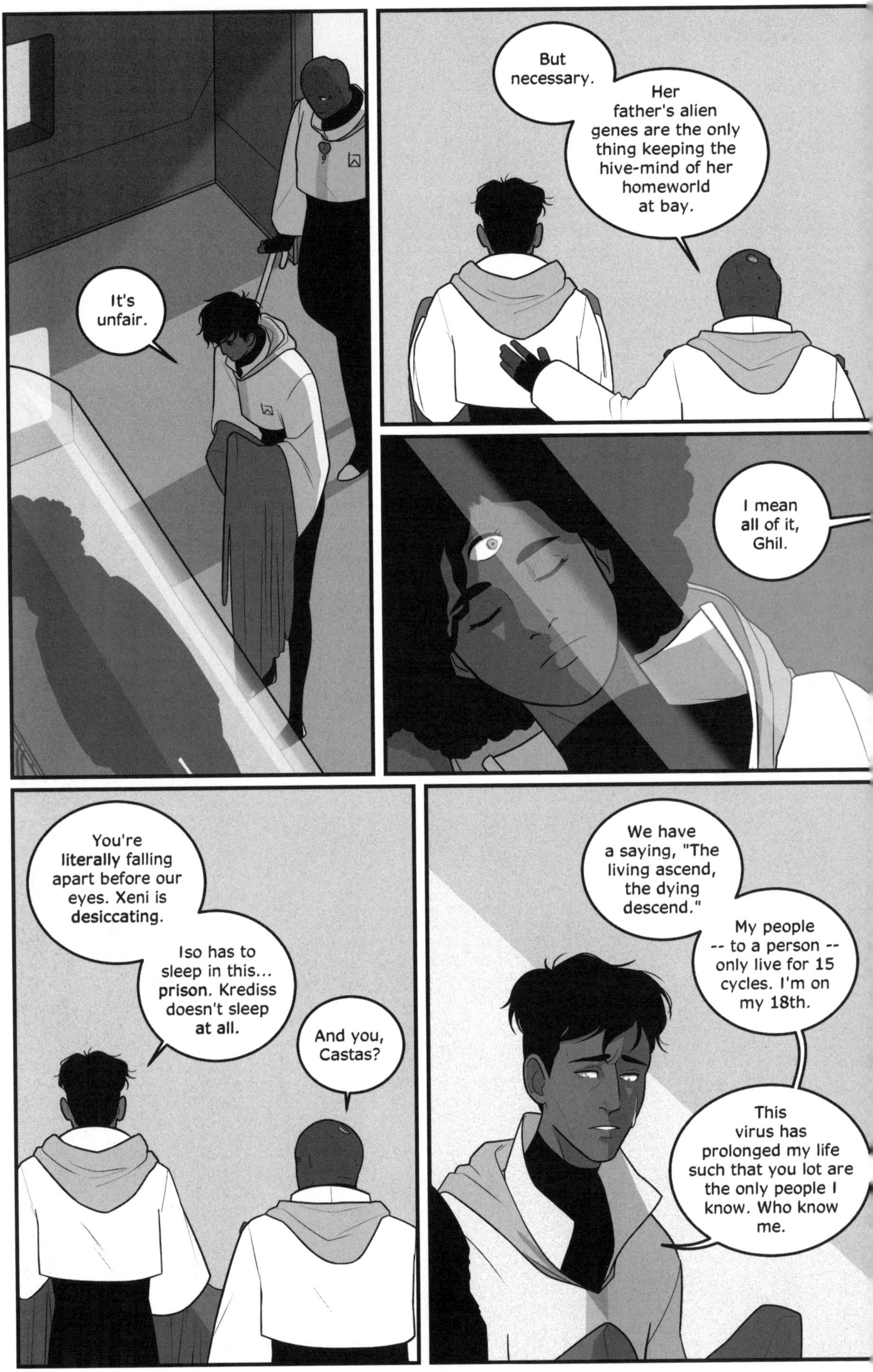
It's unfair.
But necessary.
Her father's alien genes are the only thing keeping the hive-mind of her homeworld at bay.
I mean all of it, Ghil.
You're literally falling apart before our eyes. Xeni is desiccating.
Iso has to sleep in this... prison. Krediss doesn't sleep at all.
And you, Castas?
We have a saying, "The living ascend, the dying descend."
My people -- to a person -- only live for 15 cycles. I'm on my 18th.
This virus has prolonged my life such that you lot are the only people I know. Who know me.

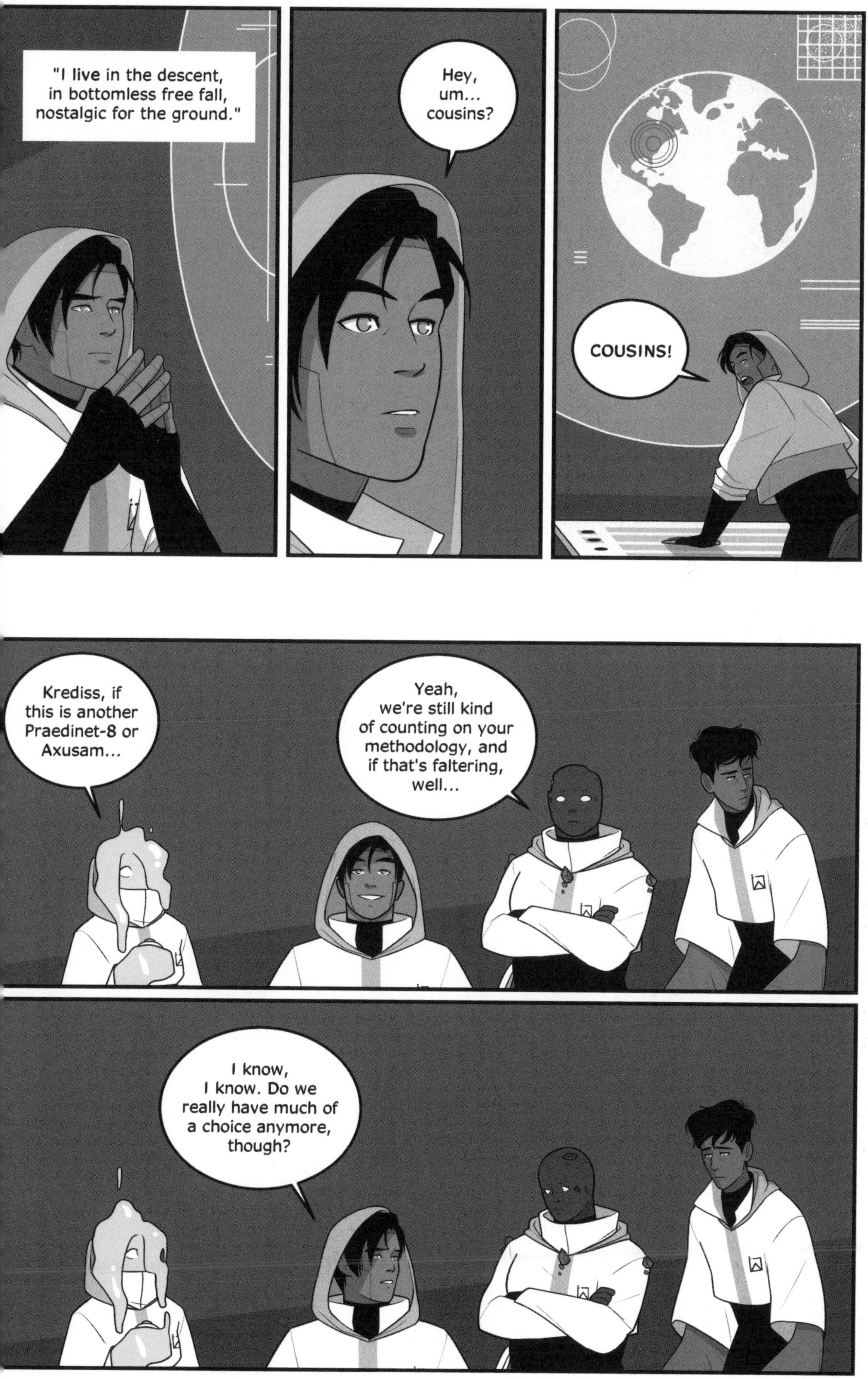

"I live in the descent, in bottomless free fall, nostalgic for the ground."
Hey, um... cousins?
COUSINS!
Krediss, if this is another Praedinet-8 or Axusam...
Yeah, we're still kind of counting on your methodology, and if that's faltering, well...
I know, I know. Do we really have much of a choice anymore, though?

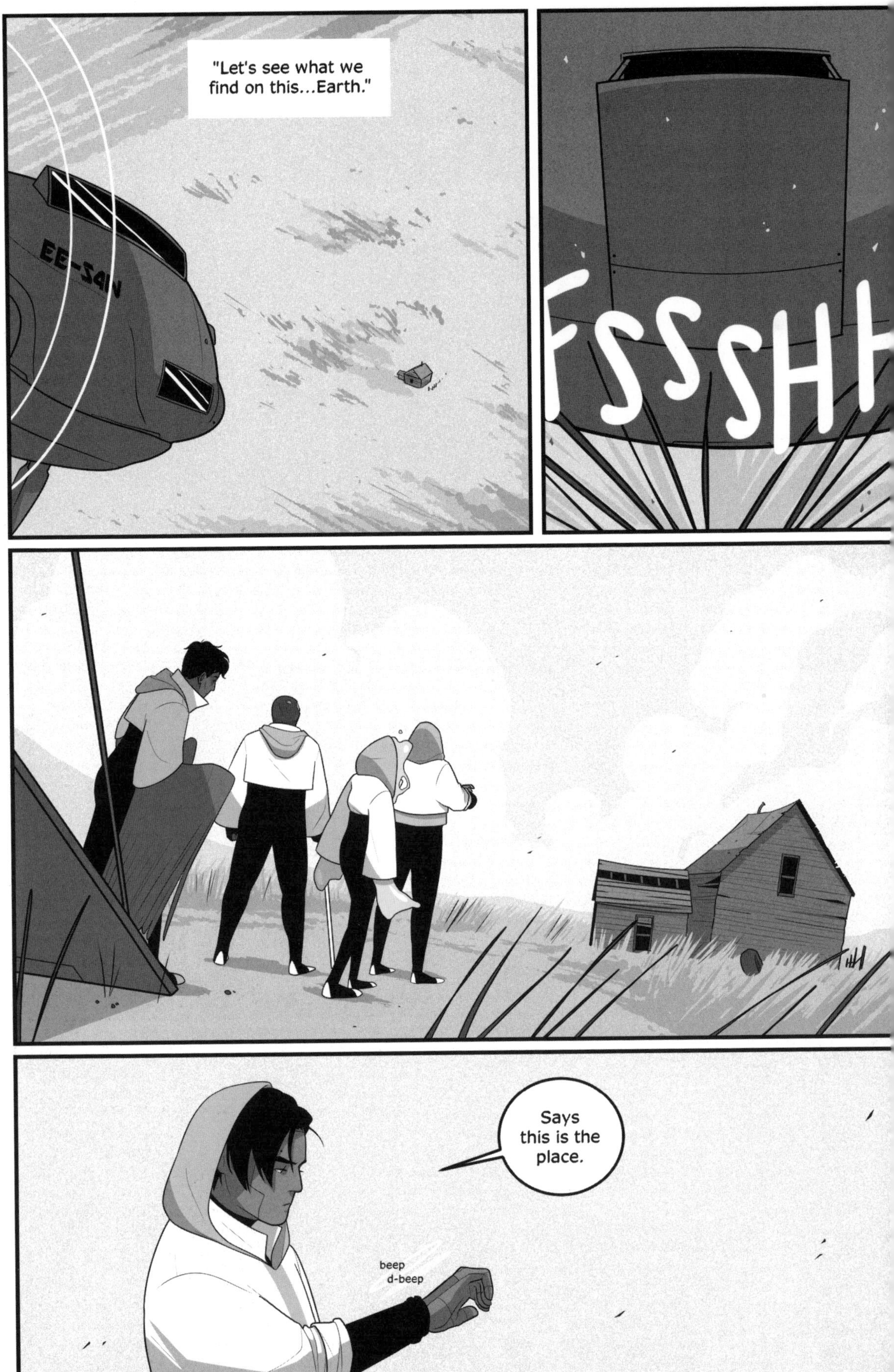
"Let's see what we find on this...Earth."
EE-S4N
FSSSHH
Says this is the place.
beep
d-beep

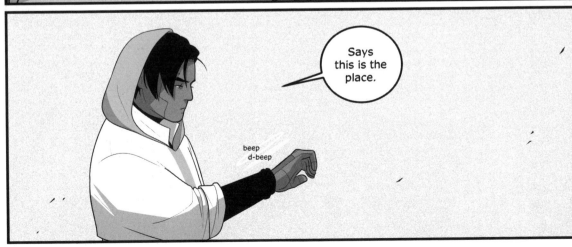

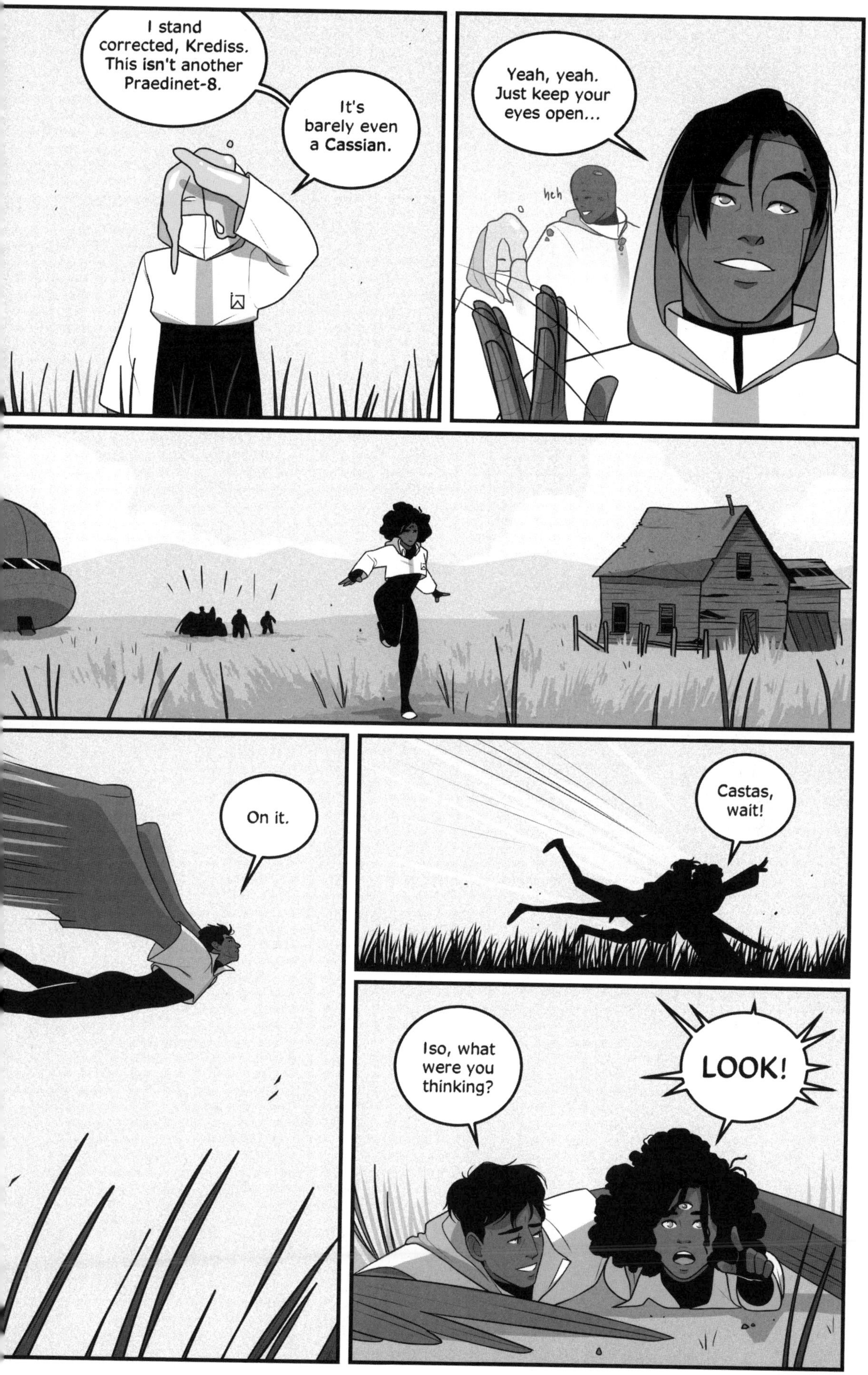
I stand corrected, Krediss. This isn't another Praedinet-8.
It's barely even a Cassian.
Yeah, yeah. Just keep your eyes open...
heh
On it.
Castas, wait!
Iso, what were you thinking?
LOOK!

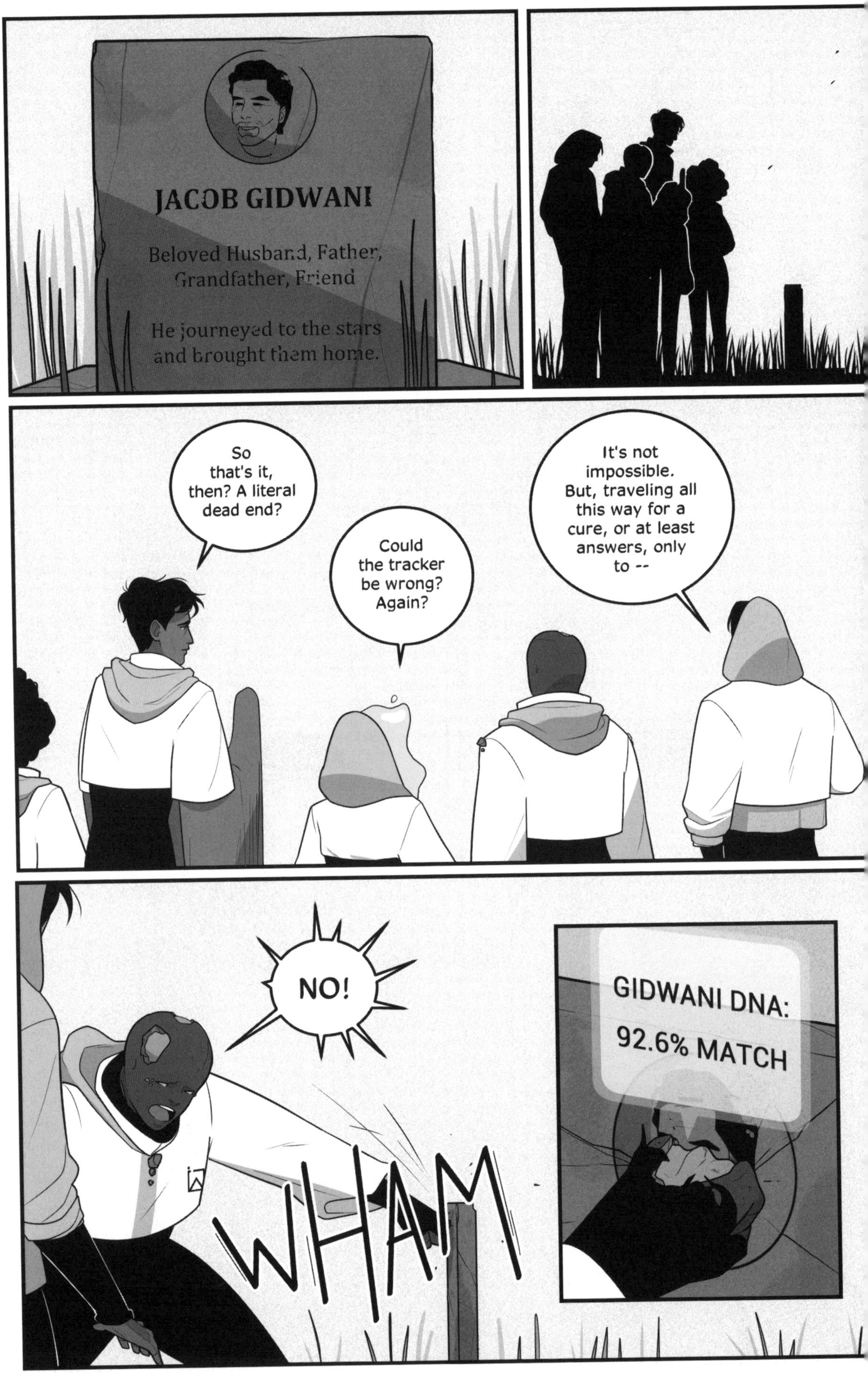
JACOB GIDWANI
Beloved Husband, Father, Grandfather, Friend
He journeyed to the stars and brought them home.
So that's it, then? A literal dead end?
Could the tracker be wrong? Again?
It's not impossible. But, traveling all this way for a cure, or at least answers, only to --
NO!
WHAM
GIDWANI DNA: 92.6% MATCH

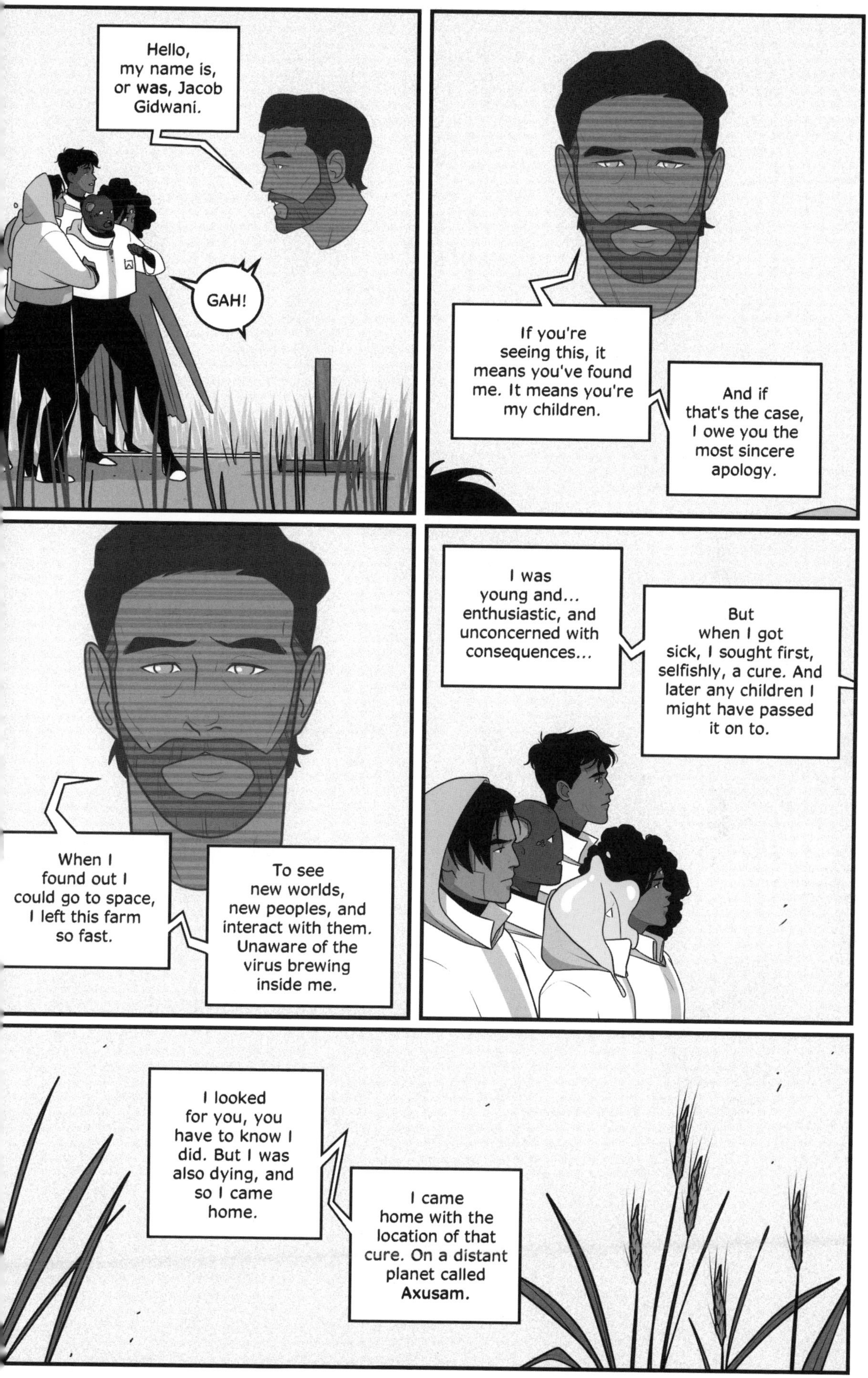
Hello, my name is, or was, Jacob Gidwani.
GAH!
If you're seeing this, it means you've found me. It means you're my children.
And if that's the case, I owe you the most sincere apology.
When I found out I could go to space, I left this farm so fast.
To see new worlds, new peoples, and interact with them. Unaware of the virus brewing inside me.
I was young and... enthusiastic, and unconcerned with consequences...
But when I got sick, I sought first, selfishly, a cure. And later any children I might have passed it on to.
I looked for you, you have to know I did. But I was also dying, and so I came home.
I came home with the location of that cure. On a distant planet called Axusam.

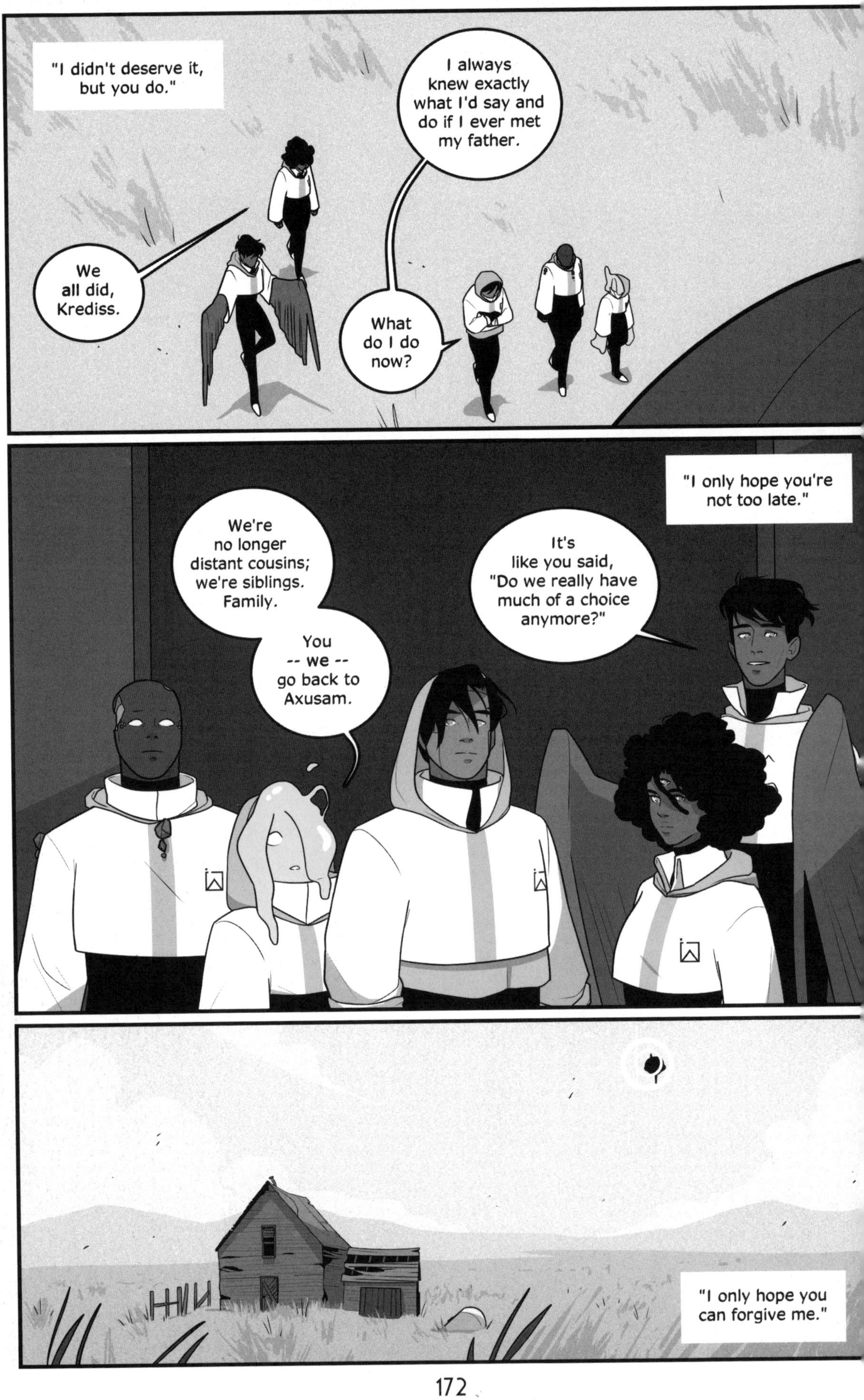
"I didn't deserve it, but you do."
I always knew exactly what I'd say and do if I ever met my father.
What do I do now?
We all did, Krediss.
"I only hope you're not too late."
We're no longer distant cousins; we're siblings. Family.
You -- we -- go back to Axusam.
It's like you said, "Do we really have much of a choice anymore?"
"I only hope you can forgive me."

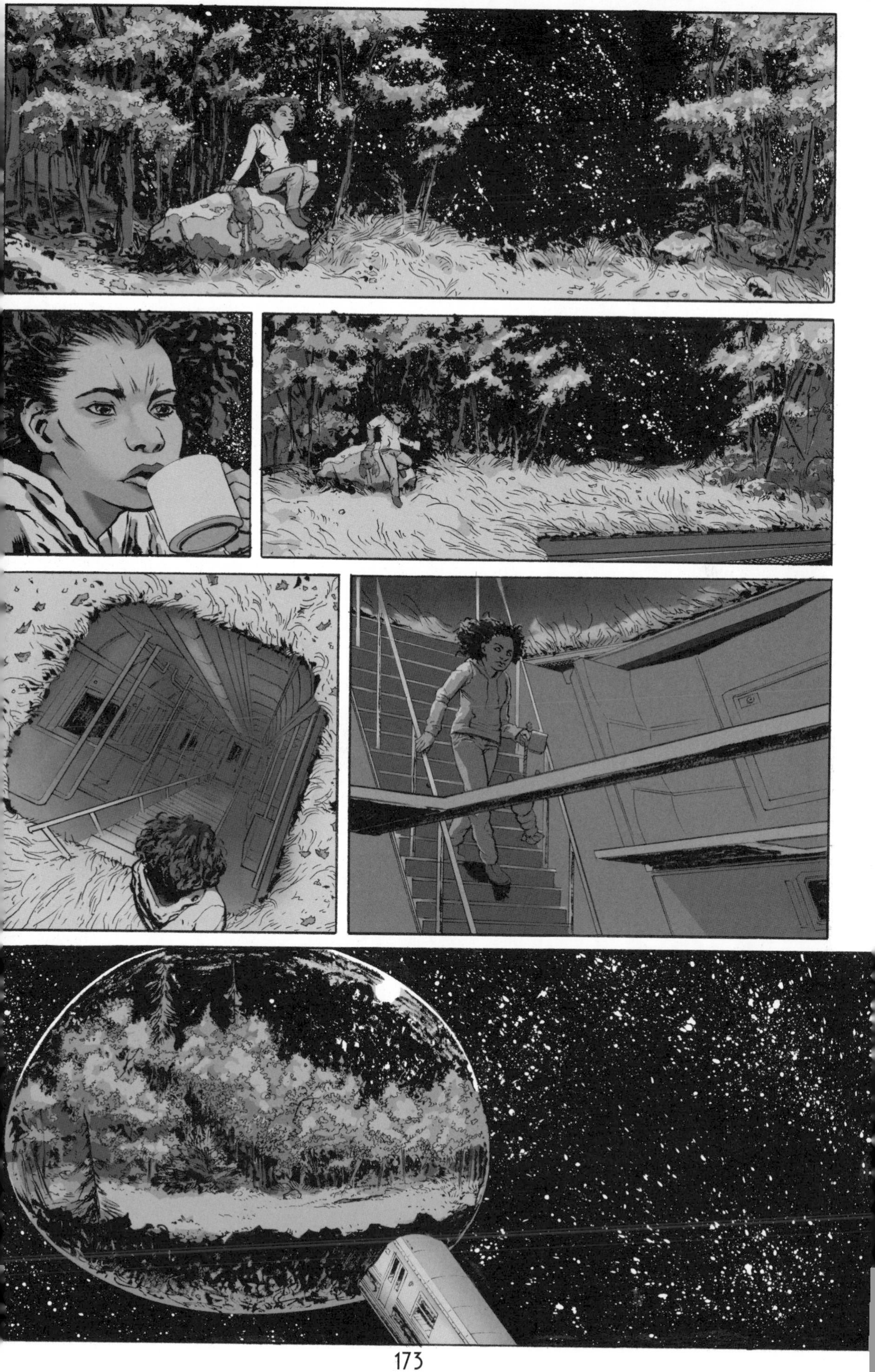

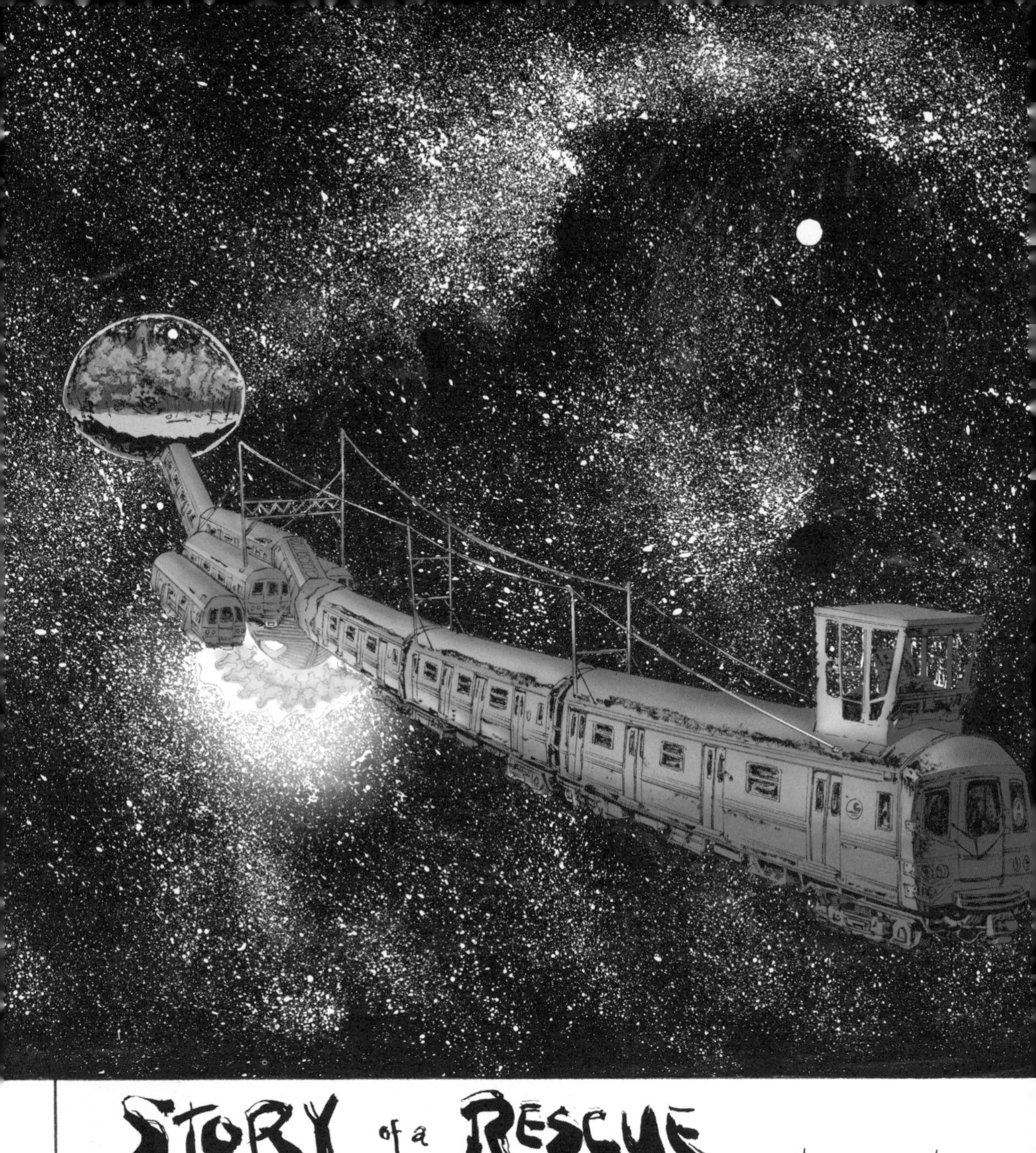

STORY of a RESCUE

NATHANIEL WILSON

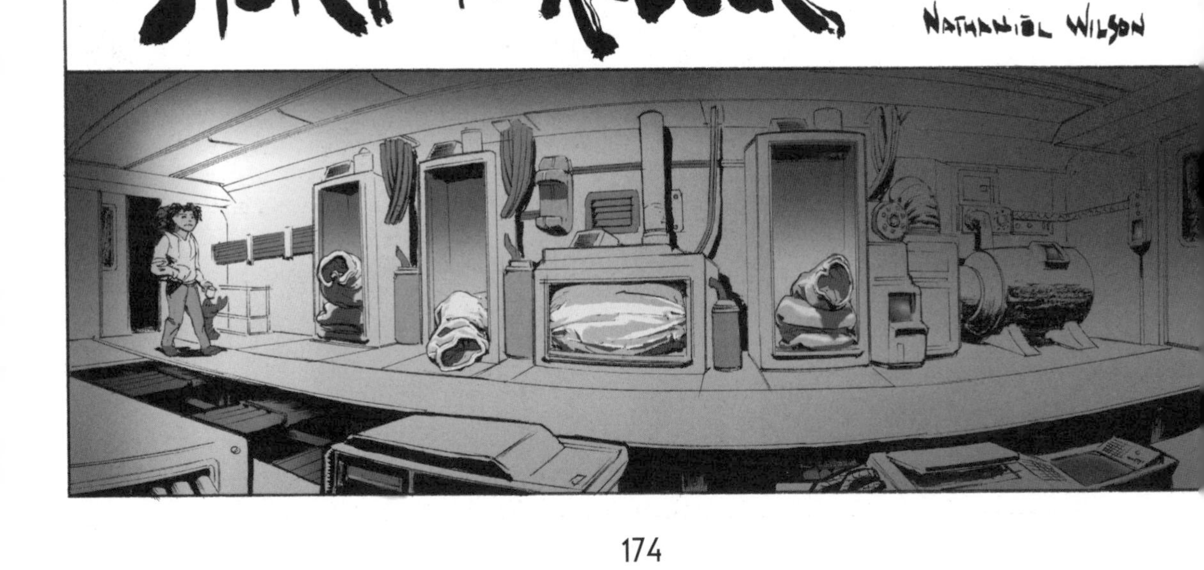

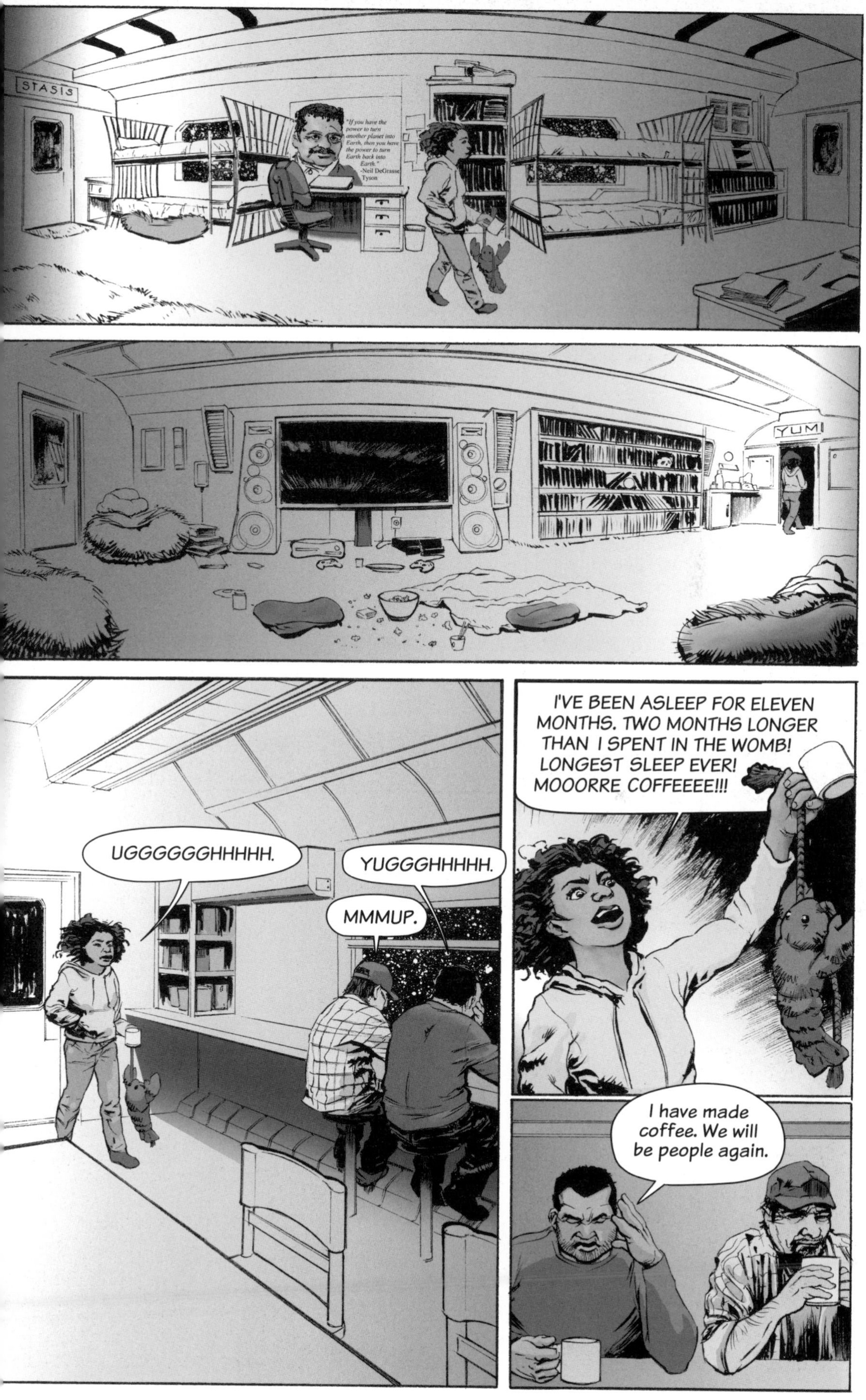
STASIS
"If you have the power to turn another planet into Earth, then you have the power to turn Earth back into Earth."
-Neil DeGrasse Tyson
YUM
UGGGGGGHHHHH.
YUGGGHHHHH.
MMMUP.
I'VE BEEN ASLEEP FOR ELEVEN MONTHS. TWO MONTHS LONGER THAN I SPENT IN THE WOMB! LONGEST SLEEP EVER! MOOORRE COFFEEEE!!!
I have made coffee. We will be people again.

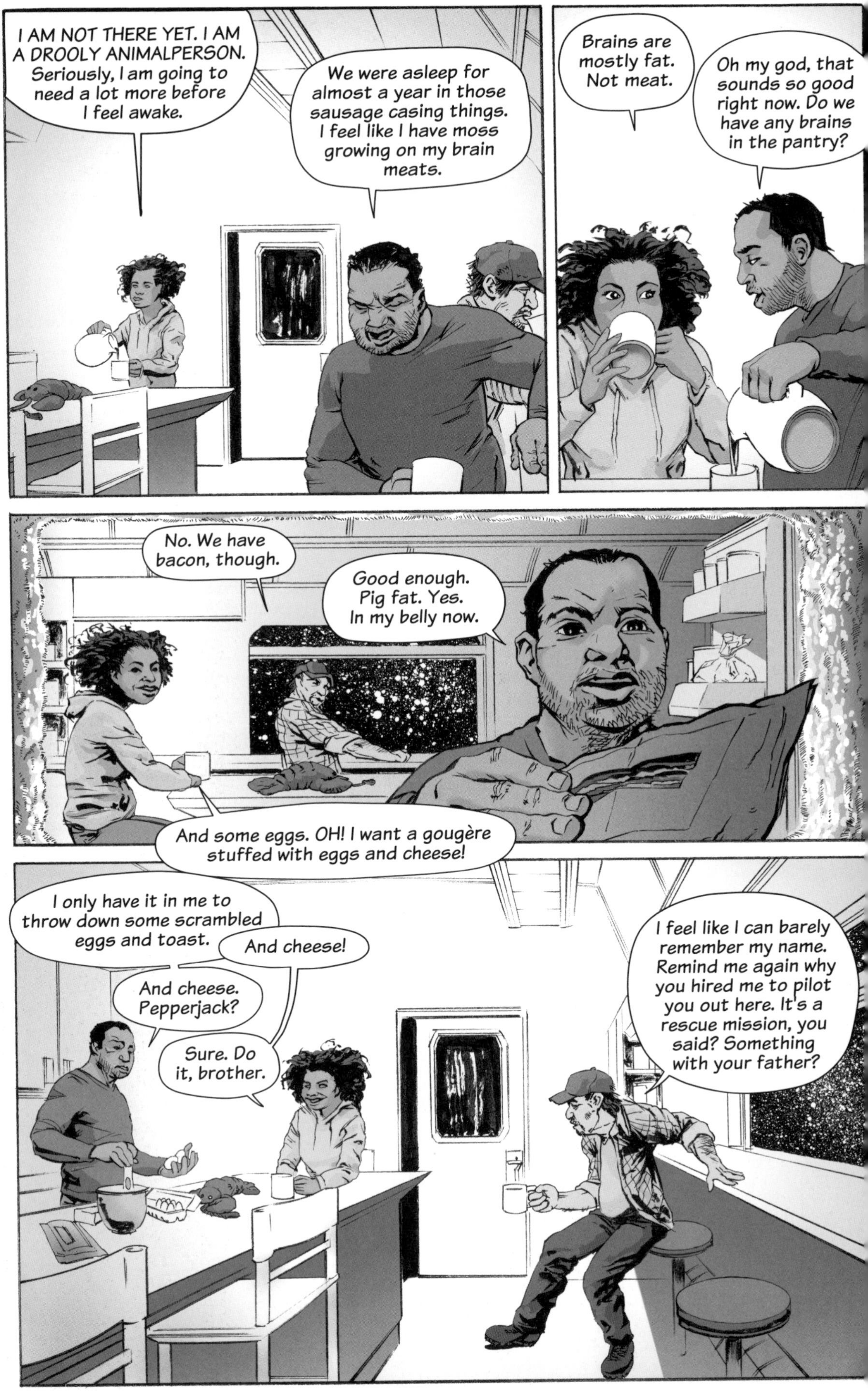
I AM NOT THERE YET. I AM A DROOLY ANIMALPERSON. Seriously, I am going to need a lot more before I feel awake.
We were asleep for almost a year in those sausage casing things. I feel like I have moss growing on my brain meats.
Brains are mostly fat. Not meat.
Oh my god, that sounds so good right now. Do we have any brains in the pantry?
No. We have bacon, though.
Good enough. Pig fat. Yes. In my belly now.
And some eggs. OH! I want a gougère stuffed with eggs and cheese!
I only have it in me to throw down some scrambled eggs and toast.
And cheese!
And cheese. Pepperjack?
Sure. Do it, brother.
I feel like I can barely remember my name. Remind me again why you hired me to pilot you out here. It's a rescue mission, you said? Something with your father?

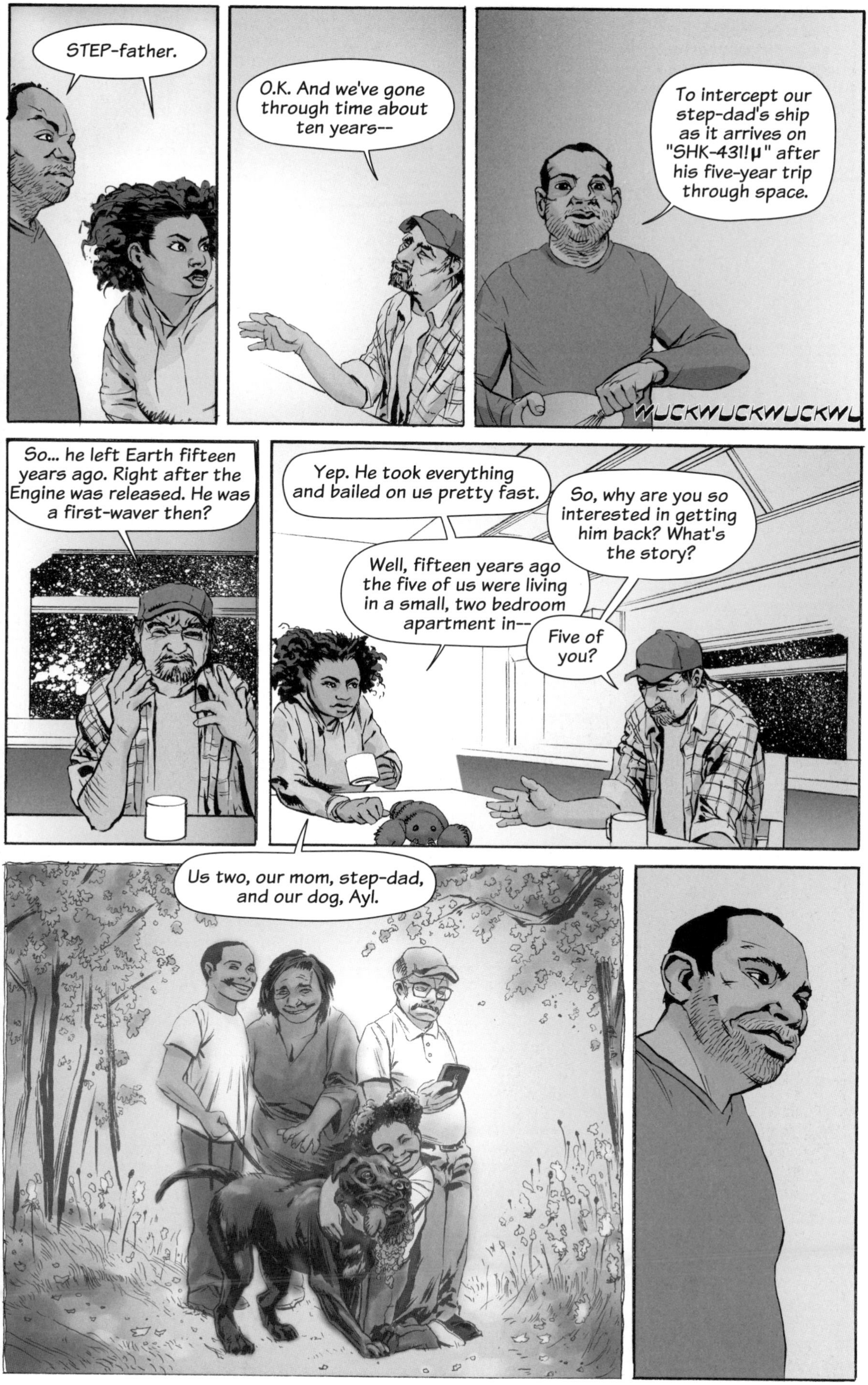
STEP-father.
O.K. And we've gone through time about ten years--
To intercept our step-dad's ship as it arrives on "SHK-431!µ" after his five-year trip through space.
WUCKWUCKWUCKWU
So... he left Earth fifteen years ago. Right after the Engine was released. He was a first-waver then?
Yep. He took everything and bailed on us pretty fast.
So, why are you so interested in getting him back? What's the story?
Well, fifteen years ago the five of us were living in a small, two bedroom apartment in--
Five of you?
Us two, our mom, step-dad, and our dog, Ayl.

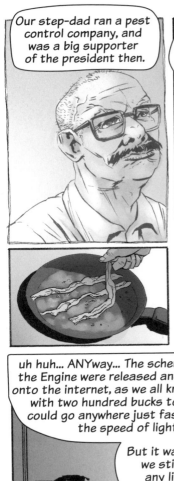

Our step-dad ran a pest control company, and was a big supporter of the president then.

Yeah, he was. Wore the hat. Went to rallies. All that stuff.

I still can't believe that was ever a thing.

Y'know, he won the election, and people never really gave him a chance. They just jumped on the hater bandwagon, y'know. They didn't give him a chance. That's all I'm sayin'.

uh huh... ANYway... The schematics for the Engine were released anonymously onto the internet, as we all know. Anyone with two hundred bucks to build it could go anywhere just faster than the speed of light.

But it was early 2018, and we still hadn't found any life-supporting planets,

let alone ones you could just walk out onto like in an episode of Star Trek.

Despite that, you'll always get a few reckless jackasses. In the first weeks, there were more than a handful of Lawnchair Larrys.

Lawnchair whos?

178

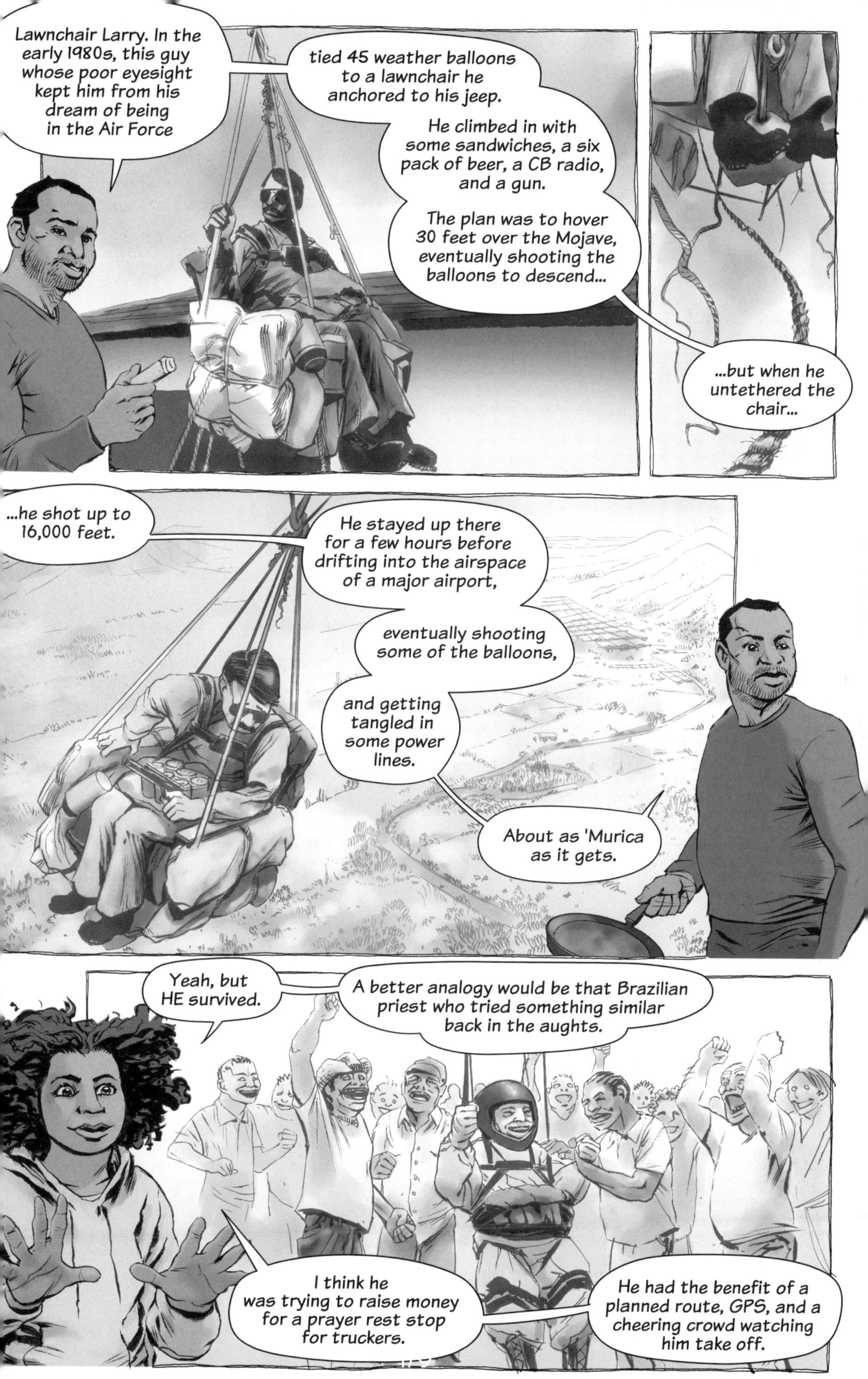
Lawnchair Larry. In the early 1980s, this guy whose poor eyesight kept him from his dream of being in the Air Force
tied 45 weather balloons to a lawnchair he anchored to his jeep.
He climbed in with some sandwiches, a six pack of beer, a CB radio, and a gun.
The plan was to hover 30 feet over the Mojave, eventually shooting the balloons to descend...
...but when he untethered the chair...
...he shot up to 16,000 feet.
He stayed up there for a few hours before drifting into the airspace of a major airport,
eventually shooting some of the balloons,
and getting tangled in some power lines.
About as 'Murica as it gets.
Yeah, but HE survived.
A better analogy would be that Brazilian priest who tried something similar back in the aughts.
I think he was trying to raise money for a prayer rest stop for truckers.
He had the benefit of a planned route, GPS, and a cheering crowd watching him take off.

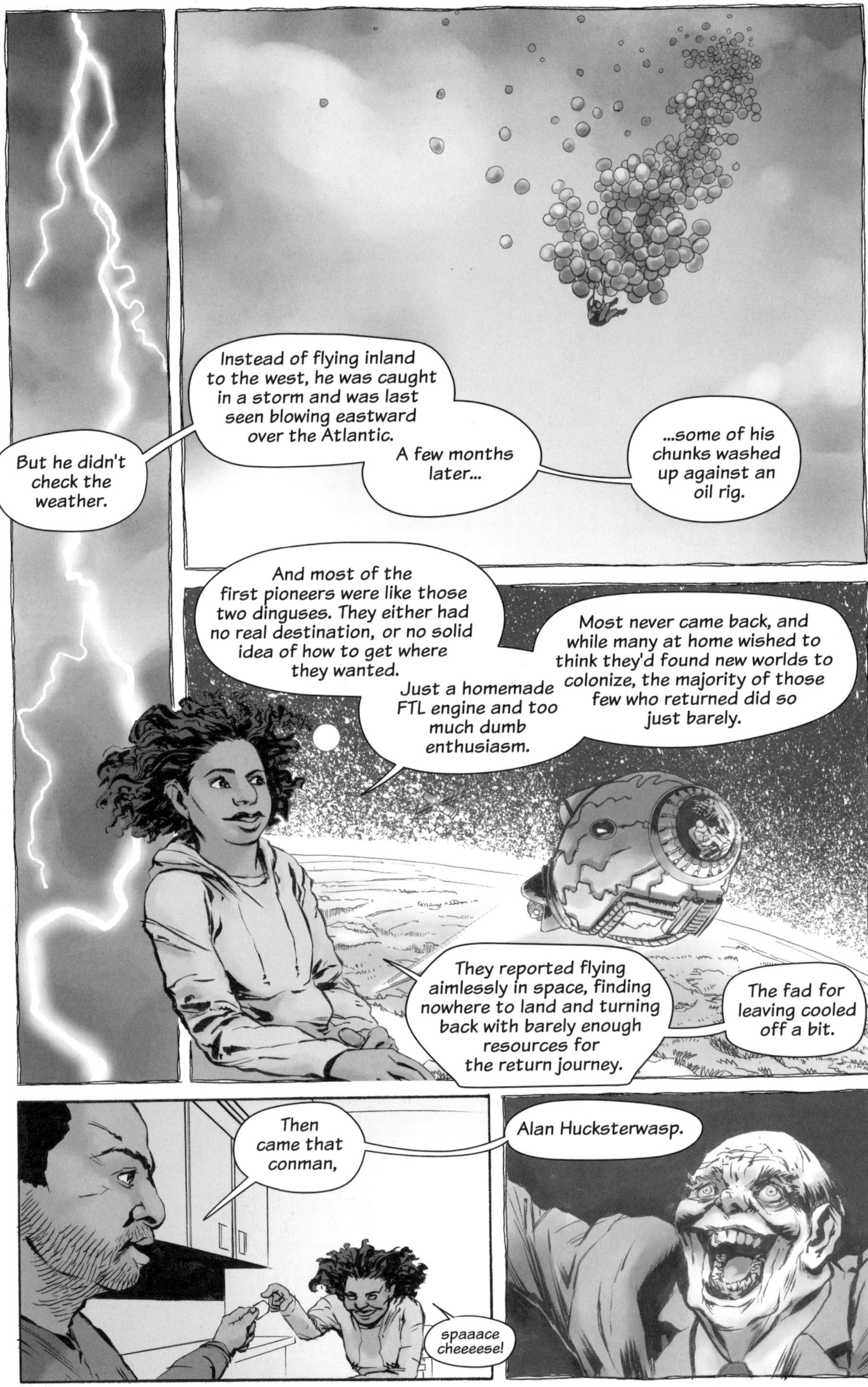
But he didn't check the weather.
Instead of flying inland to the west, he was caught in a storm and was last seen blowing eastward over the Atlantic.
A few months later...
...some of his chunks washed up against an oil rig.
And most of the first pioneers were like those two dinguses. They either had no real destination, or no solid idea of how to get where they wanted.
Just a homemade FTL engine and too much dumb enthusiasm.
Most never came back, and while many at home wished to think they'd found new worlds to colonize, the majority of those few who returned did so just barely.
They reported flying aimlessly in space, finding nowhere to land and turning back with barely enough resources for the return journey.
The fad for leaving cooled off a bit.
Then came that conman,
Alan Hucksterwasp.
spaaace cheeeese!

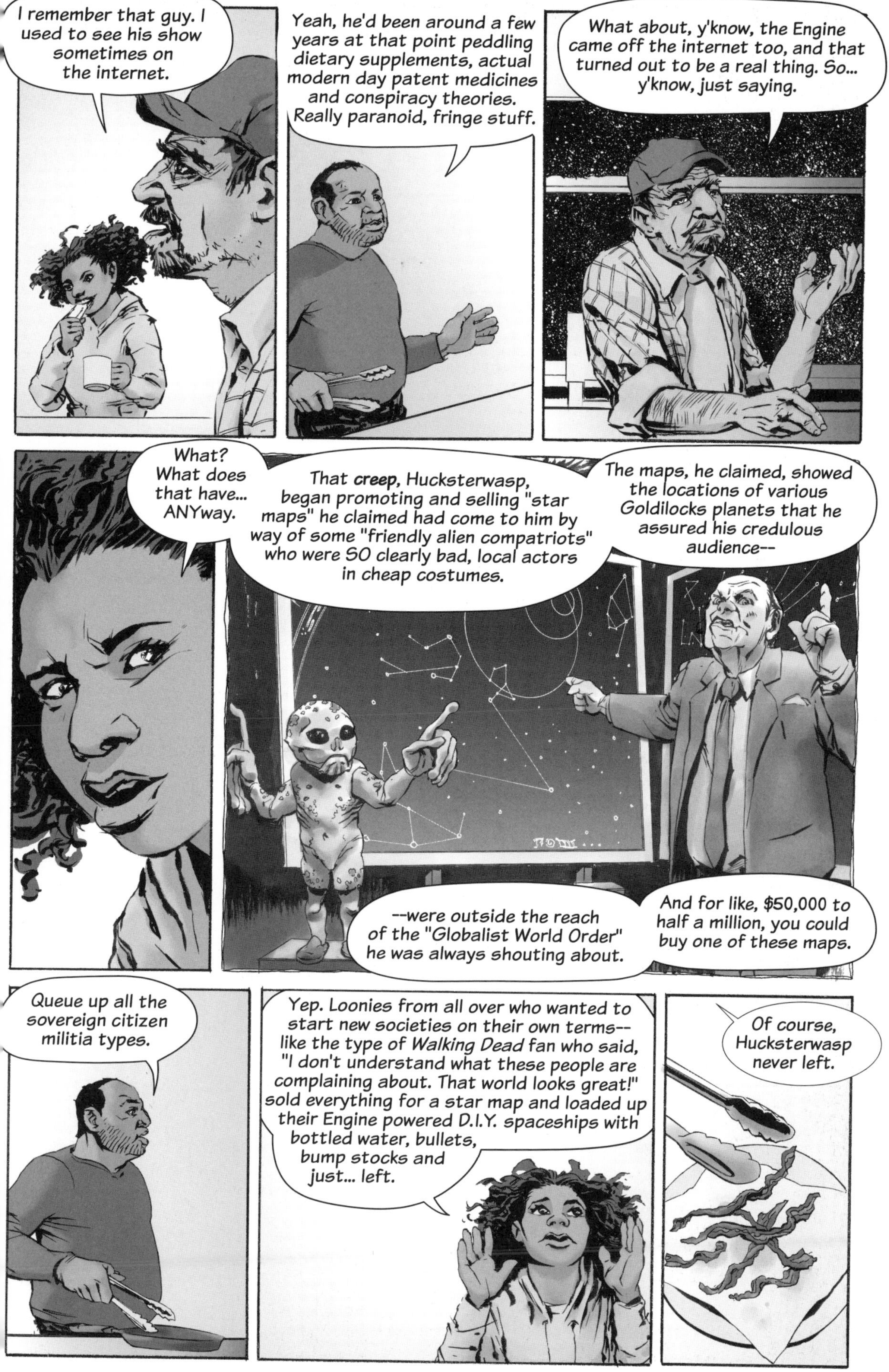
I remember that guy. I used to see his show sometimes on the internet.
Yeah, he'd been around a few years at that point peddling dietary supplements, actual modern day patent medicines and conspiracy theories. Really paranoid, fringe stuff.
What about, y'know, the Engine came off the internet too, and that turned out to be a real thing. So... y'know, just saying.
What? What does that have... ANYway.
That **creep**, Hucksterwasp, began promoting and selling "star maps" he claimed had come to him by way of some "friendly alien compatriots" who were SO clearly bad, local actors in cheap costumes.
The maps, he claimed, showed the locations of various Goldilocks planets that he assured his credulous audience--
--were outside the reach of the "Globalist World Order" he was always shouting about.
And for like, $50,000 to half a million, you could buy one of these maps.
Queue up all the sovereign citizen militia types.
Yep. Loonies from all over who wanted to start new societies on their own terms-- like the type of *Walking Dead* fan who said, "I don't understand what these people are complaining about. That world looks great!" sold everything for a star map and loaded up their Engine powered D.I.Y. spaceships with bottled water, bullets, bump stocks and just... left.
Of course, Hucksterwasp never left.

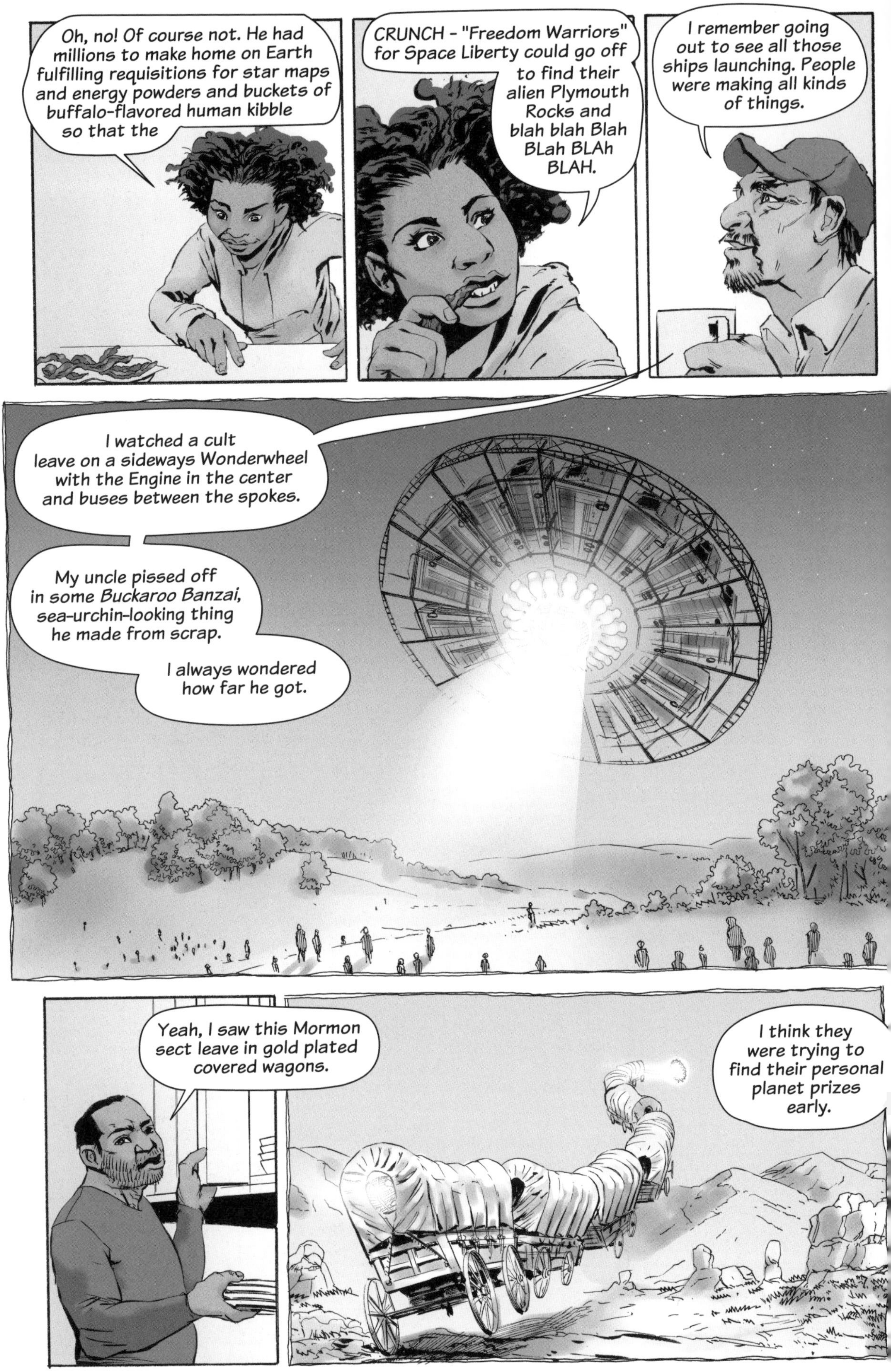

Oh, no! Of course not. He had millions to make home on Earth fulfilling requisitions for star maps and energy powders and buckets of buffalo-flavored human kibble so that the
CRUNCH - "Freedom Warriors" for Space Liberty could go off to find their alien Plymouth Rocks and blah blah Blah BLah BLAh BLAH.
I remember going out to see all those ships launching. People were making all kinds of things.
I watched a cult leave on a sideways Wonderwheel with the Engine in the center and buses between the spokes.
My uncle pissed off in some *Buckaroo Banzai*, sea-urchin-looking thing he made from scrap.
I always wondered how far he got.
Yeah, I saw this Mormon sect leave in gold plated covered wagons.
I think they were trying to find their personal planet prizes early.

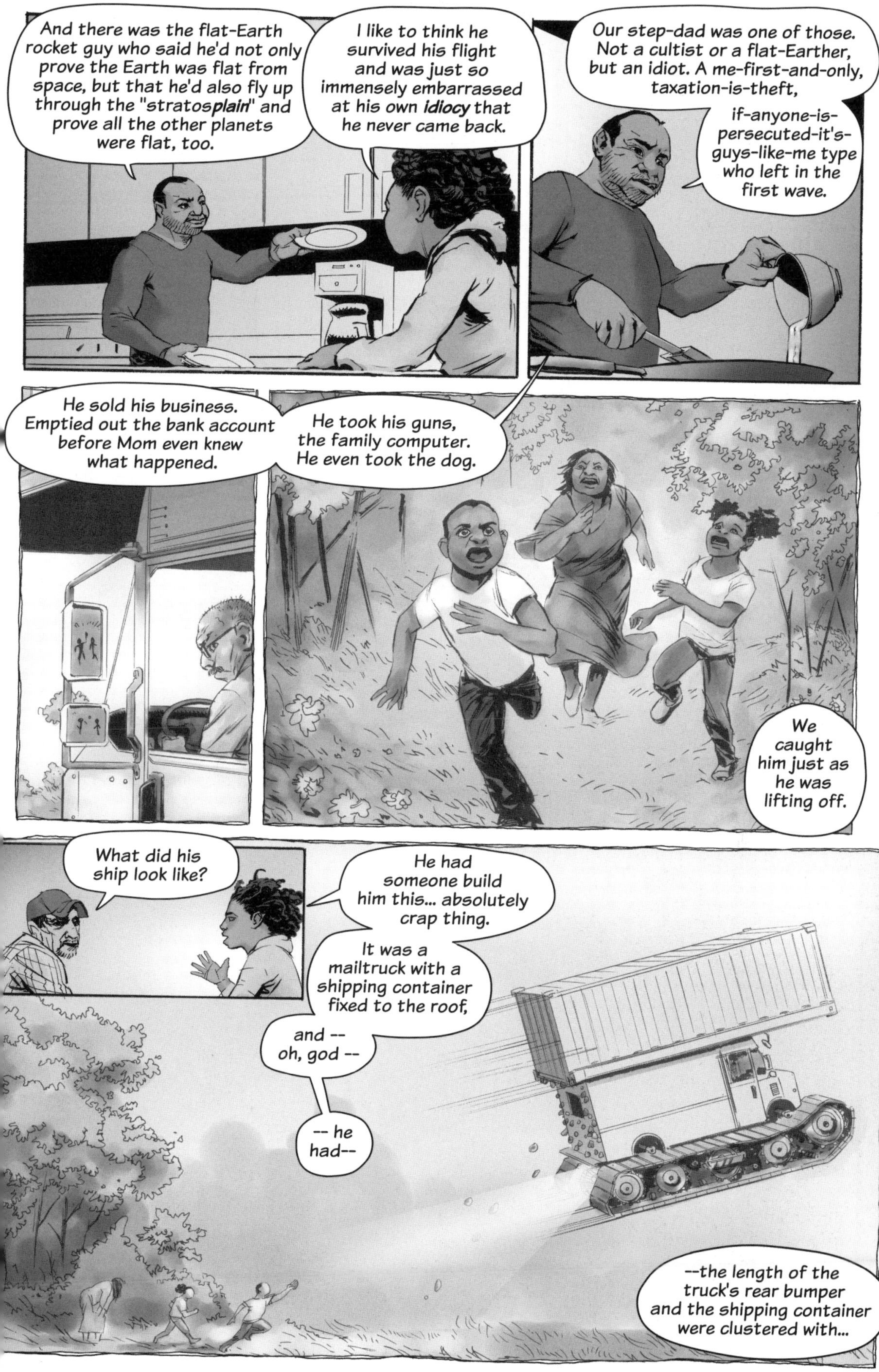
And there was the flat-Earth rocket guy who said he'd not only prove the Earth was flat from space, but that he'd also fly up through the "stratos*plain*" and prove all the other planets were flat, too.
I like to think he survived his flight and was just so immensely embarrassed at his own *idiocy* that he never came back.
Our step-dad was one of those. Not a cultist or a flat-Earther, but an idiot. A me-first-and-only, taxation-is-theft,
if-anyone-is-persecuted-it's-guys-like-me type who left in the first wave.
He sold his business. Emptied out the bank account before Mom even knew what happened.
He took his guns, the family computer. He even took the dog.
We caught him just as he was lifting off.
What did his ship look like?
He had someone build him this... absolutely crap thing.
It was a mailtruck with a shipping container fixed to the roof,
and -- oh, god --
-- he had--
--the length of the truck's rear bumper and the shipping container were clustered with...

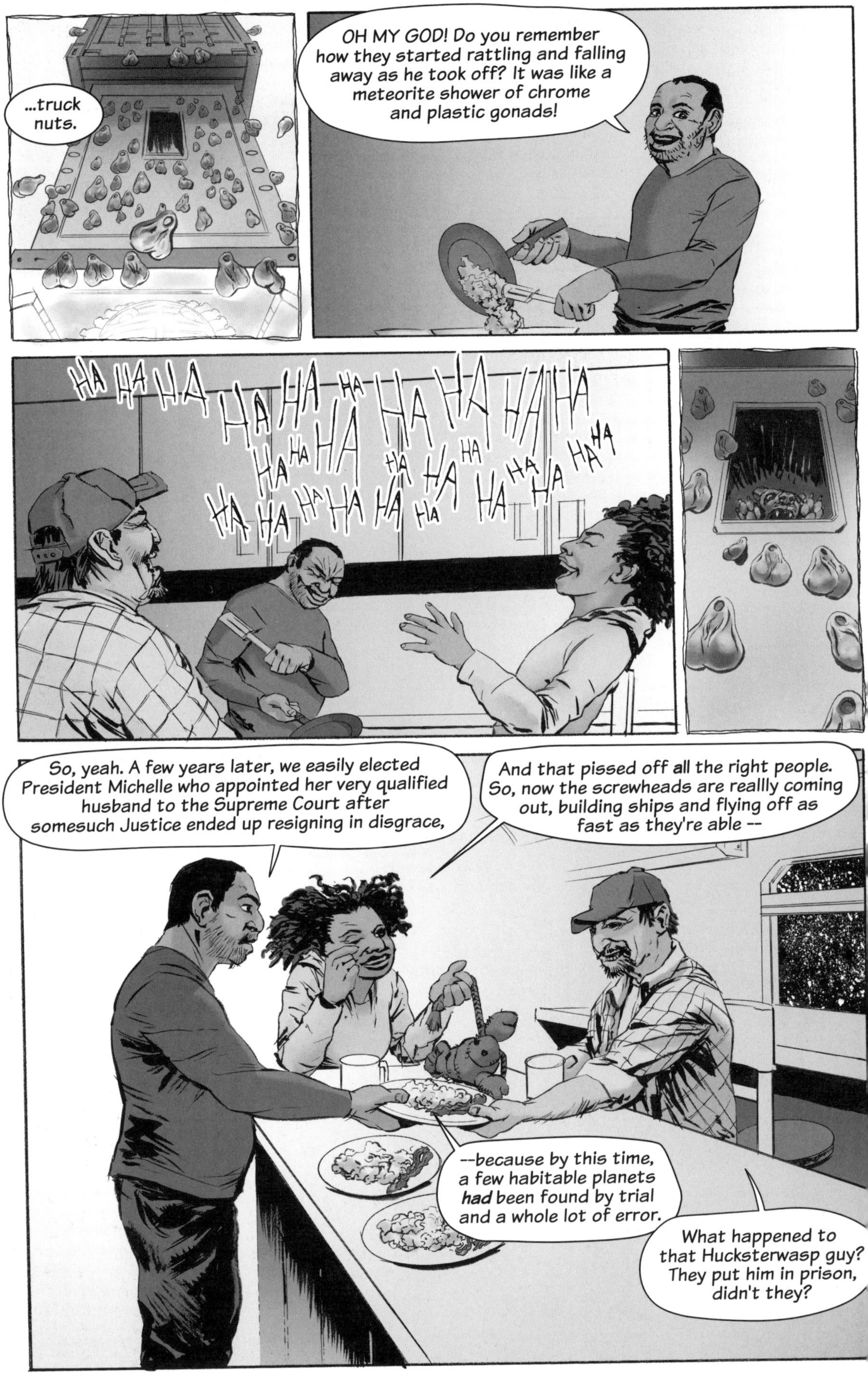
...truck nuts.
OH MY GOD! Do you remember how they started rattling and falling away as he took off? It was like a meteorite shower of chrome and plastic gonads!
HA HA HA HA HA HA HA HA HA HA HA HA HA HA HA HA HA HA HA HA HA HA HA HA HA HA HA HA HA HA HA
So, yeah. A few years later, we easily elected President Michelle who appointed her very qualified husband to the Supreme Court after somesuch Justice ended up resigning in disgrace,
And that pissed off all the right people. So, now the screwheads are reallly coming out, building ships and flying off as fast as they're able --
--because by this time, a few habitable planets *had* been found by trial and a whole lot of error.
What happened to that Hucksterwasp guy? They put him in prison, didn't they?

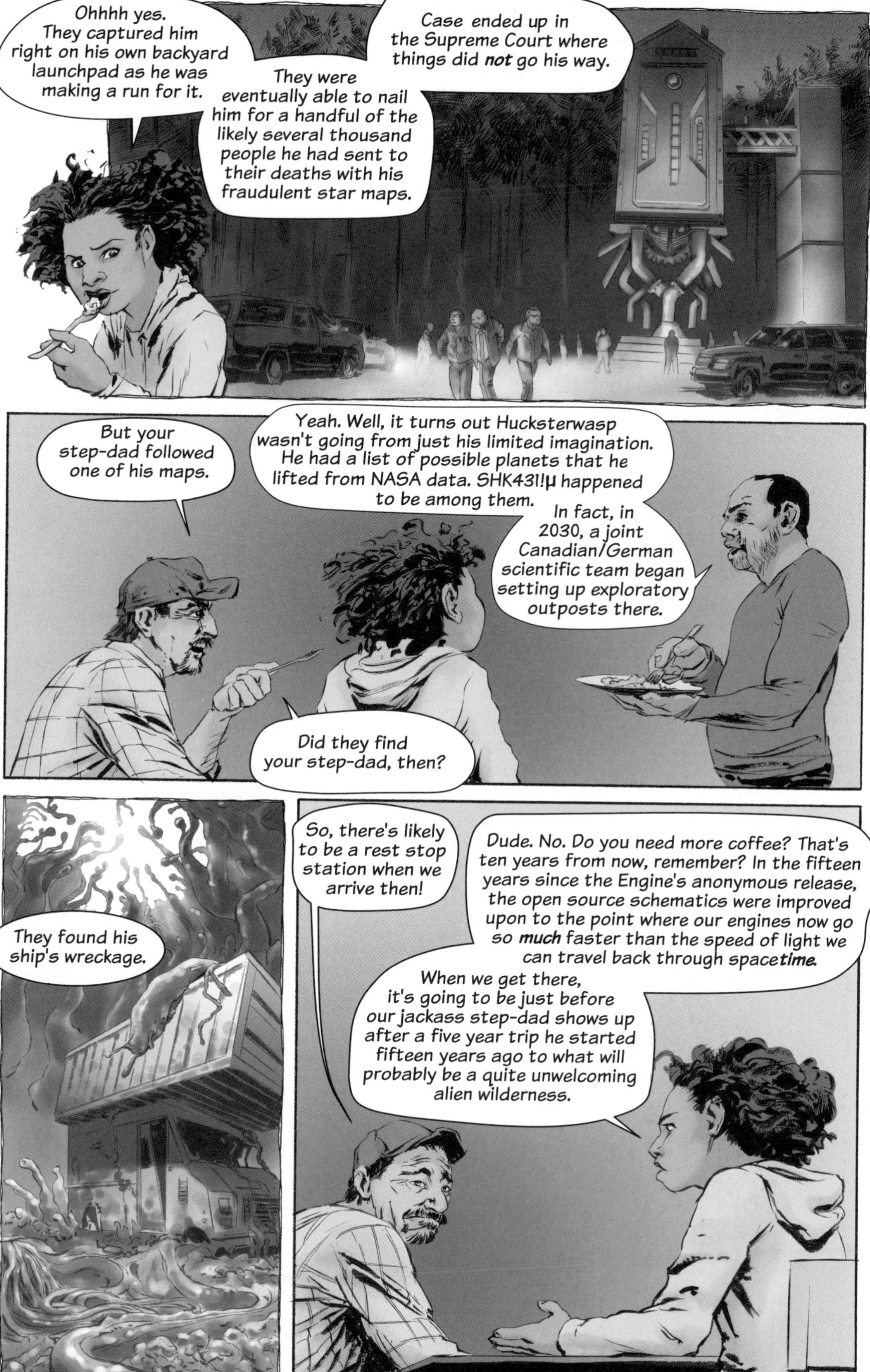
Ohhhh yes. They captured him right on his own backyard launchpad as he was making a run for it.
They were eventually able to nail him for a handful of the likely several thousand people he had sent to their deaths with his fraudulent star maps.
Case ended up in the Supreme Court where things did *not* go his way.
But your step-dad followed one of his maps.
Yeah. Well, it turns out Hucksterwasp wasn't going from just his limited imagination. He had a list of possible planets that he lifted from NASA data. SHK431!μ happened to be among them.
In fact, in 2030, a joint Canadian/German scientific team began setting up exploratory outposts there.
Did they find your step-dad, then?
They found his ship's wreckage.
So, there's likely to be a rest stop station when we arrive then!
Dude. No. Do you need more coffee? That's ten years from now, remember? In the fifteen years since the Engine's anonymous release, the open source schematics were improved upon to the point where our engines now go so *much* faster than the speed of light we can travel back through space*time*.
When we get there, it's going to be just before our jackass step-dad shows up after a five year trip he started fifteen years ago to what will probably be a quite unwelcoming alien wilderness.

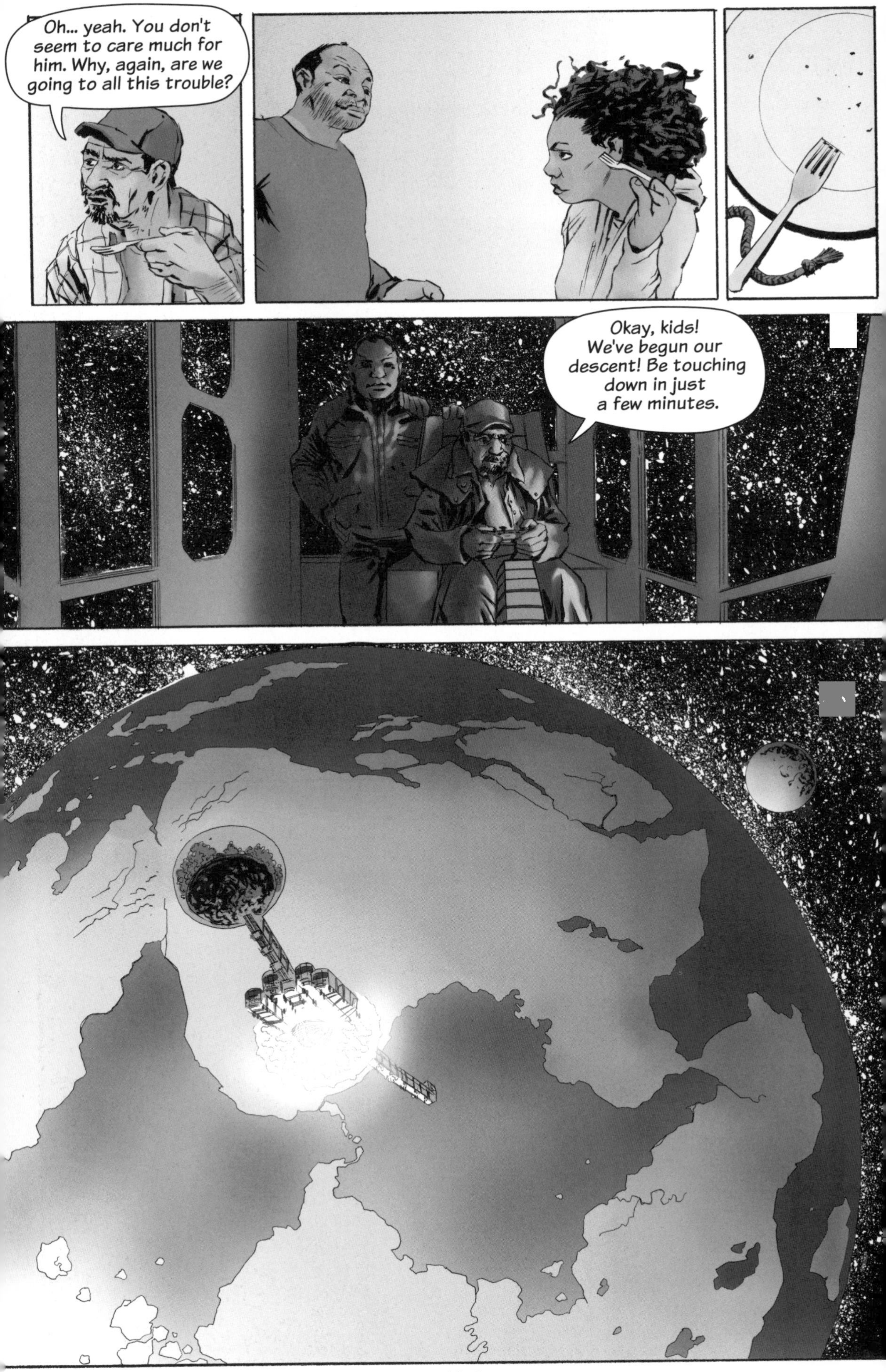
Oh... yeah. You don't seem to care much for him. Why, again, are we going to all this trouble?
Okay, kids! We've begun our descent! Be touching down in just a few minutes.

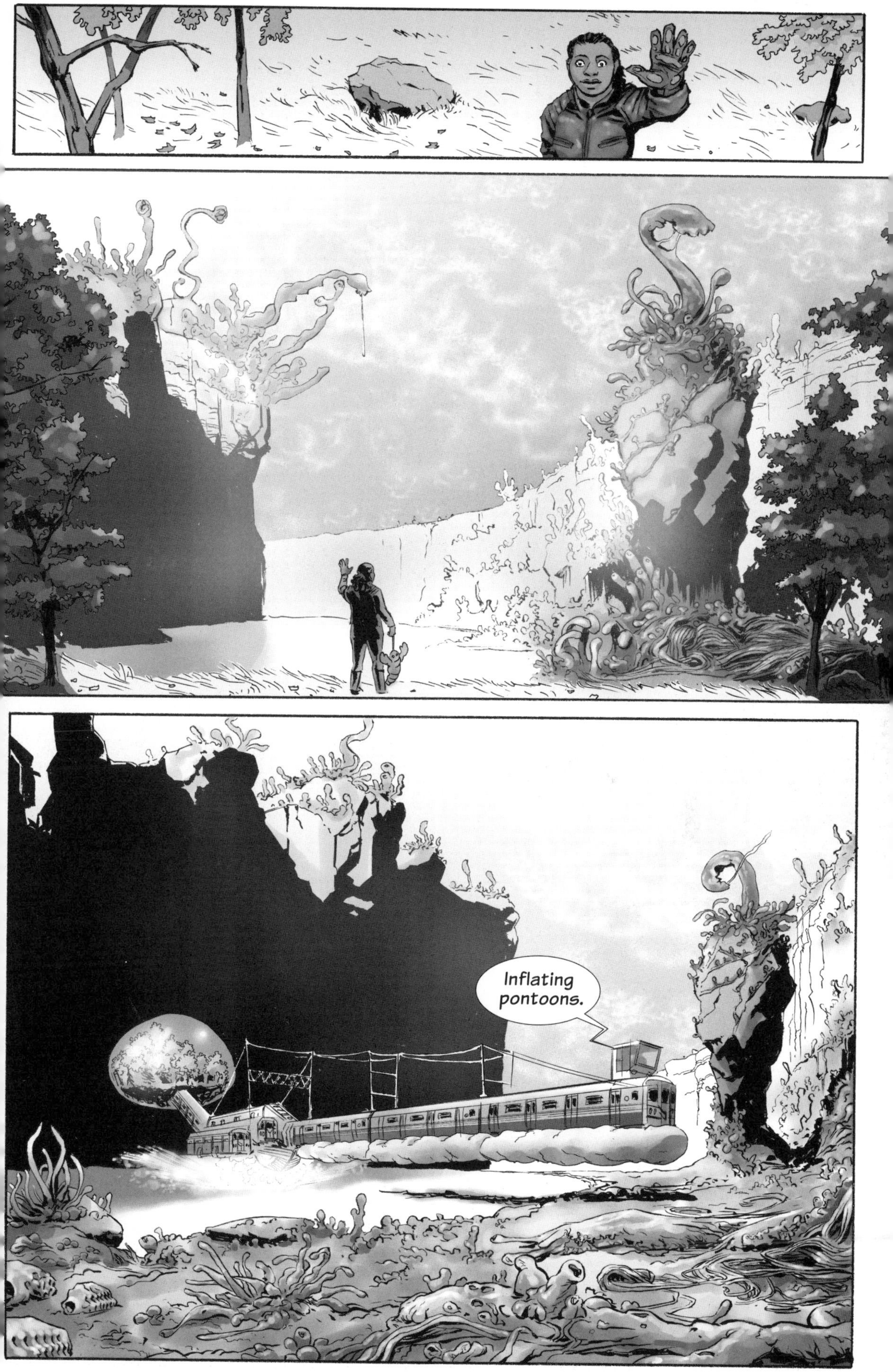
Inflating pontoons.

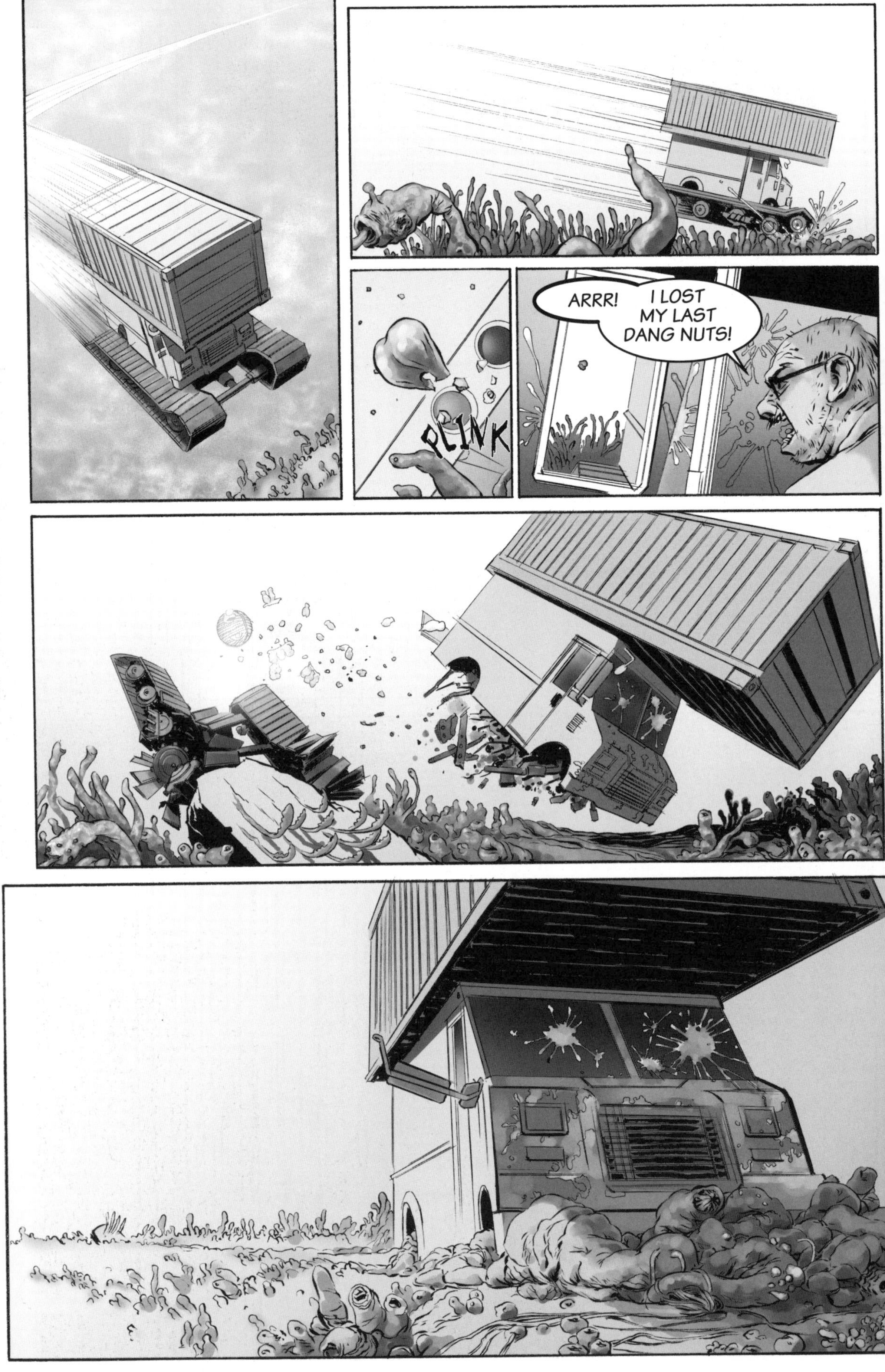
PLINK
ARRR!
I LOST MY LAST DANG NUTS!

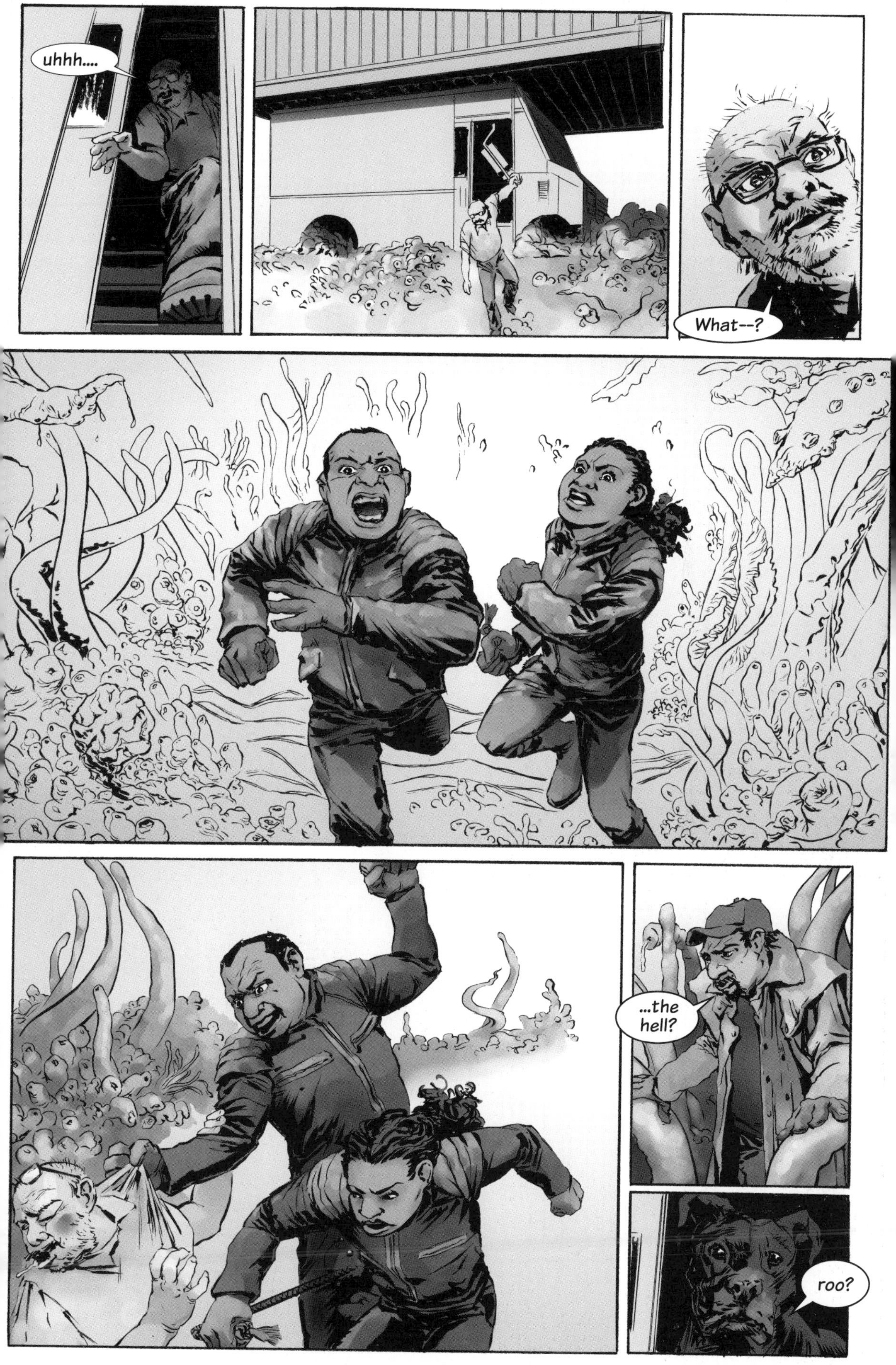
uhhh....
What--?
...the hell?
roo?

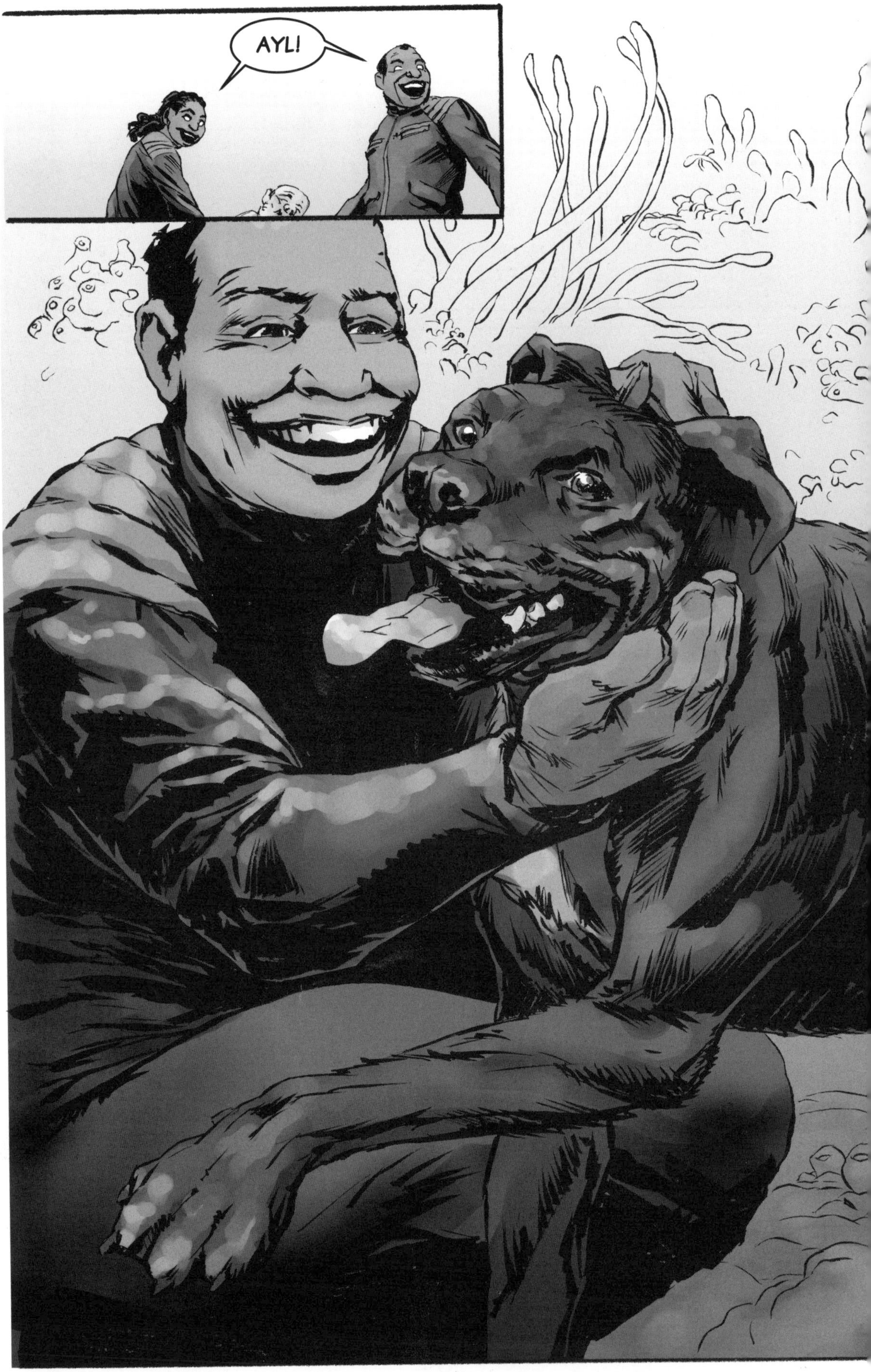
AYL!

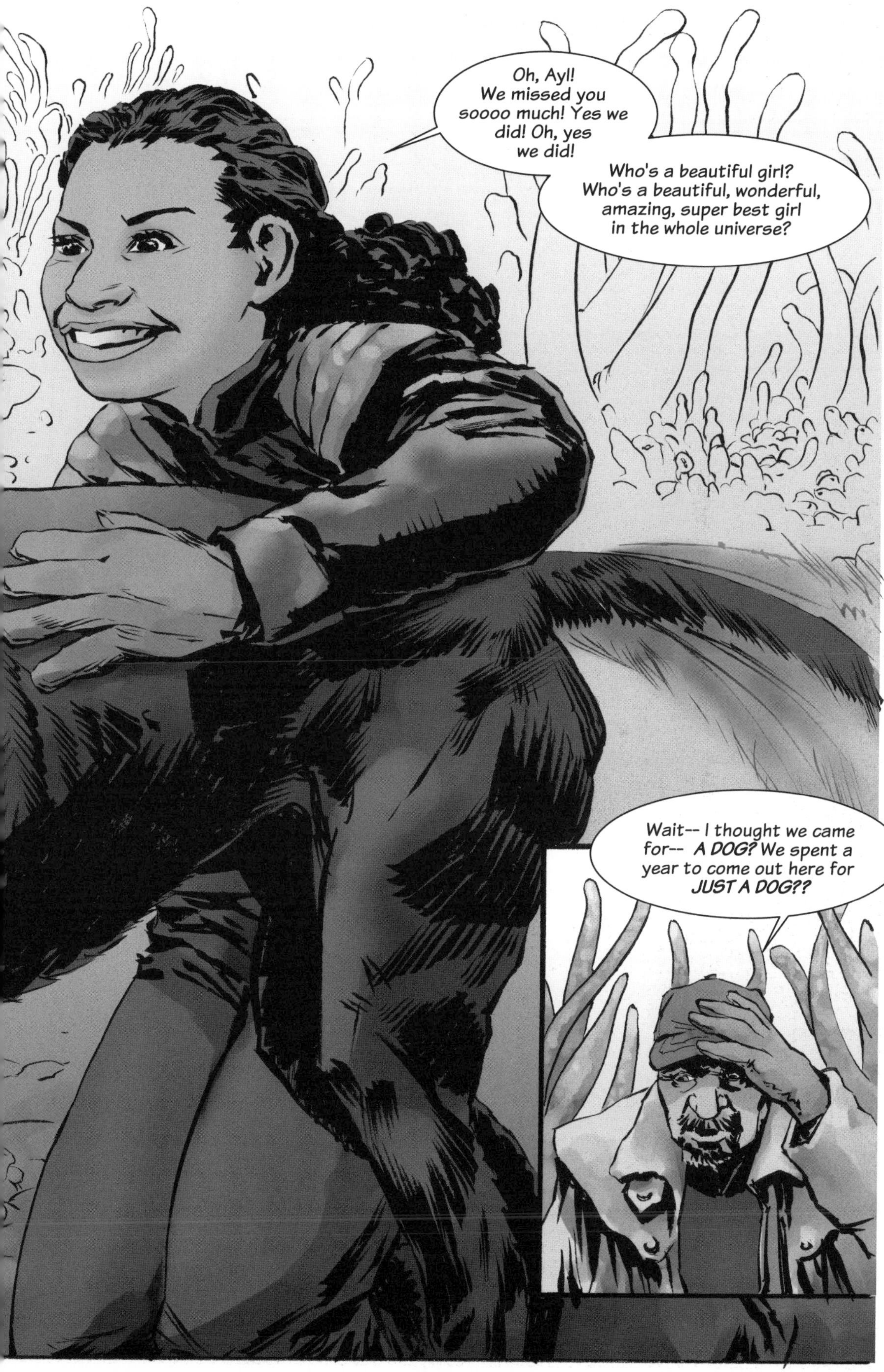
Oh, Ayl! We missed you soooo much! Yes we did! Oh, yes we did!
Who's a beautiful girl? Who's a beautiful, wonderful, amazing, super best girl in the whole universe?
Wait-- I thought we came for-- A DOG? We spent a year to come out here for JUST A DOG??

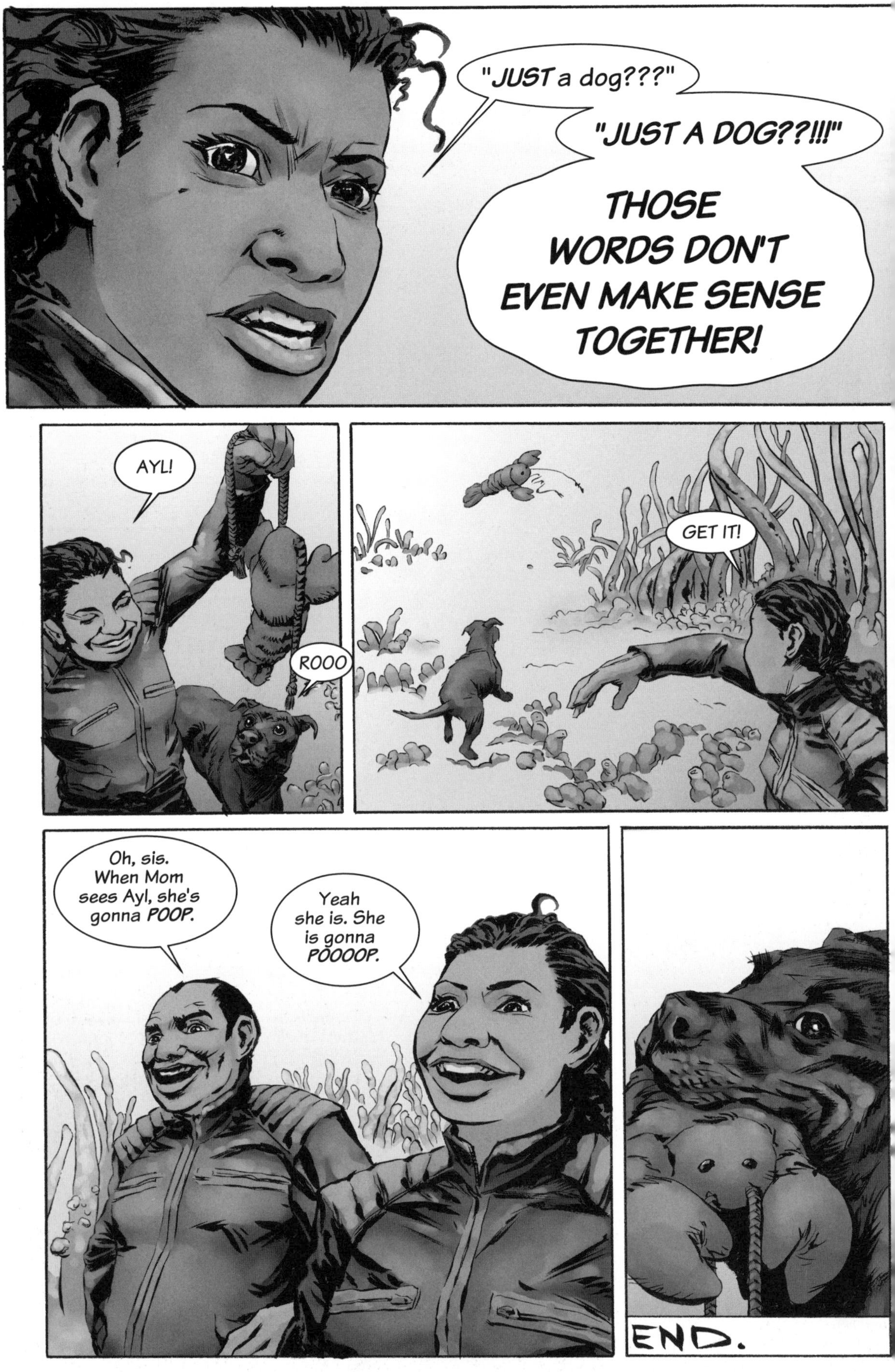
"JUST a dog???"
"JUST A DOG??!!!"
THOSE WORDS DON'T EVEN MAKE SENSE TOGETHER!
AYL!
ROOO
GET IT!
Oh, sis. When Mom sees Ayl, she's gonna POOP.
Yeah she is. She is gonna POOOOP.
END.

BY JONATHON DALTON
WORDS FROM THE DEAD

K2-3f (137 light years from home).

Just a little more...

Here it is. It's a plastic artifact, again, a widget.

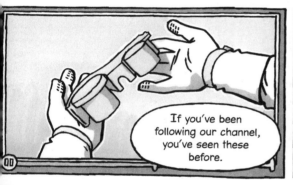

If you've been following our channel, you've seen these before.

Taucetian sites are littered with widgets of all shapes and sizes.

Everyone's got their own theory about what they're for, but none of us knows for sure.

We can't even carbon-date them, since we don't know what planet they were made on.

Next episode I think we're going to spend some time digging around the main structure.

Until then, thank-you to all our supporters. We couldn't do this without you.

Subscribe, leave a comment... Oh! And don't forget to check out the new T-shirts that Gabriel designed for us.

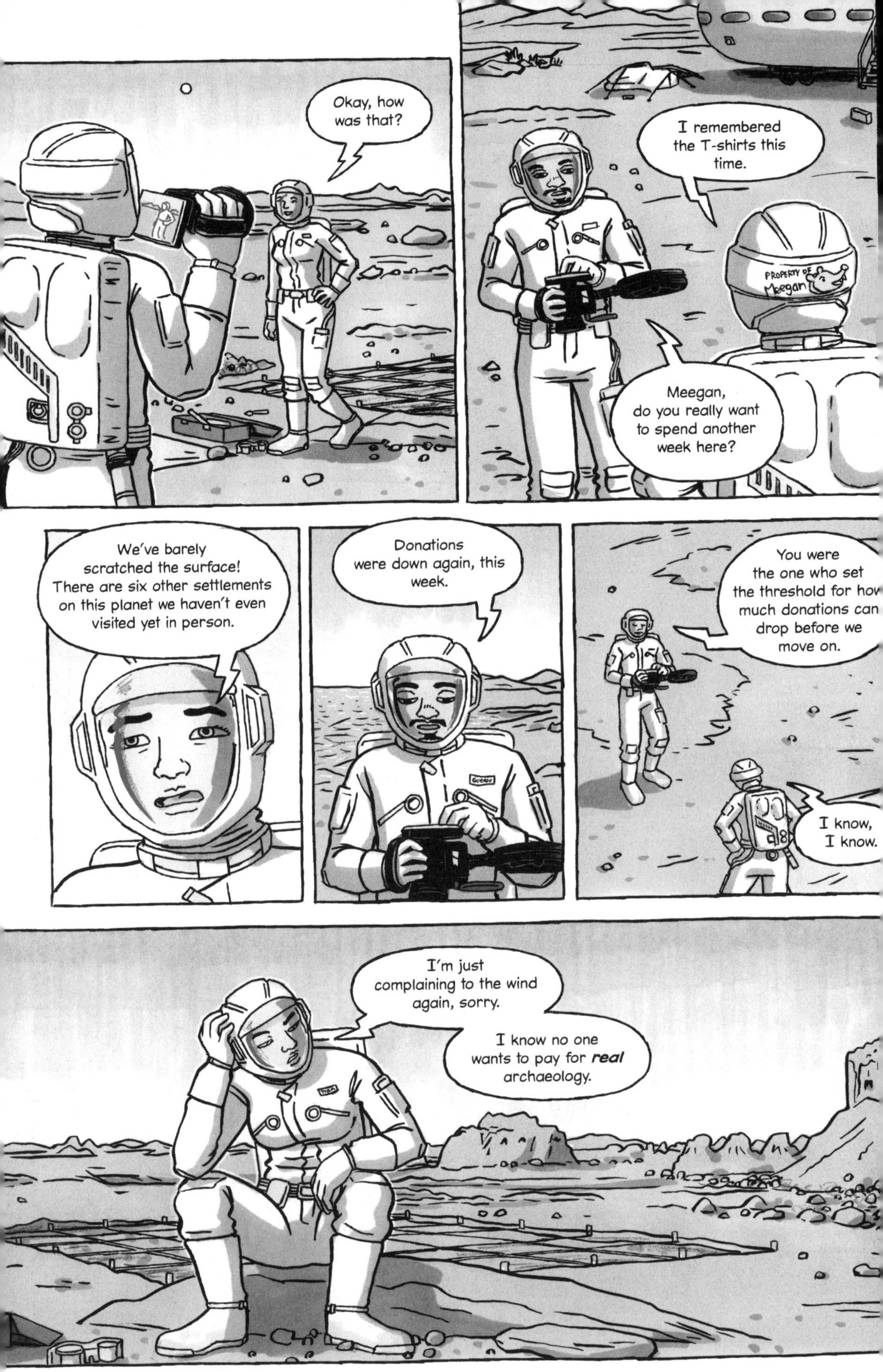
Okay, how was that?
I remembered the T-shirts this time.
PROPERTY OF Meegan
Meegan, do you really want to spend another week here?
We've barely scratched the surface! There are six other settlements on this planet we haven't even visited yet in person.
Donations were down again, this week.
You were the one who set the threshold for hov much donations can drop before we move on.
I know, I know.
I'm just complaining to the wind again, sorry.
I know no one wants to pay for ***real*** archaeology.

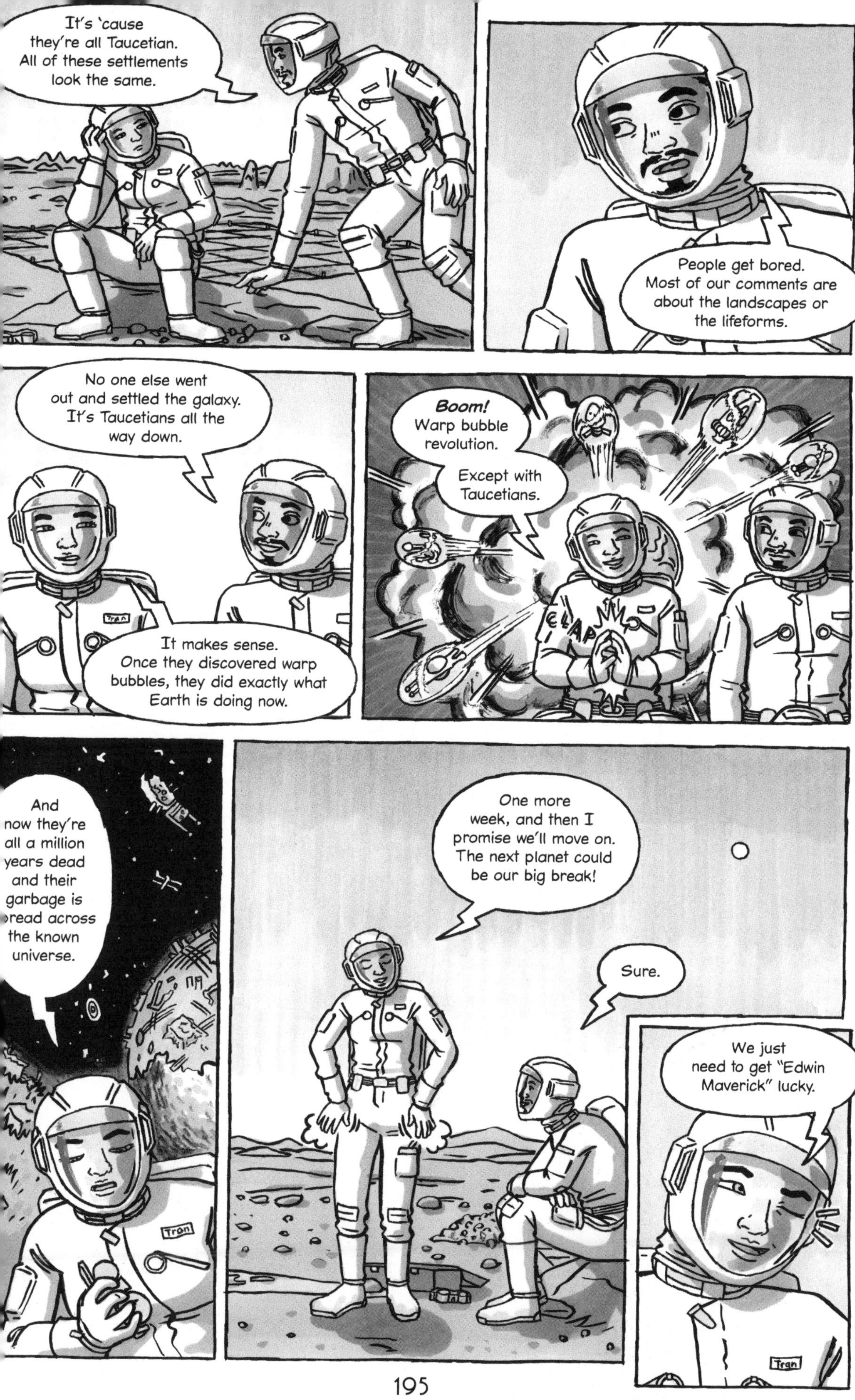
It's 'cause they're all Taucetian. All of these settlements look the same.
People get bored. Most of our comments are about the landscapes or the lifeforms.
No one else went out and settled the galaxy. It's Taucetians all the way down.
Tran
It makes sense. Once they discovered warp bubbles, they did exactly what Earth is doing now.
Boom! Warp bubble revolution.
Except with Taucetians.
CLAP
And now they're all a million years dead and their garbage is spread across the known universe.
Tran
One more week, and then I promise we'll move on. The next planet could be our big break!
Sure.
We just need to get "Edwin Maverick" lucky.
Tran

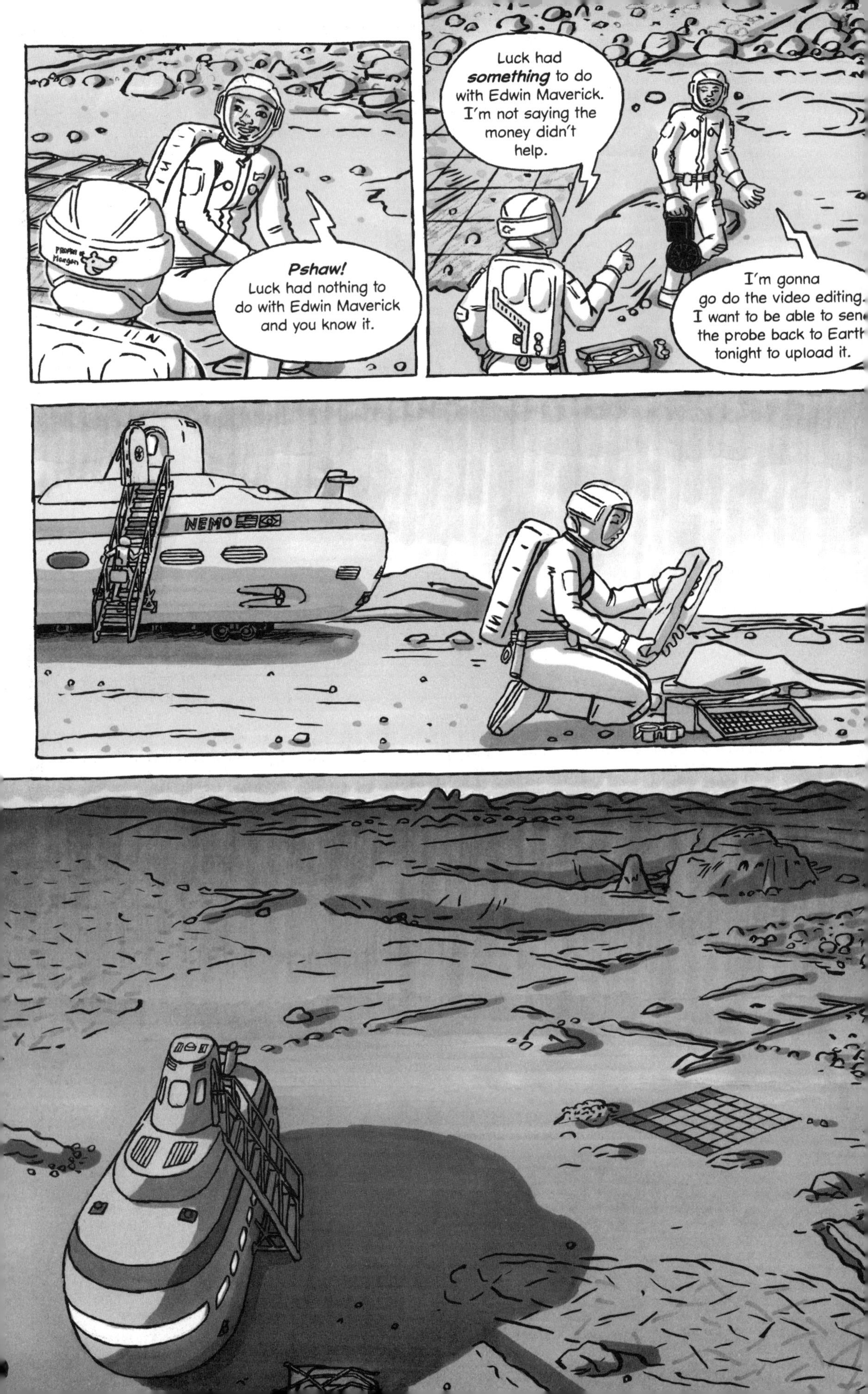
Pshaw!
Luck had nothing to do with Edwin Maverick and you know it.
Luck had something to do with Edwin Maverick. I'm not saying the money didn't help.
I'm gonna go do the video editing. I want to be able to sen the probe back to Earth tonight to upload it.
NEMO

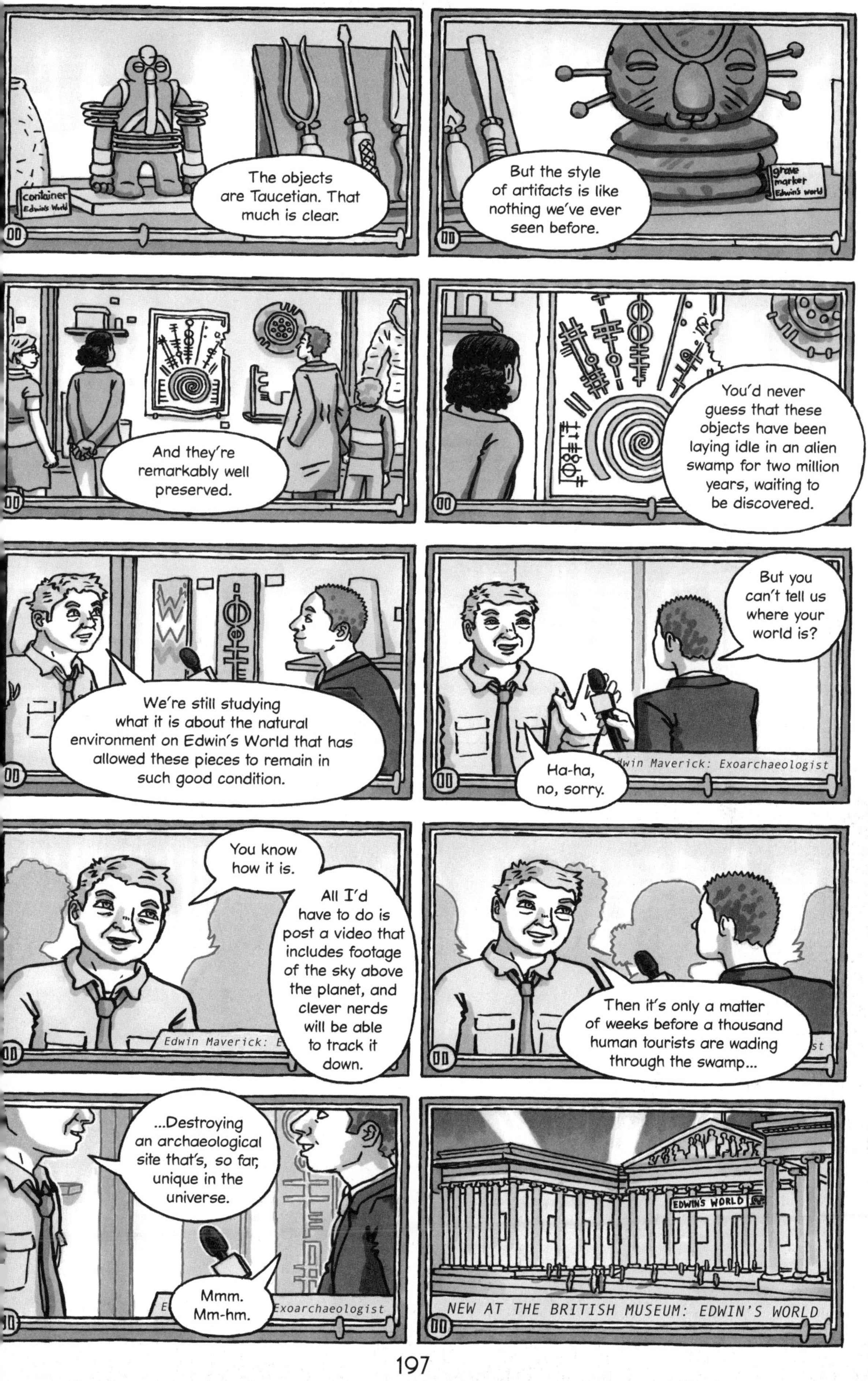
container
Edwin's World
The objects are Taucetian. That much is clear.
But the style of artifacts is like nothing we've ever seen before.
grave marker
Edwin's World
And they're remarkably well preserved.
You'd never guess that these objects have been laying idle in an alien swamp for two million years, waiting to be discovered.
We're still studying what it is about the natural environment on Edwin's World that has allowed these pieces to remain in such good condition.
But you can't tell us where your world is?
Ha-ha, no, sorry.
You know how it is.
All I'd have to do is post a video that includes footage of the sky above the planet, and clever nerds will be able to track it down.
Then it's only a matter of weeks before a thousand human tourists are wading through the swamp...
...Destroying an archaeological site that's, so far, unique in the universe.
Mmm. Mm-hm.
EDWIN'S WORLD
NEW AT THE BRITISH MUSEUM: EDWIN'S WORLD

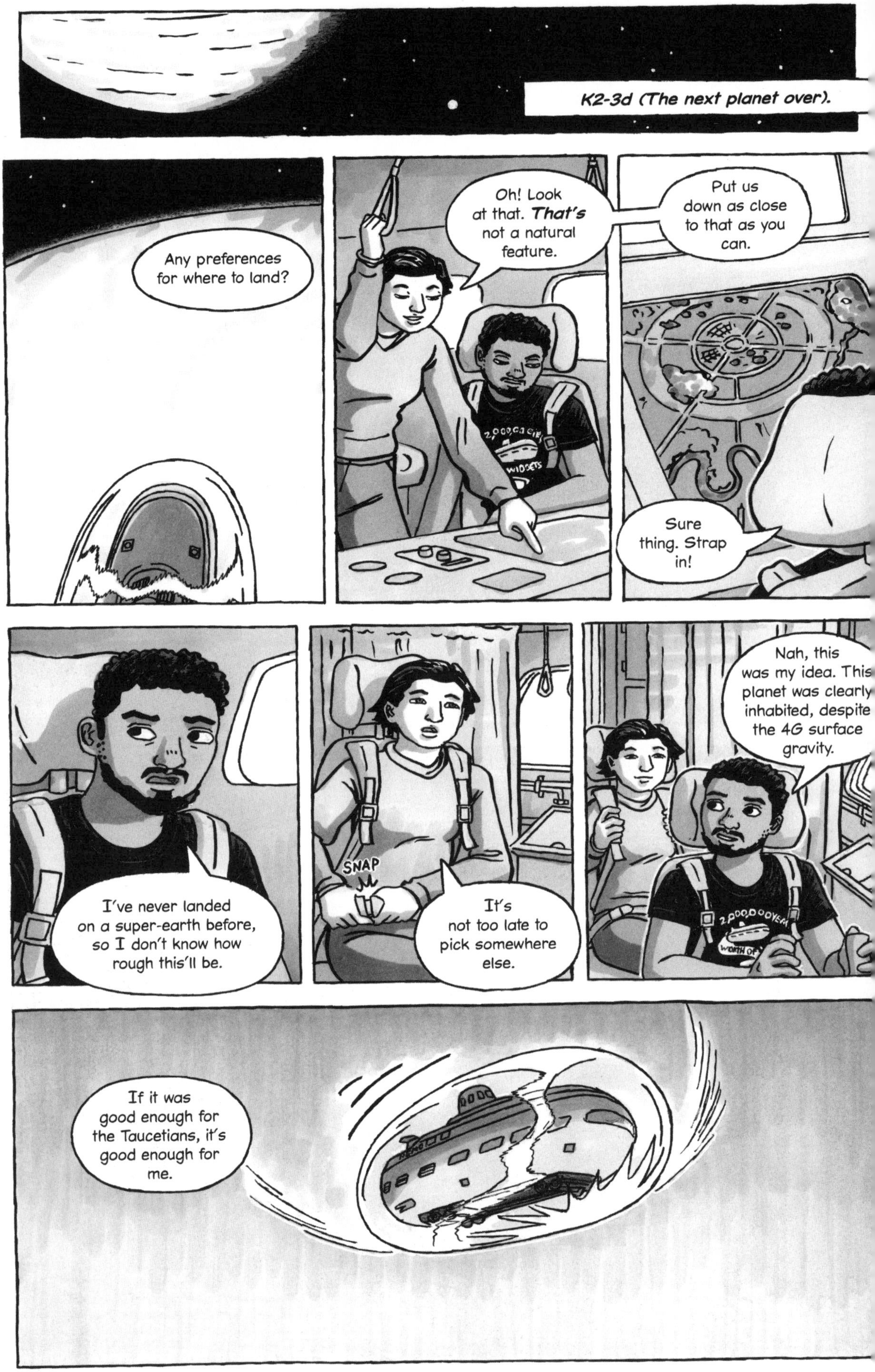
K2-3d (The next planet over).
Any preferences for where to land?
Oh! Look at that. *That's* not a natural feature.
Put us down as close to that as you can.
Sure thing. Strap in!
I've never landed on a super-earth before, so I don't know how rough this'll be.
SNAP
It's not too late to pick somewhere else.
Nah, this was my idea. This planet was clearly inhabited, despite the 4G surface gravity.
If it was good enough for the Taucetians, it's good enough for me.

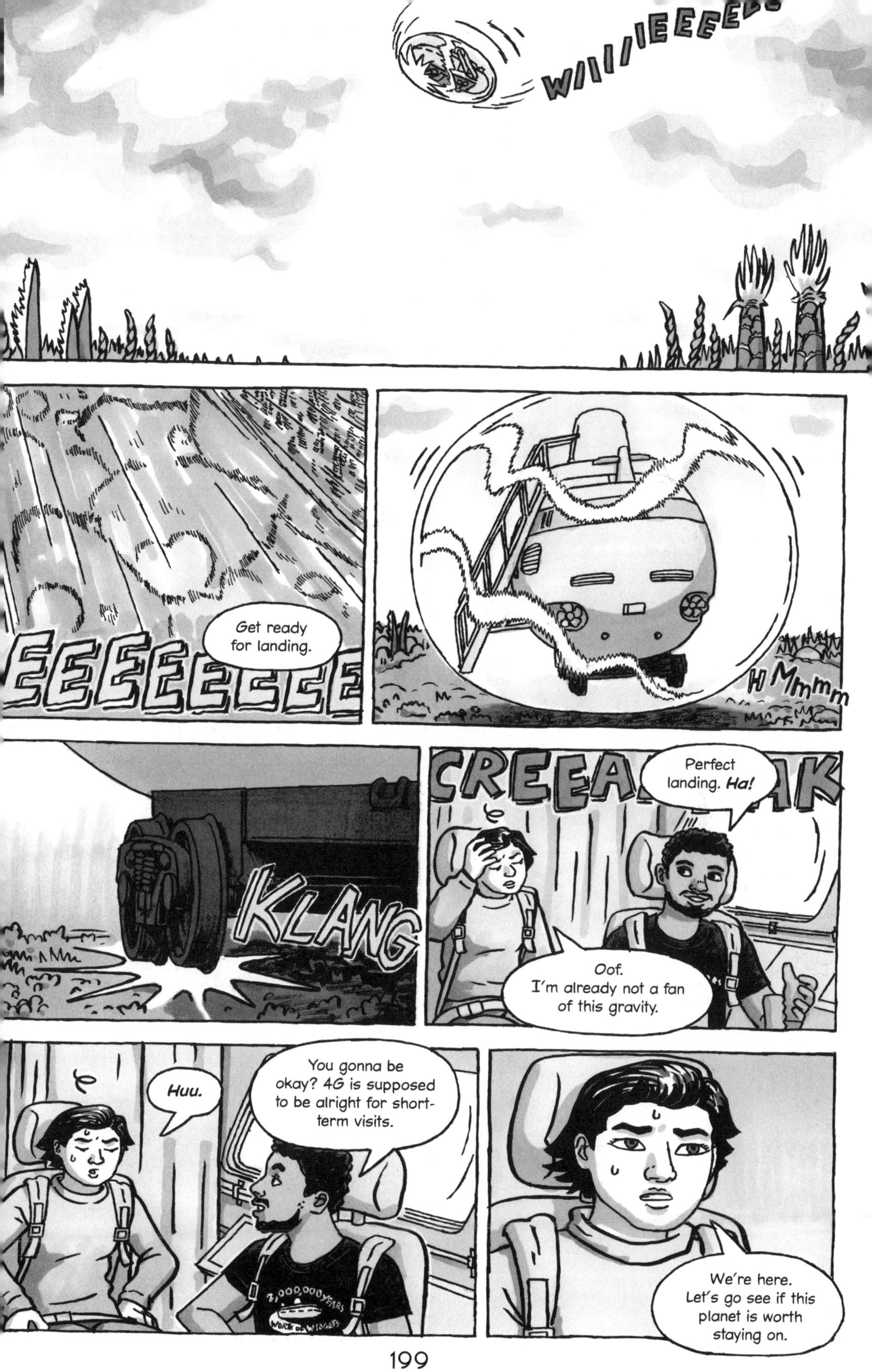
WIIIIEEEEE
EEEEEEEEE
Get ready for landing.
HMmmm
KLANG
CREEAK
Perfect landing. Ha!
Oof. I'm already not a fan of this gravity.
Huu.
You gonna be okay? 4G is supposed to be alright for short-term visits.
We're here. Let's go see if this planet is worth staying on.

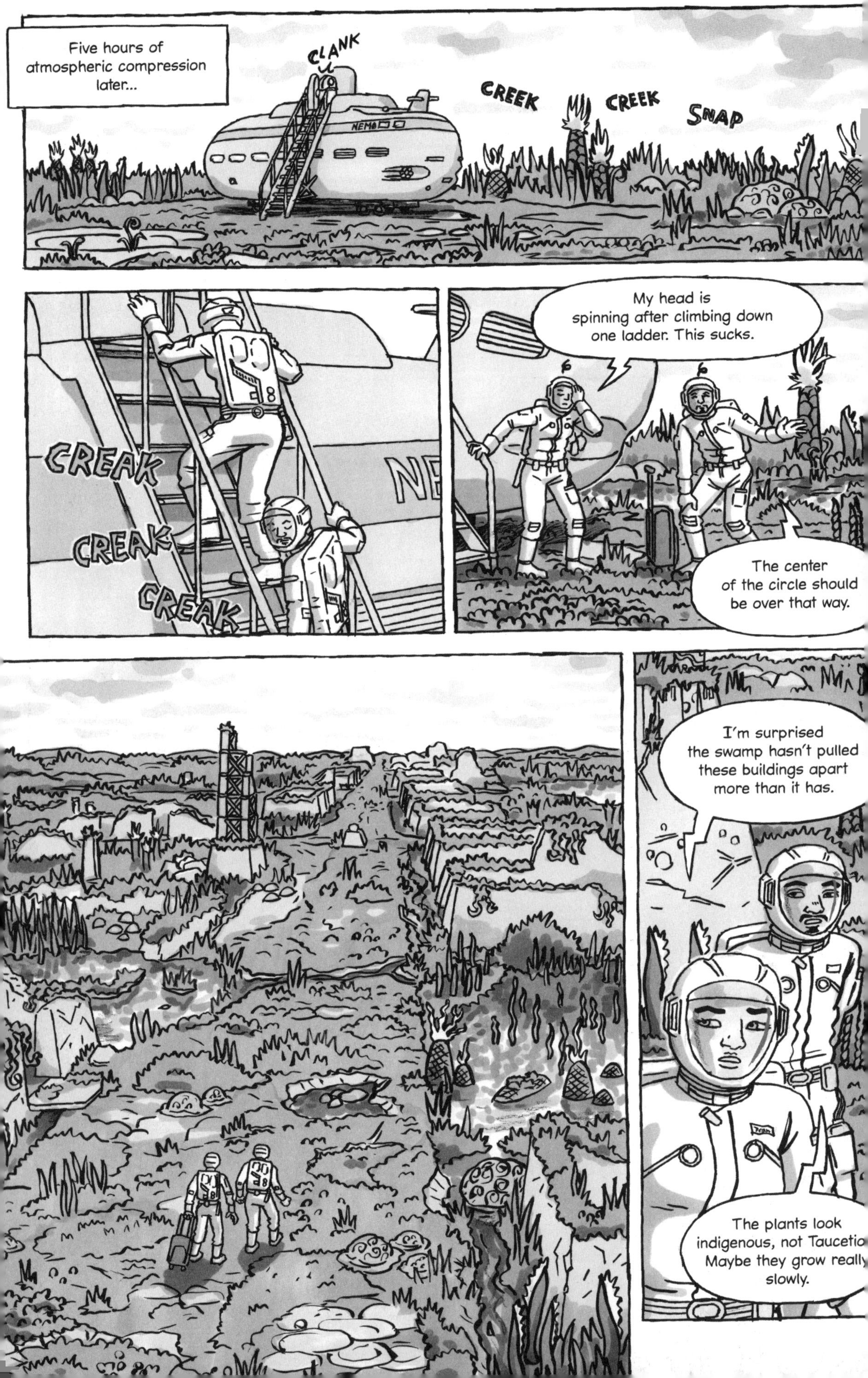
Five hours of atmospheric compression later...
CLANK
CREEK
CREEK
SNAP
CREAK
CREAK
CREAK
My head is spinning after climbing down one ladder. This sucks.
The center of the circle should be over that way.
I'm surprised the swamp hasn't pulled these buildings apart more than it has.
The plants look indigenous, not Taucetio
Maybe they grow really slowly.

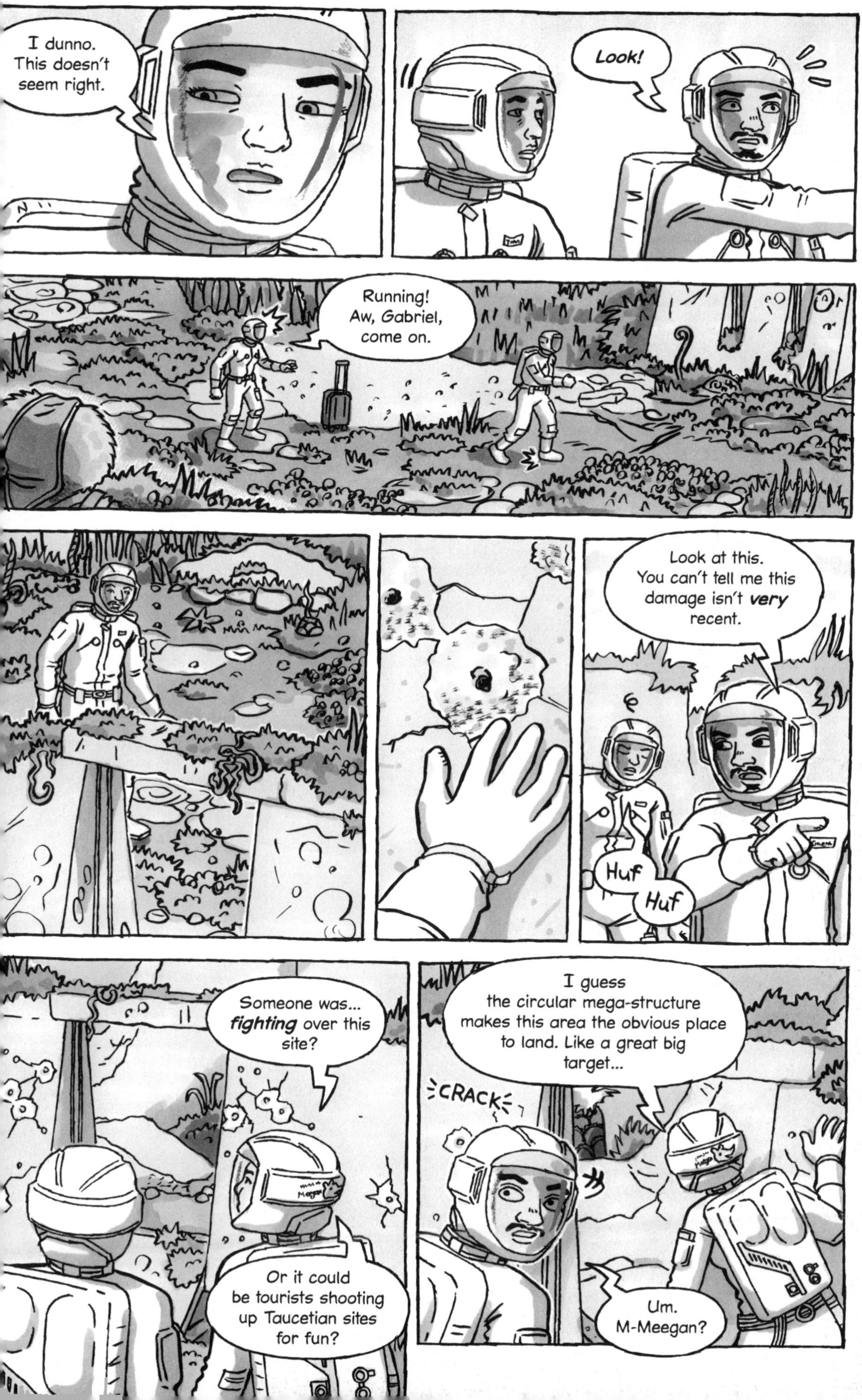
I dunno. This doesn't seem right.
Look!
Running! Aw, Gabriel, come on.
Look at this. You can't tell me this damage isn't *very* recent.
Huf
Huf
Someone was... *fighting* over this site?
Or it could be tourists shooting up Taucetian sites for fun?
I guess the circular mega-structure makes this area the obvious place to land. Like a great big target...
CRACK
Um. M-Meegan?

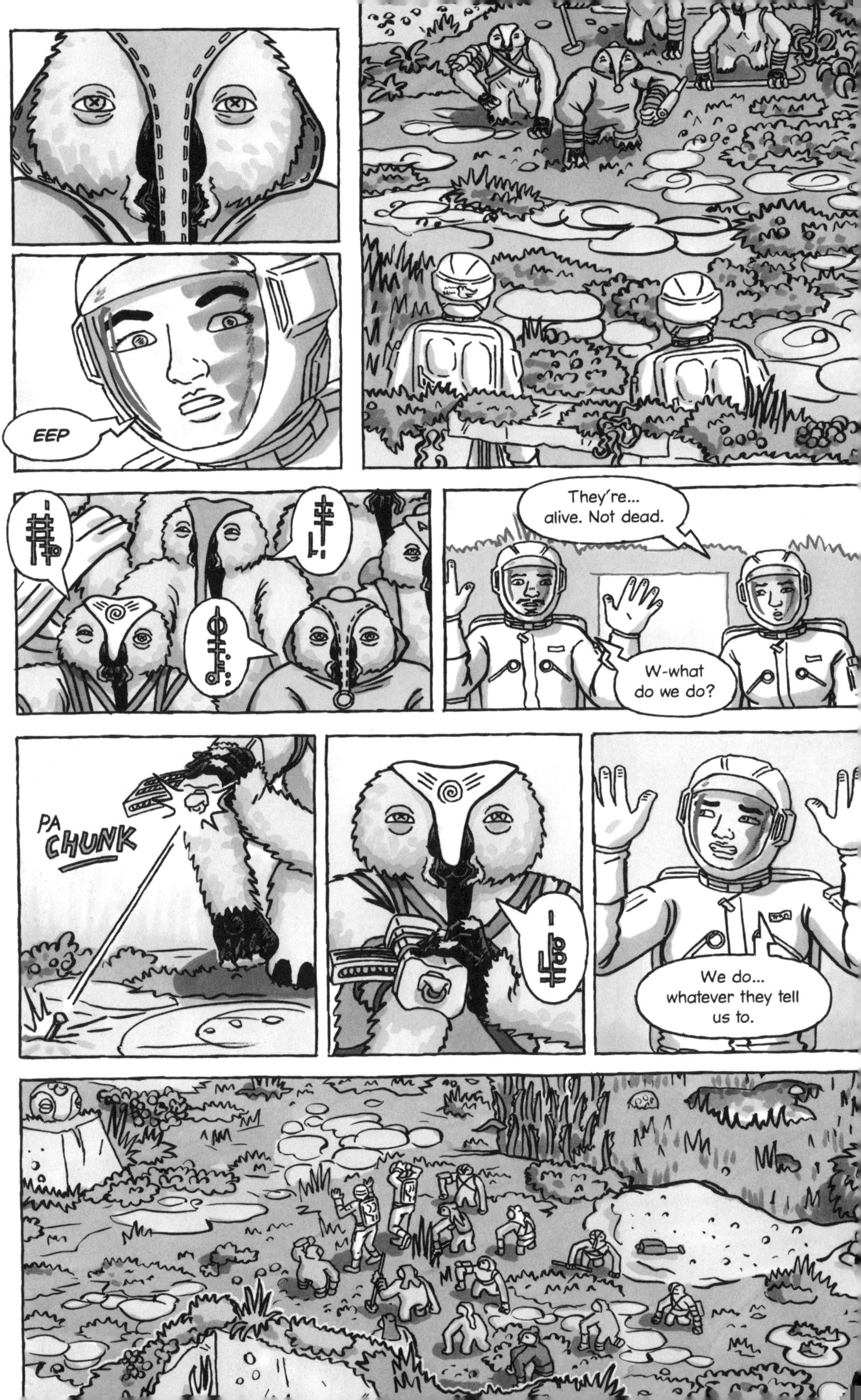
EEP
They're... alive. Not dead.
W-what do we do?
PA CHUNK
We do... whatever they tell us to.

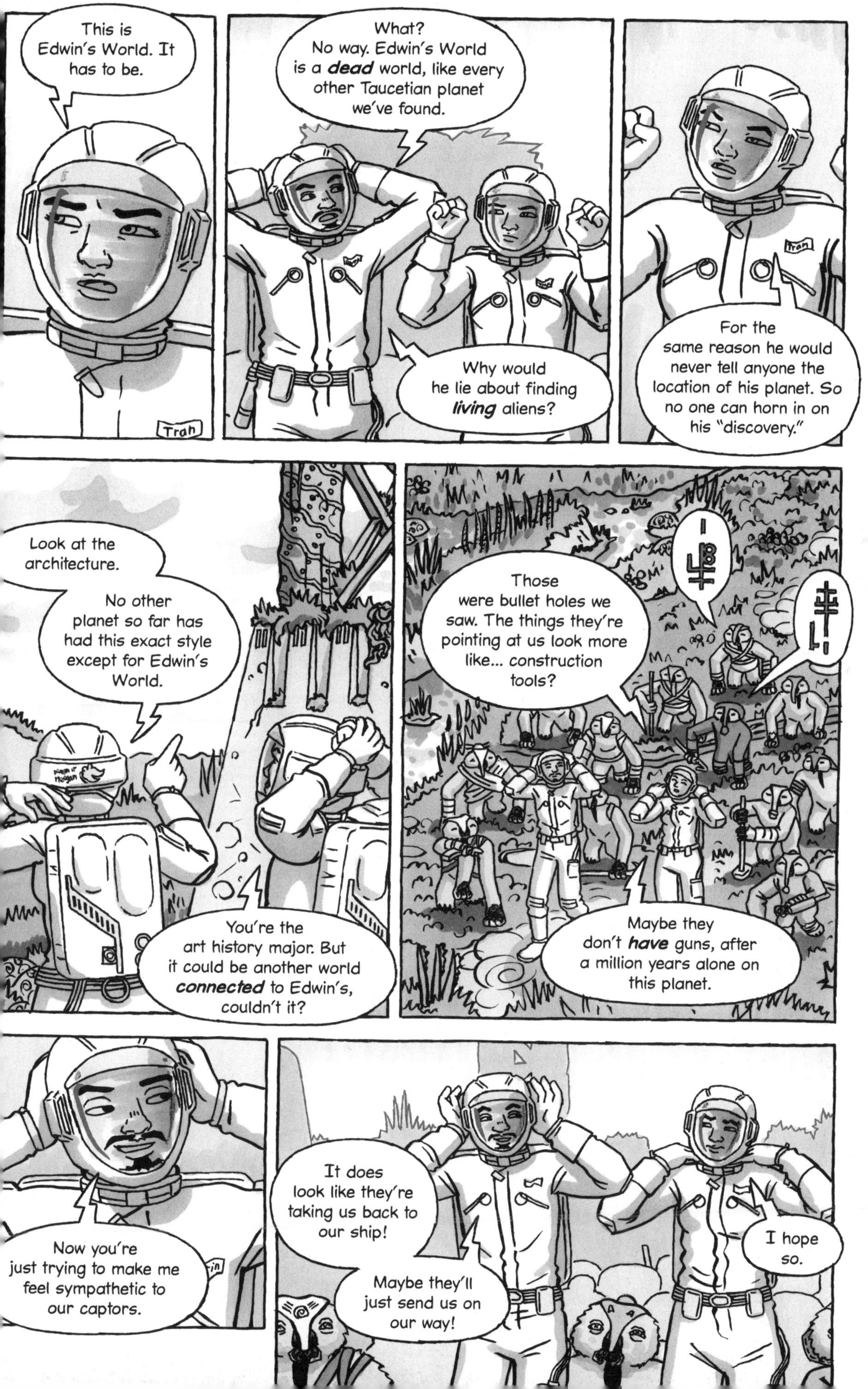
This is Edwin's World. It has to be.
What? No way. Edwin's World is a *dead* world, like every other Taucetian planet we've found.
Why would he lie about finding *living* aliens?
For the same reason he would never tell anyone the location of his planet. So no one can horn in on his "discovery."
Tran
Tran
Look at the architecture.
No other planet so far has had this exact style except for Edwin's World.
You're the art history major. But it could be another world *connected* to Edwin's, couldn't it?
Those were bullet holes we saw. The things they're pointing at us look more like... construction tools?
Maybe they don't *have* guns, after a million years alone on this planet.
Now you're just trying to make me feel sympathetic to our captors.
It does look like they're taking us back to our ship!
Maybe they'll just send us on our way!
I hope so.

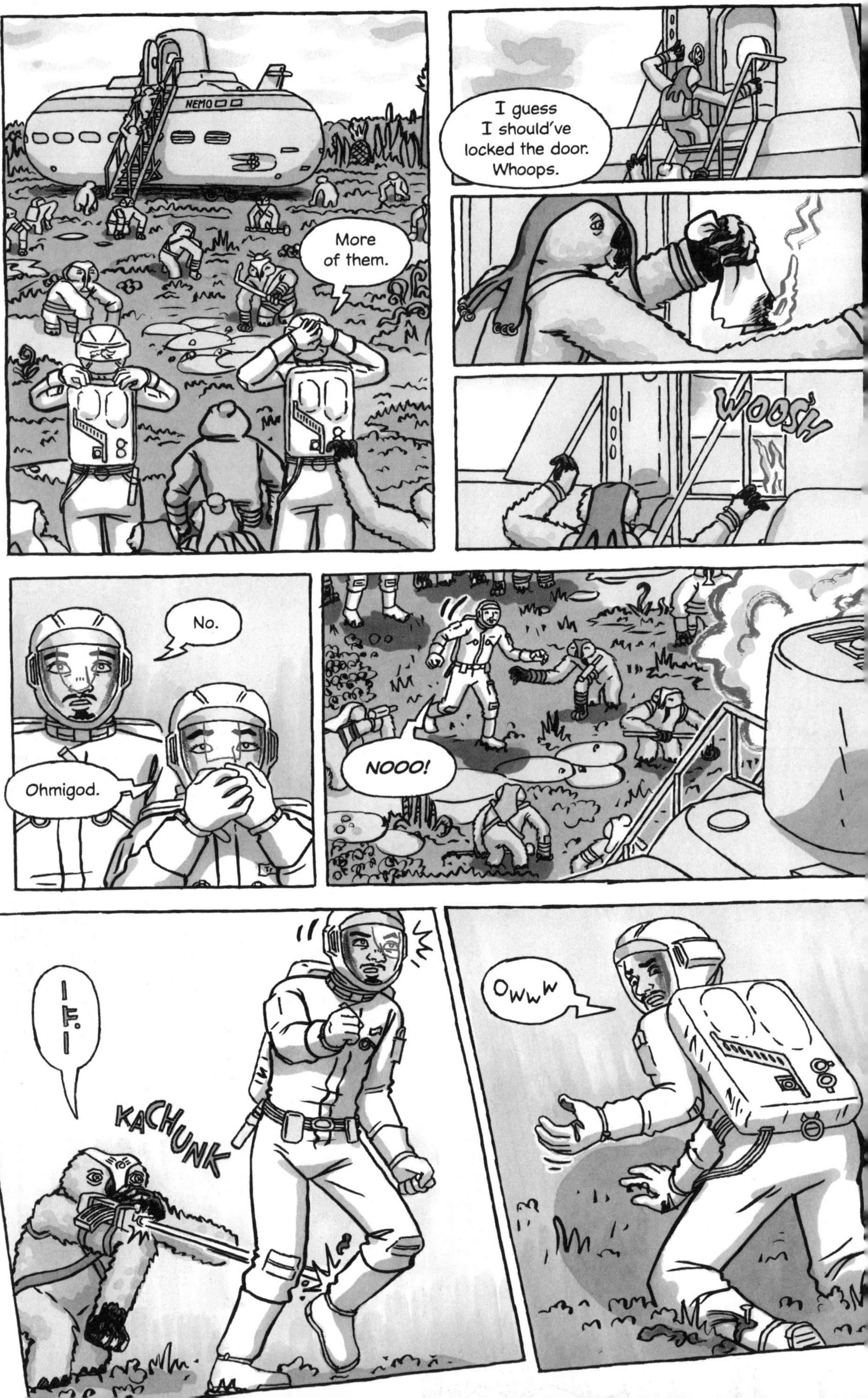
NEMO
More of them.
I guess I should've locked the door. Whoops.
WOOSH
No.
Ohmigod.
NOOO!
KACHUNK
Owww

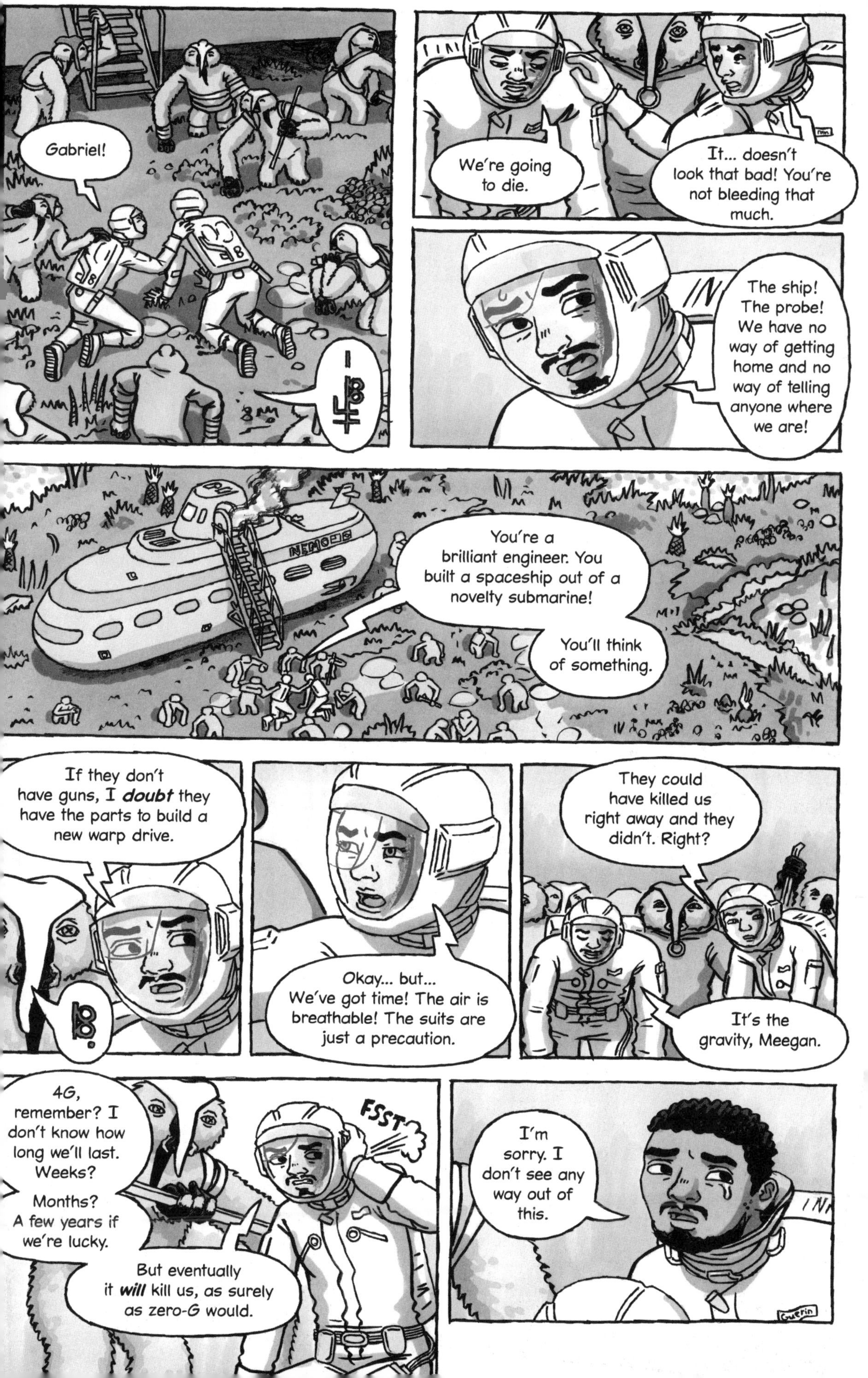
Gabriel!
We're going to die.
It... doesn't look that bad! You're not bleeding that much.
The ship! The probe! We have no way of getting home and no way of telling anyone where we are!
You're a brilliant engineer. You built a spaceship out of a novelty submarine!
You'll think of something.
If they don't have guns, I *doubt* they have the parts to build a new warp drive.
Okay... but... We've got time! The air is breathable! The suits are just a precaution.
They could have killed us right away and they didn't. Right?
It's the gravity, Meegan.
4G, remember? I don't know how long we'll last. Weeks?
Months? A few years if we're lucky.
But eventually it ***will*** kill us, as surely as zero-G would.
FSST
I'm sorry. I don't see any way out of this.
Guerin

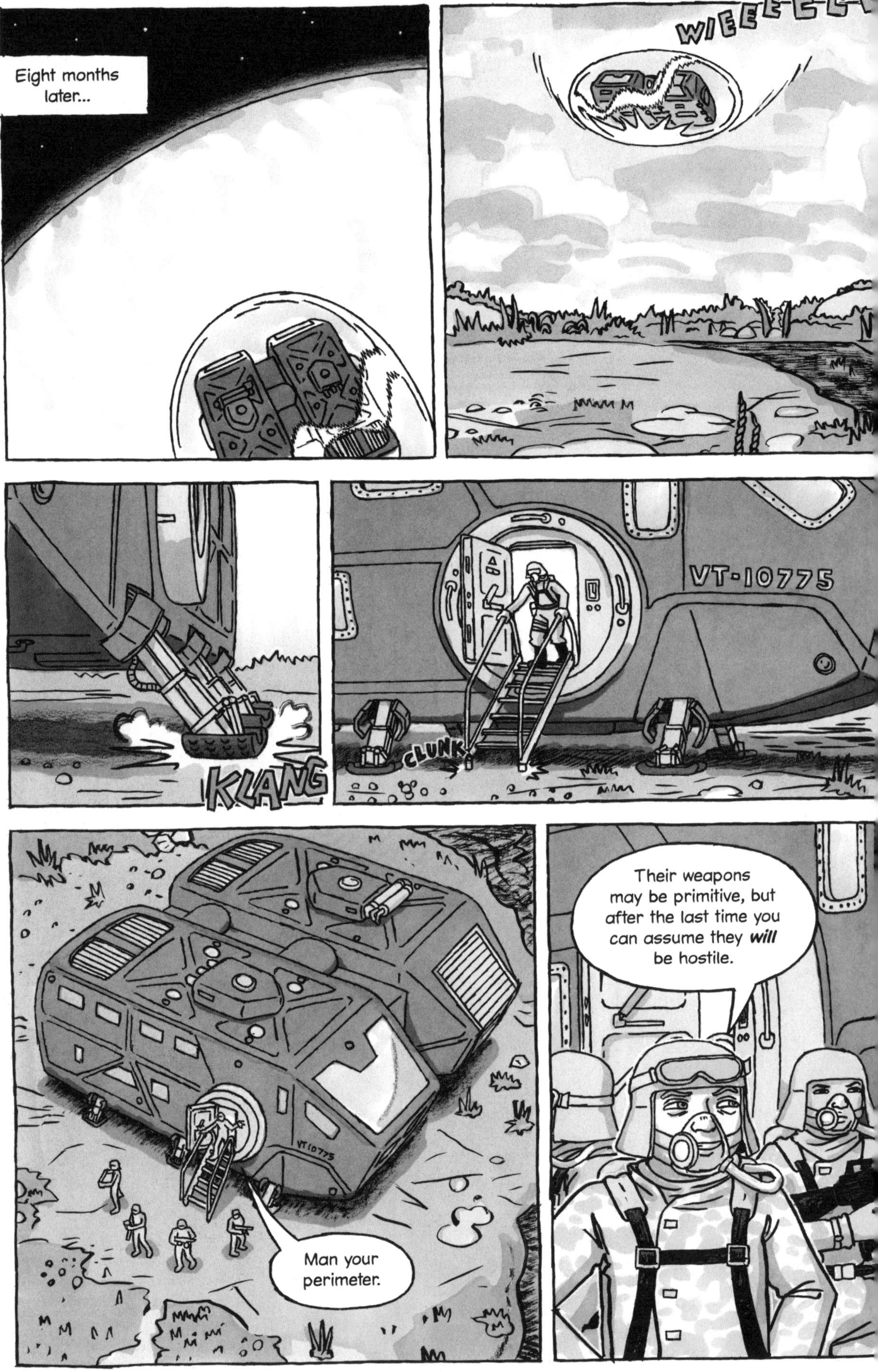
Eight months later...
WIEEEEE
KLANG
VT-10775
CLUNK
Man your perimeter.
Their weapons may be primitive, but after the last time you can assume they *will* be hostile.

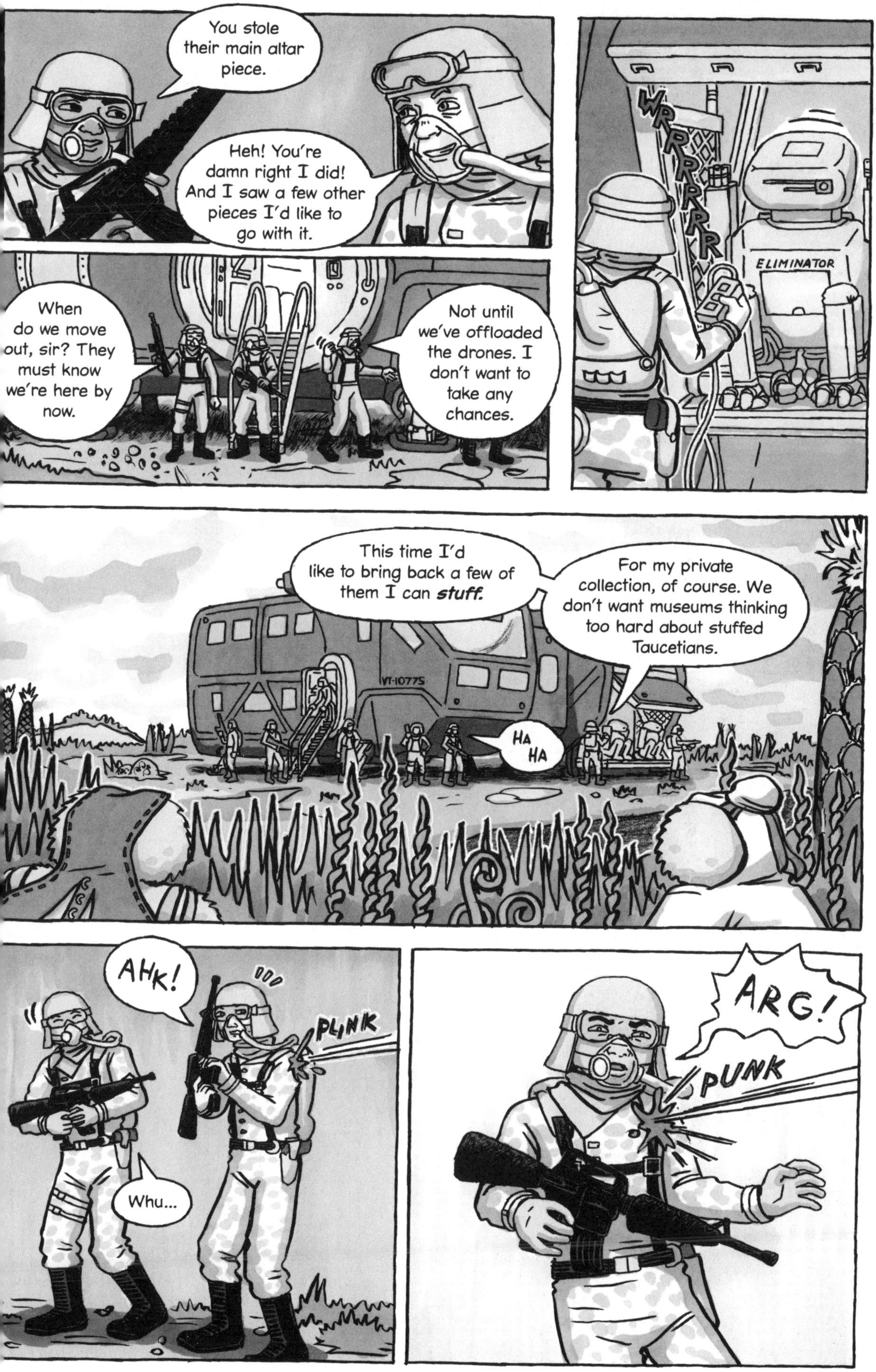
You stole their main altar piece.
Heh! You're damn right I did! And I saw a few other pieces I'd like to go with it.
WRRRRRRR
ELIMINATOR
When do we move out, sir? They must know we're here by now.
Not until we've offloaded the drones. I don't want to take any chances.
This time I'd like to bring back a few of them I can *stuff.*
For my private collection, of course. We don't want museums thinking too hard about stuffed Taucetians.
VT-1077S
HA HA
AHK!
PLINK
Whu...
ARG!
PUNK

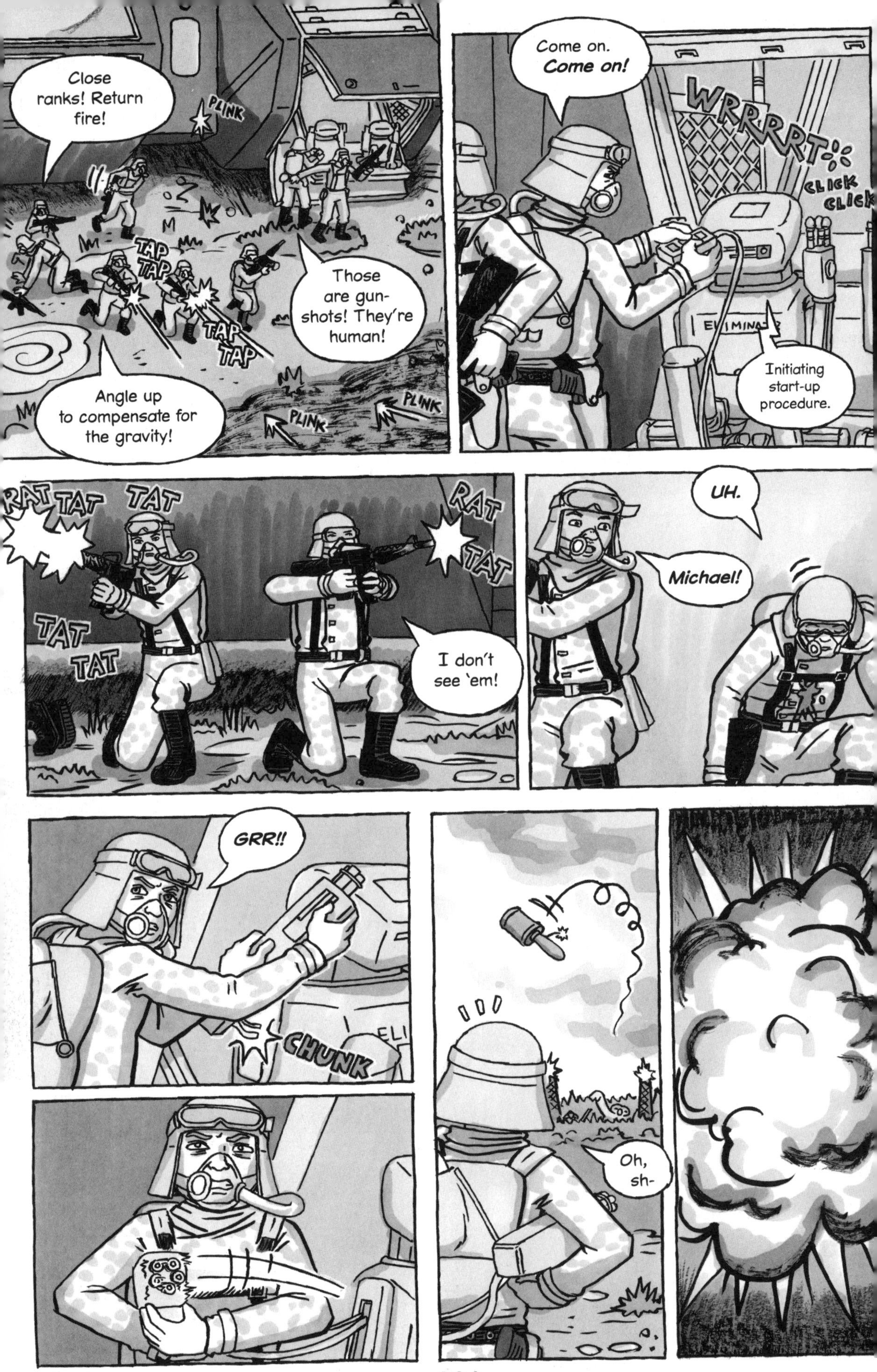
Close ranks! Return fire!
PLINK
TAP TAP
TAP TAP
Those are gun-shots! They're human!
Angle up to compensate for the gravity!
PLINK
PLINK
Come on. **Come on!**
WRRRRRT
CLICK CLICK
Initiating start-up procedure.
RAT TAT TAT
RAT TAT
TAT TAT
I don't see 'em!
UH.
Michael!
GRR!!
CHUNK
Oh, sh-

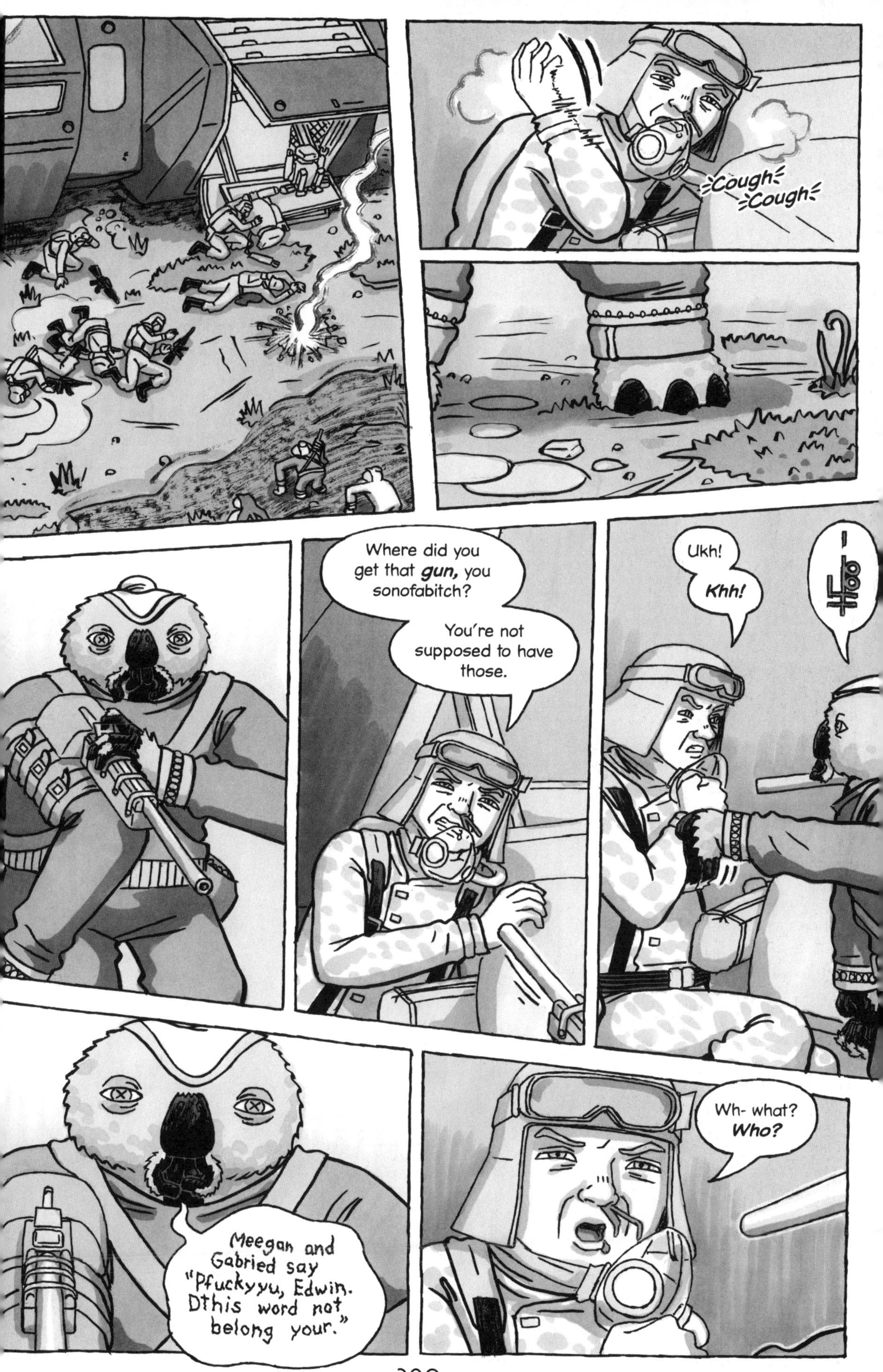
Cough
Cough
Where did you get that gun, you sonofabitch?
You're not supposed to have those.
Ukh!
Khh!
Meegan and Gabried say "Pfuckyyu, Edwin. Dthis word not belong your."
Wh- what? Who?

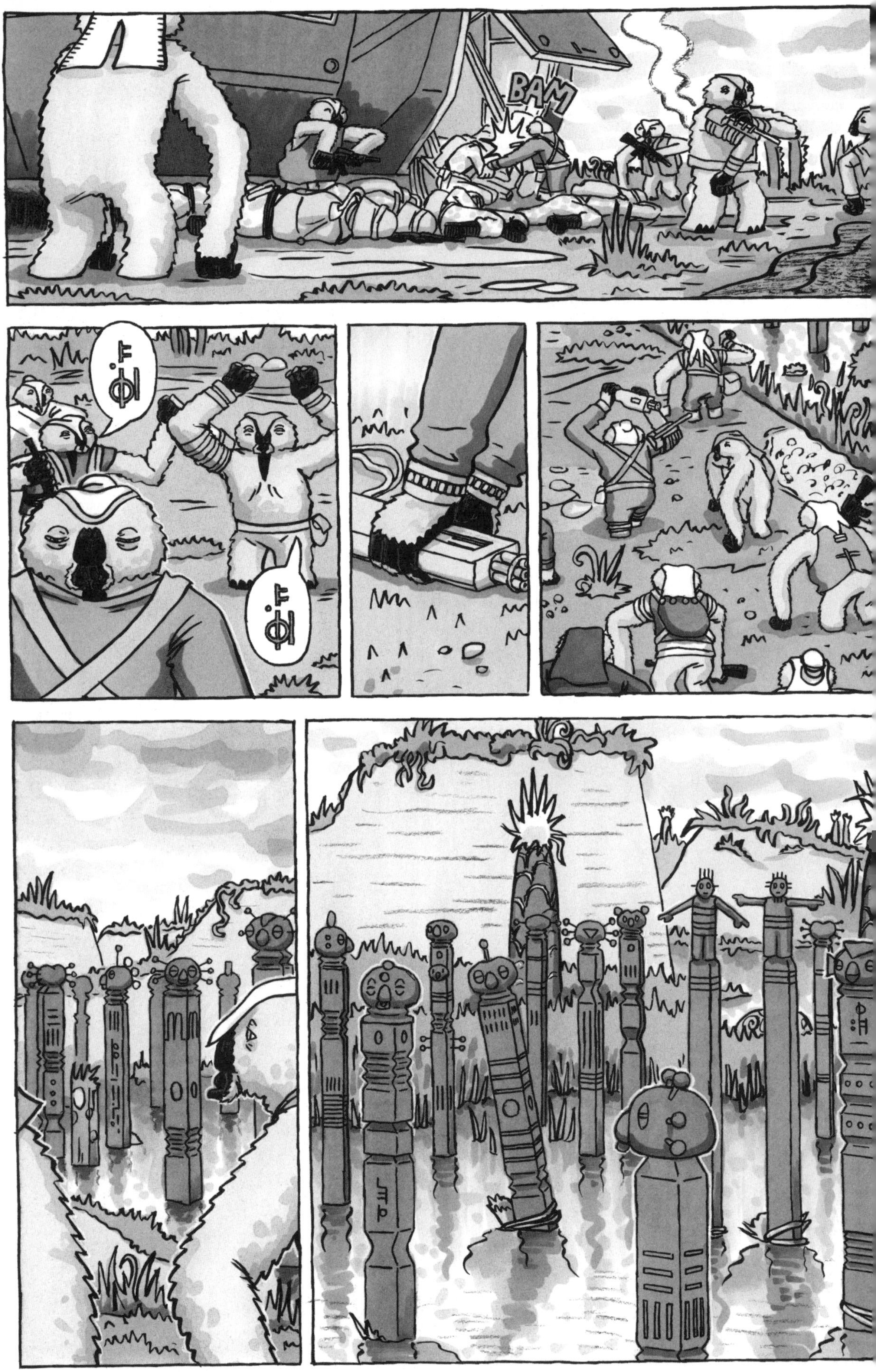
BAM

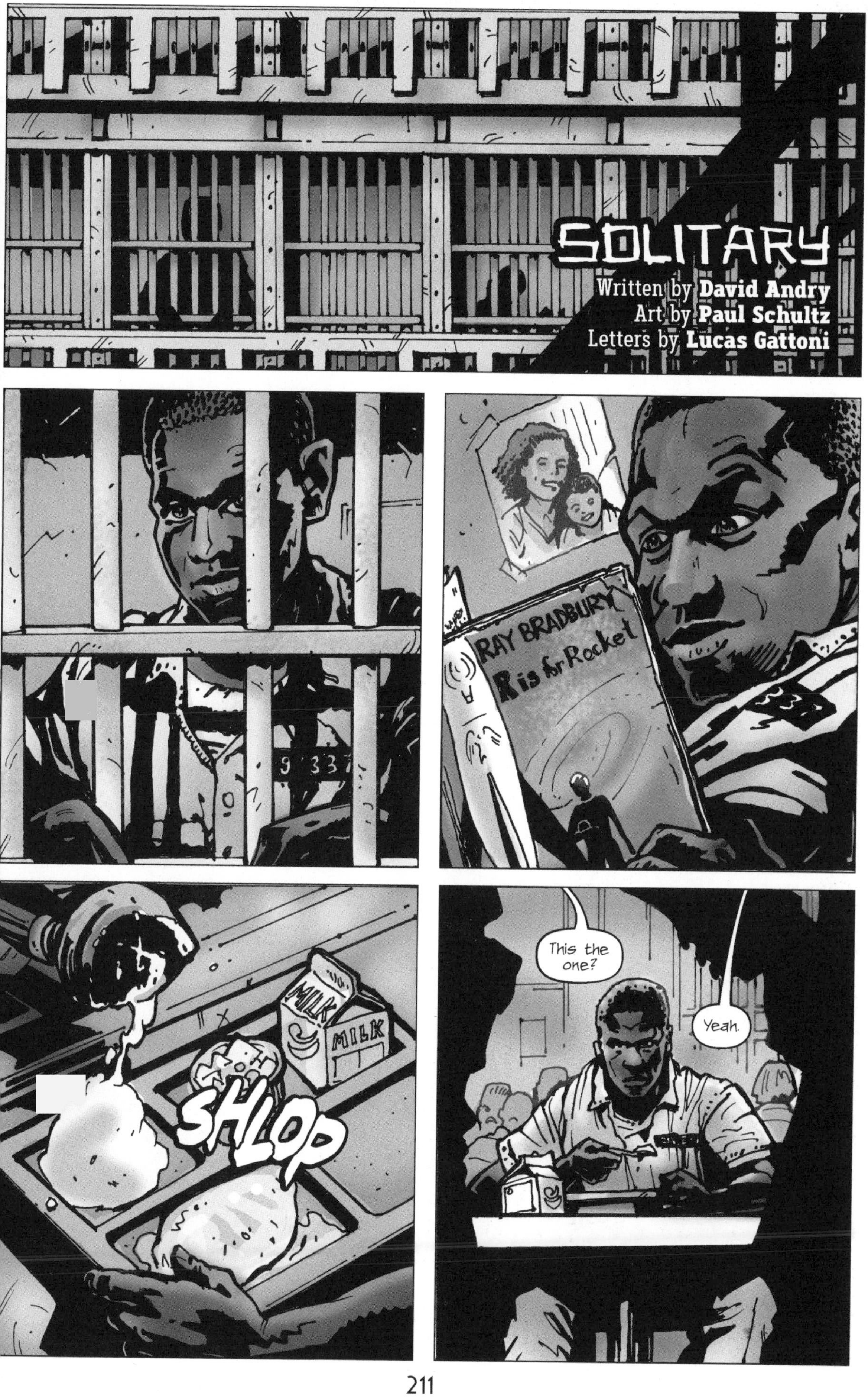
SOLITARY
Written by David Andry
Art by Paul Schultz
Letters by Lucas Gattoni
9337
RAY BRADBURY
R is for Rocket
MILK
MILK
SHLOP
This the one?
Yeah.

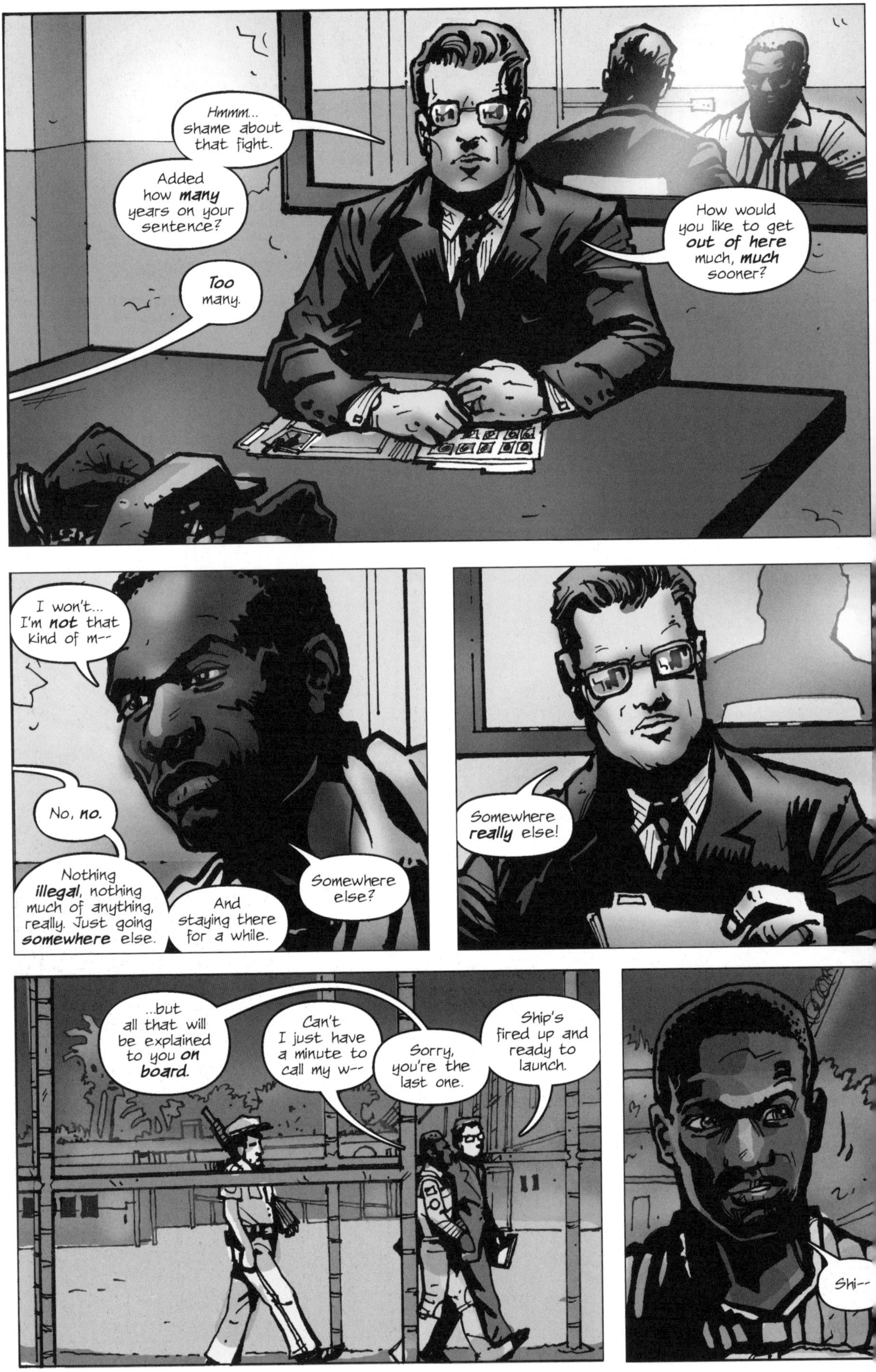
Hmmm... shame about that fight.
Added how many years on your sentence?
Too many.
How would you like to get out of here much, much sooner?
I won't... I'm not that kind of m--
No, no.
Nothing illegal, nothing much of anything, really. Just going somewhere else.
And staying there for a while.
Somewhere else?
Somewhere really else!
...but all that will be explained to you on board.
Can't I just have a minute to call my w--
Sorry, you're the last one.
Ship's fired up and ready to launch.
Shi--

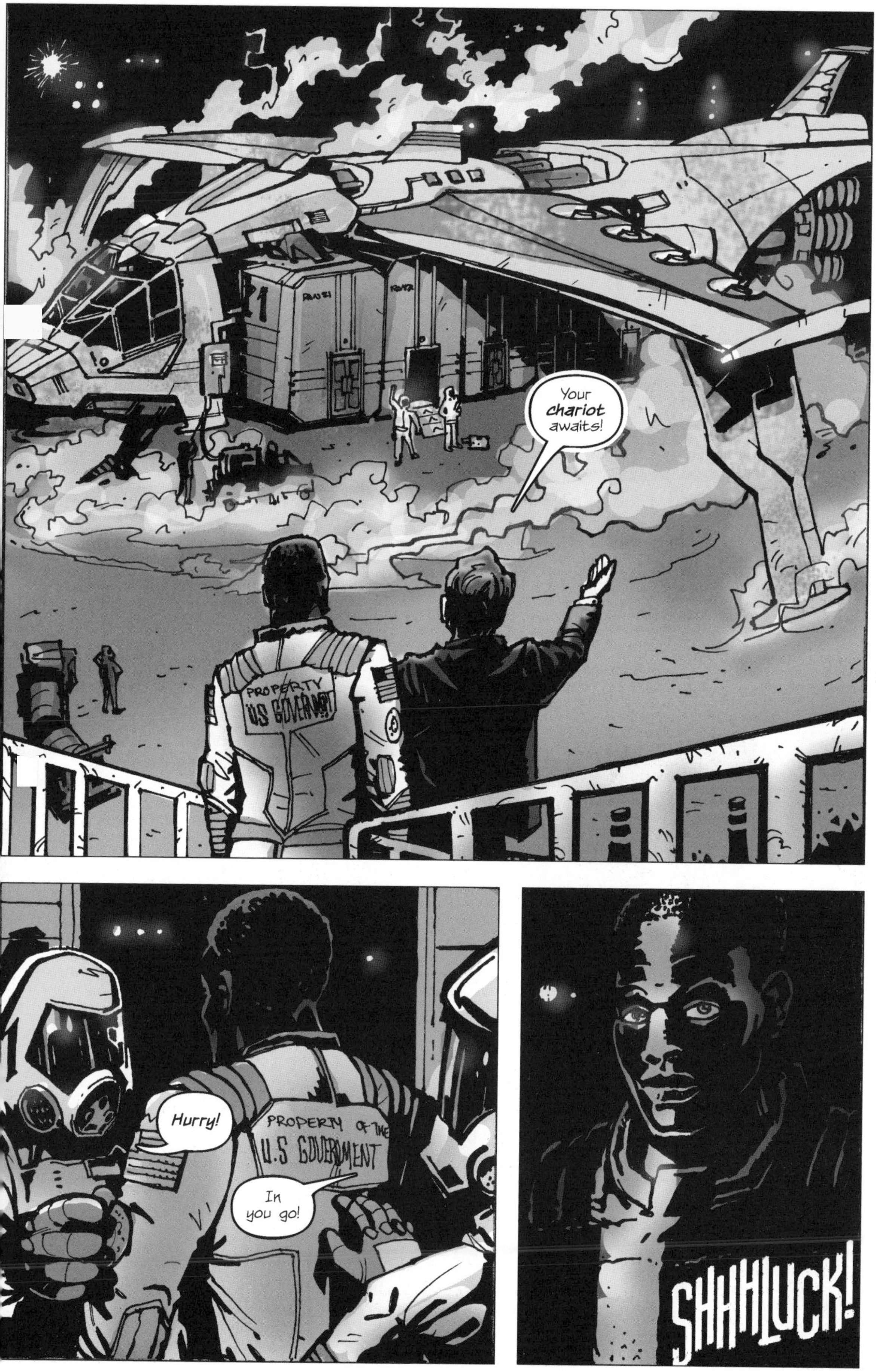
Your chariot awaits!
PROPERTY
Hurry!
PROPERTY OF THE
U.S GOVERNMENT
In you go!
SHHHLUCK!

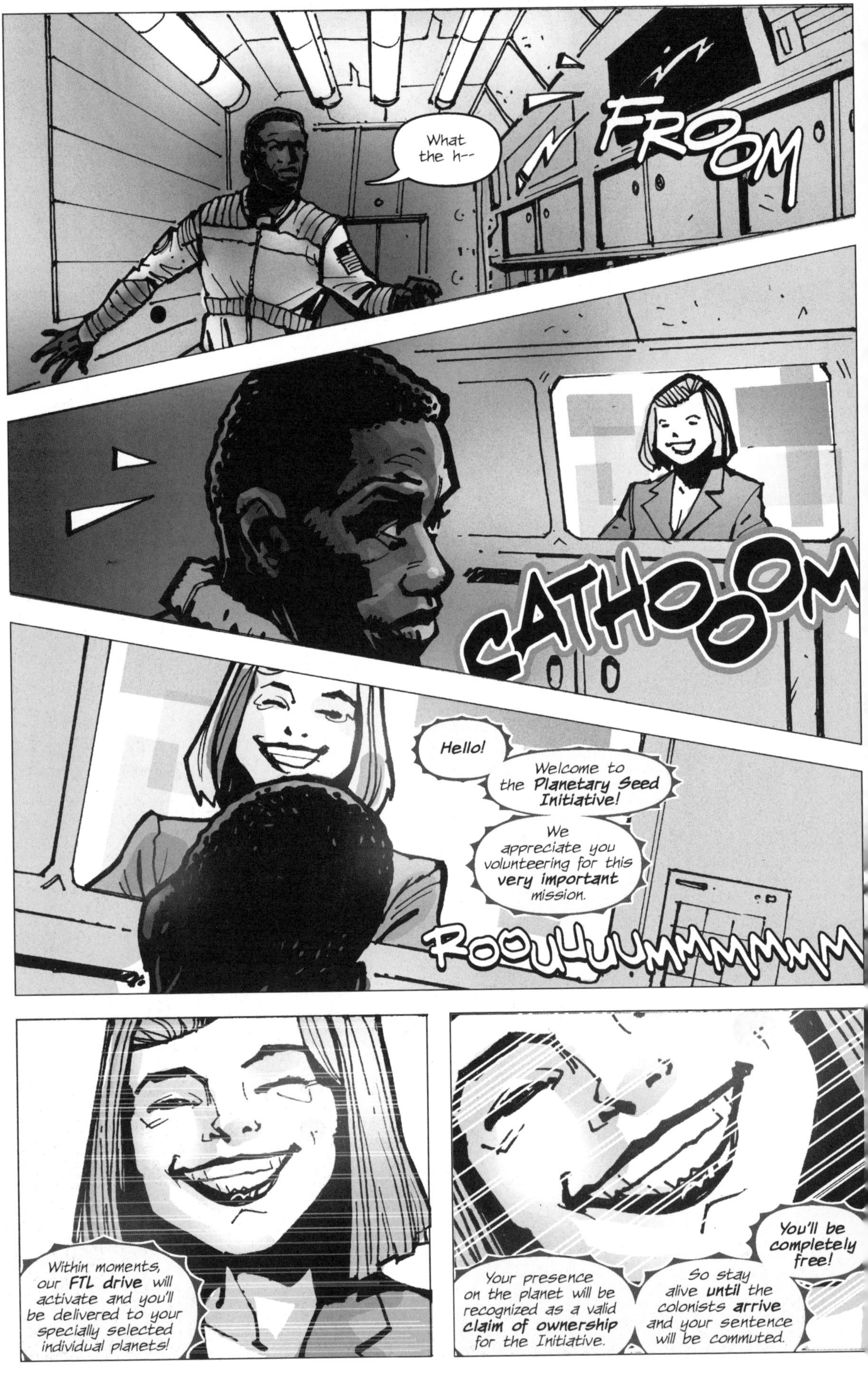
What the h--
FROOM
CATHOOOOM
Hello!
Welcome to the Planetary Seed Initiative!
We appreciate you volunteering for this very important mission.
ROOUUUUMMMMMMM
Within moments, our FTL drive will activate and you'll be delivered to your specially selected individual planets!
Your presence on the planet will be recognized as a valid claim of ownership for the Initiative.
So stay alive until the colonists arrive and your sentence will be commuted.
You'll be completely free!

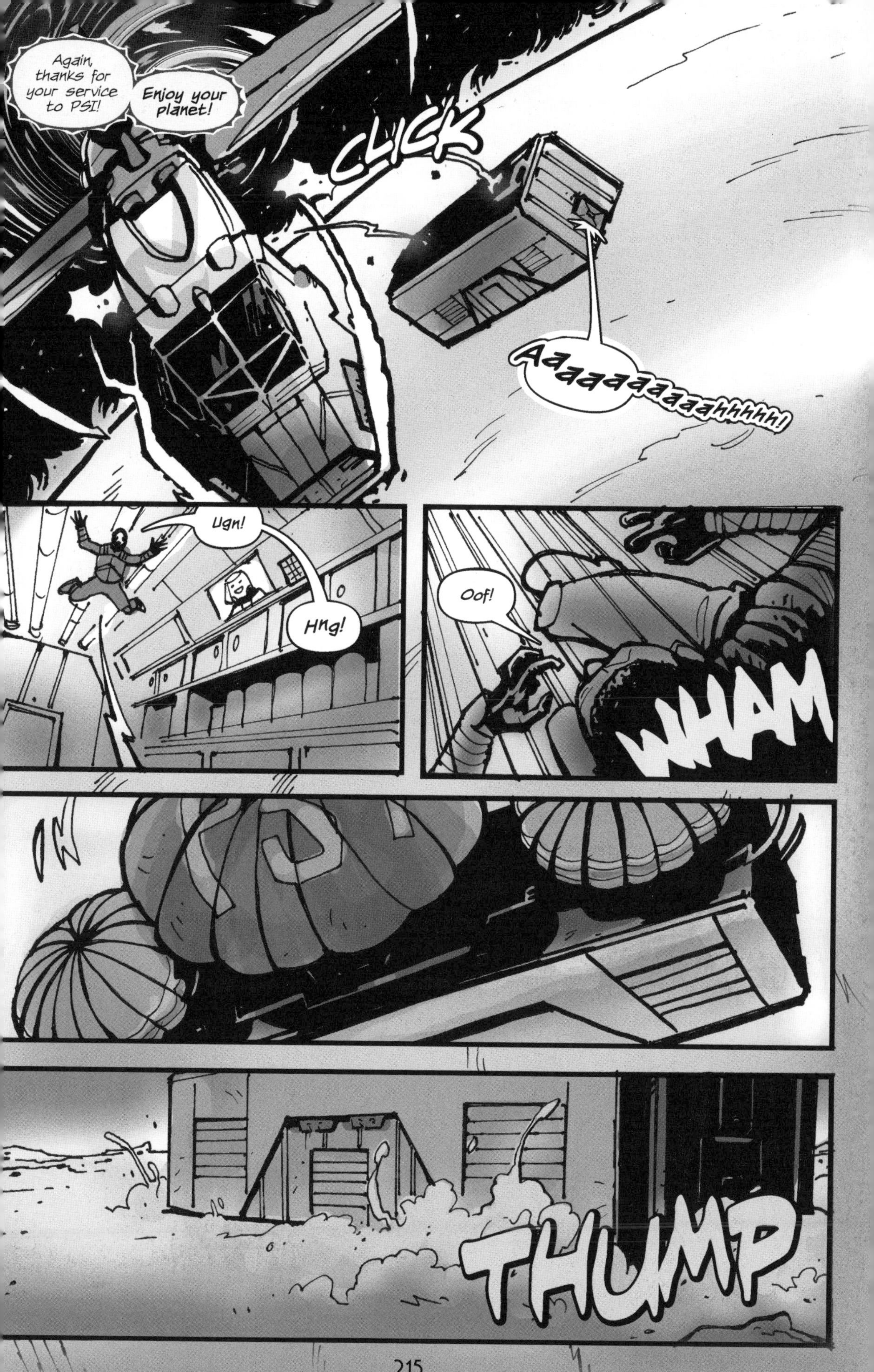
Again, thanks for your service to PSI!
Enjoy your planet!
CLICK
Aaaaaaaaaaaaahhhhh!
Ugn!
Hng!
Oof!
WHAM
THUMP

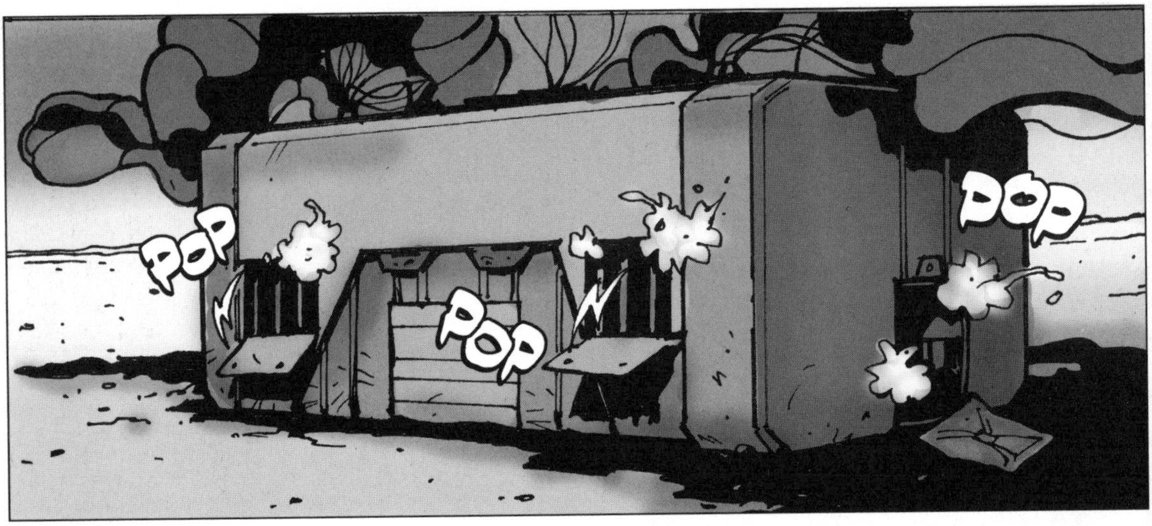
POP
POP
POP

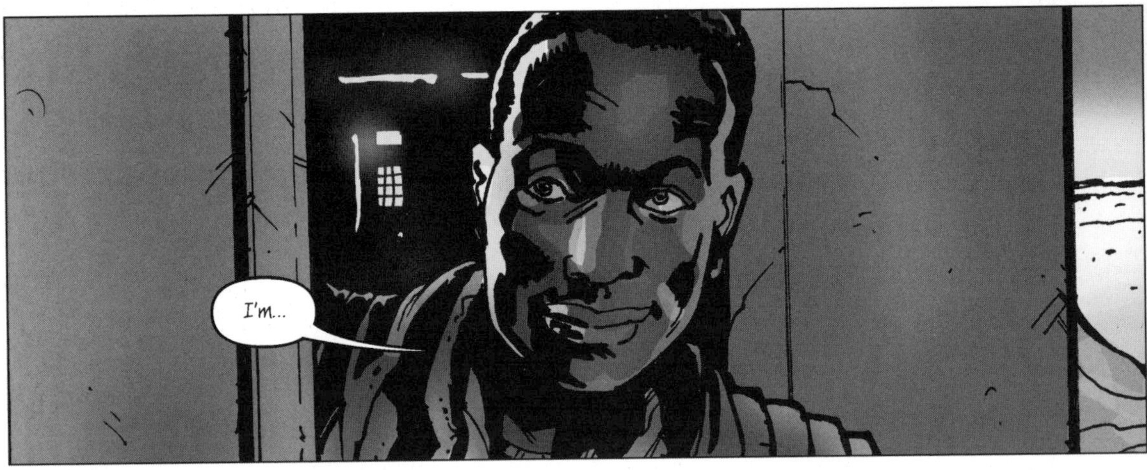
I'm..

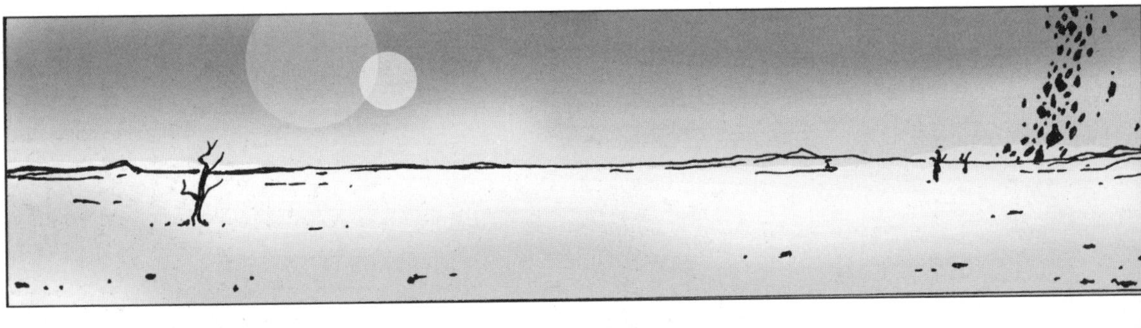

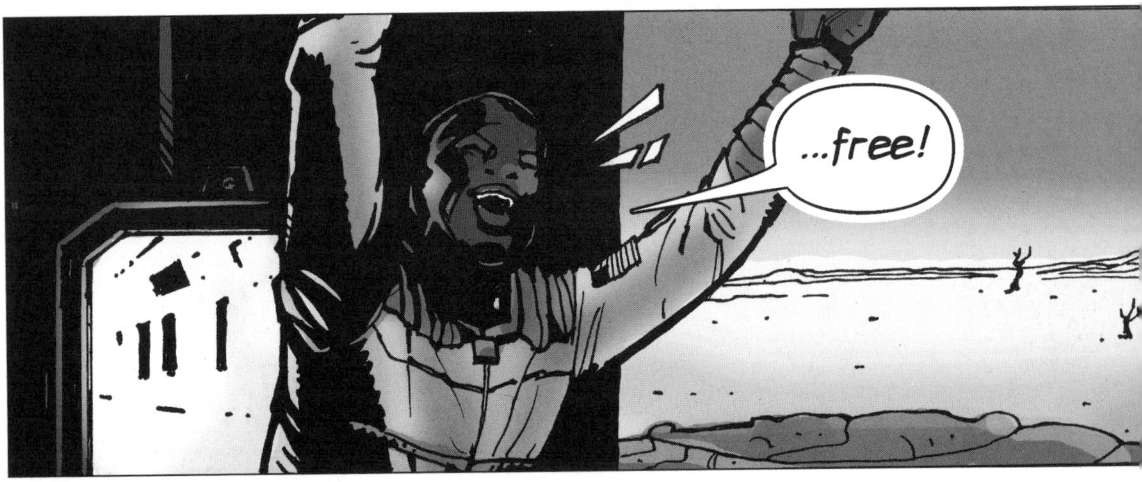
...free!

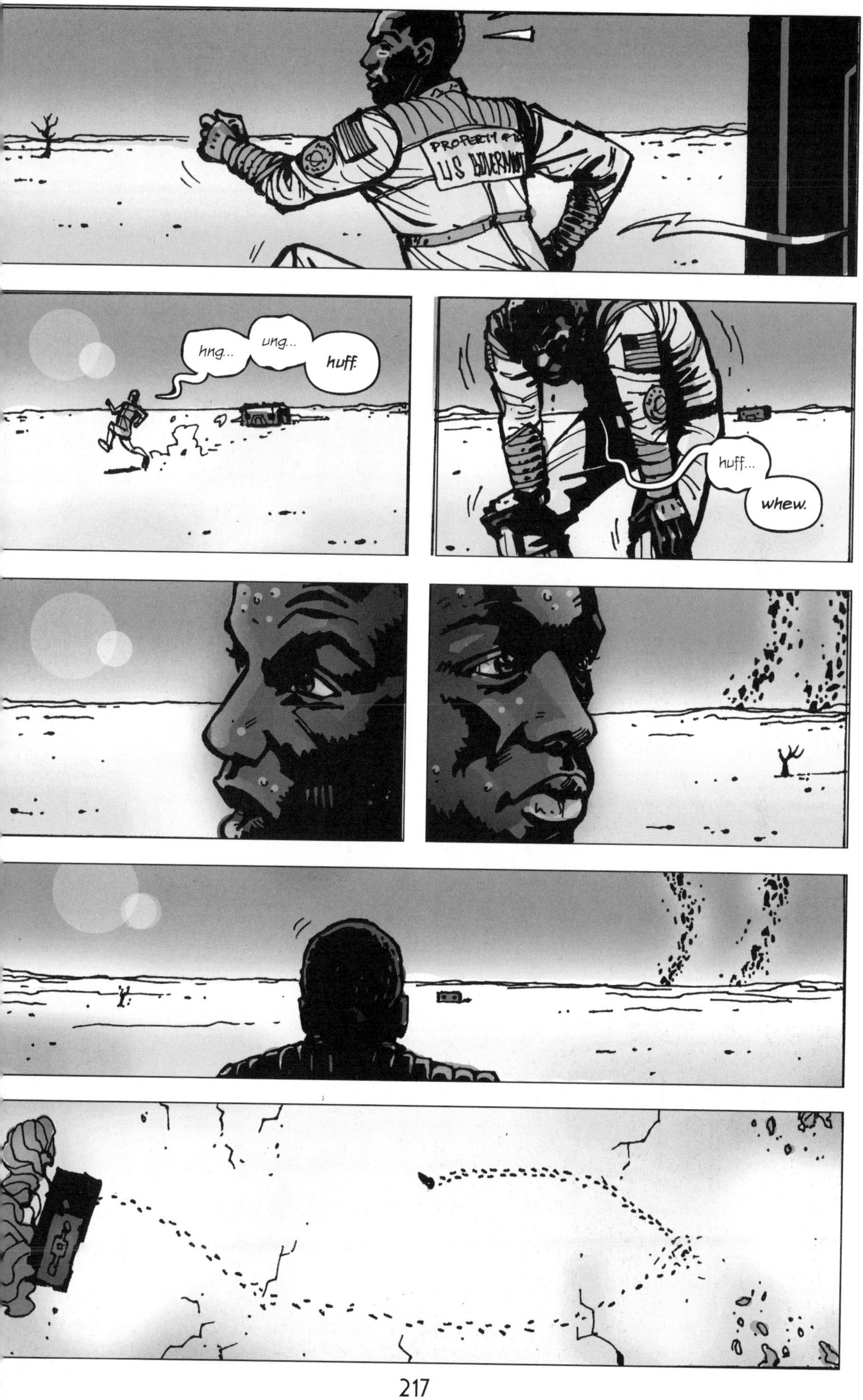
hng...
ung...
huff.
huff...
whew.

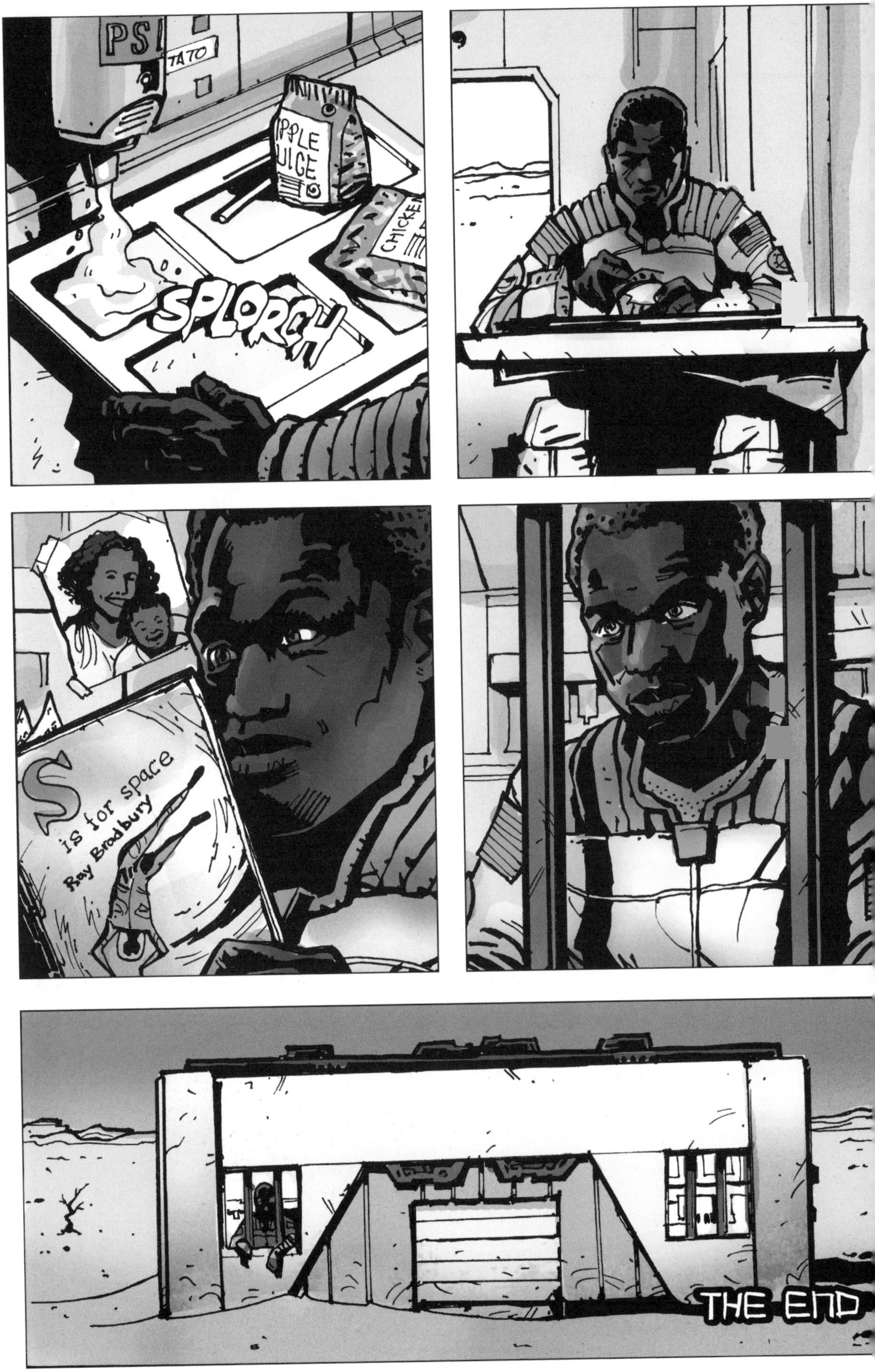
SPLORCH
CHICKEN
S is for space
Ray Bradbury
THE END

Granddad's Second Wife Cheez Hayama and Earl T. Roske

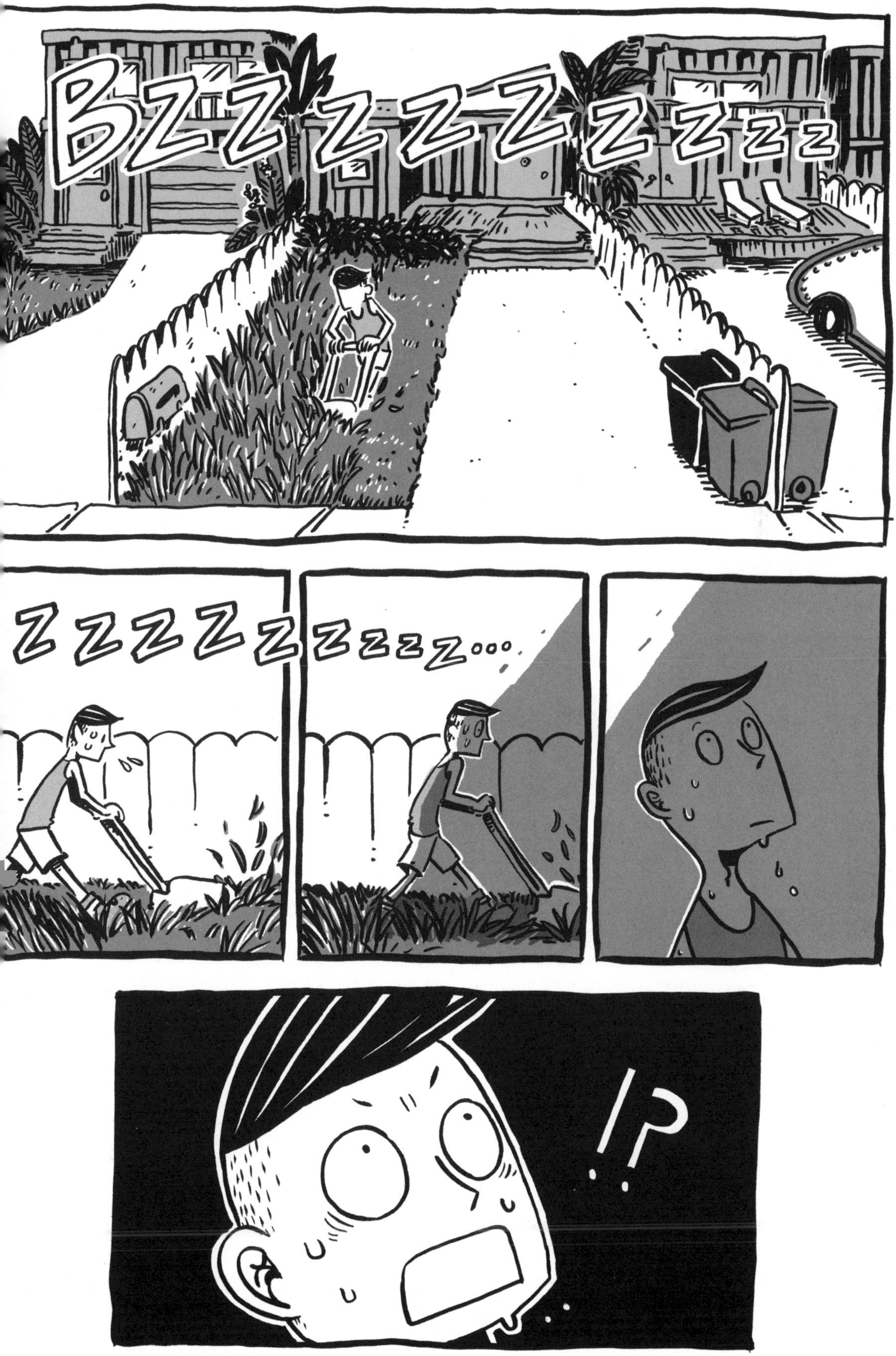
BZZZZZZZZZ
ZZZZZZZZZ...
!?

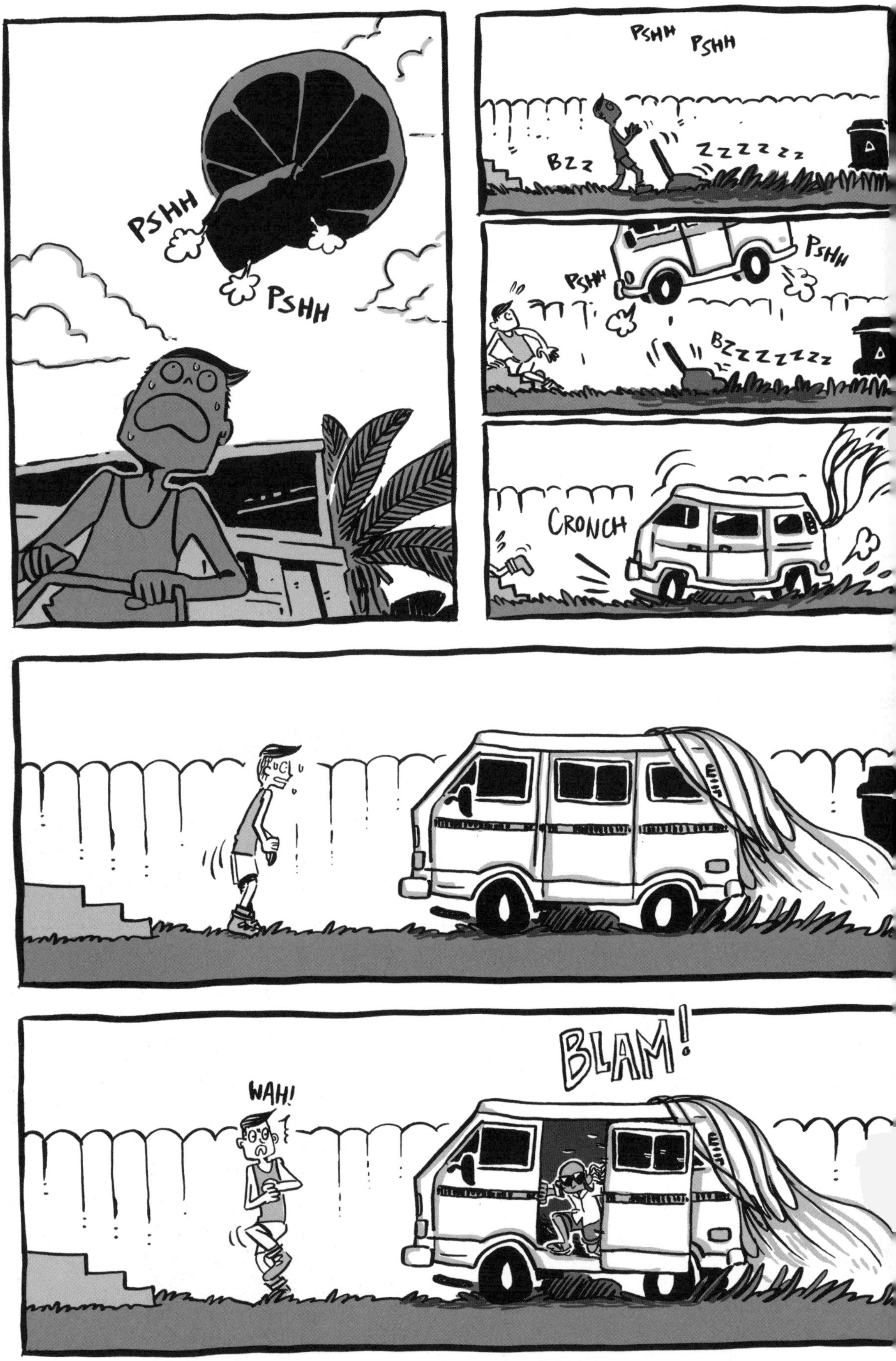
PSHH
PSHH
PSHH PSHH
BZZ
ZZZZZZZ
PSHH
PSHH
BZZZZZZZZ
CRONCH
WAH!
BLAM!

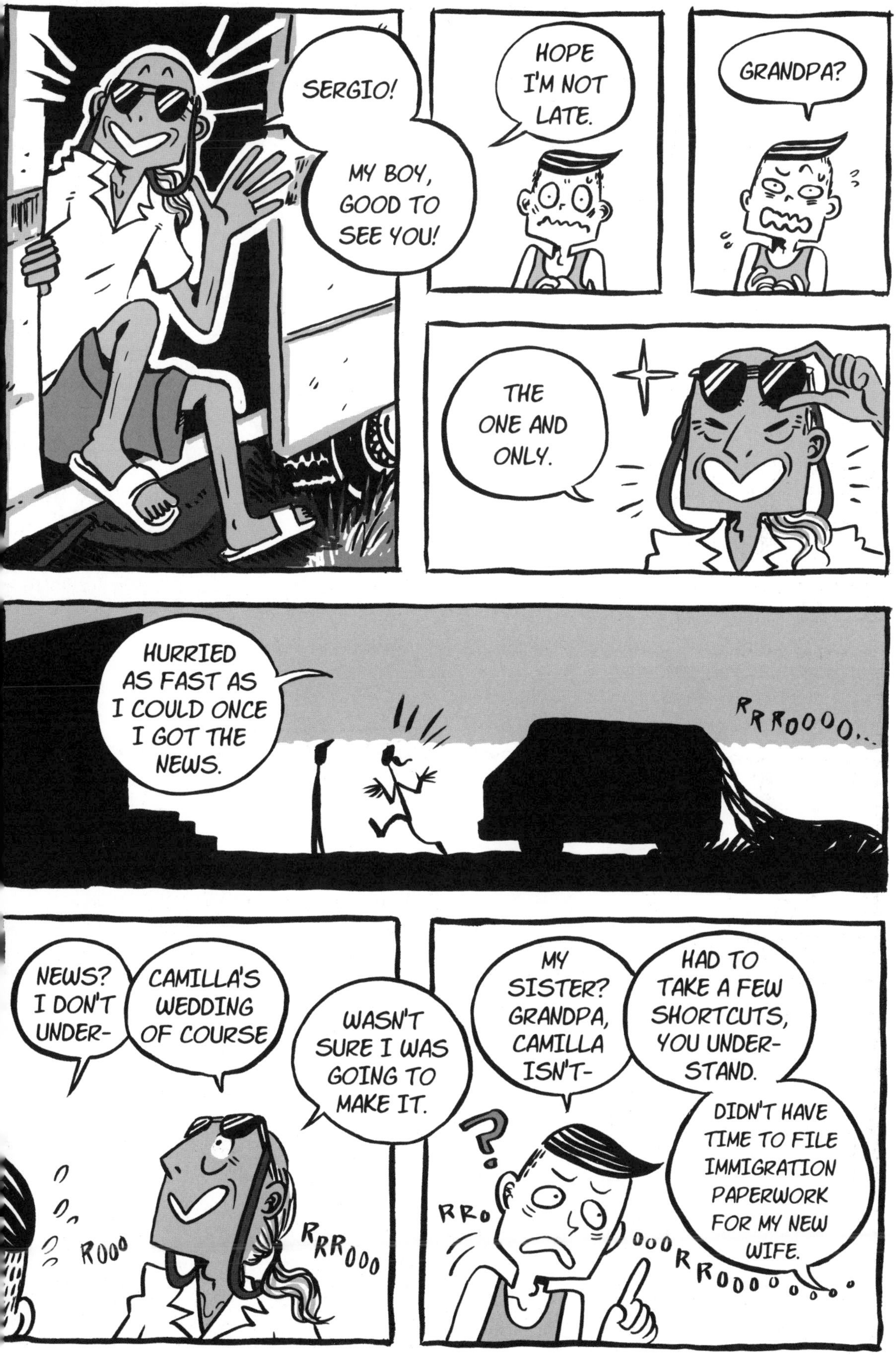
SERGIO!
MY BOY, GOOD TO SEE YOU!
HOPE I'M NOT LATE.
GRANDPA?
THE ONE AND ONLY.
HURRIED AS FAST AS I COULD ONCE I GOT THE NEWS.
RRROOOO...
NEWS? I DON'T UNDER-
CAMILLA'S WEDDING OF COURSE
WASN'T SURE I WAS GOING TO MAKE IT.
ROOO
RRROOO
MY SISTER? GRANDPA, CAMILLA ISN'T-
HAD TO TAKE A FEW SHORTCUTS, YOU UNDERSTAND.
DIDN'T HAVE TIME TO FILE IMMIGRATION PAPERWORK FOR MY NEW WIFE.
?
RRO
OOORROOOOOOOOO

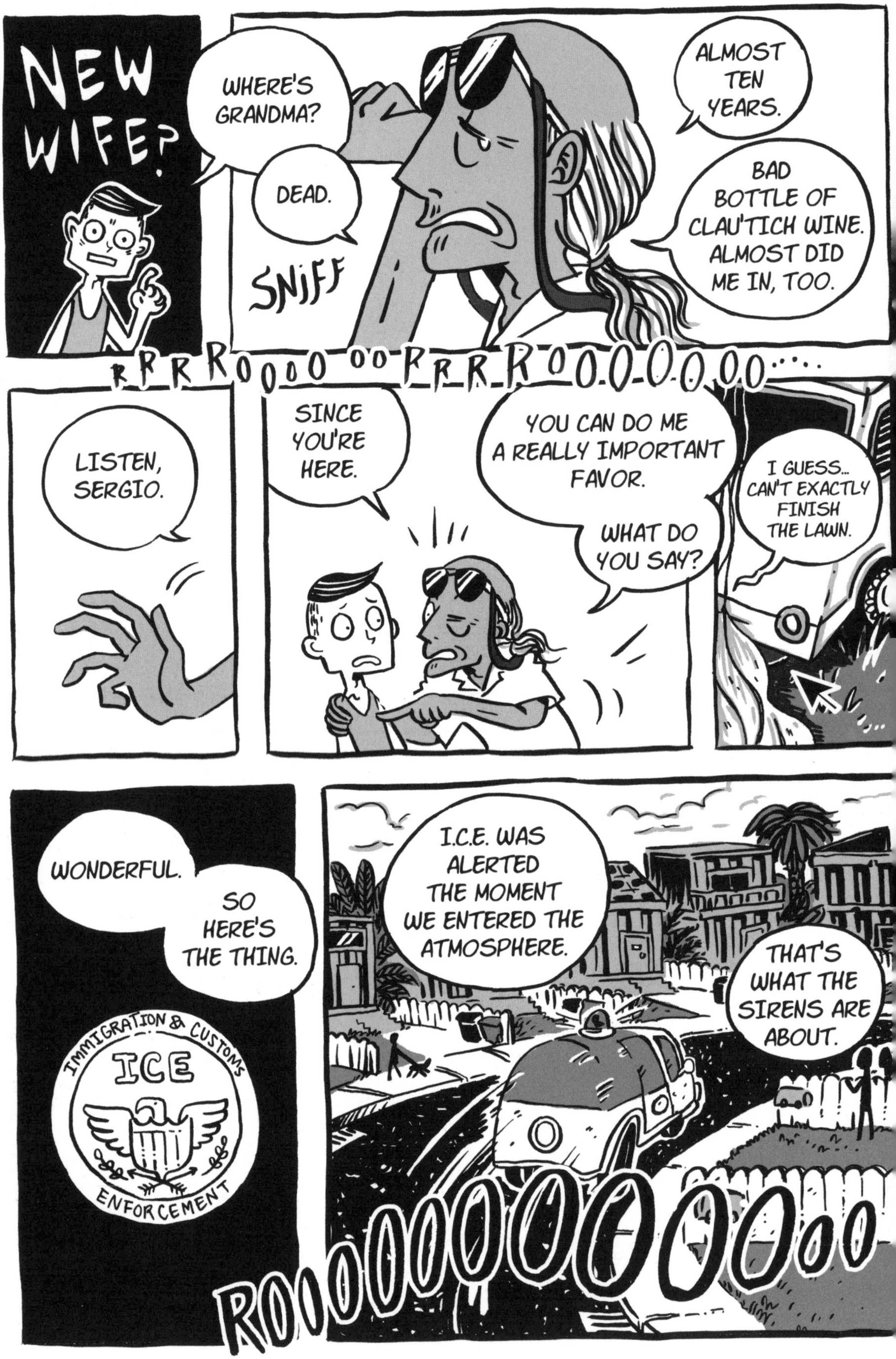
NEW WIFE?
WHERE'S GRANDMA?
DEAD.
SNIFF
ALMOST TEN YEARS.
BAD BOTTLE OF CLAU'TICH WINE. ALMOST DID ME IN, TOO.
RRRROOOO OO RRRROOOOOOO.....
LISTEN, SERGIO.
SINCE YOU'RE HERE.
YOU CAN DO ME A REALLY IMPORTANT FAVOR.
WHAT DO YOU SAY?
I GUESS... CAN'T EXACTLY FINISH THE LAWN.
WONDERFUL.
SO HERE'S THE THING.
IMMIGRATION & CUSTOMS ICE ENFORCEMENT
I.C.E. WAS ALERTED THE MOMENT WE ENTERED THE ATMOSPHERE.
THAT'S WHAT THE SIRENS ARE ABOUT.
ROOOOOOOOOOOOOOoo

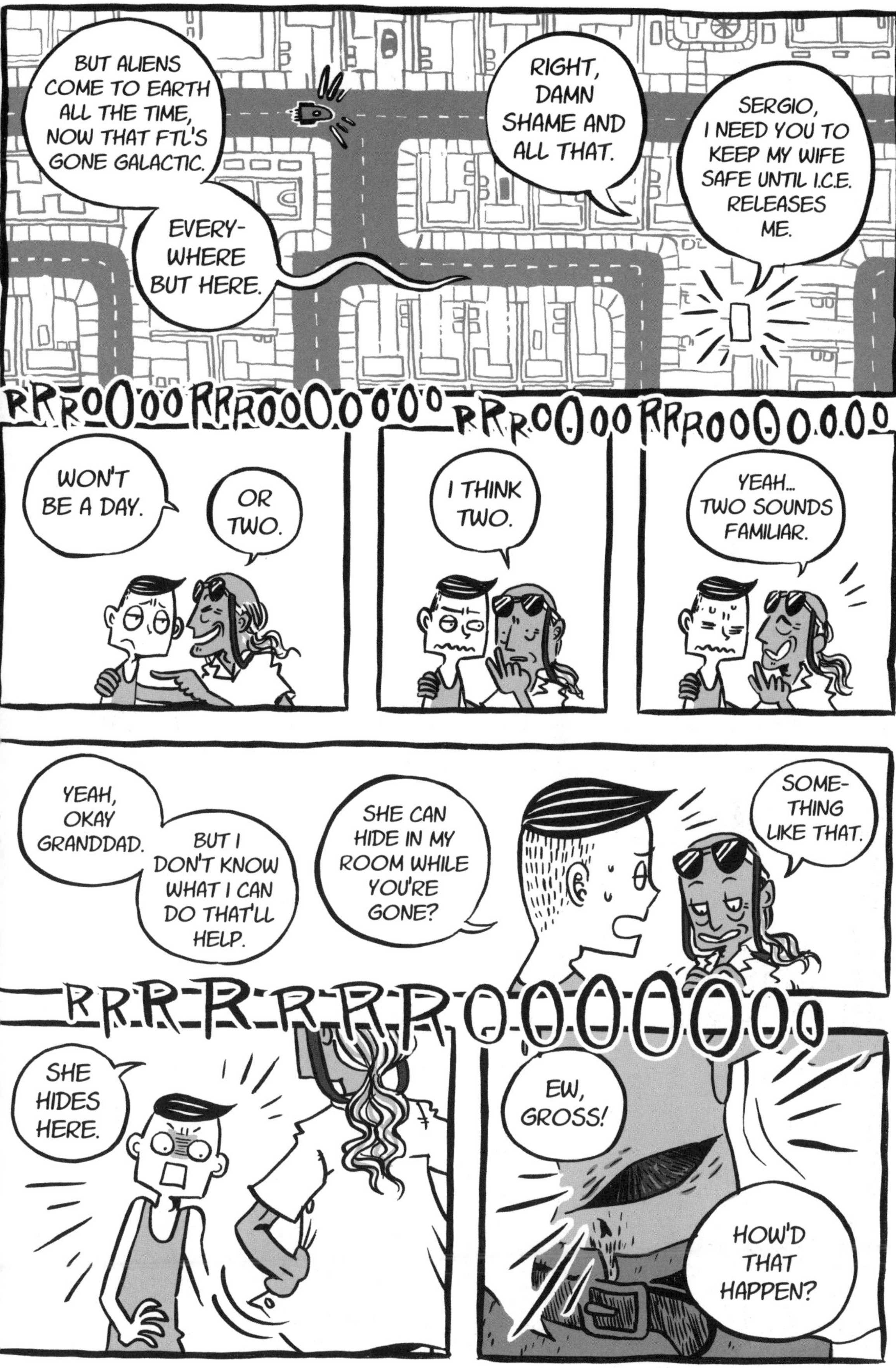
BUT ALIENS COME TO EARTH ALL THE TIME, NOW THAT FTL'S GONE GALACTIC.
EVERY-WHERE BUT HERE.
RIGHT, DAMN SHAME AND ALL THAT.
SERGIO, I NEED YOU TO KEEP MY WIFE SAFE UNTIL I.C.E. RELEASES ME.
RRROOOOORRROOOOOOO RRROOOOORRROOOOOO
WON'T BE A DAY.
OR TWO.
I THINK TWO.
YEAH... TWO SOUNDS FAMILIAR.
YEAH, OKAY GRANDDAD.
BUT I DON'T KNOW WHAT I CAN DO THAT'LL HELP.
SHE CAN HIDE IN MY ROOM WHILE YOU'RE GONE?
SOME-THING LIKE THAT.
RRRRRRROOOOOOO
SHE HIDES HERE.
EW, GROSS!
HOW'D THAT HAPPEN?

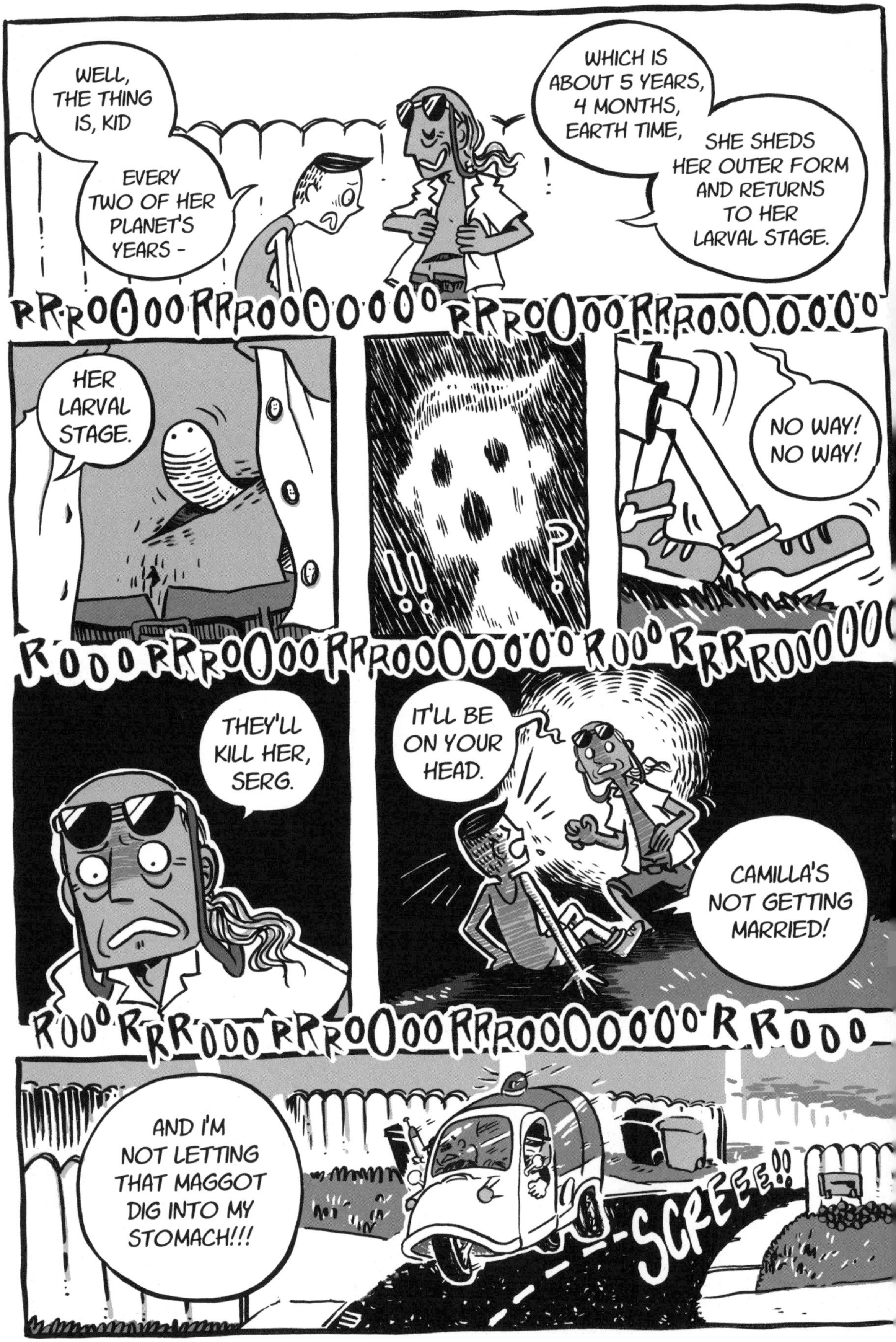
WELL, THE THING IS, KID
EVERY TWO OF HER PLANET'S YEARS -
WHICH IS ABOUT 5 YEARS, 4 MONTHS, EARTH TIME,
SHE SHEDS HER OUTER FORM AND RETURNS TO HER LARVAL STAGE.
RRROOOOORRROOOOOOO RRROOOOORRROOOOOO
HER LARVAL STAGE.
!! ?
NO WAY! NO WAY!
ROOOORRROOOOORRROOOOOOOOROOOORRROOOOO
THEY'LL KILL HER, SERG.
IT'LL BE ON YOUR HEAD.
CAMILLA'S NOT GETTING MARRIED!
ROOORRROOORRROOOOORRROOOOOOOORROOO
AND I'M NOT LETTING THAT MAGGOT DIG INTO MY STOMACH!!!
SCREEEE!!

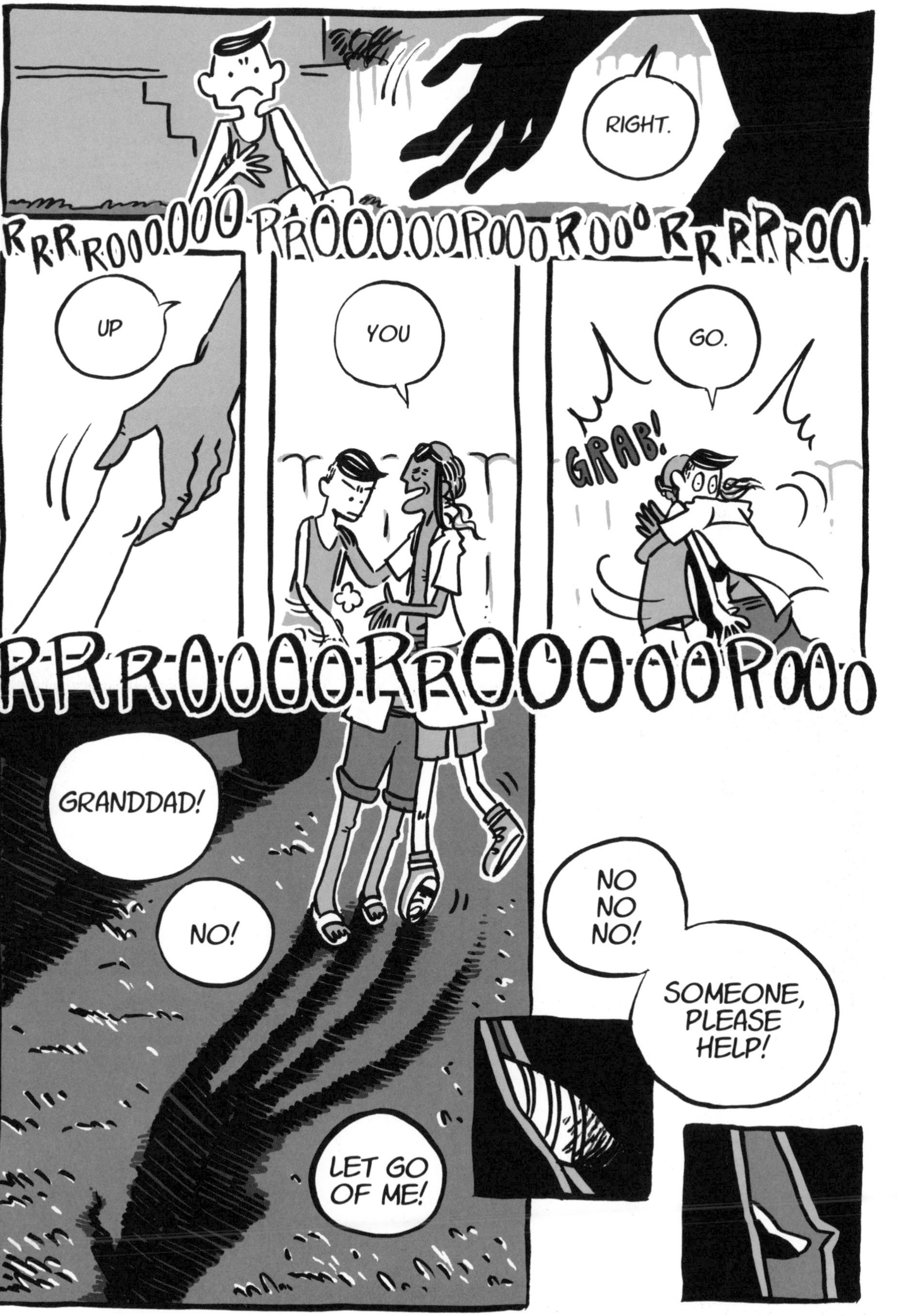
RIGHT.
RRRROOOOOORROOOOOROOOROOORRRRROO
UP
YOU
GO.
GRAB!
RRRROOOORROOOOOOROOO
GRANDDAD!
NO!
NO NO NO!
SOMEONE, PLEASE HELP!
LET GO OF ME!

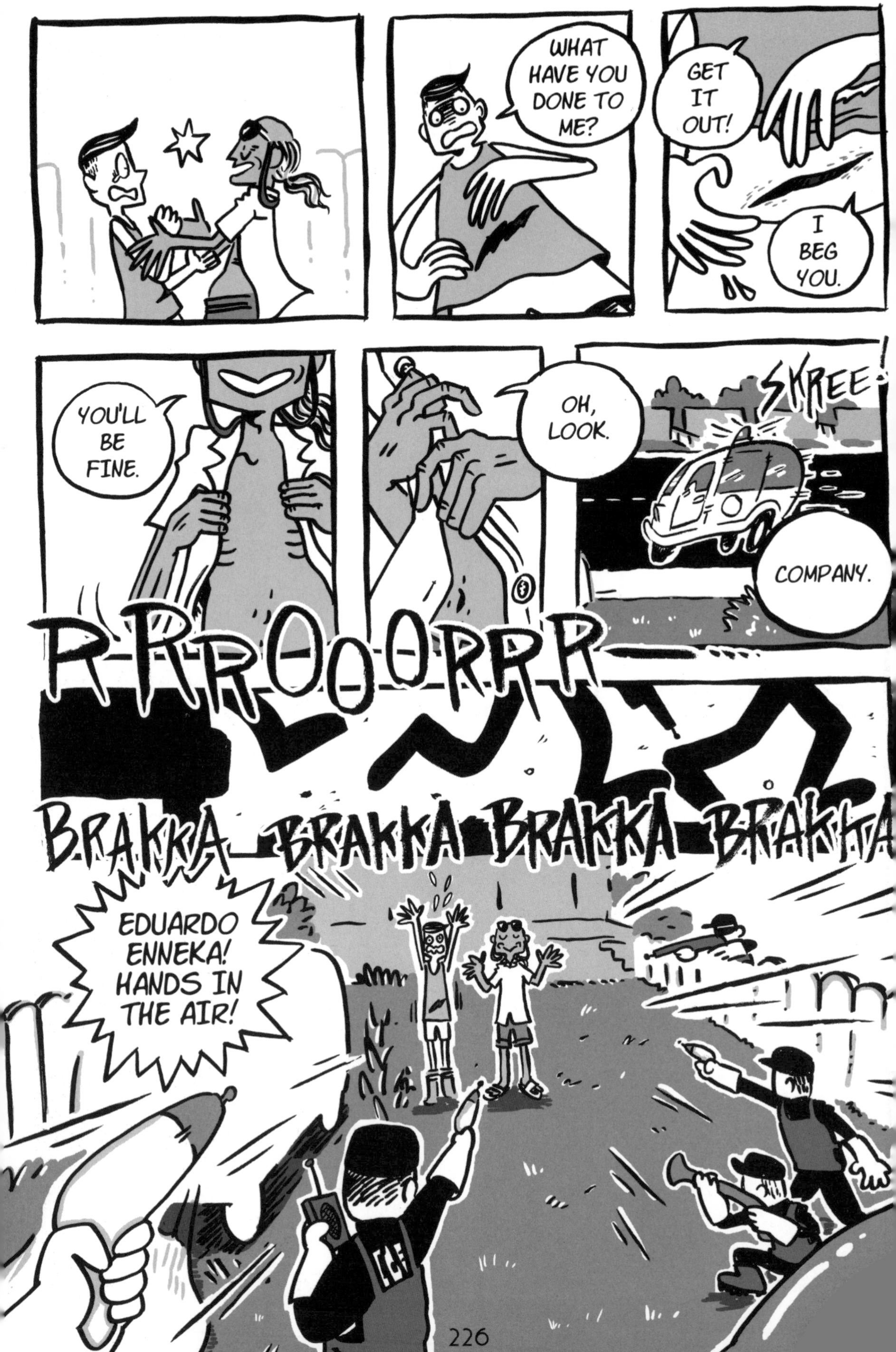
WHAT HAVE YOU DONE TO ME?
GET IT OUT!
I BEG YOU.
YOU'LL BE FINE.
OH, LOOK.
SKREE!
COMPANY.
RRROOORRR
BRAKKA BRAKKA BRAKKA BRAKKA
EDUARDO ENNEKA! HANDS IN THE AIR!

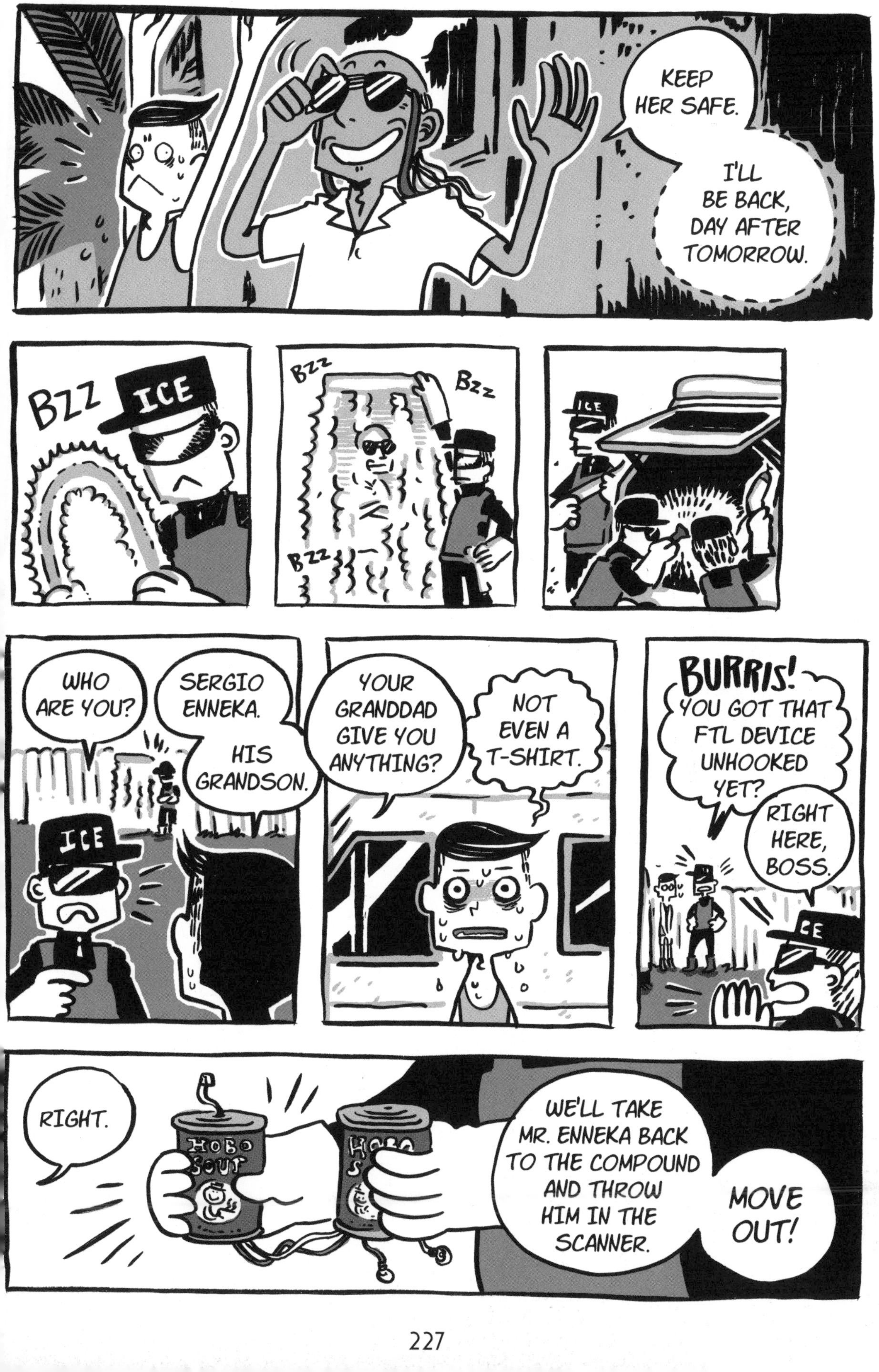
KEEP HER SAFE.
I'LL BE BACK, DAY AFTER TOMORROW.
BZZ
ICE
BZZ
BZZ
BZZ
ICE
WHO ARE YOU?
SERGIO ENNEKA.
HIS GRANDSON.
ICE
YOUR GRANDDAD GIVE YOU ANYTHING?
NOT EVEN A T-SHIRT.
BURRIS! YOU GOT THAT FTL DEVICE UNHOOKED YET?
RIGHT HERE, BOSS.
RIGHT.
HOBO SOUP
WE'LL TAKE MR. ENNEKA BACK TO THE COMPOUND AND THROW HIM IN THE SCANNER.
MOVE OUT!

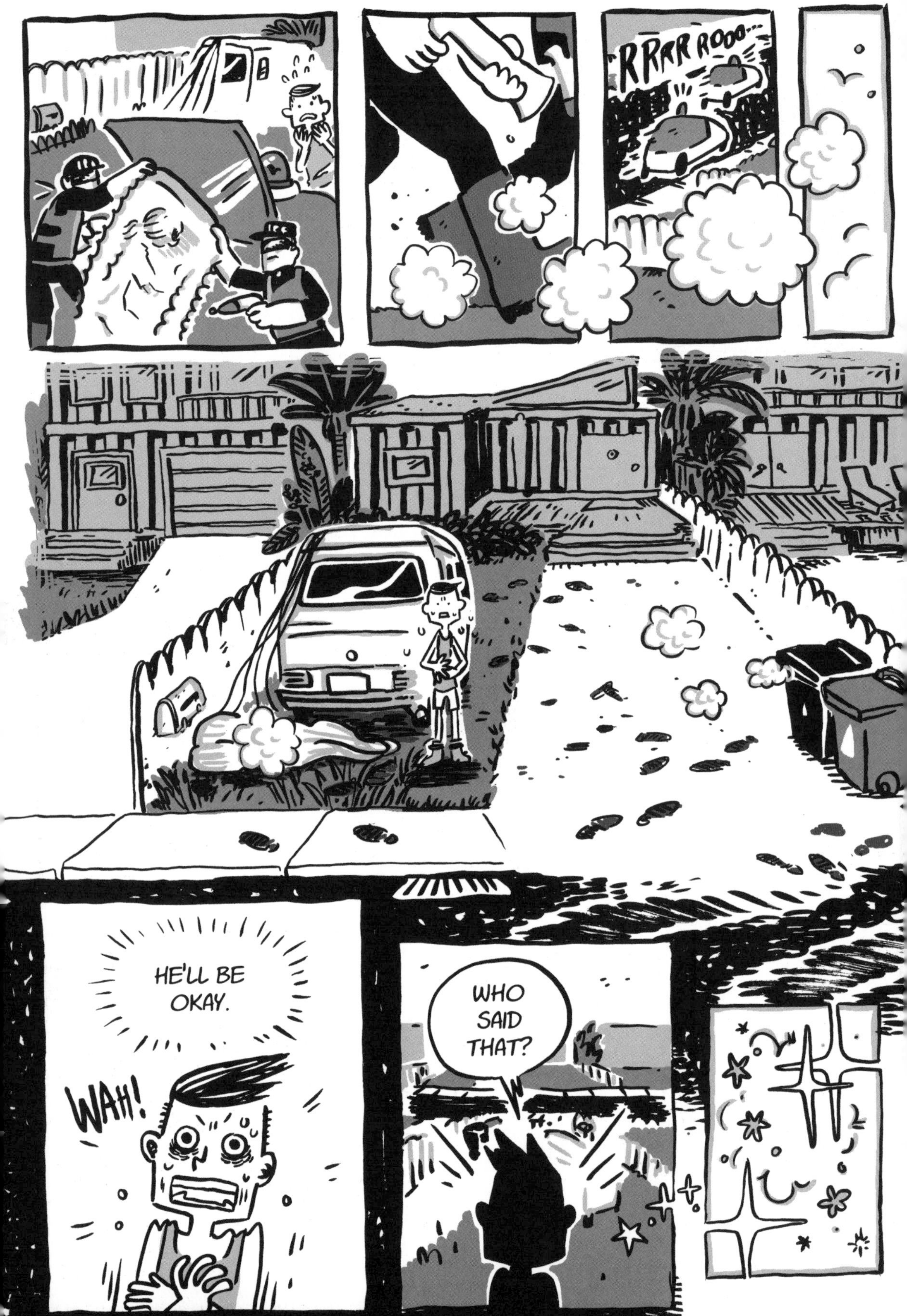
RRRR ROOO
HE'LL BE OKAY.
WAH!
WHO SAID THAT?

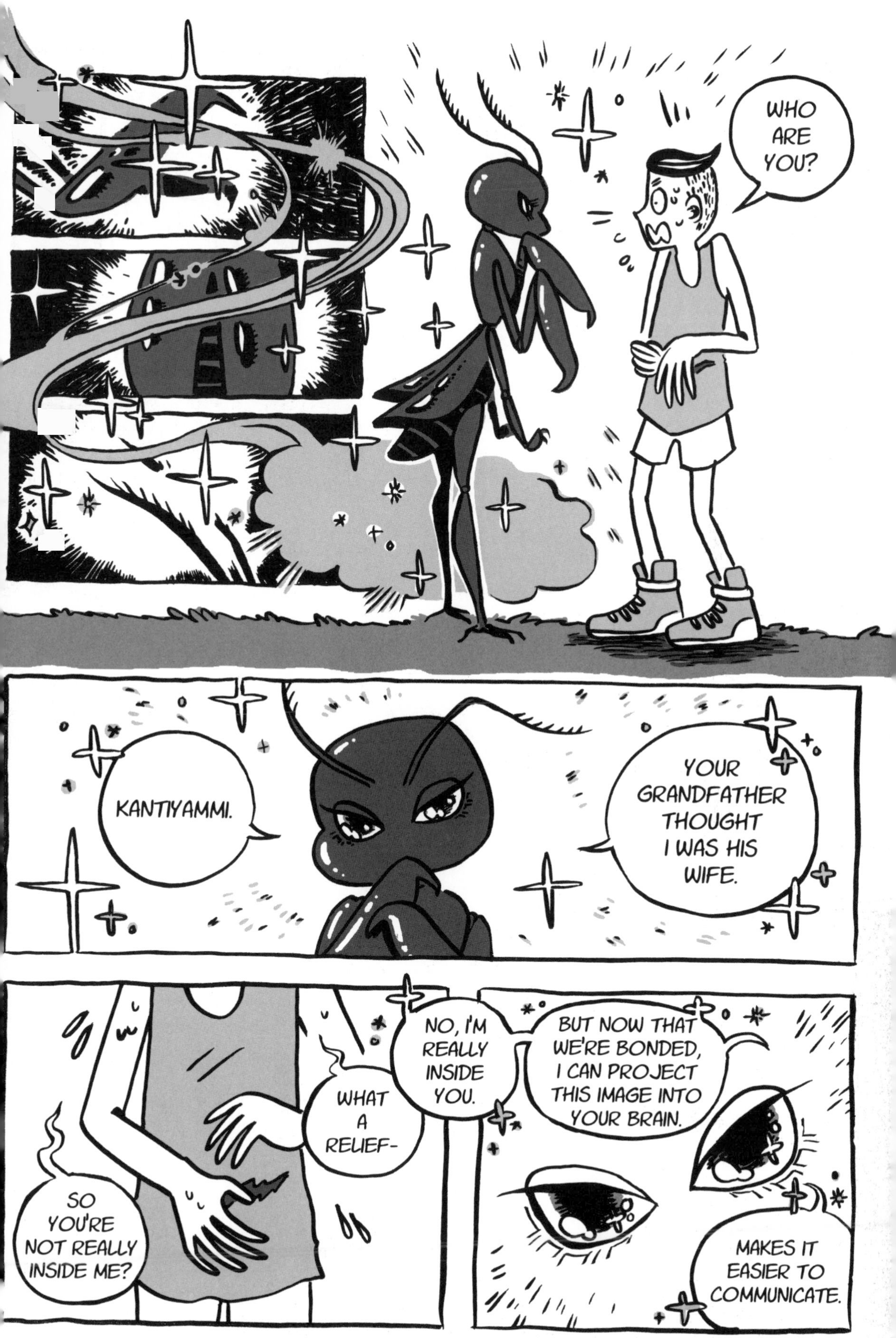
WHO ARE YOU?
KANTIYAMMI.
YOUR GRANDFATHER THOUGHT I WAS HIS WIFE.
SO YOU'RE NOT REALLY INSIDE ME?
WHAT A RELIEF-
NO, I'M REALLY INSIDE YOU.
BUT NOW THAT WE'RE BONDED, I CAN PROJECT THIS IMAGE INTO YOUR BRAIN.
MAKES IT EASIER TO COMMUNICATE.

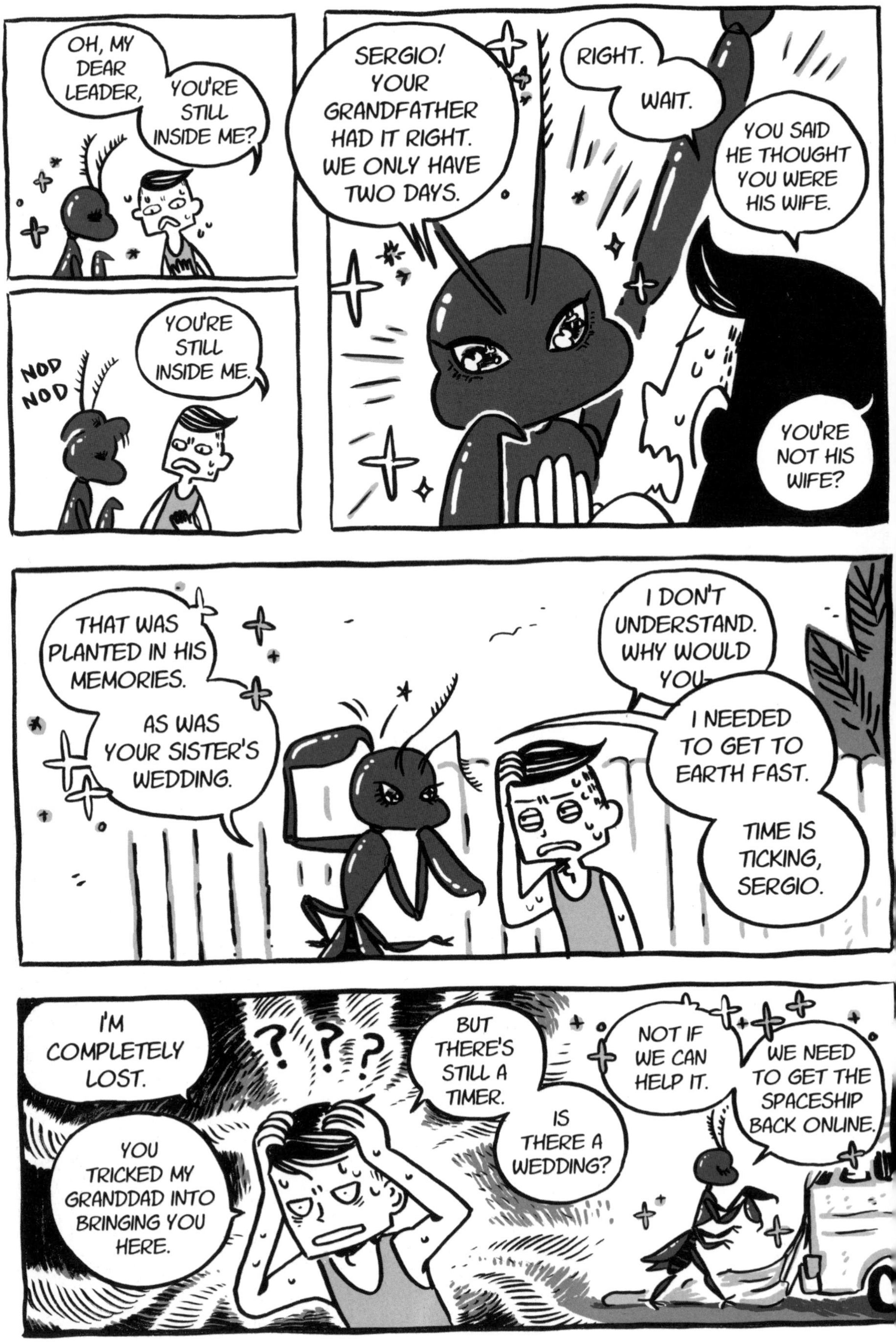
OH, MY DEAR LEADER,
YOU'RE STILL INSIDE ME?
NOD NOD
YOU'RE STILL INSIDE ME.
SERGIO! YOUR GRANDFATHER HAD IT RIGHT. WE ONLY HAVE TWO DAYS.
RIGHT.
WAIT.
YOU SAID HE THOUGHT YOU WERE HIS WIFE.
YOU'RE NOT HIS WIFE?
THAT WAS PLANTED IN HIS MEMORIES.
AS WAS YOUR SISTER'S WEDDING.
I DON'T UNDERSTAND. WHY WOULD YOU—
I NEEDED TO GET TO EARTH FAST.
TIME IS TICKING, SERGIO.
I'M COMPLETELY LOST.
YOU TRICKED MY GRANDDAD INTO BRINGING YOU HERE.
???
BUT THERE'S STILL A TIMER.
IS THERE A WEDDING?
NOT IF WE CAN HELP IT.
WE NEED TO GET THE SPACESHIP BACK ONLINE.

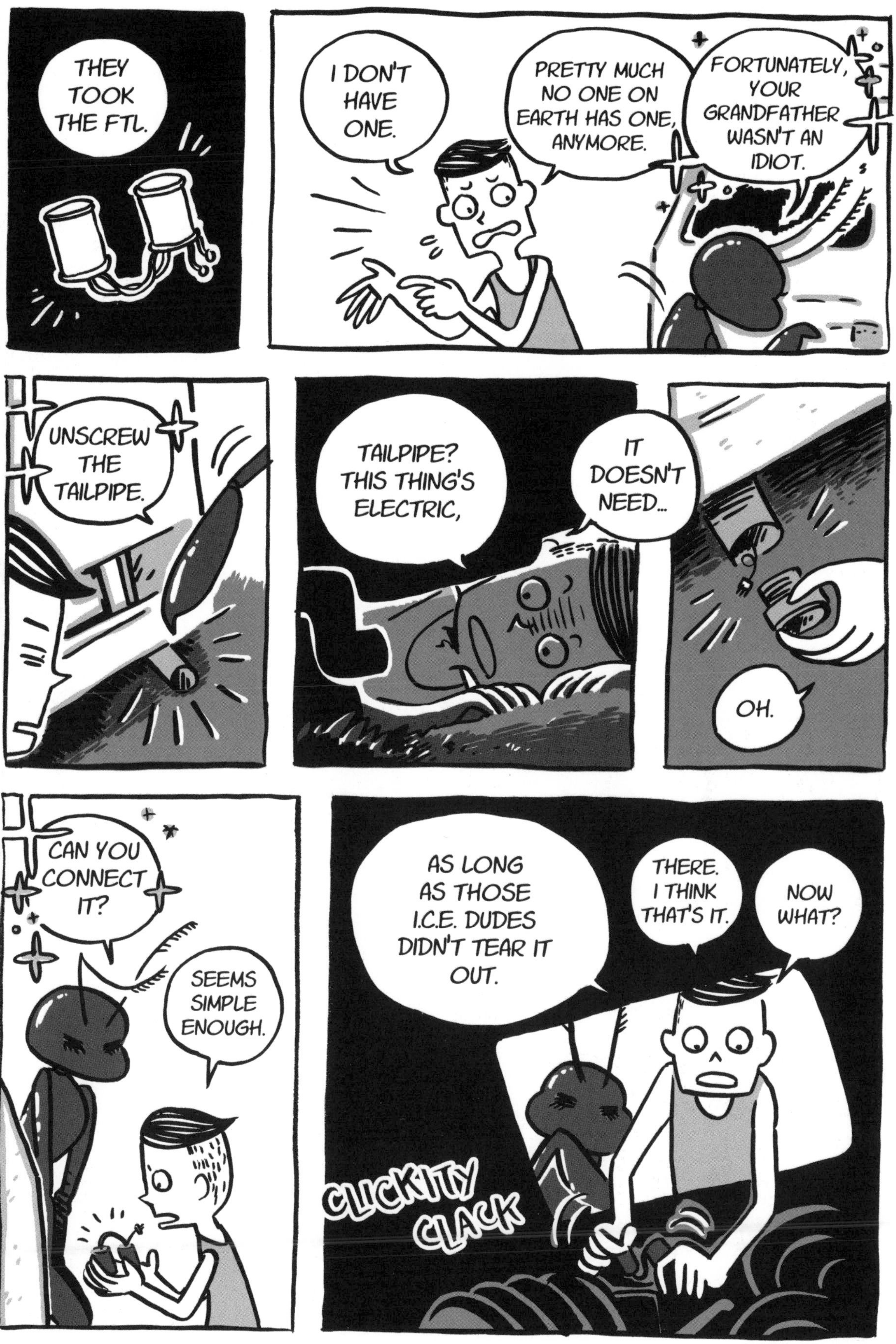
THEY TOOK THE FTL.
I DON'T HAVE ONE.
PRETTY MUCH NO ONE ON EARTH HAS ONE, ANYMORE.
FORTUNATELY, YOUR GRANDFATHER WASN'T AN IDIOT.
UNSCREW THE TAILPIPE.
TAILPIPE? THIS THING'S ELECTRIC,
IT DOESN'T NEED...
OH.
CAN YOU CONNECT IT?
SEEMS SIMPLE ENOUGH.
AS LONG AS THOSE I.C.E. DUDES DIDN'T TEAR IT OUT.
CLICKITY CLACK
THERE. I THINK THAT'S IT.
NOW WHAT?

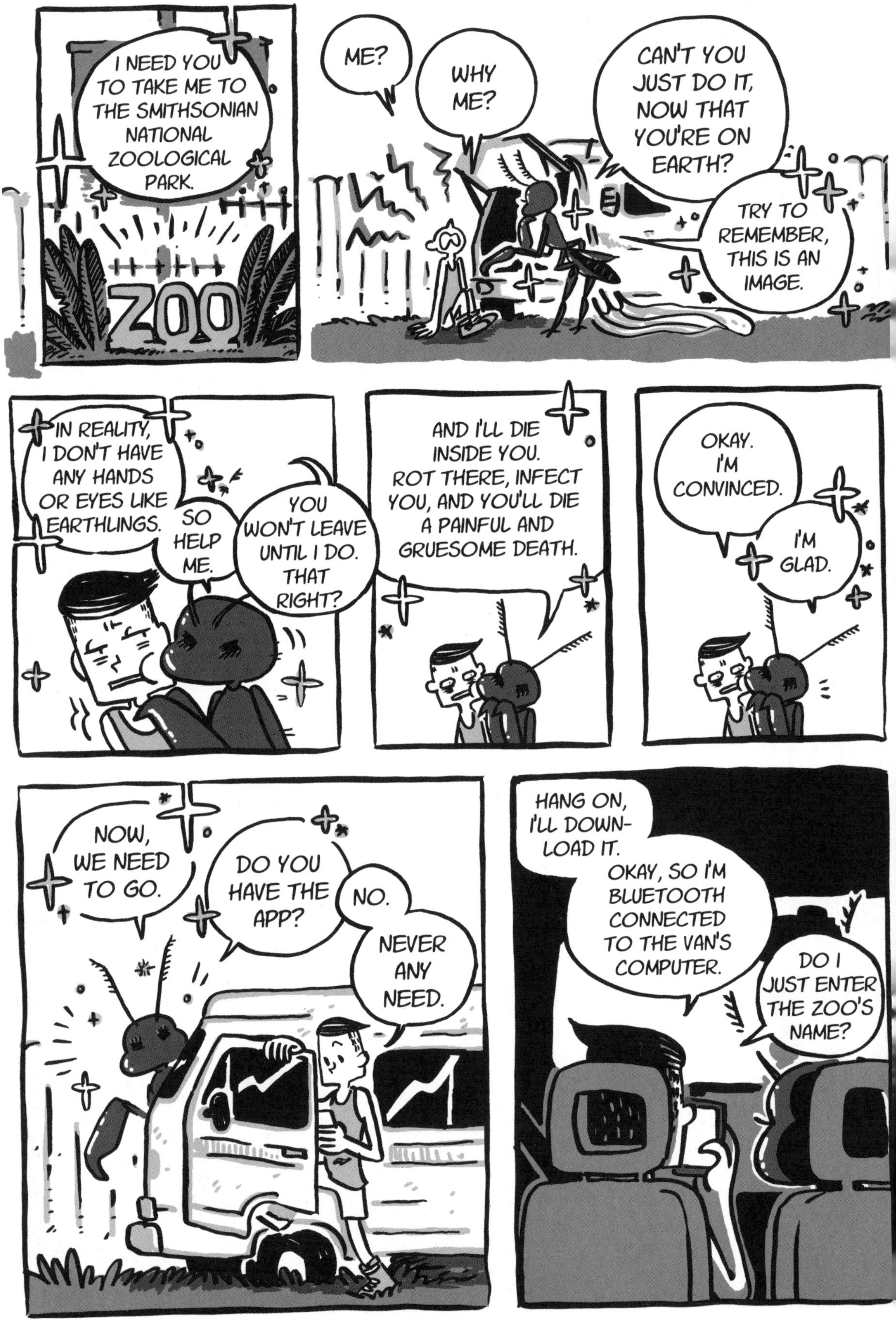
I NEED YOU TO TAKE ME TO THE SMITHSONIAN NATIONAL ZOOLOGICAL PARK.
ZOO
ME?
WHY ME?
CAN'T YOU JUST DO IT, NOW THAT YOU'RE ON EARTH?
TRY TO REMEMBER, THIS IS AN IMAGE.
IN REALITY, I DON'T HAVE ANY HANDS OR EYES LIKE EARTHLINGS.
SO HELP ME.
YOU WON'T LEAVE UNTIL I DO. THAT RIGHT?
AND I'LL DIE INSIDE YOU. ROT THERE, INFECT YOU, AND YOU'LL DIE A PAINFUL AND GRUESOME DEATH.
OKAY. I'M CONVINCED.
I'M GLAD.
NOW, WE NEED TO GO.
DO YOU HAVE THE APP?
NO.
NEVER ANY NEED.
HANG ON, I'LL DOWNLOAD IT.
OKAY, SO I'M BLUETOOTH CONNECTED TO THE VAN'S COMPUTER.
DO I JUST ENTER THE ZOO'S NAME?

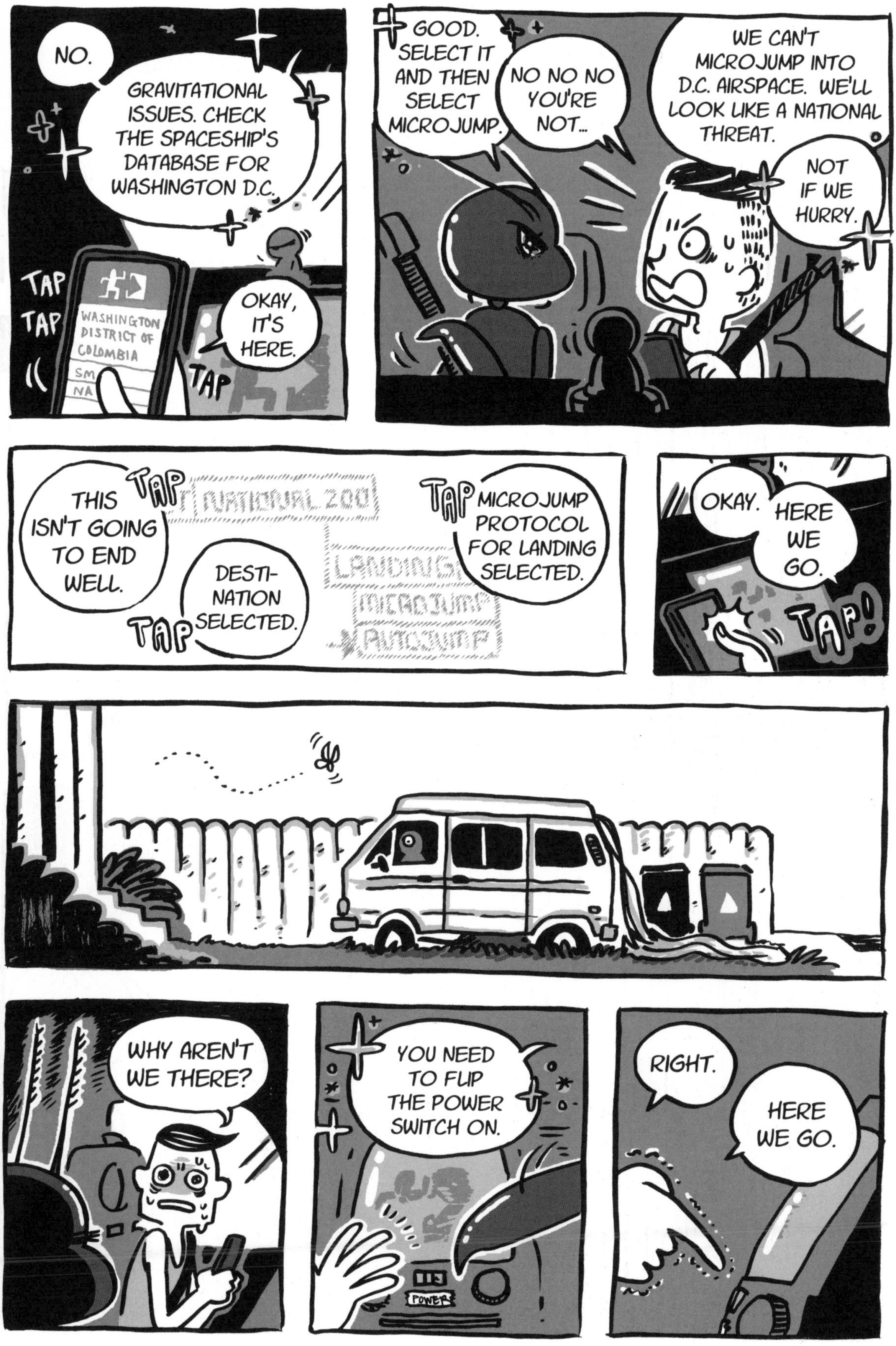
NO.
GRAVITATIONAL ISSUES. CHECK THE SPACESHIP'S DATABASE FOR WASHINGTON D.C.
TAP TAP
WASHINGTON DISTRICT OF COLOMBIA
OKAY, IT'S HERE.
TAP
GOOD. SELECT IT AND THEN SELECT MICROJUMP.
NO NO NO YOU'RE NOT...
WE CAN'T MICROJUMP INTO D.C. AIRSPACE. WE'LL LOOK LIKE A NATIONAL THREAT.
NOT IF WE HURRY.
THIS ISN'T GOING TO END WELL.
TAP
NATIONAL ZOO
TAP
DESTI-NATION SELECTED.
LANDING
MICROJUMP
AUTOJUMP
TAP
MICROJUMP PROTOCOL FOR LANDING SELECTED.
OKAY.
HERE WE GO.
TAP!
WHY AREN'T WE THERE?
YOU NEED TO FLIP THE POWER SWITCH ON.
POWER
RIGHT.
HERE WE GO.

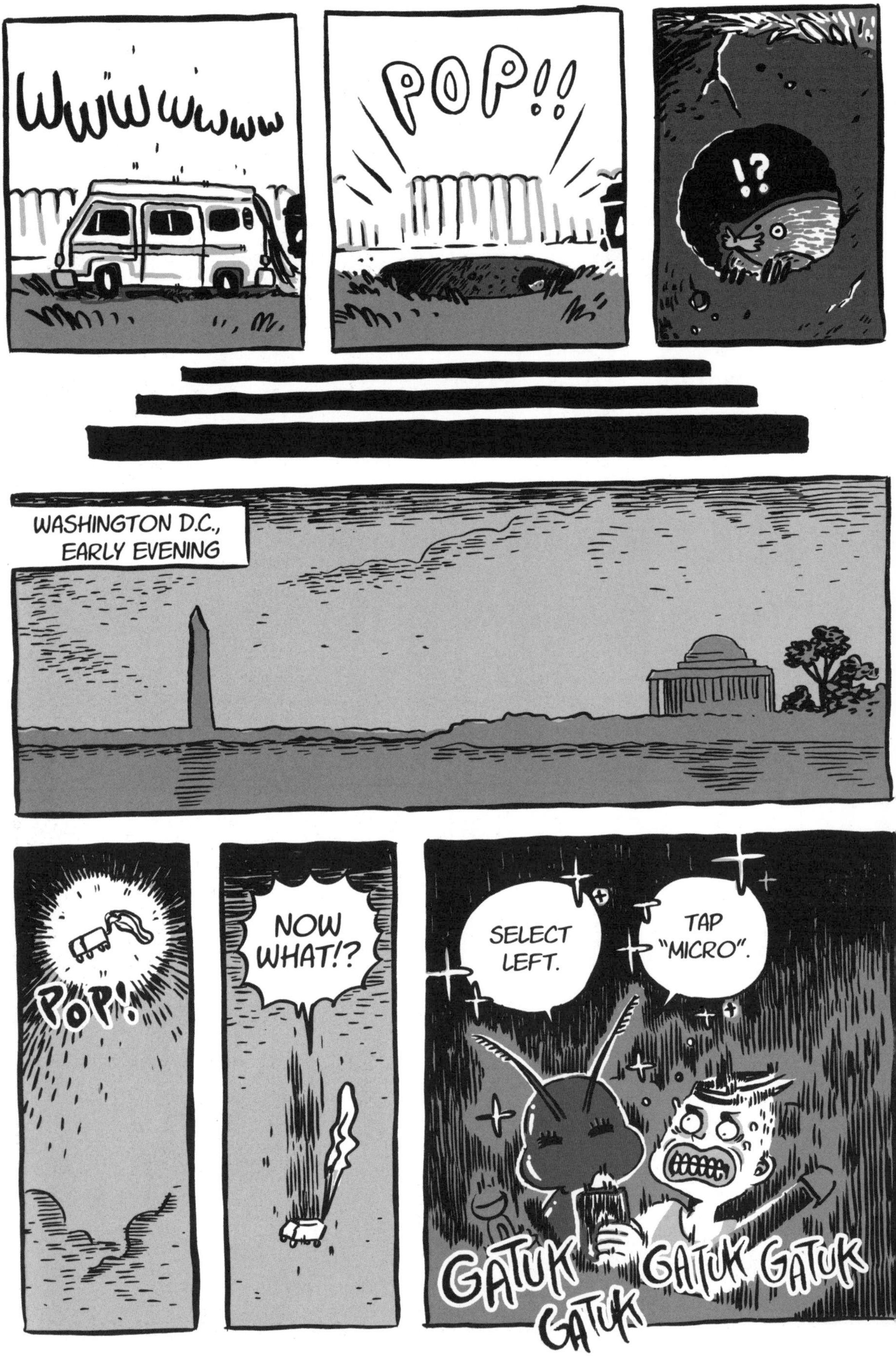
POP!!
!?
WASHINGTON D.C., EARLY EVENING
POP!
NOW WHAT!?
SELECT LEFT.
TAP "MICRO".
GATUK GATUK GATUK GATUK

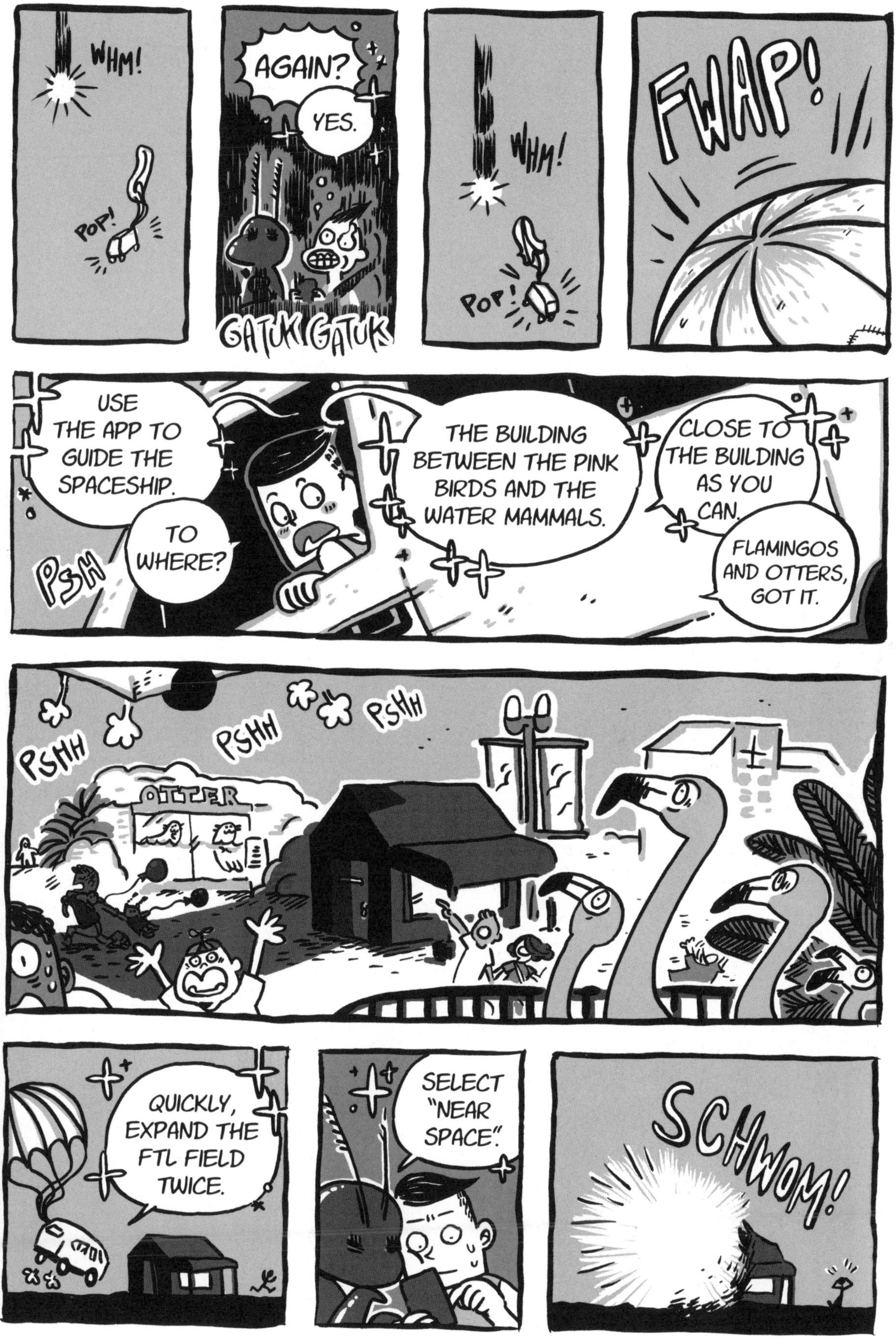
WHM!
POP!
AGAIN?
YES.
GATUK GATUK
WHM!
POP!
FWAP!
USE THE APP TO GUIDE THE SPACESHIP.
TO WHERE?
PSH
THE BUILDING BETWEEN THE PINK BIRDS AND THE WATER MAMMALS.
CLOSE TO THE BUILDING AS YOU CAN.
FLAMINGOS AND OTTERS, GOT IT.
PSHH
PSHH
PSHH
OTTER
QUICKLY, EXPAND THE FTL FIELD TWICE.
SELECT "NEAR SPACE".
SCHWOM!

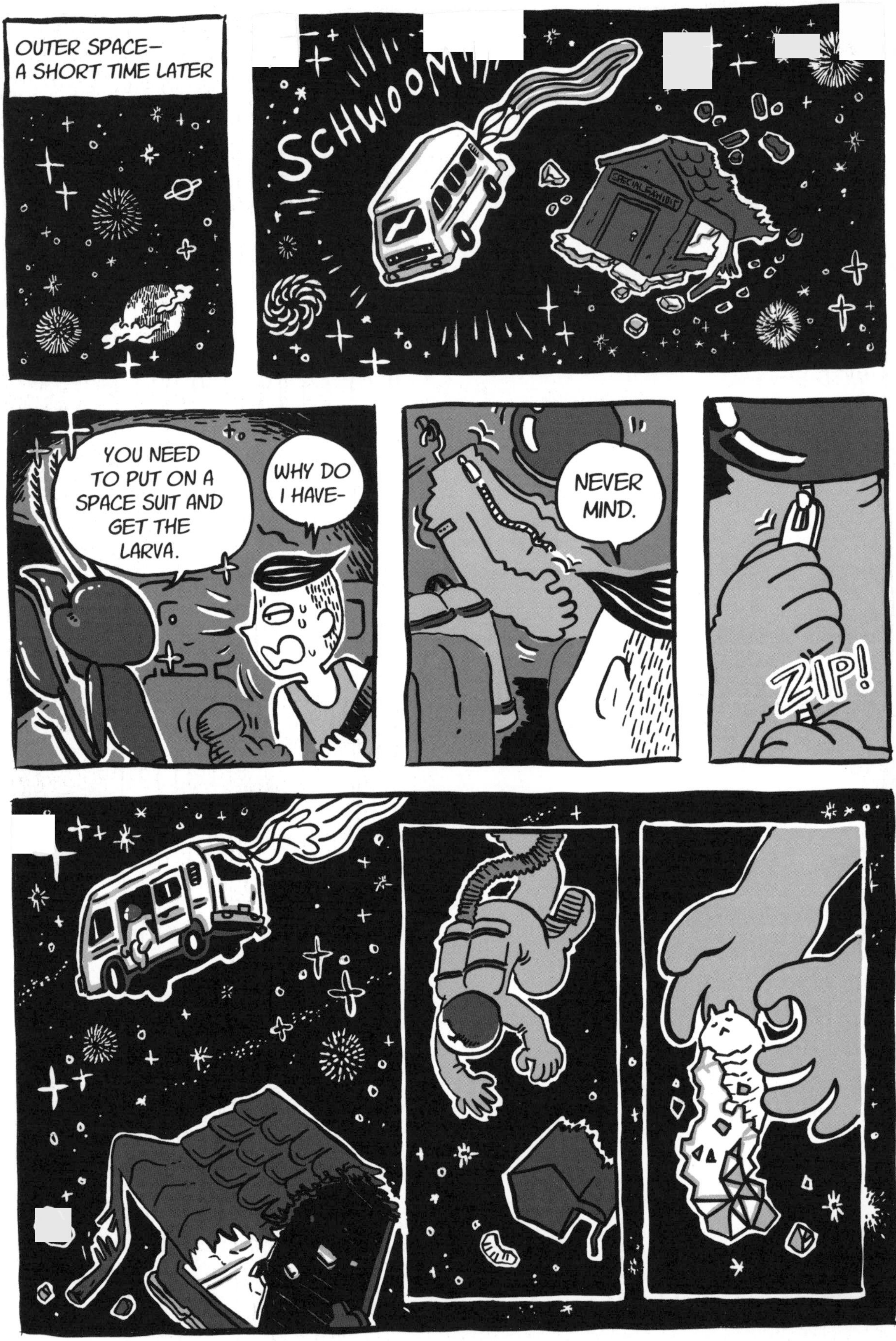
OUTER SPACE— A SHORT TIME LATER
SCHWOOM
SPECIAL EXHIBITS
YOU NEED TO PUT ON A SPACE SUIT AND GET THE LARVA.
WHY DO I HAVE-
NEVER MIND.
ZIP!

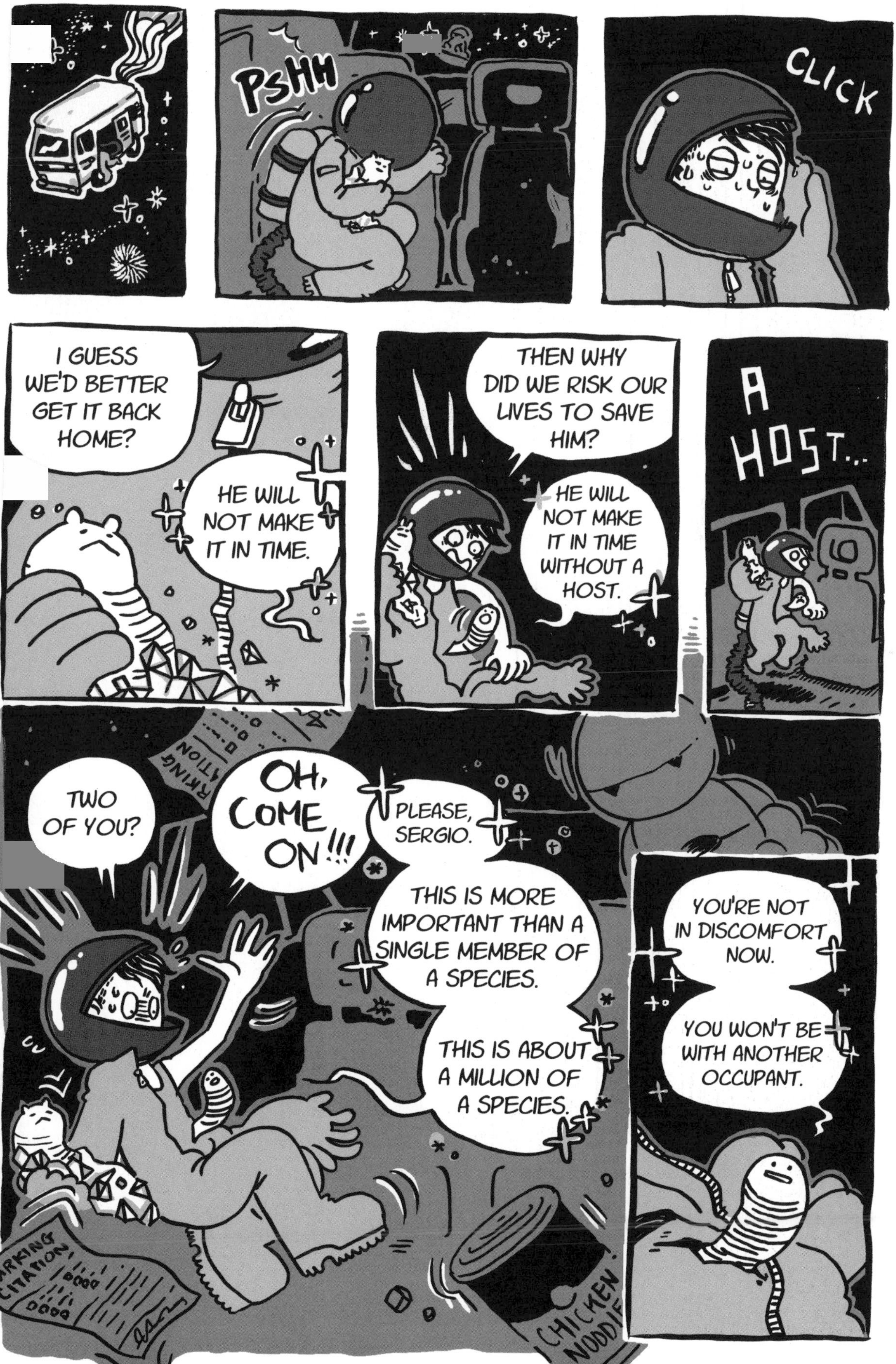
PSHH
CLICK
I GUESS WE'D BETTER GET IT BACK HOME?
HE WILL NOT MAKE IT IN TIME.
THEN WHY DID WE RISK OUR LIVES TO SAVE HIM?
HE WILL NOT MAKE IT IN TIME WITHOUT A HOST.
A HOST...
TWO OF YOU?
OH, COME ON!!!
PLEASE, SERGIO.
THIS IS MORE IMPORTANT THAN A SINGLE MEMBER OF A SPECIES.
THIS IS ABOUT A MILLION OF A SPECIES.
YOU'RE NOT IN DISCOMFORT NOW.
YOU WON'T BE WITH ANOTHER OCCUPANT.
PARKING CITATION
CHICKEN NOODLE

I CAN'T BELIEVE I'M DOING THIS.

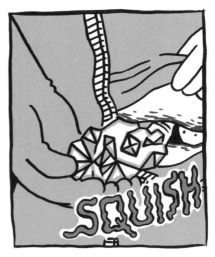

SQUISH

SQUISH

SQUISH

THANK YOU, KANTIYAMMI.

THANK YOU, SERGIO.

MY HONOR, CLAERDRACC.

GREAT, WONDERFUL.

CAN WE JUST GO SOMEWHERE THAT I CAN UNLOAD YOU TWO.

I FEEL LIKE I'M GOING TO THROW UP.

ACCESS THE SPACESHIP'S FOLDERS AND LOCATE THE ONE NAMED "NEW PLACES"

MY HOME WAS THE LAST PLACE YOUR GRANDFATHER VISITED.

WELL, I'D TELL YOU TO BUCKLE IN, BUT...

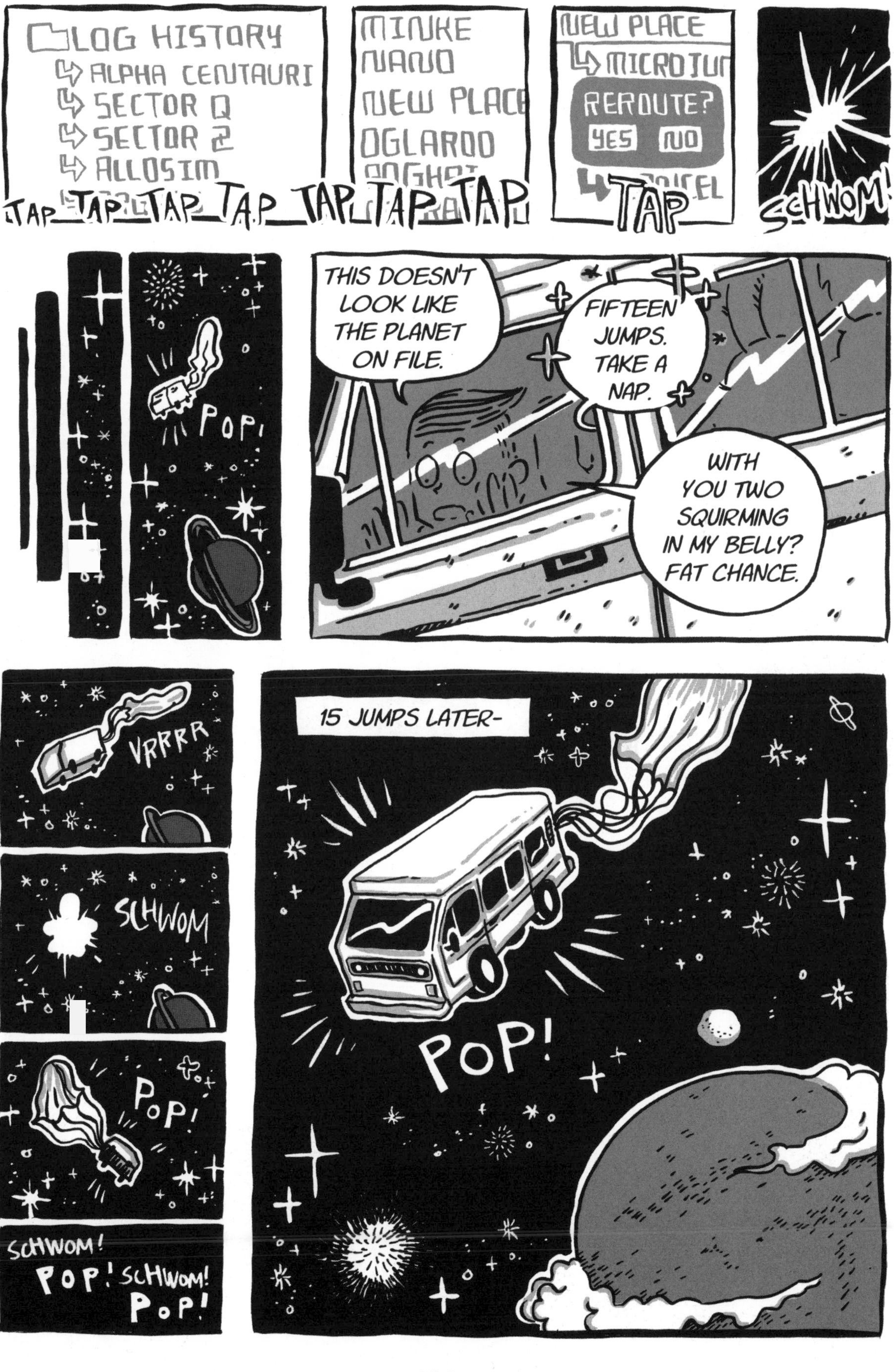
LOG HISTORY
ALPHA CENTAURI
SECTOR Q
SECTOR 2
ALLOSIM
TAP TAP TAP TAP TAP TAP TAP
MINKE
NANO
NEW PLACE
OGLAROO
NEW PLACE
REROUTE?
YES NO
TAP
SCHWOM!
POP!
THIS DOESN'T LOOK LIKE THE PLANET ON FILE.
FIFTEEN JUMPS. TAKE A NAP.
WITH YOU TWO SQUIRMING IN MY BELLY? FAT CHANCE.
VRRRR
SCHWOM
POP!
SCHWOM!
POP! SCHWOM!
POP!
15 JUMPS LATER-
POP!

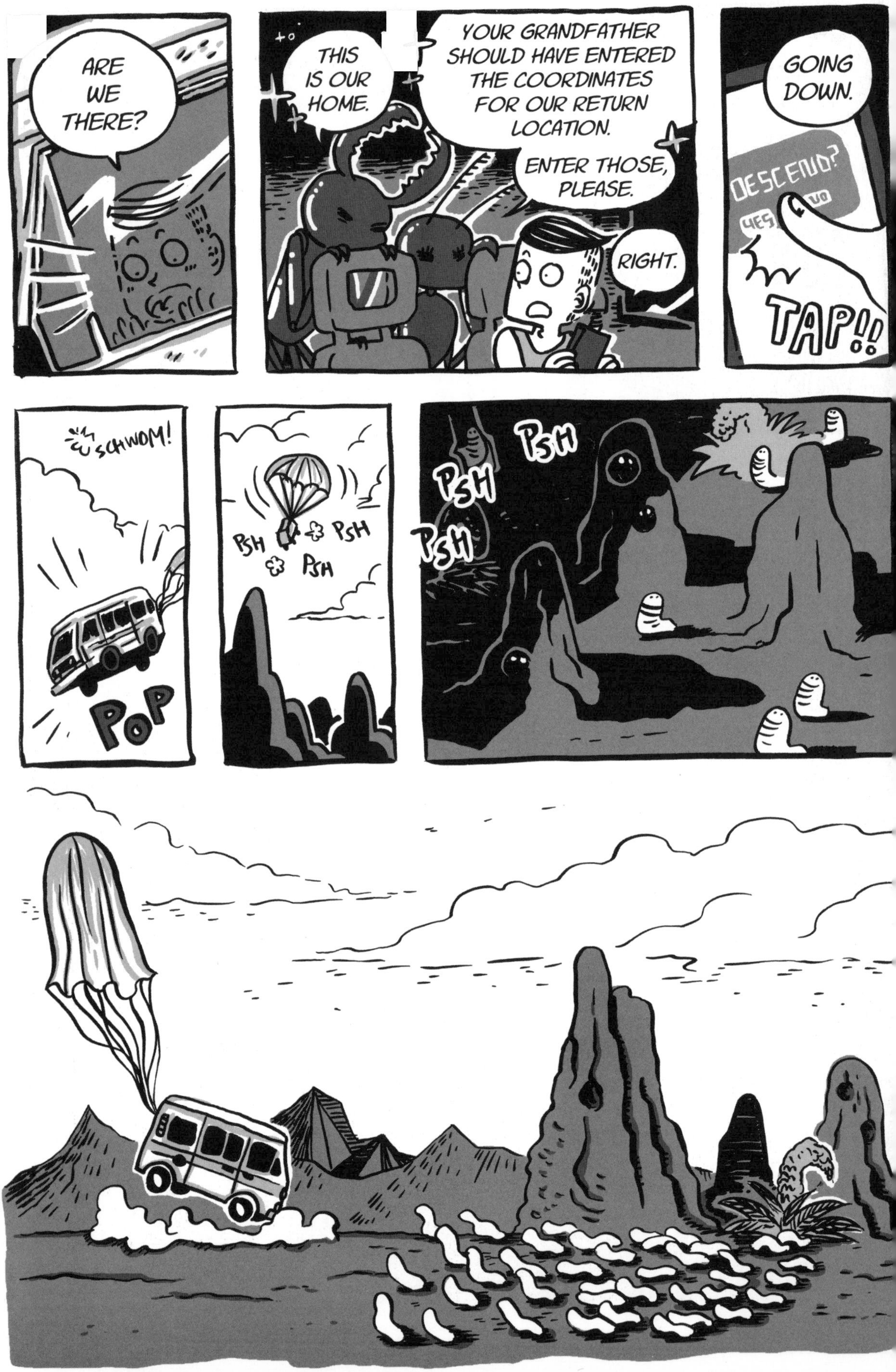
ARE WE THERE?
THIS IS OUR HOME.
YOUR GRANDFATHER SHOULD HAVE ENTERED THE COORDINATES FOR OUR RETURN LOCATION.
ENTER THOSE, PLEASE.
RIGHT.
GOING DOWN.
DESCEND?
YES
NO
TAP!!
SCHWOM!
POP
PSH
PSH
PSH
PSH
PSH
PSH

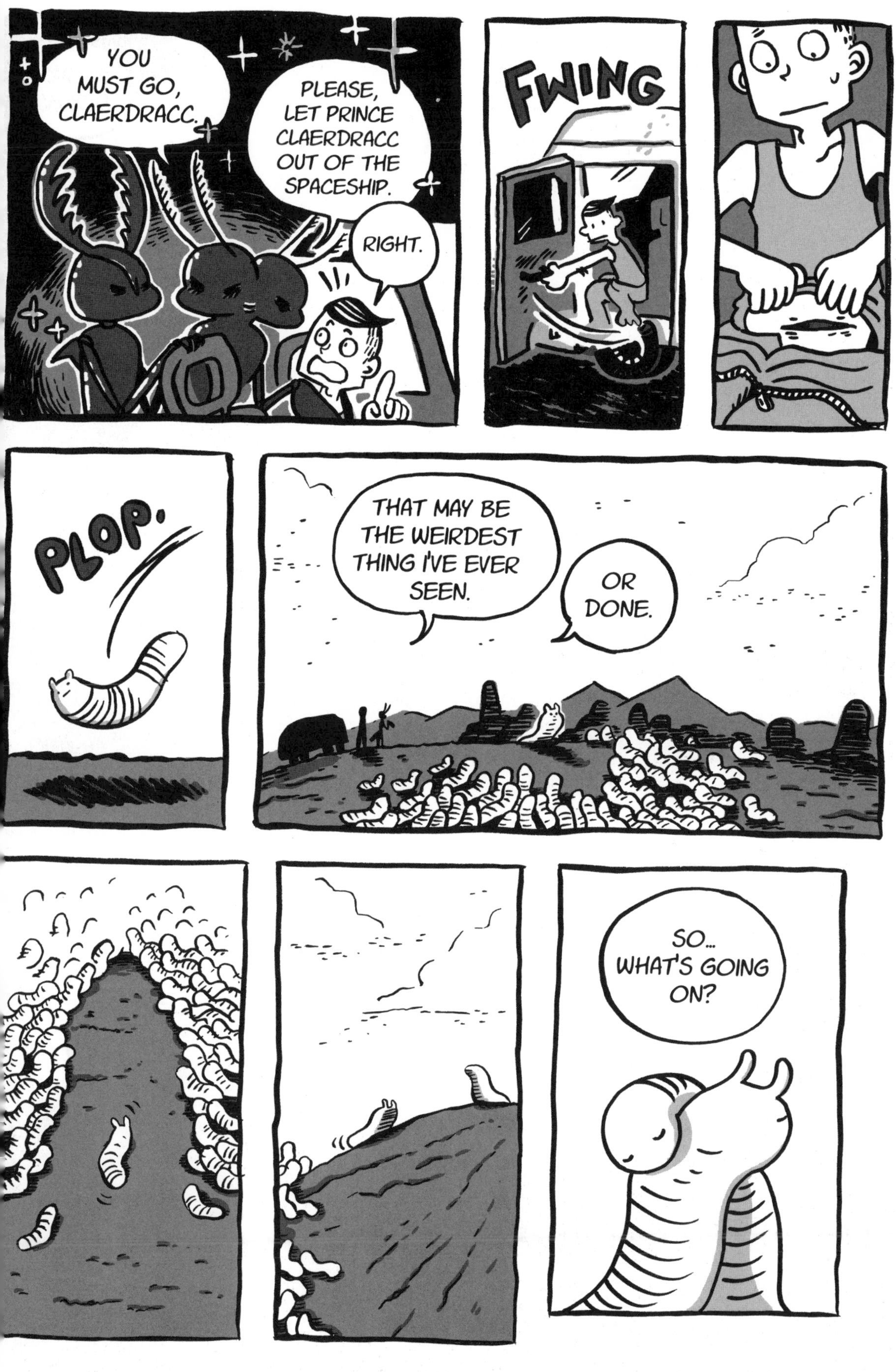
YOU MUST GO, CLAERDRACC.
PLEASE, LET PRINCE CLAERDRACC OUT OF THE SPACESHIP.
RIGHT.
FWING
PLOP.
THAT MAY BE THE WEIRDEST THING I'VE EVER SEEN.
OR DONE.
SO... WHAT'S GOING ON?

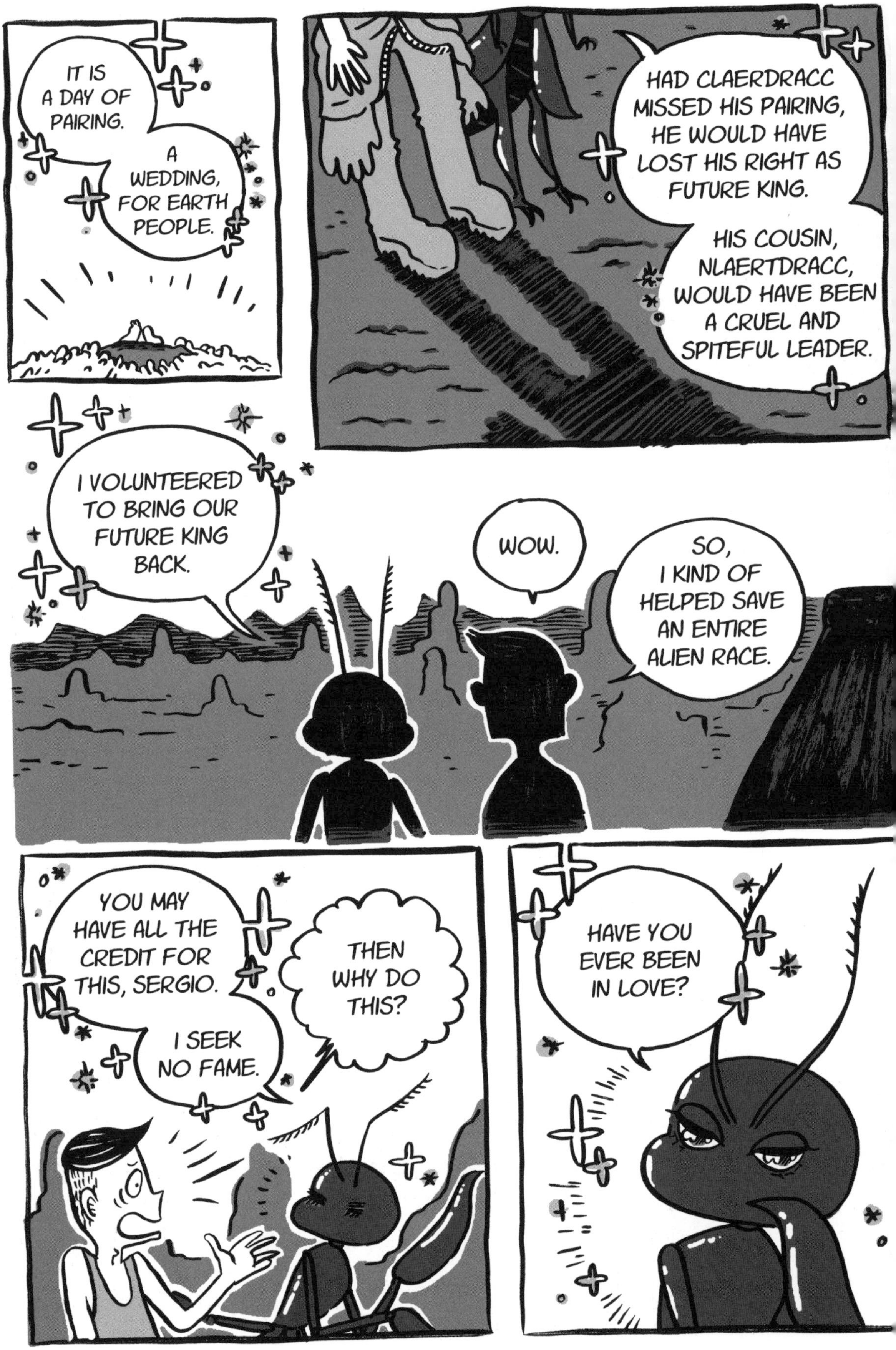
IT IS A DAY OF PAIRING.
A WEDDING, FOR EARTH PEOPLE.
HAD CLAERDRACC MISSED HIS PAIRING, HE WOULD HAVE LOST HIS RIGHT AS FUTURE KING.
HIS COUSIN, NLAERTDRACC, WOULD HAVE BEEN A CRUEL AND SPITEFUL LEADER.
I VOLUNTEERED TO BRING OUR FUTURE KING BACK.
WOW.
SO, I KIND OF HELPED SAVE AN ENTIRE ALIEN RACE.
YOU MAY HAVE ALL THE CREDIT FOR THIS, SERGIO.
I SEEK NO FAME.
THEN WHY DO THIS?
HAVE YOU EVER BEEN IN LOVE?

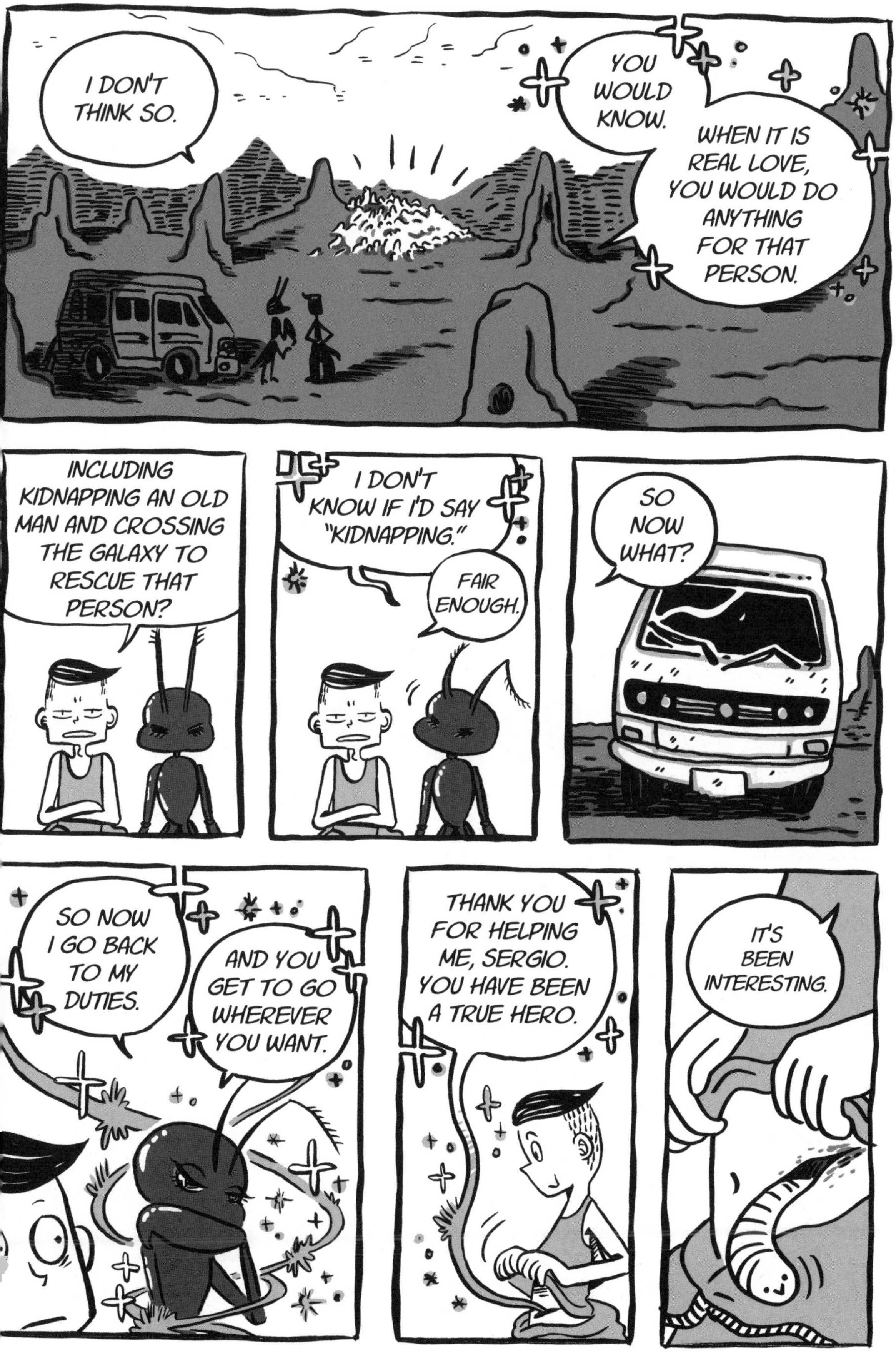
I DON'T THINK SO.
YOU WOULD KNOW.
WHEN IT IS REAL LOVE, YOU WOULD DO ANYTHING FOR THAT PERSON.
INCLUDING KIDNAPPING AN OLD MAN AND CROSSING THE GALAXY TO RESCUE THAT PERSON?
I DON'T KNOW IF I'D SAY "KIDNAPPING."
FAIR ENOUGH.
SO NOW WHAT?
SO NOW I GO BACK TO MY DUTIES.
AND YOU GET TO GO WHEREVER YOU WANT.
THANK YOU FOR HELPING ME, SERGIO. YOU HAVE BEEN A TRUE HERO.
IT'S BEEN INTERESTING.

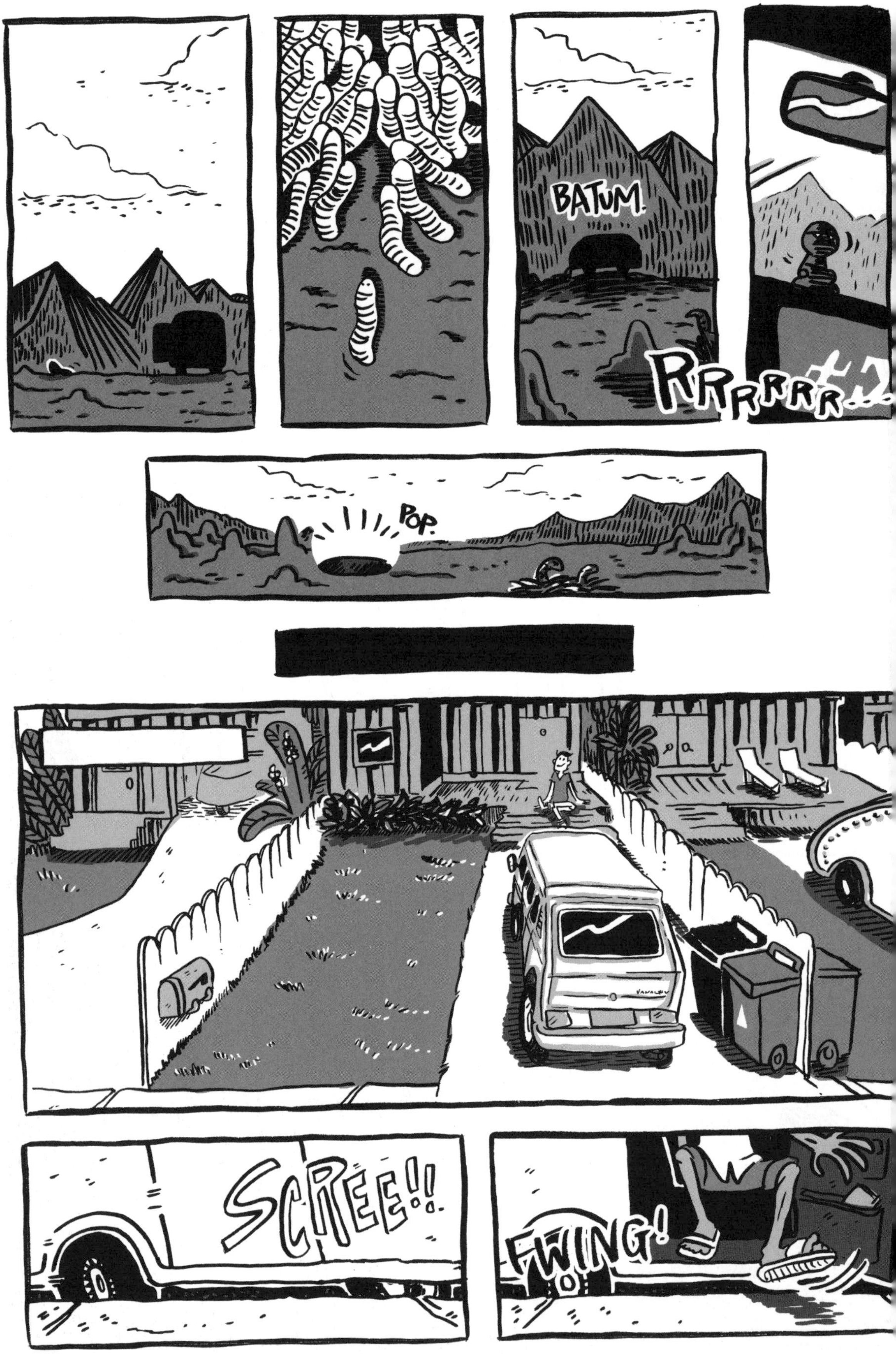
BATUM
RRRRRR...
POP.
SCREE!!
FWING!

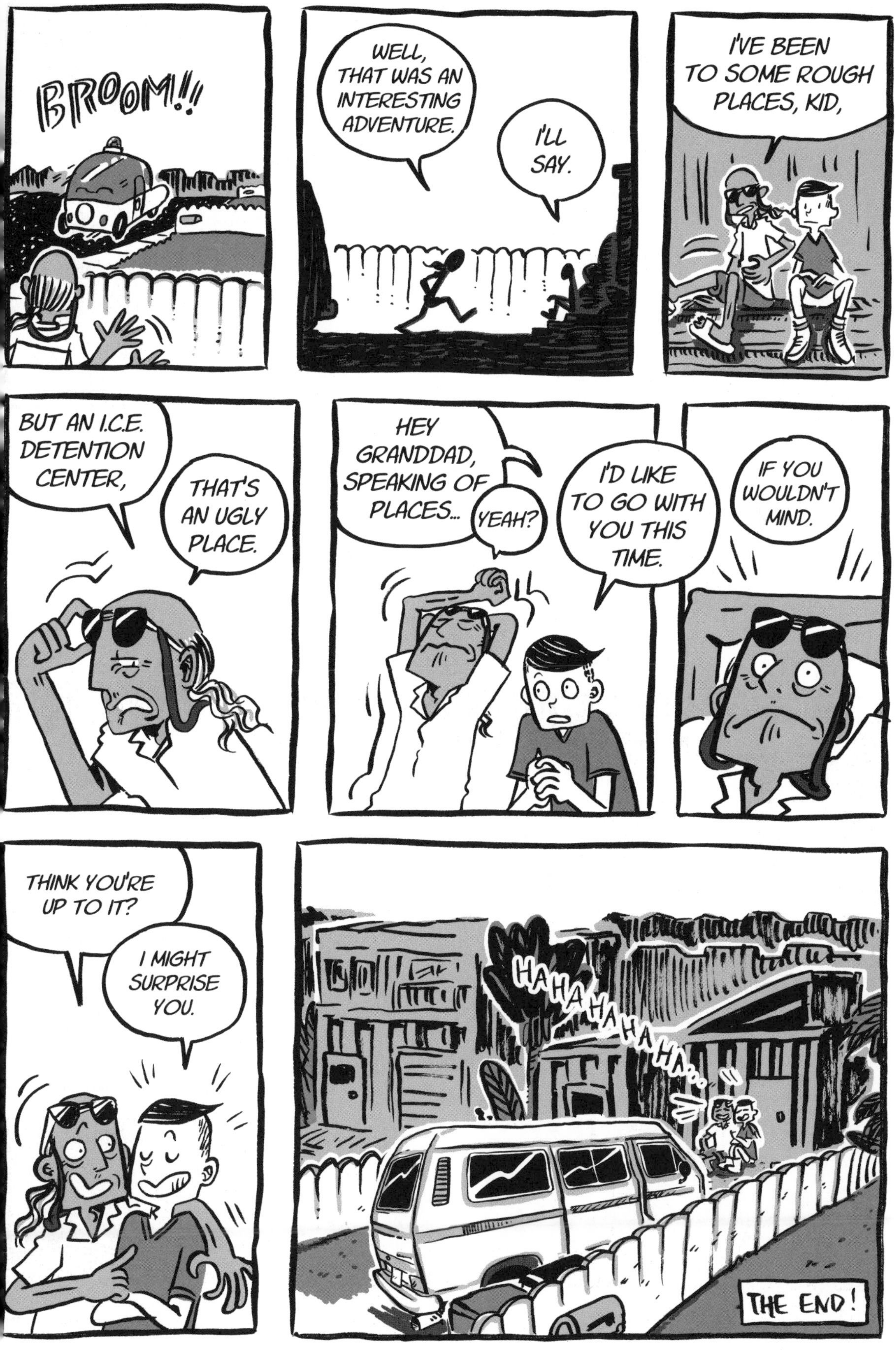
BROOM!!!
WELL, THAT WAS AN INTERESTING ADVENTURE.
I'LL SAY.
I'VE BEEN TO SOME ROUGH PLACES, KID,
BUT AN I.C.E. DETENTION CENTER,
THAT'S AN UGLY PLACE.
HEY GRANDDAD, SPEAKING OF PLACES...
YEAH?
I'D LIKE TO GO WITH YOU THIS TIME.
IF YOU WOULDN'T MIND.
THINK YOU'RE UP TO IT?
I MIGHT SURPRISE YOU.
HAHAHAHAHAHA...
THE END!

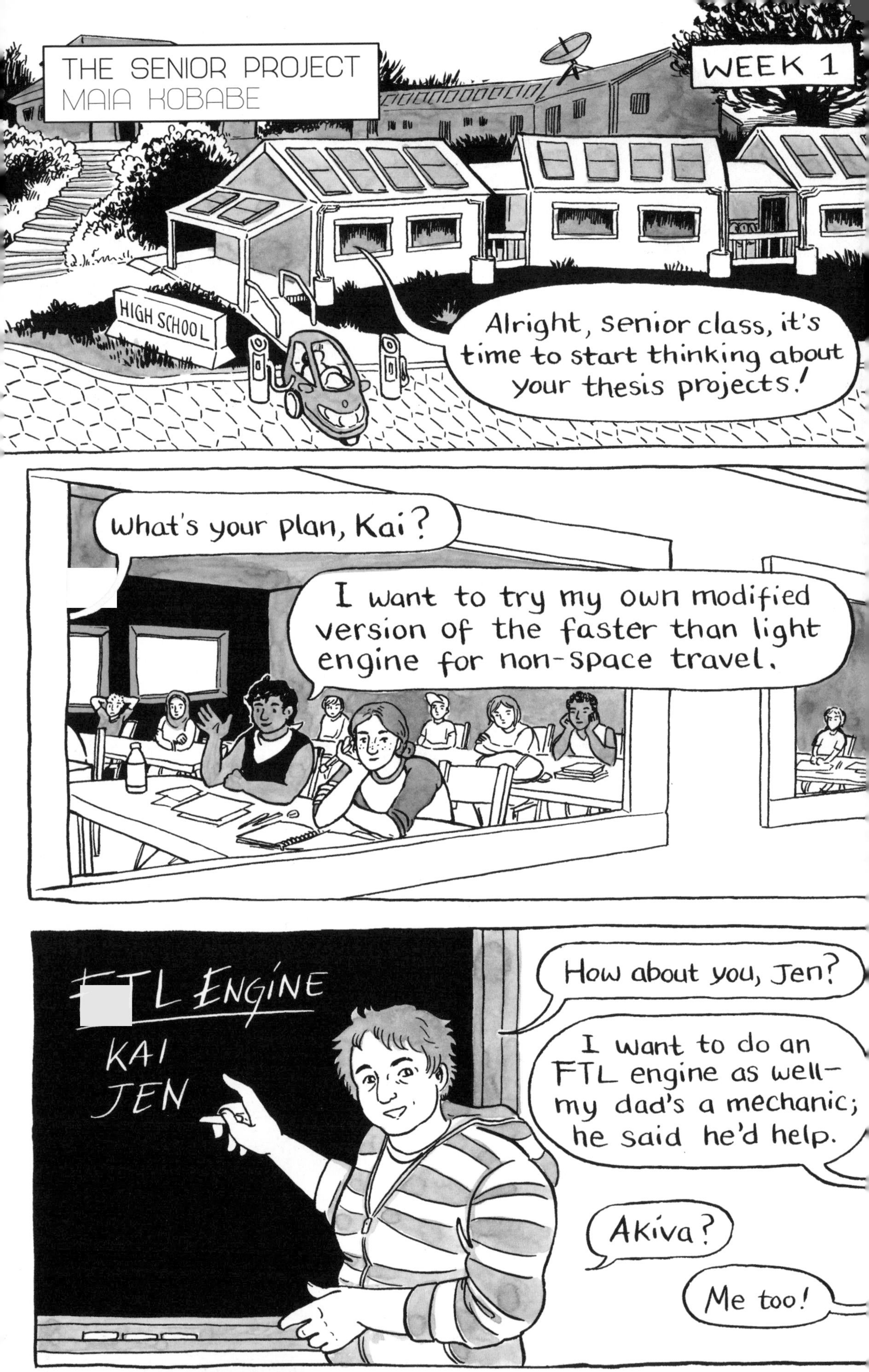
THE SENIOR PROJECT
MAIA KOBABE
WEEK 1
HIGH SCHOOL
Alright, senior class, it's time to start thinking about your thesis projects!
What's your plan, Kai?
I want to try my own modified version of the faster than light engine for non-space travel.
FTL ENGINE
KAI
JEN
How about you, Jen?
I want to do an FTL engine as well- my dad's a mechanic; he said he'd help.
Akiva?
Me too!

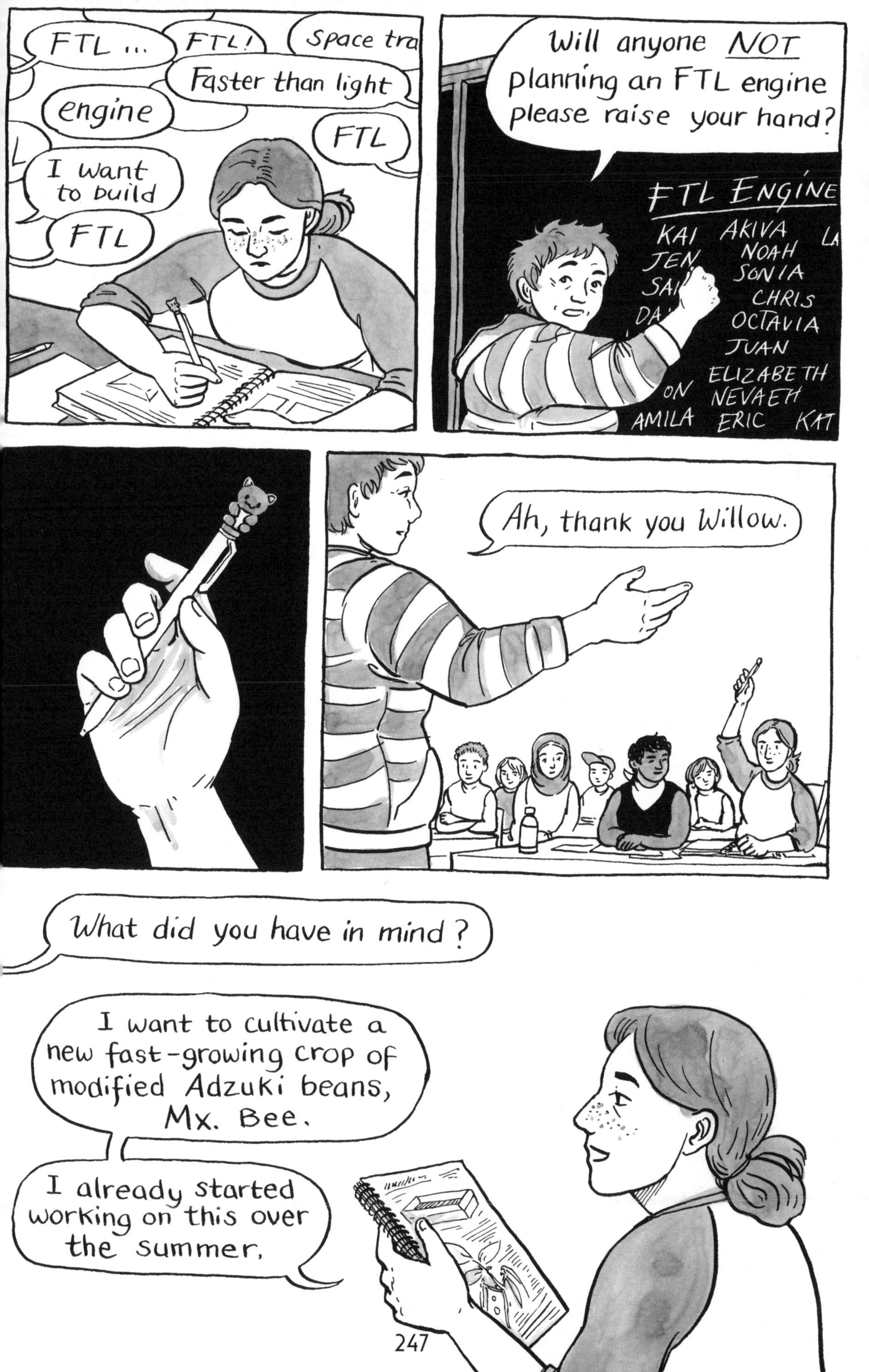
FTL ...
FTL!
Space tra
Faster than light
engine
FTL
I want to build
FTL
Will anyone NOT planning an FTL engine please raise your hand?
FTL ENGINE
KAI
AKIVA
JEN
NOAH
SONIA
CHRIS
OCTAVIA
JUAN
ELIZABETH
ON
NEVAEH
AMILA
ERIC
KAT
Ah, thank you Willow.
What did you have in mind?
I want to cultivate a new fast-growing crop of modified Adzuki beans, Mx. Bee.
I already started working on this over the summer.

Everyone is so excited about life in the colonies, but I think feeding our population on Earth is equally important...

If I get started right away, I can grow 4 harvests in 36 weeks, which should be enough for some solid data.

SEE TRAPPI SYSTEM

Thesis

Wonderful idea! I have a few articles that might help – I'll give you some resources after class.

Before tomorrow I want all of you to come up with a list of supplies and where you plan to buy them – FTL engine builders, no pre-fab kits allowed!

And don't forget, weekly entries in your project journals!

FTL INE
KAI
TEN ARA
EVE
ON

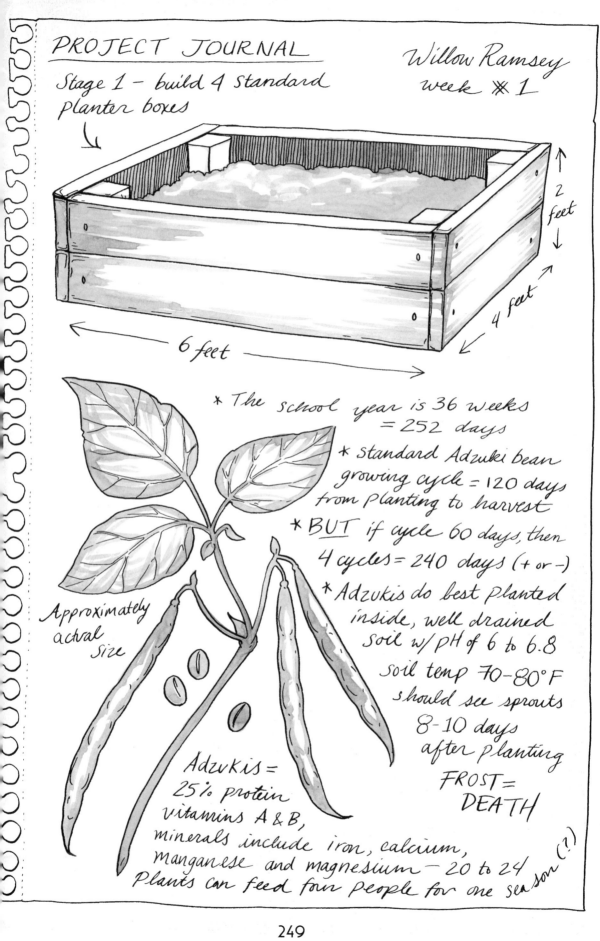

PROJECT JOURNAL

Willow Ramsey
week ✳ 1

Stage 1 — build 4 standard planter boxes

2 feet

4 feet

6 feet

* The school year is 36 weeks = 252 days

* standard Adzuki bean growing cycle = 120 days from planting to harvest

* BUT if cycle 60 days, then 4 cycles = 240 days (+ or −)

* Adzukis do best planted inside, well drained soil w/ pH of 6 to 6.8

soil temp 70-80°F should see sprouts 8-10 days after planting

FROST = DEATH

Approximately actual size

Adzukis = 25% protein vitamins A & B, minerals include iron, calcium, manganese and magnesium — 20 to 24 Plants can feed four people for one season (?)

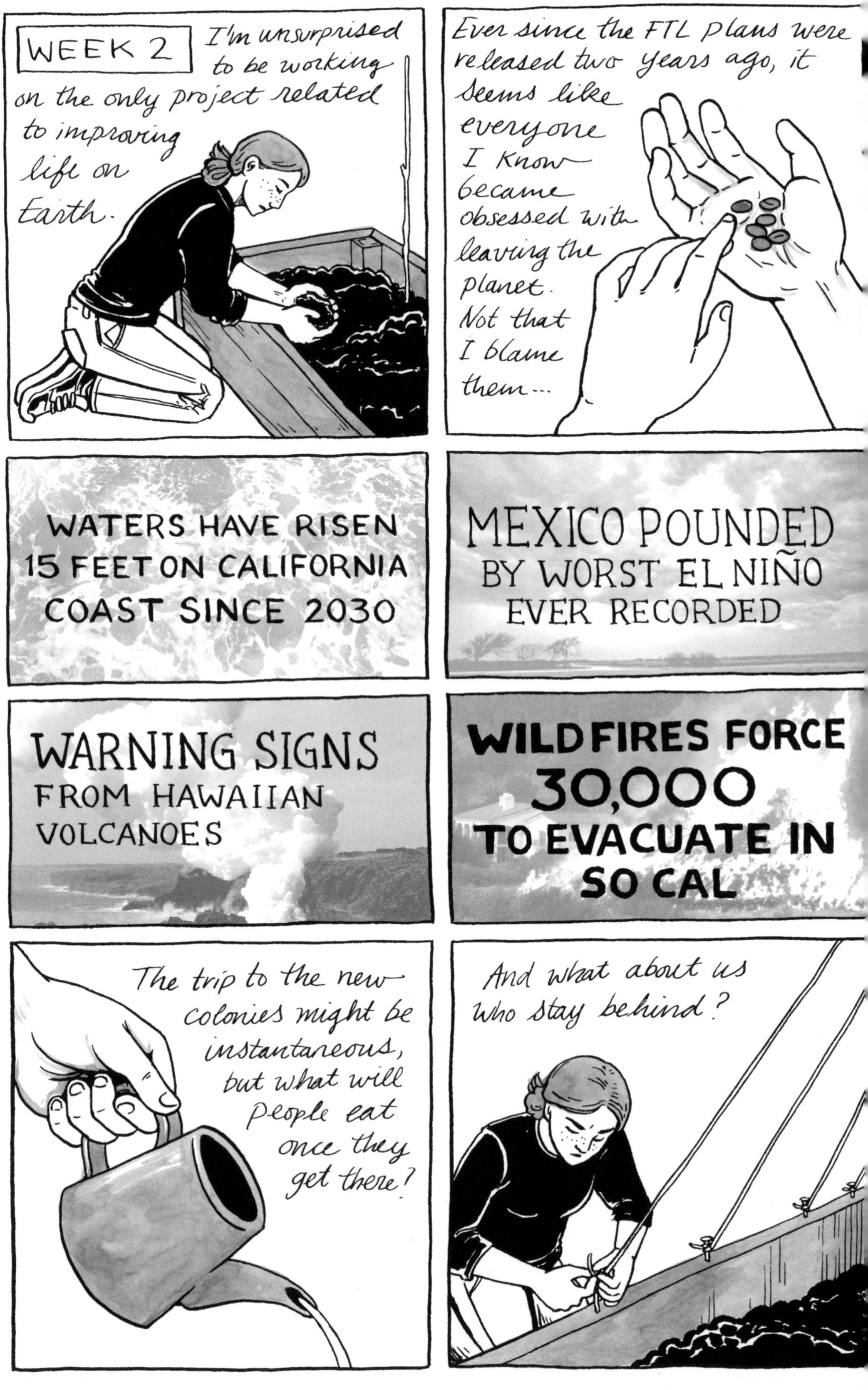
WEEK 2
I'm unsurprised to be working on the only project related to improving life on Earth.
Ever since the FTL plans were released two years ago, it seems like everyone I know became obsessed with leaving the planet. Not that I blame them...
WATERS HAVE RISEN 15 FEET ON CALIFORNIA COAST SINCE 2030
MEXICO POUNDED BY WORST EL NIÑO EVER RECORDED
WARNING SIGNS FROM HAWAIIAN VOLCANOES
WILDFIRES FORCE 30,000 TO EVACUATE IN SO CAL
The trip to the new colonies might be instantaneous, but what will people eat once they get there?
And what about us who stay behind?

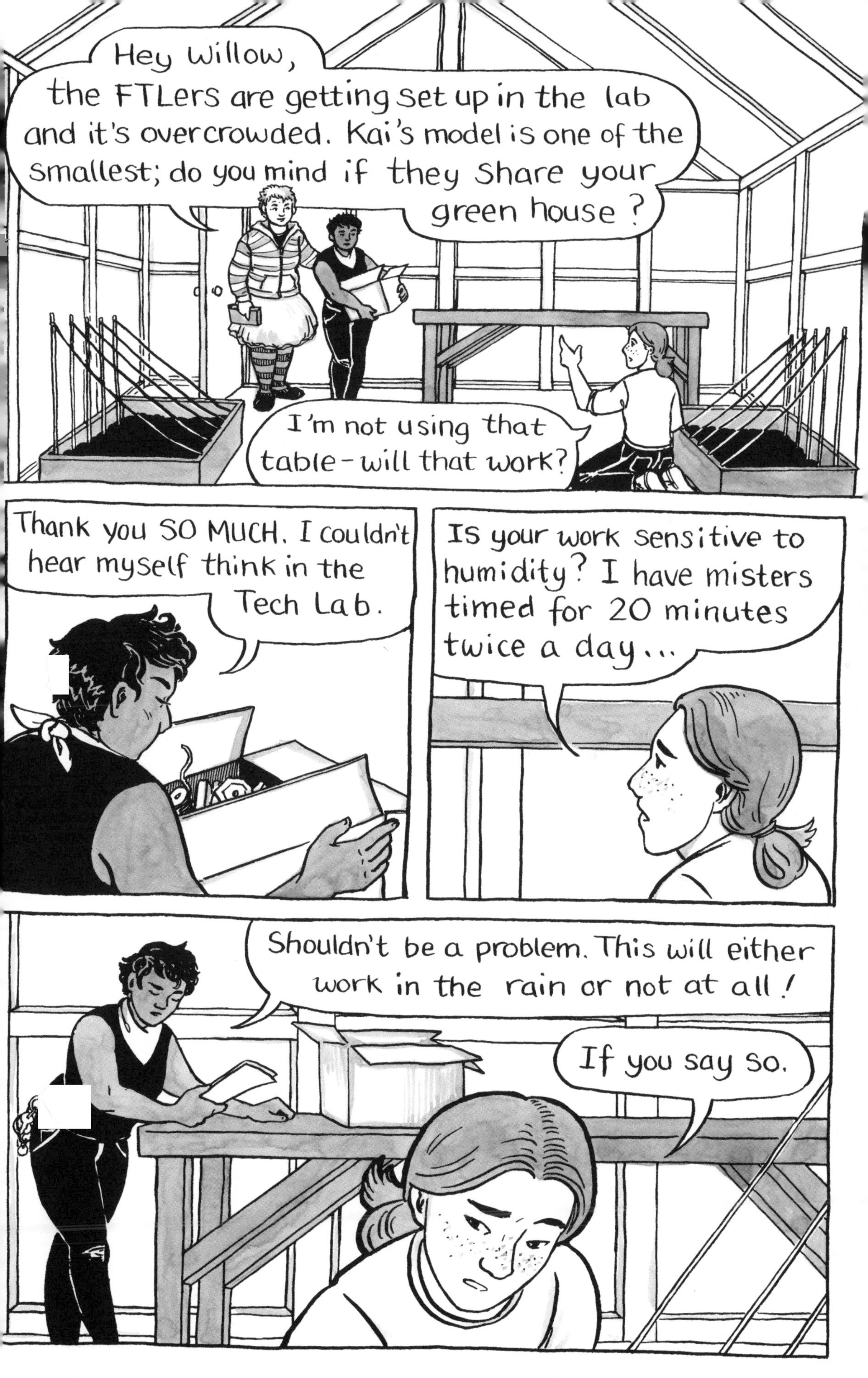

Hey Willow, the FTLers are getting set up in the lab and it's overcrowded. Kai's model is one of the smallest; do you mind if they share your green house?
I'm not using that table - will that work?
Thank you SO MUCH. I couldn't hear myself think in the Tech Lab.
Is your work sensitive to humidity? I have misters timed for 20 minutes twice a day...
Shouldn't be a problem. This will either work in the rain or not at all!
If you say so.

PROJECT JOURNAL

aka The Bean Log

Willow Ramsey
Week #3

To be honest, the hardest part of this project is what I did over the summer—I had access to my mom's bioengineering lab, where I spliced together DNA from two bean types into a completely new bean.

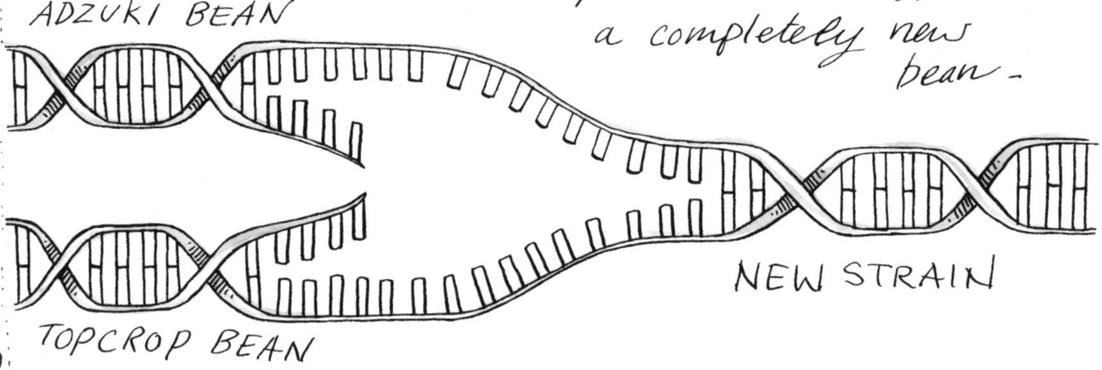

ADZUKI BEAN
NEW STRAIN
TOPCROP BEAN

Topcrop Stats =

Grow cycle of as little as 57 days! They grow into a 2 foot bush—Planted 1 to 2 inches deep, 4 inches apart, a 100 foot row can yield 120 pounds of beans. However need 6-8 hours of Sunlight per day—do less well under grow lights, and have less % protein and less minerals than Adzukis. They cannot be trained to grow up a pole/lattice (like Adzuki)

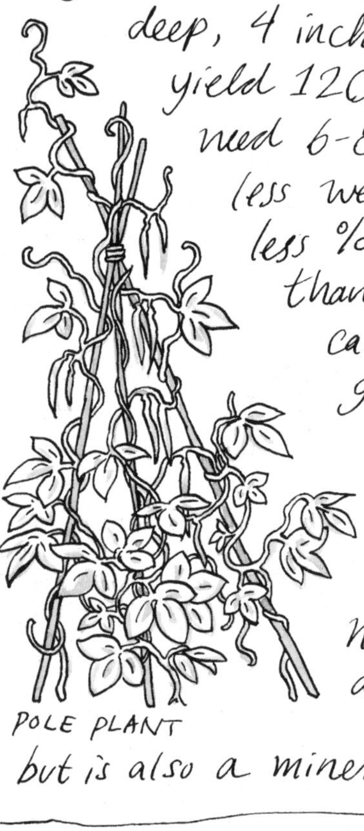

POLE PLANT

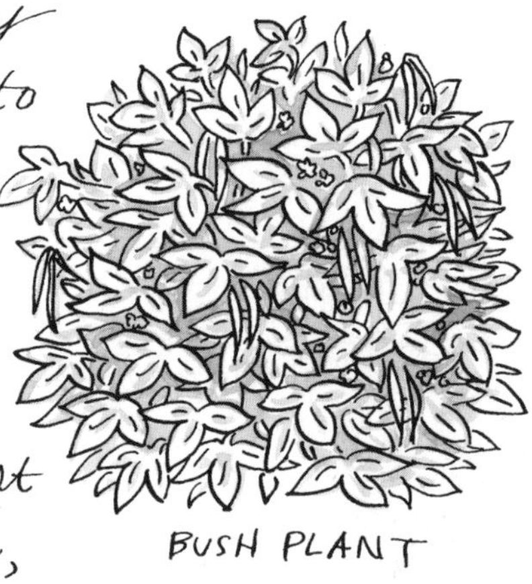

BUSH PLANT

My hope is that the New Strain is just as fast-growing, but is also a mineral rich pole-climbing SUPERBEAN

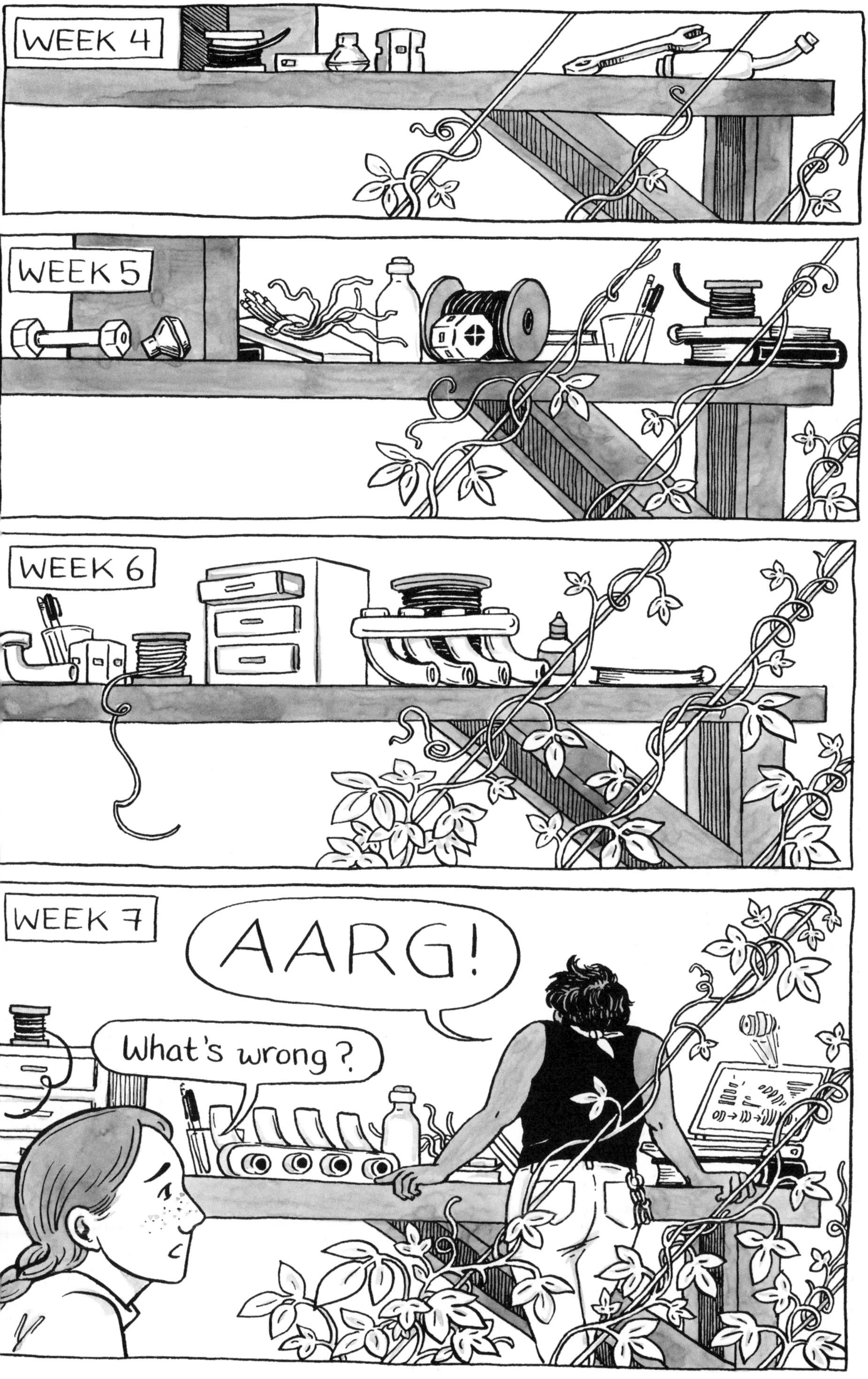
WEEK 4
WEEK 5
WEEK 6
WEEK 7
AARG!
What's wrong?

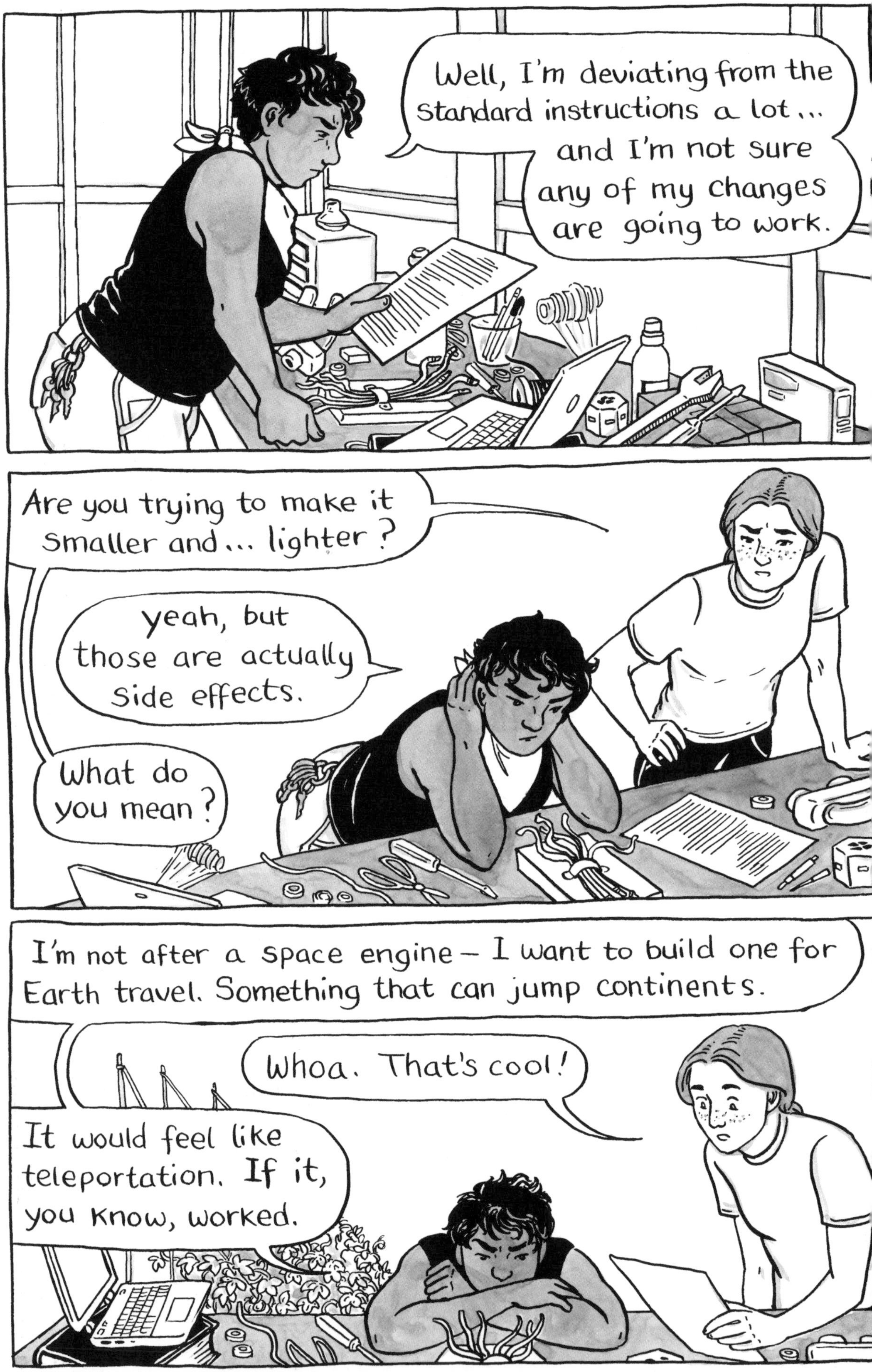
Well, I'm deviating from the standard instructions a lot... and I'm not sure any of my changes are going to work.
Are you trying to make it smaller and... lighter?
yeah, but those are actually side effects.
What do you mean?
I'm not after a space engine – I want to build one for Earth travel. Something that can jump continents.
Whoa. That's cool!
It would feel like teleportation. If it, you know, worked.

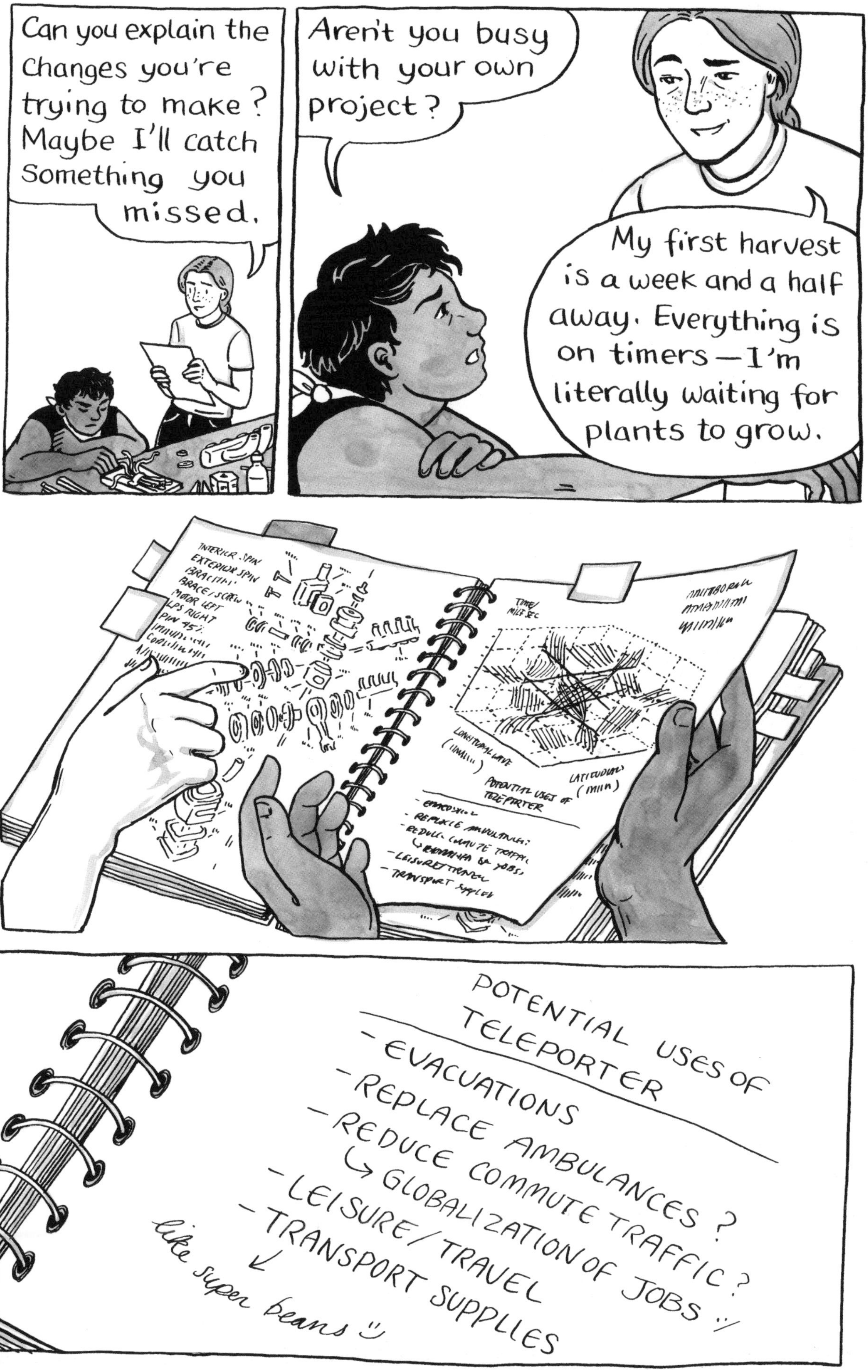
Can you explain the changes you're trying to make? Maybe I'll catch something you missed.
Aren't you busy with your own project?
My first harvest is a week and a half away. Everything is on timers—I'm literally waiting for plants to grow.
POTENTIAL USES OF TELEPORTER
-EVACUATIONS
-REPLACE AMBULANCES?
-REDUCE COMMUTE TRAFFIC?
↳ GLOBALIZATION OF JOBS :/
-LEISURE/TRAVEL
-TRANSPORT SUPPLIES
like super beans :)

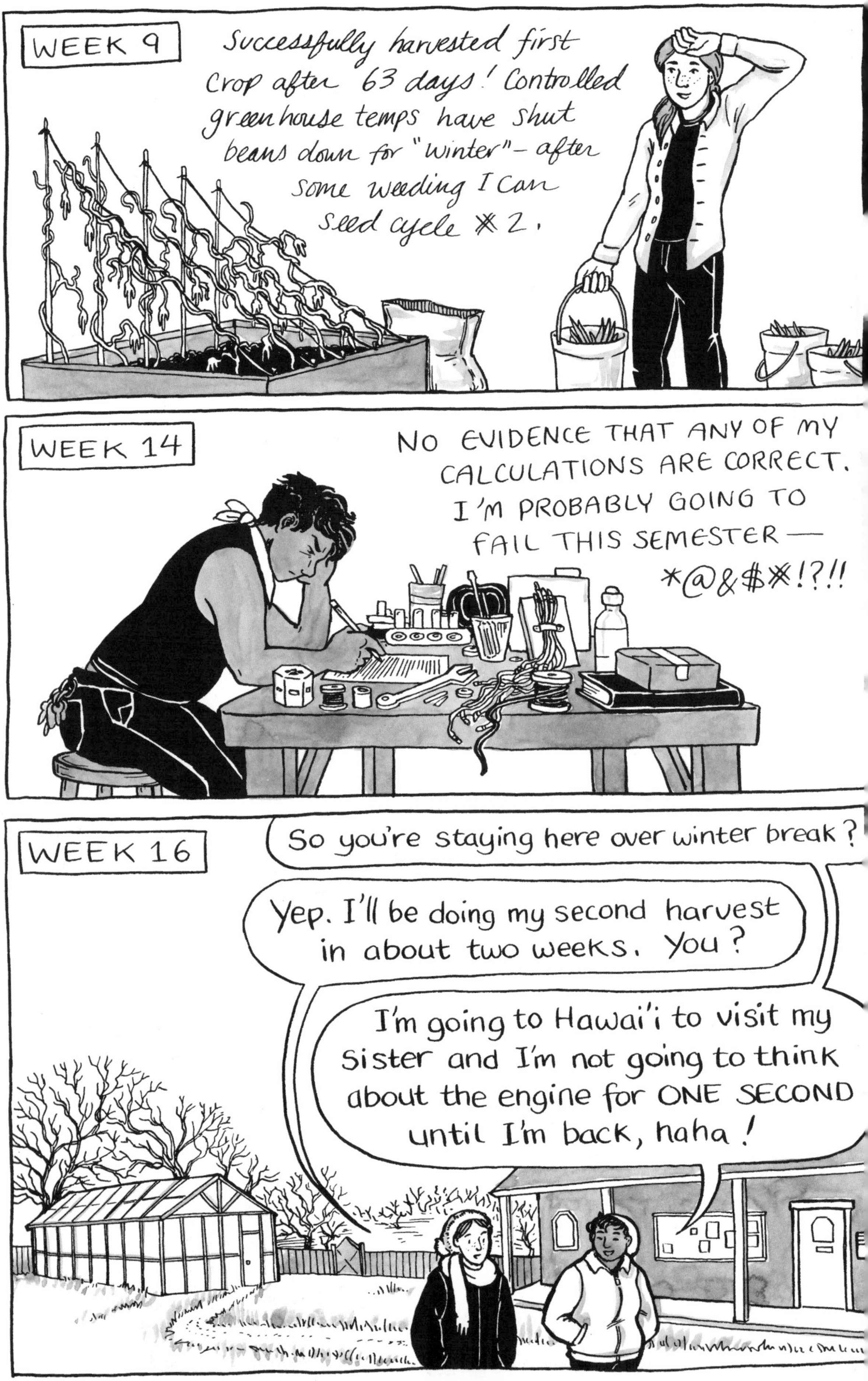
WEEK 9
Successfully harvested first crop after 63 days! Controlled greenhouse temps have shut beans down for "winter"– after some weeding I can seed cycle ※2.
WEEK 14
NO EVIDENCE THAT ANY OF MY CALCULATIONS ARE CORRECT. I'M PROBABLY GOING TO FAIL THIS SEMESTER— *@&$※!?!!
WEEK 16
So you're staying here over winter break?
Yep. I'll be doing my second harvest in about two weeks. You?
I'm going to Hawai'i to visit my sister and I'm not going to think about the engine for ONE SECOND until I'm back, haha!

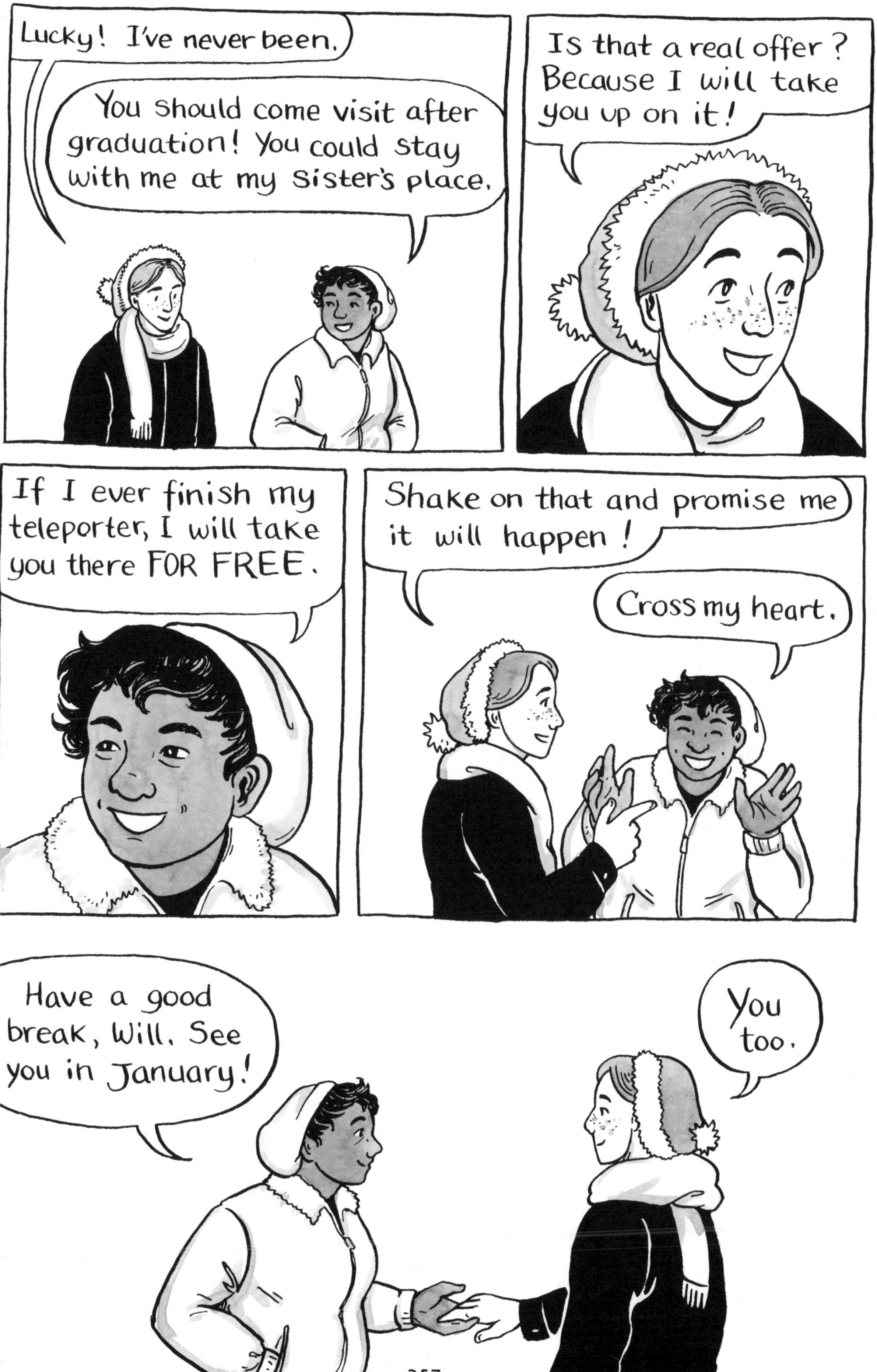
Lucky! I've never been.
You should come visit after graduation! You could stay with me at my sister's place.
Is that a real offer? Because I will take you up on it!
If I ever finish my teleporter, I will take you there FOR FREE.
Shake on that and promise me it will happen!
Cross my heart.
Have a good break, Will. See you in January!
You too.

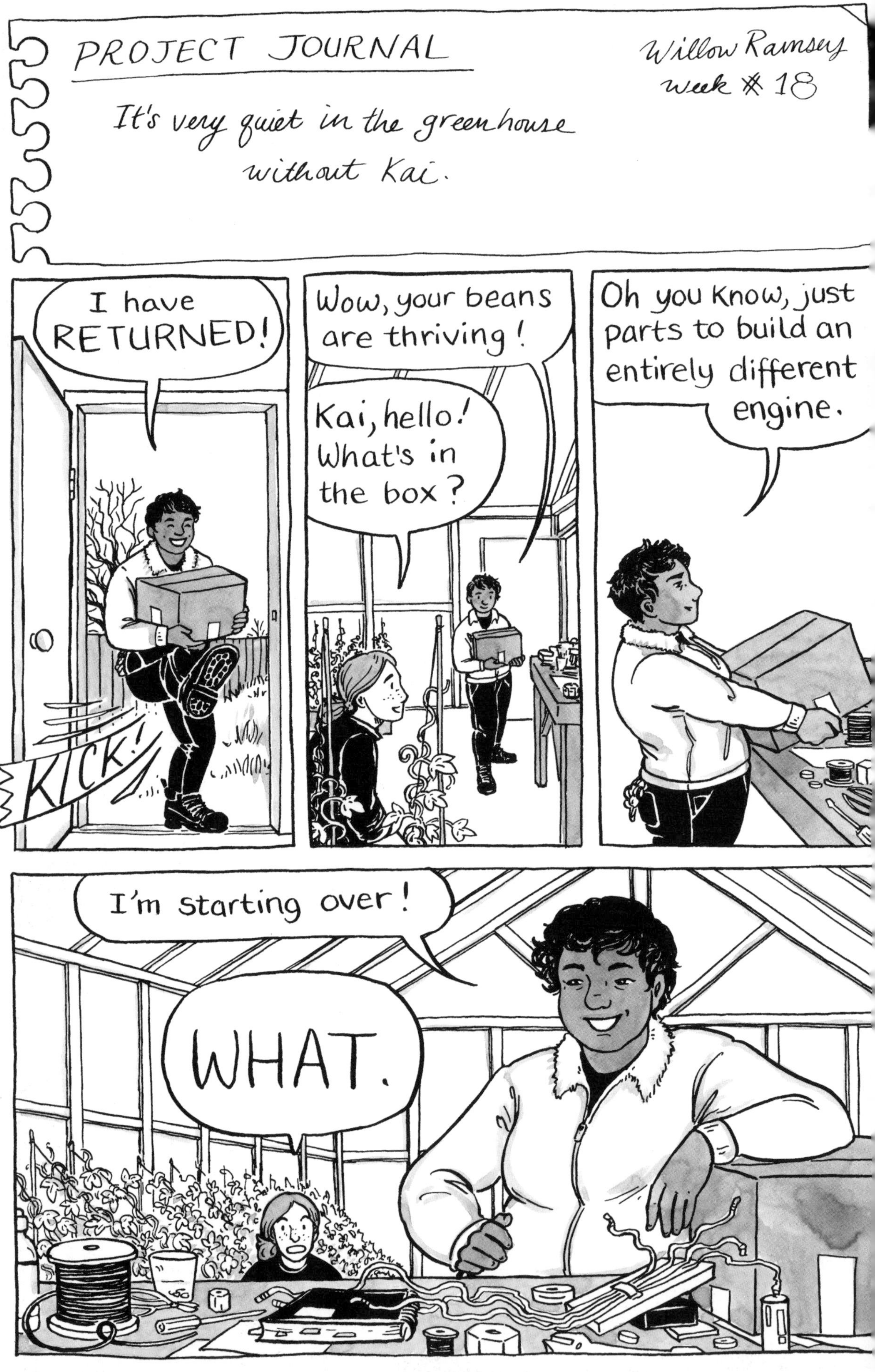
PROJECT JOURNAL
Willow Ramsey
week #18
It's very quiet in the greenhouse without Kai.
I have RETURNED!
KICK!
Wow, your beans are thriving!
Kai, hello! What's in the box?
Oh you know, just parts to build an entirely different engine.
I'm starting over!
WHAT.

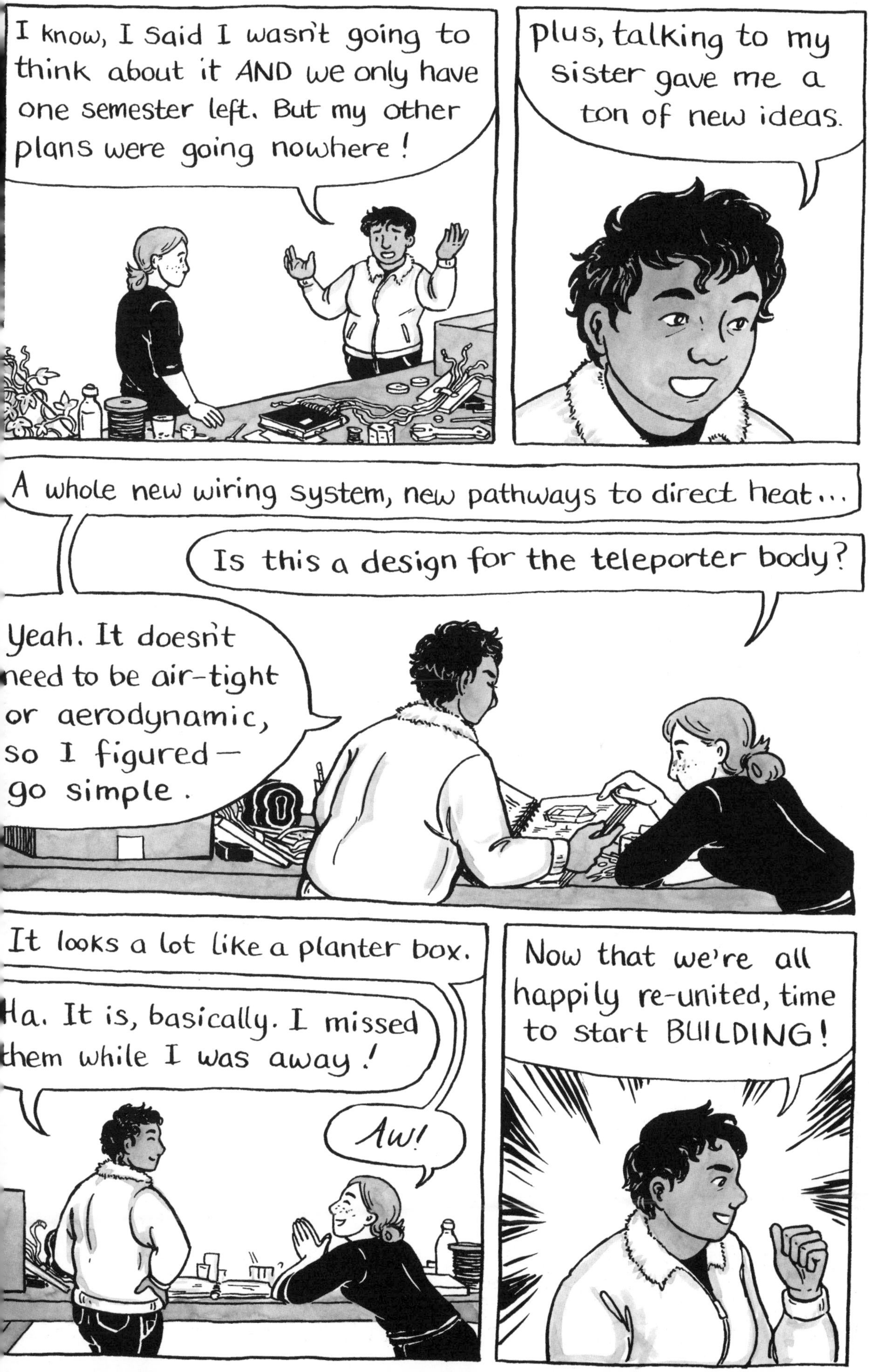

I know, I said I wasn't going to think about it AND we only have one semester left. But my other plans were going nowhere!
plus, talking to my sister gave me a ton of new ideas.
A whole new wiring system, new pathways to direct heat...
Is this a design for the teleporter body?
Yeah. It doesn't need to be air-tight or aerodynamic, so I figured— go simple.
It looks a lot like a planter box.
Ha. It is, basically. I missed them while I was away!
Aw!
Now that we're all happily re-united, time to start BUILDING!

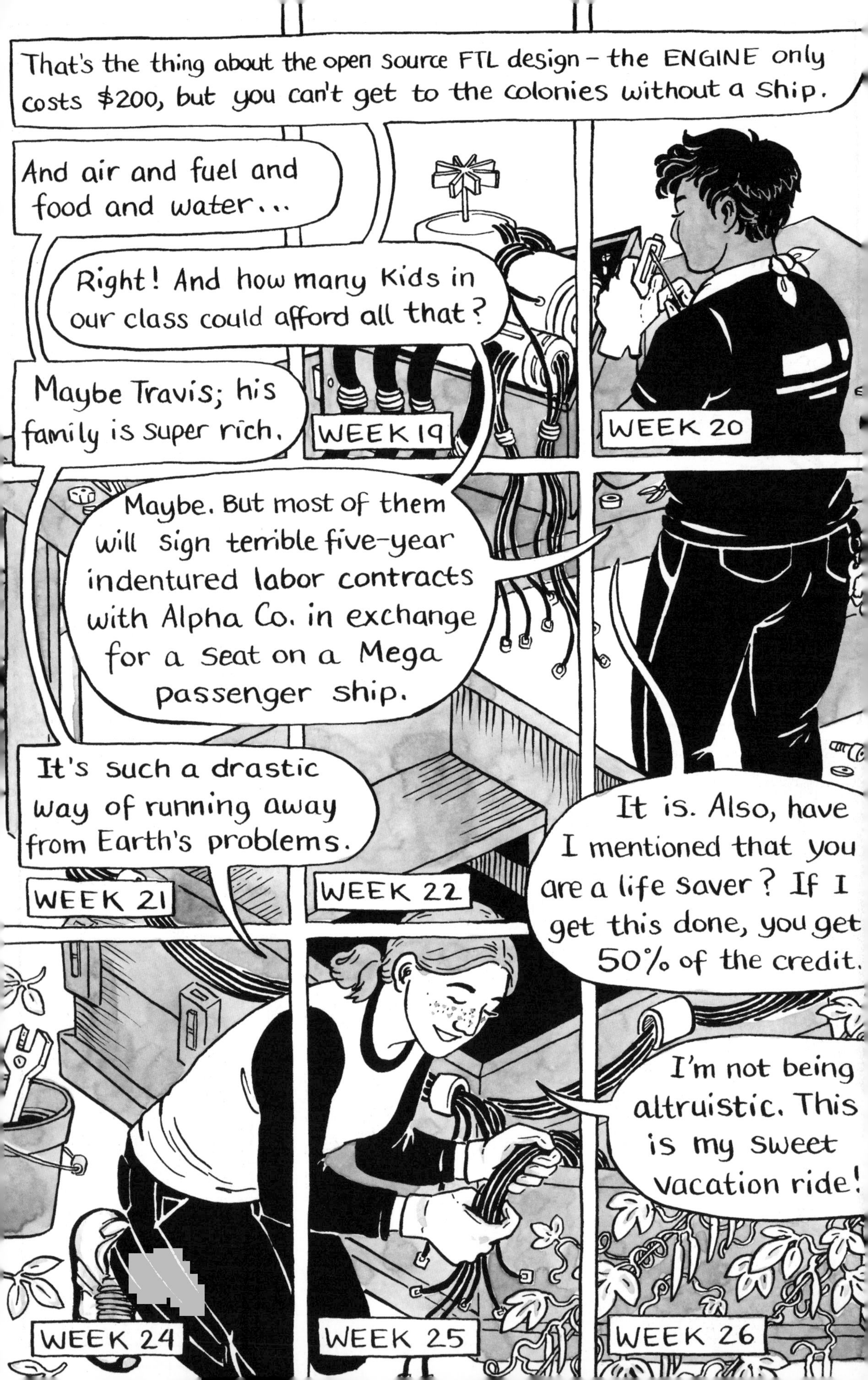

That's the thing about the open source FTL design – the ENGINE only costs $200, but you can't get to the colonies without a ship.
And air and fuel and food and water...
Right! And how many kids in our class could afford all that?
Maybe Travis; his family is super rich.
WEEK 19
WEEK 20
Maybe. But most of them will sign terrible five-year indentured labor contracts with Alpha Co. in exchange for a seat on a Mega passenger ship.
It's such a drastic way of running away from Earth's problems.
WEEK 21
WEEK 22
It is. Also, have I mentioned that you are a life saver? If I get this done, you get 50% of the credit.
I'm not being altruistic. This is my sweet vacation ride!
WEEK 24
WEEK 25
WEEK 26

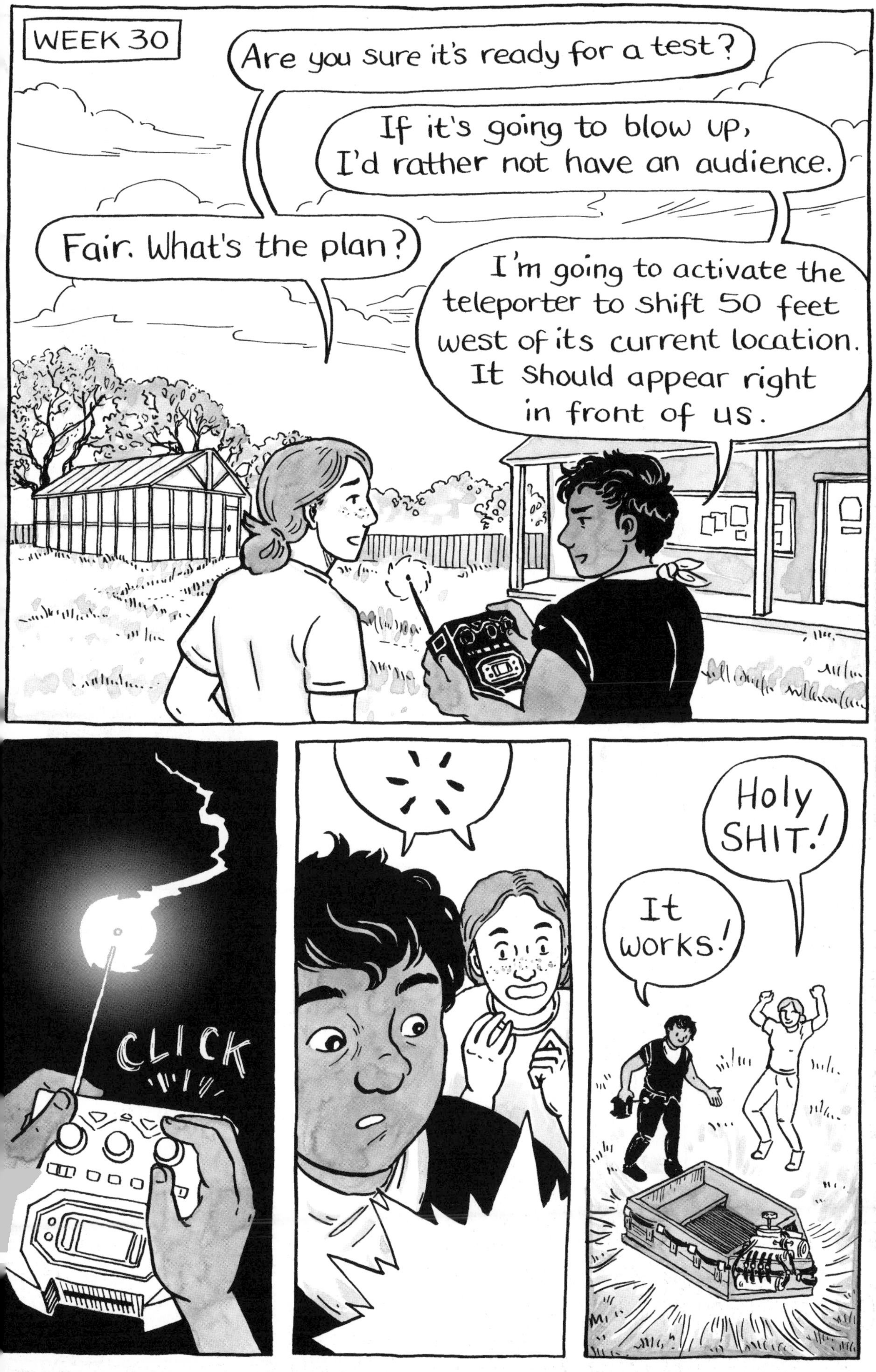
WEEK 30
Are you sure it's ready for a test?
If it's going to blow up, I'd rather not have an audience.
Fair. What's the plan?
I'm going to activate the teleporter to shift 50 feet west of its current location. It should appear right in front of us.
CLICK
Holy SHIT!
It works!

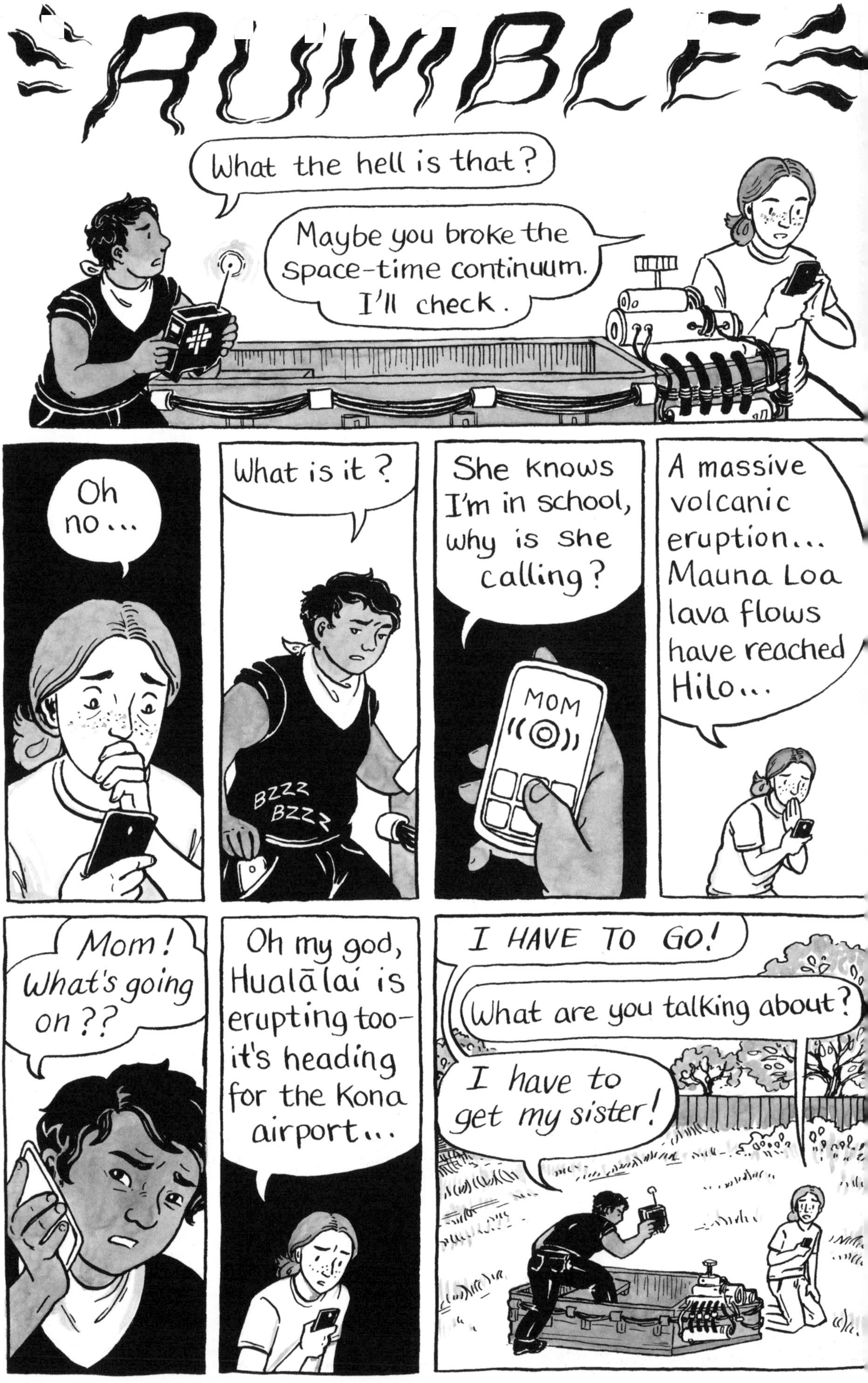
RUMBLE
What the hell is that?
Maybe you broke the space-time continuum. I'll check.
Oh no...
What is it?
BZZZ BZZZ
She knows I'm in school, why is she calling?
MOM
A massive volcanic eruption... Mauna Loa lava flows have reached Hilo...
Mom! What's going on??
Oh my god, Hualālai is erupting too- it's heading for the Kona airport...
I HAVE TO GO!
What are you talking about?
I have to get my sister!

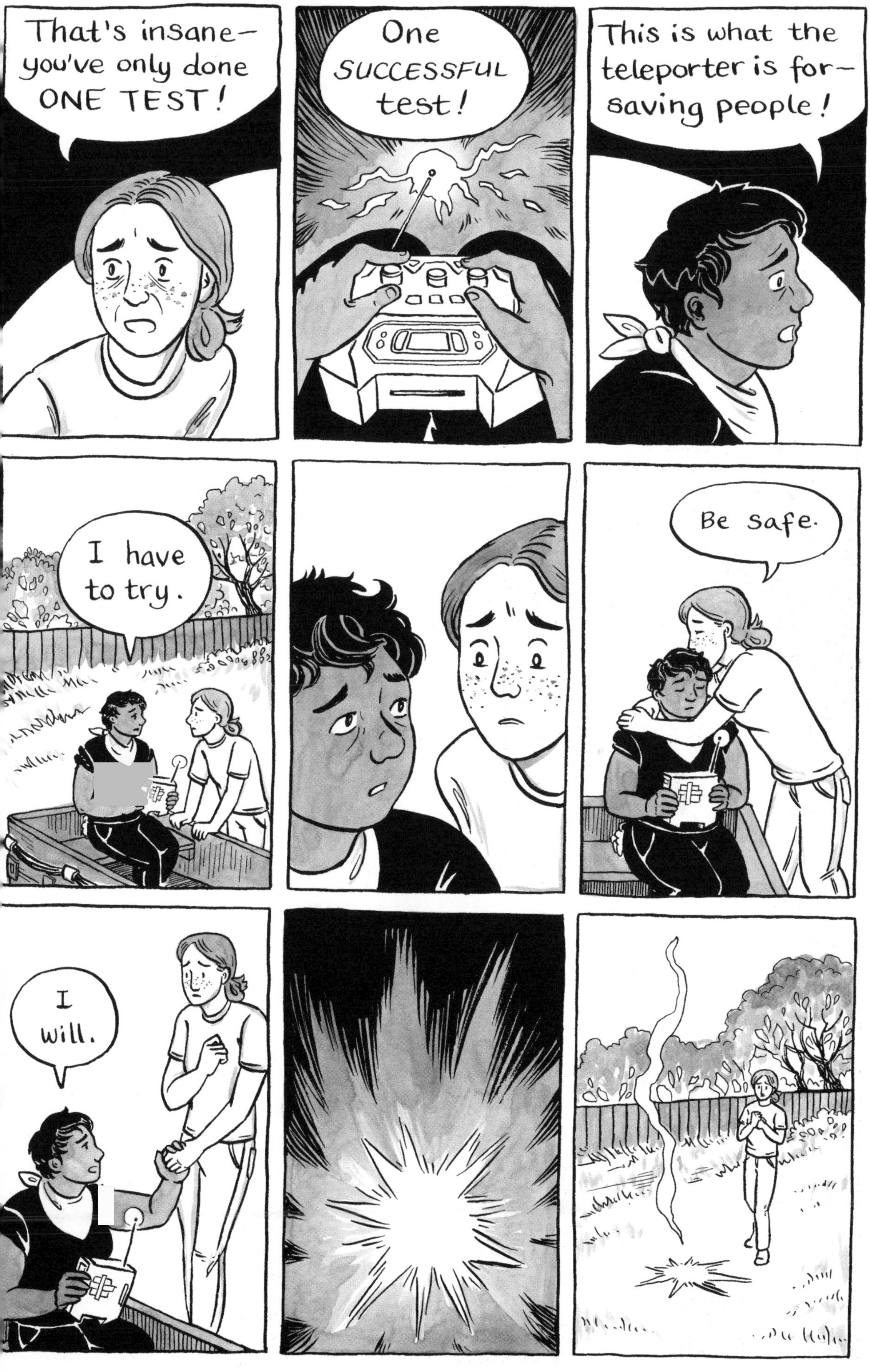
That's insane—you've only done ONE TEST!
One SUCCESSFUL test!
This is what the teleporter is for—saving people!
I have to try.
Be safe.
I will.

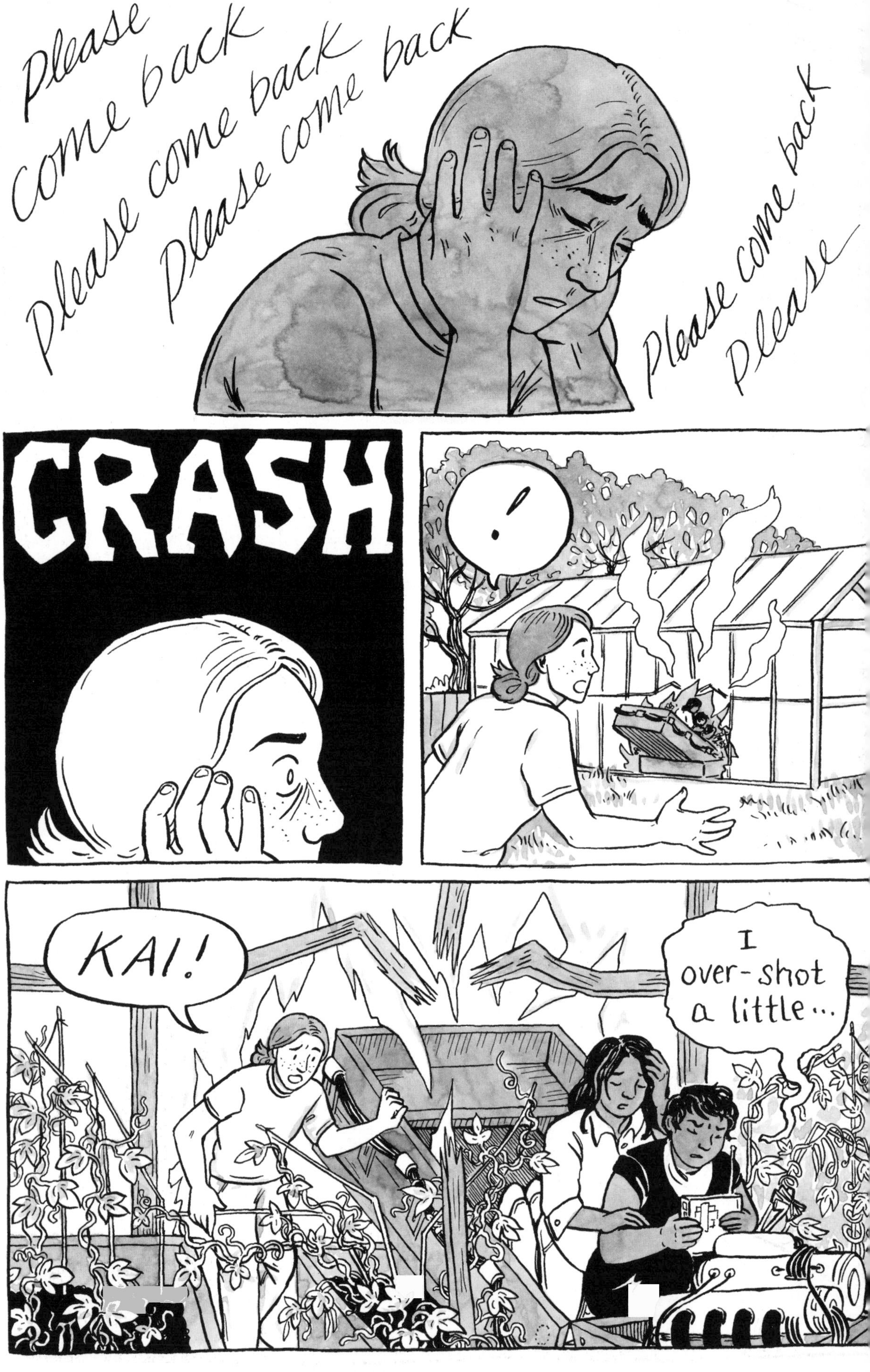
Please come back Please come back Please come back
Please come back Please
CRASH
!
KAI!
I over-shot a little...

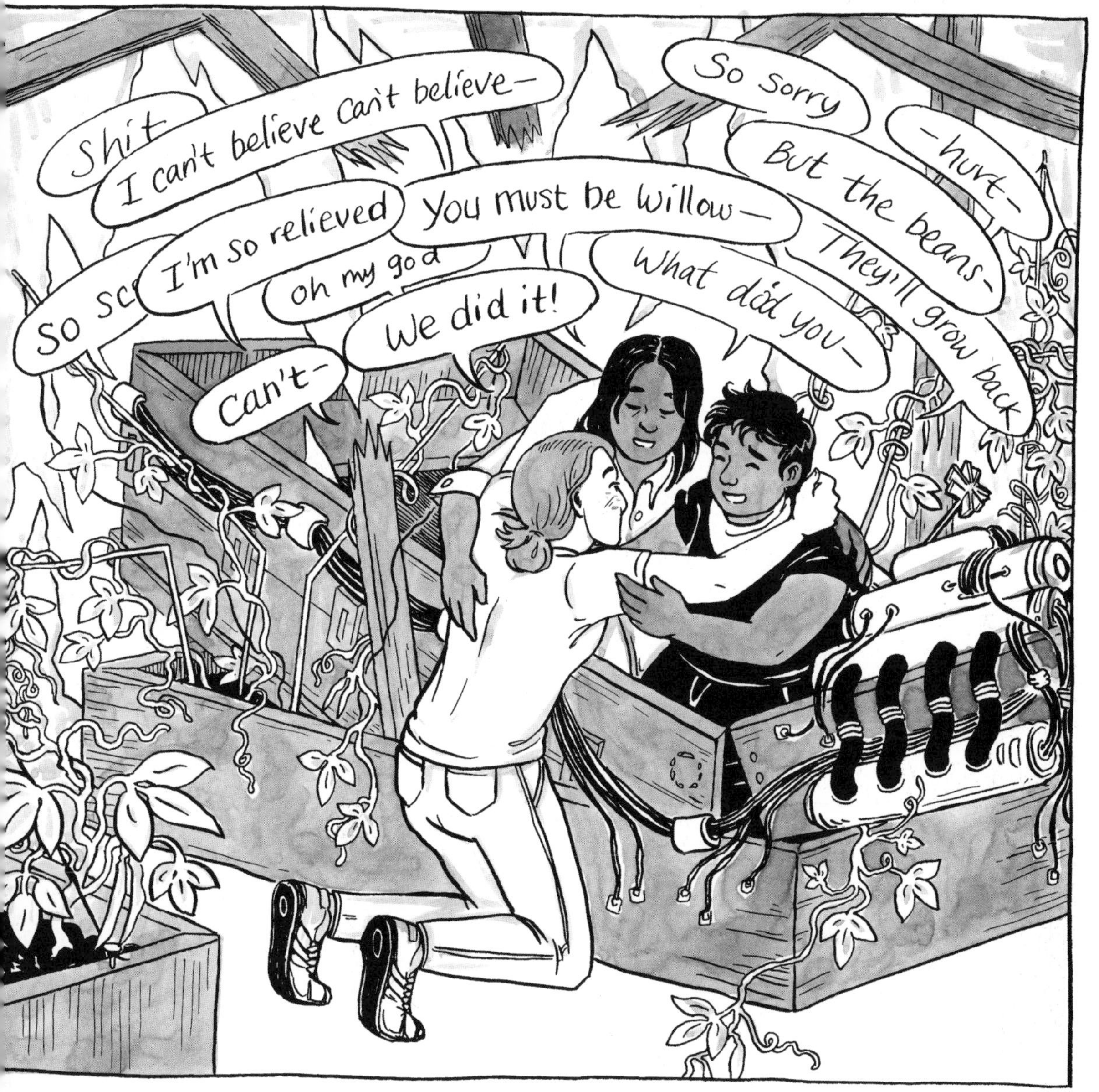
Shit
I can't believe can't believe-
So sorry
-hurt-
You must be Willow-
But the beans-
I'm so relieved
So sc
oh my god
What did you-
They'll grow back
We did it!
Can't-

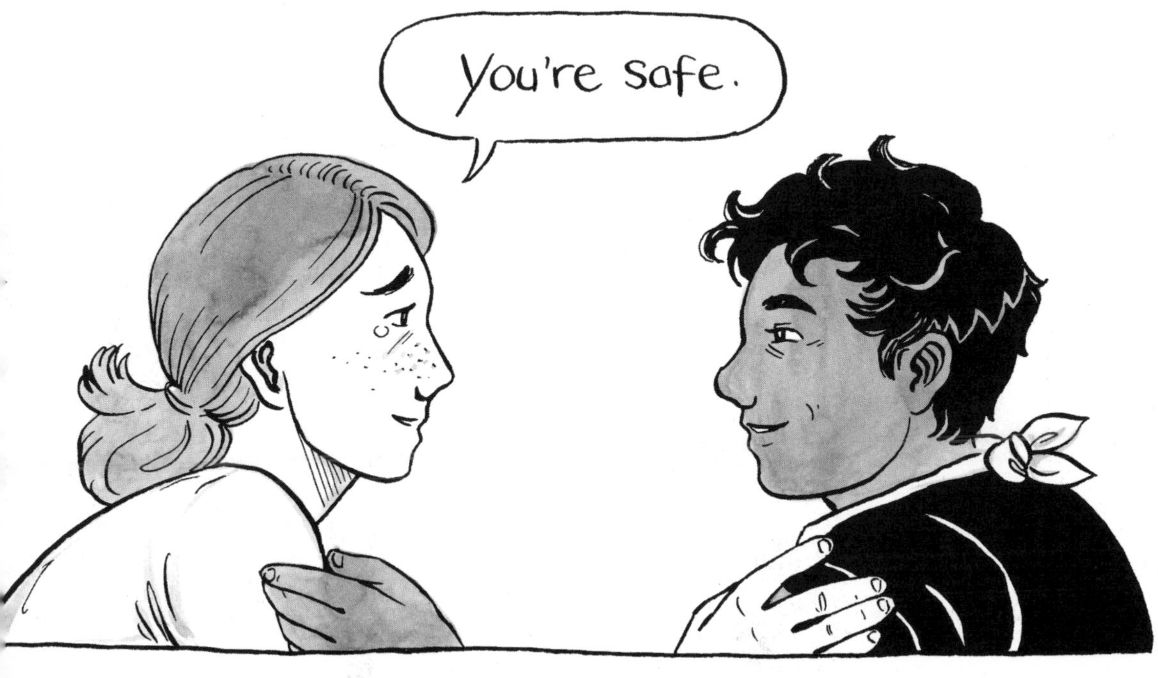
You're safe.

MY STARS AND GARTERS

AINSLEY SEAGO

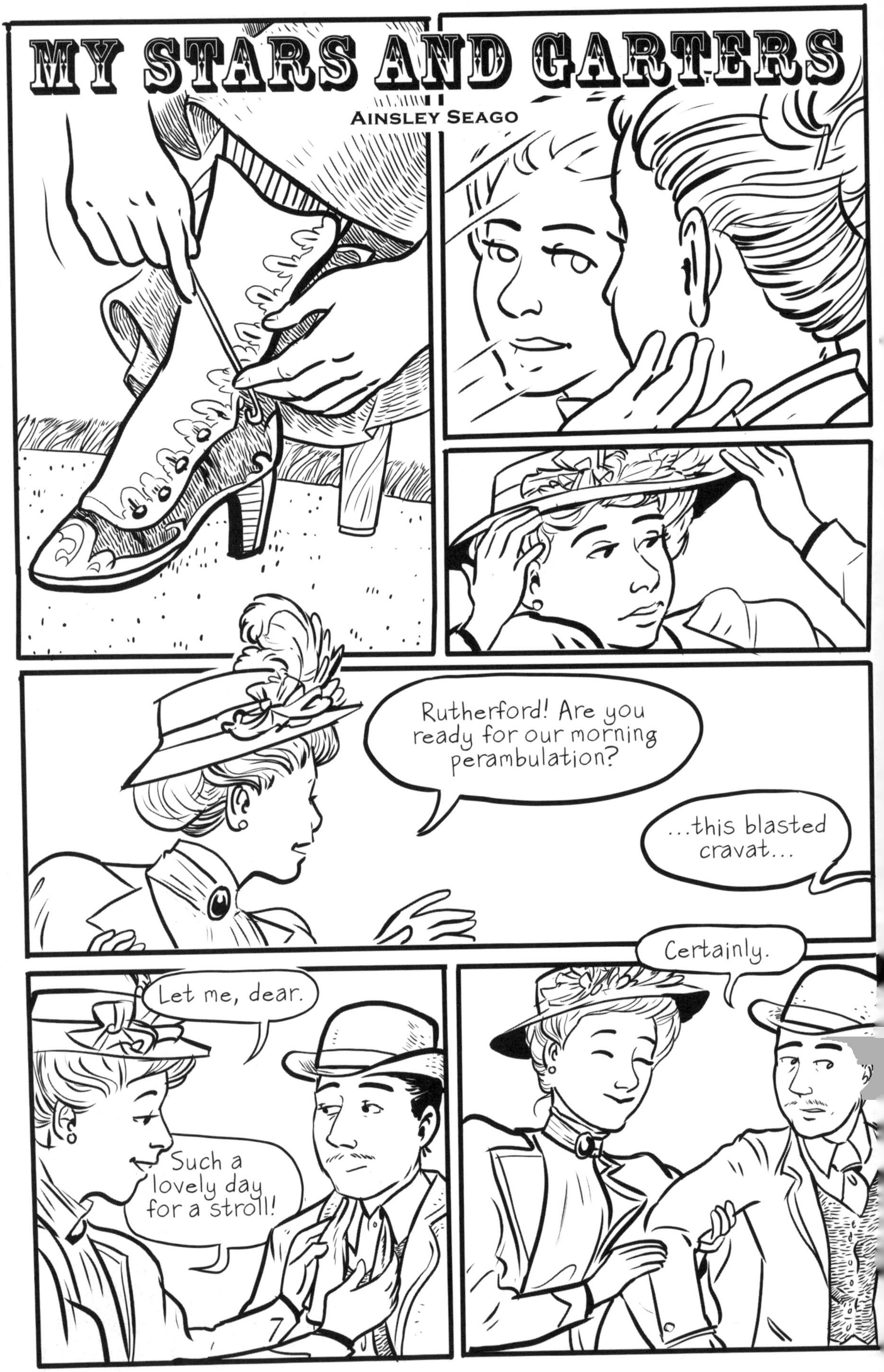
Rutherford! Are you ready for our morning perambulation?
...this blasted cravat...
Let me, dear.
Such a lovely day for a stroll!
Certainly.

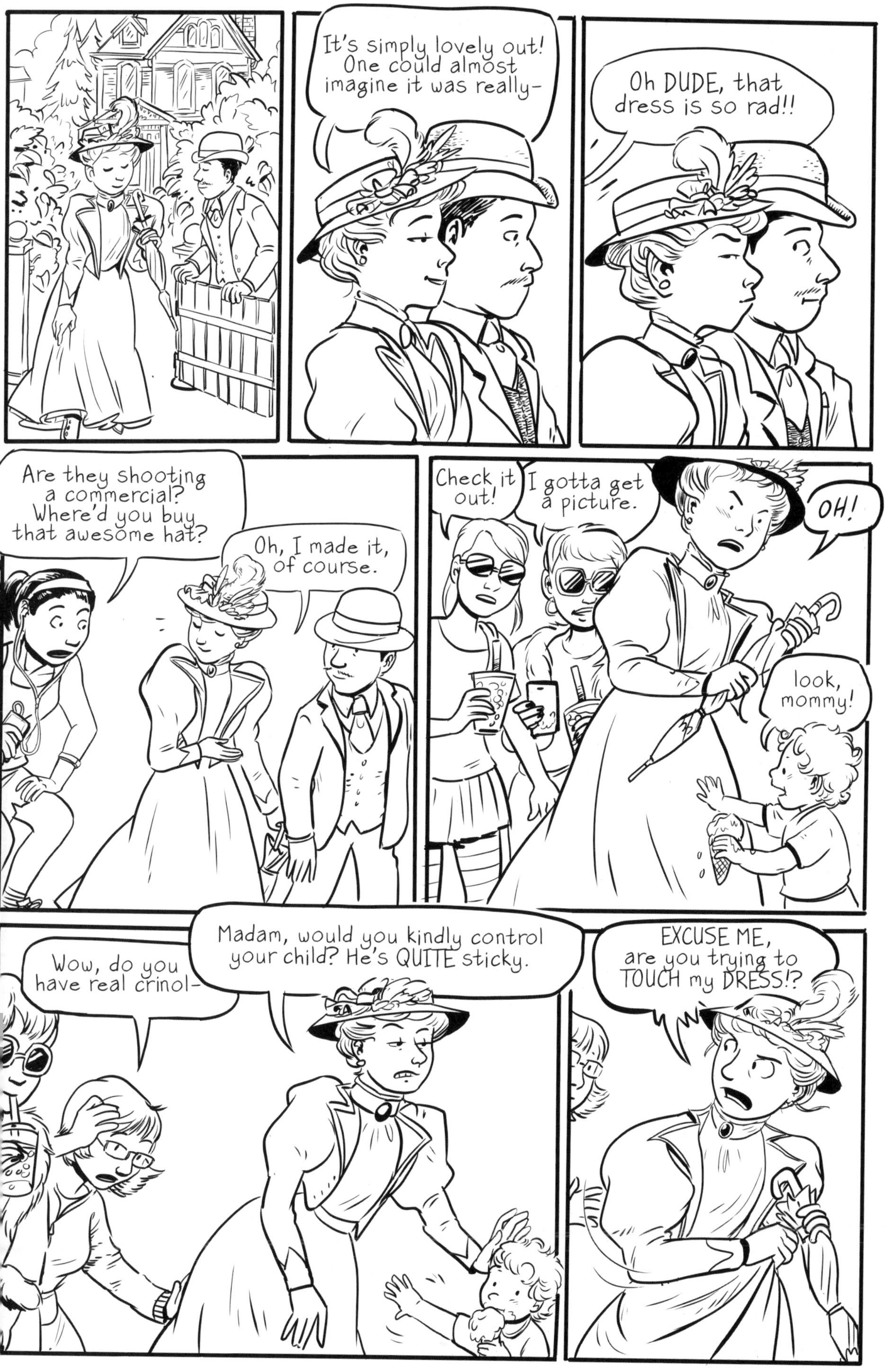
It's simply lovely out! One could almost imagine it was really-
Oh DUDE, that dress is so rad!!
Are they shooting a commercial? Where'd you buy that awesome hat?
Oh, I made it, of course.
Check it out!
I gotta get a picture.
OH!
look, mommy!
Wow, do you have real crinol-
Madam, would you kindly control your child? He's QUITE sticky.
EXCUSE ME, are you trying to TOUCH my DRESS!?

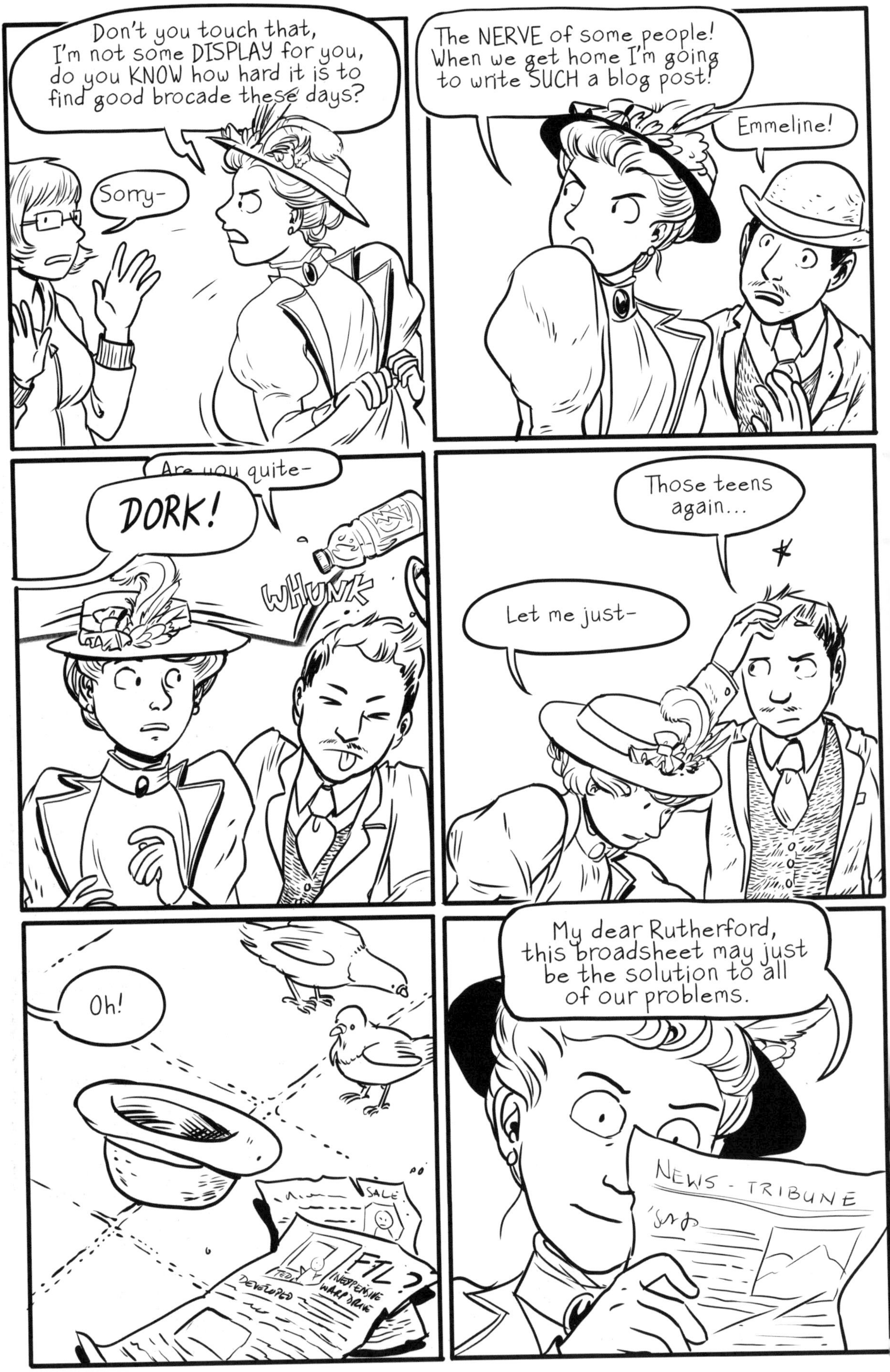
Don't you touch that, I'm not some DISPLAY for you, do you KNOW how hard it is to find good brocade these days?
Sorry-
The NERVE of some people! When we get home I'm going to write SUCH a blog post!
Emmeline!
Are you quite-
DORK!
WHUNK
Those teens again...
Let me just-
Oh!
SALE
FTL?
INEXPENSIVE WARP DRIVE
DEVELOPED
My dear Rutherford, this broadsheet may just be the solution to all of our problems.
NEWS - TRIBUNE

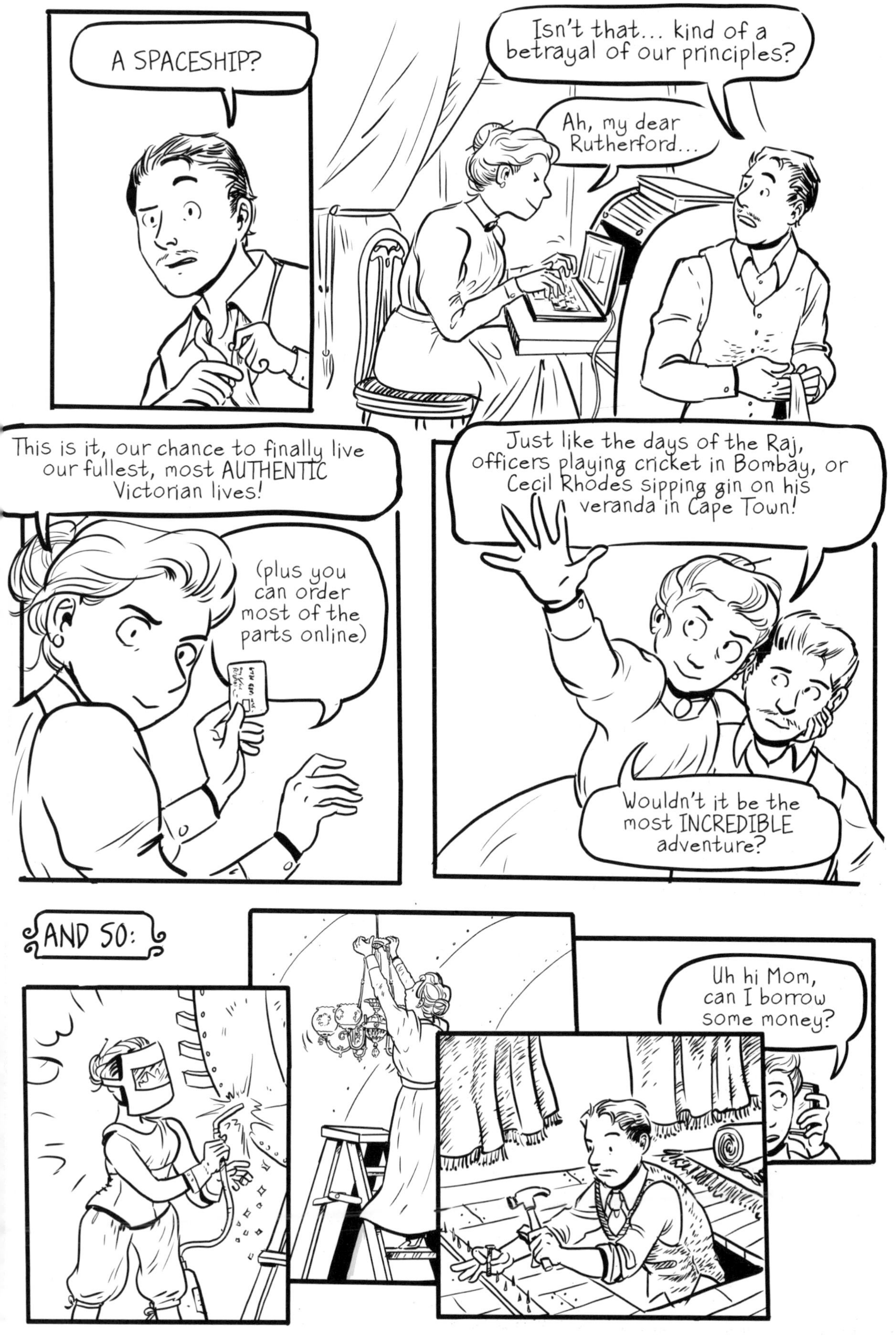
A SPACESHIP?
Isn't that... kind of a betrayal of our principles?
Ah, my dear Rutherford...
This is it, our chance to finally live our fullest, most AUTHENTIC Victorian lives!
(plus you can order most of the parts online)
Just like the days of the Raj, officers playing cricket in Bombay, or Cecil Rhodes sipping gin on his veranda in Cape Town!
Wouldn't it be the most INCREDIBLE adventure?
AND SO:
Uh hi Mom, can I borrow some money?

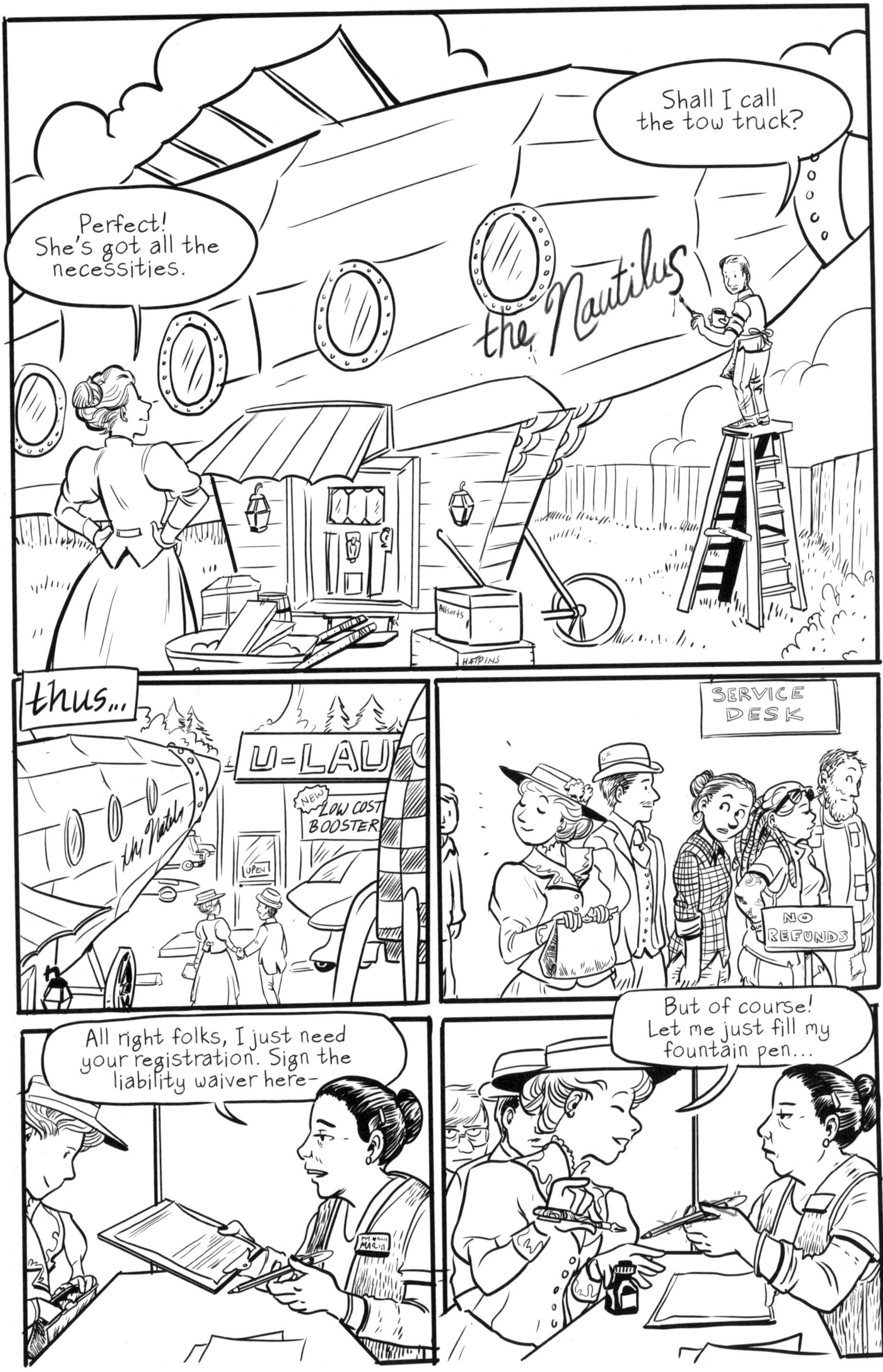

Shall I call the tow truck?
Perfect! She's got all the necessities.
the Nautilus
Allsorts
HATPINS
thus...
U-LAU
NEW LOW COST BOOSTER
OPEN
the Nautilus
SERVICE DESK
NO REFUNDS
All right folks, I just need your registration. Sign the liability waiver here-
But of course! Let me just fill my fountain pen...

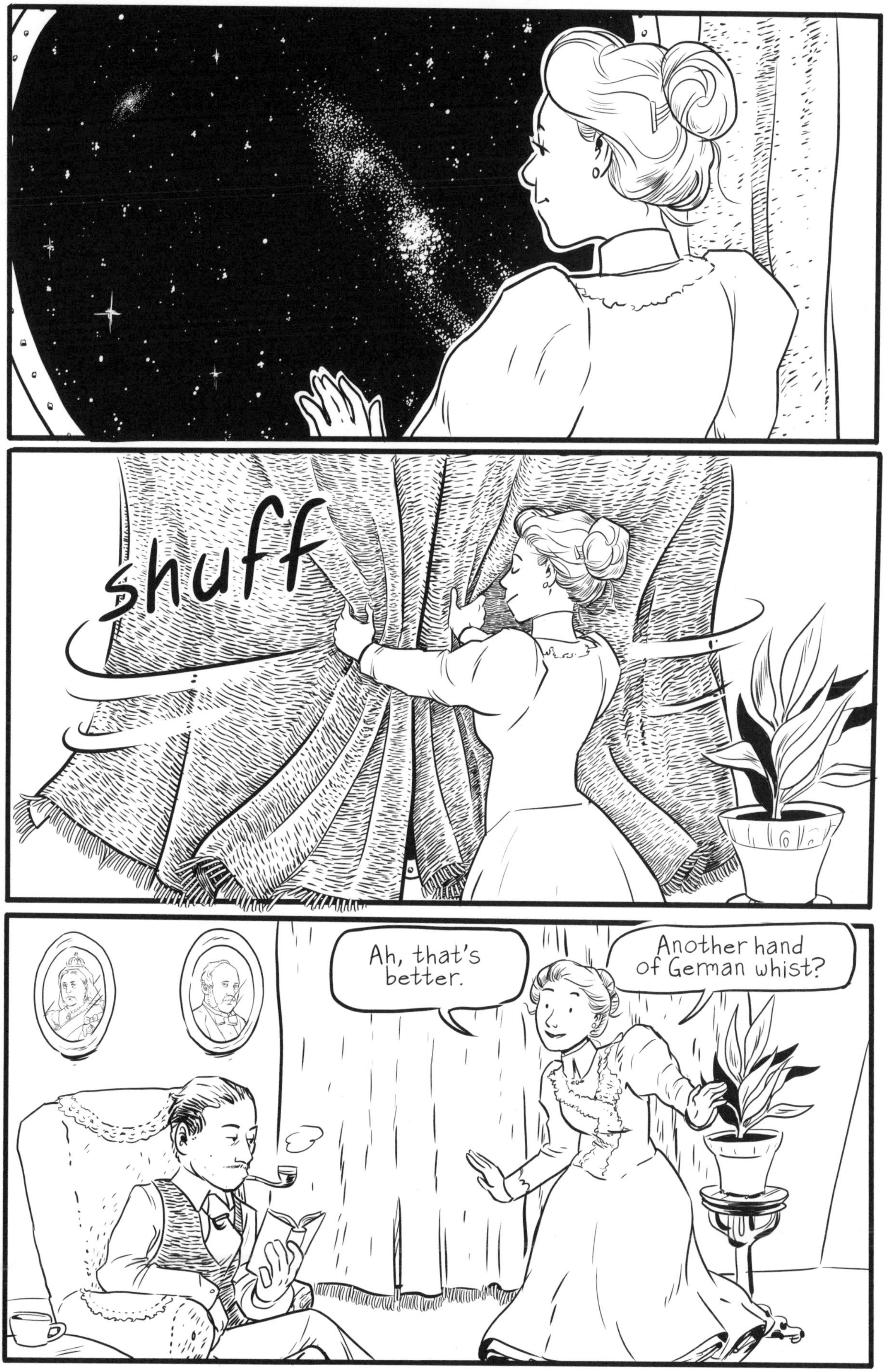
shuff
Ah, that's better.
Another hand of German whist?

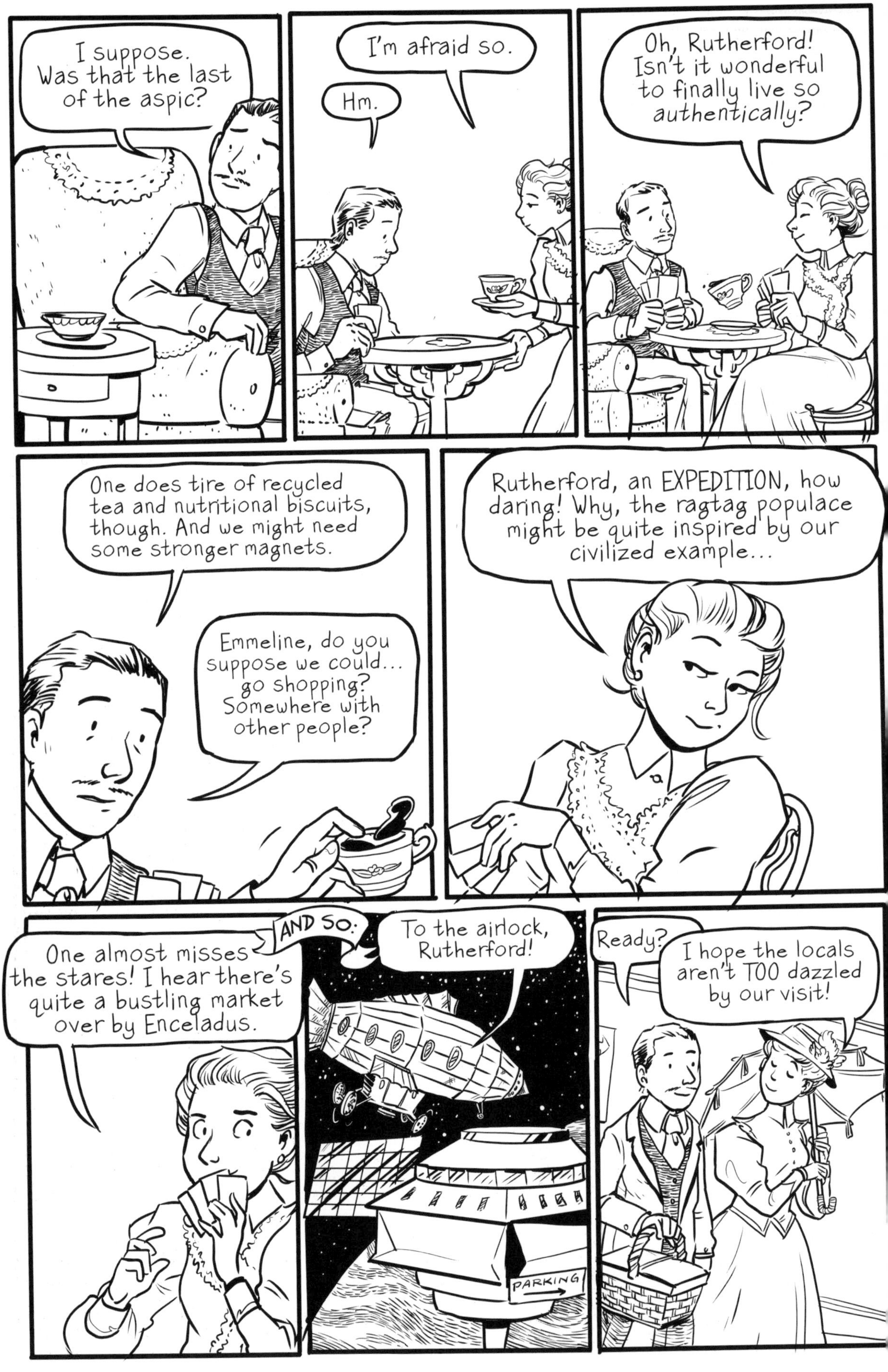
I suppose. Was that the last of the aspic?
I'm afraid so.
Hm.
Oh, Rutherford! Isn't it wonderful to finally live so *authentically*?
One does tire of recycled tea and nutritional biscuits, though. And we might need some stronger magnets.
Emmeline, do you suppose we could... go shopping? Somewhere with other people?
Rutherford, an EXPEDITION, how daring! Why, the ragtag populace might be quite inspired by our civilized example...
One almost misses the stares! I hear there's quite a bustling market over by Enceladus.
AND SO:
To the airlock, Rutherford!
PARKING
Ready?
I hope the locals aren't TOO dazzled by our visit!

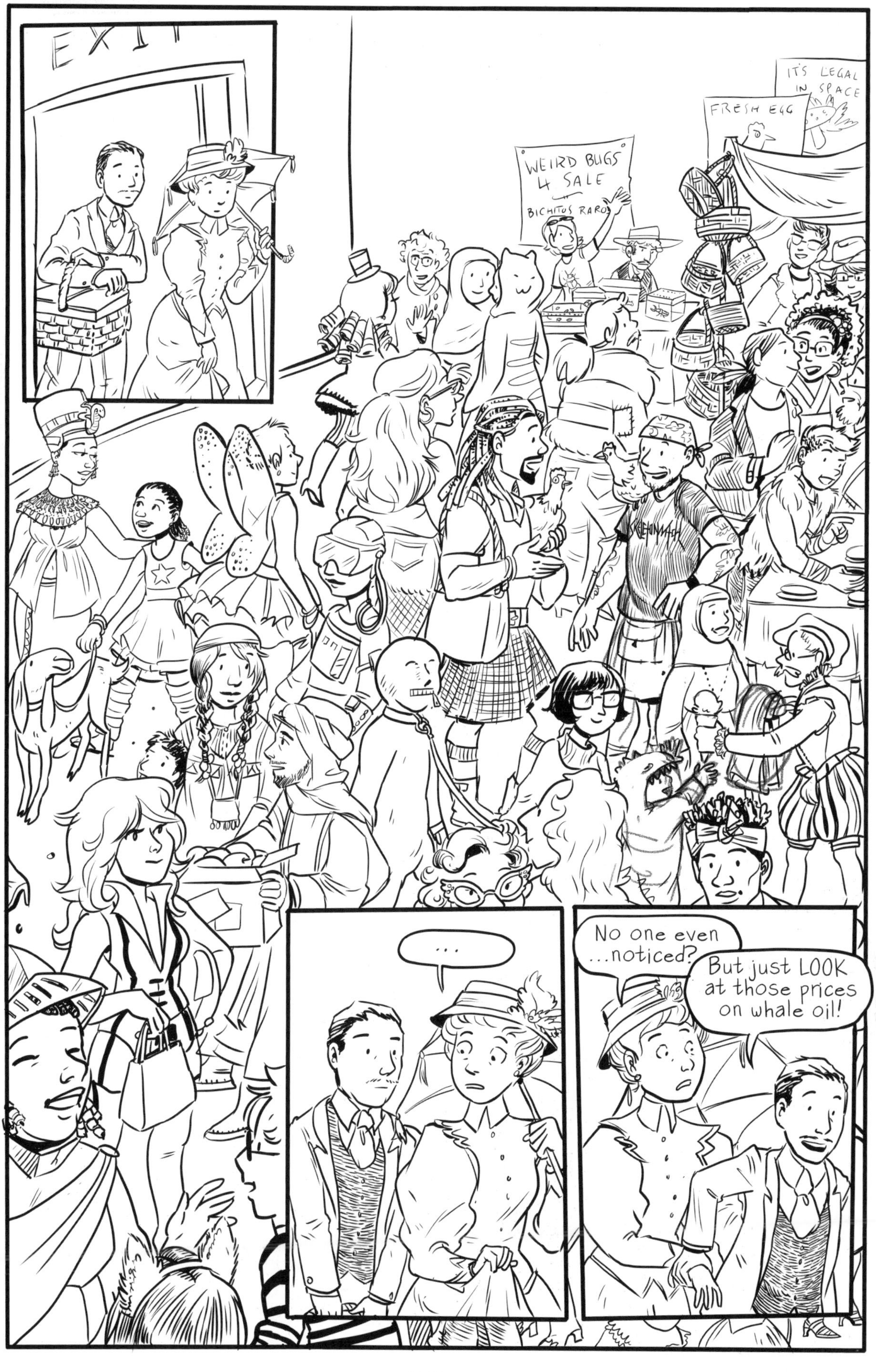
EXIT
IT'S LEGAL IN SPACE
FRESH EGG
WEIRD BUGS 4 SALE
BICHITOS RAROS
...
No one even ...noticed?
But just LOOK at those prices on whale oil!

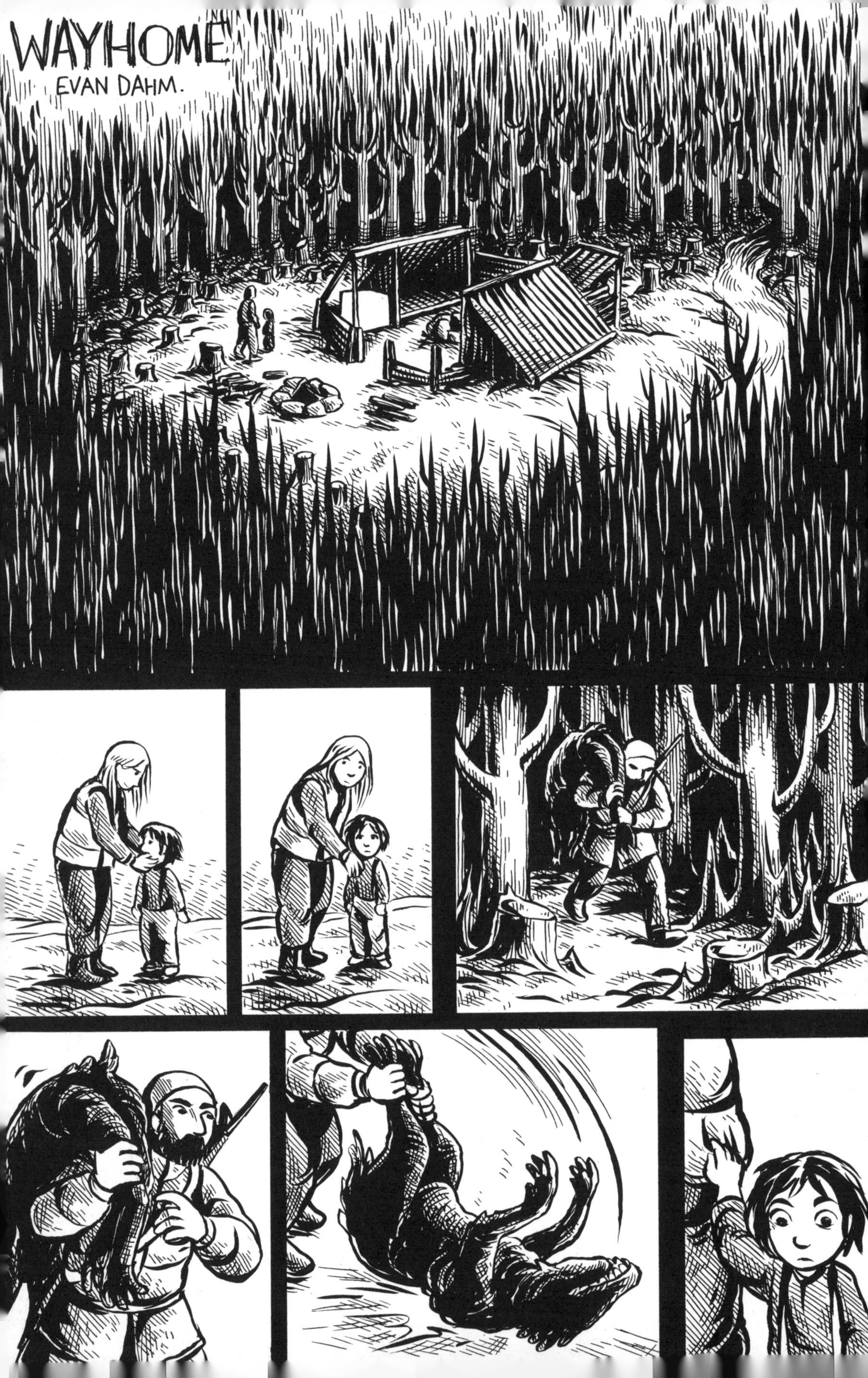
WAYHOME
EVAN DAHM.

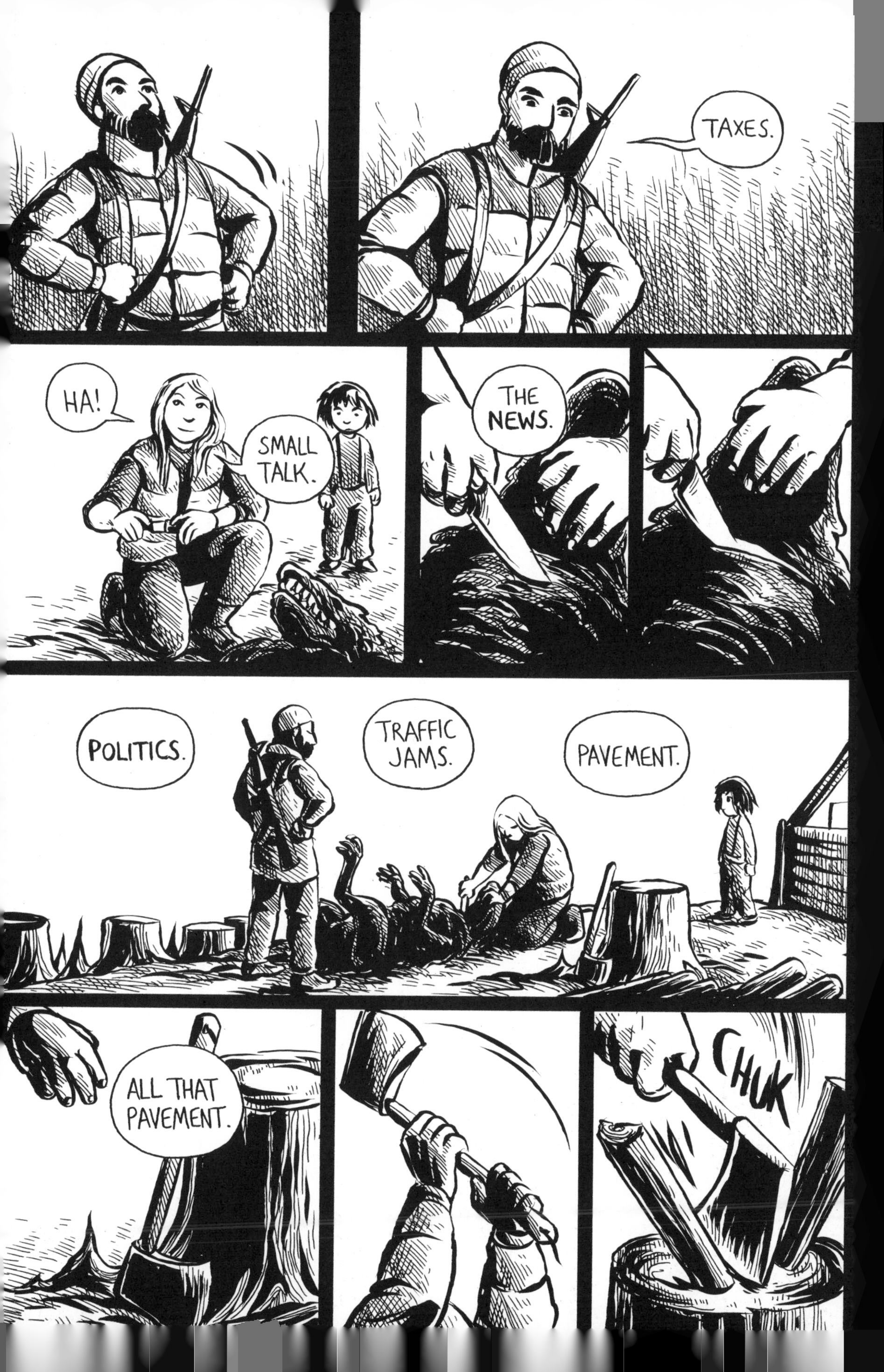
TAXES.
HA!
SMALL TALK.
THE NEWS.
POLITICS.
TRAFFIC JAMS.
PAVEMENT.
ALL THAT PAVEMENT.
CHUK

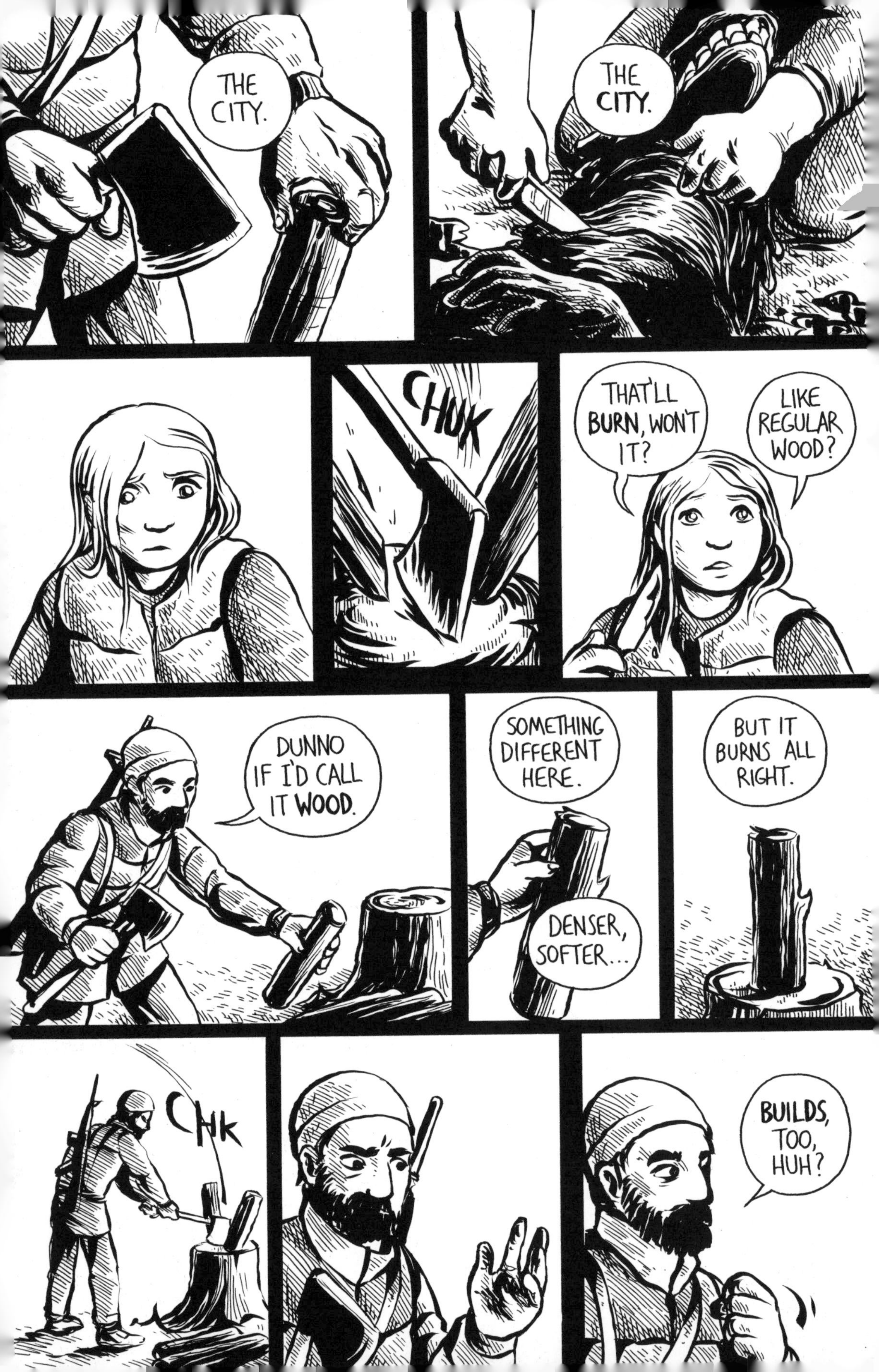
THE CITY.
THE CITY.
CHUK
THAT'LL BURN, WON'T IT?
LIKE REGULAR WOOD?
DUNNO IF I'D CALL IT WOOD.
SOMETHING DIFFERENT HERE.
DENSER, SOFTER...
BUT IT BURNS ALL RIGHT.
CHK
BUILDS, TOO, HUH?

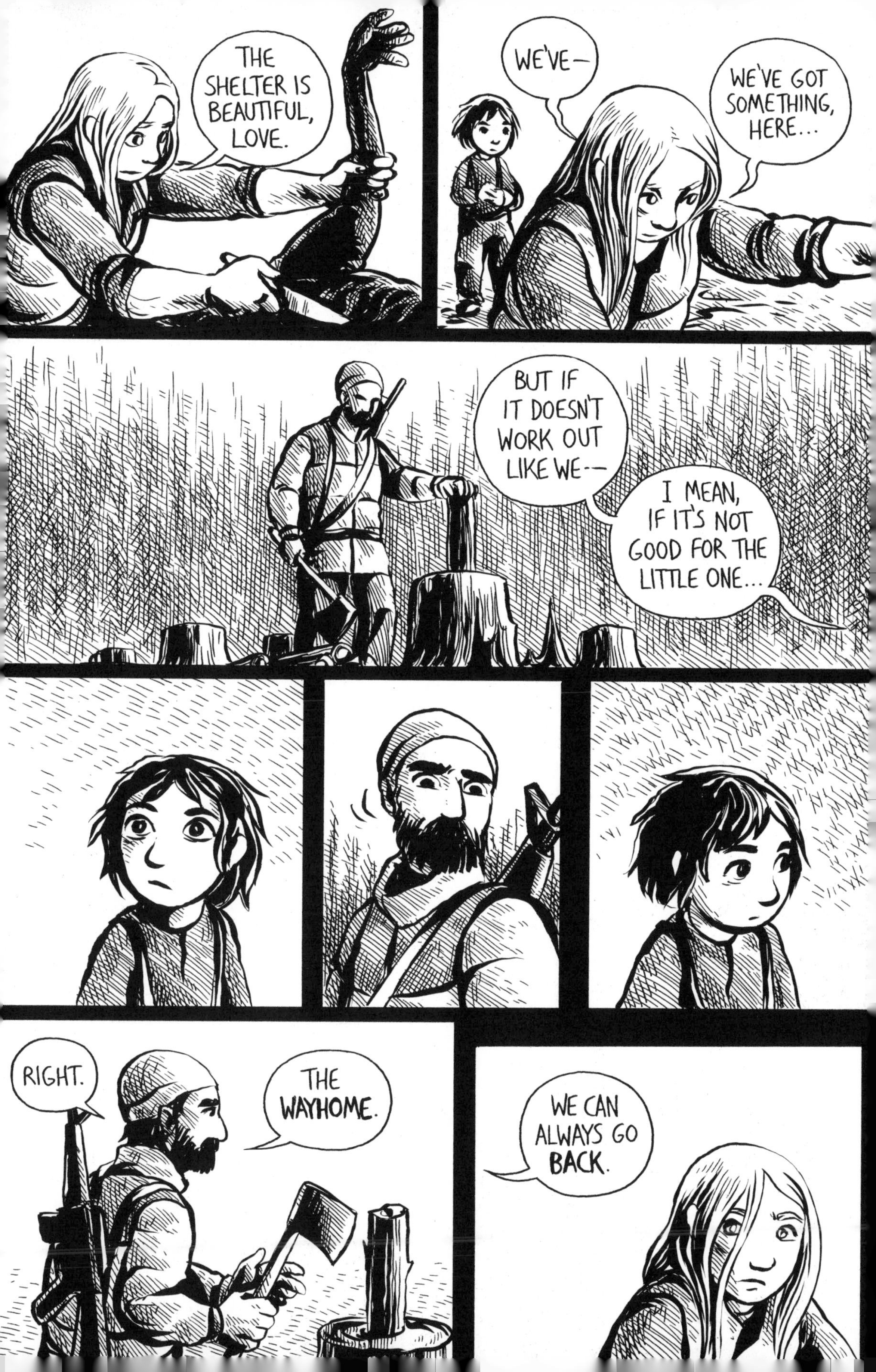
THE SHELTER IS BEAUTIFUL, LOVE.
WE'VE—
WE'VE GOT SOMETHING, HERE...
BUT IF IT DOESN'T WORK OUT LIKE WE--
I MEAN, IF IT'S NOT GOOD FOR THE LITTLE ONE...
RIGHT.
THE WAYHOME.
WE CAN ALWAYS GO BACK.

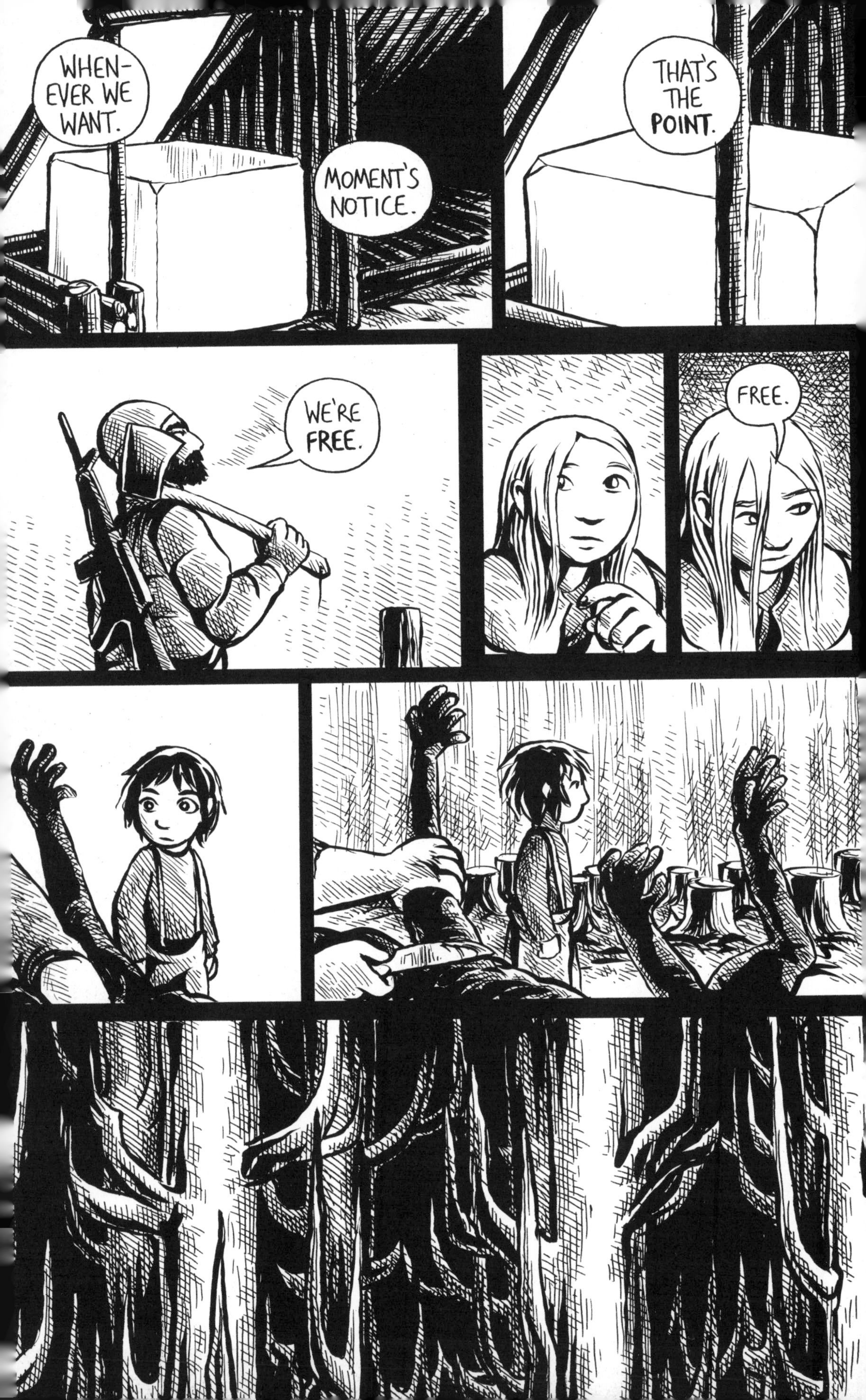
WHEN-
EVER WE
WANT.
MOMENT'S
NOTICE.
THAT'S
THE
POINT.
WE'RE
FREE.
FREE.

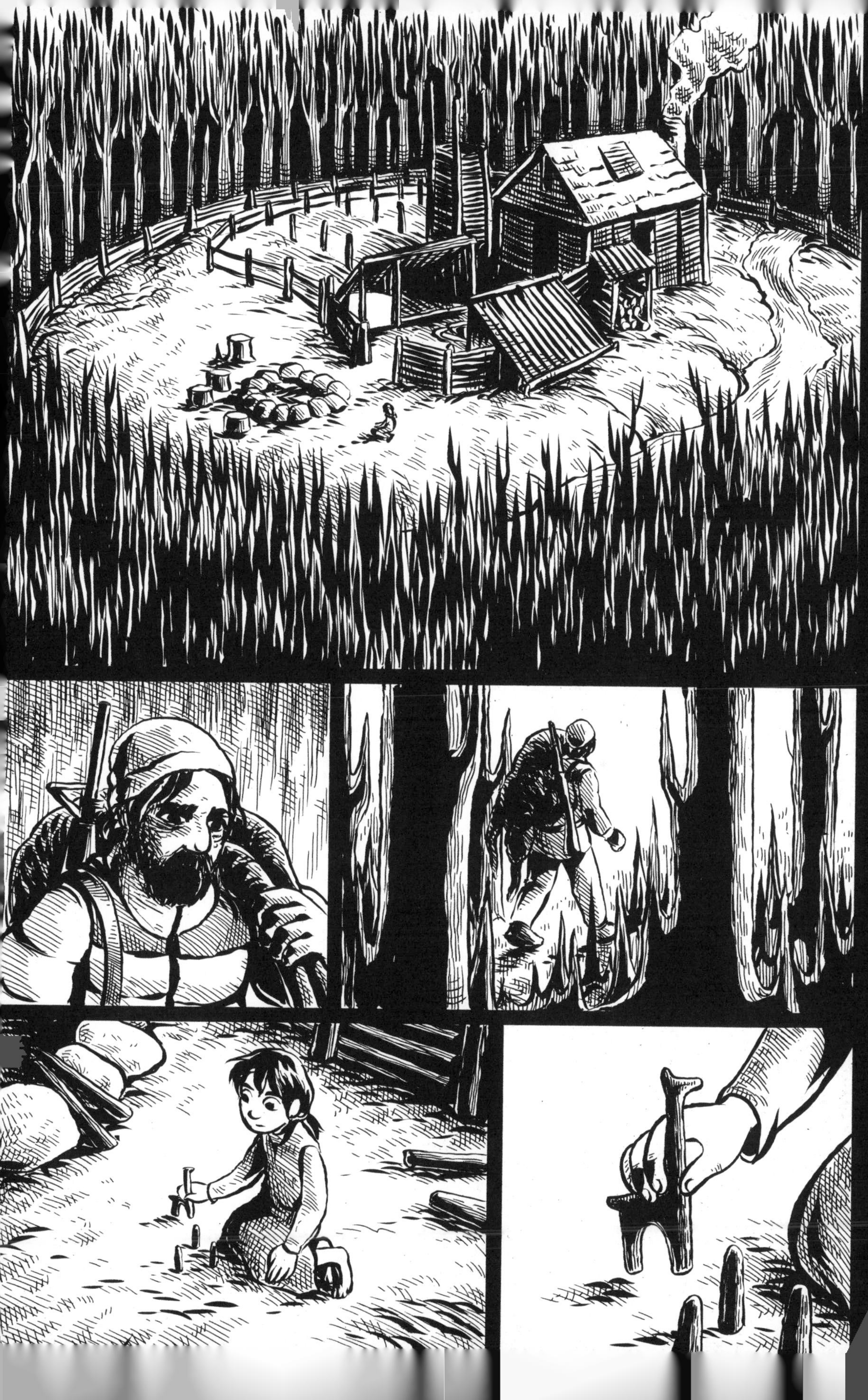

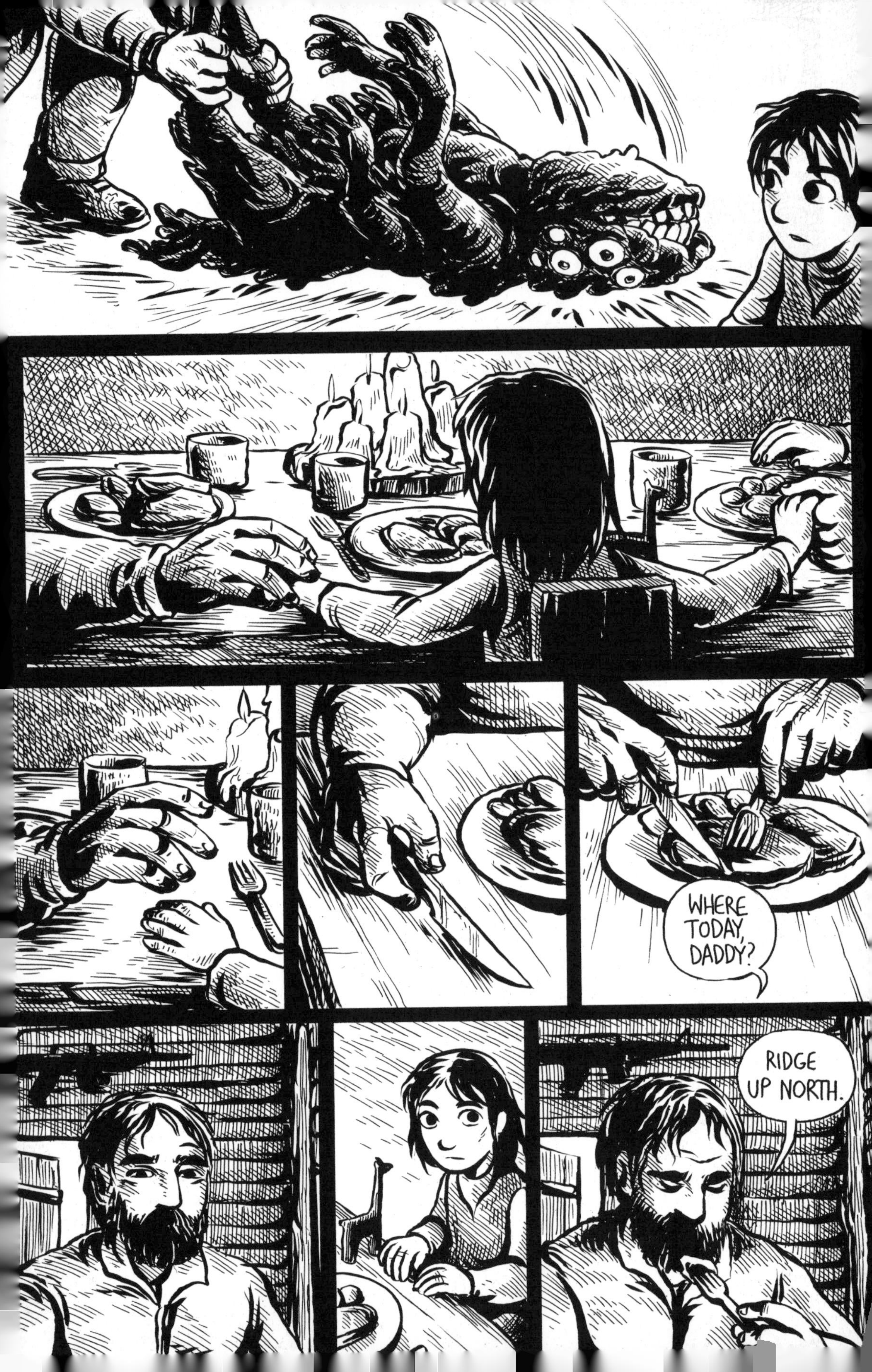
WHERE TODAY, DADDY?
RIDGE UP NORTH.

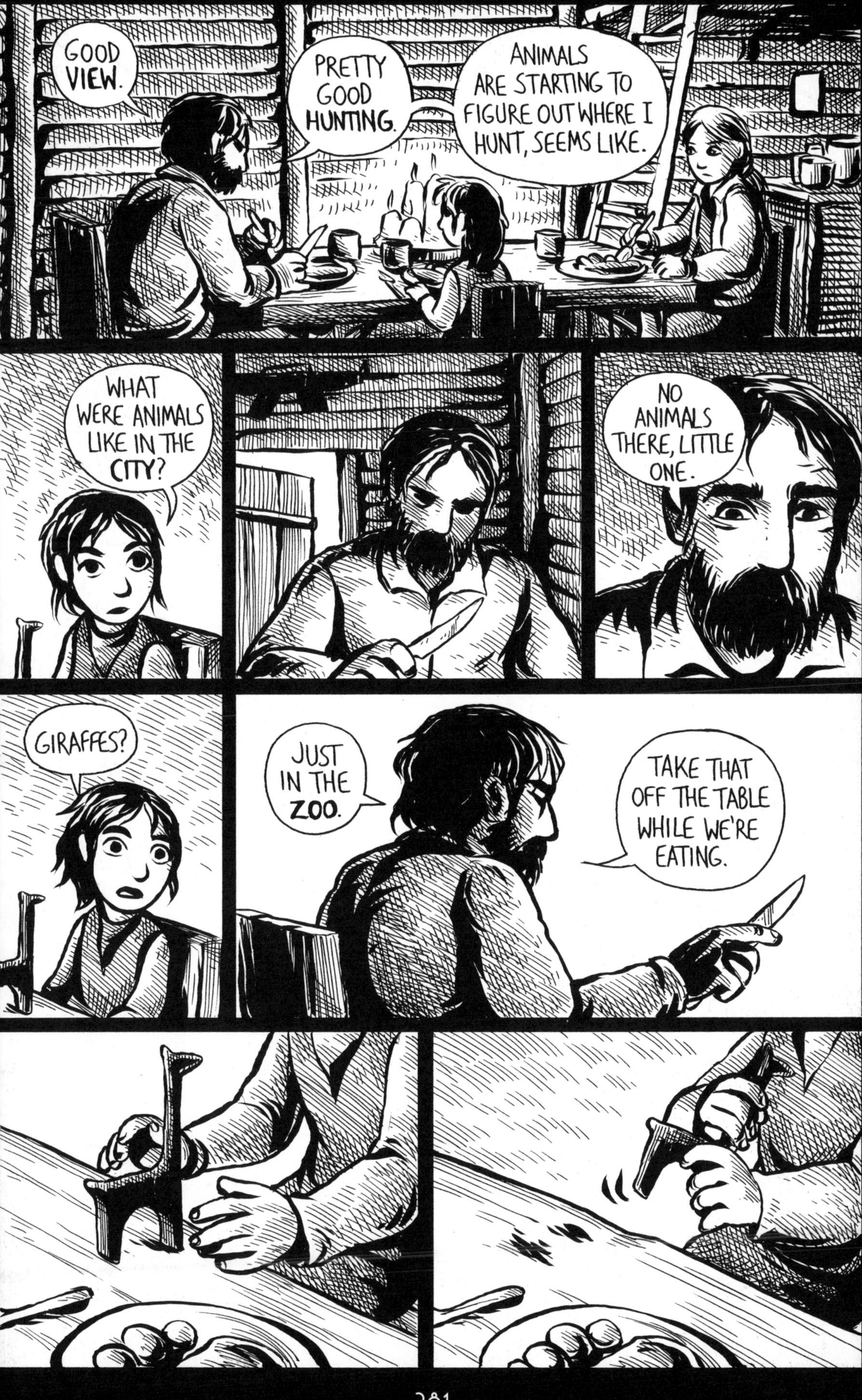
GOOD VIEW.
PRETTY GOOD HUNTING.
ANIMALS ARE STARTING TO FIGURE OUT WHERE I HUNT, SEEMS LIKE.
WHAT WERE ANIMALS LIKE IN THE CITY?
NO ANIMALS THERE, LITTLE ONE.
GIRAFFES?
JUST IN THE ZOO.
TAKE THAT OFF THE TABLE WHILE WE'RE EATING.

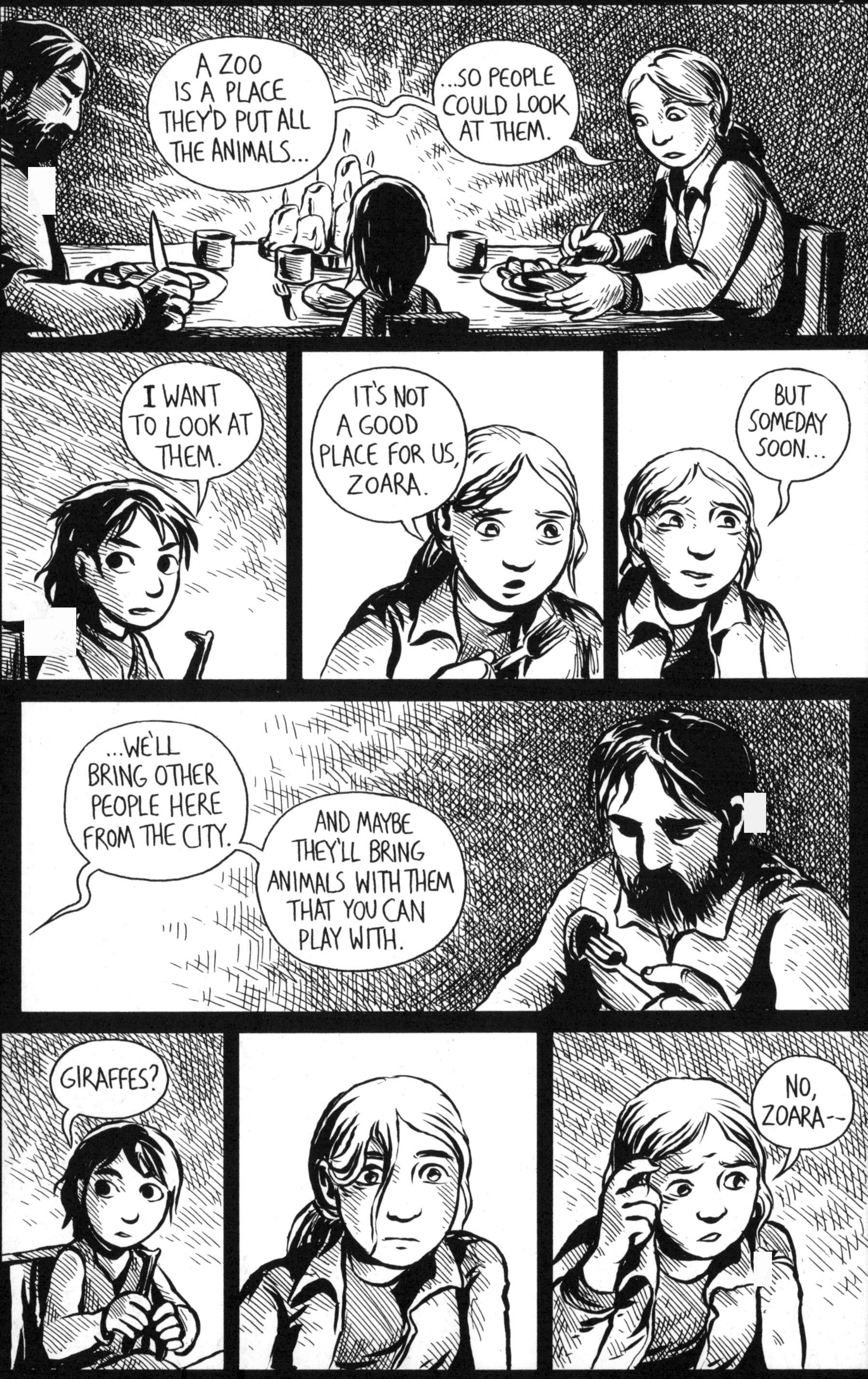
A ZOO IS A PLACE THEY'D PUT ALL THE ANIMALS...
...SO PEOPLE COULD LOOK AT THEM.
I WANT TO LOOK AT THEM.
IT'S NOT A GOOD PLACE FOR US, ZOARA.
BUT SOMEDAY SOON...
...WE'LL BRING OTHER PEOPLE HERE FROM THE CITY.
AND MAYBE THEY'LL BRING ANIMALS WITH THEM THAT YOU CAN PLAY WITH.
GIRAFFES?
NO, ZOARA--

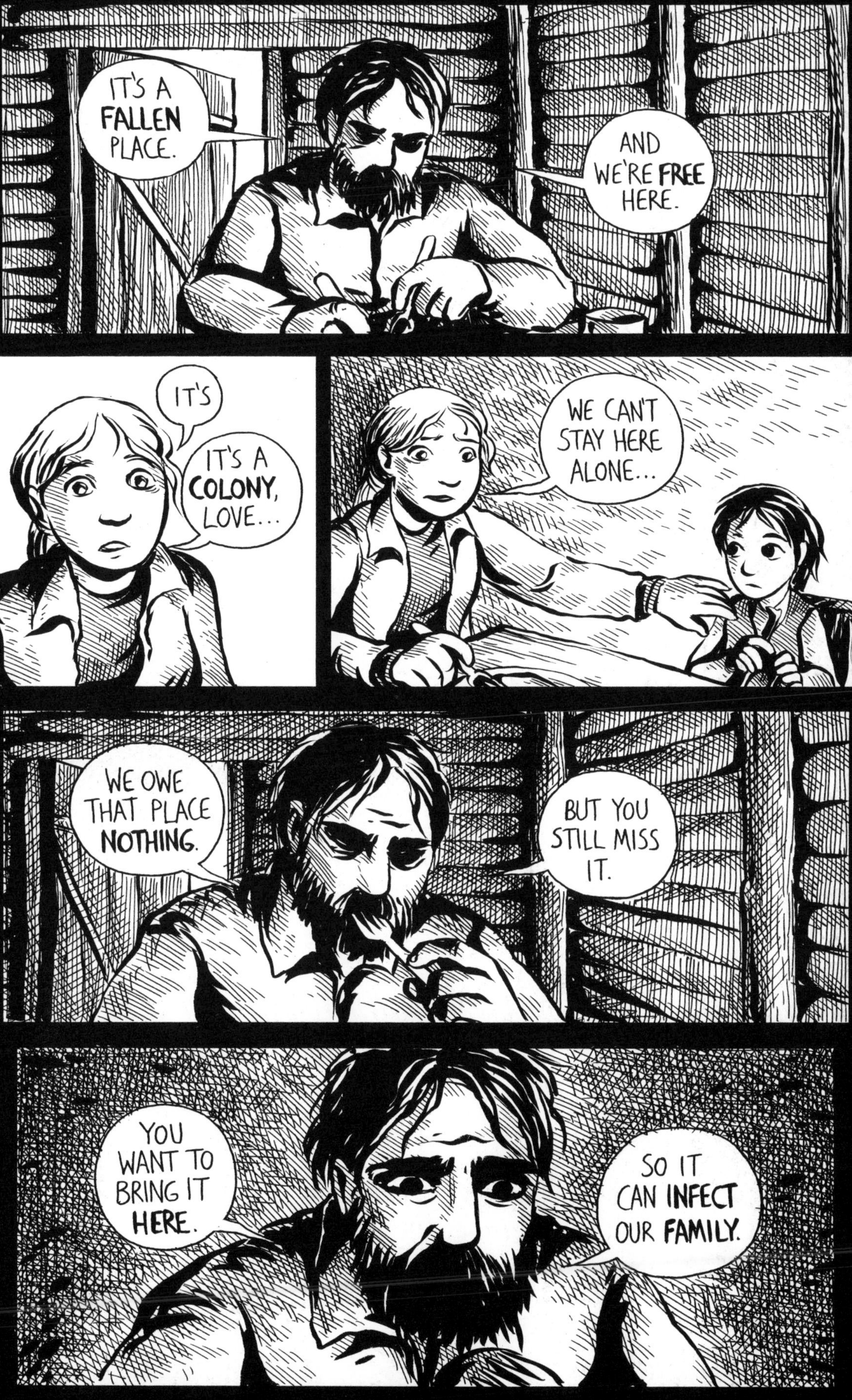

IT'S A **FALLEN** PLACE.
AND WE'RE **FREE** HERE.
IT'S
IT'S A **COLONY**, LOVE...
WE CAN'T STAY HERE ALONE...
WE OWE THAT PLACE **NOTHING**.
BUT YOU STILL MISS IT.
YOU WANT TO BRING IT **HERE**.
SO IT CAN **INFECT** OUR **FAMILY**.

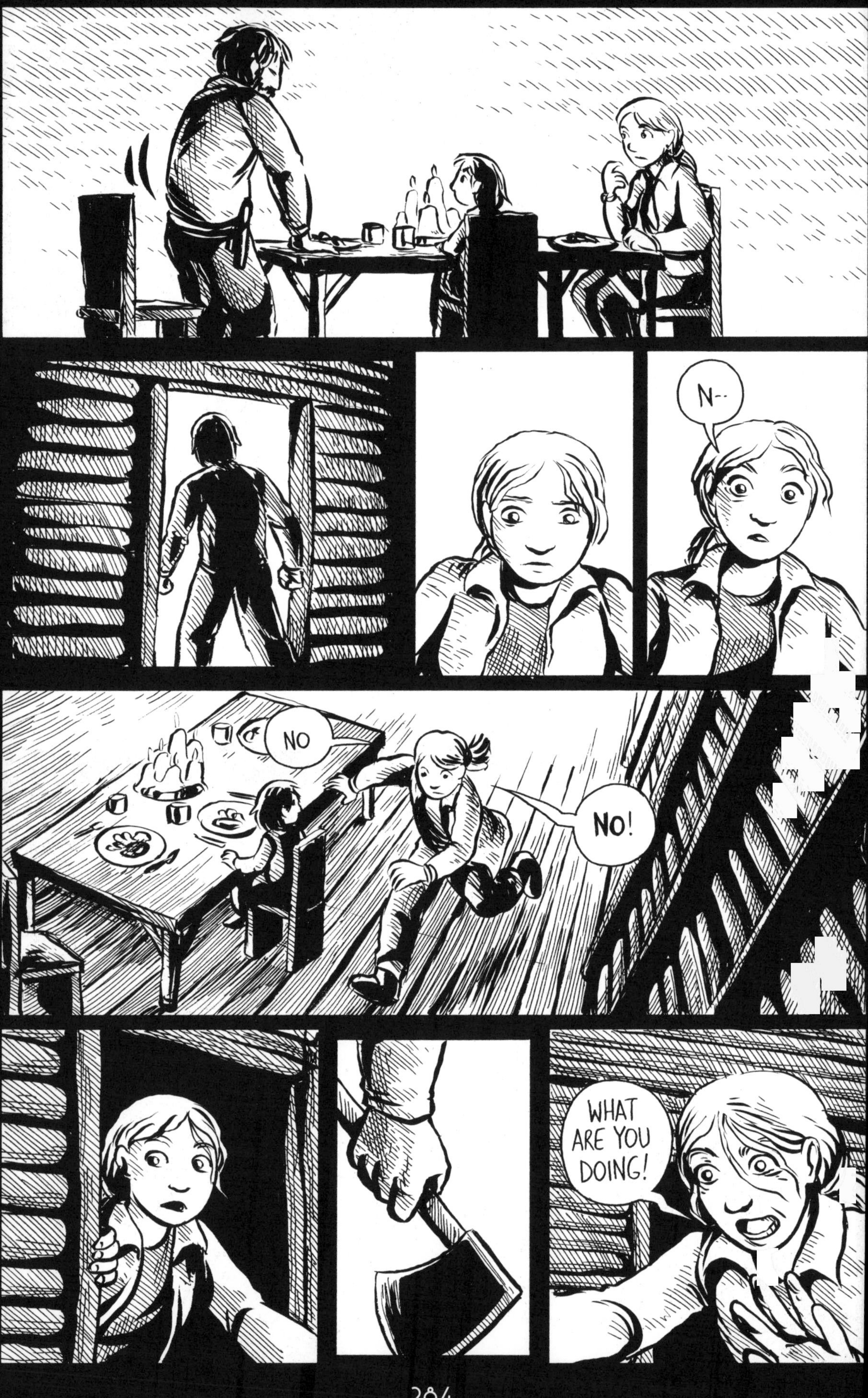
N--
NO
NO!
WHAT ARE YOU DOING!

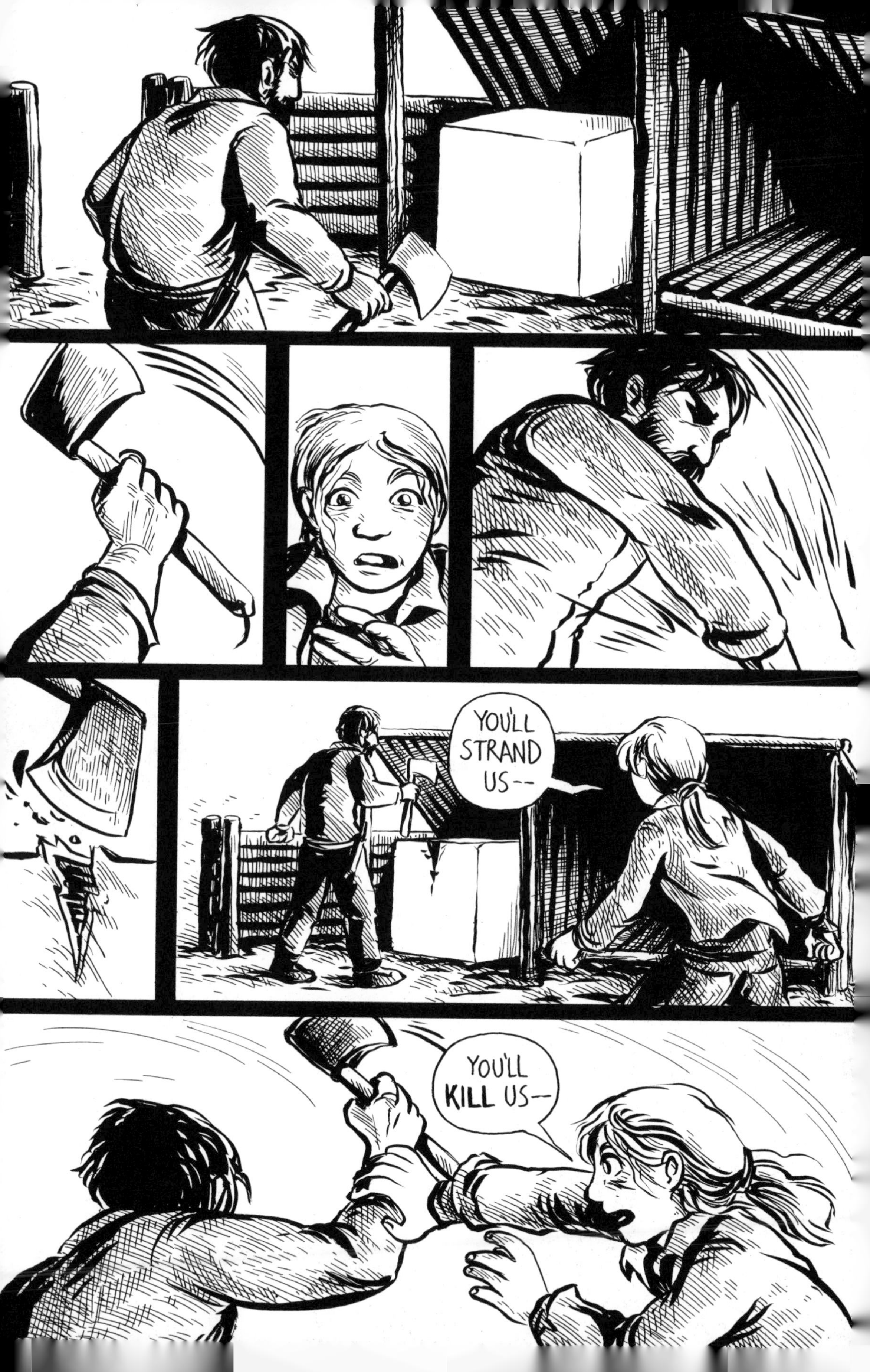
YOU'LL STRAND US--
YOU'LL KILL US--

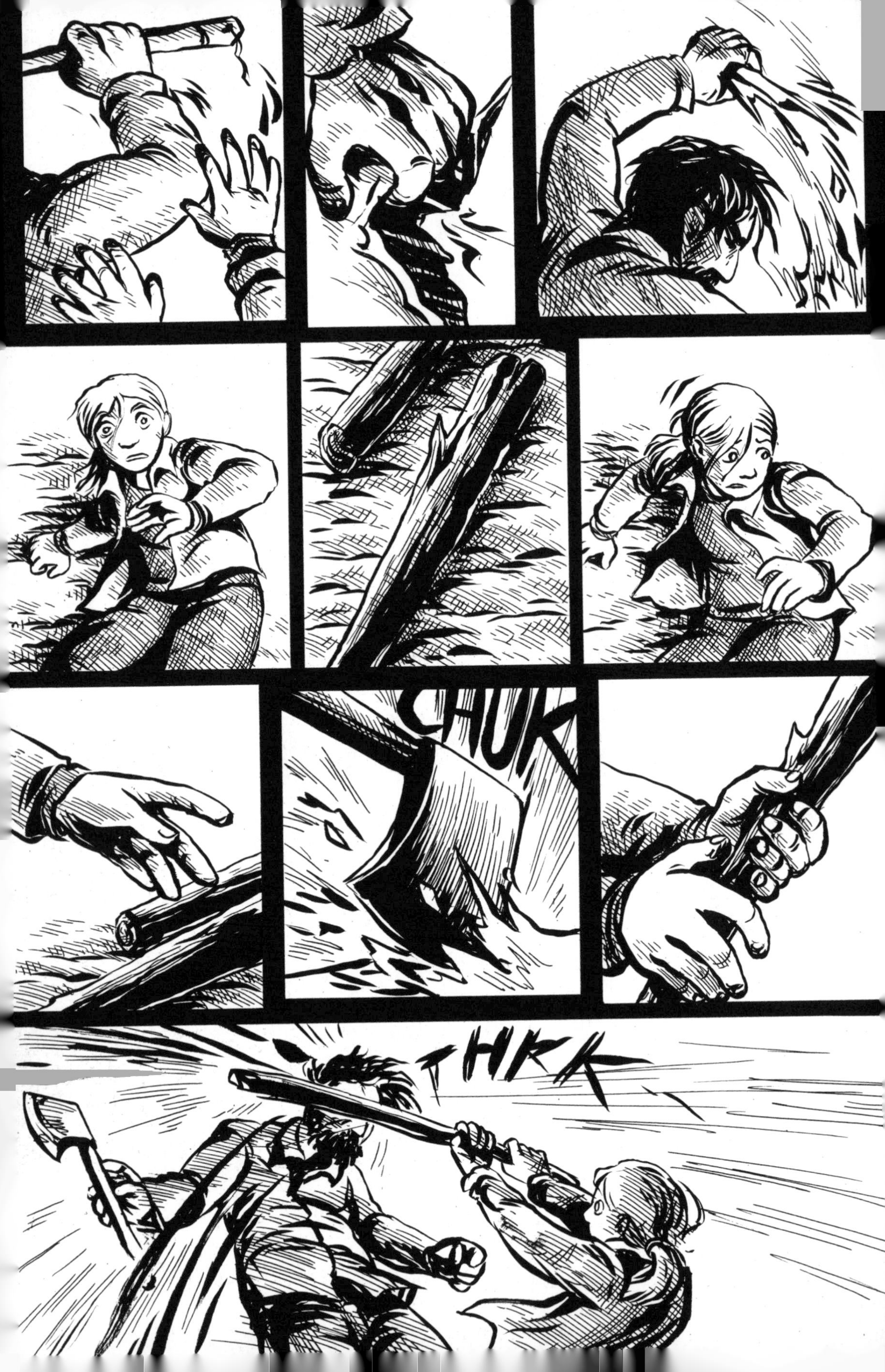

CHUK
THRK

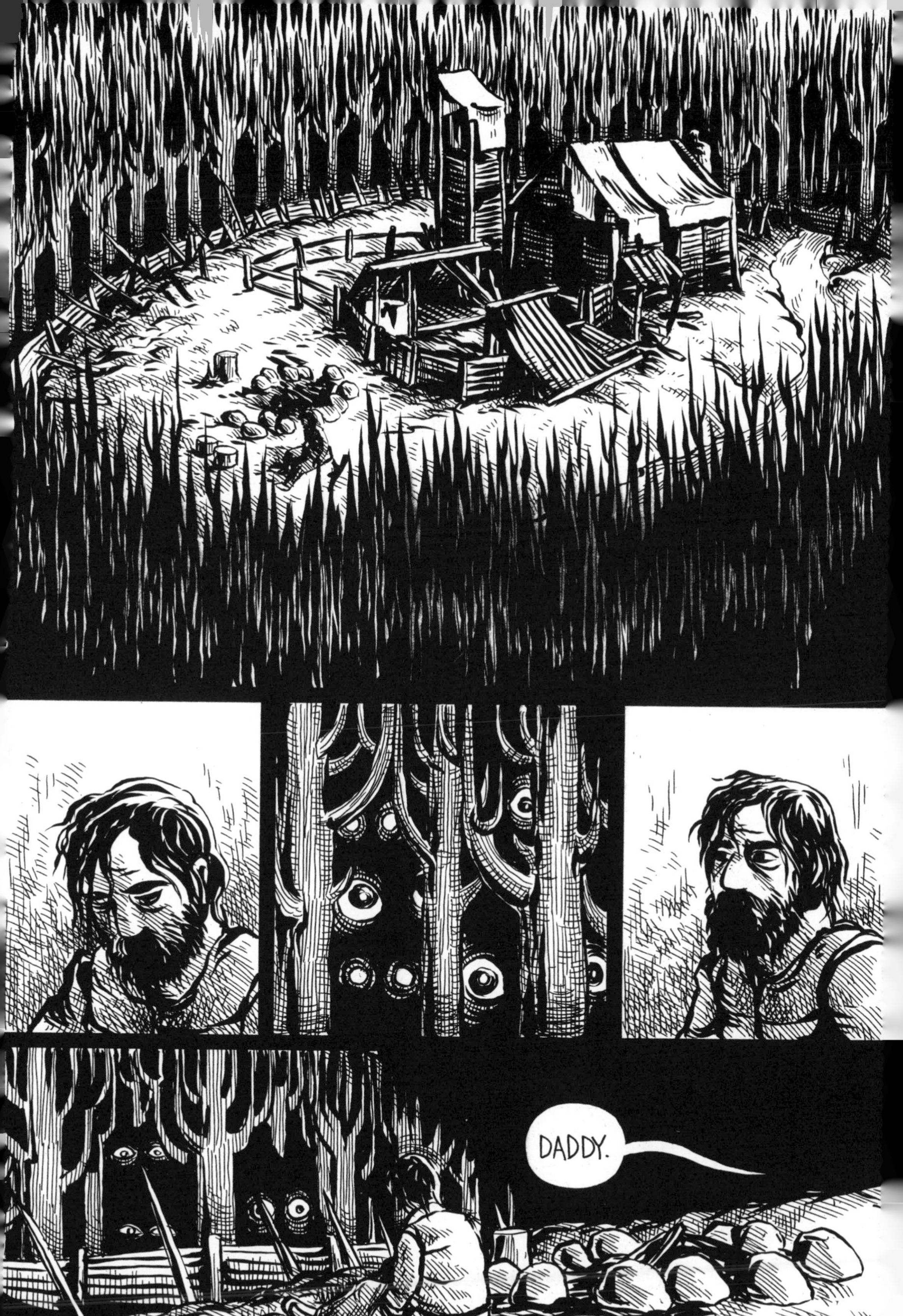
DADDY.

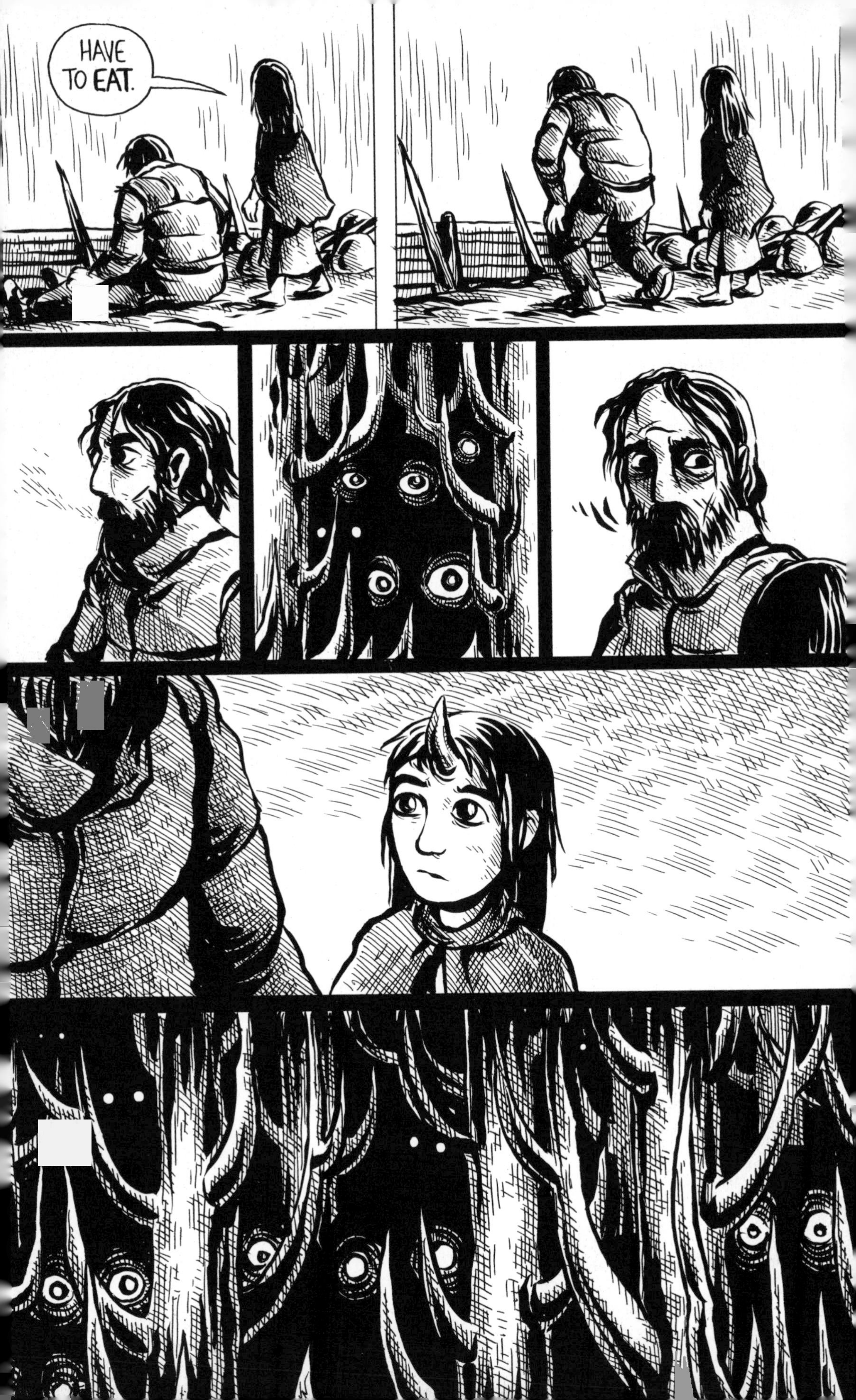
HAVE TO EAT.

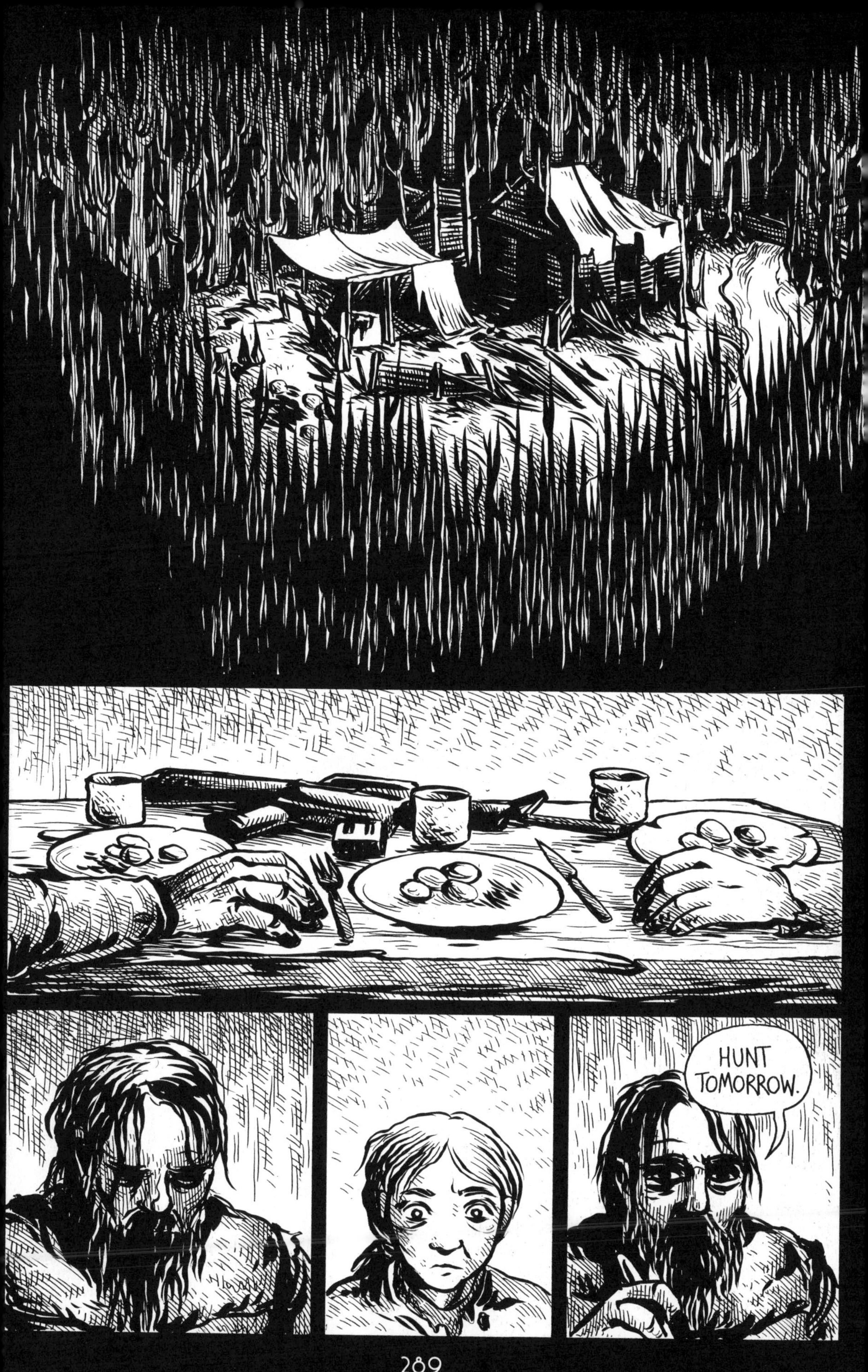
HUNT TOMORROW.

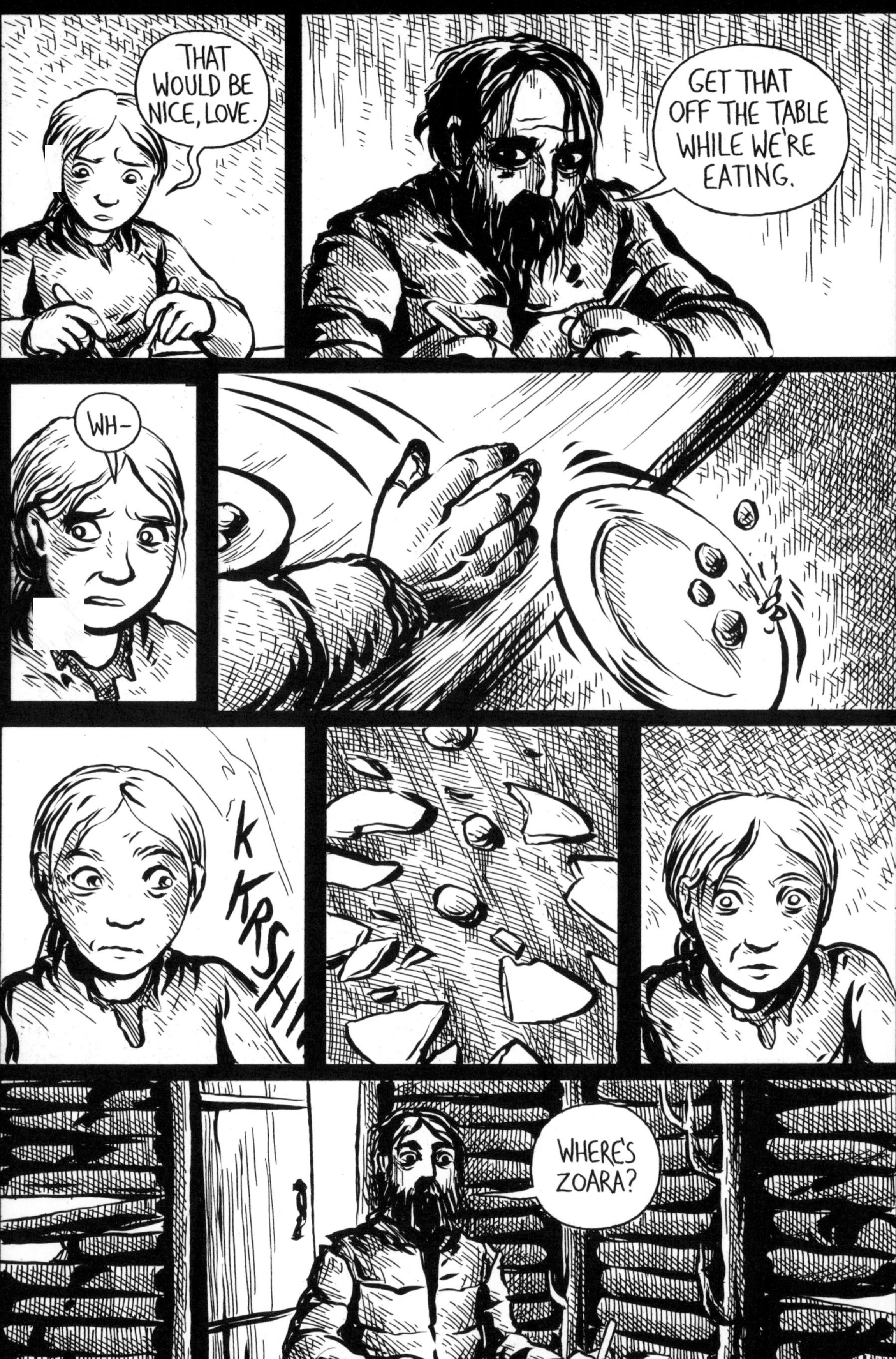
THAT WOULD BE NICE, LOVE.
GET THAT OFF THE TABLE WHILE WE'RE EATING.
WH-
KKRSHH
WHERE'S ZOARA?

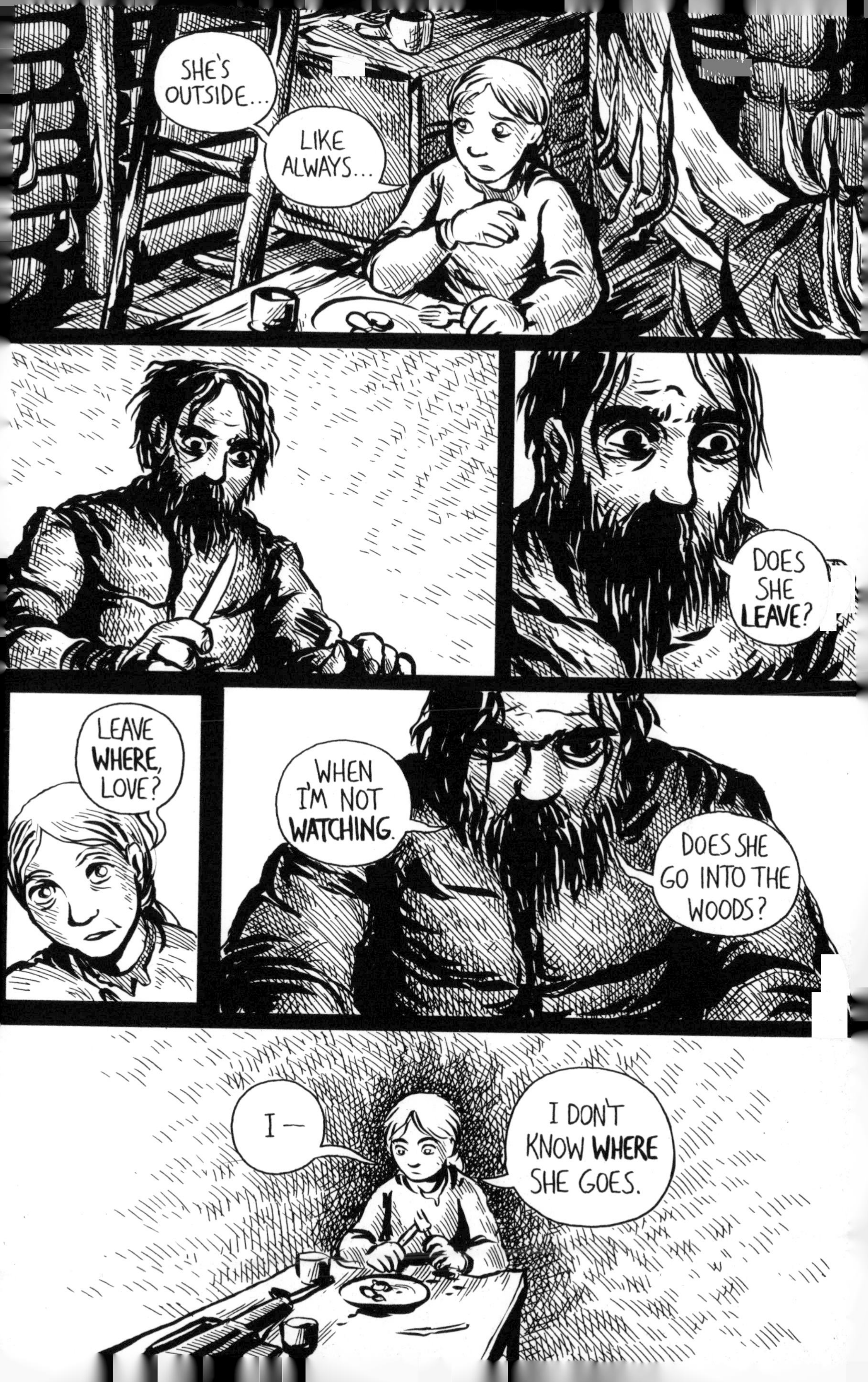
SHE'S OUTSIDE...
LIKE ALWAYS...
DOES SHE **LEAVE**?
LEAVE **WHERE**, LOVE?
WHEN I'M NOT **WATCHING**.
DOES SHE GO INTO THE WOODS?
I—
I DON'T KNOW **WHERE** SHE GOES.

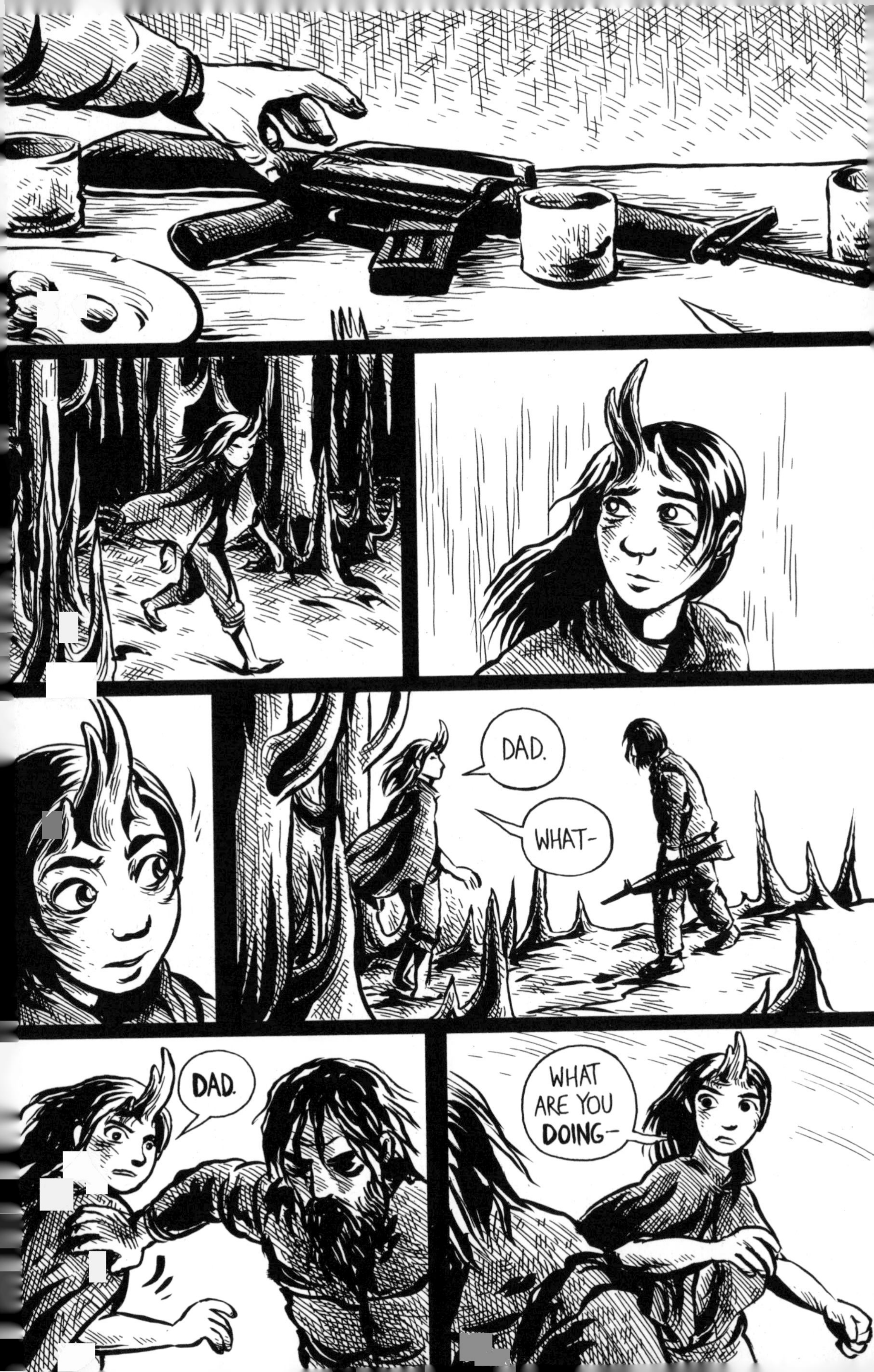
DAD.
WHAT-
DAD.
WHAT ARE YOU DOING-

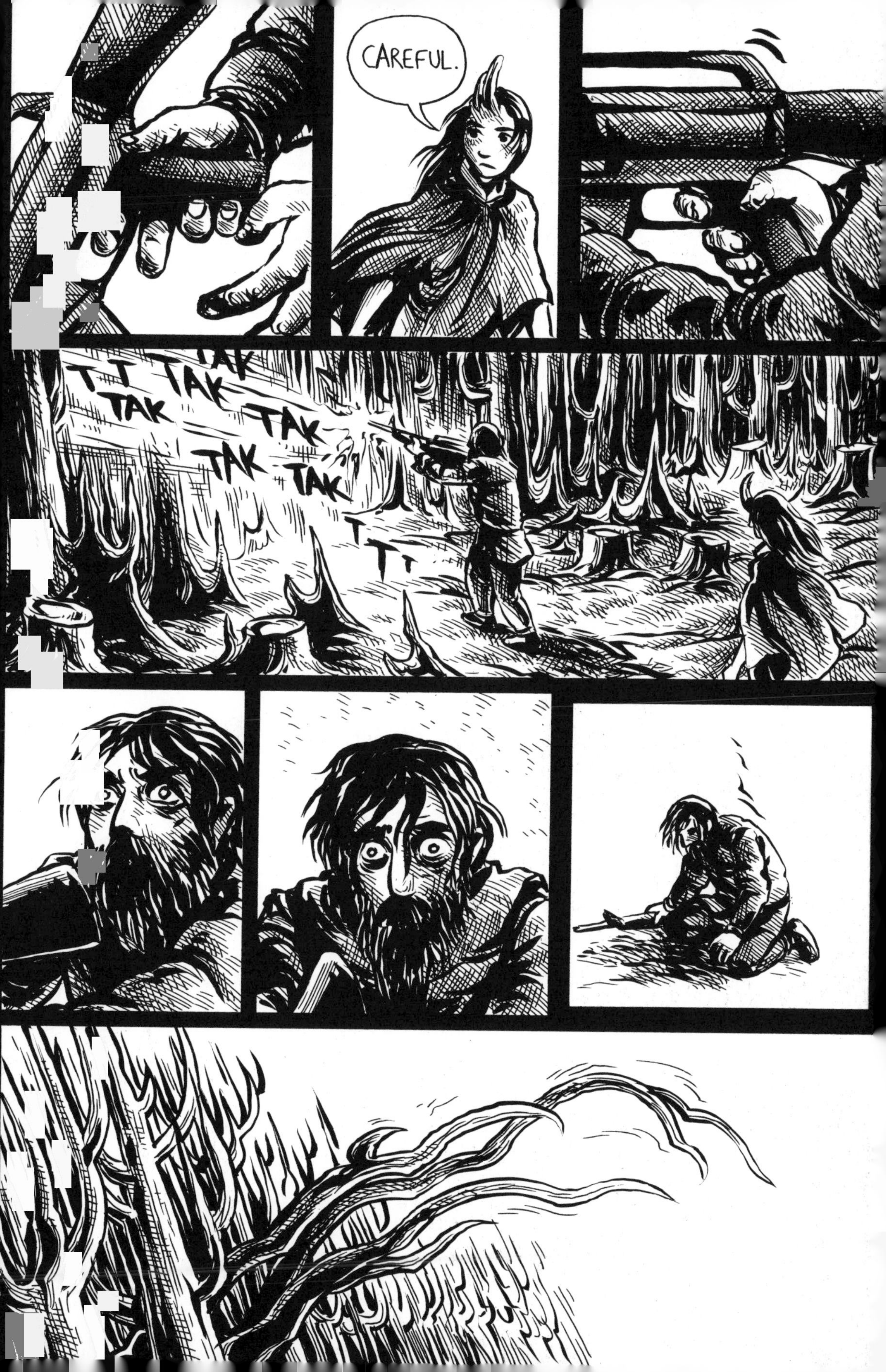
CAREFUL.
T T TAK TAK
TAK TAK
TAK
TAK TAK
T T T

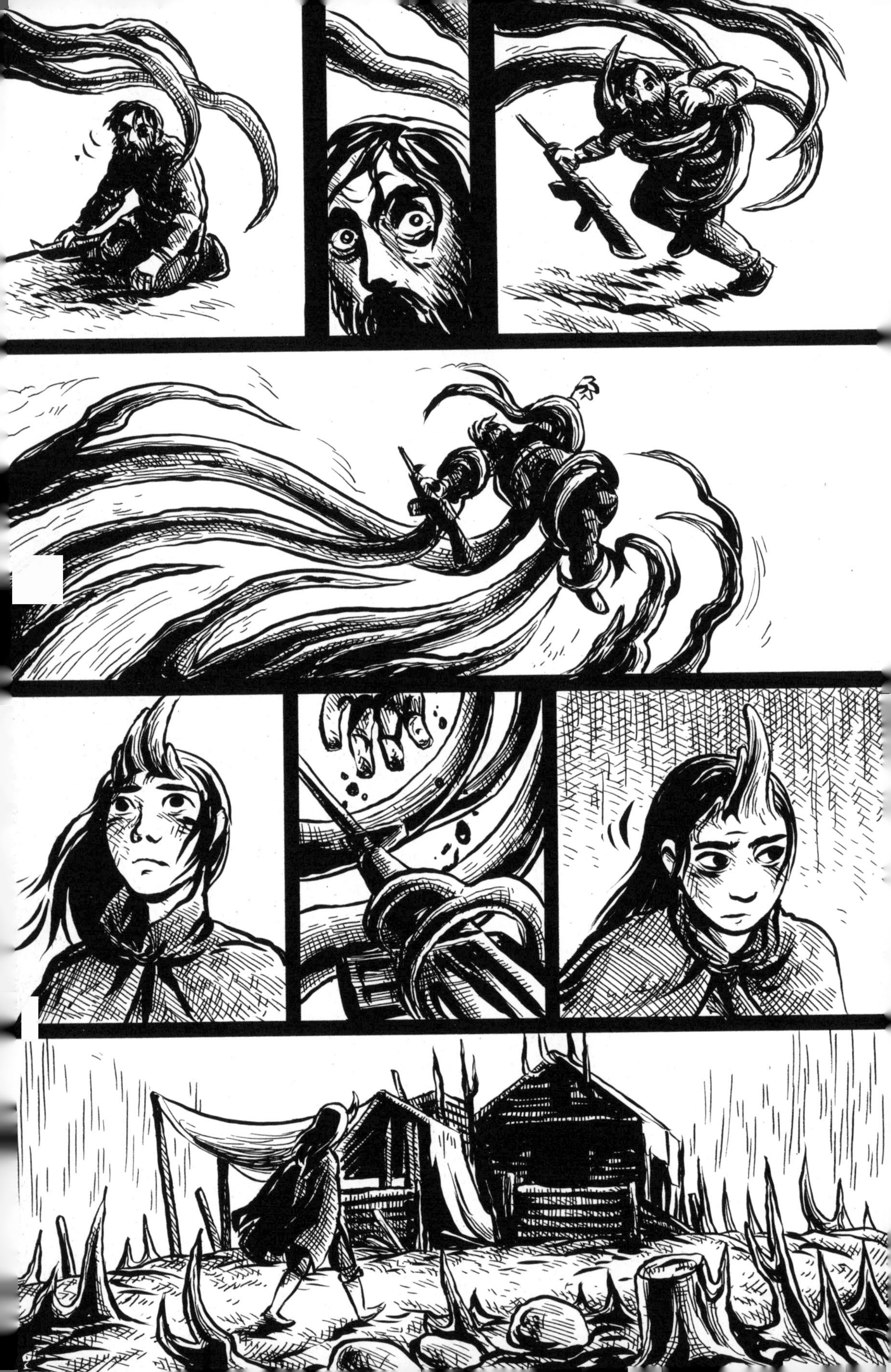

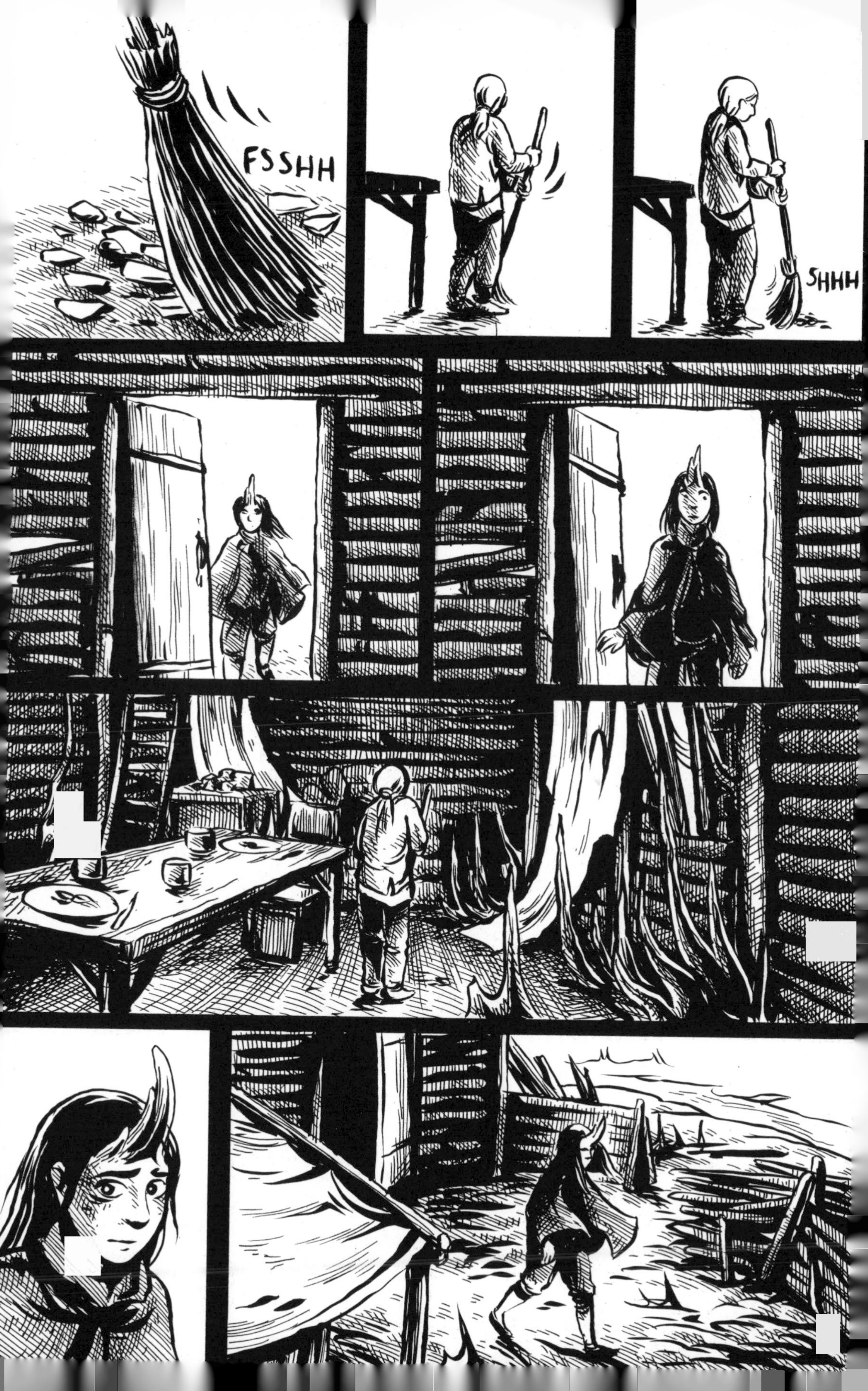
FSSHH
SHHH

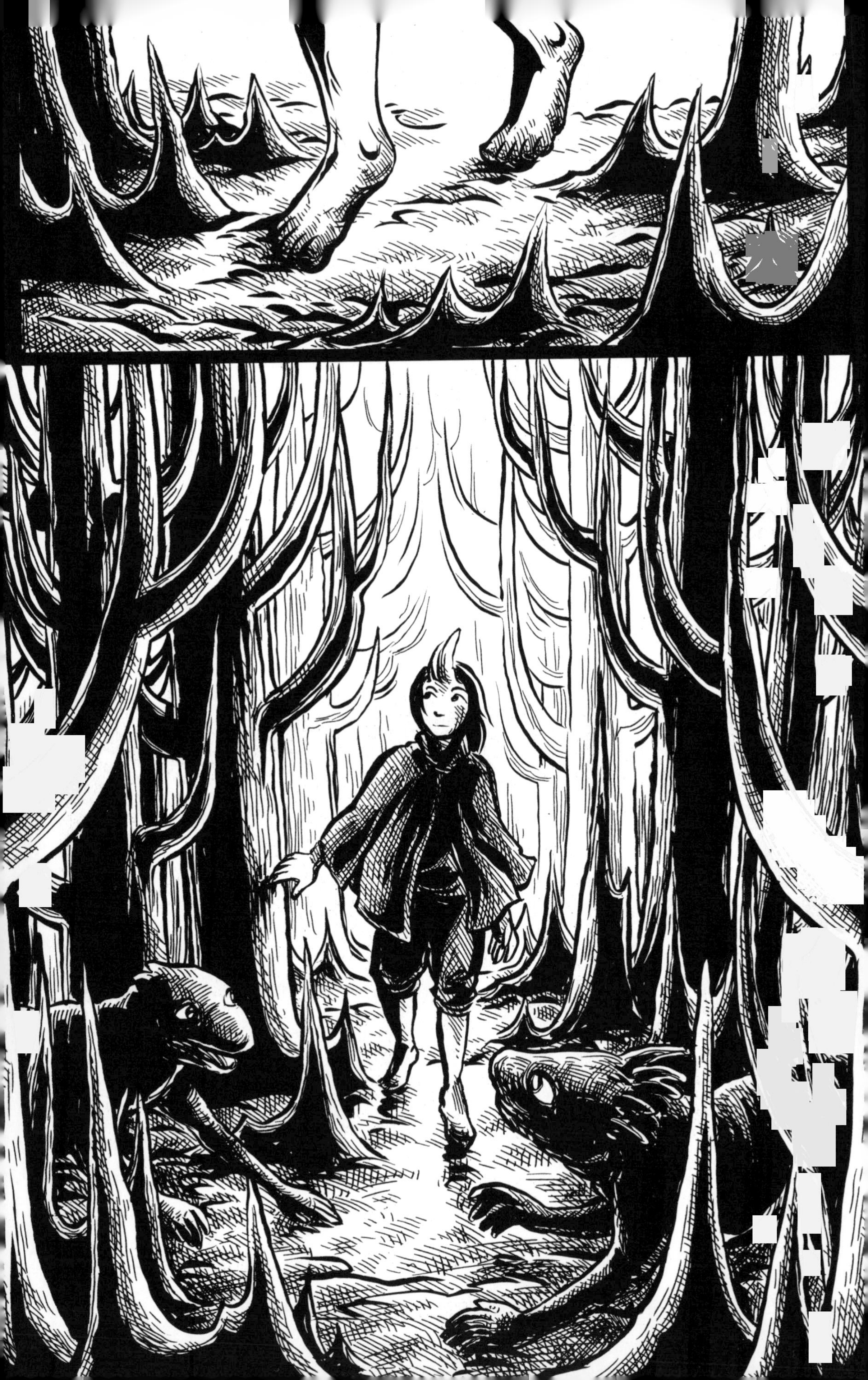

CREATORS

AHUEONAO (1989–2045?) was a reclusive hermit known to reside somewhere in Santiago, Chile. Details of their life have been reconstructed through scattered illustrations and comic pages occasionally published online. Though this output came to a sudden halt in 2045, some historians [citation needed] believe Ahueonao might have lived well past that date. It's been theorized that Ahueonao was the anonymous creator behind some of Chile's most critically celebrated memes during the tumultuous 2050–60s decades.

ahueonao.tumblr.com

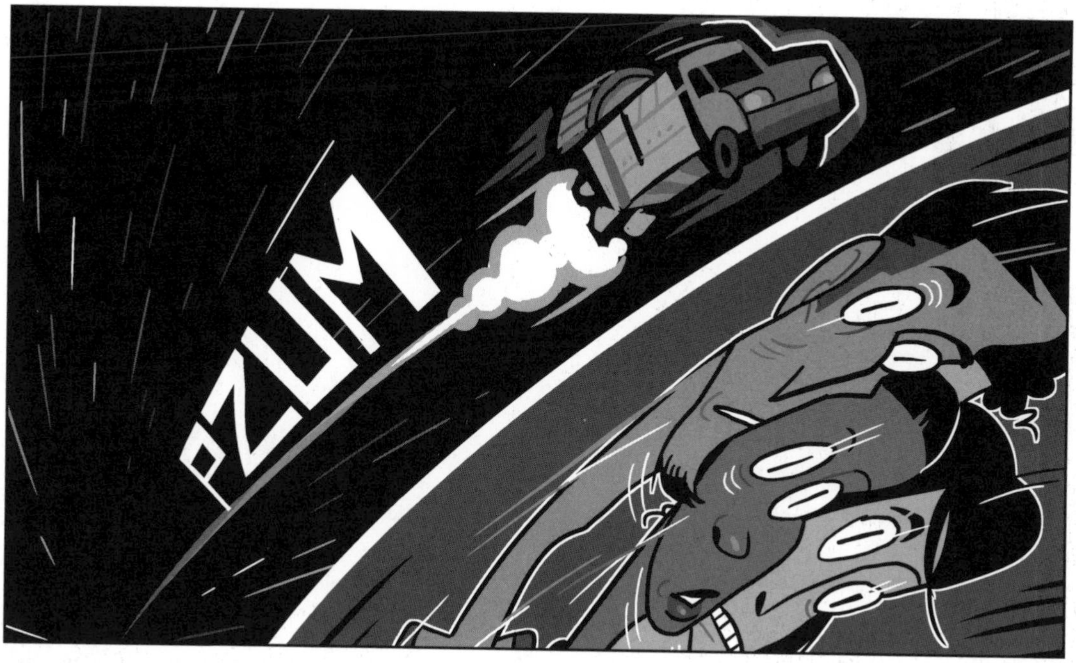
¡ZUM

AINSLEY SEAGO is a professional bug identifier and occasional cartoonist living in Australia. More of her nonsense can be found at **@americanbeetles** on Twitter.

ALEXXANDER DOVELIN is

a comic creator living in Portland, OR. Draws fantasy to help shape the everyday. Still learning, still growing. Contributor to **Beyond Anthology II**. Makes the webcomic **VALLONO**, playing with space-time magic.

xxdovelin.com

BLUE DELLIQUANTI is a comic artist

based in Minneapolis and the creator of the sci-i webcomic **O Human Star**. Blue worked with **Soleil Ho** on **Meal**, a graphic novel about eating bugs, and her work has also appeared in comic anthologies such as **Beyond**, **The Sleep of Reason**, and **New World**.

ohumanstar.com

CB WEBB is a painter, illustrator, and graphic designer

in California who recently discovered that making comics is really heckin' cool. When she's not spending her free time painting or making her magical realism webcomic, **Blanco**, she's busy petting every dog. So very, very, many dogs.

blancocomic.com

CHEEZ HAYAMA is an independent

manga artist who lives in the San Francisco Bay Area. She is best known for her comic *Eggs, Butter, and a Pinch of Ghost (Last Supper)*, which was a finalist in the 38th Morning Manga competition. Her favorite cheese is the Devil's Gulch by Cow Girl Creamery.

hayamaya.com

CINDY POWERS is a science editor

currently enjoying the good life in Tokyo, Japan. Often found in the company of her favorite karakuri-ningyo, she's been known to dabble in an occasional bit of science fiction.

DAVID ANDRY is a former competitive roller

skater and current comic book writer. He has self-published a relationship drama series with frequent collaborator **Paul Schultz** and several volumes of an anthology with his **GhostThunder** partners. He spends most of his time at a real job so he can, y'know, pay bills 'n' stuff? *FTL, Y'all* is his first published work (thanks **Iron Circus!**).

ghostthunder.com

EARL T. ROSKE is a San Francisco Bay Area

writer and playwright, author of the novels *Tale of the Music-Thief* and *Last Wave*. His stories have appeared in a variety of genre magazines and anthologies. His plays have appeared in festivals around the world.

earltroske.com

EVAN DAHM is a cartoonist and illustrator living in Brooklyn, New York with his spouse and their small dog. Since 2006, he's been creating and publishing comics online and in print, including *Rice Boy* and the Ignatz award-winning fantasy-biographical epic *Vattu*. His upcoming work includes *Island Book* with **First Second Books**, and *The Harrowing of Hell* with **Iron Circus Comics**.
rice-boy.com

IRIS JAY (she/they) has been putting comics online for over a decade. Her current projects include co-creating the erotic comic *Golden Trick* with her partner **Nero O'Reilly**, helping organize various publications from **Fortuna Media**, and working on her two solo comic series, *Crossed Wires* and *Double Blind*. If she had an FTL drive, she'd probably have a really high-minded idea of what to do with it, but she'd most likely end up using it to find weird alien porn and exotic space dessert recipes.
irisjay.net

JAMES F. WRIGHT is a queer comics writer based in Los Angeles, probably(?) best known as the writer of the culinary coming-of-age crime comic, *Nutmeg*, with artist **Jackie Crofts**. He also wrote the Eisner-nominated sci-fi one-shot *Contact High*, and contributed to the Eisner-winning *Elements: Fire*. He digs genre-mixing, Taiyo Matsumoto, and has way too many thoughts about ramen and pie.
jamesfwrites.com

JAMIE KAYE is an illustrator, character designer, and comic artist in Houston, TX who spends an awful lot of time being enthusiastic about video games and comic books. She is currently a concept artist for *Line*, a whimsical indie video game.

missjamiekaye.com

JAY EATON is a biologist and comic artist of the California bay area. When they aren't putting innocent families through harrowing transport accidents, Jay draws made-up animals, bothers local wildlife, and co-edits for *Almost Real: A Speculative Biology Zine*.

jayrockin.tumblr.com

JONATHON DALTON has completed two graphic novels, *Lords of Death and Life* and *A Mad Tea-Party*, and is working on the third, *Phobos and Deimos*. He has

also contributed stories to *New World*, *Cautionary Fables and Fairy Tales*, *Comics in Transit*, and drew some of *The Legend of Bold Riley*. He is the president of **Cloudscape Comics**. Jonathon lives in Vancouver, and when he's not making comics, he teaches elementary school.

phobos-comic.com

KAY ROSSBACH is a graphic designer

and comic creator from Minneapolis, MN who grew up in the woods of northern Minnesota. Kay produces a fantasy webcomic called **Ingress Adventuring Company** and works full-time as an internet marketer. During her free time she plays tabletop board games, lurks in the woods, and thinks about wizards.

kayrossbach.com

LITTLE CORVUS is an Eisner-nominated

queer, nonbinary, latinx comic artist and illustrator based in Seattle. A graduate of the School of Visual Arts with a BFA in Cartooning, they love positive, diverse stories and the color pink.

littlecorvusart.com

MAIA KOBABE is a nonbinary, queer comics

author/illustrator with an MFA in Comics from California College of the Arts. Eir first full length comic book, **Gender Queer: A Memoir**, is forthcoming from **Lion Forge** in May 2019. Eir work focuses on themes of identity, sexuality, fairy tales, and homesickness.

redgoldsparkspress.com

MULELE JARVIS, who publishes under

Mulele Redux, is an indie comic creator. Born in Manhattan and transplanted to Japan, he cut his artistic teeth drawing comics inspired by ukiyo-e, film, and the back alleys of Tokyo.

mulele.com

NATHANIEL WILSON is a comic

artist and illustrator in New York City who has wisely stopped feeding fig turkey meatloaf to the screaming raccoons outside his bedroom window. His first published comic story, "Green Man's Tunnel," appeared recently in the anthology **Built on Strange Ground** from **Peppermint Monster Press**. He is currently filling a Squarespace template up with black goo at **sourflesh.com** so that there will be something to pluck and peel and chew when this book is released.

NN CHAN

(a.k.a. Queenie) is an artist from Toronto who loves comics, video games, and baking. Her other hobby is eating what she bakes. She's worked for **BOOM!** as a comic artist and has also been a part of several indie game teams.

nnchan.ca

PAUL SCHULTZ has been a freelance illustrator for over 10 years. A graduate of the Sheridan Illustration program, he has worked on children's books, comic books, logo designs, tattoo designs, and many one-offs commissions. He lives and works in Burlington, Ontario.

freelanced.com/paulschultz

RACHEL ORDWAY is a freelance cartoonist and letterer who usually does sillier stuff than this. In addition to various self-published comics, her work appears in the acclaimed anthologies *Chainmail Bikini*, *Sweaty Palms* (volume 1), *Dirty Diamonds* (#8), and *Lilies* (volumes 1 and 4). She is also a former contributor to **Comic Book Resources**' sketch group **The Line It Is Drawn**.

rachelordway.com

SKOLLI RUBEDO is a jerk-of-all-trades dabbling in traditional & digital illustration, print & web design, writing, music, motion graphics, and occasionally, arcane practices intended to bring about the end of the world. They have been more or less in the orbit of the furry scene since the late '90s.

skolli.org

SUNNY is a writer, creative developer, and human-sunflower hybrid entity based out of the Bay Area, CA.